NAMED ONE OF THE BEST BOOKS OF 2022

The New Yorker | *Publishers Weekly* | *The Financial Times*
Words Without Borders

"*Solenoid* . . . is a novel made from other novels, a meticulously borrowed piece of hyperliterature. Kleist's cosmic ambiguity, the bureaucratic terror of Kafka, the enchantments of García Márquez and Bruno Schulz's labyrinths are all recognizable in Cărtărescu's anecdotes, dreams and journal entries. That fictive texture is part and parcel of the novel's sense of unreality, which not only blends the pedestrian and the bizarre, but also commingles many features of the literary avant-garde. Although the narrator himself is largely critical of literature . . . he also affirms the possibility inherent in the 'bitter and incomprehensible books' he idolizes. In this way, he plays both critic and apologist throughout, a delicious dialectic whose final, ravishing synthesis exists in the towering work of *Solenoid* itself."

Dustin Illingworth, *New York Times*

"Instead of delivering a sharp, succinct punch, *Solenoid* goes the way of the oceanic—rejecting brevity because the author, a Romanian Daedalus, is laying the foundation for a narrative labyrinth . . . The writing itself is hypnotic and gorgeously captures the oneiric quality of Cărtărescu's Bucharest . . . Cotter's translation is attentive to the efficiency of Cărtărescu's ornate but surprisingly approachable prose, gliding from sentence to sentence and calling little attention to itself. The sheer immensity of Cotter's undertaking combined with the unfailing evenness of the translation's quality is nothing short of remarkable."

Ben Hooyman, *Los Angeles Review of Books*

"[S]omething of a masterpiece . . . *Solenoid* synthesizes and subtly mocks elements of autofiction and history fiction by way of science fiction. The result is unlike any genre in ambition or effect, something else altogether, a self-sufficient style that proudly rejects its less emancipated alternatives . . . The mesmerizing beauty of creation, of reality giving way to itself: that, above all, lies behind the doors of *Solenoid*."

Federico Perelmuter, ***Astra Magazine***

"The great fun of this teeming hodge-podge is the way that Mr. Cărtărescu tweaks the material of daily life, transmuting the banal into the fantastical."

Sam Sacks, ***Wall Street Journal***

"[T]his is one of those rare books you should have in your library because its shelf life will endure as long as literature lasts."

Alta Ifland, ***Brooklyn Rail***

"*Solenoid* is the real thing—an honest-to-god novel of ideas, concerned with old fashioned, big picture philosophizing . . . It is a masterpiece in a league of its own."

James Webster, ***Full Stop***

"A masterwork of Kafkaesque strangeness, brilliantly conceived and written."

Kirkus Reviews

"Cărtărescu weaves a monumental antinovel of metaphysical longing and fabulist constructions . . . This scabrous epic thrums with monstrous life."

Publishers Weekly

Praise for *Nostalgia*

"Cărtărescu's themes are immense. They reveal to us a secret Bucharest, folded into underground passages far from the imperious summons of history, which never stops calling to us."

Edgar Reichmann, ***Le Monde***

"A wonderful labyrinth of language and color. Cărtărescu, one of Romania's foremost poets and novelists, gives us a novel filled with surprises and the unexpected."

Peter Constantine, author of *The Purchased Bride*, translator of Isaac Babel

"Read this book, then read it again."

Christopher Byrd, *San Francisco Chronicle*

"Gripping, impassioned, unexpected—the qualities that the best in literature possesses."

Thomas McGonigle, *Los Angeles Times Book Review*

Praise for *Blinding*

"Cărtărescu's fluid formalism translates all into some of the most imaginative literature since that of the masters mentioned by name in the text (Borges, García Márquez, and Cortázar, among others)."

Joshua Cohen, Pulitzer Prize–winning author of *The Netanyahus*

"*Blinding* expands inward, plumbing the infinite depths of an individual imagination. It's as though Cărtărescu has chosen to withdraw from any topical literary or cultural conversation, and that rather than attempting to stitch together a fragmented contemporary reality, he is returning to a time that never actually existed, an imaginary time when all genres were one genre and all discourses one discourse, before everything broke into parts."

Martin Riker, *London Review of Books*

"If George Lucas were a poet, this is how he would write."

New York Sun

"Cărtărescu's phantasmagorical world is similar to Dalí's dreamscapes."

Kirkus Reviews

"[Cărtărescu is] a writer who has always had a place reserved for him in a constellation that includes the Brothers Grimm, Franz Kafka, Jorge Luis Borges, Bruno Schulz, Julio Cortázar, Gabriel García Márquez, Milan Kundera, and Milorad Pavić, to mention just a few."

Andrei Codrescu, author of *The Poetry Lesson*

"His novel is nothing less than a cathedral of imagination and erudition . . . This masterwork of mannerism is guaranteed to catapult Mircea Cărtărescu to the highest echelons of European literature."

Neue Zürcher Zeitung

"Stitched into the multi-stranded fabric of *Blinding* is a tender, mesmerically precise account of a humble Bucharest upbringing and its formative effects . . . Above all, *Blinding* insists that memory can make a world . . . Cărtărescu has fashioned a novel of visionary intensity."

Boyd Tonkin, *The Independent*

"The reader is invited to embrace this feeling of overwhelming comprehension, this comprehensive vision exceeding life and imagination. As Borges said when Joyce's *Ulysses* was published, this text does not aspire to be a novel, but a cathedral."

Bogdan Suceavă, *Los Angeles Review of Books*

"Visionary, surreal, convoluted, far-reaching (perhaps overreaching), Cărtărescu's first volume concludes with a spiritual call-to-arms, in which creativity and fertility are one and the same. This vision imparts beauty to this destiny, but there are also intimations throughout of power misused, of violence, of beings struggling for connection in the face of obstacles."

The Quarterly Conversation

MIRCEA CĂRTĂRESCU

Solenoid

TRANSLATED BY SEAN COTTER

DEEP VELLUM PUBLISHING
DALLAS, TEXAS

Deep Vellum Publishing
3000 Commerce St., Dallas, Texas 75226
deepvellum.org · @deepvellum

Deep Vellum is a 501c3 nonprofit literary arts organization
founded in 2013 with the mission to bring
the world into conversation through literature.

Originally published as *Solenoid* by Editura Humanitas in Bucharest, Romania, in 2015.

First US Edition, 2022
THIRD PRINTING

Support for this publication has been provided in part by grants from the National Endowment for the Arts and the Romanian Cultural Institute's Translation and Publication Support program.

LIBRARY OF CONGRESS CATALOGING-IN-PUBLICATION DATA
Names: Cărtărescu, Mircea, author. | Cotter, Sean, 1971– translator.
Title: Solenoid / Mircea Cărtărescu ; translated by Sean Cotter.
Other titles: Solenoid. English
Description: First US edition. | Dallas, Texas : Deep Vellum Publishing, 2022.
Identifiers: LCCN 2022004772 | ISBN 9781646052028 (trade paperback) | ISBN 9781646052035 (ebook)
Subjects: LCGFT: Novels.
Classification: LCC PC840.13.A86 S6713 2022 | DDC 859/.334--dc23/eng/20220204
LC record available at https://lccn.loc.gov/2022004772

ISBN (TPB) 978-1-64605-202-8 | ISBN (Ebook) 978-1-64605-203-5

Cover design by Anna Jordan

Interior layout and typesetting by KGT

PRINTED IN CANADA

A man of blood takes clay from the peak
And creates his own ghost
From dreams, scents, and shadows
And brings it living down to us.

But his sacrifice is pointless,
However charming the book's speech.
Beloved book and useless,
You will answer no question.

Tudor Arghezi, "Ex Libris"

A fragment of his eye socket was removed. The sun and everyone could see inside. It angered him and distracted him from his work; he was furious that he in particular could not see this marvel.

Franz Kafka, *Diaries*

PART ONE

1

I HAVE LICE, AGAIN. IT DOESN'T SURPRISE ME anymore, doesn't disgust me. It just itches. I find nits constantly, I pull them off in the bathroom when I comb my hair: little ivory eggs, glistening darkly against the porcelain around the faucet. The comb collects bunches of them, I scrub it with the worn-out bristles of an old toothbrush. I can't avoid lice—I teach at a school on the edge of town. Half the kids there have lice, the nurse finds the bugs at the start of the year, during her checkup, when she goes through the kids' hair with the expert motions of a chimpanzee—except she doesn't crush the lice between her teeth, stained with the chitin of previously captured insects. Instead, she recommends the parents apply a cloudy liquid that smells like lye, the same one the teachers use. Within a few days, the entire school stinks of anti-lice solution.

It's not that bad, at least we don't have bedbugs, I haven't seen those in a while. I remember them, I saw them with my own eyes when I was about three, in the little house on Floreasca where we lived around 1959–60. My father would hoist up the mattress to show them to me. They were tiny black seeds, hard, and as shiny as blackberries, or those ivy berries I knew I shouldn't put in my mouth. When the seeds between the mattress and the bedframe scattered into the dark corners, they looked so panicked that it made me laugh. I could hardly wait for my dad to lift the heavy mattress up (as he did when he changed the sheets), so I could see the chubby little bugs. I would laugh with such delight that my mother, who kept my curly hair long, would scoop me up and spit on me, so I wouldn't catch the evil eye. Dad would get out the pump and give them a foul-smelling lindane bath, slaughtering them where they hid in the wooden joints. I liked the smell of the wood bed, the pine that still reeked of sap, I even liked the smell of lindane. Then my father would drop the mattress back in place, and my mother would bring the sheets. When she spread them over the bed, they puffed up like a huge donut, and I loved to throw myself on top. Then I would wait for the sheet to slowly settle over me, to mold itself around my little body, but not all of the sheet, it also fell in a complicated series of folds and pleats. The rooms in that house seemed as big as market halls to me, with two enormous people wandering around, who for some reason took care of me: my mother and father.

But I don't remember the bites. My mother said they made little red circles on your skin, with a white dot in the middle. And that they burned more than itched. That may be, all I know is that I get lice from the kids when I lean over their notebooks; it's an occupational hazard. I have worn my hair long ever since my attempt to become a writer. That's all that's left of that career, just the hair. And the turtlenecks, like those worn by the first writer I ever saw, the one who is still my glorious and unattainable image of a Writer: the one from *Breakfast at Tiffany's*. My hair always hangs down onto the girls' downy, lice-filled hair. Along these semitransparent cables of horn, the insects climb. Their claws have the same curvature as the strands of hair, and they attach to it perfectly. Then they crawl onto the scalp, dropping excrement and eggs. They bite the skin that has never seen the sun, immaculate and parchment-white: this is their food. When the itching becomes unbearable, I turn on the hot water and prepare to exterminate them.

I like how the water resounds in the bathtub, that chaotic churning, that spiral of billions of twisting jets and streams, the roaring vertical fountain inside the green gelatin of infinitesimally rising water conquering the sides of the tub with checked swells and sudden invasions, as though countless transparent ants were swarming in the Amazon jungle. I turn off the faucet and there is quiet, the ants melt into each other, and the soft, jelly sapphire lies silent, it looks at me like a limpid eye and waits. Naked, I slide into the water. I put my head under right away, feeling the walls of water rise symmetrically over my cheeks and forehead. The water grasps me, it presses its weight all around me, it makes me float in its midst. I am the seeds of a fruit with green-blue flesh. My hair spreads toward the sides of the bathtub, like a blackbird opening its wings. The strands repel each other, each one is independent, each one suddenly wet, floating among the others without touching, like the tentacles of a sea lily. I pull my head from one side to the other so I can feel them resist; they spread through the dense water, they become heavy, strangely heavy. It is hard to pull them from their water alveoli. The lice cling to the thick trunks, they become one with them. Their inhuman faces show a kind of bewilderment. Their carcasses are made of the same substance as the hair. They become wet in the hot water, but they do not dissolve. Their symmetrical respiratory tubes, along the edges of their undulating abdomens, are completely shut, like the closed nostrils of sea lions. I float in the bathtub passively, distended like an anatomical specimen, the skin on my fingertips bulges and wrinkles. I am soft, as though covered in transparent chitin. My hands, left to their own will, float on the surface. My sex rises vaguely, like a piece of cork. It seems strange that I have a body, that I am in a body.

I sit up and begin to soap my hair and skin. While my ears were underwater, I could clearly hear the conversations and thumps in the neighboring apartments, but as though in a dream. My ears still feel plugged with gelatin. I pass my soapy hands over myself. My body is not, for me, erotic. My fingers, it seems, move across not my body but my mind. My mind dressed in flesh, my flesh dressed in the cosmos.

As with the lice, I am not that surprised when my soapy fingers come to my navel. This has been happening for a few years. Of course I was scared when it started, because I had heard that sometimes your navel could burst. But I had never worried about mine, my navel was just a dent where my stomach "stuck to my spine," as my mother would say. At the bottom of this hollow there was something unpleasant to the touch, but that never worried me. My navel was no more than the indentation on top of an apple, where the stem comes out. We all grew like fruits from a petiole crossed with veins and arteries. But starting a few months ago, whenever I poked my finger in to clean this accident of my body, I felt something unusual, something that shouldn't have been there: a kind of protuberance scraping against my fingertip, something inorganic, not part of my body. It lay within the pale knot of flesh, like an eye between two lids. Now I looked more closely, under the water, pulling the edges of the crevasse apart with my fingers. I couldn't see well enough, so I got out of the tub, and the lens of water flowed slowly out of my navel. Good lord, I smiled at myself, here I am, contemplating my navel . . . Yes, there was the pale knot, sticking out a little more than usual, because as you approach thirty the stomach muscles start to sag. A scab the size of a child's fingernail, in one of the knot's volutes, turned out to be some dirt. But on the other side, a stiff and painful black-green stump stuck out, the thing my fingertip had felt. I couldn't imagine what it could be. I tried to catch it with my fingernail, but when I did, I felt a twinge that frightened me: it might be a wart that I should leave alone. I tried to forget about it, to leave it where it had grown. Over the course of our lives, we excrete plenty of moles, warts, dead bones, and other refuse, things we carry around patiently, not to mention how our hair, nails, and teeth fall out: pieces of ourselves stop belonging to us and take on another life, all their own. I have, thanks to my mother, an empty Tic-Tac box with all my baby teeth, and also thanks to her I have my braids from when I was three. Photographs on cracked enamel, with little serrations along the edges like a postage stamp, are similar testimonies: our body really was once in between the sun and the camera lens, and it left a shadow on the film no different than the one the moon, during an eclipse, leaves across the solar disk.

But one week later, again in the bath, my navel felt unusual and irritated again: the unidentified piece had grown a little longer, and it felt different, more disturbing than painful. When we have a toothache, we rub our tongue against our molars, even at the risk of hitting a livid pain. Anything unusual on the sensitive map of our bodies makes us unsettled, nervous: we'll do anything to escape a constant discomfort. Sometimes, at night, as I'm going to bed, I take off my socks and touch the thickening, hornlike, transparent-yellow flesh on the side of my big toe. I pinch at the growth, I pull it, and after about a half hour I have the edge up, and I keep pulling, with the smarting tips of my fingers, as I become more irritated and more worried, until I remove a thick, shiny layer, with fingerprint-like striations, a whole centimeter of dead skin, now hanging disgracefully from my finger. I can't pull off any more, since I have already reached the living flesh underneath, the part where I feel pain, but still I have to put a stop to the irritation, the unease. I take a pair of scissors and cut it in half, then I examine it for a long time: a white shell that I made, without knowing how, just as I don't remember how I made my own bones. I fold it between my fingers, I feel it, it smells vaguely like ammonia: the piece is organic, yet dead, dead even while it was a part of me, adding a few grams to my weight; it still makes me uneasy. I don't feel like throwing it out, I turn out the light and go to bed, still holding it between my fingers, only to forget everything the next day. Still, for a little while after that I limp slightly: the place I pulled it from hurts.

I tugged on the hard sliver coming out of my navel, until, unexpectedly, it was in my hand. A small cylinder, a half centimeter long and about as wide as a matchstick. It looked to have gotten darker over time, worn and sticky and tarnished with age. It was something ancient, mummified, saponified, who the hell knows. I put it under the faucet and washed away the layer of grime; I could see the thing had been a yellowish-green color, long ago, perhaps. I put it in an empty matchbox. It resembled, more than anything, the stub of a burnt match.

A few weeks later, my navel, again softened in hot water, yielded another fragment, twice as long this time, of the same hard substance. I realized that it was the flexible end of a piece of twine, I could even see its multitude of twisted fibers. It was string, ordinary string, the kind used for packages. The string with which, twenty-seven years earlier, they had tied my navel in the decrepit workers' maternity ward where I was born. Now my navel was aborting, slowly, a piece every two weeks, every month, then another after three more months. Today I'm removing the fifth piece, carefully, with a certain pleasure. I flatten it out, scrape it clean with my fingernail, wash it in the bathtub water. It is the longest piece so far, and I hope the last. I put it in the matchbox, alongside the others: they lie there politely, yellowish-greenish-black, their ends raveling. Hemp, the same material as homemade shopping bags, the kind that cut into your hands when filled with potatoes, the same material you use to tie packages. On Holy Mary's Day, my father's family in Banat would send me packages: poppy-seed and apple pastries. The brown-green string was my favorite part: I would tie the doorknobs together, so my mother wouldn't have another child. On each knob, I tied tens, hundreds of knots.

I stop worrying about the string from my navel and, as the water runs off my body, get out of the tub. I take the lice solution from behind the toilet and pour a little of the pungent substance over my head. I wonder what class gave me lice this time, as though it matters. Maybe it does, who knows. Maybe different streets in the neighborhood and different classes in school have distinct species of lice, different sizes.

I rinse the revolting solution off my head and comb my hair, hanging over the brilliantly clean porcelain of the sink. And the parasites begin to drop out, two, five, eight, fifteen . . . They are tiny, each one in its own drop of water. Squinting, I can see their bodies, with wide abdomens and three still-moving legs on each side. Their bodies and my body, wet and naked, leaning over the sink, are made of the same organic tissues. They have analogous organs and anatomical functions. They have eyes that see the same reality, they have legs that take them through the same unending and unintelligible world. They want to live, just as I do. I wash them off the sides of the sink with a stream of water. They travel through the pipes below, into the sewers underground.

With my hair still wet, I go to bed beside my meager set of treasures: the Tic-Tac box with my baby teeth, pictures from when I was little and my parents were in the prime of their life, the matchbox of fibers from my navel, my journal. As I often do in the evenings, I pour the teeth into my hand: smooth little stones, still bright white, that were once inside my mouth, that I once used to eat, to pronounce words, to bite like a puppy. Many times have I wondered what it would be like to have a paper bag with my vertebra from when I was two, or my finger bones from age seven . . .

I put the teeth away. I would like to look at some of the pictures, but I can't stay up any later. I open the drawer in the nightstand and put everything inside, in the yellowed "snakeskin" box that used to house a razor, a shaving brush, and a box of Astor razor blades. Now I use it for my lowly treasures. I pull the blanket over my head and try to fall asleep as fast as I can, perhaps forever. My scalp doesn't itch anymore. And, since it's happened so recently, I hope it won't happen again tonight.

2

I meant my dreams, the visitors, all that insanity, but this is not the time to talk about it. For now, let me turn again to the school where I've worked more than three years already. "I won't be a teacher all my life," I told myself, I remember like it was yesterday, when I was taking the tram home, late one summer night under rosebud clouds, from the end of Şoseaua Colentina, where I had been to see the school for the first time. But no miracle has happened; I very likely will be a teacher all my life. In the end, it hasn't been all that bad. The afternoon I visited the school, just after I received my assignment, I was twenty-four in years and maybe twice as many kilograms in weight. I was incredibly, impossibly thin. My mustache and long hair, slightly red at that time, did nothing but infantilize my appearance, such that, if I glanced at myself in a shop or tram window, I would think I was looking at a high school student.

It was a summer afternoon, the city was brimming with light, like a glass whose water arches above its lip. I took the tram from Tunari, in front of the Directorate General of the Militia. I passed my parents' apartment building on Ştefan cel Mare, where I lived too, and as usual I searched the endless facade for my window, lined with blue paper to keep out the sun, then I passed the wire fence of Colentina Hospital. The hospital wings were lined up over the vast grounds like brickwork battleships. Each one had a different shape, as though the tenants' various diseases had determined their building's bizarre architecture. Or perhaps each wing's architect had been chosen for his disease, and he had attempted to create an allegory of his suffering. I knew each one and had stayed in at least two of them. At the right end of the grounds, I shuddered at the sight of a pink building with paper-thin walls, the neurology wing. I had stayed there for a month, eight years earlier, for a facial paralysis that still bothered me from time to time. Many are the nights in which I wander in my dreams through the wings of Colentina Hospital, I enter unknown, hostile buildings, their walls covered with anatomical diagrams . . .

Next, the tram passes along the former ITB workshops, where my father worked for a while as a locksmith. Some apartment blocks have gone up in front of them, you can barely see the workshops from the street. The ground floor of one block was once a clinic, right at the Doctor Grozovici stop. For a time, I went there for my injections, vitamin B1 and B6, following my facial paralysis at age sixteen. My parents would put the vials in my hand and tell me not to come back with them unopened. They knew me too well. At first, I would drop them down the elevator shaft and tell my parents I had done them, but this didn't work for long. In the end, I had to get it done for real. I would set off for the clinic, at dusk, my heart full of dread. I walked the two tram stops as slowly as I could. Like when I had to go to the dentist, I would hope that some miracle would happen and I would find the office was closed, the building demolished, the doctor deceased, or that there was a blackout and the drill couldn't run or the lights above the chair would go out. No miracle ever happened, however. The pain waited for me, all of it, with its blood-colored aura. The first nurse at Grozovici who, late one night, gave me the injection was pretty, blonde, very neat, but I soon became terrified of her. She was the type who treated your bare bottom with complete disdain. Not the thought of the pain that was to come, but this woman's disdain for the kid with whom she was about to have an intimate relationship (albeit just sticking a needle in his butt cheek) quickly eliminated the vaguest excitement, and my sex gave up its efforts to lift its head and take a look. I waited next for the inevitable wetness on the soon-to-be martyred flesh, the three or four smacks of the back of her hand, then the shock of the needle stuck into flesh, its tip always sure to hit a nerve, a vein, to hurt you somehow, a lasting, memorable pain, then increased by the poison that traveled down the channel of the needle to spread, like sulfuric acid, throughout your hip. It was horrible. The blonde nurse's injections would make me limp for a week.

Luckily, this nurse, who was probably into S&M in bed, traded off with another nurse at the clinic, this one just as difficult to forget, though for different reasons. She scared you to death when you first saw her because she had no nose. But she did not wear a bandage or a prosthetic, she simply had, in the middle of her face, a large orifice vaguely partitioned into two compartments. She was as small as a gosling, brown-haired, with eyes whose tenderness might have seemed attractive if the skull-like appearance of her face did not overwhelm you. When I came on the blonde nurse's night, I was seen right away. The wind whistled through the waiting room. But the noseless little person seemed unusually popular: the waiting room was always full of people, as full as a church on Easter. I wouldn't get home from the clinic until two in the morning. Many of the patients brought her flowers. When she appeared in the doorway, everyone smiled happily. I could understand why: no one, probably, had ever had a lighter touch. When my turn came and I sat with my pants down on the rubber of her examination table, I would become dizzy from the smell of flowers, a row of seven or eight bouquets, still in cellophane, along the wall. That extraordinary brunette woman spoke calmly and measuredly, then touched my hip for a moment and . . . that was about it. I didn't feel the needle, and the serum diffused through my muscle with nothing but a gentle warmth. Everything happened in a few minutes, and I went home happy and full of energy. My parents looked at me suspiciously: maybe I had thrown out the vial again?

Next came the Melodia movie theater, just before Lizeanu, and I got off at the next stop, Obor, where I transferred to a tram going perpendicular to Ştefan cel Mare, from Moşilor toward the depths of Colentina.

I knew these places well, it was, in a way, my neighborhood. My mother used to shop at Obor. She would take me with her, when I was little, into the sea of people filling the old market. The fish hall that stank until you couldn't take it anymore, then the great hall, with bas-reliefs and mosaics showing unintelligible scenes, and finally the ice plant, where the workers handled blocks of ice that were white in the middle and miraculously transparent on the sides (as though constantly dissolving into the surrounding air)—to my child's eyes these were fantastical citadels of another world. There at Obor, one desolate Monday morning, I saw a poster that stayed with me for a long time: a giant squid in a flying saucer reached out its arms toward an astronaut walking a red, rocky terrain. Above, the words *Planet of Storms*. "It's a movie," my mother said to me. "Let's wait for it to come somewhere closer, to the Volga or the Floreasca." My mother was afraid of the center of town, she didn't leave her neighborhood unless she had no choice, for example when she had to go to Lipscani to buy my school uniform, with the checkered shirt and pants already sagging in the knees, as though someone had been wearing them at the factory.

Even Colentina looked familiar to me, with its run-down houses on the left and the Stela soap factory on the right, the place where they made Cheia and Cămila laundry detergents. The smell of rancid fat spread from here over the entire neighborhood. Next came the brick building of the Donca Simo textile factory, where my mother once worked at the loom, then came some lumberyards. The wretched and desolate street drove toward the horizon, in the torrid summer, under those enormous, white skies you only see above

Bucharest. As it happened, I had been born in Colentina, on the edge of town, in a decrepit maternity ward thrown together in an old building that had been half gambling house, half bordello in the years before 1944, and I had lived my first years somewhere on Doamna Ghica, in a tangle of alleyways worthy of a Jewish ghetto. Much later, I went back to Silistra with a camera, and I took a few pictures of my childhood home, but they didn't turn out. Now Silistra isn't even there, it was bulldozed, my house and everything else wiped off the face of the earth. What took its place? Apartment blocks, of course, like everywhere else.

Once tram 21 passed over Doamna Ghica, I entered a foreign country. There were fewer houses, more dirty ponds where women with pleated skirts washed their rugs. Seltzer shops and bread shops, wine stores, fish stores. An endless, desolate street, seventeen tram stops, most without wind shelters or any reason to be there, like the whistle stops trains make in the middle of a field. Women in print dresses, a daughter on each arm, walking nowhere. A cart full of empty bottles. Propane tank centers where people lined up in the evening for the store to open the next day. Perpendicular streets, dusty, like a village, lined with mulberries. Kites caught in the electric lines, strung between wooden poles treated with gasoline.

I reached the end of the line after an hour and a half of rocking in the tram. For the last three or four stops I may have been the only one in the car. I exited into a large circle of track, where the trams turned around to go again, like Sisyphus, toward Colentina. The day was tilting toward night, the air was amber-colored and, on account of the silence, ghostly. Here, at the end of line 21, there was not a soul in sight. Industrial halls, long and gray, with narrow windows, a water tower in the distance, and in the middle of the tram turnabout, a grove of trees literally black from the heating oil and exhaust fumes. Two empty trams stood one beside the other, without drivers. A closed ticket booth. Marked contrasts between the rosy light and the shadows. What was I doing there? How was I going to live in such a remote place? I walked toward the water tower, I came to its base to find a padlocked door, I tilted my head back to look toward its sphere glittering in the sky, at the end of a white, plastered cylinder. I walked farther toward . . . nothing, toward the emptiness . . . This wasn't, it seemed to me, where the city ended, but where reality ended.

A street sign to the left had the name I was looking for: Dimitrie Herescu. Somewhere on this street should be the school, my school, my first job, where I should appear on the first of September, more than two months from that moment. The green and pink building of an auto mechanic did nothing to destroy the rural atmosphere of the place: houses with tile roofs, yards with rotting fences, tied-up dogs, tacky flowerpots. The school was on the right, a few houses down from the mechanic, and it was, of course, empty.

It was a small school, an L-shaped hybrid, with an old central section, plaster cracking, broken windows, and at the other end of a small courtyard, a new section, even more desolate. In the yard, a basketball hoop without a net. I opened the gate and entered. I took a few steps on the courtyard pavement. The sun had just begun to go down, a halo of rays settling on the roof of the old building. From there, it sprayed out sadly and, in a way, darkly, since rather than illuminate anything it increased the inhuman loneliness of the place. My heart grew worried. I was going to enter this school that looked as stiff as a morgue, I was going to walk, the register under my arm, down its dark green halls, I was going to go upstairs and enter an unknown classroom where thirty strange kids, stranger than another species, were waiting for me. Maybe they were waiting for me even at that moment, sitting silently on their benches, with wooden pencil boxes, their notebooks with blue paper covers. At the thought of this, the hair on my arms stood up and I practically ran into the street. "I won't be a teacher all my life," I told myself as the tram took me back into the known world, as the stations passed behind me, the houses became more frequent, and people repopulated the earth. "A year at most, until some literary magazine asks me to be an editor." And in the first three years I taught at School 86, I truly did nothing but feed on this illusion, just as some mothers breastfeed their children long after they should have been weaned. My illusion had grown as large as myself, and still I couldn't—and in a way I can't even today—resist opening my shirt, at least now and then, and letting it voluptuously cannibalize me. The first years passed. After another forty, I'll retire from this same school. In the end, it hasn't been that bad. There were long stretches when I didn't have lice. No, if I stop to think about it, it hasn't been bad at this school, such as it is, and maybe even a little bit good.

3

Sometimes I lose control of my hands, from the elbows down. It doesn't scare me, I might even say I like it. It happens unexpectedly, and luckily, only when I'm alone. I'll be writing something, correcting papers, drinking a coffee, or cutting my nails with a Chinese nail trimmer and suddenly my hands feel very light, as though they were filled with volatile gas. They rise on their own, pulling my shoulders up, levitating happily through the dense, glittering, dark air of my room. I smile, I look at them as though for the first time: long, delicate, thin-boned, some black hair on the fingers. Before my enchanted eyes, they begin to make elegant and bizarre gestures of their own accord, to tell stories that perhaps the deaf can understand. My fingers move precisely and unmistakably, making a series of unintelligible signs: the right hand asks, the left responds, the ring finger and thumb close in a circle, the little fingers page through some text, the wrists pivot with the supple energy of an orchestra conductor. I should be scared out of my mind, because someone else, within my own mind, directs these movements, skilled motions desperate to be deciphered, and yet I am seldom ever so happy. I watch my hands like a child at a puppet show who doesn't understand what is happening on the minuscule stage but is fascinated by the agitation of wooden beings in crepe dresses with yarn for hair. The autonomous animation of my hands (thank God, it never happens when I'm in class or on the street) quiets down after a few minutes, the motions slow, they begin to resemble the mudras of Indian dancers, then they stop, and for two or three minutes more I can enjoy the charming sensation that my hands are lighter than air, as though my father had used the gas line to inflate not balloons but two thin rubber gloves, and put them in place of my hands. And how can I not be disappointed when my real hands—crude, heavy, organic, chafed, with their striated muscles, the white hyaline of the tendons, and their veins throbbing with blood—reenter their nail-tipped skin gloves, and suddenly, to my amazement, I can make my fingers move as I want, as though I could, through concentration alone, break a twig from the ficus in the window or pull my coffee cup toward me without touching it.

Only later does the fear come, only after this fantasy (that happens about once every two or three months) becomes a kind of memory do I begin to wonder if somehow, among all the anomalies of my life—because this is my topic—the fantastical independence of my hands is further proof that . . . everything is a dream, that my entire life is oneiric, or something sadder, graver, weirder, yet truer than any story that could ever be invented. The cheery-frightful ballet of my hands, always and only here, in my boat-shaped house on Maica Domnului, is the smallest, least meaningful (and in the end the most benign) reason for me to write these pages, meant only for me, in the incredible solitude of my life. If I had wanted to write literature, I would have started ten years ago. I mean, if I had really wanted to, without the effort of consciousness, the way you want your leg to take a step and it does. You don't have to say, "I order you to step," you don't have to think through the complicated process by which your will becomes deed. You just have to believe, to have belief as small as a mustard seed. If you are a writer, you write. Your books come without your knowing how to make them come, they come according to your gift, just as your mother is made to give birth, and she really does give birth to the child who grew in her uterus, without her mind participating in the complicated origami of her flesh. If I had been a writer, I would have written fiction, I would have had ten, fifteen novels by now without making any more effort than I make to secrete insulin or to send nourishment, day by day, from one orifice of my digestive system to another. I, however, at that moment long ago when my life still could have chosen one of an undefined multitude of directions, ordered my mind to produce fiction and nothing happened, just as futilely as if I had stared at my finger and shouted, "Move!"

When I was a teenager, I wanted to write literature. Even now I don't know what happened—if I lost my way somehow or if it was just bad luck. I wrote poems in high school, I have them in a notebook somewhere, and I wrote some of my dreams as prose, in a large school notebook with a thick cover, full of stories. Now is not the moment for me to write about that. I took part in the school competitions for Romanian, on rainy Sundays in unknown schools. I was an unreal young man, almost schizophrenic, who, during the breaks between classes, would go into the schoolyard to the long-jump pit, sit on the edge, and read my poems out loud from ragged notebooks. People looked right through me, they didn't listen when I talked, I was a decoration to them, not even a good one, on an enormous and chaotic world. Since I wanted to be a writer, I decided to sit for university entrance exams in Letters. I got into the major without any problem, in the summer of 1975. At that time, my solitude was all-encompassing. I lived with my parents on Ştefan cel Mare. I would read for eight hours a day, rolling from one side of the bed to the other, under a sweaty sheet. The book pages would adopt the ever-changing color of the Bucharest skies, from the gold of summer dawns to the dark, heavy pink of snowy evenings in deep winter. Dark would come and I wouldn't even notice. My mother would find me reading in a room sunk deep into darkness, where the paper and print were nearly the same color and I wasn't reading anymore, I was dreaming farther into the story, deforming it according to the laws of dream. Then I would shake it off, stretch, get out of bed—the whole day I had only gotten up to go to the bathroom—and, invariably, I would go to the large window in my room, where I could see, poured out under clouds of fantasy, all of Bucharest. Thousands of lights were lit in the far-off houses, in those nearby I could see people moving like lazy fish in an aquarium, much farther away the colored neon signs turned on and off. But what fascinated me was the giant sky above, the cupola higher and more overwhelming than any cathedral. Not even the clouds could rise to its apex. I pressed my forehead against the cold, yielding window, and I stood like that, a teenager in pajamas with holes in the armpits, until my mother called me to eat. I would come back to the vision of my solitude, deep under the earth, to read farther, with the light on and with another, identical room, extended into the mirror of the window, until I was overwhelmed with exhaustion.

During the day, I would go for walks in the endless summer. First, I would look for two or three different friends, who were never home. Then I would go down unknown streets, I would find myself in neighborhoods I didn't even know existed, I would wander among strange houses that looked like bunkers from another planet. Old, pink houses, merchant-style, their facades loaded with stucco cupids, chipped all over. There was never anyone on these streets, beneath the arches of old plane trees. I would go into the old houses, wander through their kitsch-filled rooms, climb bizarre exterior stairways to the second floor, discover vast, empty rooms where my footsteps sounded indecently loud. I went down into basements with electric lights and opened doors of rotten wood to find hallways that smelled of earth, with thin gas lines along the walls. On the pipes, affixed to the wall with sloppy foam, beetle pupae pulsed slowly, a sign that their wings were forming under their husks. I would pass into the basements of other houses, climb other stairs, enter other barren rooms. I would sometimes end up in houses familiar to me, rooms where I had once lived, beds where I had slept. Like a child stolen by nomads and found many years later, I would go directly to the dresser, where I would find a silver fifteen-lei coin (placed in my cradle after my first bath, now so tarnished you couldn't see the king's face), the bag with the lock of hair cut at age one (the same age when I was presented a tray of objects for me to choose my destiny, and I chose, so they tell me, a pencil), or my poor little baby teeth, a complete set, which I've already written about. Still wandering, every day in the summer of '75, down the streets and into the houses of that torrid city, which I came to know so well, to know its secrets and turpitudes, its glory and the purity of its soul. Bucharest, as I understood it at the age of nineteen, when I had already read everything, was not like other cities that developed over time, exchanging its huts and warehouses for condominium towers, replacing horse-drawn trams with electric ones. It had appeared all at once, already ruined, shattered, with its facades fallen and its gargoyles' noses chipped, with electric wires hung over the streets in melancholic fixtures, with an imaginatively varied industrial architecture. From the very beginning, the project was to be a more human, a more moving city than, for example, a concrete and glass Brasília. The genius architect planned the narrow streets, the uneven sewers, the houses slouched to one side, overrun with weeds, houses with their fronts fallen in, unusable schools, bent and ghostly stores seven stories tall. And, more than anything, Bucharest was planned as a great open-air museum, a museum of melancholy and the ruin of all things.

This was the city I saw from my window on Ştefan cel Mare, and the one, if I had become a writer, I would have described endlessly, page after page and book after book, empty of people but full of myself, like a network of arcades in the epidermis of some god, inhabited by a sole, microscopic mite, a transparent creature with strands of hair at the end of its hideous, stumpy legs.

That fall I did my military service, and those nine months knocked the poetry or any hazy literary dream out of my head. I know how to disassemble and reassemble the modernized Kalashnikov. I know how to fume the scope with a burning toothbrush so it won't glint in the sun at the firing range. I loaded, one after another, twenty cartridges into a clip in winter, negative twenty degrees Celsius, before standing guard at a far-off corner of a military compound, in the wind and wilderness, from three in the afternoon until six in the morning. I pulled myself a kilometer through the mud, with a gas mask on my face and a thirty-kilo pack on my back. I inhaled and exhaled mosquitoes, five or six per cubic centimeter of bunk room air. I cleaned toilets and polished tiles with a toothbrush. I broke my teeth on army crackers and ate potatoes, peels and all, from a mess kit. I painted every apple tree on the compound. I beat up another guy over a can of tuna. A third was ready to stick his bayonet in me. I did not read a book, not a word in fact, for nine months. I did not write or receive any letters. Only my mother visited me, every two weeks, to bring some food. The army did not make me a man, but it did increase my introversion and aloneness. Looking back, I wonder how I survived.

The first thing I did the next summer, when I was "liberated," was to fill a tub with hot water as blue as a gemstone. I let the water fill over the overflow, up to the lip of the porcelain tub, to arch in tension gently above the rim. Naked, I climbed in, while the water flowed onto the bathroom floor. I didn't care, I had to get the grime of those nine military months off of me, the only dead time, like a dead bone, of my life. I sank completely into the holy substance, I held my nostrils shut and let my head go far underwater, until the top of my head touched the bottom of the tub. I lay there, at the bottom of the tub, a thin adolescent with his ribs pathetically visible through his skin, with his eyes wide open, looking at the way, many kilometers above, light played over the surface of the water. I stayed there hour after hour, without needing to breathe, until whatever was on me detached, pinching off in pleats—a darkened skin. I still have it, hanging in the wardrobe. It looks like a sheet of thin rubber, dimpled by the shape of my face, the nipples of my chest, my water-wrinkled sex, even the prints from my thumbs. It is a skin of ash, agglutinated, hardened ash, gray as Plasticine when you mix all the colors together, the ash of those nine months in the army that nearly did me in.

4

The summer after my army service, the one I dreamed of while I was curled up in a trench under nighttime barrages, my future paradise of endless freedom, civilian life with its mystic-sexual aura, but which proved to be just as lonely and barren as the previous summer—no one calling on the phone, no one home, no one to talk to, days on end (aside from my ghostly parents)—I wrote my first real poem, what would remain the only literary fruit of mine to ever mature. At the time, I would learn the meaning of those lines from Hölderlin, "O fates, permit me just one summer / and an autumn to ripen my fruit . . ." I also felt like the gods for those few months in 1976 when I was writing *The Fall*, but afterward my life—which should have turned toward literature with the naturalness of opening a door and, once in the forbidden room, finally discovering your deepest, truest self—took a different path, suddenly, almost grotesquely, the way you throw a railway switch. Instead of Hölderlin I became Scardanelli, locked for thirty years in his tower, raised high above the seasons.

The Fall was not a poem, but The Poem. It was "that unique object through which nothingness is honored." It was the result of the ten years of reading literature. For the past decade, I had forgotten to breathe, cough, vomit, sneeze, ejaculate, see, hear, love, laugh, produce white blood cells, protect myself with antibodies, I had forgotten my hair had to grow and my tongue, with its papilla, had to taste food. I had forgotten to think about my fate on Earth and about finding a wife. Lying in bed like an Etruscan statue over a sarcophagus, my sweat staining my sheets yellow, I had read until I was almost blind and almost schizophrenic. My mind had no room left for blue skies mirrored in the springtime pond, nor for the delicate melancholy of snowflakes sticking to a building plastered in calcio-vecchio. Whenever I opened my mouth, I spoke in quotes from my favorite authors. When I lifted my eyes from the page, in the room steeped in the rosy brown of dusk on Ştefan cel Mare, I saw the walls clearly tattooed with letters: they were poems, on the ceiling, on the mirror, on the leaves of the translucent geraniums vegetating in their pots. I had lines written on my fingers and on the heel of my hand, poems inked on my pajamas and sheets. Frightened, I went to the bathroom mirror, where I could see myself completely: I had poems written with a needle on the whites of my eyes and poems scrawled over my forehead. My skin was tattooed in minuscule letters, maniacal, with a legible handwriting. I was blue from head to toe, I stank of ink the way others stink of tobacco. *The Fall* would be the sponge that sucked up all the ink from the lonely nautilus I was.

My poem had seven parts, representing the seven stages of life, seven colors, seven metals, seven planets, seven chakras, seven steps in falling from paradise to hell. It was supposed to be a colossal, astonishing waterfall from the eschatological to the scatological, a metaphysical gradation on which we set demons and saints, labia and astrolabes, stars and frogs, geometry and cacophony, with the impersonal rigor of the biologist who delineates the trunk and branches of the animal kingdom. It was also an enormous collage, since my mind was just a jigsaw puzzle of citations, it was a summum of all that could be known, an amalgam of the church fathers and quantum physics, genetics, and topology. It was, in the end, the only poem that would make the universe good for nothing, that would banish it to the museum, like the electric locomotive did to the steam engine. Reality, the elements, galaxies would no longer be needed. *The Fall* existed, within which Everything flickered and crackled with an eternal flame.

The poem was thirty handwritten pages, the way I wrote everything back then, obviously, since my long-standing dream of a typewriter was impossible to realize, and I reread the poem every day, I learned it by heart, or better said I caressed it, I checked in on it, I cleared the dust off of it every day as though it were a strange machine from another world, a machine that came, who knows how, through the mirror, into our own. I still have it, on the pieces of paper where I created it without erasing a letter, that summer when I turned twenty. It looks like an old piece of scripture, kept under a bell jar in a great museum, in controlled temperature and humidity. It too is an artifact; I have surrounded myself with them until I feel like a god with a thousand arms in the middle of a mandala: my baby teeth, the threads from my navel, my pale pigtails, the black-and-white photos of my childhood. My eyes as a child, my ribs as an adolescent, my women from much later. The sad insanity of my life.

That fall, a luminous fall like no other I can remember, I went to the university for the first time. When bus 88 crossed Zoia Kosmodemianskaia toward Batiştei, I was bubbling with happiness like champagne: I was a college student, something I had never dared to dream, a student of Letters! From now on, I would see the center of Bucharest every day, what seemed to me at the time the most beautiful city in the world. I would live in the splendor of the city that unfurled, like a peacock, its Intercontinental Hotel and National Theater, its university and Ion Mincu Institute of Architecture, its Cantacuzino Hospital and four ministering statues behind it, with hypnotic eyes of churning waters. Gossamer cobwebs drifted through the air, young women rushed toward their studies, the world was new and warm, just out of the oven, and it was all for me! The building that housed the Department of Letters had inhuman proportions: the marble hall looked like a barren, cold basilica. Below, in the chessboard of the floor, the white tiles were more worn than the black ones. Thousands of footsteps had dug into the agate-soft surface. The library was a ship's belly loaded with books. But I had already read all of them, every one; in fact I had already read every letter ever written. Still, the height of the library took me by surprise: twenty floors lined with numbered oak cases, connected by ladders, where the librarians climbed up and down, their arms full of books. The head clerk, a bearded, antipathetic young man, sat at all hours like a robot behind a raised desk at the front of the room, receiving and sorting book requests from the line of waiting students. Along the walls, as though in another castle, heaps of books awaited sorting, constantly tipping over, startling everyone at their tables.

Because it will become important later in this text (which is not, thank God, a book, illegible or otherwise), I want to record a detail here: the first time I walked into the library—a place I never stayed for long, since I never read at a table but in my bed (that piece of furniture which, aside from the book itself, is the essential part of my reading tool kit)—a thought came into my mind and never left. In the center of the reading room there was a massive card catalog, from the last century, full of drawers labeled in an antiquated hand. I knelt before one of them, since the letter V was at the very bottom, in the first row up from the floor, I pulled the drawer out to reveal, like a whale's baleen, hundreds of yellowed, typewritten cards showing the name, author, and other information about the ever more numerous and ever more useless books written in this world. Toward the back of the drawer, I found the name I wanted: Voynich. I had never known exactly how it was spelled, but I'd found it here.

This name had been stuck in my head ever since the seventh grade, when I cried while reading a book. My mother heard me and came running into my room, in her fuzzy bathrobe, smelling like soup. She tried to calm me down, to hold me, thinking that my stomach hurt or I had a toothache. It took her a long time to understand I was crying because of the tattered book lying on the rug, missing its cover and first fifty pages. Many of our books looked like that: the one about Thomas Alva Edison, the one about the Polynesians, and Fr*om the North Pole to the South*. The only complete (and unread) books were *Battle en Route* by Galina Nikolaeva and *How the Steel Was Tempered* by N. Ostrovsky. In between my inconsolable sobs, I told my mother something about a revolutionary, a monsignor, a girl, a story so tangled that I didn't really understand it (especially since I had started it halfway in), but which had made a strong impression. I didn't know what the book was called, and at that time I didn't care about authors. When my father came home that evening, leaving his briefcase on the table as usual (I always took his *Sport* and *The Spark* newspapers to read the sports pages), he found me with red eyes, still thinking of the scene in which the young revolutionary finds out his father was the very monsignor he despised! "What book is this, dear?" my mother asked him at dinner, and my father, wearing just his underwear, as he usually did around the house, said, with his mouth full, something that sounded like "boyish," to which he added, *The Gadfly*. Yes, the young man was known in Italy as the Gadfly, but I didn't know what that word meant. "One of those big gray flies, with big eyes," my mother explained. I had never forgotten that night, when I cried for four hours straight while reading a book, but I had never had the chance to learn more about it or its author. The first surprise was that the author was a woman, Ethel Lilian Voynich, as I read her full name on the card, alongside the year that *The Gadfly* was published: 1909. I felt I'd achieved a small victory, I had cleared up a mystery almost ten years old, but, in fact, my frustration would only increase. I didn't know at the time that the name I looked up in the catalog—my earlier tears turned out to be a kind of odd premonition—would connect two of the most important areas of my searching, since the displeasure of not becoming a writer had, paradoxically, released me (and I hope that this will not be yet another illusion) to follow the path toward my life's true meaning . I never wrote fiction, but this released me to find my true calling: to search in reality, in the reality of lucidity, of dreams, of memories, of hallucinations, and of anything else. Although it rose from fear and terror, my search still satisfies me completely, like those disrespected and rejected arts of the flea circus and prestidigitation.

I threw myself into my new life like a crazy person. I studied old literature with inept professors, reading monks and nuns who wrote three lines each in Old Slavonic, based on foreign models, since we had to explain the gap in the history of a culture that had come to life somewhat late. But what did I care? I was a student of Letters, as I had barely dared to dream. My first paper, on psalm versification, was almost one hundred pages long. It was monstrous, containing all possible references, from Clément Marot to Kochanowski, the psalms of Verlaine and Tudor Arghezi. All my examples were translated by me, preserving the original verse forms . . .

How lonely and hopeless I was! I would leave the university at dusk, when the asphalt, wet from the day's rain, reflected the illuminated billboards along the street. Instead of taking the bus, I often walked home among the grand apartment buildings on Magheru from before the war, past the Scala bookstore and Patria movie theater, then as the evening turned as yellow as kerosene, I sank into the little streets full of stucco houses, as they turned dark blue then black as pitch, on Domnița Ruxandra and Ghiocei; I was amazed again and again that I could go into any house, into any of the old rooms, dimly illuminated by the stump of a candle, into the rooms upstairs with an Italian piano, with cold hallways with pots of dusty oleanders withering in the shadows. Mysterious from the outside, with their cohorts of stucco figurines, these ancient houses were even more mysterious on the inside. Empty and silent, without a speck of dust on their macramé-laden tables, they seemed to have been suddenly abandoned in a terrible panic, as if in escape from a devastating earthquake. The inhabitants had taken nothing with them, they had been happy to escape with their lives.

My parents were waiting for me at home, and that was it, my entire life. I left them by the TV and went into my room that faced Ştefan cel Mare. I curled up in bed and wished that I could die—I wished it so intensely that I could feel at least a few of my vertebrae agree. My bed turned into an archaeological site, where, in the impossible shape of a crushed being, lay the yellow and porous bones of a lost animal.

5

The Fall, the first and only map of my mind, fell the evening of October 24, 1977, at the Workshop of the Moon, which met at that time in the basement of the Department of Letters. I have never recovered from the trauma. I remember everything with the clarity of a magic lantern, just as a torture victim remembers how his fingernails and teeth were pulled out, when, many years later, he wakes up screaming and drenched in sweat. It was a catastrophe, but not in the sense of a building collapsing or a car accident, in the sense of a coin flipped toward the ceiling and falling on the wrong side. Of one straw shorter than the others that decides your fate on the raft of the Medusa. With every move we make in our lives, we make a choice or we are blown by a breath of wind down one aisle or another. The line of our life only solidifies behind us, it becomes coherent as it fossilizes into the simplicity of destiny, while the lives that could have been, that could have diverged, moment by moment, from the life that triumphed, are dotted, ghostly lines: creodes, quantum differences, translucid and fascinating like stems vegetating in the greenhouse. If I blink, my life forks: I could have not blinked, and then I would have been far different from the one who did, like streets that radiate out from a narrow piața. In the end, I will be wrapped in a cocoon made of the transparent threads of millions of virtual lives, of billions of paths I could have taken, each infinitesimally changing the angle of approach. After an adventure lasting as long as my life, I will meet them again, the millions of other selves, the possible, the probable, the happenstance, and the necessary, all at the end of their stories; we will tell each other about our successes and failures, our adventures and boredoms, our glory and shame. None of us will be more valuable than any other, because each will carry a world just as concrete as the one I call "reality." All the endless worlds generated by the choices and accidents of my life are just as concrete and real as any other. The millions of my brothers I will talk to at the end, in the hyperspherical summation of all the stories generated by my ballet through time, are rich and poor, they die young or in deep old age (and some never die), they are geniuses or lost souls, clowns or entrepreneurs selling funeral banners. If nothing human is foreign to me, by definition, I will embrace, through my real-virtual brothers, all possibilities, and fulfill all the virtualities meshed in the joints of my body and mind. Some will be so different from me they will cross the barrier of sex, the imperatives of ethics, the Gestalt of the body, becoming sub- or superhumans or alternative-humans, others will only differ from me in unobservable details: a single molecule of ACTH that his striated body released while your striated body did not, a single extra K cell in your blood, an odd glint in his eye . . .

I don't know what I would have been like now, writing here in this cobweb-filled room in my boat-shaped house, in this semidarkness with only a yellow glow around the old windows, if my poem had been better received on October 24, 1977. Perhaps behind me I would have had a bookshelf (I'm ill just thinking about it) lined with my own books, with my name on the spine, with titles I cannot imagine. Over thirty years, volume after volume, these would have constituted a complete investigation of my interior world, since I can't imagine I would have ever written about anything else. Perhaps I would have become, as written in Scripture, a man clothed in soft raiment, before whom the multitudes will prostrate themselves. If we were to meet now, after seven years, the one whose *Fall* found success at the Workshop of the Moon, and I, whose *Fall*, although identical to his letter by letter, was reviled, it could only be at some meeting between teachers and a well-known author, during a Saturday training session at Iulia Hasdeu High, or at Caragiale. We would have waited for him patiently, a herd of instructors, bitter about their inadequate salaries, the tyranny of state inspections, the old textbooks with reading passages about children who are torn apart by vultures or blown up on a bridge, with the attributes and complements and divisions of sentences, while he would have peacefully sipped his coffee in the principal's office, made jokes and heard servile laughter, then they all would have proceeded, like a group of dignified statues, down the hallway lined with portraits of writers toward the auditorium, and the colleague on my right would have leaned toward the one in front of her and whispered in her ear: He looks so nice . . . Because for them, all writers are dead, and the deader they are, they better they sound. In fact, the writer on stage would have looked younger than me. He would have had that self-assurance that prestige and a body of work will give you; the chorus of literary world naysayers may dispute it, but it remains incontestable. He would have spoken simply, although his books spoke in complexities and subtleties. He would have allowed himself to be modest and warm toward this little world that he didn't know and couldn't know anything about. Afterward, he would have signed autographs (good Lord, signing autographs!), and I would have waited in a long line, holding his book, thinking it could have been my own. He would have asked my name, when I reached him, and he would have looked into my eyes just for a moment. He wouldn't have been surprised that our names were identical, everything would have been—or is now, as I am writing—like a trance, like a dream. He would have written my name, then something like, "with best wishes," he would have signed the same name, its shape deformed by the habit of hurried autographs. He would have moved on to the teacher from School 84, who gazed at him as happily as she would a fiancé. I would have gotten my coat and walked home in the wintry slush, with his book in my bag, along with a stack of seventh-grade homework. I would have read his book all at once, all night, because, whatever may be said, I love literature, I still love it, it's a vice I can't put down, a vice that will destroy me.

That evening at the workshop, I was wearing a dirty-yellow mohair sweater with a thick collar that my mother had knitted. Both my white turtleneck and my sweater were meant to seem bookish: I knew what a writer looked like. A few years earlier I had seen *Breakfast at Tiffany's*, and the author in that film wore a turtleneck, a little frayed around the neck. All he did all day was hammer at the typewriter in this kind of uniform, and, as a result, beautiful girls came in through the window, via the fire escape. I couldn't imagine what creatures would appear in my panoramic window on the fifth floor, where I would see the Balkan expanse of the city, its old walls, its facades, its baroque pediments drowning in vegetation. I was twenty-one, I was as skinny as a shadow, with a bowl cut and a precarious red mustache with a bare patch on the left. My dark face, with rings under my eyes, with all my life gathered in my eyes, looked like a charcoal sketch. But I had written *The Fall*, the insane spiral, broad as a maelstrom in the first cantos, then more and more frenetic, more hysterical, as the divine transformed into the obscene, geometry into chaos, angels into demons worthy of a medieval bestiary. I walked into the shabby classroom, an ordinary classroom with tables and benches, with brown paneling, along with ten or fifteen other college students. There, between dark walls hung with mold-stained portraits of linguists, the rest of my life would be decided. I knew the moment the workshop began, when the young professor and literary critic, endowed with a greater authority than humanly possible, with an oracular voice, with judgments no one could ever contest, announced the poems to be read. Seated beside the critic was a woman I didn't know, dressed in pink, like one of those camouflaged mantids who hunt in the cups of flowers, disguised as harmless petals. Everyone else was a classmate, most of them poets, already accustomed to the Workshop of the Moon. It was a young workshop, founded only the year before, named for the huge, perfectly round moon that floated over the university the first night, covering a quarter of the sky. With only two or three windows lit, the dark university building groaned beneath it, compressed in the middle like under a marble of incalculable weight.

First to read was a guy with a mustache, someone I had not seen before. His collection of poems was called *Autumnal Technology*: dense, bizarre poems, each with an unexpected twist. I went next. My sheets of paper, thirty or so, were written by hand. I read through them, one after the next, in an impersonal voice. My reading lasted almost an hour, while my thin shape probably disappeared completely into the air of the room. I, in any case, no longer had a body or paper covered in handwriting. I was inside my poem that had replaced the world. I twisted inside its lines in an ever-tightening spiral. I plummeted from line to line, torn by its rough reptilian skin, its thorny scorpion tails. For me, the recital lasted just a moment, as though the first lines:

Golden lyre, pulse your wings 'til I conclude this song
Hide your horse's head deep under silence
Golden lyre, pulse your wings 'til I conclude this song

had turned themselves over in another dimension and adhered to the last, becoming identical, indiscernible:

mud so versatile
mud of crates
mud of muds
mud of mists
mud
mud

The last word of the poem, in capital letters, was FINIS.

As was customary, a break followed the readings, with commentary to come after that. During the break, no one came near me. They were probably all in the thrall of the sacred horror of a magisterial work. I, in any case, was covered in goosebumps. I had been in the center of my skull, I had seen the living, chryselephantine statue that completely filled its dome of pale bones, and yet I had escaped with my life. Now, all I felt was the unfortunate itching of mohair on my bare neck. I was so tired my eyes went in different directions. The shapes of the room and of the people sitting on the benches blended together in the ashen light, until they turned into golden skeletons floating ghostly through the air. I inhaled my glory, steadily, through dry lips. A canonization would follow: I, the unknown kid who looked like a hairshirted friar with a rope belt, I would become the hope of world poetry, achieving in a single bound what others needed a lifetime to accomplish. I would never have to write another word. I would always be the author of *The Fall*, he with an eternal, marble cathedra in posterity's Eden. Toward the end of the break, the great critic, the mentor of the workshop, came over to me and asked one thing, "What's your real name, in fact?" That evening, he was wearing an impeccable gray suit and a cold blue tie. He was not yet forty. We would have to go back to another epoch to find someone who had garnered such authority and power at such a young age. I rose to my feet and responded that it was just as I had said when I introduced myself. "Oh, I thought that was a pseudonym . . ." Then he turned his back and went to the front of the room, as a sign the meeting would resume. Beside him, with the stony face of a Kabuki actress, was the floral woman.

I don't know if Akasha exists, the universal memory of the anthroposophists, where every gesture ever made and every word ever spoken is recorded, and every nuance of green ever seen by the compound eye of every locust, but in my meager memory, rent and consumed by misfortune's flames, nothing of what I experienced that evening has been lost. The train turntable of my life. In that hour of not even ferocious slaughter—offhand slaughter, scornful and smiling—the coin fell on the wrong side, I drew the short straw, and my career as a writer continued, perhaps, within another possible world, wrapped in glory and splendor (but also in conformism, falseness, self-deception, superbia, disappointment), but here all that was left was an unfulfilled promise. I have poisoned my nights, for the seven years since, in a masochistic effort to remember the grimaces, the sounds, the movements of air in that basement room that turned into the tomb of my hopes. Someone spun a pen around their fingers. Someone turned to the girl behind him and gave a knowing smile. Someone was wearing suede moccasins. The mohair collar itched, my cheeks burned.

They talked about my poem as though it were a specimen of literary disease. A mixture of poorly digested cultural detritus. A pastiche of . . . (here a list of about twenty names). The first reader was a real poet, I was an eccentric. "We have discovered a valuable addition to our contemporary cabinet of poetic curiosities." "'To aim for a thousand, to hit just a six,' Arghezi can be so devastating." As more and more people spoke, my amazement and my shame spun out of control, exceeding all limits. It wasn't possible, I couldn't be sitting in a congress of the blind. I clung to every positive nuance, I tried to ignore the sarcasm and not to hear the judgments raining down with careless severity. Surely things would turn around. The first speakers were mistaken, they were small fry without any taste. When someone new took a turn, I fixed my mind on him, under the illusion I could make him say what I wanted to hear, the way you push your entire body against the steering wheel when passing someone on a two-lane road. This time it will be okay, things will change starting now, I told myself, but the young man commenting, a classmate of mine, proved just as independent and impliable and brutal as a surgeon with a trepanning drill. And this was just what was happening: the vivisection of my martyred body. Cutting out my heart on the temple-top altar. Amputation without anesthetic, but also without hate, the way children pull the legs off flies. I screamed too, as inaudible as a fly and just as futile. Pompous, baroque, with an ambition suited to a higher goal, my poem was passed from hand to hand, they read aloud from its impossible prosody and "obvious" aesthetic inconsistencies. At times, "by the law of large numbers," one could find a formulation "that, considering the author's age, might give us some hope for the future." As the evening went on, they talked less and less about *The Fall*, and more about the other poet's work, mature and brutally masterful, elliptical and enigmatic. In the end, I was forgotten completely, in a pitiful, shadowy corner, where my turpitude was camouflaged.

I felt ashamed, more ashamed than I had ever been. At the start I had been shocked and indignant, but now I only wanted to disappear, to stop existing, to have never existed. I stopped hoping, stopped defending myself, my thoughts stopped fighting against theirs. I was like a rat left to float in a bucket without escape, losing hope and letting himself sink to the bottom. Still, charred as I was by their stubbornness and scorn, I held on to my last shard of hope: the great critic. With some regularity, he would overturn, without the right to appeal, the sentences handed down by those in the room, and his statements were chiseled in immortal granite. Like a medium, he could make no mistakes, because a daimon lived inside him, and if he did make a mistake, everyone would ignore the evidence and follow in his mistaken footsteps. The critic, who always spoke last and always to great effect, would restore to *The Fall* its initial grandeur, its marvelous depth and ecumenicism. The cathedral had been turned into a public toilet, but with his thin, playful voice, making caveats yet full of power, the critic could douse it again with holy water. Feverish, my head sank to my chest, I was waiting for nothing more than the evening's final speech, as were the others in the room. And he began to speak, after a long pause that showed no one else had anything more to say.

He began with me and described my poem as "a pointless whirlpool of words." Interesting, even moving in its intentions, but an obvious failure in its actual outcome, "because the poet has no feel for language and nowhere near the talent needed for such an undertaking." It was precisely its boundless ambition that made the poem ridiculous. "You need to learn to walk before you can run. The poet who read here tonight is like a toddler who wants to not only run a marathon, but to win." He continued in the same vein, quoting here and there, recalling earlier comments, always to agree with them, and in the end, before turning to the second author, he turned his thumb down with one last line: "The poem reminds me of those cartoons where the fuse burns down to the powder and the cannon swells up as much as it can, but then the ball rolls out and falls, flop, onto the ground, just in front of the barrel . . ."

I have no idea what he said about the other poet.

The manuscript of *The Fall*, still today, bears the fingerprints of those who spoke that night. Hundreds of sleepless nights since then have I ruminated over the same rocambolesque scenario: I track down and punish all of those who mocked my poem and destroyed my life. But especially, after so many years, I take my revenge on the single person who—bound and helpless, a simple, living anatomical specimen, made for torture—has fallen into my hands forever: me, no one but me.

6

I am, thus, a Romanian teacher at School 86 in Bucharest. I live alone in an old house, "the boat-shaped house" I have already mentioned, on the street called Maica Domnului, in the Tei Lake neighborhood. Like any other teacher in my field, I dreamed of becoming a writer, just the same way that, inside the café fiddler playing from table to table, a cramped and degenerate Efimov still lives who once thought himself a great violinist. Why it didn't happen—why I didn't have enough self-confidence to overcome, with a superior smile, that evening at the workshop, why I didn't have the maniacal conviction in my beliefs in spite of everyone else, when the myth of the misunderstood writer is so powerful, even with its concomitant measure of kitsch, why I didn't believe in my poem more than I did the reality of the world—I have searched for an answer to all these questions every day of my life. Starting in the depths of that damp autumn night when I walked home, blinded by headlights, in a state of paranoia I had never felt before. I couldn't breathe for rage and humiliation. My parents, who opened the door for me as always, were left speechless. "You looked like a ghost, you were white as lime and didn't hear a word we said," my mother would tell me later. I didn't sleep at all. I reread the poem several times, and every time it seemed different: wonderful, imbecilic, imbecilically wonderful, wonderfully imbecilic, or just pointless, as though the pages were blank. I had just read Dostoevsky's *Netochka Nezvanova,* and I thought it was his best work, unfinished because it couldn't be continued, because the young author had reached one of his world's extremes too early. I often thought about Netochka's father, Efimov, the self-taught violinist who, consumed with passion and inspiration, had become famous in his far-off province. The pride of a lowly man in the throes of a fantastic power knows no limits: Efimov came to think of himself the greatest violinist in the world. Up until, as Netochka writes (but can we believe her? What did that girl know about art, about music, about the violin? How her father must have tortured her with his furious insanity, with his crises of pride followed by despair, illness, and drink?), a "real" violinist came from Moscow to give a concert in the provincial capital. Of course, of course, after he heard "the real one," Efimov never touched the violin again and disappeared from his own fantasy world, his daughter's world, and even Dostoevsky's world, leaving behind only the fumes of wincing tragedy and a scherzo damnation. A poor man deceived by the shabby, provincial devil. I am sure that no one who reads *Netochka* ever doubts Efimov's mediocrity, the risible glory of the one-eyed man in the land of the blind, his pitiful self-deception. But I—who had lived, for several months in the summer of '76, like him and like the gods, terrified by my own greatness, by the all-encompassing power of the one who took my place and drove my hand across the paper, so that my poem ran for pages, without erasing, without revising, without adding, without rewriting, as though I had pulled away, line by line, a white strip covering the letters and words—I knew that Efimov truly was a great violinist, too great and too new and too out of nowhere to be truly understood, that the governor and those around him, although they had felt the power of his art, could never perceive more than a great, boundless light, and they could never explain why that music, so different from its birthplace, had moved them so deeply. I knew that it wasn't him, who was manipulated like a doll by a hand from another world, who was the imposter, but "the great," "the real," successful Muscovite violinist, who was world-famous, who had played for crowned heads in Paris and Vienna, and who had deigned, at the end of his career, to descend to the end of Russia to perform for the barbarians' pleasure out of the grace and nobleness of his art. An art that followed the rules, the centuries-old canons, a successful kind of music, of course, but a human one. And just this humanity was the coin that passed everywhere, in palaces and hovels alike, because the weight of the coin feels so nice in the palm of your hand. But inhuman, disordered art that didn't follow even the construction of the human ear, nor the construction of the violin, that knew not the limits of fingers on the strings, art from another world that magically penetrated Efimov's body, that art presses against your hand like the icy blade of a razor, it slices down your life line, leaving you scarred forever.

Of the thousands of answers I've given myself—during painful, feverish nights or nightmare-filled days, while I'm teaching and the students are writing an essay, or in a shoe store, icy bus stations, or waiting outside a doctor's office—to the question of why I never became a writer, one answer seems truer than any other in its paradoxicality and ambiguity. I have read all the books, and I have never known a single author. I have heard all the voices, with schizophrenic clarity, but no real voice has ever spoken to me. I have wandered through thousands of rooms of the museum of literature, charmed at first by the art with which a door was painted on every wall, in trompe l'oeil, meticulously matching each splinter of wood with a pointed shadow, each coating of paint with a feeling of fragility and transparence that made you admire the artists of illusion more than you've ever admired anything, but in the end, after hundreds of kilometers of corridors of false doors, with the ever-stronger smell of oil paints and thinners in the stale air, the route ceases to be a contemplative stroll and becomes first a state of disquiet, then a breathless panic. Each door fools you and disappoints you, and the more completely you are fooled, the more it hurts. They are wonderfully painted, but they do not open. Literature is a hermetically sealed museum, a museum of illusionary doors, of artists worrying over the nuance of beige and the most expressive imitation of a knocker, hinge, or doorknob, the velvety black of the keyhole. All it takes is for you to close your eyes and run your fingers over the continuous, unending wall to understand that nowhere in the house of literature are there any openings or fissures. But, seduced by the grandeur of the doors loaded with bas-reliefs and cabalistic symbols, or by the humility of a peasant's kitchen door, one that has a pork bladder stretched in place of a window, you don't feel like closing your eyes, on the contrary, you'd prefer a thousand eyes for the thousand false exits arranged before you. Like sex, like drugs, like all the manipulations of our minds that attempt to break out of the skull, literature is a machine for producing first beatitude, then disappointment. After you've read tens of thousands of books, you can't help but ask yourself: while I was doing that, where did my life go? You've gulped down the lives of others, which always lack a dimension in comparison to the world in which you exist, however amazing their tours of artistic force may be. You have seen colors of others and felt the bitterness and sweetness and potential and exasperation of other consciousnesses, to the point that they have eclipsed your own sensations and pushed them into the shadows. If only you could pass into the tactile space of beings other than you—but again and again, you were only rolled between the fingertips of literature. Unceasingly, in a thousand voices, it promised you escape, while it robbed you of even the frozen crust of reality that you once had.

As a writer, you make yourself less real with each book you write. You always try to write about your life, and you never write about anything but literature. It is a curse, a Fata Morgana, a falsification of the simple fact that you are alive, you are real in a real world. You multiply your worlds, but your own world would be enough to fill billions of lives. With every page you write the pressure of the enormous house of literature on top of you grows, it forces your hand to make movements it doesn't want to make, it confines you to the level of the page, even though you could burst through the paper and write perpendicular to its surface, just as a painter is constrained to use color and a musician sound and a sculptor volume, endlessly, until they feel disgusted and hateful, and only because we cannot imagine any other way. Could you get out of your own cranium by painting a door on the smooth, yellow interior of your brow? The despair you feel is that of one who lives in two dimensions and is trapped inside a square, in the middle of an infinite piece of paper. How can you escape this terrifying prison? Even if you could cross one side of the square, the paper extends endlessly—but that's not the real reason the side can't be crossed; rather, the two-dimensional mind cannot conceive of rising, perpendicular to the level of the world, between the prison walls.

One answer, perhaps truer than the others, would be just this: I never became a writer because I never was, from the start, a writer. I loved literature like a vice, but I never truly believed that it was the way. Fiction does not attract me, it was not my life's dream to add a few false doors to the walls of literature. I was always aware that style (the hand of literature inserted into your own hand as if it were a glove), so admired in the great writers, is nothing more than raptus and possession. That writing eats up your life and brain like heroin. That at the end of your career you have to admit that you, with your own mind and mouth, haven't said anything about yourself, about the minor events that shaped your life, but always about a reality foreign to you, whose intentions you followed because it promised you salvation, a bidimensional, symbolic salvation that has no meaning. Too often literature constitutes the eclipse of the writer's mind and body.

Since I have not written anything (I have kept a diary, true, over all these years, but who cares about the diary of an unknown person?), I can see my body and my mind. They are not beautiful or worthy of public attention. But they are worthy of my attention. I look at them from day to day and they seem as fresh as transparent potatoes, without chlorophyll, grown in the dark. Precisely because they were not turned over on every side in twenty books of short stories, poetry, novels, precisely because they were not deformed by calligraphy. I began writing in this notebook (and I haven't breathed a word about it to anyone) under special circumstances, just the kind of book no one would ever write. It is a text condemned from the start, and not because it will never become a book, will remain a manuscript, will be tossed on top of *The Fall* in my drawer with my baby teeth and navel thread and old photos, but because its topic is so foreign to literature and so closely wrapped around life, feeding on life like a weed, more foreign than any text that was ever spread upon the page. Something is happening to me, within me. Different than all the writers of the world, precisely because I am not a writer, I feel I have something to say. And I will say it poorly and truthfully, the way anything worth putting down on paper should be said. I often think that this is what should have happened: for me to be taken apart in that far-off night at the workshop, to completely withdraw from any literary space, to be a Romanian teacher in an elementary school, the most obscure person on Earth. See me writing now, writing just the text that—as I read those sophisticated and powerful and smart and coherent books, full of madness and wisdom—I always imagined and never found anywhere: a text outside the museum of literature, a real door scrawled onto the air, one I hope will let me truly escape my own cranium. A text that he—the one giving autographs and meetings with teachers and who knows what in other countries—never dreamed of.

7

I am usually one of the last to arrive in the teachers' lounge, long after the bell has rung. The olive-drab room (the color of schools, hospitals, and army camps) is pitiful and desolate. On the long table, almost the only piece of furniture in the room, the tablecloth has been worn thin by the friction of countless elbows. I usually find a sole teacher in the lounge, sitting at the table with a class's grade register open in front of him, making changes in blue pencil. He won't raise his eyes to see who comes in. The drawing teacher. The Latin teacher. The physics teacher. A melancholy fog will wander through, especially in winter, when the light is still dim and snow sticks to the windows with peeling sills. You are inside a dream, but whose?

I take a grade register from the pile on the table and exit into the school's empty hallways. They are narrow with low ceilings, like mole tunnels, illuminated by a diffuse light from the interior schoolyard. I pass countless white doors, behind which unknown things occur. I can hear voices—sharp, hysterical, authoritarian. They yell, they explain, they plead. Suddenly, a door flies open against the wall, like a flower in a time-lapse film exploding from a bud, and a child shoots out beside me. Then the shouting teacher is ten times as loud. The door closes again and the murmuring returns. The child disappears around a corner and never shows himself again.

The halls seem to have no end, even though the school is fairly small. You are constantly turning at right angles, constantly going up or down stairs that haven't been properly washed. You pass bathrooms with their doors wide open, you pass the nurse. I have been wandering through this mirage for three years, and I have yet to understand its layout. To this day, I will pick up the wrong register and end up in a strange room. The lab rooms seem to change location constantly, the portraits of star students are sometimes at the front door, sometimes in the secretary's office, sometimes at the back end of the furthest hall. Occasionally, I'll stop in front of them: the thirty photos, in six rows, photos of boys and girls, they seem so ghostly in the Nile-green air that I always get a chill: these are larval faces, all the same and yet each one different, as though the gallery of star students were an insect collection on the walls of a natural science museum. It is hard to pull myself away and continue down the corridor, the Romanian teacher with an enormous register under his arm.

I go up one floor, then another, then another. I know the school only has two floors, that I haven't woken up yet (it's 8:15 AM), but still, I climb the stairs, I climb for centuries. It is an infinite tower of superimposed classrooms and hallways. I stop one afternoon in a wide and dark space (very little light comes in here from the schoolyard) with the same white doors around me. Grade 5-A, 5-B, 5-C . . . As the hallways continue, the class names exhaust the Latin alphabet and change to Greek, Hebrew, Cyrillic, then Arab and Indian signs, hideous Mayan heads, and, eventually, signs that are completely unknown. I have never learned how many groups there actually are for each grade in School 86.

It is foggy and desolate. Forty children are waiting for me in a room, but which one? I almost always get it wrong. I uncertainly open a door, the students in their seats turn toward me, the teacher interrupts her explanation of fractions (if it's the lovely Florabela) or reptilian paralysis (if it's the timid Gionea) or the tics of a Tourette's patient (if I come upon Vintilă, the geography teacher). "Pardon me," I say and close the door contritely, feeling like someone who, without wanting to, has witnessed a shameful, secret event. I have always felt that whatever happens there between the children and the teachers, behind the countless white doors, is sealed under a taboo just as powerful and as unbreakable as the door of the women's restroom. During the break between each class, I sweat and tremble, not at the thought that I won't find the right room again, but that I will constantly open the wrong door, again and again, onto places I have no business going.

In the end, the children in the most improbable room seem to be expecting me. In front, at the teacher's desk, there is no one. Still, my uncertainty continues: what if the real teacher is also late? Only when I see them open their books and notebooks, as a sign they will accept me there, in the little space in front of the rows of desks, do I calm down somewhat: it is my class, I am, at last, where I should be. But what grade is this, sixth? eighth? All the children look the same to me. I strain to recall, from the three or four faces I recognize, if I am in the Rădulescu class or the group that has homeroom with Uzun. I walk to the teacher's desk, put the register down. I sit, I take attendance. I rise and walk among the rows of benches and desks, looking at their textbooks out of the corner of my eye: what in God's name am I supposed to be teaching? Grammar or literature? I am the worst teacher that has ever been. "How far did we get?" I ask them. A girl responds from the row beside the window, "We identified the principal ideas of *Childhood Memories from Broșteni*, part three." Okay, sixth grade, probably 6-B; good, I know this much at least. I can take it from here. I look at my students with something approaching gratitude. I start to speak automatically, my mind elsewhere. They write down what I tell them, also automatically, their minds also elsewhere. They were likely also wondering what class they had next, what strange and inexplicable animal would come into the room, what adult (therefore foreign and monstrous) person would be their master until the next break. We are now face to face: my face, the one I know from the mirror and hate the way I've never hated anything else in the world, and their forty faces, their small, unformed features, the faces I have always feared. "Suffer little children to come unto me," the phrase comes into my head every time I walk into the classroom—that is, five times a day—"for of such is the kingdom of heaven." The faces of children, faces that are not of this earth but from a foreign, faraway kingdom. I could tell them many things, I could carefully construct a bridge between our two cultures or two civilizations (two species?), but instead, I talk to them about Irinuca's goats and explain what sarcoptic mites are, because I have to look out for myself, because I've spent three years doing everything I can to escape and run away, to not call attention to myself, to not be cornered.

There are good classes and bad ones, classes where I can enter calmly and others where I do not dare to go. There is one of those for every grade, a group of all the problem children, the unstable, recalcitrant, and dyslexic. And Gypsies, whom teachers up to their gills in prejudice regard as nothing but psychopaths. Children who cannot bring their teachers flowers and candy.

In the lower school, these children had stupid teachers—drunks the school keeps on out of pity—but now, when they have different teachers for each subject, they cannot do the work, and neither can their teachers. "Class 5-D is like a lion's den, I fend them off with the register and a ruler," someone in the teachers' lounge will say. Women, especially first-year teachers, come back from these groups in tears. Everyone beats the kids up, and in the next class they start all over again. There's nothing to be done. I go into this kind of classroom like I'm entering a torture chamber, one of many waiting for me in my life (and my life is one torture chamber after another). There's nothing to be done: it's best if you don't think ahead. You walk automatically, the register under your arm, toward that corner of hell. You will be tortured for an hour and then escape. For an hour, you will be challenged, defied, and mocked by creatures who come up as high as your chest, but who are many and attack in waves. You can't defend yourself with the vastness of your knowledge of the world. Your world is not theirs. Your authority ends at the classroom door, where theirs begins. You'll get off most easily by not making eye contact, taking your seat at the front of the room, and sitting there catatonic until the bell rings, unmoved by the chaos, shouting, and running around the room, the battles of erasers and pencils, the glue they put on your chair. You'll want your senses to shut down, one by one, like somnolent eyes, to become a statue of yourself late in life, when the heroism of former teachers will be repaid with their image in stone, placed at the head of a class of forty stone children, as a memorial to the education system's double agony.

The bell always takes me by surprise: I don't know if the trumpets of the apocalypse will blow any louder, but the bell at the end of every class is enough to raise the dead from their tombs. Every time it rings, I am so shattered I can barely put myself back together. The children all run out of the room long before I do, leaving me alone among the empty benches and tables, a sight so sad that I look up, toward the ceiling, for a beam from which to hang myself. The walls around me are hung with absurd posters: pictures of pigs and cows for the younger kids, the periodic table and the digestive tract of a dissected pigeon for the older. Pieces of a world we will never understand. I take the register and walk with it tucked under my arm toward the teachers' lounge. This time the way seems short and utterly simple, as though the lounge were around the corner. But it takes me just as long to get there, because the space is packed with children swarming like hornets in their hive, without rest, their screams piercing your eardrums like a needle. You can't get through them, they are stuck together like conjoined twins, but you can launch yourself on top of them in a particular vault that all the teachers know—those that didn't learn it did not survive—and the children will pass you hand by hand over their lice-filled heads, feeling under your dress if you're a woman, picking your pocket if you're a man, but conveying you safely in the end to the door of the teacher's lounge. There you can pat your clothes smooth, wipe the despair from your face, and enter the room affably, ready for jokes and chat, as though nothing had happened.

My colleagues sit around the table. On the walls around them are large, moldy photos of defunct historical figures. Through the window, the water tower is visible, as well as an ancient disused factory, its roof broken and trees growing from seeds blown by the wind into its brick cornices. The neighborhood kids play there, slipping into the abandoned industrial halls through entrances only they know. When I finish teaching and walk past the mechanic's toward the end of the tramline, I come upon groups of two or three children, all with that look that says, "I went there again." At each corner of the schoolyard, before they can go into class, the children go through uniform checks. Teachers put their hands through the boys' hair, and if it is longer than the width of their fingers, they are sent away for a haircut. The girls have two vulnerabilities: the headband (white fabric, not plastic, always on) and the length of their sundress, which has to come to the knees. And there are those who have another sign of scholarly slavery: their school registration number, which used to be sewn with yellow thread beside the name of the school, on a scrap of muslin tacked to the left sleeve of the uniform. The number is used to identify those students whose behavior in public spaces is lacking, who go to the movies or hang out in bars when school is in session. I don't remember when the tag was replaced with a tattoo, but I remember it was because the students stapled their numbers on, so they could be removed when they left school, when the girls ripped off their headbands as though they burned. For many years, on the first day of school, when the nurse checked their torsos for hives and their heads for lice, and when everyone had to ingest their vaccines—a squirt of pink liquid onto a sugar cube—the shop teacher (boys studied locksmithing, the girls dressmaking) appeared with his pyrography tool red hot. One by one, their sleeves rolled up, the children's left shoulders were subjected to the meticulous inscription, in crude figures, of the number that identified them as students of School 86. The haircut check, the dresses (the girls knelt in the aisle between the benches, their hems could not touch the floor) and the numbers were invariably followed by the principal's warning: "And don't let me catch you going to the old factory. Whoever I see there will get three day's suspension studying in the library!"

Mentioning the library had an immediate effect: few children would take that chance. The school library is also the detention hall. A narrow cement staircase next to the nurse's office leads far below the earth, like the public toilets in an old train station. The librarian is the math teacher, who, since she has diabetes, teaches only part-time and spends a few hours on guard duty. She is wide, she spans the width of the table in the little entryway, and her face is full of warts. The children barely have room to pass the barbarian idol who blocks the entrance. On her rough wood desk covered in red ink doodles, she keeps a jar of cloudy liquid. Inside are her algae. She uses them to treat not only her diabetes but also her vision, bladder, bowel movements, ovarian cysts, memory, snoring, warts, indigestion, and boredom. Her algae are the panacea humanity has been waiting for, the revelation of a Russian scientist named Naumov. They appeared in the school a few months ago, introduced by Mrs. Bernini, the music teacher. Her mystical jar shone in the sun like the holy grail. There were a few pallid, translucent creatures inside, with delicate internal anatomies, floating in a hyaline liquid that resembled sperm. With her colleagues gathered around, Mrs. Bernini gravely unfolded a piece of paper, the mimeograph of many mimeographs, wherein, one after another, in almost illegible, ink-soaked letters, were typed the words of the great, wise man. They explained that the algae, of a complicated scientific name, grew and multiplied in the jar without needing to be fed, and their liquid should be consumed once a week and replaced with tap water. The miraculous algae treatment should be followed for at least a year, after which one was guaranteed perfect health in this century and, in the next, eternal life. The music teacher sent her colleagues for some cups of water, in each of which she poured a portion of the lazy, whitish animals from the primordial jar. The teachers now piously followed Professor Naumov. The algae did in fact multiply, and the cloudy liquid, while a little disgusting, could be consumed in the bathroom, while holding your nose. The teachers had completely forgotten their numerous past attempts at youth without age and life without death, for example, keeping a teaspoon of oil under your tongue for six hours every Monday, as prescribed by the Czech professor Němeček, or holding in their urine for three days, once a month, in terrible pain, as a cure for nostalgia.

The library has no books. There were at one time hundreds of children's books, but the damp underground air has covered them with mold. The covers are now rotten, stained green, and smelling like penicillin, and their pages teem with minuscule scorpions that have no stingers. Most of the old books lie, piled with dust, on rotting shelves. The room is small, the light comes from a high window behind a wire screen, like all the windows in the school. The worst-behaved kids are punished with afternoons spent here, sitting until it turns dark, with nothing else to contemplate but the librarian's elephantine, overflowing backside. Even when she falls asleep, her head on the table, watched over by the jar in strange illumination from the window's rays, the student cannot escape her custody, since it is impossible to pass between the librarian's fat, hairy legs, where varicose veins climb up and down like soft worms.

The other teachers are always writing in the registers, putting in grades, changing them, erasing them with hard erasers that wear through the paper, and they whisper when they speak, their mouths clenched or covered by a notebook, like the students do in class. And also like them, the teachers are pathologically afraid of the principal, Borcescu. When called to his office, they turn white as lime, as though an enormous tarantula had invited them to visit its lair. I am scared of Borcescu too. I never really want to see him, even though I know he has a certain weakness for the Romanian and math teachers. His whole office smells of makeup powder and foundation. It is his characteristic scent, it saturates his clothes, his hands, his face and hair. When this sweet air wafts into the lounge, the teachers automatically leap to their feet—they know that in two or three seconds the master of the school will appear. And look, really, look at his short, obese body, his disproportionately large and perfectly round head that looks like the top of a snowman. His appearance is unforgettable, because the brownish-pink powder that masks his sweaty skin never obscures his strangeness sufficiently, rather it replaces it with something just as strange. He has vitiligo, his face and hands (maybe the rest of his body, as well) are covered with spots, pale in some patches, others densely pigmented, giving his body the appearance of a soccer ball sewn from variously colored skins, over which someone has spread a thick layer of disgustingly perfumed makeup. Placed beneath three mustache threads the color and texture of tobacco, his toothless mouth cannot pronounce sibilants and is helpless before fricatives. Borcescu is as feared as his words are unintelligible. He is constantly giving orders that the person receiving strains to understand, terrorized that he could misinterpret the marble-mouthed principal. The poor teacher might stand with his head against the window for a quarter hour, turning over in his mind the words that lack any of their essential consonants.

Some time ago, in the 1970s, Borcescu's specialty was inviting the young female teachers on a trip to the mountains. He was a gallant then, courteous, with thicker hair and a paler illness. And above all, he had a Fiat 600, unusual for the time and irresistible to more than a few women. They would set off happily, and in the middle of nowhere he would stop, and he would tell his passenger that he would kick her out of the car if she didn't let him . . . Many of the teachers were subjected to this. He taught biology, which he turned into a tidy business: when he taught the anatomy of a rabbit, all the children had to bring a rabbit in. Borcescu would dissect one of them, with evident pleasure, on the large tile work surface placed over the desk, and the others he would take home, where his rabbit nursery prospered. If he taught about fish, each child had to buy him a carp from the neighborhood grocery. He dissected one, the children saw the gills, intestines, the pearly bladder, the eggs in dense packets, and the other carp were for the principal, who sold them from his apartment door, holding a scale as old as the hills. Shortly before I came to the school, he fell into the hands of one Mimi: poor old Borcescu paid for all his outings in a single day of suffering. He had picked up a hitchhiker and stopped a few kilometers on, plying his usual extortion. The woman said nothing, she let herself be encroached on in the tiny Fiat, but afterward she wouldn't let him go until they celebrated a civil union: it turned out that Mimi, an old crone as ugly as a pig, a teacher somewhere near Berceni, outranked the future principal—the blackmailed blackmailer who in the end capsized. From that moment on, Borcescu lost not only his sexual escapades, but also control over his own life, since seldom was a man ever as terrorized by his wife as he was by the one who now, with an iron hand, governed his home. In the first two years of my time there, I was occasionally called into his office, and if he was in a good mood, our conversation would invariably end with him calling me around to his side of the desk, as though he needed to tell me something very important. I was loath to do so, the smell of his powder almost made me faint. He would bring his pink lips to my ear, almost touching, and with his eyes wide in irrepressible fear he would whisper: "My young man, really . . . don't ever get married! Do you hear me?" I would play along and ask, innocently, "But why shouldn't I, sir?" "Eh, you, do you know what marriage is like?" "What's it like, sir?" "Worse than being hanged!" He looked in my eyes and went on, as though he were joking, "Not much worse. But a bit . . . Don't forget what I'm telling you . . ." None of the older teachers missed the chance to tell me the story, one hard to believe but true and endlessly repeated in the thirty years Borcescu had taught in the neighborhood, the last twenty as principal, about the time this Mimi, mad with rage, had burst through the front door of the school, breaking its windows with her shoulder, and had kicked the secretary's door flat against the wall, bowling over the student assistant with pompoms in her hair, and had blown like a blizzard into the principal's office. Teachers and students alike gathered outside to watch through the office window as Mimi, finding the office empty, stopped for a moment, disoriented, then looked everywhere for her unhappy husband, finally plucking him out from under his desk by his ear, like a bad kid, and began to pound his round head while he, red as fire, babbled unintelligibly.

I usually sit near the radiator, looking out the window at the old factory, the water tower, and the dusty Bucharest sky. I don't gossip with the other teachers, I don't drink liquids from a jar, I don't try to get as close as possible to giant Florabela, whose breasts and mound of Venus are always evident and damp, no matter how decently she dresses. I am, in the teacher's lounge, an absence, a shadow of a man: the Romanian teacher who comes and goes so unobtrusively he might have never been. After my last class, I only go to the lounge to drop off the register. I go downstairs and exit the front door. No matter the month, when I leave school it is always autumn: the cold wind blows a thick, shiny dust, it sticks to my eyelashes and hair. I come to the tram turnaround. The tram cars look like they came from another century: their sides are rusted through, their lights are broken. A sea of people are at the stop, all looking in the same direction. Far, far away, from the depths of Şoseaua Colentina, tram 21 clambers toward us. Three times as many people as it can handle try to board. Some ride on the back bumper, others hang from the door handles. I let it and its load of human polyps go without me, and since it will be half an hour until the next, I decide to walk home, setting off along the pipe factory. The wind pushes me from behind, tosses my hair, blows paper and other street trash against my body. I pass minuscule seltzer shops, bread distributors, tire repair shops, lumberyards. The sun goes down, the world turns scarlet, and every passing person feeds my loneliness.

8

I bought my house in 1981 for the price of a Dacia automobile. I was living with my parents at the time, on Ştefan cel Mare, in a wide apartment block with eight entrances, right next to the State Directorate General of the Militia. I grew up near the sunny State Circus Park, and later, as a teenager, I often went back to sink inside its sparkles and shadows, near the reed-filled lake shaded by weeping willows. I would walk, during frightening evenings of monstrous clouds, down to the lake to sit on a bench. I would stare at the brown waters for hours on end, muttering the lines of poetry that filled my mind: Apollinaire, Rimbaud, Lautréamont . . . I would borrow books from the neighborhood library, the one beside the grocery, where it seemed no one aside from me ever went. Sometimes I took my load of potatoes, tomatoes, and cucumbers to the library. I would leave them in the entryway and pass into the shadowy, book-filled chambers. The librarian was a reserved man, as inconsequential in reality as he was concrete and corporeal in countless later dreams of mine. The books, in alphabetical order, were for me like those rows of apartment building mail-boxes that covered an entire wall. When I was a child, I always wanted the key to every box! I would have spent my mornings reading the letters, entering everyone's sad, run-down lives. I did sometimes, with great effort, manage to pull an envelope out through the narrow slot, using a stick and poking my fingers as far as I could into the dark space, frightened to death I might get caught. Then I would read about diseases and burials, appeals for money, shameful propositions, and estate arrangements. And now I finally had all the keys! Each book was a slot where I could look into another person's skull. They were all brains with organs of intelligence, courage, pride, melancholy, and evil outlined and numbered in permanent marker. I opened each book like a trepanning surgeon, with the additional amazement of a doctor who, instead of the same circumvolutions and the same ashy-brown substance irrigated by the arborescence of veins of blood, would find something different in every dura mater he pried open: a child, curled up and ready to be born, an enormous spider, a city in the first hours of dawn, a giant, fresh grapefruit, a doll's head with its eyes rolled back. What strange osmosis occurred between my brain and an author's, what bizarre process turned our brows transparent! How our foreheads stuck together, like conjoined twins, how their cerebral substances melted into mine! I looked into their minds, I read their thoughts, I could feel their trials, their silences, their orgasms. Their moments of illumination. I poured the contents of my mind over them the way a starfish digests a nest of snails. We joined, we mixed, Apollinaire and me, T. S. Eliot and me, Valéry and me, until, like a holograph, an unreal hybrid was born, one that made your spine shiver: the book. Poetry. The insanity of dissolving into a cistern filled with the liquid gold of poetry.

I would watch the lake, the reflections of clouds and the apartment blocks on the other shore, until dark fell and the park emptied itself of people completely. I would no longer notice my unhappiness, the way we are not aware that we are billions of cells, a cluster of lives. Only once the surface of the lake reflected nothing but the stars did I stand up, all pins and needles, and sink again into the network of park paths. One night, I found the circle of the lake floating a half meter over the ground. On another, I saw I could walk across the pitch-black surface, passing diagonally to the other shore. But the Circus Park at night, as different from the daytime park as a woman is from a man, never ravished me as much as it did the night I suddenly came upon an area I had never seen before, not even as a child, although I knew it existed: it was very far, toward Tei Lake, where the serpentine paths opened suddenly onto a vast space of terrible loneliness. In the center was a pool filled with black water. A statue rose from the pool, a naked young man, his arms raised to defend himself from a terrible threat. His fear, carved in silent marble, overwhelmed me: obviously, I was that young man, and his eyes wide with terror were my own.

I have always been afraid, purely afraid, with a fear that sprang not from the thought of some danger, but from life itself. I live in a blind person's fear, in the uneasiness of one who does not hear. I have never truly slept, because I know the moment I close my eyes, someone is in the room, watching me, slowly moving toward my sleeping face. How could I protect myself when my senses closed down, when I gave myself over to enormous worlds? My fear came especially from the fact that we don't know what the world is like, we only know that facet our senses illuminate. We only know the world our senses construct inside our minds, the way you might build a dollhouse under a bell jar. But the enormous world, the world as it really is—indescribable even if there were millions of senses open like sea anemones in the untamable flux of the ocean—surrounds us and it crushes us, bone by bone, in its embrace. When I turned twelve, my fear of the world became acute and focused. I understood for the first time that the source of my fear was not the jaws, tusks, claws, or hooks of beastly monsters, not the specter of my fragile body being torn open: it came from the void, the nothing, the unseen. I was at the time an avid reader of fantasy and adventure stories, printed in paper pamphlets. Every Thursday I would get up at the break of dawn and run to the newsstand so I wouldn't miss an issue. The paper was poor, the illustrations cheap and amateurish, but the stories filled me with wonder, enchantment, and passion, or with horror and anguish. Whether they told of temples and bars of gold in the jungles of southern continents, cities beneath the sea, experiments performed by psychopathic scientists, incomprehensible extraterrestrials, self-aware viruses that took over the world, or spirits that entered your mind and took over the reins of your will, the stories took up my hours of loneliness and, naturally, flowed into my dreams, becoming homogeneous with my interior life. Two of these stories made a deep impression, still there today.

In the first story (who wrote it? I never knew; the authors' names on the cover were just hieroglyphs I could ignore), a muzhik in faraway Siberia is sleeping next to his wife, while a biting wind blows in snow through the cracks of their wooden hut. The peasant wakes a little before dawn and notices his wife is not beside him in bed. He decides she must have gone outside for something and falls back asleep. But when it becomes light and she hasn't returned, he goes out onto the porch, pulling his nightshirt to his chest against the cold. What he sees outside leaves his mouth gaping: on the fresh snow that fell overnight, so pure that God himself wouldn't dare to step on it, he sees his wife's footprints go from the porch to the middle of the yard, where they suddenly stop. The snow all around them is untouched. The last lines of this story, which like so many others gave no explanation for what had happened, describe the muzhik looking dim-wittedly toward the sky.

The second was about a convict left to rot in his cell. He was sentenced to life and is guarded so closely that he is sure he will die in prison. But one night, he hears a weak tapping from one of the walls. He presses his ear against it and hears it even better: clear, intelligible, repeating at certain intervals in an elaborate series of taps. Amazed, the prisoner decides it is just another of the many hallucinations of his miserable seclusion. But the next day, at the same time, he hears the taps again, and then again, consistently, day after day. He memorizes the series of taps, he makes notes on the bit of wall hidden behind his bed. From time to time, the pattern becomes more complicated, as though newer and newer "words" are appearing in this code from his neighbor beyond the wall. It takes the prisoner months to guess the first connections in the secret fabric of taps, and then years until he can master the language. In the end, a dialogue begins, the prisoner responding in the same code (which he wrote in an invented hand, with crescents, gears, crosses, and triangles scratched into the plaster of his cell wall). His neighbor, as he now understands, is sending him an escape plan, one of a breathtaking brazenness and incredible simplicity. One night, after he has made all the necessary preparations, the prisoner escapes, following the instructions to the letter. Many years later, rich and well known under a false identity, he asks for permission to visit the prison, intending to meet, finally, the one to whom he owes everything, and to attempt to save him too. The man is taken to the cell where his youth was wasted, and he asks the guard about the prisoner on the other side of the wall. But on the other side, he learns to his amazement, is only the sky and sea. It is an exterior wall, dozens of meters above the waves crashing against a rocky shore . . .

That same holy terror, that same feeling that something beyond the pasteboard model of the world was staring at you, its prey, and this something was slowly approaching with its thousands of sticky hairs, and you were unaware because you have only a couple antennae when you need organs to perceive Everything, I felt it that night in Circus Park beside the silent pool with concrete edges where the stars were reflected, and I had that same feeling of hopeless loneliness much later, in the autumn of 1981, the first time I walked down Maica Domnului. It was a putrid and luminous autumn. I was twenty-five and had no future on Earth. I had been a teacher at the end of Colentina for a year, and I knew then (as I do now) that I would be there until I retired. Then I would die, without leaving any trace of my passage through the world, a fact which gave me a kind of dark contentment. One Sunday in October, my unhappiness—the very air I breathed—pulled me out of the house. It had been raining furiously all morning, but it became suddenly quiet that afternoon, and the apartment blocks across the street became suddenly clear and translucent, vested in a light that came from nowhere. I left my building and walked through the glittering wind and across Circus Park. The lake was muddy and trash floated on its surface. I had never, not as a child nor later, gone to the far other side of the lake, beyond the line of those four blocks the lake reflected, the "diplomats' blocks," on whose balconies girls with chocolate-colored skin or boys with slanted eyes played with tops and mirrors. I knew that beyond them was the Tei Lake neighborhood, whose geography was for me mythical, because my godmother lived there on an endless little street bordered by construction sites where people dumped their wash-water. In their fenced yards, you could see stakes for tomatoes and beans, each with a colored glass ball on top, mirroring the clouds. Galvani High School was there too, and a half-collapsed elementary, and a large lumberyard that filled the neighborhood with the smell of fresh sap. But Maica Domnului didn't lead directly to this neighborhood, it went diagonally toward Colentina.

After the park, I crossed railroad tracks where I had never seen a train, and there, as I had imagined, I came upon a place unlike any other in the world. When you are four years old, every new place is like this. You move in the field of hallucination and vision, until the trails of memory are worn into your brain. Any new sight feels like a fable, however banal it might be, because expressions such as "in reality," "truly," or "as it is" are meaningless to one who sees reality the way that later we relive our earliest memories or live within our dreams. Maica Domnului always seemed to me like the tentacle of a dream stretched into the waking world, or, if everything is interior and reality is only an illusory artifact, a glimmer of a deep and sunken childhood.

Maica Domnului had no normal houses, because here normality itself ended. The weather wasn't even normal. When you arrived in this zone, this channel from another world and another life, the climate changed and the seasons turned upside down. Here it was always, as I wrote, a putrid and luminous autumn. The splinter of asphalt, lain who knowns when over the old gravel road, had faded and torn like an old rag. It was full of bumps from the powerful plant seeds germinating underneath. On either side of the road were old houses, merchant-style, including some built between the wars, little villas that once were modern and attractive. But how odd they were! Each one had some monstrous, or at best out of place, addition, the excessive imagination of an architect who seemed to have planned part of the building in the daytime, and the other part when awoken in the middle of the night, compelled to draw on his slanted table by the light of the full moon.

All the houses have round windows that glow brightly in the sunset. All have wrought iron gates, art nouveau vine works over stained-glass portals of flickering orange, azure, and lilac. All are covered in an age-worn, discolored calcio-vecchio. But every facade has at least half its plaster missing. The flayed wall reveals its dusty brick. Between the bricks are ancient gaps in the mortar. Most of the windows do not have glass: they are covered over with ragged, yellow newspapers. Rising over the roofs—like stumps raised toward the sky, in reproach and indignation, by giant amputees—are bizarre, rusty ornaments: towers and cupolas made of tin, vulgar cement statues, their faces chipped, clusters of pale pink angels like larvae on parade. One of the houses has ramparts, like a medieval fortress, another looks like a tram depot, a third is, pure and simple, a solemn crypt in the middle of the yard, without a single flower. At sundown, the scene soaks up the scarlet like tissue paper and becomes unbearable.

Most of the yards grow nightshade flowers, white and pale purple, that darken the evening air with their scent. Other yards are all weeds. At dusk, the people who live here come out and squat in front of their strange houses, people even stranger and more enigmatic than the houses themselves. Mountains of sunflower seed shells collect in front of them. Most of the ruins are home to Gypsies. They don't have running water or electricity, they don't pay any bills or taxes. There are also Romanians from the slums, carpenters who make funeral banners, pattern-makers at some factory, ticket-takers on a tram. They idle their days away with their shirts hanging open. You can see them on the balconies: young girls dressed like prostitutes hanging undershirts, bras, underpants, and other, unidentifiable, brightly colored rags out to dry. Tattooed men, with a dangerous air, smoke while staring toward the end of the street. All talk loudly, in what seems an endless argument, and yet all of them have an air of melancholy that makes them, you might say, the most fitting residents of my street.

You have to go down the street quite a way to reach the boat-shaped house. It is the only one with no fence, and it doesn't need one, enthroned and somber at the end of a lot full of rusted springs and ancient refrigerator carcasses. Whoever wants to, even those that don't, will throw out their old things in front of my house. It isn't, actually, boat-shaped, but a shape that stubbornly resists description. The bottom should have been a cube, but, no one knows how, it ended up an upside-down pyramid, like a paper boat. From this platform a crooked and asymmetrical watchtower rises, with a bare concrete staircase winding tightly around it, leading up to a single door, worn by the wind and rain. The lower level, the house itself, has an almost monumental entrance: a wrought iron gate in the form of two young women with their hair down, each with a lamp in her thin hands. To their left are two square windows, with wrought iron lattices, black, thin bars that seem convulsively twisted. The facade is gray, ancient, and worn, like all the other houses on the street. The tower's round window glows manically in the sun, at any moment of the day. Set against a clear sky, full of white, puffy clouds, on a summer morning, the tower has an unearthly beauty, but in the deep evenings, the window's scarlet flame is petrifying. This demented, desperate brilliance, this cry for help, made me, on that October evening, want this ugly, sad house more than anything in the world. I immediately strode across the lot to the front door. Behind the black bars, the glass was broken, like every other window. A cold breeze came from inside and it smelled like debris. A piece of paper was pasted beside the door, with "For Sale" written in pen. Below was a telephone number, and below that, "Ask for Mikola." I walked around the house, in the thickening dusk. Behind it was another street, with ashen apartment blocks, as though it was only on Maica Domnului that the neighborhood's arborescence produced these fruits of an exuberant, creole sadness. The windowless back wall of the house had once had a door, now bricked over. At that moment, looking at the outline of the door, I could see myself living there my whole life. If a house is the image of the one who lives there, as anamorphic and deceptive as it may be, I knew that there, in that ashen tesseract, I had found my ideal self-portrait. I could already see myself in the narrow tower room, watching the sky through the round window, while on the horizon, the sky turns dirty yellow and, all across this gaslight hue, the first stars emerge.

That same evening, when I came home, I spoke with my parents about buying the house. My mother knew Maica Domnului very well: nothing but whores and switchblades. They began to shout at me: "Is this why you went to college? To live with Gypsies? Tomorrow are you going to bring me a daughter-in-law in a gaudy dress? Tell me she's not going to leave you out on your bare ass, you little dog!" "You don't know them, listen to me," my father threw gas on the fire. "How are you going to sleep? All night it'll be shouting, fiddle, accordions, insults, like, like Gypsies are . . . Put a shirt out to dry, when you come back the next day it's gone." They kept on like that until I ran out of patience and left, went down to the phone booth, and called Mikola.

The man's voice on the phone made him seem very old, an impression confirmed when we met. He had built the house, he said, during the previous regime. So it was about a half century old. Since he had been away a long time (in prison, I was more than certain), the house had not been cared for after the war, and bit by bit it had fallen into disrepair. It needed a little structural work, and the plumbing and wiring had to be redone. Otherwise it was a good house, he had designed it and built it there, in a part of the city that seemed to have a future. It had lain empty about six years, after the last inhabitant had left for Israel, and the Gypsies couldn't or hadn't wanted to move in. The interior was relatively functional. I could, if I wanted, buy it with the furniture included. After he told me all of this in a single breath, in a hoarse voice, I asked him the price, and Mr. Mikola, pulling his beret farther back on his head, looked at me with his round, blue eyes, which the unusually deep folds on his forehead gave an expression of permanent surprise. Through the window of the narrow kitchen, where we were talking beside a plastic tablecloth, you could see the grassy banks of the Dâmbovița. "Eh, we'll settle on something," he told me. I seemed like a decent guy, and that was more important to him than money. He wasn't going to leave his house in just anyone's hands. Then, with a sort of senile inspiration, he told me a story that was, at first, quite confused. I was supposed to teach second period, I had already missed drill practice, and I couldn't let myself miss my first actual class. But in the end I did, because the old man's story, as incredible as it was, captivated me, and I didn't have the heart to rush or interrupt him.

What the man had been was hard to define: as an inventor, physicist, architect, even a kind of doctor, he had been known as Nicolae Borina, if that meant anything to me. I looked at him blankly. Among other things, he had invented the "Borina solenoid" but never patented it, because in the first place he didn't have any real education. He had only gone to the first few grades in Abrud, or Aleșd, "where I ought to have a statue!" Ten years he spent in the United States, where he had caught Tesla (for me at that time, the name was a brand of radio), and his solenoid was, as far as I understood, a continuation, an extension of his master's research into electromagnetism. Returning to Bucharest in 1925, he had wandered from one thing to another, modernizing the electric trams, studying escalators, trying to produce electricity at almost no cost by combining coils and magnets . . . He had built three or four industrial halls and even appeared in the circus, where he did a stunning (as he said) number with voltaic arcs. "We made electric sparks eight meters long, we did, until that stupid tent caught fire and they kicked us out." He peppered his story with, if you believed him, tens and hundreds of other achievements, including the famous Two-Wheel Maria, a sophisticated grisette who performed at the Grand Palace on Christian Tell; he mounted a dynamo to the front wheel of her pink Dorlay bicycle, apparently the first in Romania. He was subsequently hired by an Austrian firm that produced medical equipment, primarily chairs and other tools for dentist offices. He built the house during this period, the most productive of his life, when the famous solenoid was perfected and Mr. Mikola was about to conquer the world. He had been living in a hotel, like everyone in Bucharest high society, but in those years, especially once he began to practice "unipolar medicine," he saved up enough to construct the house. At this point in the story, I asked him what kind of therapy it was, how it treated illness. "Don't think I was one of those quacks from Flacăra. I actually healed people, I did. Don't ask me how, but I healed them. The best people came to me and they all left satisfied. Here was what we did: we used a device I invented (based on master Tesla's sketches, if I'm honest, but with my original contributions) which consisted of a pink spiral and a blue one (made of a very pure copper that we painted and insulated) in a double helix. This double spiral was two meters tall and wide enough inside for a person. So we had people stand in a chalk circle on the floor, and then we lowered the spiral down over them from the ceiling. Then we sent magnetic unipoles through the spirals, in opposing directions, the greatest secret science ever had. Not even the great Tesla could get to the bottom of it. The treatment lasted two hours, and the patient left healed of every sickness of the soul and body. Hepatitis, tuberculosis, melancholy, syphilis, hangnails, loving the wrong person, bad dreams, even some types of cancer were eliminated from the organism, which blossomed again as it had at age twenty." Of course, the envy of his guild was not slow to arrive, and within just a few years, the practice became the target of terrible attacks. In the end he was put in prison as a charlatan, and only interventions from high-placed people saved him from losing his fortune.

He had chosen his house's location through a complicated process. I listened to the old man, up to this moment, with interest and amusement. From here on the story became difficult to follow, with a lot of technical details I could not comprehend and which did not interest me. I understood the main idea of his discourse only later: Mr. Mikola seemed to believe in a planetwide magnetic network, which had, here and there, points of great intensity (nodes) and, in the opposite sense, inert points (valleys). His house was supposed to be over a node, the closest one on the map. You could find these points through either geomantic sensibility or a dizzying series of numerological calculations. The old man had followed both paths: when, through the art of combination, he found one of the Bucharest nodes, he checked the accuracy of his calculations with his own supersensorial faculties. "There, in the Gypsy neighborhood, in that vacant lot, was the magic place. I felt it as soon as I arrived. In that moment I perceived a silence as pure as white snow, I did, a silence from before there were ears, before the idea of sound. Or a silence from before the world appeared."

He purchased a tract of about five hundred square meters, taking care to cover the entire node. He dug a deep, wide foundation for the house, discovering some very old ruins from the abyss of history. There, in the grave of fresh clay, Nicolae Borina put his solenoid. It had cost a fortune. It was a torus shape, nine meters in diameter. Around the iron core were placed—in an incredibly complex pattern, in alternating directions and orientations calculated in an obtuse numerological system—sixteen layers of copper coils, each five millimeters thick. The giant spool had been manufactured in Basel and brought into the country by rail, on a special train. It was transported from the Filaret station at night and installed in secret, onto a socket with hydraulic cylinders and bearings, in the pit in Maica Domnului, where the medieval remnants were scooped out and dumped without much discussion into the landfill. A layer of concrete went over the solenoid, and the house was built on top.

My life had included, even before that moment, a fair amount of insanity, but the old man's story left me breathless. Second period at school had come and gone, and the rest of the day was not far behind. I could not care less. The old man seemed delirious, but I knew better than anyone that delirium is not the detritus of reality but a part of reality itself, sometimes the most precious part. In addition to the house, as a kind of advertising brochure or instruction booklet, I was buying a story. From then on, I would be the owner of a house that had been constructed, even if only in the senile imagination of a nonagenarian, on top of a gigantic coil buried in the earth. It was as though Mr. Mikola, in an inexplicable magnanimity, had given me a bell jar containing his own brain, with a boat-shaped house built upon its hemispheres.

"On the twelfth of September 1936, young man, I finished the house. It stood alone, beautiful as a pearl, amid the empty lots and tin shacks. And inside it was painted and furnished, framed paintings and photographs were on every last wall, precious carpets (today worn down to their discolored webbing) glistened in vivid hues . . . In the windows, black stems of wrought iron sprouted buds and tender branches . . . It was a wonder, as lovable as a woman with wide hips and generous thighs . . . I had a house and land, but I didn't enjoy it, I didn't . . ." The woman proved to be frigid. The solenoid, whatever the hell it was supposed to do, never worked. It was the greatest disappointment and defeat of the inventor's life. He had started the machine on the very first night. Aside from the large coil, it had a number of motors and other devices, many he had invented himself. The air began to buzz, the floor vibrated gently, but the wonder (which the old man, unexpectedly stubborn after so many revelations, refused to explain in the slightest) did not appear. He advised me, therefore, to take a look at the coil and, if I still wanted the house, to enjoy it as though it were a normal building, even though . . . Even though, he added with remorse, it's too bad . . .

Mr. Mikola did not even get to enjoy the normal parts of the house. Immediately after the change of regime, he was imprisoned for political reasons (a former fascist? member of one of the historical parties?) and not released until 1964. After a difficult struggle, he regained his right to own the house, with the help of a friend at the highest levels of the party. Luckily, it had not attracted the greedy eyes of any of the new vultures, since it was in a rundown neighborhood of ill repute. After it had sat empty a while, worn by rain and snow, the old man had rented it to one person or another, but lately he had not been able to find renters. Now, as he was living what might be his last years, he thought to sell it, even though he did not believe he could. "Only a person like yourself sees my house as worthy of desire. I can tell you want to live there. It's clear you didn't choose the house, it chose you. I can only wish you more luck with it than I had. This is why I said (it's so seldom I talk to anyone) you should fix it up for yourself and the woman you choose to live with. It's a good house, it is, you'll be comfortable there."

He sold it to me for seventy-five thousand lei. In the end my parents gave me the money, what else could they do? The borrowed it from the Banca

CAER, and they are still making payments. I had looked at the inside of the house with the old man the weekend after we talked, but still, when I set off for the first time down Maica Domnului, with the closing papers in my briefcase and the key in my pocket, it was like I was going there for the first time, and, in fact, it has been like that every time since: I am always surprised and charmed by the melancholic smell of rot around me, the silence and distance, as though I were in another realm, so different on that street than on any other. No more do I have that feeling of rending happiness, except in the afternoons, when I am about to fall asleep and see flashes from my most important dreams.

Every time I enter my house, I feel as though I am entering an enormous stomach. I can almost hear, around it, the whispering intestines. At night, when I look at the stars through the latticed windows, I see the ganglions of the grand woman inside of whom I live. The creaks of the old furniture and the flooring sometimes seem to me, in the middle of the night, like the popping vertebrae of an enormous column of spongiform bone. I am happy in my home. I have come to know its interior anatomy quite well. The rooms have tilted walls, none of them is as tall as any other. The wardrobes reach the ceiling. Their wood is spongy, swollen as though puffed out by invisible breezes. The hanging light fixtures are the same wrought iron as on the doors and windows. The bathroom is always damp, the oil paint on the green walls is faded, the metal faucets look like salt has eaten them away. The tub is a deep, old-fashioned type, with lion-claw feet. At the bottom, the porcelain is worn away like the enamel off of old teeth. When I stand naked, facing the gray water that fills the tub, I sometimes feel I am in a world without time, in a photograph: I have always been, I will always be this way, frozen there, beside the toilet with a rusty handle, unable to move, looking silently at water I will never enter.

My home has tens, hundreds, or thousands of rooms. When I go through a door, I never know where I will end up. All the rooms are silent, with giant macramé tablecloths, pedestals with red crystal candy bowls, showcases where model ships sail. Sometimes there are narrow hallways between the rooms, with windows heaped with pots of pale flowers hanging over the edge. Passing between rooms always takes me up or down a few steps, always to discover behind the next door an enormous salon, with strange allegories painted on the ceiling, or the opposite, a closet with mops and rags. When I come home from school, usually at six in the evening, I start my meanderings through the house. The light is clear and rosy, like a gelatin that fills the entire space. Sometimes I feel I stay still and the house rotates around me: windows approach, hallways slowly take me in, doors swing open to greet me . . . Perspectives constantly change, and I proceed by standing still, amazed by the ever-changing views.

Finally, I come to the bedroom; of all the shifting rooms, it always stays the same: the only ordinary, dusty place, where the texture of faded sheets, the chipped finish on the dresser, and the nightstand where I keep my treasures have become transparent and in the end disappeared from my field of consciousness, the way you can't see the soft, inverted grail of jellyfish in the ocean waters. Everything in my bedroom is true: the sheet is a sheet, the plaster is plaster, I am an unimportant mammal who has lived for a moment on Earth. Beside the dresser is a ladder that leads up to the deck. It is a library ladder, one that glides along the wall. But this one has been solidly screwed into the ceiling. There is a hatch above it, awkward to open from the top of the ladder, where suddenly the blue sky appears with summer clouds, through this rift in the variable geometry of the ceiling. I climb onto the deck, which, if there were not a tilted white tower growing asymmetrically above, would resemble those white cubes where people in the Near East live. The tower's thick, white plaster is flaking off from the rain and heat. A spiral staircase surrounds it, making one complete circumference. The deck is flat, without a wall or rail; sometimes in the summer I spread out a sheet and lie in the sun, under clouds so low that I can feel them, warm and damp as sponges, on my thighs, nipples, nose, and chin. The sun reflects in the tower's round window, making it glow like a lighthouse on a craggy peak.

The tower, whose oddness and metaphysics made me buy the house, has a door at the top, just under the roof. For a long time I did not understand why it needed a spiral staircase and an entry point hanging from the side. At some point the door had been painted scarlet red, but by my time, only traces and flakes of the paint still clung to the timeworn door, covered with insect larvae and translucent cobwebs. It was always locked, but not with a key, as you might expect, rather with a code, like a briefcase. Within an iron rectangle were four wheels, each as oily as the next (thanks to this dark grease they turned easily, in spite of the rust that had nearly obliterated the numbers), which turned under your finger to show a digit. The number that opened the lock, with a click of the tumblers, was 7129. Mikola had wheezed this great mystery into my ear: the number was secret and should never be written down anywhere.

When you opened the door, the darkness inside appeared hard and dense: where could you enter, where could you fit? You had to push the door again, with a force equivalent to the volume of darkness you displaced. After your eyes adjusted to the dark, you saw you could step onto a small landing, a metal walkway suspended over the night. I remember when, my heart beating forcefully, I entered the tower for the first time: Once I closed the door, the world disappeared. It wasn't just that I couldn't see anything: sight itself disappeared. I could not remember what it was like to see. I opened and closed my eyes without any change. The other senses also disappeared, along with their worlds, except for the pressure of my feet on the metal. Terrified, I tried to open the door. There was no door. There were no walls around me. I held my hands out into the void, into nothing, and the tips of my fingers, like insect antennae, tried to latch on to reality. Or to generate reality, like tiny electric sparks. My fingertips returned inert, without any report from death and absence. I was alone, placed like a statue on my walkway, in the infinity of the night. I stayed this way for hour after hour. I felt my hands across my face and body to demonstrate the continued existence of existence. I shouted unheard, I felt, as I had in so many nights of fear and cold sweats, the terror of the end of being, the disappearance of the world. In the end, surfaces and sounds and tastes, and my internal organs, and the perception of acceleration, and ineffable aromas, these returned, or my brain re-created them, like a tireless weaver with his flying shuttle, so that out of nonbeing, first the imperceptible filaments were woven together, the infra-real strings and curls, braided into the fabric of space and time. Vague, phosphorescent, the walls remade themselves around me, as though a light had begun to flicker, growing by a single photon each minute, but growing, and ricocheting off surfaces in order to invent them, bit by bit. I began to sense things around me again, and, when my fingers found the extraordinarily vague ebony switch, I felt, for a nanosecond, that I had slipped into the refined flame of the creator. I pressed it and there was light, blinding and unbearable. It took another eternity for my eyes to become accustomed.

Hanging from the metal platform was a ladder, also made of metal. It led toward the tower floor, in the center of which, though apparently floating about halfway up, was a round, ivory-colored object occupying a quarter of the field of vision, the rest of which contained the rectangular stone tiles of the floor. The object seemed to levitate in the shaft of the tower, but once you climbed far enough down to touch it, you could see it was actually held on a metal column, also ivory-colored, stuck to the thing that now appeared clearly: an old and complicated dentist's chair, the leather headrest faded, the iron of the drill and turbine covered by a fine dust, the tray in front full of nickeled utensils. The round body above it was full of curved glass apertures, like spotlights. In front, at the same height as a patient would sit, there was a round window, like a porthole, making my dwelling look even more like a ship. The window was covered with a kind of lid, which also had a number on it, this time with several more digits. I didn't try to open the hatch for a long time, because all my attention was on the chair, waiting there for decades perhaps, bolted to the floor. Not a speck of dust, not a strand of cobweb, not the tiniest trace of mold was there to show the passage of time in that silent room. It seemed like an image from the center of your mind, clear as a camera lucida and just as enigmatic. I sat, as I would do so many times, in the yellowed, imitation leather chair. A push of a metal button turned on the lights in the giant porcelain saucer. I was bathed in light, supported from behind, with my head back on the headrest, like a navigator in a ship set to cross the void between galaxies.

What was this vision? The old man hadn't told me anything about a "dentist's office," as I imagined the tower originally was. But what kind of office could this have been; in order to get to the dentist, you had to go through a bedroom, climb a ladder, cross the porch, go up another stairway, a narrow and dangerous one made of cement, around a tower, and then climb down like you were in a submarine? Who would ever enter this claustrophobic and sinister trap? And where was the waiting room? I thought about all of this in the hours when, having retreated to my tower, under the clear light of the bulbs adorning the ivory cap, I toyed with the instruments on the porcelainized tray: strange, narrow pliers, snippers, grinders shaped like tops . . . It was only missing the substances that give dentist offices their special smell: filling paste, plaster, anesthetics. There was no smell at all in my tower.

Was it possible that Mr. Mikola, in who knows what moment of trial and penury in his life, would have worked as a dentist? Could he have used this chair to study dentistry? Who would have been his guinea pig? Or was he trying, as an inventor, to make these chairs better, to improve their circuitry, transmissions, rheostats? But there was no sign of handiwork, no trace of oil, no loose screws: the mechanism was as perfect as an insect with a hard carapace and flawless mechanical joints. It all worked, even though it was an older model and therefore a little strange-looking: every turn of a button lit a dim bulb and whirred the tips of mechanisms hanging from thick cables of twisted metal. A button raised and lowered the chair, with a sound like an old elevator. Another caused a pink rubber tube, with a metal tip, to suck up imaginary saliva.

I was, for a long time, a guest in my own house. Because the times were terrible and the stores had nothing but jars of floating, livid vegetables you could not possibly eat, and because I suffered from loneliness like a dog, I preferred to stay on with my parents, on Ştefan cel Mare. My mother knew where to get her ration of eggs, where "they stashed" the cheese. We went to stand in line at dawn, sometimes while it was still night, behind the apartment block across the street, in an awful winter wind, in an animalistic crowd, for a speck of chicken or a bottle of milk as thin as water. Still, it was food, and, still, I was with my folks; I had someone to talk to. But sometimes I went straight home after school and spent the night in my silent bedroom on Maica Domnului. How many times, in that period of unending sadness, did I wake in the dead of night with the feeling that I was inside a cell as narrow as a tomb, buried deep below the earth? How many dozens of times did it seem to me that through the walls I could hear the tap-tap of an impossible escape? How many notebooks did I fill with crescents, gears, crosses, and triangles, an obscure language and yet the only important one, resembling logical notation? The terror of being in the world, my animalistic fear of the nothingness of our lives, displayed itself in all its desperation. But the taps on the wall stopped before I could decipher them, to be replaced by the endless night.

9

I want to write a report of my anomalies. In my obscure life, lying outside any version of history, placeable perhaps within the taxonomies of a history of literature, things have happened that do not happen, not in life and not in books. I could write novels about them, but a novel would muddy the facts, would make them ambiguous. I could keep them to myself, as I have until now, and ponder them until my head cracks open every night that I spend balled up under my blanket while the rain beats furiously against my window. But I don't want to keep them to myself. I want to write a report, even though I don't know what kind of report or what I'm going to do with these pages once I'm done. I don't even know if this is the right moment. I haven't come to any conclusion, I don't have a coherent story, the facts of my life are vague flashes over the banal surface of the most banal of lives, little fissures, small discrepancies. These unshaped shapes, allusions and insinuations, topographical irregularities are sometimes insignificant by themselves, but taken together they become strange and haunting, they need a new and unusual form in which their story is to be told. Not a novel, not a poem, because these anomalies are not fiction (or at least not entirely), not a scientific study, because many of these events are singularities that even the laboratory of my mind cannot reproduce. In the case of my anomalies, I can't even separate dreams from ancient memories from reality, the fantastic from the magical, the scientific from the paranoid. My hunch is that, in fact, my anomalies come from that part of the mind where these distinctions do not hold, and that this zone of my mind is nothing but another anomaly. The facts of my report are going to be phantasmic and transparent, but that is the nature of the worlds in which we simultaneously live.

Since I was seven, I have kept a cheap medallion I received from some foreign tourists whose buses stopped at the State Circus. Whenever we heard that a bus was nearby, we dropped whatever we were doing into the sand, jumped off the swings, left the frogs alone in the reed-filled lake at the end of the park, and ran toward the circus building, with its enormous prismatic windows and its azure, corrugated cupola, under which I had lived my whole life. We gathered around the massive bus and, in spite of our parents' warnings ("Don't let me catch you begging from the foreigners! What, are we beggars now? What are people going to say?"), we held out our hands to receive a stick of gum or an Eiffel Tower keychain or a brightly painted metal car . . . I was about seven when a woman stepped out of the bus in a printed dress and pink hoop earrings, smiled at me, and put this gilded copper coin in my hand. I ran off to the heavy chestnut tree that hung over the fountain; here, a big kid wouldn't take it from me. I looked more closely at the gift: it shone brightly in the summer sun. It was a round, gilded coin set in a metal frame. There were letters on both sides of the coin: A, O, R on one side, M and U on the other. Several days passed before I solved the mystery when on a whim I flicked the coin and it spun so quickly in its metal frame that it became a gold sphere, as free and transparent as a dandelion, with the ghostly word AMOUR in the middle. This is what my life is like, how it has always seemed: the singular, uniform, and tangible world on one side of the coin, and the secret, private, phantasmagoric world of my mind's dreams on the other side. Neither is complete and true without the other. Only the rotation, only the whirling, only vestibular syndromes, only a god's careless finger spins the coin, adds a dimension, and makes visible (but for whose eyes?) the inscription engraved in our minds—on one side and the other, on day and night, lucidity and dream, woman and man, animal and god, while we remain eternally ignorant because we cannot see both sides at the same time. And it doesn't end there, because you need to comprehend the transparent inscription of liquid gold in the middle of the sphere, and in order to understand it with your mind, not just to see it with your eyes, your mind must become an eye in a higher dimension. The dandelion sphere must itself be spun, on a plane impossible to imagine, in order to become, in relation to the sphere, what the sphere is in relation to the flat disk. The meaning lies in the hypersphere, in the unnamable, transparent object that results from spinning the sphere in the fourth dimension. But here I've come, much too quickly, to Hinton and his cubes, to which my anomalies seem in some obscure way to be connected.

My facts will be, therefore, ghostly and transparent and undecidable, but never unreal. I have always felt them touch my own skin. They have tortured me much more than necessary. In a way, they have stolen my life from me, in the same way my books would have, if I had managed to write them. Furthermore, there is another reason to regard these facts as dubious and undecided: they are not finished, they are ongoing. I have some signs, I've made some connections, I've begun to see something that resembles coherence in the charade of my life. Clearly, something is speaking to me, insistently, constantly, like a continuous pressure on my skull, on certain organs, but what is this message, what is its nature, from whom does it come? What does it ask of me? I sometimes feel like a child in front of a chessboard. You've grabbed the pawn, wonderful. But why are you sticking it in your mouth? Why are you tilting the board so all the pieces fall off? Or could this be the solution? Maybe the game is won by the person who suddenly understands its absurdity and throws it to the ground, the one who cuts through the knot while everyone else is trying to unravel it?

I will, therefore, put a story of my life together. Its visible part, as I know better than anyone, is the least spectacular, the tamest of lives, the life that fits my timidity, my introversion, my lack of meaning and lack of future. A matchstick burned almost to its end, leaving behind a gray-white line of ash. A Romanian teacher at School 86 at the end of Colentina. In spite of that, I have memories that tell another story, I have dreams that solidify and confirm these memories, and together, there, in the underground caverns of my mind, they have built a world full of fantastical events, indecipherable facts that, nonetheless, demand deciphering. It is as though a floor of my life collapsed: the cables snapped and the connections broke off the building on the surface. My memories of childhood and adolescence contain chains of events I can barely place and cannot understand, like puzzle pieces tossed into a box. Like dreams awaiting interpretation. I have thought about them often; they appear so clearly before my eyes (I hold a shining piece of cardboard in the light, it has round or invaginated edges; its illustrations are clear as a mirror: a few blue flowers, part of a lampshade, a string of pearls on a throat with no body, a cat's paw . . .) that my mind is full of images and allegorical figures, all of them enigmatic, because enigma is a sign of incompleteness: a god is only the visible part of a world with one dimension more than our own. Each of my memories and dreams (and dreamed memories, and remembered dreams, because my world has thousands of hues and shades) contain indications that they belong to a system, like puzzle pieces that stick out and poke in: this coupling mechanism is the most salient part of their "abnormalities"—of "my anomalies"—because, to the extent of my knowledge of people, literature, and life, no one has noticed the interlocking system, the hooks and eyes, of certain ancient memories and dreams. When I was a child, my parents would buy me, at the Little Red Riding Hood store on Str. Lizeanu whose floors smelled so powerfully of kerosene cleaner, the cheapest and most banal toys: a tin cart with crude decorations, a dwarf that came out of a rubber egg, a mechanical goose with a key that turned to make it hop across the shining table, cubes with pictures of cows, horses, and sheep, and the "Jumbled Pieces" game with pictures from fairy tales. This last one made me the happiest. On one side were parts of a picture as shown on a separate piece of paper, and on the other side, each tale had a decoration, a backing paper with colors and shapes. Naturally, I would first put the squares together according to the pictures: Snow White's left eye goes with her right. The dwarf's elbow connects to his shoulder and a part of his chin. But soon, assembling the picture from the jumbled fragments seemed too easy, too boring. I began to put the puzzle pieces together by their backs. I would sort them by color and follow their logical connections: the circle continuing out of one piece connected to a circle cut from the shining square of another. Sometimes it was very hard, but the difficulty increased my satisfaction and gave the game new meaning.

I cannot help but wonder whether our oldest memories—the limpid memories that flow through our lives while thousands of other, perhaps more important, moments have left our memory—and likewise, our dreams of haunting clarity that seem made from the same substance as our haunting memories, are not this kind of a game; a test, a challenge we have to pass through in the inexplicable adventure of this life. Perhaps the beating of our hearts is only the stopwatch that measures the time we have to find the answer. Perhaps, if we get to the last beat without understanding any part of the immense puzzle in which we live, it will be bad for us. Perhaps, if we find the solution, if we give the right answer, we will be released from our cell in the great penitentiary, or at least ascend one level closer to release. The white mouse running through plexiglass hallways doesn't know its memory is being tested—it's just living its life. Its brain is not capable of asking: Why am I here? How did I end up in this maze? But isn't the maze, with its symmetries, its piece of cheese at the farthest end, itself the marker of a higher realm, of an intelligence, in comparison to which my poor little mind is just babbling in the darkness?

The fact that I have not become a writer, the fact that I am nothing, that I have no importance to the world outside, that nothing outside interests me, that I have no ambitions or needs, that I don't fool myself by painting doors "with sensitivity and talent" on the maze's smooth walls, doors that will never open, gives me a unique opportunity, or perhaps the opportunity available to all those who are alone and forgotten: I can explore the odd artifacts of my own mind as they appear during the endless series of evenings when, as my silent room darkens, my mind rises like the moon and glows brighter and brighter. Then I see palaces and hidden worlds on its surface, things never revealed to those running inside the maze, obsessed by the piece of cheese, without a moment's rest, convinced that this is all the world holds, that beyond the white, curving walls there is nothing. I wonder how many lonely and insignificant people, how many clerks and tram drivers, how many unhappy, mourning women without an inheritance or a university title, without power and without hope, are actually excavators working the thick earth of autumn evenings, an earth of pupae and worms, an earth that trembles with beetles scurrying through their tunnels?

Since the autumn of 1974, from the age of seventeen, my life has had a double, a paper wrapping, and, until now, I have paid it no more than the careless attention a beggar gives the newspapers he puts over himself so he won't be cold. I am talking about my diary, where, for thirteen years, I have recorded, without any intentions, in a pure reflection of my inner voice, happenings, literary exercises, reactions to books I have read, frustrations and sufferings, unusual states and dreams. I have written in old school notebooks with ruled or graph paper and flimsy, turquoise cardboard covers with an idiotic dwarf on the front and a multiplication table on the back, I've also written in expired day planners with cracked plastic covers, in wire-bound student notebooks, in notebooks as long and narrow as train tickets, whatever I could find, whatever I had on hand, with pens and markers (some pages have faded beyond legibility) . . . All these notebooks are in a disordered pile in the bottom drawer of my nightstand. Today I am going to put them in chronological order, so I can pull out those fragments that are interesting to me, that I almost know by heart. Many of my anomalies are recorded there, in pages that feel almost soldered together. Each entry is dated and sometimes recorded in passing, sometimes shaking with a terror that runs transparently through the text. At least these facts I cannot doubt, at least these were embedded within the irreal reality of my life. If it weren't for the diary, I doubt I would ever have begun to write these pages. First, because I would have fallen out of the habit of writing, of writing even nonliterary texts, of filling pages with inky curls. It is impossible to imagine how stultifying the profession of teaching is, how much you degenerate, year after year, correcting homework and goading students to learn, repeating the same phrase dozens or hundreds of times, reading the same text aloud "with feeling," talking to the same colleagues in whose eyes you perceive the same desperation and helplessness that they see in yours (and which you see in the mirror, every morning as you shave). And you know you are decaying, that your mind is a pool of bombastic vomit and clichéd quotations, and still you can do nothing but scream, silently, like someone being tortured in an underground cell, alone with his executioner, watching in complete lucidity as the fabric of his body is rent, as he is eviscerated alive and unable to object. Second, because I would have forgotten what has happened to me. These pages are living folds of my memory, the curls and braids of the letters are flexible, raw synapses, like tendrils of vines. I haven't written any novels, but if I had, they would have only been ramifications of my diary, my veins and arteries branching into further networks of tunnels where each node is an umbilical cord where a chubby fetus grows, whose face looks like mine. My diary is my witness, it is proof that at a particular moment, in a place with precise coordinates, the world opened up, there was a breach, and the charming and terrifying pseudopods arrived from another world, not the world of fiction, not the world of a feverish brain, but a world embedded in what we still call reality. Not in a dream, not in hallucinations did the visitors arrive, not in hypnagogic or hypnopompic states was I hurled against the wardrobe after I was yanked, sheets and all, from my bed by an irresistible force, and not within the secondary game of fiction did I dissolve in flames of mad ecstasy, not in overexcited fantasies was I forced into horrible, horrible couplings . . . Everything was real, everything lay on the same plane of existence where we eat and drink and comb our hair and lie and go to work and die from longing and loneliness. Dreams are also real, our first memories our real, and fiction is real (so real!), yet we feel foreign to our ashen homeland, we feel hard, prickly, stubborn, unimaginative, meaningless, or unsalvageable, the cell where we were tossed after we sipped the dark waters of Lethe. The real—our legitimate homeland—ought to be a fabulous realm, but it is instead an oppressive prison. Our destiny ought to be escape, if only to escape into a bigger prison that connects to an even larger one in an endless line of cells, but for this to happen the doors in the yellowed wall of our brow bone must burst open. I will scratch, with a rusty nail, for months and years of miserable, animal strain, on this door in the wall that in the end (I have my signs) must fall.

I know no one does this; people are resigned and stay quiet. This prison is inescapable. The walls, definitely, are infinitely thick, it is the night before our birth and after our death. "What's the point of pondering the infinity of the nonbeing to come? I will darken my life for no reason. I still have a few years until then, I can still enjoy this blessed light, the full moon rising over the forest, the discrete functioning of my gallbladder, my ejaculations into happy wombs, the productivity of my work, the bug that climbs toward my fingertip to spread its crumpled cellophane wings. No one knows what lies beyond the grave." We have the same attitude as the ancients: let's eat and drink, for tomorrow we die. And within the logic of the prison with infinite walls, we can't think any differently. Is there another way, aside from digging like a mite through the wall's endless dermis?

As long as I can remember, I have had a strong feeling of predestination. The very act of opening my eyes in the world made me feel like I was chosen—because they weren't a spider's eyes, they weren't the thousands of hexagons of a fly's eye, they weren't the eyes on the tips of a snail's horns; because I didn't come into the world as a bacterium or a myriapod. The enormous ganglion of my brain, I felt, predestined me to an obsessive search for a way out. I understood I must use my brain like an eye, open and observant under the skull's transparent shell, able to see with another kind of sight and to detect fissures and signs, hidden artifacts and obscure connections in this test of intelligence, patience, love, and faith that is this world. As long as I can remember, I have done nothing but search for breaches in the apparently flat, logical, fissureless surface of the model within my skull. What am I supposed to think, what am I supposed to understand, what are you saying to me, what are you whispering in an unknown language?

"As long as I exist, as long I have been given the impossible opportunity of being," I have often told myself, "I am, without a doubt, chosen." We are all chosen in this sense, we are all illuminated, because the sun of existence illuminates us all. And I am chosen twice over because, unlike a wasp or crustacean, I am able to think in logical space and I can make models of the world in which I can move on their reduced, virtual scale, while my arms and legs move through the inconceivable real world. And I am thrice chosen because unlike shopkeepers and plumbers and warriors and whores and clowns and other groups of people who look like me, I can ponder my choices and think of myself thinking. The object of my thought is my thought, and my world is the same as my mind. My mission is, thus, that of a surveyor and cartographer, an explorer of organs and caves, of the oubliettes and prisons of my mind, as well as its Alps, full of glaciers and ravines. Walking in the footsteps of Gall, Lombroso, and Freud, I also attempt to understand the colossal, intricate, imperial, and, in the end, inextricable Gordian knot that fills the forbidden room of the brain, its braids of wire and hemp, its spider silk and strands of saliva, its obscene lace of garters and fine scales of gold chains, its flexible bindweed ductwork and anthracite black whips of a beetle's antennae.

Up to this point, our chosen status is natural, like a gift we assumed would come, although it still feels like a wonder. If I had been a writer, I would have stopped here and been happy, ultrahappy, with my power of invention, with the beauty and singularity of my books. We live in a charming jail, no less magical than anything else we can imagine. At the end of my life, I could have proudly pointed to a line of novels or books of poetry, arranged like so much bread sliced from the world in which I lived. To be human, to live the life of a person, to bring new people and new beings formed by your mind into the world, to rejoice in the seventy rotations of your world around the ball of lava that gives it life—we may call this happiness, even if every life adds some blood, sweat, and tears to the mixture. But there is a fourth level of chosen, in comparison to which all of the world's literature is just as volatile as dandelion puff.

Our school's porter, Ispas, is an old Gypsy man, always smoking, eternally unshaven, with the dry skin of those who were born in the unhealthy air of the big and ugly city. He sits in between the two latticed entrance doors at a minuscule table dusted with the dandruff that falls from his hair. No one takes any notice of him, not even the kids. No one sees him come or go. He sits there, like a rag doll, stuffed into his brown uniform, in the lowliest job in the world. But his watery, chestnut eyes are as human as those of a stray dog. No one looks at him, but he looks at those who pass as though he were counting them, classifying them, giving them purpose. The only people who sometimes stop and chat are the janitors, usually the voluble and overweight Aunt Iakab, with her mongoloid face and pronounced mustache, who constantly butts in on chatter in the teachers' lounge. She's the one who told everyone about the porter's crazy idea. He lives alone, splitting his life between school and a stairway in an apartment block on Râul Colentina, where he sleeps on a mattress. The tenants let him stay there out of pity, they even let him sleep in their apartments when they are traveling, because the old man tries hard but can't earn two coins to rub together. "But guess what he thinks," Aunt Iakab says, bursting with laughter. When she laughs, her olive cheeks poke out left and right like she's holding bread buns. "He thinks that one day a flying saucer's going to come and take him to another world. 'Obviously,' I say to him, 'it'll be you, of all people.' I mean really . . ." At night, Ispas walks through the neighborhood, stopping in the middle of intersections. He stands there for hours on end, ready, his old, dirty suitcase swollen like an accordion, and the neck of a bottle with a corncob plug sticking out one side. He looks at the sky and yells to "them" that he's ready. "I mean, they've found the right person," a bored teacher will mutter, before she tucks the register under her arm. They've been making fun of the porter for years, but he, silent and humble in between the doors, knows better. He has time to wait, he has his faith. At night he looks up from our minuscule world at the star-filled sky, and even if he will never be taken, this hope alone makes him better than those around him, people who mock others and run around the plexiglass maze day after day, looking for the cheese. At least he looks at the stars, he, the lowliest person who has ever lived on Earth; at least he wants to get out.

Any definition of "the chosen" is controversial. It has nothing to do with a person's face, his actions or ideas. Being chosen is unimaginable, and for a rational mind built for this world, it is complete insanity. When a Christian says, "I will be saved," the skeptic recalls that there is no reason an unimportant mite—living for a nanosecond on a speck of dust in one of a billion billion galaxies—should be noticed, in particular, by an eye from another world and in the end be saved. We cannot pretend that we will be saved any sooner than a single bacterium in our intestinal flora. Why should I be saved, in particular, of all the people on the planet? What is precious in me, what fruit could be picked, and who could do it, from the seed of light that is my consciousness?

I never laugh at the porter and his flying saucers. He, like others, feels foreign to our world. Like others, he writhes, searches, and waits. I think that the discomfort of those like him, however ridiculous, is a sign of being chosen. Because no one in this world, where everything conspires in the construction of perfect illusions and a corresponding despair, no one can hope if it wasn't given to him to hope, and they cannot search if they do not have the instinct for seeking engraved in the flesh of their mind. We search like idiots, we look in places where there is nothing to find, like spiders that weave webs in the corner of a bathroom where flies don't come, where not even mosquitos can reach. We shrivel in our webs by the thousands, but what doesn't die is our need for truth. We are like people drawn inside of a square on a piece of paper. We cannot get out of the black lines, we exhaust ourselves by examining, dozens and hundreds of times, every part of the square, hoping to find a fissure. Until one of us suddenly understands, because he was predestined to understand, that within the plane of the paper escape is impossible. That the exit, simple and open wide, is perpendicular to the paper, in a third dimension that up until that moment was inconceivable. Such that, to the amazement of those still inside the four ink lines, the chosen one breaks out of his chrysalis, spreads his enormous wings, and rises gently, leaving his shadow below in his former world.

10

Sometimes Irina comes over. She is the physics teacher, skinny and pale, with the face of a martyr illuminated by her incredible blue eyes. I have never seen eyes like hers. Irina is like an old, worn photograph, a sepia portrait of an anemic creature, the very image of resignation, but her eyes look like someone poked holes in the photo to let the blue sky show through. I remember the first time I saw her in the teachers' lounge. It was winter, the winter of '81. I had come to school while it was still dark outside, and I was standing at a window half-covered with frost blossoms. I was quietly enjoying the last ten minutes before class began. I was still half-asleep, alone in the room, when the door opened and Irina appeared. From the first moment, her eyes surprised me: she seemed like a collage, like a magic trick. It wasn't just that the eyes did not fit the woman's then jaundiced face: they didn't even fit reality itself. They were beautiful, but not as you would say, "A flower is beautiful," or, "A child is beautiful," rather as you would say, "It is beautiful that there are flowers and children." The word "beautiful" didn't fit her except as a substitute for a word that doesn't exist. She didn't greet me, although I nodded toward her. Only after a few minutes, when others started coming into the lounge, did I overhear her say she was the new physics teacher. Of course, over the following weeks, Irina became part of the living furniture of the teachers' lounge. I saw her during the breaks between classes, when she, like all the others, tossed the register into the cupboard and sat at a corner of the table. As soon as she lowered her eyes, and she spent most of her time looking at the floor, Irina disappeared. She melted, pure and simple, into the background. She was extremely shy, she usually sat alone, only seldom joining in the endless conversations among teachers who had small children: how hard it was to find powdered milk, where she could find a stroller that didn't look like a wheelbarrow . . . We took the same tram home, number 21. It was the only tram toward the city, so I knew where she lived: she got off each time near the Suveica dress shop, as did I, and lost herself among the apartment blocks across the way. It took two years before I came to know her, if you can ever know someone. In all this time we never exchanged more than a couple words, as was true of many of my fellow teachers, the way that, while you might see the same clerk at the bread shop every day, a whole lifetime may pass and you still won't be sure if she is a human being like you or a bizarre coloration that inexplicably appears from time to time on your retina. It took two years for us to wait for the tram together under a pale sky last spring, alongside other teachers, all of us dressed lightly for the first time although the air was still damp and cold, to stand silently in the tram full of passengers, to get off at Suveica and go to my place, almost in a single motion, almost without a thought, seemingly as we had done countless times before. As we stood next to each other in the tram, pushed together by the animal crowd, she suddenly turned her face toward me and said, "Aren't you a poet?" I decided in a split second to take this as a joke, so I smiled and answered, "What makes you think that?" "I thought that poets acted like you do: in the lounge you're always staring out the window, never making a sound... I've never seen anyone so silent." She kept smiling, she looked in my eyes, and she did it for the first time, maintaining this absurd story: "I think you and I, in a way, are a lot alike."

That's how it all started, not between us, since there is no "between us," that's just how it started. Things happened to begin with this conversation, but I think everything would have been the same if she had said to me, at that moment in the tram, "These are the first warm days we've had this March," or "Look how the sun is reflecting off the windows." I felt, suddenly, as I stepped off the tram behind her, straightening my jacket the crowd had crumpled, that there was no border between us, and I could have taken her hand then if I had known that there were no other teachers, parents, or children in the tram. Suddenly, where there had been nothing, a portal opened, suddenly the door to a house you've passed hundreds of times is wide open, waiting for you in the night with all its windows lit. It's not magic, because it is just as natural as a dream of embracing, on the street, a woman you don't know. In a dream, nothing is magic, the dream itself is magic. It's natural, but in a suddenly unnatural world. It's normal, but in a life that is sweet and sad and not your own. I walked alongside Irina down Str. Suren Spandarian, talking about Krishnamurti, while the overflowing trash bins began to stink, the way they did every spring after the thaw . . . A rag here and there had fallen from an apartment and landed in a tree's bare branches, a skeletal dog curled up at the foot of a stairway here and there reflected us in its yellow eyes . . . When she said, "Here's where I live," pointing to one of the blocks without slowing her steps and without turning to say goodbye, my certainty that we would end up at my house and in my bed simply became a reality, as though we were already in bed and this were nothing unusual. I know—and she confirmed it later—that in all that ten-minute walk together, from the tram stop to the front of her block, as opposed to a love story where they make all the decisions, we didn't make a single one, as we had never not decided anything in our lives, but even more so: the way you don't decide to float downstream when you fall into a rain-swollen river that bears you along with an uprooted tree and bits of a roof, or the way a beetle encased in amber doesn't decide to stay there for eternity. We are embedded in existence, we are woven into its great tapestry, we are not expected to make decisions, since everything is decided ahead of time, the way the rungs on a chair don't decide to make up the chair, they just do. That is how it is with things you don't feel every day, but just like what happened to me with Irina—when you shouldn't be there and yet you are, when everything should be different and yet it is as it is, and you have the quiet feeling that this is how it should be, how it was supposed to be.

"It's crazy that I teach physics," she said to me, "Me, when I don't believe in reality at all . . . I talk to the kids about matter and physical laws, when I know everything is an illusion . . ." Irina was reading theosophy and anthroposophy, teaching herself English so she could read Krishnamurti, but for now she had to guess at half of the words, and she had invented, pure and simple, her own Krishnamurti, guessing meanings that never existed and mistranslating the already disconnected and vague phrases into luminous and exalted textual whirlpools that, in her eyes, were sacred and as indisputable as sensory data.

I have never been interested in ecstatic blather about Madame Blavatsky and her white cat, about Rudolf Steiner and Gurdjieff, about Templars and Rosicrucians, it never spoke to me; at most, I've paid them unconscious attention, the way you notice a woman's perfume at a party. And this was basically the story: Irina's fragrance was her meager originality—without any connection to either her real life or her otherworldly eyes, more metaphysical and more insane than any writings of the Illuminati or alchemists. "I want to believe that things exist," she once said, while with the same lazy, unhurried steps we walked from Nada Florilor toward Tei Lake Boulevard, "but honestly, I can't. I touch them and say to myself, 'it's an illusion, these aren't real.' I touch myself and I cannot believe I am wrapped inside this body. Do you understand what it means to live like this? To feel, in every moment, that you are someone else, that you come from somewhere else, that you have no connection to those around you, to your job, that everything around you is foreign?"

On Maica Domnului the houses shed their plaster facades in the violent, frozen sun. I knew them all well, in their teratological succession. It was like we were living inside an insect collection, and we were walking down the space between two lines of enormous coleoptera with metallic shells and extravagant appendices. As the dusk grew deeper, each chip of their porous plaster left a rosy shadow, pointed like a needle, across the facade. And we spread our rosy shadows, like the hands of a clock, across the street. When we came to the front of my house, Irina stopped in the middle of her sentence about the pain a past offense had left in her brain. We stood for a moment face-to-face, with the empty lot behind us full of rusty pipes and springs from who knows what bed frame. Before I had time to wonder how she knew I lived precisely there, precisely in the boat-shaped house at the back of the blurry optical field where we were standing, the pale and tired but smiling woman (without her detached and strange eyes, like the stars above a battlefield, taking part in her smile) took me by the hand, and like that, hand in hand, we walked the fifty or so paces to the building. A moment later, we came to the bedroom, and there was nothing more for us to say, as though we had not been colleagues at 86, and also that the world really was an arbitrary illusion, and words like *suffering, Gurdjieff, spirit, psychology*, even *biology*, had melted like a sugar cube in water. Her vulva, her breasts, even the muscles of her exhausted body, even the dizzying power of her sexual mind were familiar to me, as though our bodies had danced their somber rite hundreds of times before. I don't want to write about Irina's sexuality now, but I will later; this manuscript needs it, because I have never had a darker, more fantastic, more incarnate, or more bittersweet experience, and I believe that in this world, where we live enveloped in sensitive flesh, there is no drug more powerful. During our first evening in bed, while the room got darker and darker, her whispers in my ear also became darker, until both of us saw nothing else. I accepted her fantasies—from the first moment, as though they had always been mine too—as naturally as I accepted her lips and tongue, her moans and writhing. Not even when we were completely quiet, lying on our backs one beside the other in the semishadow, passively regarding the stripes of light crossing the ceiling as cars passed down the street, did I wonder, as I had often done almost at random while making love with other women: what, in fact, am I doing here? who is this person beside me? The way a homeless person must wonder, moment by moment, looking at the fellow who ends up sharing his campsite.

I remember I showed her, that first night, pictures of me when I was a kid, and my baby teeth shining in the luminous dark of the lamp like milky crystals. But I didn't tell her about the diary, the dentist's office, or my ex-wife, who played a strange role in our bed and our fantasies but whom Irina didn't need to know more about. I chose to keep a secret, impenetrable place in my relationship with the physics teacher, because, even if she would never think of disrupting my search, she could still be replaced at any moment with someone identical yet somehow different, a stranger with the same eyes and same erotic energy but subordinated to a power more terrible than sex or the mind. This had happened to me before. My experience with Ştefana forced this prudence upon me, to surround myself with multiple crenelated walls, because even if they fell one after another, at least the central tower would remain secure. My baby teeth and my photos defend my diary, they create diversions from what is just as confused as it is fundamental, because there, there is no more fiction, but truth, in all its implausibility and unbearableness.

When I came back from the bathroom, I found Irina in the middle of the room. And not because she had gotten out of bed and started to wander around the house, but because she was floating, naked and glistening, a meter above the bed, her hands under her head and her blond hair running through her fingers toward the floor. "I should go," she said, "it's enough for one day." I couldn't make a sound. Glassy, semitransparent, her internal organs undulating softly in the dark under her skin, Irina floated in the coffee-colored air and everything had the atmosphere of an old memory, impossible to place. She extended her finger toward the ebony button above the bed, which I noticed now for the first time, pushed it gently and began to sink slowly, flickering like a light bulb and undulating like a silk scarf, onto the crumpled sheet. "You have a very pleasant house," she said, sitting up. "I would like to live like this." It's the solenoid, the thought flashed through my mind. How had I never noticed the button, especially since, in the golden spot of the wall lamp, it was as scarlet as a woman's nipple surrounded by a darker areola? From that night on, when I pushed the button immediately after Irina left, I always slept aloft, floating between the bed and ceiling, occasionally turning over as if I were swimming in the lazy, glittering light.

When I visited my aunt as a child, in Dudești-Cioplea—always an adventure, because it didn't happen often and we had to get up early, and mornings in the summer were unexpectedly cool, especially because my mother would only put me in an undershirt to wear all day, and because the trip through the city, changing trams three times, passing through places with magical names: Obor Market, Fire Watchtower, Endocrinology Institute, which always made me imagine crinum lilies hidden in its strange name, was long and winding—the first thing I did when we arrived and my seamstress aunt opened the door with broad gestures of exaggerated pleasure was to explore the hidden places of her house, to open the drawers of her treadle sewing machine, and to work on the wonders of her buffet display case: fish made of glass, a box of rummy tiles, lovers and drunks in porcelain, the usual inhabitants of living rooms on the periphery. From the drawers in the sewing machine, from among all the buttons, thimbles, elastic, and pieces of colored cloth, I took out two curved, black magnets, full of needles stuck by their points to the magnets' shiny coal, as though I pulled two prickly hedgehogs out of their dens. I cleaned off the stubborn layer of needles and began to play with them, sticking chains of coins together, or moving a nail across the table with the magnet underneath. The strong metallic click the magnets made whenever I brought them together, or the fact that they could pull ferrous metals: paperclips, staples, needles, coins, didn't seem so strange to me—they were magnets, after all, and I knew all about them from the Electrospooling Cooperative on Ghiocei; when I was in the sixth grade, I would jump over the fence to investigate the heaps of scrap in the yard. The miracle, as well as a slight panic, began in the moment when you turned the magnets around, and suddenly there was an unseen, elastic cushion between them; no matter how you tried to bring them together, they would, at best, slide to one side or the other, as though the cushion were a transparent floe of melting ice. It was the first evidence I had that there were things in the world you cannot see with your eyes, yet were there, preventing your progress and occupying space with the same bored legitimacy as a table or a glass. The two magnets detected a phantom between them, an unreality, they opened a portal to a world of concrete and palpable impossibilities. You wanted to hold that chubby pillow of air in your hands, like a sick sparrow, to play with it like a rubber ball, but its existence seemed connected to the two magnets, just as powerfully and inseparably as reality itself seemed to be connected to the miraculous magnets of our own eyes. The blind—I thought then, while my aunt, kneeling, took pins from her lips to hem my mother's new skirt, and everything was framed by the door like in an old painting—spent their lives playing with invisible things like these, palpable things, with unrealities, with the electromagnetic, metaphysical, and existential fields of things in the world, without sight or light. For hours on end I would handle the unseen face of my world, suddenly caught, unveiled, and shamed by the two magnets that did not want to and could not come near each other, because coming near would have crushed the unknown mystery of our lives.

In the same way, I float at night, in my bedroom, in the blue light of the moon, on the unseen mattress of the magnetic field, more relaxed than a yogi, more voluptuous than a cat curled up asleep in its special spot with a paw over its eyes. The solenoid under the floor fills the room with an almost inaudible buzzing. Four times per night, I slide down the stages of sleep until the paradoxical sleep robes me in its light of melted gold. Four times I rise again, gradually, to the surface, with my skin still dully shining in the night of the chamber with the glimmer of flames in the deep. I spend much of my time in decompression, like deep-sea divers, so that the dense foam of dreams doesn't explode my mind. When I open my eyes in the gray cold of the morning, I am startled by the sight of myself in the mirror: an unshaven man, with damp hair, floating face down like a drowned body, in the middle of a silent room.

Irina, without whom I would have never discovered my bedroom's little secret—I could swear that the ebony button wasn't there before her first visit—comes by once a week, or every other week, unpredictably but fairly regularly. Our sex life has gained an incredible amount thanks to levitation; we make love in the air, without the awkwardness of people handicapped by a bed. We close the drapes, lie down naked across the bed, push the button, and we rise gently through the total, unblemished darkness, such that it doesn't matter if we open our eyes or keep them closed. We embrace without knowing who is above and who is below; suddenly space has no point of orientation. We are only bodies, with dry parts and wet parts, with warm parts and rough parts, with hairinesses and smoothnesses, with acrid tastes and fatty tastes, with softnesses and tumescences. We devour each other, we cleave to each other, we enter and exit each other's cavities, we lose ourselves in the dark and find ourselves, ever sweatier and more ardent, after our fingers claw through nothing and nevermore to find other fingers, or a foot, or a shoulder, or hair, or a mouth, or the eyelashes of the other person, so we can approach and touch and come close. We almost make a metallic click, like two curved magnets, but our click, which culminates in a physic aura and an unimaginable jet of light, is never the end of our encounters over the undisturbed bed. After our epileptic screams subside and our membranes calm down, we turn on the light, and the image, violently mirrored, of our bodies floating, surrounded by droplets of sperm and sweat, Irina's soaked hair, our membranes, our starving sexes, fill the suddenly alien, unbearable reality. We insert ourselves between the sheets, we land and the bed creaks beneath us, we feel heavy, as though we were wearing lead armor, and, turning out the light again, we sink (the moment I've been waiting for ever since, hours before, we began to undress) into our true, secret life, in comparison with which our physical love has been a weak and insignificant prelude.

11

I haven't had time to write here for the past ten days or so, since I've been grading, buried under heaps of thin notebooks, stacked by class. I grade, I fill up the pages with underlining and corrections, then with a violent twitch of my hand I toss a grade into the corner. I read mechanically, my mind elsewhere, although I know all the children well. As soon as I open the notebook, I know who I'm dealing with. The handwriting itself shows his nature, the grease and ink stains on the cover are as revealing as any personality test. I don't even need to read their compositions and grammatical analyses to know what grade I'm going to give them, and how unfair, how mistaken, this grade is. How unfit I am, the judge set above them, a risible god, with my obscene red pen. Here's Palianos: he never knows when to write *sa* as a separate word and when to hyphenate, but he has to take care of his five brothers, to cook, wash, iron, even though he's only twelve. Here's Mădălina Teşoiu: she's in the seventh grade and already her cheap perfume stinks up the classroom. She's always surrounded by boys from the high school, they pull on her clothes, they touch her at parties and she never says no, that's what they call her, "Mădă who won't say no." And Mădă here has written a fairly accurate study of Alecsandri's poetry. Chinţoiu is the scruffy kid in the last row: so far this year, I've taken at least four pornographic magazines away from him, but once, when I promised extra credit to whoever came to the next class and recited a long poem from memory, I'll be damned if the runt didn't do it, in a mumbled rush of words, without missing a line. Since his triumph with the Eminescu poem in class, he recites it at Christmas in the trams, then he gets off at a snowy tram stop to wait for the next one: Eminescu makes him a lot of money. And with Valeria Olaru, the chunky and pimply girl from class 7-C, there's an embarrassing story: last year, I stayed behind with her one evening in late autumn to tutor her for the Romanian literature Olympiad that Sunday, and I was just explaining how we study characters in the short story and the novel, when the door suddenly opened and the girl beside me jumped with a yelp, and Aunt Iakab came in holding a bucket. "Why are you sitting here in the dark?" she said offhandedly, frowning and suspicious, then she clicked the lights on and left, and only then did I realize I was sitting on a bench next to a young girl whose face was beet red and suddenly running with sweat, in an empty classroom without realizing time had passed, while it had gradually turned so dark that the room was almost black.

I am not a teacher and I never will be, that is the truth, even though the Gypsy girls with headscarves and crepe skirts selling sunflower seeds on Maica Domnului call me "dom profesor" when I pass. Even though the children, roughhousing in the hall during the class breaks and yelling and playing soccer with the eraser in an unbelievable swarm, will snap to the walls when I pass with the register under my arm and call me, "dom profesor!" half seriously, half sarcastically, because I am the dumb Romanian teacher who never beats them. In my first year teaching, when I was an adolescent with a straggly mustache, always wearing pleated shirts that emphasized my skinniness and Romanian jeans made from a terrible material, the children would flagrantly light up cigarettes when I went down the hall and blow smoke in my face just to show the others that I wouldn't do anything, or they would roll a ball down the hall to me and shout at me to kick it back. During class, they would put paste on my chair or send paper airplanes through the air to knock their blunt tips against the chalkboard where I was writing. Later, things settled down; I learned how to control my fear, they learned my tics, and now we function like an old machine that more or less does its job. As I look more and more like a teacher—the passing years homogenize those in the lounge until we look like dried moths in an ancient collection—the role seems stranger to me and less fitting, like a black pantyhose pulled over the face of a bank robber.

During the long break between classes, I eat at the auto shop beside the school. A cement building painted, in who knows whose idea, pink and Nile green like one of the cheap desserts from the cafeteria over the shop. In the yard there are heaps of car tires you have to walk carefully around to get to the building, where Dacias and Opels covered with dirt a finger thick await on lifts raised toward the ceiling. Workers in overalls, some of them the parents of our students, wander around the cars, or slide underneath, while talking about soccer nonstop. They don't even notice us walking upstairs to the dining room. Everything is dirty and smells like burnt motor oil, but this is the atmosphere where we eat; there isn't another option on the whole street. I wait in line, behind the young mechanics in oil-stained blue overalls, behind girls from our school who flirt shamelessly with the mechanics. Many already have a woman's figure, and when they see themselves clear of the prison of the school, they change the way they walk and talk, their hair glistens in ringlets that they all seem to let fall onto their shoulders at the same time, and they become different people, more seductive and aggressive than their age. They are little women with lips already used to their mothers' cheap lipstick, staring emptily like their older sisters into the mirror, making out under the Voluntari bridge with boys from the edge of town. The mechanics are jealous of the power I have over these girls, since just after I finish my marinated meatballs or my cardboard pork chop, I stand up and motion to the girls (who are drinking soda, giggling, pulling their hair over their eyes and talking louder than they should), and they get up to follow me, like a platonic harem. Now transformed back into students, they go to class with me in the school next door.

Exactly a week ago, just as I came back from the cafeteria, I had the displeasure of meeting Borcescu at the front door. His round head, variegated like a soccer ball, nodded for me to come to his office. Waiting there was Goia, the new math teacher, a tall young man with a tragic face, pale as death, and a slow, reptilian manner. His face seemed to have been carved into his flaccid, puffy flesh, and his brown, exophthalmic eyes reflected everything as clearly and cuttingly as a soap bubble. He might be the most intelligent teacher in the school—we talk whenever we have a few minutes, because he likes to read, poetry in particular, and I yearn for knowledge of certain areas of mathematics. With Goia, you feel awkward and fearful at first, you avoid looking at him too much, as though he were ill. But now that a few months have passed and he has settled in, the women teachers all like him because he is modest and incapable of sarcasm or irony, and the children feel he is one of them, because although he is tall, floating like an enormous lobster over their heads, the new math teacher speaks to them the way he does to everyone: directly, without particular emphasis, and crystal clear. "We don't even have to go over it again at home," the students say, and it's true. I didn't need books on topology or nonlinear equations: Goia knew how to make the most incomprehensible and abstract things simple and straightforward. He transformed the counterintuitive into the familiar, without grotesquely popularizing the subject like some books do. He found the most natural explanation.

We glanced at each other, enough for me to understand that he didn't have any idea what this was about and was just as surprised by the meeting as I was. Borcescu didn't usually call teachers into his office. Perhaps he was embarrassed by the bags full of wine bottles or the boxes of cigarettes that lined the walls, burnt offerings from the parents, or perhaps the smell of his foundation and powder seemed too strong in his office, in any case he preferred to install order in the classrooms, like an old constable, happy to be king of his street corner, where passersby looked at him with fear and respect.

"My young man," he declaimed at me from his chair, with warm eyes and a toothless smile, "my young man, as I was saying to this kid . . . you tell him what I've always told you since you came here . . ." "What do you want me to say, sir?" "What else? What being married is like . . ." "Like what, Mr. Borcescu?" The principal's face lit up. The foundation on his eyelashes seemed to melt and streak across the inside of his glasses. "Worse than being hanged, Mr. Goia, you listen to me! Not much worse, but nearly . . ." And the principal indicated how much worse by separating two discolored, powdered fingers of his right hand. Goia smiled crookedly, but we both relaxed, because it was clear we hadn't been called in to be dressed down.

No, as many times before, the principal wanted to talk about the old factory. The children skipped class from time to time, in groups of three or four, and when their teacher noted the absences in the register, the other kids in the class would chorus, along with "He's sick" or "He's skipping," the enigmatic phrase, "They're at the old factory!" This had been happening for a long time, with the same regularity with which people ate at the auto shop. The kids went to the water tower where the trams turned around, or they went on organized trips to the pipe factory where almost all the neighborhood parents worked. There were school investigations, generations of children had been questioned, herded into the principal's office to have their palms smacked, their heads knocked against the wall, their cheeks slapped and hair yanked, but aside from ordinary things, like smoking together in the abandoned industrial halls, they provided no revelations. It was one of those secrets smaller people have, with their large heads balanced on thin necks and their shining, black eyes; people different than us, the adults, as different as women and men, but even more so, because they lived in their tiny, enclosed world, without a past or future but full of myths and strange rituals. They were tiny, with narrow shoulders and fragile bones, they jealously guarded their secrets, and the big people forgot them, once they discovered the mystery of sex, drugs, and fantasy. In their irreducible hostility, the two human species thought differently, dreamed differently, and secreted different neurotransmitters across their synaptic gaps; they faced off in an unending game of secrets, and the tall and arrogant ones often forgot how vulnerable they were in this war. Because the children were human larvae, they must be kept in a state of slavery and ignorance. I was an unwilling mercenary in the eternal, the ambiguous and treacherous war between the species. Under the shell of a dominant species, always faced with dozens of members of the other group, always imparting, like the gods, rudiments of a strange wisdom, always forced to endure, with poorly disguised fear, their hatred and mockery while they in turn smoldered under a false oppression, I hid a child, still intact, dressed like

Charlot in my own skin, now grown too big for him. On the last day of school, I saw my colleagues in the lounge, a pantheon of decrepit gods, trembling at the windows, where they watched the children running around, pushing each other, almost knocking down the school's fence and singing their savage hymn of liberation from captivity:

Now it's summer vacation
All across the nation,
The schools are all knocked down,
The teachers are all drowned!

No uprising, no revolution, however bloody, was ever so radical, because in this case they wanted the gods to die and to destroy the magic tools that forced the children of light to listen. In millions of dusty, poorly lit rooms, cold as the chilled chambers of slaughterhouses, a lonely adult confronted thirty pygmies wading in their crude dreams and fantasies. Who were these beings with hypnotic, beelike eyes? Why must they be tamed, year after year, and eventually transformed into beings like us? Was it only to keep them from devouring us?

Borescu talked on for a while behind his desk, bobbing his pink noggin, but neither Goia nor I was listening anymore. To understand what splattered forth from the two yellow teeth remaining in his lower gums, you would have needed a superhuman level of concentration. You felt for poor Mrs. Idoraş, the secretary who had to pound his dictation out at the typewriter: the echoes of his whistling teeth kept her up at night, and usually you would find her asleep with her cheek on the pearly gray metal of her typewriter in the cold, sad main office, brightened only by the benighted ficus tree in the corner. No woman ever had such watery eyes: a liquid quivered between her eyelids, and her pupils, like the bubble of a level, slid slowly from one side to the other, glittering sleepily in the gray chamber. We were given to understand we should take a trip to the old factory across the lot behind the school to see what was going on. "You'll see that those demons are doing more than smoking. Drugs, or . . . I don't have to explain. These seventh- and eighth-grade girls are like goats, their tits are already huge and they've got a fire between their legs, why beat around the bush. These older Romanians, you know, the ones that tan a little deeper, they'll get married in the eighth and stop coming to school. If you go around to see why, some fourteen-year-old punk comes out to the fence in his indispensables and he tells you, 'I'm supposed to go to school, dom profesor? I'm a married man, it's too embarrassing . . .' You have to go see what's going on, they're not going to tell you. This is the neighborhood, these are the troops, lucky some of our kids come from simple people with common sense . . ."

I knew these common-sense people. They came to me in the evening, after school, with a pack of cigarettes, even though they knew I didn't smoke, and they tried to convince me to hit their kids, whenever I could, with holy fury: "Smack the back of their necks, dom profesor, don't go easy or they'll walk all over you! Give 'em the back of your hand! You know I won't get mad. My dad used his cane on me, the big one he kept behind the door, and now I thank him for beating some sense into me, for not letting me play ball in the lot." No one knew why, but the men in the neighborhood—the lathe-operators, machinists, planers, millers at the pipe factory—all grew out the nails of their little fingers, on both hands, and this gave them a dangerous, criminal air, in spite of their beer guts and undershirts, their shirts unbuttoned to show their chest hair, the slippers they wore to parent meetings. If you didn't accept their little bribes—bottles of rachiu with corncob stoppers, plates with a kilo of meat, packs of cigarettes and coffee, cartons of eggs—they would be offended to the depths of their souls and stomp out of the lounge cursing your mother. The wives were almost always pregnant, with empty eyes and slack jaws, holding a two-year-old by the hand. They dressed their little ones, another strange thing in this neighborhood, with their underpants over the pink crepe shorts, and they always put at least two hats on, one over the other. The mothers also asked me to beat their stinky little scholars, who only understood physical violence—if you spoke to them nicely you'd get nothing out of them.

School 86 beat its kids. It beat them with the register, it beat them with a ruler, it knocked them on the head with a man's gold ring. It yanked their hair and smacked the backs of their necks with the side of the hand. It gave them nosebleeds with a well-aimed slap. It called them to the front of the class at the smallest infraction and whipped their hands with an electric cord. It jabbed the pointer into their ribs. Any classroom door you opened, you always saw the same line of kids against the wall with their hands raised like surrendering soldiers: they stood like this the entire period, their arms shaking terribly. Kids who failed had their legs bruised like prostitutes. Naughty boys caught playing with a rabbit from home had their heads knocked together so hard you could hear it in the schoolyard. The children defended themselves savagely, and woe betide the teacher who got ambushed in some far-off part of the school, in the yard, in back of the school, or on the second floor between the dentist's office and the chemistry lab. At the end of every year, someone, usually one of the men who beat their kids the most, would be stalked on his way out of the brightly lit school one winter evening, and through the darkness full of thick snowflakes, he would feel the heavy, dirty folds of a blanket thrown over his head. There followed a rain of fists and steel-toed boots, because some of the eighth-graders were veterans, sixteen or seventeen years of age, already neighborhood terrors.

We left the principal's office some twenty minutes before the start of classes. Walking with Goia down the dirty, Nile-green hallways with unfamiliar faces hung on the walls—they might have been Slovenian writers or Latvian physicians—was unpleasant and strange: he was two heads taller than me. His intelligent, mothlike face floated beside the ceiling on a dark and slow, almost threadlike body. It was like walking next to one of those fake circus tall men who is actually a coat with three men on each other's shoulders inside. We took our registers from the empty lounge and parted in front of the stairway. I went up alone, feeling the old lump in my throat, up the stairs to the melancholy, frightening upper story, where the classrooms lined a pillared hallway, one so long that the doors were barely visible in a Nile-green fog. Through a few of the windows at the end, slants of light fell, breaking up the dark pattern of the floor tile. I was suddenly blinded as I passed through them, my clothes and hair in flames, because the next moment I would dissolve into the deep darkness. Every time I came to this floor, I would leave reality. I didn't know and didn't dare imagine what happened behind the doors of the physics, chemistry, or biology laboratories, or, especially, the door to the dentist's office. Behind the painted plywood doors, I could imagine a dense wall of ancient brick, sealing off who knows what crypt. Along one side of the hall stood a line of children, boys and girls, silent and pale. Through some of their bodies, as they stood in the liquid amber of a light pillar, you could see their little hearts beating and their lungs drawn with a pencil, like in the bodies of water fleas or aphids. A nurse I didn't recognize at first put a drop of a thick, pink liquid on a bit of sugar and then put it on the tongue of each child in the slowly advancing line. Those who had already received this strange communion, with their hair in bangs or pinned under plastic headbands, returned to the back of the line, meaning this process would never end. The cubes of sugar and the viscous liquid from the pipette multiplied miraculously, and the nurse seemed to whisper to each student as she set the friable cube on their tongue, the same words, in the same concentrated, almost passionate intonation. Of course, I went to the wrong class again—Florabela, Mrs. Rădulescu, Preda, Bernini, Spirescu, shouting and ranting in front of the same children, interrupting themselves and staring at me with disapproval, and thirty pairs of eyes sticking into me suddenly, like thirty pins—until I found, finally, the room where my children (the same that all the others had, the same Anghel, Arăşanu, Avram, Boşcu, Bunea, Bogdan, Calalb, Corduneanu, Cană, and so on, up to Zorilă and Ion, the new kid) were waiting for me beside their benches, with glassy eyes and their hands clasped behind their backs. None of them showed the slightest movement the whole time I spoke to them about pronouns and relative adjectives. I could have taught them *zvidrida* and *hohabira*, it would have been just the same. When the bell rang, I left them motionless, as though they were submerged in silver nitrate, and I went out with the register under my arm, almost running down the stairs toward our world. I threw myself into a chair in the lounge, where an ancient, phantasmagoric cloud of cigarette smoke floated.

Goia was one of the last to arrive, coming through the door with the music teacher. We put on our coats and set out together into the dusky neighborhood. We had come to know it fairly well: a modest village at the edge of the city, beyond it were only the train line and empty fields. Perfectly straight streets that went on forever, nostalgic like all paths through poor neighborhoods, with multicolored kites stuck in the electrical wires, with rusty cars on bricks in the yards, with little kids digging worms out of the ground and gray-haired people eating outside under a walnut or cherry tree by the light of a single bulb surrounded by moths and transparent flies. In the sky, a low crescent moon, with its tips pointing up, yellow as a slice of squash. Here, the idiot who always sat on the fence and wore a gray wool hat even in the middle of summer, shaking hands with whoever passed. There, the kiosk where the children bought juice and ice cream. You could walk all night along these streets without finding any place other than the grocery where all our children's parents bought potatoes, cheese, and cigarettes. In the store's endless lines we'd run into the little kids, who'd say hello.

Turning at the propane tank exchange, you went down Depozitului, through lines of those same houses with trellises of grapevines in front, with the same cats with black fur spots over their eyes and nose, until you came to the edge of the lot where the factory rose. Evening had come, a homogeneous, dirty-pink evening, against which the ruined industrial halls looked black as pitch. The math teacher went first, sinking into the waist-high grass and laurel trees. It was the only place in the field where you could cross to the factory: a barely visible trail led across a reedy ditch toward the closest, thick-looking wall, without an opening down its entire length. The endless brick wall was black with soot. The factory was ancient, built in an empty field, and the neighborhood assembled around it only as an afterthought, no more than four decades ago, because it was just after the war that Colentina was extended toward Voluntari, lined along both sides with lumberyards and cement factories, seltzer shops and low-ceilinged bars, military barracks and hideous funeral homes with black banners and freshly polished coffins propped against the wall and ebony hearses with glass windows and horses with blinders waiting eternally on the pavement in front. And in back, like patches on the blankets of agricultural fields, courtyards spilled down silent streets, with houses cobbled together from tin and tarpaper at one end, flanked by chicken coops and rabbit hutches. Here, the new city-dwellers lived, those who left the countryside after the war and the famine, and then again after the change of regime. The new residents, who made their brick or mud houses by themselves, with their own hands, never worked at the old factory, because when they arrived it was already abandoned and ruined. A smaller hall, set like a chapel in front of the principal building, had been demolished by the first settlers, and its bricks, clay rectangles still bearing the petrified mortar, had been hauled off in carts, pulled by bony horses with bridle sores, to build the surrounding houses. No one, however, had touched the main building. Its main wall, with a large, circular hole in the middle, still loomed over the fragile model of the neighborhood in a dramatic foreshortening, so tall and so melancholy that, especially in the summers, when clouds in a glinting sky crossed the great rosette, the building tore at your heart, it made you feel your loneliness more than ever. Like the water tower where tram 21 turned around, and all the warehouses, halls, covered markets, disused factories, steam-puffing mills, and tanks of gas in our crepuscular city, the industrial architecture of the old factory was paradoxical and fascinating. It had massive walls, flat and functional, from which the ends of metallic ramps covered in bolts poked out, windows made of thick, bubbly glass letting little light in, bas-reliefs and friezes buttressing the heavy volumes that combined, improbably, absurdly, in a way touchingly (like a corpulent woman bound in the satin ribbons of a corset that does nothing but make her fat behind and love handles overflow), with grotesque and pointless decorations of cheap stucco, born of the frustrated aesthetics of an age as refined and heroic as it was languorous and dreaming. The factory walls were adorned with oval windows framed by plaster angels with yellowed wings, now missing an arm or a head, holding the window frames as you might a large, heavy mirror; with crenelations and moldings, human faces in plaster, unending trusses marked with indentations; with a single, chlorotic virgin, almost breastless and hipless, her hair pouring down two floors over the wall's broken brick, and a philosopher in a toga, plucking an unknown instrument. Aside from the unusual proportions of the building, now so black it looked like it had survived a fire—when in fact it had not been touched by anything but the devastating gusts of time—that looked, in fact, with its triangles, squares, and circles, like one of the toy block constructions I would make as a child, only to knock it down with a flick of my finger, the hallucinatory ornamentation, both neoclassical and art nouveau, gave the factory the air of an artifact from another world. We were sure, however, that the real surprises were waiting for us inside.

No one knew what the factory had made. Perhaps pipes, to make the city sewer system, or to help the war? Maybe the pipe factory was nothing but the modern avatar of the factory we were now walking around, through mud full of mortar fragments. But we knew, from what other teachers or a child's father had said, that nothing of what could be found in the bowels of the halls could have come from any pipe production line, in fact it didn't fit any production line they were familiar with. More probably, like all of Bucharest, the saddest city on the face of the earth, the factory had been designed as a ruin from the start, as a saturnine witness to time devouring its children, as an illustration of the unforgiving second law of thermodynamics, as a silent, submissive, masochistic bowing of the head in the face of the destruction of all things and the pointlessness of all activity, from the effort of carbon to form crystals to the effort of our minds to understand the tragedy in which we live. Like Brasília, but more deeply and more truly, Bucharest was born on a drawing board from a philosophical impulse to imagine a city that would most poignantly illustrate human destiny: a city of ruin, decline, illness, debris, and rust. That is, the most appropriate construction for the faces and appearances of its inhabitants. The old factory's production lines, driven by long-immobile motors, had produced—and perhaps, in a quiet isolation beyond humanity, continued to produce—the fear and grief, the unhappiness and agony, the melancholy and suffering of our life on Earth, in sufficient quantities for the surrounding neighborhood.

On turning the corner we saw the entrance, since the front of the building was much narrower than the sides. We reached it in a few steps. It was a wide and very tall entryway with two scarlet doors. A thin rail line extended beneath it, out into the lot's weeds. The front wall was so tall and narrow that it seemed ready to topple onto us. Over the door, at an extraordinary height: the wings of a large chimera. I couldn't see it well since the light had faded to an oily brown. It might have been any winged creature, an owl, falcon, or bat, chiseled into gray rock. Its glass eyes filled with the yellow hues of dusk.

The door was, naturally, locked. A dense layer of rust covered the padlock mechanism, rising in relief around the four tumblers. The slanted light fell onto the rust, turning it into the surface of an uninhabited planet, only just revealing the characters on the tumblers: a cross, a crescent, a gear, and a triangle pointing up. It was clear that no one, for decades, had unlocked the frozen mechanism. This was not the real entrance. We needed to go around the next corner, to the north side of the building, to that wall we saw extend endlessly without an entrance. Large, copper-colored braces held up the walls in places where the bricks ballooned out dangerously. Flakes of mica glittered in the penumbra, like a field of snow. Here and there among the bricks, a damp and fragile branch grew out: a poplar seed wrapped in its delicate fuzz had been carried here by the wind, into a crack, and opened its little vegetable stem. A pale leaf rose and fell in the weak breeze of dusk.

We saw no holes in the wall, and yet the children somehow got into the building from the side facing Str. Arbustului. Borcescu had gotten at least that much from his gestapo interrogations. There might be a small group inside right now. As everyone knew, every child went into the factory at least once; it was just as natural to visit this ancient ruin as it was to go to school. Walking ahead of me, Goia's gnomon-shaped shadow fell across the enormous wall. But the wall, the only one without any tacky, chipped plaster sculptures, the only one that, on an inhuman scale, rose as high as the invisible roof, was impenetrable. Not even the outline of a door, not even a piece of metal sticking out that could have been a handle or hinge.

We stood for a good fifteen minutes in front of this blind wall, looking at each other in confusion. We might have given up, because it was already getting cold and the sun had disappeared behind the outlines of the extremely distant blocks lining Şoseaua Colentina. The field was dotted with twisted wires, crooked carburetors, truck tires, dead animals with dirty fur. The sky was now as scarlet as nail polish, with a single cloud, like a lunula, floating over the neighborhood. We didn't have more than another hour of light.

We would have never found the entrance, or at least not that evening, if a rat hadn't appeared, one of the many that had invaded the neighborhood in the past few years. They were incredibly intelligent and brazen. They weren't afraid of cats or people. The rat came around the corner, stopped when it saw us, frozen for a moment, its translucent ears catching the light, its golden whiskers trembling, and then it ran off through the reeds and umbelliferous wildflowers, chamomile and snapdragons, until their rustling stopped suddenly, as though the animal had disappeared into a burrow. The lot was just as desolate and immobile as it had been before, a simple, neutral background for the construction in its center.

"I think there's something there." Goia turned toward me and we peered down the trodden sprigs of grass. "A circular thing, do you see it? About fifteen meters or so. Could be a truck tire . . ." The light continued to dim, but this intensified the contrast between what was lit and the shadows. After I came home, I wondered for a week if it was only at a certain time of day, just in the moment of crepuscular light, that the entrance appeared. More than this, I began to wonder if somehow the dusk light created the entrance, pure and simple, out of nothing, just as the immaculate face of photographic paper, in a bath of revealer, draws the outlines of a building or the eyes of an unknown being. We walked through the waist-high bay trees and grass, harassed by hundreds of mosquitoes, and before we had taken twenty steps we saw, in a small pit in the earth, the end of a large cement tube, its reinforced lip protruding a little above the vegetation and disappearing, at a steep slant, into the earth. The pit, about a meter deep, was revolting: hardened human feces with stained newspaper thrown on top, burnt rags, and three or four metal curlers, with elastics full of hair, were scattered about and hard to avoid. The tube was massive, with walls as thick as your palm, and there were letters printed along the lip. It was big enough that you could walk in it bent over, or at least crawl. As it pointed toward the wall, and as we couldn't see its end, melted into the dark, we realized that the entrance couldn't be anywhere but there. "The problem is," Goia said, "that judging by the angle of the tube, by the time we come to the middle of the building, we will be several meters deep. Maybe there'll be a place to climb up." But this wasn't the real problem, my colleague knew as well as I did. The problem was we were afraid. We were alone in a barren field, beside a ruined building. Night was falling. The pit stank horribly. The mouth of a sewer pipe was waiting for us, one that could lead smack into a filthy mud of urine and feces, or a swarm of snakes or rats. Or it could be barred by a grate with lime-eaten bars and a dog had who decided to die there, unknown, mummified, with its teeth bared, almost embedded in the bars. In the end we decided to climb in, with uncontrollable horror and fear, but at least there were two of us, and that meant a lot in this kind of situation.

The sewer pipe was not blocked. It only became slimier as it descended into the ground. After a few more meters we were slipping and sliding so much, we realized we would not be able to get back up. The steep slope would be impossible for us to climb, as the tube became more and more covered with a thick, black gel that stank of mold. We didn't have time, however, to become more scared than we already were. About halfway down, we started to slide, pure and simple, like we were on a sled, covering ourselves top to bottom with the green-black slime. Then the mouth of the tunnel threw us onto a hard, bad-smelling surface that scraped against our hands.

We were inside the building. It was a realm of emptiness and melancholy. We were, as we realized before we stood up, inside a huge pit, excavated along one wall in a corner of the factory who knows when, a kind of archaeological dig site or an ancient cemetery. All around us, half emerging from the dry earth, were tombs, crypts, and funeral monuments sculpted in the delicate transparency of marble, travertine, chalcedony, and malachite. There were broken columns and statues with shining arms, there were crosses decorated with porphyry wreaths. There were winged children with sweet faces, lying with their cheeks in their hands on the slab of a grave. There were cenotaphs resembling enormous wardrobes, covered with large letters chiseled with mechanical precision. Everything glowed enigmatically in an olive light, falling in thick bands that contrasted violently against the shadow of these depths. The source of these transparent bars of light was the half-collapsed roof of the hall, at a disproportionate height. There were the same thick windows, with their wire reinforcements, through which the light filtered and took on this cadaverous color in the huge pit. But in the roof there were also large gaps where we could see, even paler in color than the walls, the sky. We walked for a while around the pit, we peered closely at the faces of the stone children, asexual and pure, with pronounced, anatomically perfect muscles, and wrinkled clothing without a trace of a chisel, as though the rocks had once been soft and been poured into forms of an unmatched smoothness. We contemplated the perfect corners of the tombstones, we passed our fingers along the soft piping carved into the marbled agate or the onyx darker than the night itself. Crossing the light that came from above, beyond the rim of the pit, two long, thin metal ramps rose toward the surface, propped up here and there in the loose dirt floor. "Should we go up?" I whispered to my colleague, who stood there amazed by the fantastic sight. We climbed one of the pitch-black ramps, and a minute later found ourselves in the hall itself.

The light was green-olive, clear, and uniform. The walls of the hall, lined with long metal bars, cables, and girders in complicated shapes made to guide carts now resting at one end, rose smooth and straight, the farthest of them dissolving into the light. Everything shone dimly, everything had the aura of an indescribable loneliness, as you find in great cathedrals. Fastened to the floor by enormous bolts, along a centerline of the hall running from the locked entryway to the other end of the factory, five pieces of machinery rose almost to the ceiling. Each sat on a circular base as high as my chest, in the shape of a ring. Each base was a different color that in daylight must have been much brighter. As far as we could tell, in the olive shadow that denatured everything, the first base was a dirty pink, the second dark blue, the third scarlet, the fourth a kind of orange-sienna, the fifth a yellow so bright it seemed to glow in the distance. The concrete rings must have been six or seven meters in diameter. The mechanisms or equipment on top, all identical as far as we could tell, were completely unknown to me. They were all made of polished metal and comprised enormous parts that could change position, sliding along round rods and racks with tiny, sharp teeth. Everything seemed recently oiled and completely outside of time. The floor was full of debris, bits of rope, burnt oil, dead rats, metal filings, and rusty scraps, but none of that touched the machinery, not a shard, not a black splash, not a speck of dirt. It was as though we were under the hood of a brand-new car, with the motor glimmering in cleanliness. Neither Goia nor I could identify the technology behind the enormous machinery. They didn't seem powered by steam or electricity. There were no cables; however, strange conveyor belts, on either side of the five monstruous mechanisms, connected them like engorged veins across the floor. Around them the air was vast and gelatinous, and we seemed as unimportant and black as two minuscule insects inside the carcass of an ancient radio.

Truly, the hall resembled nothing so much as the tube radios and televisions that my family had owned. When stripes began to roll across the minuscule black and white screen, with a contrast so weak that everything was drowned in a dance of gray shadows, my irritated father, always in his cotton shorts like he played for Dinamo Moscow, first would give the veneered carcass a few quick slaps and then take reprisals. One of my great pleasures was to help him take the TV apart, a ceremony always held with the solemnity of a complicated operation, the patient open and all its organs exposed. First, we moved the surprisingly heavy television onto the gateleg table in the kitchen, where my dad and I often played ping-pong, then we went for the tools. We took out our old "turnscrew," with its broken ebony handle, and the old pair of narrow tongs that he would use as pliers. Then my father undid the pressboard back, swearing like a cab driver because the soft metal screws had stripped out long ago. Inside was an incredible amount of dust and a kind of lint felt that had to be cleaned off to get to the electronic components. He would untwist the colored wires and carefully pull out the trays of tubes. He would let me have the burnt-out one to play with, and then he would put a new one in. Nothing fascinated me more than the sight of the diodes and triodes under their glass capsules—like vials for injections—with tiny gray letters and numbers printed along their base. And now I found myself just there, inside the place I would have wanted to explore as a child. I almost expected a wall of the factory to come off suddenly and to see my father's colossal face, red with irritation, and watch his blackened lathe-worker fingers enter the hall, feeling for the burnt-out tube.

We walked around the five metal monoliths for a long time, investigating them with an almost maniacal minuteness. What were our little scholars doing in this giant hangar? Had they found something that we could not—either because we weren't kids anymore, or because no one had initiated us, through who knows what mystical hopscotch or symbolic number system, into the mystery of the old factory? Or perhaps we had forgotten, the way we forget everything, and more than once, over the course of our lives, when our brain molts like a crab and must quickly find another, more spacious world to house its soft stomach? Through enormous cracks in the roof, we could see the first stars, pale in the still-rosy sky, even if its rose color, here inside, turned a dense amber, holding sinister insects in its glass forever. Goia had gone somewhere toward the end of the hall. I heard him shout in a choked voice while I was busy following the thick veins, damp and lilac-colored like the ones under your tongue, that carved through the floor between the machinery and the conveyor belts. I ran toward the far corner, veiled in green light, and I saw Goia, taller than ever, more like a wise praying mantis than ever, but also more menacing, gesturing with a hand that appeared to hold a small, soft object. "Look at this," he said, opening his enormous, acromegalic hand to reveal a square of black canvas with yellow letters crudely sewn into its surface. "I found it on the ground, it must have come from one of the children." The tag had the name of the school and, underneath, a number. Of course, I didn't recognize the number, I never paid attention to this aspect of the student uniform. When I was on duty, I would sometimes line the students up in the schoolyard, but the principal did all the work, seconded by the history teacher, the famous Mrs. Rădulescu. And once the children had their school numbers tattooed directly onto their arm, where their fathers had mermaids and hearts crossed by crooked, misspelled words, no one sewed the numbers with yellow thread anymore. The canvas square that Goia held must have been a few years old, and whoever had worn it on his left sleeve was, almost certainly, no longer a student.

I added this object to my collection of treasures, and since the factory visit, I take it out every day. It is a kind of proof, a witness to the reality of that world, which remains foreign no matter how much we would like to understand it through reality. In a way, the school ID number is like a lily with its petals curving open, found one morning on a pillow by a person who just dreamed he had received such a flower from a winged being. It is an object taken from its world, but abnormal in ours, an amphibious object, paradoxical like marine mammals that breathe air but look like fish, because even if the tag had once been the most banal accessory of an empire of slavery, its number hadn't belonged and didn't belong to this world, because it was larger than the total number of atoms inside itself, so large that my colleague, when he read it out loud, felt a mental strain. "Nine hundred fifty-two to the power of seventy-six . . . it makes no sense . . . Maybe the mother sewed it on wrong and folded it over. But the last numbers are clearly exponents." Cantor's mind was shattered when he imagined infinity to the power of infinity. For the ganglions in our skulls, there was no difference: the number on the tag was, practically speaking, just as inconceivable.

I think we never would have noticed the entrance if Goia hadn't found that tag, in the corner where the walls were covered with mechanisms of an unknown technology. They were all metal, the same silvery metal as the large machines that dominated the hall, and they were also lubricated with a thin oil that stayed on your fingers after you touched it. There were intricate pieces inside strangely cut-out frames—Maltese crosses, pushrods and flywheels, worm drives, and, of course, gears and racks—and yet most of it was other shapes, unknown mechanisms resembling clockworks. If you stood in front of these panels for a few minutes, you saw the pieces slowly change shape, as though the metal was in fact a dense liquid that made elaborate waves across the surface. Together, all the frames of coupled mechanisms formed a wall of technology, like the command center of an electric plant or a dam. In the center was the luminescent blue outline of a door. It took a while for us to notice, in the lower-right corner of the door, just above the floor, a box with movable numbers, like the lock on a briefcase. Each of the five tumblers was set to the most enigmatic number a human ever imagined, one that eternally bites its own tail, as it does not delimit but excludes the infinity of the world: zero. Meanwhile, it had become so dark that only the light of the stars painted the lines and contours of the panel surfaces, as they slowly glided into new configurations. The numbers on the box were still visible, since they were engraved in a gray metal that glinted even in total darkness.

We played with the numbers, spinning the five wheels through their ten facets, for a good long time. No combination would open the blue outline of the door. And yet it must be true that every child in our school knew the code, because we were sure that there, in the secret room of the old factory, things happened—scandalous, strange, and frightening, or only juvenile?—things that everyone knew about, but which, like the ancient mysteries of sunken worlds, they could not or would not divulge. "Maybe there isn't a single combination, but one for each person who wants to enter. Maybe it's a personal number that has to be used in conjunction with your fingerprint on a phone, or your face projected onto the photosensitive material of the door, or simply your breath. And the code could serve as proof you are called, or chosen. In this case, you would have to have received the combination from somewhere, it must be somewhere in your data, in your memory, in your world." But I believed that the five numbers could be connected to the colors of the enormous concrete rings where the mechanisms were mounted. Everything in the sinister darkness of the building was gray, vast, and desolate, like an empty visual field. A feeling came over me, as I looked around, disoriented and frightened: that I was within the visual field of a strange being. Goia kept rotating the tumblers. He crouched at the base of the door, and I could hear the soft clicks of the tumbler mechanism, obscured now by the dark body of the math teacher. And suddenly, the door slid open and the ray of intense and pure blue outlining the door became the rectangular frame of a hallway of azure fog. "I don't get it, I just played with the numbers," Goia said as he stood up, but when I saw the number on the box that looked like a metal pencil case, I understood how marvelously his unconscious memory had functioned. The number that opened the door was 95276.

In the enormous factory hall, now it was completely dark. Night had fallen quickly, before we could notice, like the time when the janitor had surprised me, in that dark, empty classroom, sitting on the bench next to the girl I was tutoring. The milky light that flowed from the secret door almost blinded us. Without a word, Goia walked into the corridor, which, I could now see, had glass display cases along both sides. The light eroded his outline, making him thinner and taller, as if he were loops of black wire. His movements became more careful, his triangular head tilted toward the right and then to the left, glimmering in the blue fog. "Amazing," he said from time to time, in a broken, almost inaudible voice. I didn't budge until the outline of his body had almost completely disappeared. Vague, brown traces toward the end of the corridor, visible only in their slow movements, were all that indicated someone's presence, the way the tips of a spider's feet are visible, dark bits of mist in his cotton lair. I was suddenly very afraid. I remembered that we hadn't found the entrance, more so we had been drawn toward it, guided by the terrifying ruin, and now we were in its belly and there was no escape. My panic grew to an unbearable intensity, and I fled through the darkened hall, under the stars blazing in the holes in the roof, I tripped over the bumps of veins in the floor several times, I almost fell into the pit of tombstones—their solitary forms, soft and round, glinted rosily in the deep—and suddenly I thought that I was dreaming, that I was having a nightmare, so I threw myself onto the cement floor, into the scraps of twine and metal filings and black grease. I rolled around and hit my face to wake myself up, but the pain proved that everything was real—because pain is another word for reality. The surfaces were hard, indeed. My eyes were wide open and my mind lucid, but fear had deformed everything, it had driven me into hallucination and delirium. I stood up, shook the industrial refuse from my clothes, and went back, my heart beating more strongly than it should have, to the door gaping open in the great building's wall. I knew full well that on the outside, the building was perfectly rectangular, that there was no way for the door to open into a room, and yet it led into a virtual depth, as inexplicable as the depth of a photograph, or the depths of perspective that create a third, and false, dimension in paintings on a wall. If you could go inside a trompe l'oeil mural, you wouldn't descend into its fraudulent depths, you would only get smaller as you moved along unseen lines of perspective. You wouldn't move through constantly changing spaces, with porphyry arches and columns and unintelligible Biblical images opening and closing behind you; rather, they would change their shapes constantly, rectangles would become parallelograms and trapezoids, the arcs of circles would change into hyperbolas, and circles into ellipses, becoming thinner and thinner as they tried to look deeper and farther away. I often thought that the world, along its three dimensions, is an equally deceiving trompe l'oeil for the infinitely more complex eye of our mind, with its two cerebral hemispheres taking in the world at slightly different angles, such that, by combining rational analysis and mystical sensibility, speech and song, happiness and depression, the abject and the sublime, it will make the amazing rosebud of the fourth dimension open before us, with its pearly petals, with its full depth, with its cubic surface, with its hypercubic volume. As though an embryo didn't grow in its mother's womb but arrived, from far away, and only the illusion of perspective made it seem to grow, like a wayfarer approaching along an empty road. A wayfarer who, after he passes through the iliac portal, continues his illusory rise, first an infant, then a child, then an adolescent, and in the end, when he is face-to-face with you and looks you in the eyes, he smiles at you like a friend from the other side of the mirror, having found you again, at last.

In the end, I entered the picture in the wall loaded with strange technology. The air in the corridor beyond was sweet and cool, and its walls glistened with reality. Here and there, their surface became glassy, and suddenly I found myself in a kind of natural science museum, with showcases, dioramas, and aquaria lining the corridor. After no more than ten meters, the corridor ramified into a labyrinth of rooms and smaller rooms teeming with items on display, artificially colored biological specimens and hideous creatures in jars, with explanatory wall texts celebrating the exobiology of these nightmarish creatures. Far away, from another section of the museum, I could hear, like slow drips into a fountain, my colleague's footsteps, lost among the spectral exhibits. I dared to look at the large dioramas.

Monsters, monsters that the mind can neither conceive nor house nor accept, suspended like spiders on glittering threads, monsters out of our ancestral reflexes, with pale skin, clattering teeth, eyes drooping from their sockets. That make our piloerector muscles fire, that send cold sweat running over our already cadaverous bodies. Fear, horror, petrification, terror, fascination, dread, screams, and insanity. Torture beyond our brain's capacity to imagine the contents of hell. Not fangs, not claws, not rending, not the perineum tearing during birth, not the living dismemberment of cancer, not being buried in a mound of tropical ants, not being bound to the mouth of a cannon, not the plucking out of eyes and tongue in a barbaric oubliette, not heaps of red and black demons ulcerating in the terror of demonic joy around mournful and pure white bodies with virginal breasts and unblemished braids in their hair, or olive bodies with broad shoulders and beards fresh from the scissors sunk into lava up to the waist. Instead, these were absolute monsters, monsters of the psyche; forms made to suffer eternally in the eternal life of the mind, like regret, like remorse, like embarrassment, like dishonor, like the memory of things that shouldn't have happened and yet burn in your memory like red-hot iron. Like horror beyond horror, the greatest horror, the mother of all our fears: the fear of an eternity in which you no longer exist.

Excessively huge, as big as tigers, buffalo, giant tortoises, and polar bears from the dioramas in ordinary museums, the great display cases held creatures I knew well. When I was sixteen, my parents sent me to a village along the Danube, so I could have something to do during my endless summer vacation, when three weeks might pass without my speaking to anyone; I was eager for any adventure, even a trip through hell. I was an adolescent on the threshold of insanity. I read the greater part of every day, and often my parents found me still reading at dawn. Only when I heard the first trams on Ştefan cel Mare would I close my book and go to sleep. I had no friends. When my loneliness and desperation became unbearable, I would go out for walks, taking side streets I didn't know, lined with old, merchant-style houses covered in plaster putti and gargoyles. I would leave in the morning and return late in the evening, as the moon rose. At lunch, with the money my parents gave me (a single three-lei coin with a tractor heading nowhere), I would buy myself a soda and a cheese pastry. When I got tired, I would go to a park and sit on a bench, in the summer's paradoxical cool. I would sometimes look in on other kids from the high school, but I never found them at home. I would take the tram fourteen stops, rocking back and forth in the rear car, until it came to a distant periphery of the city filled with empty streets, where I imagined one of the girls I liked was living. But the address was always wrong. And June, July, August, full of dust and sweat in the desolate city, refused to pass. Every summer seemed immobile and eternal. When the fifteenth of September finally came and I went back to school, it felt like salvation. My classmates looked at me like I was crazy, the teachers were mean and uncaring, but at least I could see people's faces, at least I could talk with someone. I could never understand how I had survived the summer that had just passed, how my aloneness hadn't suffocated me completely.

At the time, I read almost two hundred books a year. On my bedstead, I had heaps of books I would read simultaneously. I would go to the B. P. Hasdeu Library, located across the street in an old block that, when they widened the street, was put on rollers and shifted ten meters back. To the left of the library was the grocery, I knew its sections so well: cold cuts, cheeses, and in another area, candy. To the right was the fruit and vegetable shop, whose clerks kept their thumbs on the scales. The library was minuscule. It was actually just two rooms: one where the librarian sat, the only entirely gray person I have ever met (gray hair, gray eyes, gray skin), and another with bookshelves on every side. I may have been the library's only patron; at least, I never saw anyone else. Sometimes I imagined that the library and the quiet and lonesome man at its helm existed only for my sake. Every few days, I would read the author's name and title on the spines and choose a few books to take home. The register on the librarian's table, where I signed the books out, never showed another patron's name: only mine, from top to bottom, on every page. I read a lot of poetry, sometimes out loud on the street, making people turn their heads toward me sympathetically, and I read novels and essays. I was especially interested in books about people as alone as I was, with whom I could have, finally, an actual dialogue: *The Notebooks of Malte Laurids Brigge*, *Alone* by Strindberg, *Hunger* by Hamsun . . . Reading in my room, until I didn't know if it was night or day. I would only turn on the light when I couldn't make the letters out at all.

So this trip to the shores of the Danube, where I would stay for a month with an agricultural engineer and keep records of the trucks hauling the grain harvest away, was manna from heaven to me. I still didn't talk to anyone, I was still alone from morning to night, listening to Los Paraguayos records and walking in the sunflower fields, but the landscape was new, and this meant a lot. I was breathing fresh air, under enormous skies. At night, I would go into the backyard filled with flowering poppies and look at the stars: I had never seen them so glorious, so blazing, never had they arranged themselves so clearly into constellations. Never had they scared me so much.

The agricultural engineer did not have many books. After I finished the ones I had brought with me (*Return to Tipasa* by Camus, *The Dwarf* by Pär Lagerkvist, *Doctor Faustus* by Thomas Mann), I began to look through his cabinets, while he was gone all day. He only came back in the evening, when, without losing a moment, he would get drunk, show me his diplomas, cry, and go over to see his neighbor, who was also his lover. I wouldn't see any more of him until morning. He mostly had specialized books: agricultural treatises, old university textbooks about the care of grape plants and raising sheep . . . and I read these too. I read the articles on the square pieces of newspaper stuck on a nail in the bathroom in place of toilet paper. I read the labels off cans of liver pâté and jars of honey, I read the vacuum cleaner instructions. One night, however, in the cupboard where he put old letters, postcards, and all kinds of notebooks, I made an amazing discovery, one which marked my life more deeply than any book of literature.

It was a parasitological treatise, with a dirty, worn cover, like all my notebooks had at that time, like my high school uniform that seemed made of blotter paper soaked in faded ink. On the cover, crudely drawn in a dirty Nile green, I could just make out an odd kind of flower, which I later identified as the scolex of a tapeworm. At first, I looked through the dirty, dusty book because I was bored. When I opened it, minuscule, amber-colored beetles scurried across the pages to hide. But then I found, within the world of the animals that infest your body, devouring you from without and within, a great, somber poem. Not Dante, not Bosch, not even Lautréamont had ever seen, when they imagined their infernos, the bestial face of the louse in close-up, the visage of a larval fly, the flagellate legs of mites. They could not invent, for their subterranean caverns of flames and tears, any demons more terrible than lice and ticks, roundworms and tapeworms, eye worms and the blind armies of mites. I saw, in the book's plates—crudely drawn, and for that all the more horrible—the saga of creatures not of our world, perverse metamorphoses, improbable transits between heteroclite hosts, diabolical techniques impregnated by a malign genius that could come from nowhere but the Adversary who rules the tunnels under the earth, as well as those dug through our skin and flesh. I saw the figure of an angelic infant parasite that ate your tongue and then took its place, taking its share of what you ingested and teaching you an unknown manner of speech. I saw transparent larvae that entered your brain, rummaging their bristles through your hippocampus, that altered your memories and desires. I saw the exuberant appendices—a kind of hand and a kind of knife and a beak like a hypodermic syringe—of a parasite that dug tunnels through your eardrums, and I shuddered at the crustacean parasite with neither face nor body nor internal organs that infects the hermit crab, penetrating its thorax and abdomen, entering the thin tubes of its legs, hollowing out its flesh and replacing it with its own, until the empty shell begins to move its segments under a foreign will, and the false hermit crab spreads its eggs by mating with the true ones. Divisions of worms, minuscule arachnid phalanges, without pity and without the blessing of light, expulsing seas of eggs and oceans of feces, living in our pores and our pulmonary alveoli, invading our sex and nipples at night with the wet tubes of their stomachs borne on legs with hooks and claws; the quilted, pearly, metallic, or only damp and bloody textures of worms, speckled pink and violet—an infraworld of light and divinity, of devourers and self-devourers, real and beautiful. A world forever damned.

I saw now, in the horrifying museum in the abandoned factory, in its strangely clear dioramas, creatures from that old book, but grown as big as tigers and elephants, inhabiting environments that were hard to recognize, even though they were only our own world at an exaggerated scale. I saw in one display an enormous piece of ivory—gray flecked with pink, twisted and dense like an old string of pearls around the frame of a miraculous icon—the size of a giant tortoise. Nothing indicated that the riverstone-smooth object was alive. And yet, when I least expected it, from one edge of the shiny ivory, from a dark dent the size of a bean (the pearly skin's only irregularity), a few dots, black as anthracite, transformed into eight thin claws and a curved beak. Its black legs barely able to transport its blood-filled body, the tick that usually lived behind a cat's ear now marched across the diorama. In another display, there was a broad louse that favored the pubis and underarms, with its tiny, skeptical eyes on a pink face, with its leprous body, with the nightmarish anatomy of its claws. I walked through the maze of corridors, fascinated and pale, drenched in cold sweat. Living larvae, their gills spread open, scuttled away at my passing, tentacles stuck across the glassy transparency showed interior pharynxes and lilac veins, blind faces beat against the glass, baroque and incomprehensible appendages contracted and relaxed among the porous, striped boulders of dead skin the size of Amazonian serpents that made up the substrate of the monstrous aquaria. A cross section of a living animal's epidermis with hyaline endoplasm beating in every cell, with strands of hair as thick as trees stemming from its sweat glands, revealed, among the Golgi corpuscles and pressure-sensitive disks, the wavering tunnels of the mites that cause mange. And I saw them, large as sheep, with beak-shaped legs where twisted flagella burst out, with potbellied bodies full of hair, blindly dragging each other along, their voracious jaws biting into the gelatinous skin of the enormous animal on which they lived, mating and devouring each other, insensibly climbing over and under each other . . .

These creatures were alive, but did they really live? They doubtless sensed the world around them, but how? And what did the fact that they sensed it mean? What kind of life was that? Ever since I found, at age sixteen, the treatise in the agricultural engineer's house, I hadn't stopped wondering what it would have been like to be born as a mite or a louse, or one of the billions of polyps on coral reefs. I would have lived without knowing that I lived, my life would have been a moment of obscure agitation, with pains and pleasures and contacts and alarms and urges, far from thought and far from consciousness, in some abject hole, in a blind dot, in total oblivion. "But that is what I am, it is," I suddenly found myself saying out loud. This is what we all are, blind mites stumbling along our piece of dust in an unknown, irrational infinity, in the horrible dead end of this world. We think we have access to the logical-mathematical structure of the world, but we continue to live without self-consciousness and without understanding, digging tunnels through the skin of God, causing him nothing but fits and irritation. The mite that burrows through my skin does not know me and cannot understand me. Its ganglions of nerves are not made for it. Its sensory organs do not spread their sails more than a few millimeters around the body it does not know it has. Neither can we know the miraculous creatures that are to us what we are to the parasites in our skin and the mites on the pillow where we sleep. We cannot detect their chemical secrets, and our thought is equally powerless. All our knowledge is a stammering tactility. But just as their bodies are made of the same substance as ours, our thoughts are the same substance as those creatures who are nothing but thought. To know them, however, you need thought of another nature and on another level, thought of a body of thought we cannot conceive of, just as the mite cannot conceive of our thought and cannot, truly, think.

I toured the parasite dioramas for a long time, in the crepuscular light. I looked lice and ichneumon larvae in the eyes. I saw how, like in the bolgia of thieves in the other Inferno, the host and parasite melt into an agonic embrace, one passes into the other, they become each other's organs and limbs. With eyes that opened wider as much as I tried to close them, fighting my desire to curl up in a corner of the labyrinth and transform over time into a heap of dust, I saw myself: how strange, how unreal will I seem to the great and marvelous creatures bent deeply over our world, with my eyeballs, with my hands that end in five fingers, with my baroque lungs and intestines, with my penis and my testes and my fingernails and my brain and my blood flowing through the supple tubes of my veins! I was made of flesh, just like the flexible and compact monsters in the display cases. My fate was the same as theirs. For a long time I circled the enormous displays, perhaps for hours. Then I came out unexpectedly into a large rotunda.

A single, circular diorama, like a layer of gelatin, wrapped entirely around the room. The diorama was occupied by a fantastical, dark purple worm made from shimmering velvet, a living, moving creature of unparalleled beauty. It swam in graceful contortions and undulations through a liquid medium that it filled almost completely; it had a rose of plumage around its circular mouth, and orange demilunes and electric blue stripes on its muscular body. From the base of the bell to its apex in the ceiling, the worm moved ceaselessly, peristaltically, hypnotically, as though it was the Ouroboros serpent eating its tail for all eternity. And on the polished onyx floor—a black mirror that reflected even the smallest details of the room—there lay, with her eyes closed and breathing gently, a young girl of colossal size.

She might have been fifteen meters long. She was completely undressed, white as milk and as baby teeth, with shiny, chestnut hair held in two elastics with plastic daisies, each as big as a truck tire. Her just-budding breasts, her narrow hips and chaste thighs showed she was eleven or twelve years old. Her body warmed the first few meters of the floor surrounding her. I walked around her in amazement, brushing against her ponytails as I passed, and on the other side of her immense body, I found Goia, who gazed at her with his usual gravity. "Maybe she's the girl who wore that school number," he whispered to me. "This place is all for her." But his whispers echoed unexpectedly loudly under the large dome, enough that, before our eyes, the girl began to awaken. We stood back while the girl slowly sat up, still groggy, looking around her.

We left quickly by way of a door we hadn't noticed before, and we ran down the narrow corridor. After about a hundred meters, the corridor stopped suddenly inside a room at the base of a tower, inside which a metal stairway rose in a spiral. We kept running, climbing step after step with great effort. The tower was tall and round, with massive cement walls. Not one window disrupted the smoothness. Turning constantly in the same direction made us dizzy. My heart was beating through my ribs. The vision of the gigantic girl pursued me with a fantastic power, it drove into my mind. After a long time, we came to the top and exited, finally, to the stars, onto a metal platform that extended around a large, white sphere. Below us, in the night, we saw flickering streetlights. A few late trams were stopped at the station at the base of the tower. Across the street, beyond the few cars driving with their lights on, we could see the green-lit windows of the pipe factory. "How can this be? We're on top of the water tower," I said to Goia. "Look, there's the old factory!" The massive building we had just escaped stood, black and silent, against the rosy city sky. A few shadows, from the trees growing on its roof, just as dark, scrubbed the sky at every breath of wind. The moon, rocked onto its back with its peaks toward the top of the sky, was larger than I had ever seen, as though the tower were thousands of kilometers tall, stretching toward it. But what amazed me even more, as I stood with my back stuck to the railing and my damp hair blowing in the wind, was what I saw when I looked more carefully at my colleague, who usually loomed over me with his height. He looked around indifferently, occasionally pointing out a place in the neighborhood. "There's the seltzer shop. And the Roibulestis' house, the one with the second story that hangs off the back. The grocery is over there. And look, there's our school, do you see the basketball court?" But his legs vanished somewhere inside the staircase, as though he hadn't climbed all the steps up to the platform at the top of the water tower. I looked down into the illuminated emptiness inside the tower, and I saw, shockingly, that Goia's body was twisted like a snake down to the end of the stairs, down the length of the tower, and his feet were still at the bottom, on the ground. "Let's go back and look for an exit," he said, and he retreated, getting shorter and shorter, in a spiral, toward the bottom of the stairs. I was so tired that my mind didn't ask any questions. We left through the door at the bottom of the water tower, which we found unlocked, and we set off down Str. Dimitrie Herescu, passing the auto shop, until we came to the tram station. We got on the second of the two cars and rode to Doamna Ghica, alone in the brightly lit car. I got off at Doamna Ghica, while he continued. I arrived home exhausted, my clothes dirty and stained with oil, smelling like dog feces and fear. I soaked in the tub for an hour before going to bed.

At school the next day, the math teacher and I went to the principal's office, and I let my colleague do the talking. He said, with his weak voice and a sincerity that you could not doubt, that we went to the old factory, got inside through a crack in the wall, and found nothing but dirt, rubble, and bare walls—so what our students were doing in the dilapidated industrial hall remained an enigma. Maybe they were smoking, maybe they were daring each other to jump off the old conveyor belts . . . We agreed we would poke our heads in, "at least once a month," just to keep the situation under control.

12

I picked up the coins from under the bed, behind the wardrobe, off the carpet, from the far corner of the room. This evening, when I took off my pants, a shower of noises shattered the total silence of the house: the fistful of little objects from my pockets scattered across the floor with an unexpected harshness. It shook me out of my daydreams, like one of those times when you wake up like you've been hit with an adrenaline hammer: you're shaken, it screams in your ears, it pours a cup of cold water over your head; or, like being deep in your dreams and the heat of your blankets, when you hear your mother's far-off voice in the dark, winter morning saying it's time to get up and go to school. The coins suddenly glittered in the raw light and scattered across the floor, bouncing, spinning, and glittering, with a metallic noise that irritated my nerves. Two or three coins spun on the parquet long enough for me to wonder what side they would fall on, heads or tails, and I watched them without moving, with one bare foot in the air and the other still in its pant leg, until their spinning slowed and the final rotations became louder and more random as gravity sapped their liberty and exuberance. And then silence and dark light again, and the disks of silver and copper coins spread over the floor. Little divination machines, on one side Urim, on the other Thummim, now emptied of their premonitions and life.

I stacked them on top of each other, in a thick and uneven roll on the corner of my desk, and I tried to start working. The story of my life, as I would like to begin it today, is the story of an unknown person. This is precisely why I need to write it, because if it's not written by me, the only one to whom it means anything, then no one will write it. I am writing, not in order to read it, as its sole future reader, forgetting myself for a few hours beside the fire, but to read it while I write it and attempt to understand it. I will be the only writer/reader of this story, the purpose of which, I'll say for the tenth time, is nonaesthetic and nonliterary. I have no other pretension than being the writer/reader/liver of my own life. It could be the biography of a louse or a mite, but it would still be just as important as my own skin, because I am that obscure creature, the tunnels where I swarm are my own, the excrements: mine, the sensations: mine, the turpitude: all mine. Even if I am no one, I feel pain if I prick my hand, and the pain I feel is mine and mine alone. Even if no one else cares, I do.

I did not see daylight for the first time one June day in 1956. I see it only now, in my imagination, for the sake of the workers' child born that year in a miserable maternity ward in a dirty world. I believe, in fact, that I had seen much more light before, through my shut eyelids and through the rest of the thin skin that enveloped my little body, while I was floating in the cavernous pool of liquid diamond, embracing my mirror image. After the uterine bath of luminous oil, after the ecstasy of life budding from another life, I was brutally pulled from my cavern, pushed through the tunnel of flesh between my mother's legs, pointing my head and lengthening my body into the shape of a boat, and the land to which I was exiled seemed to be a somber, gray realm of ruins. I came into a world where reality is rotten, with holes in its fabric big enough for your finger, and I search precisely for these rips and tears in the stories. My parents were young at that time and had also arrived in a new world. They were new to the city, they had left their families behind in the country and were trying to deal with their new life of lathes, metal scrap, emulsions, fabric looms, bits of thread, and unbearable screaming in their ears. But also the world of privacy in their little rented rooms, where they made love at night, like awkward Puritans, always with a feeling of guilt. The moon of that neighborhood, filtering through the geraniums in the window, cast a pallor onto the faces turning toward each other. For a long time, even after our birth, they didn't change: two country people in the city, trying to remake the village, there between the concrete apartment blocks and rumbling factories and trams ringing their bells as they zipped through intersections. They were from different parts of the country and would never have met. But they happened to both be on a union trip to the same resort, I think it was Govora, where, as a young man and young woman, she was twenty-five, he twenty-two, they would have laughed together at the workers' parties and stepped on each other's feet while dancing, they would have kissed against the wall of the girls' dorm, a cute converted house, and they would have promised to meet again in the enormous city of Bucharest, where no one had a phone and where some couples were lost forever on account of a missed date. But my father, a brown-haired boy from Bănăt, as handsome as a prewar movie star—wherever he went, color retreated and the world turned black and white—didn't want to lose Maria and got a transfer to Bucharest, to the ITB workshops, to be with her. He spent his days working on tram couplings, tightening the bolts with a blackened wrench, he was always thinking—and even his thoughts had a Bănăt accent—of the girl who would be not only the first in his life, but the only. My mother had not, on the other hand, decided to spend her life with her "boy"; she had just recovered from a big breakup, she had loved a medical student who dumped her once he became a doctor, because my mother, as was customary in Tântava, didn't want to give herself to him before they married. What happened between a man and a woman was disgusting if it wasn't consecrated by a veil, bridal gown, and wedding, a cross kissed in the church and a crown on their heads. And she had told her older sister, an apprentice seamstress, that she didn't want to raise this boy, even if he was svelte and handsome, with the velvetiest brown eyes that ever were. Her sister was more practical and talked some sense into her: she was twenty-five, and old women needed to marry quick. What was she waiting for? Costel was a good boy, serious, he loved her, he had a trade, he didn't drink, didn't smoke. Where was she going to find another like him? And another thing, he had asked her to marry him one evening, on a little bridge in Cişmigiu Park after a photographer had posed them against the railing, she with her "Cicero" haircut and he with his hair slicked back with walnut oil . . . What else did she want? To be an old maid? To take care of other people's kids? She and her new husband could live with them for a bit after the wedding, with Ştefan and her in Dudeşti-Cioplea, they had two rooms and their boy slept with them. She kept at her so much that Maria said yes and went with Costel. I have in front of me, as I am writing, their wedding portrait, the official one, the two of them against a velvet curtain backdrop with a vase of flowers on a tall pedestal next to the bride. This picture, enlarged and framed in a plaster oval, hung above their bed for a long time, in their tiny, rented room on Silistra. It's been touched up, but you can still see—beyond the formal and certainly rented clothes—their fears and uncertainties, their embarrassment and stiffness in that double tomb, the wax dolls in the diorama of the inevitable photograph. Nothing could have made them smile: my father is frowning and clenching his teeth as though he wanted to kill someone, and my mother is already thinking, it seems, of all there was to do after the wedding, since no one had given them so much as a spoon. Not a single member of his family had come from this Bănăt of theirs on the edge of the world, and my mother's relations were poor and stingy, people from the mountains who talked sharply and held on to their money. My grandparents, in the group pictures, are complete peasants, he with his freshly trimmed mustache, she with her headscarf that barely showed the tip of her nose, both of them with country clothes and a lost look in their eyes. The clerk is my mother's brother. The other country girl is her older sister. A few city people, bald men with big bellies, brassy women with beehives, are the witnesses, friends from the dress shop, neighbors, who knows. My cousins Costeluş and Aura are little, two or three years old, staring at the camera with round eyes. They all seem to be looking toward part of the room that isn't visible; something unexpected and miraculous must have happened there, magic tricks with doves, or flowers drawn from a glove.

It was hard for me to pull myself, that June day in 1956, at eleven in the morning, from the embrace of Victor, my twin brother. We had become used to each other as we hung there, two balloons in the azure, diamond-filled cavern, each tied down by the thread of his umbilical cord. We had grown together, we had felt each other's bioelectrical field as our first sensation, two weak lights in the forms of our curled bodies. Later, when our eyes developed, we opened their lids, saw each other, and smiled. Victor, in that godly light, was the most beautiful thing in the universe. His body was transparent, like those minuscule creatures in stagnant water. For months we looked at each other's eyes, then we looked at the organic walls around us, so dematerialized by the honey-thick light of the amniotic fluid that we could see the world outside, without any clue that it would one day be ours; we heard, filtered through the beating of our mother's heart, through the gurgling of her intestines, through the rushing of her pulmonary alveoli, voices, music, sounds of trams and tears, the laughter of those outside. If I could have, I would have warned Victor to stay inside, and sometimes I cannot help but think how good it would have been to have been hidden somewhere, to have been reabsorbed into the placenta, to have regressed to the egg, to have never been born. Over the course of a quarter hour, we both arrived, one after the other, identically insecure—neither of us weighed more than two kilograms, "couple of kittens," as the doctor later said to our father—and identically unhappy. The new world seemed to be sunk in darkness, drowned like pictures in the newspaper, where the ink overflows the outlines.

For a few months, our parents did stay with my mother's sister. How they got along with us, I do not know. The times, need I say, were terrible.

My mother had no milk, since she ate nothing but pasta and jam. There was no powdered milk to be found. In the end, my father spent a third of his salary on cow's milk from someone who kept two or three cows in a yard nearby. The milk was bluish, thinned with water, and infested with tuberculosis bacteria. This caused, several years later, my intradermal reaction test to produce a saucer on my arm, and I was sent for preventative care to Voila. After half a year, my parents took us, one at a time—no one but my mother could tell us apart, and she would hesitate so long that even I am not sure who to think I am—they took us out on the trams and brought us, asleep, back to their rented room in a house with twenty or so rooms like it, on Str. Silistra in Colentina. I lived there until I was three, in the place where Victor tragically disappeared, when we were about one.

I don't remember him, honestly, even though he is always in my mind, sometimes it seems he inhabits it completely. My mother never wanted to talk with me about him, the lost one. How often did I wonder whether Victor had been an imaginary child, born out of who knows what deep need of my mother's mind, the way some forms of hysteria mimic a nonexistent pregnancy, with pains just as rending as a real birth. My locks and baby teeth are a kind of archaeological proof of my existence at that time. The pictures—even though the oldest one dates from when I was eighteen months—show that, one spring or autumn day, photons sprang from the sun and ricocheted off my eyelashes and cheeks and fell like snow onto the plastic film, corroding it, the same way that today, other photons, released by a sun thirty years older, ricochet off the eyelashes of the child in the picture and enter my pupil. But where are his locks of hair, his baby teeth, his pictures? Where are his baby clothes? At the back of a shelf in the yellow chiffonier in the front room, my mother still has mine . . . Our navels were tied, one after the other, with the same twine, in the same crude knot, there, in the delivery room with the roof that let in the wind and rain, that dripped water full of grit and rust onto the white stomachs of pregnant women. I am still pulling out stiff, blackened pieces of the thread; he may have been buried with the string still in his navel, and together they rotted in the earth.

What I do know is that, according to what my relatives said, when we were about a year old, an ambulance came and took us to the hospital, burning with fever like a pair of furnaces. We both had double pneumonia. It wasn't hard to get sick: the room had a cement floor, like a prison, my parents were as poor as could be, the winter had been hard, with snow up to the windowsill, and wood was expensive. Both of us ended up with lung infections. A few cold and rainy days were enough for all the motley crowd in that Cour des miracles (thieves, prostitutes, trash men, simple tradesmen, and all the dirty-mouthed types from the outskirts of town, who all made a constant racket) to be overwhelmed with colds and flu. Since everyone wanted to kiss our cheeks, like we were little local princes, and our mother was so proud, it's no surprise that we were sick most of the time. Our little bodies were so tortured with fever you could barely touch us.

The hospital was a yellow building beneath yellow clouds, as though the clouds had been constructed and painted at the same time as the building. In the children's ward there were thirty beds with white, iron frames, but so old and broken it was a wonder they could hold all the sick girls and boys. The nurses were ugly and unkempt. They wore a cheap perfume that came in bottles shaped like cars. There, in two neighboring beds, my brother and I lay in agony for several days. From time to time, they gave us shots, pitilessly, with one of the stubby needles that would continue to terrorize me my whole life. Sometimes, I would feel the frozen disk of a stethoscope on my burning skin, red as a stove top. We agonized there, alongside thirty other children, days on end, until my fever broke, my eyes cleared up, and I could see, clearly and in every detail, the empty bed next to me. Even though I don't remember, I will never forget it.

When they brought us to the hospital, my mother told me, they examined both of us with a stethoscope. They began with me, without much interest, even though I was almost fainting with fever. When they came to Victor, there was some confusion. The doctor, an older, bald man, moved his stethoscope all over the child's reddened skin, without seeming to notice his screaming, and then he walked out of the ward, a tiled room like a public toilet. Our mother sat with us for about a quarter hour, despairing because she couldn't help us (how many times did she tell me later, whenever I was sick, that she had prayed that the sickness would pass to her or that something bad would happen to her, if it meant I would get better), until the doctor came back with two of his colleagues, and instead of giving him anything to soothe his suffering, they examined Victor again. They acted like they couldn't believe what they found, as though there was something not right in his little body. Our mother waited with her heart in her throat for the doctors to say something, but they acted like she was invisible. And so she was, as were all the patients; aside from asking "where does it hurt" out of the corner of their mouths, the doctors said nothing to the patients, as though the patients were not people who could understand, but dogs or cats. They would quickly and illegibly write a prescription, then depart with the same acrid and bored expression. But this was different. Our mother heard something like "impossible" or "a highly unusual phenomenon," and a few expressions in their lingo that she pointlessly strained to understand. In the end, all the more scared by the doctors' agitation, she dared to ask if it was really that serious, if her boy was sicker than he seemed to be. The three didn't even turn to face the young socialist worker, unslept and tear-stained, her hair a mess; the first doctor only said, over his shoulder, that Victor was "anormal." At first, he had thought that Victor didn't have a heart, or that it wasn't beating. In the end he found it, but it was upside down, pointing toward the right. Then, little by little, tapping on his ribs and pushing his stomach, he had found that the liver was on the left, and it seemed overall that Victor was, in every organ and every asymmetrical element in his body, a mirrored child. Everything that was supposed to be on the left was on the right, and vice versa. A different doctor said a phrase he had found in a fat and well used vade mecum, a phrase our mother didn't remember, aside from something that sounded like "inverse" and "total." It took me a long time to locate it, but now I know that the doctor had said, "situs inversus totalis," meaning an extremely rare condition in which all of a person's organs are inverted along the vertical axis of our body. None of this meant anything to our mother—Victor could have two heads as long as he was healthy and not tortured by the hell of fever.

Victor was not—is not—identical to me, in the sense of twins born from the same zygote, but inverse to me, my avatar flipped inside another dimension. We didn't grow in our mother's womb in an embrace, but stuck to a warm mirror, like two shark pups writhing in their mother's parallel uteri. We would never know how far this mirroring went, if it was only the organs that were inverse or also the depths of our biologies, inverted amino acids, exchanging the dextrorotatory for the levorotatory in inverted spirals of DNA. On the outside, we seemed identical, only our mother could tell us apart, but in the depths of our biology we were as different as two people could ever be.

Victor disappeared, and he took with him perhaps the only reason, the only brilliance, the only beauty, the only opportunity of my life. Lacking him, I have always felt mutilated, like one of those half-people who push themselves along the street by their hands, planted on a dolly. A child born without a hand or an eye could not be more confused by the actions of the gods than I have felt, without Victor, my entire life. I have gazed with half my gaze, I have listened with half my hearing. There are mental patients who no longer perceive half their body or even half the world. Starting at age one, this is how I have lived.

I don't remember anything of what followed, but my parents must have spent months in agony. The hospital told them my brother had died, they showed them papers with stamps and signatures. But they didn't show them a body. Where was he buried? Who was to blame for his death? No one knew. My father hollered and marched down the hospital halls, he knocked down the plaster model of a pregnant woman, with her womb viewed in section and the infant turned head-down in her uterus, he grabbed the doctor by the neck and tried to choke him. First the guards came, then the militia. My mother was screaming like crazy at the end of the bed, its sheets already changed for the next child. She was scared of losing me too. Everyone was very patient with my parents, one nurse even teared up, but they had no answer for their cries. They charged my father for the model he broke, and he had to repay them, month by month, for almost a year. My parents wrote petitions and requests all the way to the Central Committee, but who were they? They never got a response, were never given an audience anywhere. At the ATB workshops, a few days later, my father was visited by a man with a surly expression. He showed his ID discreetly and advised my father to calm down. Nothing he did would bring the child back to life. Doctors make mistakes, they're human, what would happen if they put all of them in jail? Where would you get replacements? My father came home not consoled, but frightened. We all slept in the same bed at that time, in the little room on Silistra, Victor and me in between our parents.

Now it was just me, back home after a week, healthy but skeletal and my thighs covered in needle marks. Everyone along that courtyard, all the neighbors, even the most criminal, were mourning. Once my brother disappeared, I became the absolute master of the place, because I was the only small child in the revenue house teeming with people. The thieves and prostitutes melted for me, they never came home without some candy for "the girl." I was constantly held, and, according to my mother's wishes, dressed like a girl in dresses, my hair long and curly, dark blond at the time. Workers who stank of motor oil and were as hairy as gorillas took me for rides on their mopeds or bikes, carrying me around the slums like a trophy. Time passed, and Victor, once so present, especially because we were two kids of one kind, more spectacular than one could be alone, faded from everyone's memory, faded like the double being of our family's twins. I was alone, beloved as I never would be again, held in my mother's arms, spoiled and protected, never let out of their sight, suffering from too much love and too much fear. After what happened that autumn, I was forced to wear two or even three hats on my head, one on top of the other, I was smothered all winter under the thickest clothes we had, they saturated me with penicillin and streptomycin at the smallest sniffle, in such quantities that I stank like mold from a mile away. Those were the years when they destroyed my health, out of love; and also out of love, they tortured me horribly, decade after decade.

Penicillin and streptomycin. I heard these words hundreds of times in my childhood. I couldn't cough without a doctor appearing. Even though he wore white, he was the darkest figure of my childhood, until he was replaced by the dentist. Has anyone else described childhood as a torture chamber? And yet that is what it was, for any child of the 1950s and '60s. At least polio and its fears had passed a few years before, leaving its victims among us: kids like us, full of life, running around behind the apartment block, but with one leg strapped into a metal brace. I saw them later at school, during gym: one normal leg, the other as thin as a walking stick, ribcage puffed out like a bird's, the crooked movement of the hip; poor crippled children, the more stunningly sad, the more their eyes were as clear as ours and their minds just as good. It may have been the case that the neighborhood idiots—the two or three children with dim, deformed faces who were walked up and down the Aleea Circului all day, under the chestnuts, by their mothers all dressed in black as though they were in permanent mourning for the quick-witted daughter or son that they never had—were happier because their minds were incapable of understanding their own tragedy. The sight of them, which some of my colleagues enjoyed, always caused me revulsion and terrible suffering, like the sight of the dwarves when our paths crossed almost every day on Aleea Circului. How they must have suffered, these little people with a grown person's head on the body of a rickety child, how much hate, powerless fury, and despair must they have felt: why did it have to be them? Why did they have to live in hell, without the hope of the eternally condemned, in the only life on Earth they were given? You must feel the same way when suddenly hit with a devastating illness.

A few years ago, one of my students was a girl like all the others, a hard-working kid who, even though she was taking care of two or three little brothers at home, never lagged in her schoolwork. She had a pure face, framed by straight red hair that shone like a mirror. A beautiful child who, in the eighth grade, began to acquire the colors, shapes, and longings of an adolescent. During a break one day, the boys in her class took the handle off the door to use as a toy gun. The girls made up a game: one at a time, they looked through the round hole in the door, watching the kids act out something on the other side. No one could understand how it happened, what insanity had momentarily invaded our world, when it came time for the red-haired girl to look through the hole. On both sides of the door, kids were yelling, pushing each other, laughing, the boys were trying to lift up the girls' skirts or hitting each other "right in the gearbox," and in the middle of this mandala of arms and faces and motions and teeth and buttons and collars and shoes and braids, suddenly someone slammed the doorknob back in as hard as they could, and the girl's eye burst and blood sprayed onto the door and the ground, and the kids' faces went from red to pale. The girl was left disfigured. She came back two months later, with gauze over her right eye. It was very hard for me to teach with her there, with that gauze held to her face with pink tape. When I had to teach her group, it felt like the sky was falling around me. She would be like this all her life, one-eyed, alone, with a horrible, motionless glass eye like a stuffed animal, a one-eyed worker bent over her machine, gluing on soles in a shoe factory then taking the tram home, a woman who would have been attractive if she weren't missing an eye, who could have had a husband and child. Then summer came and the girl left for break, with her gauze pad and her fate and everything.

But there's no need for a nickeled brace on your breadstick leg, or a piece of bloody gauze, for you to feel the hideousness of life. The doctor that visited our modest, working-class home at the smallest sign of a cold or swollen tonsils always came with a nurse. And the nurse carried a metal box that mirrored my narrow, dark face. "It's like she thinks you're Saint Sisoes, she can't stop looking at you," my mother would say. "Your child is rachitic," the nurse would butt in. "Sunshine, fresh air, good food, that's what he needs. Take him outside. Enough with the books, he's not going to be a philosopher." But I couldn't care any less about what they were saying, because while they chattered my eyes were glued to the frightening ritual: the cheerful nurse with bleached hair and lipstick on her teeth would take a syringe from the box, attach the needle and then—and this is what scared me the most—take out two tubes of cloudy, white liquid, their rubber stoppers held on by a thin strip of metal. I would not be the first victim of that long, thick needle's angled tip. First, she stuck it through the stopper. The needle sucked up the slobbery liquid, the tube hanging from the needle in the air, until the entire dose traveled into the barrel of the syringe, then she pulled the tube off and pushed the piston, making the needle spit a moldy-smelling spray. The air filled with mold—puffy, green mold, like a moth's wings, condensing on the walls. A slime of sharp-smelling mold covered the window like frost. The mold spread over my mother's eyes and the nurse's, over the drum of the stethoscope, which hung like a fish's bladder from the doctor's neck. There was mold on the roof of my mouth and in my lungs, I could feel it clearly everywhere, especially on my fear-paralyzed brain. A spider, a royal cobra, a transparent scorpion approached me with venom dripping from its stinger, I had no escape, and, even worse, my mother, my eternal refuge, pulled down my pants and my waffle-weave underpants, holey and yellow from being boiled, she herself was accomplice to my smiling and lipsticked executioners who touched my tensed buttock and said with a smile, "Don't clench, I won't kill you!" And then, as a sinister prelude, they rubbed a pad of terribly cold alcohol on my skin. The damp, blue pad was thrown into a corner: I saw it there, balled up and bearing the nurse's white fingerprints, I felt three or four quick smacks on the muscle, more martyred by fear than it would be by pain, and then the penetration of the needle, breaking the skin and flesh, diving into the marbled muscle tissue through which I myself flowed—my spirit that reacted to cold and heat, pressure and scrapes, burns and breaks, itches and pains—and releasing a pocket of moldy sap, to be infiltrated by a thin arborescence of blood. I yelped, my mother holding my shoulders; her betrayal hurt the most. Everyone was smiling—it was very strange to find yourself in the hands of a smiling executioner. Then they left, leaving behind the penicillin and streptomycin tubes "for me to play with." Feeling humiliated, I got up from the bed, pulled up my pants, and began to limp around the room. That was the first dose, the first red, swollen dot on my buttock. There would be another twenty-three, every six hours, day and night, on the right and on the left. When they woke me up for shots in the middle of the night, everything became a thousand times more horrible. I wasn't really awake, the sudden light blinded me, evil people with their needles and glass tubes cast long shadows onto the walls, I would start to scream like I was having a nightmare, I would writhe, desperately trying to protect myself, but I was held by the shoulders and subdued, like a pig whose time had come, my face pushed into the sheet (by my father, mother, the doctor, whoever was around), and the venomous insect again, implacably, approached its paralyzed victim. I felt the caustic incision again, my tissue dissolving in the saliva that stank of death and ruin, I could feel the long needle injecting a supple, fierce animal that would tear my interior to shreds. Then my pajama pants, printed with flowers and butterflies, were pulled back up and the living creatures in the room retreated, the light went off, and in all the darkened universe, only the pain shone brightly, like a star pulsing green-yellow, with a crumbling corona. Curled up like an animal, I sank into sleep, only to be awakened again, in the icy morning, for another dose.

I developed a fear of doctors, such that my first photograph, at eighteen months, showed me frowning and tearful. I remember the moment well. They took me into the yard, where turkeys in the pen spread their feathers and their beak wattles swelled with blood, and they sat me in front of a lilac tree. I didn't know what was going to happen. The photographer appeared suddenly, with his nickeled device around his neck, smiling like all the stethoscoped, skeletal doctors. It took a while for everyone to make me sit still, and even so, tears were running down my cheeks, and the unhappiness on my sepia face is there still, decades later, like a stigmata and like a prophecy.

For some, early childhood is a period of development with fantastic colors and dear faces; for me, it was a violent spectacle of shadows and flashes of light. I don't remember Victor, but I know that, about six months after we were born, our mother put us both in daycare because she had to go back to the factory. Production was more important than children, and at Donca Simo our mother was a leader, she oversaw eight looms that never stopped weaving. I remember, I remember, even though I have often been told there's no way I could, the blood-colored dawn in which our mother, at the first light, in a terrible cold, carried me to the daycare. The unreal succession of buildings, the great, purple sun rising directly in front of us, our pink shadows stretching behind. The frightening daycare building, its hallways, the polyp of children's faces in the bedrooms. If I examine my memory, my first, my very first and oldest memory is from that place: I am being carried, but not by anyone, I levitate through a yellow air, then there is a WC with stalls, one of them opens and I am placed on an enormous toilet seat. What was that, what was I doing there? My mother told me I almost died at the worker's daycare. "The women there would put you on the toilet and forget about you, they would forget to feed you, they didn't care about you at all. When the mothers came to pick their children up, they found them screaming, covered in poop, oh, so awful!" We didn't adapt in any way: we screamed from morning until five in the afternoon, inconsolable, until we were purple. We wouldn't eat a thing, we turned transparent from starvation and abandonment. In the end, our mother took us out of there, she confronted her bosses at the fabric factory and resigned. She never worked again. She stayed at home with both of us until the bad thing happened, then she stayed with me alone, half a child, to become the half a person I am today.

I have another extremely old memory, also linked to the lower area, to excretions and shame, but without any connection to the first memory. I am very young, barely able to stand. I am, as a consequence, as in so many other memories and dreams, in a very high room filled with dirty light. The wall in front of me is indescribable. It is the most concrete image from this illusory world that I have ever received into my skull. A green-yellow wall, concave, damp, slimy, cracked, uneven like mud in one place, smooth as a mirror in another. Rivulets of water trickle down, branch out, sink into its crust and pus. Along the base of the high, wide wall, through the floor covered in puddles, runs a gutter. The gutter holds old urine that has sat so long it has corroded the grate, and within the urine there are unidentifiable, putrid shapes that emit poison gases. Am I being punished? Am I locked inside a room for urination? Where am I? Who put me here? I see my shadow lying across the floor and wall, but I don't sense myself. I am nothing but that wall, that filthy gutter.

Our life went on there, in the revenue house on Silistra, with its thugs, tinkers, quilters, whores, and thieves. A few seasons passed, I felt them as periods of dark and light alternating on my skin under the flowing clouds. The hairy stalks of the geraniums in the windows budded as often as their flowers rotted, turned brown and pale, and tumbled onto the sills. In our single, narrow room, with a single bed, stove, and cement floor, my mother would read to me. Sometimes we went out, into the courtyard first, and then, when I was two, onto the street covered in trash and puddles reflecting the sky. Now it seems as though the years on Silistra were one continuous springtime, raw with cold winds and a sun from the dawn of time. Other kids from other courtyards came to the same street, but at that age we didn't know how to play together, we just looked at each other, not like human beings, but the way we would look at sheep, cats, stray dogs. We didn't recognize other members of our own species. We lived more inside our little crania than outside, among flowering apricot trees and brick houses. I would approach children my age, I would look at their ears, fingers, the saliva running from their mouths. Then I would look at the gigantic, translucent tulips in colors I had never seen anywhere else, then I would look at the sky in the puddles. Beside our dirt-splattered house, the bulging, blind wall of the neighboring house rose like a polyp. Across its giant surface, like a worn-out map, there was an irregular pattern of plaster and places where the plaster had fallen, allowing the ancient bricks to gleam in the sun. Perhaps that wall, blocking the horizon of my earliest childhood as though dividing one age from another, engendered my fascination for blind walls, for brick surfaces without windows, invaded by lichen, by moths the size of your hand that bask, motionless, in the sun. Abandoned who knows when, some scaffolding climbed the wall. It was, from God knows what caprice, painted pink (the intersecting metal bars that rose almost to the roof) and light blue (the motor at the base and the platform that it raised, like an elevator without walls). The machine, overcome with weeds, was the kids' favorite place to play. We were there from the morning on, in our baggy overalls and dirty undershirts. We liked that wall, we would tilt our little heads back as far as possible to see the top of the wall sticking up in the air, our vertebrae popping with the effort. We liked to put a hand on the wall to feel how hot the sun had made it. It frightened us, but we also liked it when, at our touch, from the cobweb-filled holes between the bricks, black articulated legs would poke out, belonging to an unusually large and strong spider. We could make them scoot out across our hands. The spiders were big but didn't bite, unlike the stray dogs that were a constant menace. The spiders didn't do us any harm.

Five or six of us would climb onto the platform between the pink bars (I can still see the nasty pink, with a lot of white from crow and pigeon droppings dried on the convexity of the dusty bars), and the oldest of us, Mia Gulia, who must have been four years old, pushed the broken ebony button. The motor would begin to buzz and vibrate and we rose slowly along the blind wall, while the street and houses sank underneath us, and the multicolored globes on top of pillars in the garden next door came into view, and the model of a ship on the second floor of our house, and the grocery with a balcony above, and, far away, a mixture of trees and roofs that extended without end, it surrounded us everywhere and none of us knew how large the world was. Or, better put, for each of us the world was our house, the neighboring house with the wall, the bit of street out front, the grocery where our parents carried us, and everything else was darkness and fear.

When we came to the top, we huddled together, holding tightly to each other's clothes, almost pulling them off. High above us were some crooked, rusty braces that kept the wall from falling over. Between them, among the little trees that grew there from seeds blown by the wind, a few of the bricks had been removed to make a vent for the room on the other side. There we could peep in, following the thick shaft of light that slanted down from the opening. On the other side of the wall was a large, strange room, where nothing moved. Still, we felt someone was there, someone without a face, someone outside of sight, outside of the world of shadow and light. Our fear became uncontrollable. We screamed as we finally descended on the elevator platform, from which we could have been knocked by the slightest wind, but we weren't screaming for fear of heights or danger, but because we had seen the great, frozen wasteland inside the house with the blind wall. We jumped off the platform before it thudded against the ground, and we ran for our mothers' legs and grabbed on desperately. The oleanders that filled the courtyard had more powerful smells than the chopped meats and borscht soups that simmered in twenty rooms at once, stronger than the whores' perfumes and the sweat-stained undershirts of the working men.

I now know why we were so frightened by that opening, that gap in the fortifications at the top of the wall of the neighboring house. Because that was the house's eye—because we weren't peering in through the narrow gap between weather-beaten bricks, rather the old, decrepit house was looking at us. The neighboring house, which normally saw nothing but the sky, drank in our dirty, snotty faces, our brown eyes, our teeth hanging crooked in mouths that gaped in wonder. With its one eye of unfinished brickwork, the house stole our souls to create one of its own, it tried to pull us inside, into the silent, motionless room, so we could gaze eternally at the sky through the solitary opening.

Just once, out of the dozens of times we raised ourselves toward the sky along the blind wall, did we ever see someone inside. Through the narrow gap we watched a woman, a snow queen. The summer clouds reflected in her wide, large eyes, her eyelashes—in the middle of July?—glittered with stars of snow. Her snowy hair trailed mist. I can still feel the pressure of her hand, when, without looking at the other children, she reached out an arm from her world, as though she were emerging from a mirror, and her lacquered fingers took hold of my own. I can still feel the click, like two magnets coming suddenly together, but I cannot decide whether it was our eyes or our hands that stuck together for an endless moment.

We grew up, we all grew up, as though once we threw Victor out of the basket, our balloon rose high, taking along the revenue house on Silistra, the oleanders, the street, the grocery store. Soon, the room where my mother and father, alone and miraculously young, loved each other and spoke to each other in distinct dialects, where there had been four sleeping in a bed, but then only three, that room couldn't hold us anymore and expelled us from its womb. Victor had turned into an empty grave, in Ghencea, where for years I brought him flowers on my birthday. I became the boy-girl with twin ponytails down to my shoulders, my father became a journalism student, and our life took another path. Only my mother stayed the same housewife, taking care of us all. Only her mind was always closed to me, as though all the doors and windows on her side were bricked over. Why did she wait so long to tell me I had had a twin brother? Why did she "not remember" (is that possible?) the date of his death? Why did he die sometimes at four months, other times at six months, eight, and a few times at twelve? Why was he sometimes my twin, but occasionally—to my amazement and despair—was he born a year after me? How could this mystery persist in our family? Why didn't I ask her directly to tell me, for God's sake, what happened? Why didn't I hold her blackened hands against the table and force her to tell me the truth? Why didn't I ask her to let me suck milk from her breast underneath the house, to press the house against her fallen breast and its unusually large areola, until she told me the whole truth? This is what happens in the stories she told me herself, that's how tough guys found stuff out from their sister or brother. I never did this because that's not how things were under the cool veneer of our family. We were creatures who only met at the kitchen table or in the bed. My mother and father didn't talk about anything but money. My father and I didn't talk about anything but soccer. I had to circle them, like walking around a statue in the garden, to try to understand them. If they had ever started to talk, I would have been amazed, as though a marble woman in a museum had moved her lips when I passed. We were afraid to talk to each other, we never imagined it was possible. I doubt that, even on the verge of certain death, we would start to talk to each other. As the years passed, this insulating porcelain shell covered every piece of warm skin, and when we found ourselves in the same room, we heard nothing but a ceramic clinking.

This is why I've had to invent some details, to imagine some scenes, to populate the wasteland where I lived with characters and feelings; I had to give birth to my mother, in my own image, so I wouldn't be an orphan. Today

I can't tell my hallucinations from reality, the words I put in their mouths from the clinking porcelain, the translucent facts from the opaque. I know only that Victor was the first anomaly of my life, and the uncertainty and suspicions that always follow heavenly signs were born in the same womb as I.

13

Caty taught chemistry, but she actually spent her classes telling the children stories about her fairy-tale house in Cotroceni, about its eleven rooms, about its Renaissance furniture, about her dozens of Bohemian crystal vases, about the engravings hung on her walls, originals, some of which cost as much as an apartment. She didn't even know how many dresses she had in her enormous built-in wardrobes, but she could describe them all to the children, with details that stuck in their minds. It wasn't hard: Caty wore a different dress every day, different shoes, different hair color, and she shone so brightly that even the children's ashy hair seemed to turn red, blue, or orange purely from the radiance of her skin, the effect of creams and bubble baths that rose and fell, like the tides, according to the phases of the moon. Sixty-eight shining eyes stared at her like she was a fairy while, with her self-satisfaction and airs before these poor kids from the edge of town, she talked nonstop about her fence, which cost forty thousand lei, and her artesian fountain whose waters changed color every five minutes, and her cats, and her Persian rugs, and her son who studied German with Fräulein tutor and whose beauty and intelligence amazed everyone he met. No woman had ever had a mouth like Caty's, almost perfectly round, almost a bright red circle cut horizontally in two by a sensual line of ink. All in all, she was rubicund and flowery, a liar and a braggart, as fake as only a warm, life-size doll could be, and she had velvety brown eyes. You'd eat her for breakfast, her fortysomething years and all. At twenty she must have been all fruit, like a banana in its skin, filled with the same delicious material from head to toe. Without a doubt, if you had ever penetrated her peachy flesh, that happiness-colored material would have covered you all over, would have made you one with the sweet, inflatable woman unfolded beneath you.

For the last five minutes of class, Caty suddenly moves from Chanel, Coty, Lancôme, Giorgio Armani, and Dior to other names, equally foreign to the children: fluoride, chromium, bromine, iodine. Then she leaves the room with a train of girls in tow, patting her back, touching the hem of her pastel dress, insatiably inhaling the scent of her hair and underarms. They all want to be her and to have a house in Cotroceni, a big, fat husband who works at the Ministry of the Exterior, a genius child, and tons of evanescent, perfumed, crepe, silken, slippery, transparent dresses, curly as carnations and labia, in huge chiffoniers built into the wall. Caty walks down the tiled stairs, lighting them up as she passes over their dark and sinister colors, and she comes into the lounge to be greeted by the smiling, chirping, eyelash-fluttering hatred of all her colleagues. "My darlings," she says before she passes through the door completely, "I am simply exhausted, I can hardly tell you. Imagine, yesterday I cleaned, one by one, one hundred fifty-six crystal windowpanes in the interior doors of my house. I counted: one hundred fifty-six! Doesn't it drive you crazy?" And she throws herself into the first chair, spent, but observing out of the corner of her eye what effect her declaration has had on the other teachers, whose faces only turn greener than usual. The teachers adopt their usual tactic: Caty does not exist. They won't interrupt their chatter about suppositories and talcum power to lend her an ear. Beneath the portraits of Uzbek scholars and writers, the walls' dark green paint appears to lend its hue to all their faces and teeth. Caty is a firework display that does not exist. "When you work so hard, girls, I mean what good are servants when you still have to get your hands dirty, you tell yourself sometimes you don't need a child, or a husband, or a . . . lover, they'll just drive you crazy." Caty never hesitates to insinuate that her Ministry of the Exterior clerk was not the only one to enjoy her perfect bottom and her unusually pointy breasts, and the slight pause before the word was just to make it more thrilling and her more interesting. She would have spoken in the same way to drunks in a bar, to the women sweeping the streets with tree-branch rakes, to the blind and to the deaf, perhaps even to blank walls. The verbal content of her soft and fragrant skin needed periodic emptying, like a full udder, and it didn't matter who did the milking. She lounges in the chair a few more minutes, and even though the bell has rung and the "girls" are moving toward their classrooms, she starts another story: "Last Saturday night I had such a fright . . . We were almost overrun with burglars, my darlings! Good thing we had the doorknob electrified. When the man touched it . . . that was the end of that! It doesn't kill them, just gives them a shock and burns their hands, the little bastards . . . Can you imagine, girls, for a house like ours, with two stories and eleven rooms . . . the wrought iron fence alone cost us forty thousand lei . . . My husband has a pistol, but with the electrified doorknob, which was my idea, we really do sleep soundly." The last one to leave, Băjenaru, a math teacher, forgets in her indignation that the woman in flower print who tells fat lies doesn't exist, and she spits out: "But what if a child goes and touches the knob, did you think of that?" Caty is undisturbed and makes up some story, but I go to class, leaving her to reveal to the Montenegrin scholars in the paintings the secret of her child detector.

I wouldn't waste my precious pages here with a goose like her, if she hadn't led me to the Picketists. One Sunday last summer, I was put on guard duty at the school. This never bothered me, especially during nice weather, since what I did on Sundays at home (writing in my diary) I could do just as well in the school's downstairs office. On Sunday there was no one in the entire school. Since it was the third trimester—in the summertime with brilliant light—the empty school was melancholy and enclosed in its enigma like an ancient temple, a building you are not sure is a temple. The empty classrooms howled with loneliness like an ear with tinnitus, the entire school became an actual ear that listened to its own whistles and snarls deep within its cochlea. Not even this phantomatic light was enough to tempt me to draw a map of the endless corridors. I limited my wanderings to a few moments on the first floor, and then I went quickly back to the office and set to work.

That Sunday, with summer clouds in a sky broken by the old factory and the water tower, I was deep inside my diary. I was writing down the terrifying dream that had woken me the previous night (a nuclear bomb exploded downtown, I knew the shock wave was spreading quickly, demolishing buildings, burning up trees, liquefying people, and I was running as fast as I could to the underground shelter beside our house on Floreasca), and just then the door opened and Caty appeared, as radiant as a pseudopod of the warm, trembling wind from outside. Her smiling mouth was like a poppy petal cut in two by a tremulous line of ink. She was surprised to see me there—one of us hadn't understood Borcescu's instructions, probably her, as ditsy as she is. In any case, what to do? Tony is at the park with Fräulein, Matei's work called him in . . . Caty sat in a chair across from me, the desk between us, like a Mediterranean Sea with a glowing, intangible Tangier beyond. Everything she wore was "shipped in," brands that people like us had heard of, but in the way they had heard of Graal and the Shroud of Turin. Sometimes a Neckermann catalog passes through the neighborhood, and a housewife takes a break from her pots, makes a coffee, lights a BT, and, holding the catalog, she dreams. The women and men in the thick, shiny pages are from another planet, another dimension. You can't reach them, just as you can't exceed the speed of light or travel through time. But you don't even want to go there, the same way you don't want to enter the enormous screen at the movies and talk to Robert Redford. You don't want to because you can't, and because you can't, you dream, all afternoon, holding the Neckermann, looking at dresses and blouses and shoes and purses and their deutschmark prices and, on the last pages, the pictures of resorts on the shores of all the oceans and in all the archipelagos, the swimming pools with gelatinous, blue water, with gigantic cruise ships, with young men and young women, perfect as perfection itself, sitting at a bar in a straw hut on tall chairs, drinking something Nile green, the color of jellyfish meat, from conical glasses with a little foot. Even men borrow the Neckermann to touch themselves and look at the unimaginably beautiful blondes and brunettes, in bras and panties, whose satiny hair and eyelashes are twice as long as natural—proof they are not human, that they are another species from an untouchable world. There is a difference of quantum phase between us and them, their reality is foggy and unintuitive, and on that long-ago Sunday so was Caty's reality, her musky perfume from under her chin, between her breasts, between her thighs and buttocks, dressed in waves of cloth with pink summer prints.

I was not bothered by Caty, even though I was already divorced and doing as poorly with women as humanly possible. In a way, I was glad for someone to keep me company, even though I was sorry to stop writing in my notebook; I would probably leave it closed all afternoon. It was already three and the worst of the heat was on its way, I was alone in a limitless building with a woman I had nothing to say to, but I had to rise to this occasion, like so many others.

Fortunately, of course, she carried the whole conversation. What she had purchased, what Matei had purchased for her (usually rings and necklaces: how much they weigh, how many carats the diamonds have), what smart things Tony had said . . . Today, before she came to school, she had stopped by to see a friend just back from Copenhagen. You wouldn't believe what all she had brought, the crazy girl! Caty looked in her purse, a woven beach bag, and took out a soft package wrapped in lilac-colored paper. "It's just what I needed, because here, try all you like and you'll find nothing but horrors," she chattered on, while her nails, painted to match her amazing lips, struggled to untie the package. The light in the office was patchy, like in a forest, and a hundred thousand shades of orange and rosy pink and cyclamen and green like an unripe lemon and lilac like a fig fell over the shining cheeks, snub nose, and pearly bodice of the large rubber woman, who, finally, untied the knot and revealed, packed like oranges in crinkly paper, several objects of a silky fabric that at first I couldn't identify. "Panties, darling, panties! Have you ever heard of a wackier gift? She's a nut, that Miki, but that's why I like her . . ." She took each item in turn and held it out to me, as though holding tropical butterflies by the tips of their wings. Caty expected me to take them in my hand, touch them, admire the style, maybe try them on. I knew that it would be a complete mistake to interpret it as an invitation and to make a move. I was like Tantalus: the forbidden fruit was right in front of me, but if I stretched out my hand . . . "Yes, very nice," I said, like one of her friends would have. Caty gave them a greedy look and, completely satisfied, put them back in her bag. "You can't even find the cheap ones here anymore, it's so awful . . ." She chirped on about her friends' bodies, who had put on weight, who had gone on a diet . . . Wrinkles, what can you do, it's a part of aging, even if you take care of yourself, just like crow's feet . . . Thank God she didn't have any, not yet anyway, but . . .

And here, at a certain moment, while she kept talking, looking out the window at the crows jumping between the trees on Str. Dimitrie Herescu, diced into fine cubes by the thread curtain, Caty turned toward me and looked into my eyes. Her voice stayed the same, frivolous and sexual and husky, but her face took on something male, as though she had suddenly aged a decade or two: "I can't begin to tell you how sad I was to turn forty! I felt so desperate, so upset . . . I cried the whole day, the most beautiful part of my life was gone . . . Why do we have to get older? Why do we lose our beauty, our happiness?" These were not rhetorical questions. Caty was leaning toward me, waiting for me to answer. She looked at me with such hate and despair that, if I had stolen her youth and beauty, like magical animal skins covered in precious stones, and hidden them in a cave, I would have brought them back in a second, I would have even apologized. "But Caty," I said to her, "you should be the last to complain . . ." She didn't let me continue: "I should, it's unfair that I should complain. What else am I supposed to do? To sit here defeated and fucked (pardon me, but as one colleague to another) and left without a cent?" The obscenity sounded like a gunshot inside the office walls. What the hell was going on? My erection at the sight of the underwear had passed, so the change in register was sudden and stupefying—as though your cat, who'd just been begging at the table, suddenly began to talk, not only in a human voice, but making learned allusions to Plato's Myth of the Cave. Caty was so focused and so serious that I barely recognized her. Under her pastel mask, made from the feathers of all the birds of the jungle, was the dark, sweaty face of a shaman. "Do you even care that we get old and die? Do you care about cancer or being paralyzed?" Caty, who was once the most charming creature in the universe, would wither and be covered with salt, like pearls aging in moldy treasure chests. Her cry of fear, facing the years that would, inevitably, rot her teeth and stain her skin, was the negative of her cries of pleasure in the middle of the night, the ones that all her neighbors knew, the same agony and, somehow, the same vitality. Slowly, the disfiguring fear in her eyes calmed down, and she returned to speaking with the implacable automatism of those missionaries who knocked on our doors to give us poorly printed brochures: "I am the Way, the Truth, and the Life." It seemed that even in the parallel world of the Neckermann catalog, from whence our chemistry teacher had parachuted, things were not so glamorous. The day she turned forty, alerted by the sound of her sobbing in front of the mirror, like death's-head moths whose feathered antennae sense the female's pheromones from dozens of kilometers away, the Picketists entered her life.

"My house was full of guests, a total madhouse, but I, if you can believe it, I was locked in the bathroom, sitting on the toilet seat, crying. Forty! When I was a girl, I thought any forty-year-old woman was a hag. That's what we called our teachers, in high school, shallow as we were: the math hag, the history hag . . . the Romanian hag . . . Aging was not for me. How could I imagine that I would become the chemistry hag so quickly? Yes, darling, everything passed too quickly, like a dream. I saw myself in the mirror, wailing, with a wet piece of toilet paper in my hand: I looked frightful. You know, mascara under my eyes, red face . . . Matei knocking at the door now and then, it was so bad." But the Picketists saved her and gave her the power to go on, to cover the silvery strands of her hair with dye and to choose dresses that slimmed her corpulent figure. Without them, she would have grabbed her famous electrified doorknob herself, "But I'd pump it up to ten thousand volts: we have a generator in the basement for when the electricity is out."

I was not completely unfamiliar with the name of the Picketists. Patrolmen would come to the school from time to time to talk to the children about traffic laws, about socialist ethics and fairness, and what they should do if a car stops beside them and someone they don't know offers them candy. They also talked about extremely dangerous sects that, it seemed, had recently been spreading and evangelizing throughout the city. Fat and sweaty, awkward in front of the slack-mouthed children, the patrolman shifted from side to side and read, from a crumpled piece of paper he had pulled from his pocket, the names of the most suspect of these sects, stumbling, halting, at times stopping entirely to catch his breath. The teachers also learned that in the school's neighborhood there were some emissaries of a new way of thinking "that has nothing to do with the materialist, Marxist-Leninist doctrine that, dear children, our party promotes." The most awful and perverse of these sects were the Essenes, Simonians, Meandrites, Saturnilites, Ophites (not officers, kids, ha-ha . . .), Naassenes, Perates, Barbelognostics (they don't know what a barber is), Carpocratians, Mandaeans, Elcheanites, Nicholasians, TM-ists, MISA-ists, and Picketists. Their secret messengers look the same as anyone else, maybe they're the checkout girl at the grocery, or the trash man, the guy at the propane station, maybe even a militia officer, although this the patrolman found hard to believe, but—and here all the little ones' eyes opened wide—one thing is the giveaway for all of them. "Children, if you're alone with any grown-up, even your mommy or daddy, if they open up their hand and there's an insect staring up at you, that person is in a sect. Run away as fast as you can, because they're going to put you in a sect, too, and make you kiss snakes on the mouth and eat little children and do all sorts of things that are not allowed under the morals of communism." The children were paralyzed. For weeks afterward, when they would write me essays like, "The First Day of School," "How I Spent My Summer Vacation," "Autumn Is Here," or "My Favorite Classmate," whatever the topic, the person with the insect would show up somewhere. If they were buying bread, the checkout lady would open her red hand and, with an abject grin on her face, show them a large, springy grasshopper. People walking down the street would have a metallized bug, a centipede as hard as wire, a cricket, or a tiny ladybug. The children were too afraid to come to school, where the teachers might hold out their hand to the class to reveal an imperial stag beetle. They hid in basements or climbed up trees to wait for the sects to pass, as though they were storm clouds. The person with the insect appeared in their dreams: the bug grows into the flesh of his hand and becomes a part of his body; the person holding the insect no longer sees through his own eyes and no longer thinks with his own mind: the insect sees and hears everything for him, as though he were holding, in his palm, his own head.

During her birthday party, Caty became a Picketist. It was toward dawn, after they had danced all night with the obstinacy and excessive enthusiasm of those who, having reached forty, the apex of the vault, the keystone of our life's arched back, still refuse to look toward the future. They danced in the dark, they caressed each other like teenagers, not for pleasure but as a sad, dark demonstration: I still desire you, even though I know every centimeter of your skin all too well, even though I tell the children that "love changes over time, into a kind of friendship with a lot of responsibility," that people stay together not because they are in love their whole lives, but in order to raise their children and, in general, "to do things together." They didn't just pretend that there was something left between them; they really wanted it, they would have given their own skins to feel love and tenderness again, or at least an animalistic desire for each other. They would have wanted to slip their fingers—as they had once in the thick shadow of an old house's hallway, or on a park bench late at night, or at an adolescent party—into the underwear of the good and curious girl they once knew, or the passionate and awkward boy to feel his damp, burning sex, but they knew that the lips of their vulvae were dry and their penises were only semierect, and that April, May, and June had passed without the possibility of return. The men, already balding on top and growing fine hairs in their ears, would have given anything to feel once more, yes, even their aching testicles as they rode the bus home ten stops, late in the evening, after sitting on a park bench for hours with the same girl who, now a grown woman, moved heavily in their arms, to be as sweaty and passionate as they were then, as they would never be again in this inexorably degrading life. To touch the nipples of the girl you love and desire with a tortuous madness, to feel her pubic curls and the place between her thighs, so oddly shaped in comparison to yours, to see yourself reflected in her desirous eyes as you feel her sweet tongue and her abandon in the face of your aggression, the golden sap of endorphins, the drug of falling in love that is the distillation, within a rock-crystal flask, of the other drug, of passion and erection and penetration and ejaculation, to die and to rise again in the house of love, you to melt into her body and she to melt into yours, not to hold breasts in your hand but to have breasts, not to hold the cylinder of his burning flesh in your small hands with painted nails, the man's swollen veins and moist head, but to have a penis yourself, grown on your lover's body, that is, on your own body. To see, with your four eyes with lashes that meet and interlace, the fourth dimension, the future nuptial dance, the future nights of sex, to hear the screams of the woman you love, the deep groans of the man you love, repeated hundreds and thousands of times, like links in the sexual chain of our lives . . . all of this will pass, will sink, will wither, will rot, will dry out like branches whose sap no longer runs. Caty and Matei danced all night feeling neither desire nor love, and at dawn, drunk only on Martini, with her tears still wet on her cheeks and her lipstick spread beyond her lips like an obscene stain, the inflatable woman of my dreams walked out of her house and sat on the front steps. It was cold, the clouds above were fluorescent and threatening, but underneath a little blue was already showing. She thought about taking a lover and starting a new life, of course it was just a thought, a thought emerging from her despair and fear, in fact she was thinking of her own youth in the light of many years, of her Botticellian figure, or the zephyrs that had once run through her hair grown down to her thighs, she was hopelessly in love with her younger self, she was a lesbian in love with her younger body, with her delicacy and madness, her pure, shining eyes, her dresses, her delicate shoes with the highest of heels . . . She wanted to go back there, she wanted to have never left . . .

Then, as Caty told me in that miserable office under a mottled, gelatinous light, then a man came out of her house and sat next to her on the cold steps, facing the yard, a man called Virgil, "You don't know him, of course, he's a friend of ours, a physicist from Măgurele, Matei's known him a long time, whenever he's in Bucharest he invites him over for a beer or one of our parties." He sat next to her, smoking and talking, for about two hours, they saw the purple globe of the sun rise directly in front of them, drenching everything in amber and freshness. The man looked exhausted, as though he had come on foot down a long road, drawn by the pheromones emanating from the woman on the steps. But this time, the message was not sexual, the bushy combs of the male butterfly had not sensed the infinitesimal but imperious emanations of her velvety womb. The message came instead from the great neural ganglion in the skull of the unhappy person who sat there, at dawn, looking her future in the face. They were the pheromones of unhappiness, nostalgia, a horribly intense desire to return, to swim upstream through the cold waters of time, like a salmon going back to its source. Caty was not a woman then, she was a creature stripped of her sex, a lowly human like everyone else, like absolutely everyone else; a person made of perishing flesh and self-hatred who, like a dandelion, spread the black signs of unhappiness all around herself, her new curls growing on a bald head, her new makeup on her earthly cheeks. It was a new sex, a different sex, the sex of death and waste that now searched, like a bat sending little peeps into the wind, for its dark partner. Virgil had heard these subliminal cries, inaudible to the human ear, and he had appeared in the only possible window of Caty's frightened mind, the way a seasoned Casanova knows the precise moment, exceptionally rare as it is, when the most chaste girl's icy heart might be conquered.

Virgil sat silently next to her on the cold step, looking toward the melted globe of the sun and the millions of drops of dew on the ground before him, holding a closed hand on his knees, but then he opened his fingers, like the thick petals of a carnivorous plant, to reveal, on the capital M we all have scribbled there in the middle of our palms—and which cannot stand for anything other than Mors, the Roman god of death, since all the paths across our palms lead, through the pointless whirls of destiny, through the risible games of karma, to the common boneyard—a delicate, green praying mantis, its triangular head turning in every direction, with evidently intelligent eyes, with long and supple limbs, with a spindly body covered with praying wings like rough blades of grass. Virgil lifted the insect until it fit within the melted metal circle of the sun, so that it looked now, against the incandescent amber stain, like a black shadow in prayer surrounded by a pulsing halo, an intense, hypnotic field of energy. And then he began to talk to the woman (exhausted by the lateness of the hour, her sadness, and alcohol) about the Picketists, about their response to the great questions our mind endlessly ponders, by the simple fact of its existence: Where does unhappiness come from? How is the infinite misery of our lives possible? Why do we feel pain, why do we suffer illness, why have we been given the pains of jealousy and unrequited love? Why are we wounded by the people around us? Who approved cancer, who released schizophrenia into the world? Why do amputations exist, who allowed torture machines to come into our minds? Why do people extract teeth to extract confessions? Why are bones crushed in traffic accidents? Why do airplanes crash, why do hundreds of people fall, for long minutes, knowing with absolute certainty that they will burn, they will explode, they will be torn apart and crushed? Why do people die of hunger, why are they buried under collapsing walls? Who can tolerate blindness, how can you reconcile yourself to suicide, how can you live alongside radical amputees and the incurably ill? Who can endure the screams of women in childbirth? There are millions of diseases of the human body, parasites that devour it from inside and outside, suppurating diseases of the skin, intestinal occlusions, lupus, tetanus, leprosy, cholera, plague. Why should we passively put up with them, why should we pass by, pretending not to see them, until we are impacted, as we certainly will be? Our minds will suffer, so will our flesh, our skin, our joints. Sores and pus will cover us, phlegm and sweat will drown us, injustice and tyranny will make us bow down, annihilation and impermanence terrify us.

Why do I know I exist if I also know I will not? Why was I given access to logical space and the mathematical structure of the world? Just to lose them when my body is destroyed? Why do I wake up in the night with the thought that I will die, why do I sit up, drenched in sweat, and scream and slap myself and try to suppress the thought that I will disappear for all eternity, that I will never be again, to the end of time? Why will the world end with me? We age: we stand quietly in line with those condemned to death. We are executed one after the other in a sinister extermination camp. We are first stripped of our beauty, youth, and hope. We are next wrapped in the penitential robe of illness, weariness, and decay. Our grandparents die, our parents are executed in front of us, and suddenly time gets short, you suddenly see your reflection in the axeblade. And only then do you realize you are living in a slaughterhouse, that generations are butchered and swallowed by the earth, that billions are pushed down the throat of hell, that no one, absolutely no one escapes. That not one person that you see coming out of the factory gates in a Méliès film is still alive. That absolutely everyone in an eighty-year-old sepia photograph is dead. That we all come into this world from a frightening abyss without our memories, that we suffer unimaginably on a speck of dust, and that we then perish, all in a nanosecond, as though we had never lived, as though we had never been.

The mantis turned around in Virgil's palm, as he spoke in a monotone, as though reciting a text he knew by heart, and then it shot up in flight, suddenly an enormous locust, over the dew-pearly garden. It disappeared over the fence woven with Jericho roses.

Caty nodded at every phrase, as though her frivolous being, made of pretentions and silk, had only then awoken, had at that moment escaped from the Neckermann with its perfect men and perfect women, and had entered the dictionary of skin diseases, the forensic treatises, the anatomy of melancholy, the history of infernos with their sinister illustrations of the crushed, burned, amputated, oligophrenic, hanged, starving, and paralyzed people emerging triumphant from pits of horror, showing their green lunatic faces and their eyeballs slung into the backs of their heads like broken dolls. From that morning on, the sweet, multicolored woman with her sparrowlike mind led a double life, one I heard of for the first time sitting in front of her in the deserted office where the last ficus tree rotted away. By day she was still the chemistry teacher, envied by all her colleagues for her clothes and shoes and purses, her house with 156 panes of glass, and her ministry husband, but by night, two or three times a week, dressed in black without makeup or perfume, in a headscarf and shoes the janitors wore, with tears dancing in her eyes and a dark hatred over her face like a dead god of love, and holding a crude sign made from a television box proclaiming, "Down with Aging!", she stole out of her house and went to the Saint Elefterie church, where she joined a pack of somber silhouettes, all coming from the neighborhood Cotroceni, then walked through the quiet of the ruined city, haunted by nostalgia and old trams, toward the cemeteries: Ghencea, Bellu, Andronache, Izvorul Nou, Armenesc, Străulești, Adormirea Maicii Domnului, Metalurgiei, Israelit, Eternitatea, Colentina, Berceni, Luteran, Progresul, Saint Vineri. Through the narrow streets between abandoned, empty buildings with their doors flung open, rotted like old barrel staves, with plaster allegorical statues spreading their flaking wings under the full moon, their group met up with groups from other neighborhoods, other people with shadowy faces and shining eyes. At the cemetery gates, beyond whose tall fence, profiled against the still vaguely illuminated sky, rose the stubby cupolas of the crypts and stumps of pitch-black crosses, the Picketists, sometimes a few dozen people, sometimes hundreds, took out their signs ("Down with Death!", "Down with Illness!", "Down with Agony!", "Down with Suffering!", "Protest Pain!", "Pro Eternal Life!", "Pro Eternal Consciousness!", "Pro Human Dignity!" "NO to Passivity!", "NO to Laziness!", "NO to Resignation!"), and they began to silently pace in circles, for hours, in the cold of the night, with the determination of those who, as they say, "won't go down without a fight." "We're always demonstrating, we're always fighting against the terrible things people do, in their meanness and blindness, but how can we accept the destruction of the spirit, the enormous absurdity of its life and death in flesh? How can you await your execution, as silent as sheep and just as innocent, when you are a spirit, when you are a part of the Godhead? We, the Picketists, we scream silently against this unbelievable, unqualifiable, unpardonable human genocide. We hold that it must end. As free and dignified people, we must protest fate and fatalism. We do not accept them, we will not bow down to fate, and if we must perish, at least we will know it was not without revolt, without a yell, without indignation. We are the only ones who will die on our feet, not on our guts in the dirt, or on our knees." Caty had heard these words dozens of times. Once every cemetery in Bucharest had been picketed for nights on end, the members of the sect, all in black and protesting before the blind and illiterate dead with crooked signs, moved to the crematorium, hospitals, the state militia, and the Securitate. They were arrested in droves, committed to psychiatric hospitals, locked up with political prisoners in miserable jails, but those who remained were always seen, with their signs, with their eyes bathed in tears, wherever the carnivorous flower of human suffering appeared. As though they had an intuition for pain and misfortune, they would arrive at a fire before the firemen and to serious car accidents before the ambulances. More than once, Caty came home bruised by the rubber batons of patrolmen or drenched by water cannons. But she found, in the end, her peace. In the end, she no longer feared getting older and disappearing. She fought against them, she hoped against them. The odds of winning weren't important, but the fight was. Caty had separated herself from the lazy mass of hostages who lived with bowed heads.

I looked over her shoulder at the empty street: it was Sunday, and a sweet, lazy mist encompassed the little village at the edge of Bucharest. Across the street, the neighborhood idiot, with his two knit hats, one over the other, pulled down to his eyebrows, perched on the fence around his house and shook hands with all who passed. And here, in the silent room, where Caty's voice had shimmered like a silk thread for hours, the air was a motionless, translucent gelatin, like in an antiquities museum in the evening, after the last visitors have left. How unreal it all seemed, how unexpected and how complex! What a giant shadow, what a mental shadow she cast, truer than she was herself, this creature who had seemed the embodiment of frivolity . . . But even the basest street-corner prostitute, with nothing better to do than shout obscenities, stomp around in a dirty pair of heels, and do her job for every thug and drunk in the world, has the same metaphysical blossom under her skull, the same gateway to knowledge and eternal salvation, the same castle of infinite grandeur, the same power to breathe not just the stagnant air of our world but the very Spirit, the air of Plato's heavens. Even she has the same power as Bach or Spinoza, the power to see ideas, to use *and, not, or, if,* to understand that the sun will come up tomorrow, bathing the world in its splendorous gossamer. Even the last alcoholic—brutalized, hollowed out, a compulsive liar and braggart who sleeps in the middle of the street in a puddle of vomit—houses beneath his skull a brain worthy of Kant and da Vinci; even he, moment by moment, like a fountain in the shape of a lion's head, generates space and time and the putrid breath of the world's unreality. Even he, maybe more than others, maybe deeper and with fewer words, feels overwhelming nausea at the thought of death, and perhaps that is why he stifles it in the drink that paralyzes him and turns him to ash. Because we are all the same, the venal loan shark and the naïve poet, and the serial murderer and the archivist, the sociopath politician whose career is littered with cadavers and the scholar who pushes knowledge one micron farther. Neither gorillas nor gods know they will die; only we do, here at the middle of our path, between flesh and spirit, between good and evil, between sex and brain, between existence and non-existence, our sentence is scrawled across our forehead. This extermination camp exists for us alone. Only for us, we who weave the future day by day, in our mind's eye ("the sun will come out tomorrow"), and our supreme punishment has been prepared through this same miraculous gift, just for us: we will all be exterminated, everyone, down to the last, just as surely as the sun coming out tomorrow. The fact that this will happen is not the source of our pain in our daily hell, because even dogs and elephants and eucalyptuses and fleas and lichen and paramecia will perish the same way, down to the last, along with asteroids and galaxies and the diamantine substance of our world; rather, the knowledge of our common destiny is the red-hot iron that brands us, on our brain, like cattle on their hip, before the final execution.

The rubber doll in front of me, with her mouth as round as a poppy petal cut in two by a line of ink, with the areolae of her breasts visible through her floral blouse, was moist and sexual, but a bitter substance filled her inside. Dark had fallen when we realized, at the same moment (and at the same moment rejected the idea), that now, in the school's whistling emptiness, we could melt our despairs together into one even more despairing embrace. For one moment only, we looked each other in the eyes and felt, both at the same time, a wave of excitement caused by isolation, privacy, and pheromones, and yet nothing in the world could have made me embrace her, an amphora filled with nostalgia for those times when she was a voluptuous goddess of joy, when she lived inside the Neckermann along with her perfect, immortal fellow citizens. After that moment—in which our chests had felt a sudden release of adrenaline, darkening our nipples and descending toward our abdomens—we smiled awkwardly and walked out of the office.

The night was warm and deep, the wasteland uninhabited. We talked aimlessly as we passed the mechanics and came to Şoseaua Colentina. The slanted windows of the pipe factory glinted orange. The water tower was dark. Two trams were parked in the turnaround, and another was approaching very slowly from far away, where the street narrowed between the lumberyards and tire shops. Caty sat in the seat ahead of me, and, turning round, she continued to talk about this and that, as she did in the lounge, without stopping. Only when my stop came, at Doamna Ghica, did she ask if I wouldn't like to come next month, when they were getting ready to picket the morgue, known as the Mina Minovici Institute, in the center of town. I accepted her invitation immediately. We agreed to meet in Vitan, beside the post office, and to leave for the morgue at midnight, along with the other Picketists. I left the tram and waved to Caty, who in the brightly lit tram seemed a graceful and multicolored tropical fish in an empty aquarium. I sank into the labyrinthine streets that led to Maica Domnului. It took me half an hour to reach my house.

14

The first time I felt something was happening (although everything at that time seemed stupefying and new, since I received the world day to day, not just its forms, colors, and sounds, but also its mode of use: I discovered, by holding a newspaper between my fingers, that it could rip; by touching a cup, that I could drop it against the floor; by watching my mother, that she was the odd god who protected me from all the other specters, my individual survival kit and my icon and my magic talisman and the breasts where I sucked a voluptuous liquid) was the winter morning my mother took me to the hospital for oral surgery. Nothing is strange to a child, because he lives in the strange, thus dreams and old memories seem made from the same substance. The strange at that time was just the banality of the world. My fingers were strange; I would stare at them, minute after minute. My senses were so acute, and the thin, domed glass of my cornea was so sparkly, that when I looked at my fingernails, I saw the white, cloudy crescent of the lunula rise like a cloud little by little, from the base toward the tip of the nail until, like dandelion fluff, it left the nail to dissolve into the room's green air. My curving, soft nails adhered to the flesh of my finger, but they were not a smooth wall: I could clearly see their prismatic structure, their parallel stripes, as though a multitude of horn splinters grew from the base of the nail. Nothing, likewise, was real; it was all a sketch. Nothing was sculpted in material, rather in feelings: in fear, joy, heartache, appetite, and curiosity. I lived in a mental landscape, I was still developing inside a uterus, but the uterus of my own head, which I needed to crack like an egg to extend my bones, awkwardly, into that which I would soon call reality.

But even within the general strangeness of life at age three, things do happen, if you are a chosen person—to your honor or your shame—hyper-strange things with no place in the crystallized normality of the world around you. Things that make even your dream-mind say, "This can't be happening." Because along with the forms and their methods of use (their handles and hooks and invisible buttons: grab me, tear me, untie me, fold me, chew me, taste me, hear me, cut me), we receive something else, without knowing how or from whom, the superlabel or superhandle of "This can be, this can't," "This is true, this isn't"; that is, we select, out of the hodgepodge of possibilities, probabilities, unrealities, and oddities, a single structure that we name "reality" and base our lives around it. I was never able to take as real the thing that happened that winter morning when my mother picked me up and we went, swimming though the snowdrifts, "to Doru's, so we can play with his toys." Doru was my cousin, many years older, whom we had visited a few times. The city was a brilliant white around us; I remember how his image skipped along to the rhythm of my mother's footsteps. My little hands were clasped behind her neck, and I watched behind us. Only my eyes were visible, above the scarf across my nose and mouth.

For a while, the city was gentle and familiar, I knew the streets and buildings around our house, where heavy, dry snow now fell in a gentle rustling. The headscarves and hats of the people who passed were full of snow, the trams and cars were also freighted with snow on their roofs and hoods. I squinted from so much white, so much pure light. Little flashing stars gathered on my eyelashes. After purring lazily for a while, the city began to growl like an irritated animal. I didn't know the way anymore: what had been made of tenderness was now made of fear.

The route to Doru's was clearly defined in my mind. But my mother wasn't going that way. She had lied, I clearly remember having this thought, but just for a moment, since I couldn't bear to follow it all the way to the end. The god that holds you and clutches you to its breast just cannot lie, since it is being itself, with being's certainty. I abandoned this painful and perverse thought, but the city began to roar like a lion, from all its unfamiliar buildings, from its unfamiliar streets, from the eyes of its unfamiliar people. It was like we were suddenly surrounded by a host of snarling dogs, baring their demonic teeth. The only escape was my mother, in spite of my suspicions. My mittens clung to her neck so tightly I almost choked her, and I whimpered, "This isn't the way to Doru's . . ." My mother held me out a little and looked in my eyes, "Sweetie, we went a different way. Look, we'll be there in a moment. I'll let you play with his toys, all day, I promise." Her head, framed by its scarf, occupied the entire sky. What I read in her face—I had learned her features like they were a map: the gentle valleys of her cheeks, the little veins beneath her eyes, her mouth with a very light lipstick, her tired eyelids, her eyebrows with flakes of snow—was not reassuring. She wasn't smiling. Holy water did not flow from the icon. I didn't know what a lie was, but I knew that my mother was lying when I saw the topographical map of her face, its elevation lines just as strange as the streets and houses and visions of the snow-covered city.

I was, for the first time, alone in the world. I doubted, for the first time, not just the world's sounds and colors but the very destiny that until then had smiled in my face. Where was I being carried? Toward what was I floating, in the darkness, through thick snowflakes, carried by the one who had carried me in her womb, who had been one with me, who had shared her veins and arteries, blood and food, as though I were one of her organs, like her liver or spleen? To whom, and why, was she donating her excess organ, why was she betraying it, what thought or what compulsion, or what other dimension drove my mother down the astonishing path of lies?

The next thing I remember is the starry sky. I was lying on a bed, on an unpleasantly cold, pinkish-brown mat, like all the beds in the clinic had. Above was a night sky, full of stars. I don't know if I had ever really seen stars. Yes, getting off the tram on our way back from my aunt's in Dudești-Cioplea, drowsy and yawning, since I had been asleep for ten stops, there was the starry sky above me, where sometimes the horns of the moon glowed with an extraordinary intensity. But never before had the stars truly overwhelmed me. I saw them shining now, as I was lying on the bed, without recalling my fear during the trip to the hospital and without asking myself how I ended up in this room; the stars unfurled above me, seen through a fish-eye lens; they spread over the entire sky, some as large as the pitchers of imperial lilies, bending the mathematical stem from which they hung, others scattered finely, Mandelbrotian, into the holes and folds and hollows of the night sky. The milled grains, flower seeds, and bits of gold mixed together above me, they flickered and shone over my three-year-old face, collecting on the convex glass behind my eyelids. As chaotic as they seemed when I first opened my eyes—as though for first time in the world, without a memory, as though I had come to life at that moment, on that hospital bed—the stars grouped themselves together in my mind, made to catalog and to sort everything, by force, according to the Utopian logic of dreams, into shell-shaped constellations, strings of pearls, evil dolls, silverfish, upholstery springs, apple cores, circus clowns, Mommy, Daddy, child. I was splattered all over with the ink of constellations. Where was I? There was complete silence. It was hard for my eyes to look away from the stars. I felt no emotion, just like a few years later, when my tonsils and adenoids were extracted with terrifying implements, and I sat there without fear, without myself in fact, in front of the doctor whose apron and gloves were covered in blood: he had given me a blue pill that tempered my fear, leaving me simply curious as I was taken into the torture chamber. "Open your mouth," the doctor had said, "I'm not going to do anything to you, I just want to measure your tonsils," and I had believed him; and even though I felt every brutal slice in the flesh of my throat, it was like I was feeling someone else's pain, without any connection to me. "Alright, almost done," said the shadow man, whose forehead light bulb blinded me as I sat, with blood running from my mouth, in the dentist's chair, "Now open your mouth again, wide, as wide as you can." I glimpsed the steel crook he poked into my throat and suddenly felt—I don't know if I can call it pain. What I felt, what I experienced exceeds ideas of pain the way a caress is exceeded by being flayed alive. It was a geyser of concentrated, pure pain, red and blue like an acetylene flame. As though my martyred skull were a bulb that suddenly germinated the intolerable stalk of pain. But I didn't scream, although I had never felt anything like that, although what I felt then scarred me for life, because the blue pill had separated even this shock of pain from the mind that rose above it, and which, hypnotized by itself, was no longer bothered by anything outside. With some satisfaction, the doctor held up his hook, on whose tip was the piece of bloody, red flesh he just removed from my body.

Even today, I don't know how I found myself on the bed with a rubber mat. I have tried to imagine how to fill the blank tape between my memory of the trip through the snow-covered city and my appearance on the bed, lying on my back, with my eyes open, under the stars. I don't know if I had arrived somewhere, if I had been checked into a hospital, if I had been prepped for an operation. I don't know if I was given the blue pill this time, but I know I felt the same, just the same as I felt later, in many moments in my life I can only explain, perhaps, as a sudden and elastic penetration of dream into life, or my life into dream: the total lack of fear, the mental lucidity, but also the mind itself, without its owner, a grave and somewhat curious enchantment, a fascinated wonder before the exceptional landscape, without needing to know what I'm doing there, how I got there, when I'm going home.

Later, after I had mindlessly contemplated the dizzying stars above, I turned my head and looked around. My bed was in the middle of a circular room, with milky cream-colored walls, all smooth, and above them was nothing but the dome of the sky. If there were an actual glass dome between me and the stars (and now I no longer doubt it), the glass must have been unspeakably clean and clear, all but invisible. Only differences in the grouping of the stars—more loosely spaced directly above me, at the apex, and more tightly clustered toward the edges—gave any reason to imagine a transparent bell. I looked around, while still lying on my back, at the shiny, circular walls and at the floor of the same oddly calming cream color, when suddenly I came back to myself and remembered that I was. I didn't know how I got there, but I knew I existed, I didn't remember my mother, but I was the three-year-old boy again, I could look at his fingers, knowing they were mine, whose chest, in clothes that were not his, rose slowly with each breath. I sat up quickly, my legs hanging over the edge of the bed.

That's when I heard the voice: frighteningly brutal, inhuman. Difficult for me to describe. It was not, exactly, a voice: it had nothing of the pitch, intensity, or timbre of a real voice. The human voice is a thought that passes through flesh. It is an abstract current, like melted crystal, that flows through the moisture of skin and cartilage, that turns opaque within the vocal tract lubricants (phlegm, saliva), that passes through the teeth and lips, after first being tormented by the snail's foot muscle of the tongue. The voice is sexual, it comes from the ovaries and the testicles, it is dominant or submissive, it is marred by the viscosities of the body, by the billions of bits of matter in this world. But the deafening voice I heard there, in the circular chamber, had no impurity. It was the voice that, when you are in danger, commands the release of adrenaline into the blood, the voice that incites intestinal peristalsis. It was the indistinct voice of action, of a command adhered to its execution, the entity of command-submission, question-answer. I heard it in my mind and with my mind, yet it resounded through the circular room like a bell. It commanded me to lie back down on the bed. If it had actually yelled at me (as my father sometimes did), I couldn't have been more frightened and I couldn't have lain down more quickly. I was simply thrown onto my back by the terrible wind of that interior roar. Although I cannot relive all its horror, I have never forgotten it.

What came next? That's easy: nothing. The same blank tape as before. I remember absolutely nothing from that moment. I wake on my back and everything breaks off. I don't know whether I was chloroformed, operated on, or if I left the hospital. Even today I don't know what happened on that day, in that winter of 1959. But it remains powerfully present in my mind, and clear, even with the breaks I've mentioned. My entire mind rejects the idea that it may have been an oneiric episode, or that I may be confusing memories from different places and times. No, if it is possible to know anything for sure, I knew that everything happened that day in the order of events I have given, that the circular space was the "operating room" my mother told me about later.

What operation could I have had? I have no sign of an incision anywhere on my body. I asked her about it, of course, but only later, when I was able to understand that the oldest images that appeared from time to time in my memory were not precisely memories, but vestiges of an older system of capturing the effluvia of the world, atavistic organs of the mnemonic animal housed in my skull. I would play with these mental kidney stones, the way you might roll colored marbles in your fingers for the sake of their pleasurable, crystalline clacks. These relics were not many, seven or eight fossils of an older brain, dating from the time when dreams were not yet separate from reality, when they preserved, like insects in amber, these entire detailed, disturbing truths about what had been, was, and is my true life. My mother always confirmed them, but only halfway, she would clarify and minimize them simultaneously, she pretended to think they were ordinary memories that my mind re-remembered now, as though I had had the same mind then, at eighteen months, at two or three years old, packed inside my cranium, most of which was taken up by my enormous eyeballs. Just as she had done with Victor, as she had with the mysterious doctors in our house, as she had with my baths in which she poured a deep-smelling liquid, like vulvae and chamomile, an amniotic scent that I can still sense in my nostrils. Just as she would later with eternal trips to the Mașina de Pâine Clinic. For a long time as a teenager, I thought I was seriously ill. I thought I had something horrible—that a parasite had taken control of my spinal cord or even my consciousness. I carried a germ that must not escape my sack of skin, because once it did, it would destroy the foundations of the world. My mother knew, but maybe she wasn't my mother, maybe she was a supervisor, an angel who watched me moment by moment, and then I understood why—as she carried me through the blinding winter of '59 among the old, snowy apartment blocks that slid past and rose in the rhythm of her footsteps—she had let me glimpse her true face by lying to me, in order to separate herself from me again, long after the umbilical cord had been severed. Since I couldn't ask her anything directly, for fear she would answer, I restrained myself to little allusions, to chance words at dinner, while she, sweaty and smelling like the fried potatoes and pork sizzling on the stove, battled the flies in her disgusting manner: she followed their flight with her eyes, with her hands out, and she'd suddenly smack her hands together, crushing their fat, black bodies. "Mama," I asked her when I was about ten. "Do you remember when we were supposed to go visit Doru, but instead we went to the hospital?" "When was that, sweetie?" "I was little, it was snowing, you carried me, and I told you that wasn't the way to Doru's . . ." My mother stood motionless for a moment in the smoky kitchen. It was hot, we were dying of heat even with the balcony door open. "When? When you were three? Two and a half, three? Yesss . . . I took you to the hospital for an operation, you had a tooth coming in the wrong way, they removed it. Don't you remember?" "What hospital was it?" "Oh, I don't think I know . . . so long ago." "And when did you get me from the hospital?" "I don't remember, sweetie. Don't you have anything better to ask me?" And our life goes on, with school, meals, naps, and my mother's mismatched statements and contradictions and silences and confusions pile up like a swelling boil, and I see even more clearly that I cannot rely on her to explain the enigma and melancholy of my life.

Because it's not me but my cousin, my mother's sister's son, who has a scar on his right jaw. How can my mother make such a mistake? Does she mix things up on purpose, not even hiding her attempts to derail my obsessive questioning? But doesn't she understand that her mistakes only provoke me, that they are clues, like the slips of a suspect under cross-examination? Or is my mother on my side, trying as hard as she can to send some message, desperate to communicate, even through her clumsy mistakes, that the enigma exists, that my uneasiness is justified? Maybe she is hostage to some bizarre power that keeps her under close watch, and she can only let these absurdities slip out, flagrant absurdities: not facts, not information, but warnings.

Ever since that winter morning, I have known I cannot rely on my mother, until then the body of my body, just as a hemiplegic knows he cannot rely on half his body. That—not three years earlier—was the moment when the umbilical cord between us was cut. Beginning with that moment, my mother, the symbol of my world and its central pillar, proved herself the ally of doctors and dentists, the torturers of my childhood. I remember how I wanted her to be just for me. How I learned knots, how I tied the doors shut with threads, rags, and shoelaces so a new brother couldn't get into the house. When my mother was about to go grocery shopping, I would put a fork on the threshold, so she couldn't leave. I would tie her apron strings around my waist, so we could be just us again, inseparable, forever. But my mother was now someone else, as distinct from me as a statue, as a wardrobe, as a cloud passing overhead.

Where had I been, in that room, whose reality I could not doubt any more than I do the room where I am writing now, in my house on Maica Domnului? How could I have seen that starry sky, each star a drop of molten gold, when it had been winter and the sky would have been blanketed with clouds? What happened that morning, in the winter of 1959? I don't know if this is the first anomaly of my life after Victor, but it was the first I remember. The sap that flowed from that moment irrigated my entire life, because many other anomalies have followed the trajectory from my "operation" at age three to the illnesses and hospitals that subtend the hidden side of my life. If I were a writer, they would have remained hidden forever, obscure, half-forgotten, down to the most meaningless trace, because no novel, by definition, can tell the truth, the only thing that matters, the true interior of the writer's life. Since I am not a writer and do not paint false doors on the walls, I am content to write, and this contentment takes the place of glory. When I write here, in this already enormously swollen diary, I feel a cool, blue halo surround my skull. I write in the dark, by the imperceptible light of my glory. Only this light feeds the darkness of the world, only this light does not frighten the hordes arriving from the depths.

15

The first book I requested, filling out the title and author on the library slip in the golden autumn of my first year at college, the air full of bits of gossamer, was not an anthology of old Romanian literature, not Cantemir's *Hieroglyphic History*, not *Chroniclers of Muntenia*, no textbook on phonetics and phonology. Those I had purchased long ago, and they were all in my room on Ştefan cel Mare stacked on my bedside table, untouched. I had every book on the list I got the first day of class. I remember my first trip to the Mihai Eminescu Bookstore, across the street from the university. The city center was not, for me at that time, a part of Bucharest, it was Paris, Berlin, New York, London, and Tokyo rolled into one. The people here seemed beautiful and brilliant, the buildings unreal, the days expansive and ecstatic. I wouldn't look directly at the world when I walked the sidewalks, where each tram ticket and cigarette butt glittered under a circus spotlight of constantly changing colors, rather I saw everything through the starving eye of a photographer. That is how I saw women's hair—fluttering in the dusty air, collecting bits of floating cobweb that filled the vast space between the Hotel Intercontinental and the

Fisherman's Restaurant—and the lights and wind twisting around the buses and cars that passed under the blind gazes of the four statues. Whenever a girl walked past, holding her student briefcase under her arm, her dress fastened in front, as was the style, with a large safety pin decorated with onyx and chalcedony, I inhaled deeply to experience not only her perfume but the pheromones her skin emanated, along with musk and sweat. I was twenty, and I had never embraced, not even at a dance or at a tea (as parties were called then), a girl. Women were as foreign to me as the far-off worlds of luxury villas, yachts, Western cities, and restaurants I never went into—as though they had the doors nailed shut or they were women's restrooms. They were not for me, they were not part of the reality I was given to touch.

I entered the Eminescu Bookstore, almost empty at four in the afternoon, holding my list but looking for one book in particular—a massive dictionary of ethnology and folklore, one which my new classmates, their faces as blank as balloons floating toward the ceiling of the narrow seminar rooms, had told me was hard to find. I wandered the shelves for a long time, under the charming eyes of a clerk dressed in red. The books were a buffet and made me hungry: I could have devoured every single one. I knew some of the books, had even read them, I had them noted in my address book like a libertine would write the names of women he had conquered; others were as fresh as just-opened, dew-covered flowers, and all the more appetizing. My gaze slid along their spines, I was just straining to read the vertical titles, letting my head tilt far to one side, when I suddenly saw the dictionary. It was enormous, resting on the highest shelf, by the ceiling, between other, much thinner books. I went right away to the clerk to ask for it. With the disgusted expression of many young saleswomen who feel insulted by their job, the girl in red, with a bizarre look about her (something was not right with her eyebrows), followed me, but when she saw the book, she stared me down with an expression I could not understand. I could not believe that the hate, scorn, and disgust in her heavily outlined eyes were directed at me, a kid who had asked, politely, for a book. "Get out or I call the militia," she said in a low voice, then she turned around and walked to the front of the store, where I had found her when I had entered. She stood there, leaning against a shelf, small and svelte in her red suit, without so much as looking at me.

What was this insanity? What was wrong with the dictionary? Or with me? I stood motionless in the middle of the store, embarrassed and upset like a person unjustly accused of theft or indecent behavior who wonders, like in a dream, if he isn't actually guilty. I left by another door, toward the Math Department, and I went for a long, slow walk in the luminous autumn air. A terrible feeling of humiliation was growing inside me, so heavy that I quickly realized that I would not be able to go home and spend the night with it. I went back to the bookstore, where now there were two or three customers, and I went directly to the saleswoman. "Excuse me, but I would like to ask why you didn't give me the ethnology dictionary. I need it for school, see it's here, on my list . . ." The girl looked at me with the same hostility: "You really want me to call the militia." "But I don't understand, what did I do? What happened?" She looked at me again with some doubt. "You're a student?" "Yes, in the Department of Letters. The dictionary is here, see, on my list . . ." "Okay, I'll give it to you, but I won't get on the ladder." "The ladder? I can climb up there if you're scared." "I'm not frightened of climbing, I'm afraid of your gang . . ." I couldn't understand. I went back to the rear of the store, I climbed the ladder to the ceiling and took the large book from the shelf. Only once I had paid, at the cashier in the front, did the clerk walk me to the door and apologize. "You have no idea how many weirdos there are in the world. When I started here, in the first weeks, I couldn't understand why customers would ask for books from the top shelf at the back of the store. I would climb up the ladder to get the books, and the customer—would take out . . . Then I understood what they wanted . . ."

I was appalled. Books, especially those in the sanctuary of the bookstore, were not, in my mind, compatible with sexuality. Even less with perversion. The story the girl in front of me told—whose eyebrows, I now saw, were a bit more slanted than they should be, making her beautiful, sincere face unexpectedly expressive—didn't seem sordid or obscene or revolting, rather it seemed unreal. I had never before realized that an attractive woman made of flesh and perfume wrapped in lingerie and fabric is just as strange for a bookstore as a phantom is in the real world, like a fragment of a dream that broaches reality. And that the phantasm of the saleswoman in a short skirt who climbs a ladder and stretches to the last shelf, revealing the tops of her thighs to your gaze, could be the prey of those who searched for shadowy, clandestine pleasures. I exited the store into the diesel-scented city center, looking back a few times toward the red spot in the bookstore without knowing that I would see those thighs (which I had already imagined) countless times, and that in a few years, the girl—so charming and so disgusted by all the perversions of the world—would play a frightening and unnerving role in my life.

But on the rectangular request slip, recopied a hundred times, for the reading room in the ocean liner of the Letters library, with dozens of levels and loaded with every book ever written, I wrote a title that was not on my list of required readings. Because after I finally had discovered the author of *The Gadfly*, for whom my tears had literally soaked page after page one afternoon in the sixth grade, reading in my unmade, ragged bed in my room on Ştefan cel Mare, I could only ask for this book. I filled the slip out wrong, barely able to look at it, for *The Gadfly* by Ethel Lilian Voynich, and only then could I complete other slips for the required books. I wanted to return to the body of the twelve-year-old boy who didn't know anything about the unification of Italy, or revolutions, or the church, or freedom, who in fact barely knew he was in the world, and yet who sobbed loudly, as he never had before—and would never do again—even though he didn't know why. I wanted to use that small, anemic, totally anonymous body, those dark, tear-filled eyes in his razor-thin face; like Regine Olsen, I wanted to know if repetition was possible. *The Gadfly* would become my madeleine, the irregularities of my macadam, the flash that suddenly set fire, like a billion-watt bulb, to the endless realm of my mind. I wanted to reread the book and cry again, to be shut again inside the body and mind that had disappeared from my world eight years ago. I wanted to see the aloe pot on the table, the paint with glints of mica on the walls of my room, and especially the panoramic view of Bucharest through the triple window above the street, the mixture of houses and trees spread to the edge of sight, under motionless summer clouds in the dusty sky. I wanted to pass the tongue I had then over the chapped lips I had then, to wrap myself in the sweaty sheets I had then. The long hours of that afternoon felt in my mind like a single scene, a single moment, a synthetic and motionless fragment of a kind of diffuse, unfocused, and yet precise reality, where I felt (or reconstructed) the sting of my tear-wet eyelashes, the musty, stale air of my room, the sordid bedclothes and their sweaty smell, the phantomatic fragments of the story and text of *The Gadfly*, which tore at my soul, which made my breath burn, as though I was suffering the worst of love. The library book gave me the clandestine and unnatural chance to steal again into a universe illuminated by a younger sun.

When I came home from school, I ate with my parents then threw myself into bed with *The Gadfly*. Of course I couldn't go back. I didn't have enough patience even to get to the page where I started last time, in the copy without a cover and missing the first few dozen pages. This sentimental book isn't what I want to talk about now. Disappointed and bored, I went to put the book on my bedstead, where I kept the five or six books I read simultaneously. I decided to take a glance at the preface. It was a habit I acquired while studying for my entrance exams. The writers' biographies sometimes proved more fascinating, more human, and, in any case, more surprising than their books. Some writers were superior to the novels and poems they had written, while others lived such tepid lives that you could only ascribe their literary edifices to diligent, tenacious demons who lived inside of them for decades. Ethel Lilian Voynich did not fall into either category, and the few lines about her in the preface bored me almost as much as the book. I note this here only because, re-remembered much later, they proved to be the first piece in the metaphysical motor of my writing.

I said "metaphysical motor," but just as well I could have said "paranoid motor," since all metaphysics is actually paranoia. There's a day when you see three or four blind people, after not seeing any for years, not even in a dream. You meet a woman named Olimpia, and a few minutes later you open a dictionary to the page showing Manet's *Olympia*, then two hours later, on the street, you pass Olimpia's Flowershop. These are nodes of meaning, plexuses of the world's neural system, they connect organs and events, signals that you ought to pursue until they wave a white flag—and you would, if you didn't have this stupid prejudice for reality. We ought to have a sensory organ that can tell sign from coincidence. In a single day, you see three pregnant women one after another: what does this mean? If there had only been two, would the coincidence have affected you as much? What if these three were joined by one more, suddenly emerging from a house and walking down the street in front of you? And if she stopped and quickly turned around and handed you a crumpled scrap of paper, where only this was written: "Help!"—and then she fled awkwardly up the street? How long would the ice of reality hold? When—at what moment—do you feel it crack beneath your feet? First you see the fine cracks of coincidences, these ramify and expand unsettlingly, but the ice still holds and so far you're not worried: it was just another pregnant woman, a fourth. It happens. It is not impossible that they all should cross your path in a single day. But then she hands you the note, you read it, and the ice shatters, you fall into the freezing water, and suddenly you are underneath, searching like a sea lion for a hole where you can breathe.

Ethel Lilian Voynich was born in 1864 in Cork and lived for ninety-six years, dying only eight years before I sobbed through her book. She was the youngest of five children born to Mary Everest (whose uncle had given his name to the tallest mountain on the planet) and George Boole, the famous mathematician. At fifteen, she read a book about Mazzini that made a strong impression, transforming her into a militant in search of a noble cause. She learned Russian and took part, for the two years she lived in tsarist Russia, in the Russian anarchist revolutionary movement. In 1892 she married the Polish revolutionary and antiques dealer Wilfrid Voynich, but she maintained a close connection to her teacher Stepnyak, who had introduced her to the subversive and revolutionary world of Russia's future masters, the communists. Together with her husband, she published the writings of Herzen and Plekhanov, as well as works of the nihilists; she met Engels and Eleanor Marx, as well as British sympathizers of emergent communism William Morris and G. B. Shaw (now I can understand what the torn and battered copy of the *The Gadfly* was doing in my parents' house: it had been condoned by the Soviet propaganda machine), and in the end, in London, after a tumultuous affair with the anarchist Sidney Reilly (the model for Arthur Burton, alias "The Gadfly"), Ethel Voynich began her famous novel. To research Mazzini's Italy, she traveled to Florence and Pisa. The book appeared in the United States in 1897 and became an international bestseller. It then sold millions of copies in the Soviet Union. In 1914 the Voynich family moved to New York, where Ethel lived until the end of her life, publishing novels which never enjoyed the success of *The Gadfly*, and translating Russian literature.

That's about it, the thin fishbones left at the edge of the plate after the actual content of her life has been consumed by the acid of time. Not even the author's portrait, poorly printed on the first page, told me anything more: an austere woman, her hair tied back, firm eyes and thin lips, lacking both beauty and interior light. A dark stubbornness, her face turned away from the world. Yuri Gagarin read *The Gadfly* and adopted it as his touchstone. Shostakovich wrote music inspired by the novel. Sergei Bondarchuk played Father Montanelli in the film version.

I was reading a newer edition, of course, than the one I had held in my hands twelve years before; perhaps that's why I didn't recognize it as the true book. It didn't smell like bad paper, porous, yellowed, rotting. The glue wasn't made from bones, and minuscule paper scorpions, pale and tailless, weren't consuming the paper, appearing sometimes along the spine. While I read, almost without seeing the letters, the color of the sheets didn't match the twilight precisely, like it had before. The first book had been a portal to my internal cistern of tears, while the second—just a door drawn on a wall. The first had been anonymous and title-less, and it lacked the first chapters, the way any book ought to begin and be read by an honest, nondiscriminating mind and eyes, open as they would never be again. Perhaps all we want from reading is to return to that age when we could hold a book and cry, to that time between childhood and adolescence, the sweetest era of our lives.

16

Footprints in powdery snow leading to the center of the yard, stopping there, between the country house and the well, and a sleepy peasant, his coat thrown on over his embroidered nightshirt, looking at them from the porch, not fully awake, thinking he is still dreaming but shaken by the dawn wind back to his senses. A sole strand of yellow light decorates the edge of the frost-covered barn, and the plum trees, and the three or four huts clustered under swollen clouds hanging like blintzes in the low, misty sky. And Ivan or Foma or Boris takes the two wooden steps and walks through the knee-deep snow toward the middle of the yard, but he stays to one side of the first line of footprints, afraid to touch them, and stops just where his woman had, where her path on Earth had ended. The pure snow all around him in waves with lilac shadows, with six-pointed stars glittering here and there, as though enchanted, in the overflowing dawn. The peasant stands there a long time, a rooster crows from far away, a cart driver shouts from a path close by, and, suddenly, though he has been looking at the ground in stunned incomprehension and terror, the peasant raises his eyes toward the sky. Every strand of his flaxen beard is full of ice crystals, frost is growing over his eyebrows, and his burning eyes full of red capillaries and his gaping mouth show his horror and trembling before the divine miracle. His woman has been stolen into the sky, like Our Lord Jesus Christ and Saint Ilie. This is what he said to his neighbors, who had gathered an hour later, like to see a bear in his yard, their enormous rawhide shoes erasing the evidence of her footprints' sudden end in the empty snow, said to the gendarmes who came to take him, said to the judges who condemned him to be hanged because he had killed his wife and dumped her in who knows what hole in the river, and finally said to the executioner who passed the noose over his red ears and bowl-cut hair. "When things like these start to happen, look up," he remembered the priest proclaiming, "raise your heads, because your salvation approaches." And the priest had quoted the Gospels: "I tell you, in that night there shall be two men in one bed; the one shall be taken, and the other shall be left. Two women shall be grinding together; the one shall be taken, and the other left . . ." There wasn't time for any more church memories, full of saints' faces and the smell of incense: the peasant was soon hanging, his eyes bulging and his purple, bloody tongue poking out between his lips, from the gallows that rose above the endless province.

I often think about this story, and when I do, I can never keep my hair from rising on the back of my neck like some cornered wolf. But I always feel like I am missing something. What is this story saying, what is it saying to me? It feels like an equation far too complicated for my little mind. But this isn't the right image, because it would mean that at least in theory I could understand what it's saying or what it wants to show me. A better way to put it is that I am missing the receptor, as though I were deaf and someone were intensely talking at me, looking in my eyes, pressing their forehead to mine, shaking my shoulders in the hope that I might understand, but nothing reaches me aside from their emotion, their fear, on the other side of the wall that separates us. Or I am a cat lying on the kitchen tiles, looking at you with wide, serious, green eyes. You want to show it something, a tassel for it to play with, you hold out your hand and point at the tassel in the corner, but instead the cat looks at your finger, it sniffs at it, and licks it with its rough tongue. The sign doesn't signify, the index finger does not indicate, they become, for a brain that lacks the power of thought, the thing shown. All we are left with is stubbornness—still a form of belief. We know we are in the maze, we know we have to escape, even in the absence of an angelic mind, even in our plodding reasoning, even as we improvise with what we have, even as we take the wrong turn thousands of times before we take the right turn once, and we believe that we will find the exit, if only by dumb luck, because without this belief, we could not breathe.

I have been writing for more than three months, here in my animal solitude, where I have lived as long as I remember. Just after I eat my dinner each afternoon, I take the tram to school. In the evening, I take the same tram back home. In the tram I always read, I keep a book in my bag, among the student essays and my writing utensils. I don't know if it's by accident or on purpose, but everything I've read recently is connected to my situation, to my life as a solitary and hopeless person. Over the past few months, since I began the story of my anomalies, I have read—while I swayed in the crowded tram, standing, resting my book on the shoulder or the back of the person in front of me—the great books of loneliness. Every character with whom I identify bears these stigmata. On my nightstand at the moment—because I keep reading at home, in the evening, until deep in the night—*The Notebooks of Malte Laurids Brigge*, *Alone* by Strindberg, *Shameless Death* by Dagmar Rotluft, *The Confusions of Young Törless*. And, of course, the book I hold dearest, Franz Kafka's *Diaries*. The day before yesterday, while the tram was turning around at the end of Colentina in the sunset, I remember I lifted my eyes for a moment from the Strindberg. At that moment, I had the clear sensation that the opposite was happening, that at that moment I lowered my eyes onto the page of a book, leaning against the rough rock of a Stockholm bridge balustrade, after I had looked around the hazy, martial city around me, to read more about a solitary man in an improbable and distant Bucharest.

I sometimes fantasize that I was once, in a dream or another life, a tattoo master, so abstruse and so pure that no one ever had access to my art's wonders of lacy designs, ink, and pain. Shut in my room, alone in front of the mirror, I covered my skin with minute, crooked, overlapping, unreal arabesques, like the Nazca lines and the suppurating networks produced by mange. Centimeter by centimeter, from my shaved scalp to my shoulders, not avoiding the backs of my ears, my eyelids, or the wings of my nostrils, my body was conquered by painful, fine designs, artificial flowers blooming like frost on the windows in windy nights, flowing, in painful slowness, from the metal needle with which I martyred my skin. This same network of blue ink, in which you could see all the landscapes of the world, all its objects of desire and of horror, like chimeras, like inscriptions, like sentences in a sinister calligraphy over the flexible epidermis, also covered my spine, which I decorated performing fakir-like contortions, marking each vertebra with a sun, lizard, cloud, embryo, or a calm, triangular eye, and my shoulder blades with the ambiguous, claw-tipped wings of an archaeopteryx. Forgetting to eat and sleep, almost forgetting to breathe, filled with a god of melted gold upon which my skin draped as if over a tailor's dummy in the corner of his shop, I tattooed my generous dermic surfaces with utmost care for months and weeks on end, ennobling with my art the heaviest human organ. Circles of ink descended, bit by bit, toward my chest, placing oboes, cobras, and cargo boats across my ribs, surrounding my nipples with the gaping mouths of carnivorous plants. I ornamented my stomach with cathedral arches teeming with allegorical figures, my navel surrounded in the center by sunrays and doves, then I engraved my sex and buttocks with demons, gargoyles, and trolls in foul orgies, I lowered the tattoo needle to my thighs, I engraved two cheetahs on my knees and roots on my feet. I was content in the living suffering of my skin, I felt I had no limits, that everything was possible, that I had encoded, there, in the curls, volutes, cups, and thorns of my tattoo, the algorithm of being and the formula of divinity. Swollen with the breath of continuous inspiration, the patterns didn't touch my skin anymore; they peeled off and levitated a few centimeters above it, a skin made of hallucinations and dreams. Soon, I couldn't find one square centimeter where I could stick the needle, because my soles, palms, gums, glands, and nails had all already fallen prey to the luxuriant tattoo jungle.

I sensed the limit of my art at that point, and likewise the limit of my knowledge. You have no more skin than the one in which you find yourself. You can't tattoo over old tattoos. I was still young, I had many years ahead of me: what would my life be without my sole source of meaning and happiness? It couldn't end like this. It took me years to peel the idea of tattooing away from the idea of skin.

And then, finished with the surface of my body, I descended within. I tattooed my cerebral hemispheres, my spinal cord, and my cranial nerves, numbering them like anatomical models. I tattooed my lungs, heart, diaphragm, and kidneys, covering them with unknown cities, telescopes, insects, and solar systems. I labored for years over the lace and spiderwebs with which, like a new peritoneum, I covered my knot of intestines. I engraved my bones with verses from the Koran, the Kebra Nagast, and the Hebrew Scriptures. I tattooed my trachea with the great Altdorfer. I calligraphed my bladder with galaxies bound by clouds of dark matter.

And when I was done, when my minute, illusionistic writing had filled my body with the most beautiful story in the world, told by a million mouths at once, I was immune to melancholy because I suddenly knew that, just like the unsoundable world around me, and just like my body reflecting it like a drop of dew, the art of tattooing is endless.

I moved toward the border between body and spirit, I crossed it, holding my instrument of torture, and I began to tattoo myself, knowing I would never exhaust—even if I spent eternity wounding—the infinite and infinitely stratified and infinitely glorious and infinitely demented citadel of my mind.

PART TWO

17

MY MOTHER RAISED ME AS A GIRL, UNDER the enormous skies of the slums. She let my dark gold hair grow halfway down my back, and she put it in braids. She made me fanciful dresses out of material she got from her sister, bell-shaped dresses like the pink or blue felt doll dresses that populated our dark rooms, alongside glass fish, lacquered stems in vases, and hand-colored photographs in frames of crushed glass. She changed my adornments daily: a new hairstyle, a ring of cherries for my ear; she undressed and dressed me as she had, when she was a child in her Tântava, wrapped rags around the wooden spoons that the girls used for dolls. The little icicle between my legs didn't stop her from fulfilling the dream or the fantasy hidden deep in the twisted nautilus of her mind. I needed to be a girl, since she only had me left of her two boys, and with that, *basta*. My father would frown and swear when he saw me transvested, but he didn't see much, and what he did didn't reach that deeply into his consciousness; there, where he himself should be, was nothing but an empty room. He would swear and move on, as clouds move over an empty sky. Because my father would never live, never feel true pleasure or true sorrow, he passed through life like a sleepwalker with velvety brown eyes, without knowing he was alive, without knowing that he should wonder from time to time what being in the world was about. He would have slept next to a wolf and raised a baby dragon, as long as he was left alone, as long as no one spoke to him. He would often stare off into space—this is my only inheritance—and then he would make such an unpleasant effort to leave the pitiful mysticism of an empty, comfortable mind, floating like a milk-drugged baby, that my mother and I came to the understanding that in fact my father wasn't there, even if he came home in the evening from the ITB workshop smelling of grease and lathe filings, even if we ate together, even if all three of us slept in the same bed. Everything that happened in our little room on Silistra happened between my mother and me.

The girl-boy went on bicycle rides through the edge of town with our neighbors. The child would tromp up the stairs to the second story of the U-shaped house painted a sinister purple. She would tease the turkeys in the wire pen. She would go out on the street, between puddles and mud, to play with other kids. All the flowers in the yard were taller than her. The smell of wastewater, the slum's most powerful smell, irritated her nostrils when the spring wind licked the shanties along the street. The house with the blind wall next door, the dark, low grocery at the end of the street, and the yard across the way with its colored globes stuck on bean stakes wound with tendrils, and, especially, the luminous and compact clouds above—these filled her with wonder, even though she didn't know anything else, as though she were a traveler who suddenly found an enigmatic realm of unexpected splendor, completely enclosed within its own strangeness.

I can remember how happy I was to be a girl, how proud I was of my braids tied with elastic from old underpants, I remember my red, patent leather sandals that my mother kept for a long time . . . But the feminine part of the chimera that I was disappeared the day my mother took me, along an unknown path, through the unbearable whiteness of the blizzard, "to play with Doru's toys." My dresses and braids disappeared that day, forever, and no one ever took me for a girl again. Today, it feels as though I had been a girl in a previous life, as though the girl left a hole shaped like her body in the petrified ash of my mind, like those left by the people incinerated at Pompeii. I have kept the ash-blond braids in their yellowed paper bag. One end is cut and tied tightly with a rubber band, the other is frayed, emerging from the soft braid of hair like the tip of a delicate brush. Often, at night, when I am looking at my poor little treasures, I take the braids out, I lay them across my palm like soft animals, then I go to the mirror and hold them up to either side of my head. A strange chimera looks back at me: adult-child and man-woman, happy-unhappy in his only certainty: loneliness.

Then we moved to Floreasca, to a small apartment block with a pointed roof that we lovingly called "the villa." It was a yellow building, with smooth plaster that bubbled in places like a lemon peel. In front there were always enormous roses, and above, the sky with pink veins, like resin. The sky was domed like a bell, holding the entire neighborhood under its jar. If we wanted to go somewhere, we had to cross through the sky. There were only three places we had to go: the grocery, with the bread distributor attached, the clinic, and the state militia building. I could go to the first one by myself, with coins in my hand. It was at the end of the street, just beyond the gelatin wall of the sky. I boldly pushed through the two or three meters of blue gelatin and found myself outside, where above there was no sky, just a gray void. The clerk at the bread store always marveled at the azure drops left in my hair and on my clothes after I crossed the blue gelatin wall, she gave me bread made especially for me by the baker next door—it was braided, red-brown, and always had a surprise in its puffy flesh: a little plastic biplane, a scrap of paper with a heart drawn by a trembling hand, a jade ring . . . Then she would put the change in my hand: two or three large metal coins with the national symbol on one side. This was money, it would buy you anything. It was kept in the kitchen table drawer. There was also paper money, with detailed drawings on it, but that was so crumpled and torn and stuck with chocolate and marked with permanent marker that you couldn't even make out the faces. My mother kept paper money in the chiffonier, under a stack of clothes. I only liked the coins, and I played with them endlessly. I would arrange them in flowers over the reflections of light on the dining table, and, at my aunt's, I would put them on a magnet and make chains of five or six coins, stuck to each other by their edges, since the coins also became magnets. When I moved them closer, they jumped together: *click*. And they were so hard to pull apart you'd think they were sad to say *un-click* . . .

I only went to the clinic or the militia station with my mother. The two of us, hand in hand, were much stronger, and we made such an impression on the walls of sky curving down to the asphalt that two blue, transparent creatures popped out that looked just like us, walking ahead of us holding hands, then after a bit they dissolved under the gray sky, leaving my mother and me with azure droplets in our hair, walking the twisted and unfamiliar paths under skeletal trees, through the enormous world. My mother knew the way and I knew my mother, and in the end we reached the clinic, a long, low building, divided into lots of offices inside. Each one had an examination table covered halfway in a pinkish-brown mat; a white, iron scale that also measured your height to see how much you had grown; and a white cabinet with glass shelves that held nickeled metal boxes. Each office also had a young doctor, with a stethoscope in her ears and curly copper hair falling loose down to her waist.

Likewise, the beds had half-undressed patients, their ribcages rising and falling. The doctors pressed the frozen foot of the stethoscope to the patient's chest or back and listened attentively, as though their hearts were saying something serious and important. One bed was always empty, and that's where I would lie down. My mother waited in a corner, playing with the sliding weights on the scale, or reading the pamphlets where ugly microbes bared their broken teeth. Lipsticked and perfumed, with gentle, soft movements, the redheaded doctor was ready to examine me.

She asked me to stick out my tongue and pressed a metal-tasting utensil on top of it so she could look at my throat. I would cough and feel like I would vomit. She looked quickly through my hair for lice, keeping her own away from my suspicious head. She would press on my stomach for signs of hives. She would pass her stethoscope over my ribs, clearly visible through my skin, and ask me to breathe deeply. She would ask if I had worms. Oh, I had them all the time, they really itched at night, but the worm pill looked like a bar of soap, green with fibers in it; and it was unbearably bitter, so I would say I didn't, but my mother, who could hear me writhing in my bed at night, would divulge my embarrassing secret to the doctor. Yes, I had pinworms, as the doctor said, I had even seen them once—small and thin, very white, shiny and mischievous, moving there in the jar with the fecal sample. Before becoming someone, I was my own little body, perhaps that is why I spoke about myself like I was a thing like any other: it, I would say, it. Then I understood that I wasn't a body, I *had* one, that I was its tenant and its prisoner. I didn't have worms or nits or constipation or hives, but it did, the one made of a soft and shifting material, the *it* where I lived. When I was suffering from an illness, even though the illness was not mine, but its, the cell walls where I was the prisoner seemed to become damp or to burn so hard that the fire would take my breath away, or freeze me through. My body made me suffer sadistically, it was my mortal enemy, it was a stomach that digested me, little by little. It was the trap of a carnivorous plant into which, as a winged creature, I fell to my demise. I had already heard of internal organs, and I knew that, inside my skin, I was supposed to have a heart and liver and lungs, even an entire skeleton, but I didn't believe a word. Since I hadn't seen them, they didn't exist. I preferred to believe that inside me was a uniform, glowing substance, a warm, liquid wax, with which I thought and lived, saw and heard, laughed and cried. Others, sure, maybe they had organs, like the pig I saw cut up and scorched at my grandfather's house in the country, maybe they had guts full of poop, but I was put together in an entirely different way. To this day I still believe that I am not like other people, other living creatures. I don't even use the word "living" to talk about myself, because I don't feel that I am living, I am not a part of the life that takes place in spores or bacteria. When I cut my finger, sure, there was blood, but I preferred to think that it was created on the spot, by the simple penetration of the knife blade into my finger, rather than imagine the twisted network of veins, arteries, and capillaries through which blood endlessly flowed, a network I would never see. How could this blood be? What color could it have, there inside my body, where there were no colors, because there was no light? When, much later, on the stairs of the block on Ştefan cel Mare, where we had moved two years later, I put my index finger in front of the elevator light bulb, I confirmed for myself the fact I had no internal structure, that I was completely filled with a pinkish hyaline substance, translucid, like whatever filled the bodies of jellyfish.

The idea that I live inside an animal—that even when I'm in a library, when I'm reading *Prolegomena* by Kant or *In the Shadow of Young Girls in Flower*, I house gluey guts, gurgling systems, and apparatuses, that my glands secrete hormones, that my blood carries sugar, that I have intestinal flora, that within my brain cells vesicles full of chemical substances descend through microtubes and release them into the spaces between synapses, that all this happens without my knowledge or consent, for reasons that are not my own—even today this seems monstrous to me, the product of a saturnine, sadistic mind that probably spent eons in order to imagine the most brutal ways to humiliate, terrorize, and torture a conscious mind. Yes, I live inside a compartmentalized animal, slippery, mucinous, constantly struggling for a breath of air, a tube that aspirates structured material and eliminates destructured material, that writhes for a nanosecond on a speck of dust within a grand and abject universe, looking up occasionally through the film of the atmosphere toward the nearest other speck scattered across the sky. Waiting for something to come from there, something that will never come, as long as eternity lasts.

The doctor then had me stand on the white scale, she moved the weights until the scale's pointed beak calmed down to quantify how much the earth's magnetic power pulled me in. I was stuck to it like the coins to my aunt's magnet. Every year, the earth crushed my bones a little more, pressing them against the sidewalk, bridges, the lids of sewers in the middle of the street . . . Then she measured my height, sliding the bar to the top of my head, and she noted that the animal in which I lived had somehow found a way to combat universal ruin and collapse: I was growing, while everything around me was cut down, was pushed to the ground, was made into dust and ruin. I recklessly faced off against the god who leveled everything down to the nothing that was the floor of being. Then she gave me the usual shots, without which my childhood was impossible to imagine: penicillin, streptomycin. In those days, doctors seemed to think if they didn't give shots, they had no reason to exist. I thought they somehow needed the howls, sobs, and tears of the little ones who couldn't understand why they were being punished so severely. What bothered me most was the fact that every time I was writhing on the mat, screaming like a snake had me in its jaws, while the nurse came at me with her unforgiving hornet needle, my mother always went along with it. She held me down with all her might, she yelled at me, she threatened to beat me. Sometimes she threw herself onto me, on the bed, holding my hands behind my back. Then I felt the needle in my flesh and the poison filling my buttock. I would stay on the mat, humiliated and sobbing, and it was my mother who then, incomprehensibly, would wipe my wet face and pull me up, with a tenderness that amazed and wounded me: "Enough, enough, it's over . . ." I would limp out of the office, hiking my pants up so no one would see the needle marks, the inflamed stars scattered at random over my right and left buttocks. The word "clinic" scares me even today, it has the clinking sound of nickeled tins, the clatter of glass shelves, and the moldy smell of penicillin, the true smell of my childhood.

Other times, much less frequently, we went to the state militia. My parents would have to renew their ID perhaps, who knows, the fact is that in the evenings, we would come out from under the gelatin bell, now amber-colored, that cast an unreal light onto the streets and sidewalks; bearing large drops of amber on our eyelids, we would go toward the wild world, much wilder than our trips to the clinic. We would never see a soul. The buildings were the same, the same restlessly shifting perspectives, the same copper trees dropping their leaves. We reached the iron gate in the hour when night mimicked day, when the sky was like pitch hemmed along the horizon by a yellow-green stripe the color of snake venom. The gate glided away on wheels. We entered the building with barred windows and went to the second floor. The walls were painted khaki. We entered a waiting room where they hadn't turned on the light, even though it was almost impossible to see. Only the barred windows were there, letting their sepia scenes enter through the brown air. It was an eternal dusk, into which we, my mother and I, crossed timidly. Only occasionally would someone else be in the room, sitting on a high-backed bench. We would wait a long time, two or three hours. Tired of playing with my fingers, I would keep asking my mother how much longer we had to stay, and she would whisper that I needed to be patient. I looked at the poster of criminals, then I went to look out the window . . . The wood floor creaked with every step, and like all the wood floors at that time, it reeked of the kerosene cleaner. Finally, the door would open, startling my mother, who would jump up, take her purse, and hurry to the door. She would turn around only for a moment, from the doorway, to tell me to behave, she'd be right back.

I was left the master of the darkening hall. I would walk among the benches, I would look at the paintings shining on the walls. Everywhere, in the clinic and here at the militia, or anywhere else, there was a painting on the wall, a man with a massive face, heavy eyes, and gray hair. On a bench in a dark corner, I once found a girl, younger than me, missing a front tooth, with earrings shaped like raspberries, sitting with her knees to her chest. Maybe she was waiting for her mother, too. On the bench beside her was a large seltzer bottle made of blue, polyhedral glass. If you pushed its handle, bubbly water spouted from the tin vulture's beak. We played with the bottle for a long time, then a game where we clapped our hands together, in more and more complicated ways, but our mothers were taking a long time, so we decided to crack the door open and peak through. The door was much larger than those in our houses, we could only reach the handle on tiptoe. The door opened a few centimeters, and with my head over hers, we looked into the next room.

We expected to see an office and patrolmen in uniform and our mothers sitting on chairs and taking documents from their outdated purses or responding to questions modestly. At the least, we expected to see lights. In the enormous room beyond the door there were hardly any, it was barely brighter than in the waiting room. Amazed by what we saw, we stepped finally onto the stone floor of the vast hall.

It was like an underground grotto, like a cavern with gently phosphorescent air. There were no stalactites, but we had the clear sensation that we were beneath the earth, below a mountain whose pressure we felt with specialized sensory organs, apparently. The floor was stone, and here and there were stone benches and rectangular stone basins filled with black water. The arches above were magnificent, so high we could barely see their striations, shiny and sharp like the roof of a cat's mouth. All the stone around was, in fact, shiny and semitransparent, as though it were a mucous substance that only imitated the toughness of the mountain. We moved through the large hall, void of any other objects, looking desperately for our mothers. We held each other's hand, and our tiny shadows spread over the walls and floor in a monstrous anamorphism, constantly changing like in fun-house mirrors. When we got tired, we sat on the stone benches. These felt organic, they heated up quickly from our thighs and began to pulse strangely. They seemed to meld with our flesh. Then we peeled ourselves off, like a scab from a wound, and felt farther along our way in the dim light.

Over the course of that endlessly long trip through the enormous grotto, our bodies transformed, we became adolescents, our child's clothing fell from us in rags, fluttering in patches behind us. If our mothers had survived, they would have to be old now, gray-haired, with glasses and dentures, their bodies weighed down by diseases of the liver and spleen. We might not even recognize them. But we continued, hand in hand, in our new, delightful bodies. We were already adults, we filled out the archetypical human form completely, with our brains visible through foreheads as translucid as the skin of crustaceans, with our brains just as sexual as our genitals, with our sex organs that knew as much as our brains. We were the Human in its twin instantiations, we were now as impersonal as the birds and frogs that have no name or identity beyond their species. We were examples of the human species, more beautiful than anything else on Earth, glowing from within as though life were nothing other than interior light. We communicated through our clasped hands, the way that two sides of a mountain communicate at the peak, we were conjoined twins sharing a portion of our body through which the same blood flowed in a double system of veins and arteries. Our emotions also flowed through our interlaced fingers, as well as our thoughts, our sensations, and most of all, our ecstasies that filled our bodies of melted pearl. In front of the three tunnels in the opposite wall of the stone hall—where, after decades, we had arrived—we stopped and turned toward each other. Our mothers must now be shards of bone, scattered teeth, vertebrae mixed with sand and clay. A mass of rotted hair on a bald skull. A ring too large for the fourth fingerbone.

The tunnels were colossal—three gaping maws lined with the same smooth, transparent stone. They looked like the trachea of the earth. They slanted downward toward the depths, but not those of our insignificant planet, a speck of dust in the just-as-minuscule infinity of our insignificant universe, but the depths of being, of night, of forgetting, of incomprehensible nothingness. To slide down those bottomless pits, to sink in those caverns of oblivion meant, perhaps, to regress, to become a child again, then a wise fetus with heavy eyelids, swinging on a trapeze through the clouds, then a damp, transparent embryo, then an egg in the uterus of a woman from another time and place, ready for a miraculous rebirth. I will never forget those three mouths burrowed into the cavern walls in front of me, nor my frightened intuition that in the depths, each of them branched into other dark tubes that snaked through the flesh of being, and then again into other tunnels, over and over again. Perhaps reality itself shuffled through them like a blind mole, terrified by its own aloneness.

I embraced the woman next to me, and we stood, looking each other in the eyes, like a double god of soft sapphire, emanating light deep into the tunnels. When my mother woke me, in the darkness of the waiting room, I was curled up on a brown wooden bench. Through the windows I could see the stars, and by their light I saw the girl, also being woken by her mother. We stared at each other fixedly, so we could recognize each other later, and then we each left toward our homes.

Floreasca is a separate world for me, a place like I've never found anywhere else, a place under an eternal, glinting magnifying glass. My life there in the little apartment—whose layout I no longer remember, as though it were a forbidden room in the corridors of my mind—has left me the most limpid-obscure, the most fancifully colored and sightless memories; in the lack of images, all that I remember are the emotions. I see my joys and fears like concrete objects, in all their details and from all sides at once, the way the things see themselves in order to exist. I have often thought I should go back to that neighborhood, where I spent my childhood among the sweetness of roses taller than me, reading on the windowsill with my legs hanging out. I thought I could go see the street with the musician's name, the grocery, the militia station, and the clinic, not realizing you can't revisit the imaginary neighborhood dug into the soft stone of your mind, but only the one made of brick, debris, and plaster, the one with the chestnuts that indifferently bear their spiny fruits in autumn. The neighborhoods of childhood exist nowhere on Earth. And still, I said to myself more than once: I should go there anyway. I should use the present-day buildings, clouds, and trees to project shadows onto my unshielded, sensitive brain, and perhaps in the play of their shadows I will recognize something from that time.

I did it once. I took tram 5 down Str. Barbu Văcărescu and got off at the Institute for Planning and Projects, beside the desolate bus depot full of stray dogs. In the distance, to make everything feel even more impossibly sad, the ruins of the former sulfuric acid factory ate themselves away. Floreasca started just around the corner, but I couldn't walk those streets again, because the great blue gelatin dome over the neighborhood had slowly turned to stone and now it was as hard as a half-meter piece of glass. Beyond, broadened by the curving barrier, you could see those who had remained the prisoners of the little streets, the students at Rosetti High School, those who went to the Floreasca movie theater to see, for the tenth time, *Treasure of the Silver Lake*, the clerks at the bread distributor and the grocery, the manager of the fruit and vegetable store, the patrolmen and the doctors, who had all been surprised when the dome turned to glass. They pressed their faces against the thick glass and shouted, silently, to those outside, these captives of an air bubble in the enigmatic crystal of memory.

18

Mrs. Rădulescu taught history. The children did not like her, not only because she made them learn endless lines of vaivodes, their years of coronation and decease, the years of their battles and edicts, and the "causes of rebellion" and "social conditions," but also because on the index finger of her right hand she wore an impressive golden ring, so massive and so sharp on its heavily ornamented edges that wherever Mrs. Rădulescu appeared in the khaki corridors of the school or in the teachers' lounge or in the tram that we all took toward the city, the first thing you noticed was the ring, and only then did you see her—its wide, flabby appendage wrapped in black or purple fabric. The lumpy, hammered ring, in whose complicated filigree you could see, at various angles, swans, assault cannons, naked women, xylophones, V-8 engines, hydra with seven heads, or anything else you might desire, was not so much a decoration as a weapon. Pity the child who didn't spend his nights dreaming of the year of the High Bridge Battle or the start and end of Dabija-Vodă's reign: the ring would crack against the top of his head and blood would trickle through his unwashed hair. There was no grade where you couldn't find at least one child with a scar exposed by his short hair—two or three stitches left by an encounter with Mrs. Rădulescu's ring. The smacks from the hard-backed registers that most of the other teachers doled out seemed like motherly caresses in comparison with the massive force of her fearful ring, descending unexpectedly onto their fragile skulls like an ostrich beak. "Go clean yourself up, and bring your father to school tomorrow," heard the one who suffered, as he left a trail of blood on his way out of the room. The other children would clean it up with the chalkboard erasers.

Aside from this, Mrs. Rădulescu was a decent woman. In the lounge, the teachers crowded around her because she knew countless pickle recipes. Her husband held the rank of major at an institution with a sinister reputation, and they owned a reddish-orange Škoda that they loved like their own skins. Mrs. Rădulescu drove it to school every day, since her husband had a hired car from work. She would park it on the soccer field, so the fire hose could reach it. The first thing you saw in the morning as you entered the school was three or four students from the history class washing doamna profesoră's car. They sprayed it with the fire hose until the entire yard was a lake; they wiped it with the sponges that were used for everything—cleaning up vinegar, wiping chalk—they rubbed it clean until it shone, the way doamna profesoră liked it.

Mrs. Rădulescu teaches not only history but also the constitution, a topic with an uncertain object of inquiry, even for her. Ordinarily, we teach math during the period assigned to the constitution, or we teach Romanian, as we do during the periods for art, handwriting, and music. The children take only one fact away from the constitution classes: the name of the person in the painting over every chalkboard in every room. No one actually knows who he is. He is someone who, somewhere, led the country. All anyone knows about this person, who appears on television fairly often speaking what seems to be another language, is that you are not allowed to tell jokes about him. You can joke about Gypsies, Jews, people from Olt, no problem. But not the man in the portrait. On the contrary, about him you recite poems and sing songs, but again, no one knows why. Many children are put in the choir, even if they can't sing. Those with no voice or ear for music are just supposed to make the motions. And the school choir takes part in an annual show, called *Montage*. It is put on by Mrs. Rădulescu and Mr. Gheară, the music teacher and choir director. All the songs are about the Homeland, the Party, and the man from the picture over the chalkboard. Strangely, although the lyrics and music are full of emotion, it seems impossible for the children to look like anything but cadavers. Thirty cadaver children, green and unspeakably sad, singing emotional songs for celebrations and contests. Neither the history teacher's ring nor Gheară's insults can revive them from the coma they fall into when they open their mouths. When I first came to School 86, I thought this was a local phenomenon, but then I accompanied the children to the sector-level and citywide contests. All of them, from every school, behave the same way: while they wait in the hall, they chatter and roughhouse, they shoot spitballs or throw apple cores at each other's heads. As soon as they are on stage, however, they start to decompose. Cheek to cheek, immobile olive angels with terribly sad eyes, mouths that seemed to open and sing only through magic, the way a frog's leg twitches in Galvani's experiments. The director writhes in front of them, gesturing like a crazy person in her ceremonial dress, but the children remain cadaverous and vacant, emanating a strange chill of unhappiness. *Montage* is a combination of poems and music. Doamna profesoră does not write the script. I've seen it: about ten pages, copies of copies. The poems, by now almost illegible, are filled in with red and black pen, then cut, added to, and switched around by angry arrows. It looks like the purposefully obscure work of an alchemist, or the author of a hoax. The text is supposed to be a grandiose panorama of the golden age, the story of a wise and all-knowing Party bringing progress to a blessed country. But the countless cuts and changes have mixed up the times and events to the point that you can't understand anything. The proletarian heroes of the 1950s burst into the present, and their anachronous mania and class struggles make everyone laugh. The Americans bomb everything. The Germans are condemned to be forever Nazis. The children conscientiously recite, with the same unhealthy, Nile-green faces, with the same waxen expressions, this logic- and chronology-lacking filth. It would be just as well to recite a table of algorithms, addresses out of the phone book, or the names of streets in the neighborhood. "With a little more heart, Mioara, dammit, you look like you're at a funeral," Mrs. Rădulescu would shout every five minutes in the gymnasium where they were rehearsing, and Mioara, the school's award-winner, with her white blouse full of smocking, embroidery, and tassels, cannot convince her cheeks to adopt a more luminous shade of green. "Again! Look at me," says Gheară, at the out-of-tune piano, "don't start until I raise my hand. And remember, accent on 'love': "Our be-*love*-ed Presidennnnt . . ." Gheară, in spite of being named "Claw," is a bonhomme type with a red head, eternally unshaven cheeks, and a falsetto voice like a bellhop. At least he doesn't beat the children, but this makes him suspicious in the parents' eyes and gives him a bad reputation in the neighborhood. But he has a happy personality, he like parties and drinking songs. When he is so disposed, he throws himself on the piano like he's going to break it and sings old, soulful Italian canzonette . . .

In addition to the literary-musical *Montage*, the history professor is also responsible for the Scientific Atheism Club, which gives an annual prize for "Best Atheist." The children are happy to go to the Atheism Club and want to win the prize more than anything, because it is a transistor radio in a very pretty brown leather case. Mrs. Rădulescu's husband brings one back from his trips abroad and generously donates it, every year, to the school. But winning is no small task, the tests are many and complicated. Who knows in whose aunt's or grandmother's attic doamna profesoră discovered her huge, ancient icon, its surface covered in thousands of thin cracks and set in a flowery frame of precious wood, perforated all over by wood-eating insects. It depicted the Mother of God, with rings around her wise and suffering eyes, dressed in a violet headscarf, and on her breast, where she clutches him as though afraid she will lose him before the ordained time, the chubby and sweet infant Jesus, whose brown, adult eyes bore into you, his fingers arranged in a ritual gesture of blessing, infinitely graceful. Old traces of mother-of-pearl, now removed, and precious stones line the gilded clouds of the eternal mother and her holy child. Doamna profesoră brings the icon to school every Thursday, the traditional day of the Atheism Club. She stops her car and takes the icon out of the back seat from under a stained sheet, and she carries it, unable to see and tripping on the stairs, up to the history office, whose walls are decorated with the faces of the nation's vaivodes. The children are already there, waiting impatiently for the contest to begin, their large eyes watching their teacher set the icon on her desk, propping it against a few massive dictionaries and gravely unveiling it, the way memorial plaques are placed on the walls of houses where illustrious people once lived. The old and all-holy icon dominates every meeting of the Atheism Club. Every child who goes knows it by heart and dreams of it every night, every line of ink in the folds of the Virgin's cloak, every hint of a frown between her eyebrows, every nuance of the Infant's most luminous and transparent brown eyes, every termite tunnel in the mahogany flowers on the frame. In a way, in fact, every child is present in the icon, along with doamna profesoră, because the thin layer of glass that protects the ancient painted canvas reflects them all, superimposed on the image of the holy figures.

After adjusting the icon on the desk, Mrs. Rădulescu removes the "Funny Bible" from her purse and begins to read to the children, making silly faces, or sometimes frowning and pounding the bench, as she intones the silly stories that clearly demonstrate what immoral and lying goats are in this "so-called holy book." Since there is not even a single real Bible in the school's entire neighborhood, the children can hardly wait to hear stories about Moses (who stuttered), Noah (who drank), David (who showed his shame in front of the holy altar),

Solomon (who split children in two with his sword), Abraham (who was just about to roast his own son on the grill), and many more instructive and educational stories of this type. When she comes to the story of Sodom, she explains to the uneasy students that God didn't rain down fire and brimstone over the city because—how ridiculous!—some idiots wanted to mate with angels ("but these aren't stories for your age"). Out of the question! They probably had an earthquake like the one that hit in '40, when doamna profesoră was a child, that destroyed the Hotel Carlton. Her face burns with anger and her terrible ring strikes whatever is near when the subject comes up—and it comes up strangely often—of the abject way in which, drunk as a pig, Lot, who ran from Sodom, did something extremely nasty with his daughters, since Mrs. Rădulescu also has a daughter and she would never let her be treated like that. But after all the silly and crazy stories in the book of books, when all is said and done, the children have to remember one simple fact: God, an old man with a wavy beard and a big book with strange red letters open in front of him, does not really exist, no matter what their grandparents tell them. He has been invented by priests to fool the world, to take people's money without having to work. In fact, humans are the masters of nature; they form it to their desires. Work made man: monkeys learned how to use tools.

The worst of this group of saints, martyrs, angels, archangels, and other imaginary creatures seems to be an individual named Jesus Christ, who never existed but in spite of this fact did many things he should not have. He said: "Render unto Caesar the things that are Caesar's," in other words, he was in favor of man's exploitation of man. He was in favor of adultery ("that means your daddies leave their wives and run around like idiots after other women"), since he didn't do anything about the loose woman who was caught committing adultery. They say he was born of a virgin, that means a pure woman, you see, but that is what shows Jesus Christ is a myth, the opiate of the people, because other false saints and gods appeared to be born from virgins. "In fact, children, let me tell you what happened, what a professor of philosophy taught us during training: Jesus's mom got into trouble with one Pantera, a Roman soldier, and when she ended up pregnant, she had to get married quickly, and to someone dumb enough to take her like that, so she got Joseph, the village carpenter." Still, they must remember—in spite of all these stories—that none of those people ever existed, not Mary or Joseph or their kid born in a feed trough, no more than Father Christmas (only Father Frost existed, who came to the school every year with a bag of cookies and moldy oranges), or Muma of the Forest or fairies. Yuri Gagarin had been to space, that is, to heaven, and he didn't see any gods or saints of any kind.

After this theoretical training, Mrs. Rădulescu moves on to the concrete, since "in theory, everything works, but in practice, we're dead," as the shop teacher, Eftene, wittily put it. He would from time to time, while the children were busy filing something, let unprincipled observations slip out, and there wasn't a faculty meeting where he didn't get his knuckles rapped: "Work made the man a monkey," for example, or "In capitalism, man exploits man. In communism, it's the other way around." Doamna profesoră splits the students into groups according to where they are seated, then she draws a line across the space between the benches, toward the back of the room. Row by row, the children come up to the line and, from a distance of five or six meters, they attempt to spit on the icon, as proof that they truly uphold the teachings of the Atheism Club. Mrs. Rădulescu leaves nothing to chance: the icon of the Mother of God is divided into different areas, like animals outlined at the butcher's, and each area is marked in points from one to ten, so everyone understands that pegging the two faces with saliva bullets is completely different from dampening, through the glass where gelatinous splats slide down in a fascinating way, the long fingers or wrist of a hand. For the Best Atheist contest, the power of your lungs matters, but also your precision. The girls have no chance, their spit just drizzles onto their chins, some don't even know how to spit, and the liquid doesn't escape their lips. But the class bullies, who have spent the breaks between classes spitting on each other until they were white with foam, are experts. Usually one of them wins Best Atheist and gets the radio, so he can listen every Friday to the science program, *The Compass Rose*. The participants also get points if they can prove that, during the year, they urinated on crosses in the neighborhood cemetery, put a note on the back of the priest that said, "IDIOT," or made their bigoted grandparents cry with the stories from the "Funny Bible." But the "mother and child bullseye," as Mrs. Rădulescu called the icon, always decides the winner.

Sometimes, out of all the children in the club, it comes down to two, in their undershirts and black gym shorts, egged on by the gallery of their classmates. "Spit on the eye! Come on, hit the eye!" they shout, or "Right between the eyebrows!"; "The bellybutton on the baby!"; "The thumb!"; and the champions, well-developed kids who are repeating a grade, follow the shouts and cheers, until the cleaning lady is left with a lot to clean up afterward, rubbing the icon glass with the same rag she uses for the floor. Then she dries it with toilet paper and puts the sheet back on. The children carry it to the shining, red-orange automobile parked under the basketball hoop, and they place it very carefully in the back seat. Such a precious relic of a bygone era shouldn't have to suffer the potholes that litter Str. Dimitrie Herescu, the street outside the school, where the cars are so battered they almost collapse into heaps of metal and rubber scrap.

One frozen December morning, just before the winter break, Mrs. Rădulescu lost her ring. We were making a census of the animals in the neighborhood, just as in the summer, before the school year began, teachers were tasked with going from house to house to complete a census of school-age children. In the summer and the winter, we went down long streets that, after crossing many others full of little houses with front yards, ended in open fields; silent and sonorous streets like in a village, with a grocery or lumberyard or a recycling depot on the corner, with ancient cars parked in front of the houses, with pines and fruit trees painted white up to the middle. A gang of kids with nothing better to do would follow us from house to house; they knocked on doors for us and talked to the half-dressed people who showed their confused heads through the door: "Are you here for the electricity? The gas?" Summer was a little easier, in spite of the enervating heat. The neighborhood was ghostly, a wasteland, streets narrowed in the distance, the light was intensely yellow, shadows were completely absent. We felt as though we were walking through a scale model of the neighborhood, without life, noise, or movement. A dirty kite tail hung from the electric lines stretched over the alleyways, a dove cooed far away. "Two old people live here, no school kids," the boys and girls who followed us would say. "This is where the Enaches live, from the seventh and eighth grades, their parents aren't home, they work." We recorded the Enaches in the registers we carried under our arms and went on, under the sweltering heat, along the endless fences. In the yards, through half-open doors almost solely occupied by the housecoats of chesty, unkempt women and the thick country sweaters of their husbands, who wore berets down to their eyebrows, you'd see rusty bicycles, starving dogs, pens full of goose droppings, bare-bottomed infants crying with all their might. At the end of the streets was the railway, after which the overgrown field began and then continued to the end of sight, as uncrossable as a sea without shores.

Winter was much more difficult, because there could be winds and gales, weather so bad you wouldn't take your dog out in it, yet we were forced to trudge through snow up to our knees, to be battered by gates blowing in the wind, blinded by needles of ice, frightened by howling dogs that snapped their fangs at us, to go again from door to door, to knock dozens of times before someone opened, and, finally, when a suspicious eye appeared in the crack of the door, to tell them why we were there: "Animal census. We would like to know whether you have pigs, birds, cows, sheep, etc., so we can note them down." We had to shout above the wind. Everyone left us standing at the door. It never crossed their minds to invite us in for a hot tea. "None at all, where am I going to get any animals. I had two or three geese last summer, sure, but . . . I don't keep them anymore. Pigs, I haven't had any for years . . ." They all lied, but what did we care? We weren't there to investigate. We marked a line in the register, barely holding on to the pen with our gloved hands, and we moved on, keeping away from dogs and the frightening gusts of wind. By the time evening fell over the neighborhood, all at once, like a sheet of metal, around four in the afternoon, we couldn't feel our bodies, we were frozen right through. We went back to the school with wet, red cheeks, with that dazed look that comes from the frost, to warm up a little in the teachers' lounge, before going home.

How strange the lounge looked, lit up at night, when the rest of the school howled in the dark! The ceiling fixtures dripped a brown, dirty light, they painted our faces the earthy colors of subterranean creatures, the portraits of Herzegovinian characters took on some of the sinister olive of the painted walls. And yet, there we found, in that illuminated hole inside the homogeneous pitch black of the world, a refuge from the streets of ghosts and loneliness. As we disencumbered ourselves of coats still covered in snow and stomped the snow from our feet, we felt part of a tragic fraternity, a family of moles huddled in the center room of their network of tunnels, like blind mites on the skin of a mangy dog. As the snow fell harder against the windows, we felt as though we were inside an ark, moving by chance through universal damnation.

The evening Mrs. Rădulescu lost her ring, we were all sitting around the red fabric of the long tables after spending the entire day outside for the census, drinking tea to warm ourselves since the school's the radiators were, of course, cold as ice. That was how students studied in the winter: the teachers and children were bundled in coats, Russian hats, headscarves, and gloves; every breath emerged in the frozen air like an icy, unraveling geranium. The secretary made us the tea, in her small room where I had sat with Caty when we're on guard duty. They used a hot plate improvised from a concrete block with grooves chiseled in for the red-hot elements. We were chatting aimlessly about a new diet when the history teacher burst in, shouting as loudly as she could: "My ring! My ring is gone! They stole my ring!" Florabela, the beautiful math teacher, full of charm, gold, and freckles, tried to calm her down: "Hold on, no one stole anything, it will turn up . . . Where did you leave it?" But Mrs. Rădulescu had collapsed, exhausted, into a chair, with her hand on her heart, a reaction we all thought understandable, since without her famous ring, three-quarters of her being would vanish. The wrought gold ring was her vital center, her essential chakra, the mystic eye in her forehead. Her wide and lumpy body was already turning gray, as she sat collapsed on the chair, and the light had vanished from her eyes. "I don't know, I don't know . . ." she babbled. "Maybe in the office . . . I took it off because my hands were frozen . . . and now it's goooone!" she shouted lugubriously. Yes, yes, she had put it on the corner of the secretary's desk, then she got a cup for tea, the secretary had poured the tea, and . . . she didn't know. Everyone had been around, anyone could have taken it. The porter, the janitors. "Or the shop teacher," piped up Spirescu, who taught art, and everyone's ears perked up because the shop teacher, Eftene, was a Gypsy, which for most people meant he was a professional crook; furthermore, he wasn't a quiet Gypsy who kept to his place, but he was one of those bitter, sarcastic ones, always mocking people, right or wrong, lippy, undomesticated, who already had a heap of enemies. No one dared to say to Eftene, "Come over here, Gypsy," because whoever did, the next time they came to school, had to pick their teeth up off the floor. He was always being interrogated by the militia, they all knew his type. Each year, when shop class began, he asked the children to buy a kit for fretwork. The school supply store had two kinds of kits, one made here and another, more expensive one with hardened metal saws, made in Russia. Eftene would walk calmly past the shop benches, each with a vise, and check the children's kits. The moment he saw a Russian one, he threw it out the window. Eftene also told all the anti-socialist, even anti-president, jokes, and so often that the authorities didn't know what to do with him. In the end they decided it was best to leave him alone, like someone who had a screw loose. Eftene had, additionally, some status in his clan, a kind of uncrowned king, and every street cleaner or bottle seller or flower woman stood up when he passed, because he was one of the few Gypsies who had been to school. He was actually an inventor, he had a patent for a machine that made wheels for dumpsters, and he prided himself on the fact that his machines had made part of every dumpster in the city.

The shop teacher didn't usually come to the lounge, he would stay in his workshop, full of iron shavings and grime, where the children learned to use a file, to chip-carve pieces of basswood, or to attach radio tubes to circuit boards with a soldering iron and wire, but more than anything, they learned, according to what their blue-work-coated instructor said, that "socialism is a society for lazy people," that capitalist engineers were all bald on top (because they were always scratching their heads: What to do, what to do?), but socialist engineers were bald in the front (from slapping their foreheads: Oh God, what did I do?), that capitalist managers kept their butts in the chair and their eyes on the factory, while the socialists kept their butts on the factory and their eyes on the chair . . . But above all, they learned that everything bad always came from the Russians, our great friends from the east. And that evening, after he had also gone through the neighborhood with a register under his arm, looking for ducks, geese, pigs, rabbits, cows, sheep, horses, when there were none to be found, even though you could hear the clucking, oinking, neighing, and mooing from the backyards, Eftene took off his coat and hat, took a cup of tea from the secretary, and went to his workshop without stopping at the lounge. I had always liked his personality, funny but smart, his experience of the misfortunes of the world, his old Indian skinniness, his lopsided mouth like Gandhi's, where gold teeth glinted . . . His eyes didn't show intelligence but a kind of cynical agility: "You want to know what people are like? Don't look in palaces or libraries: come into my old, lonely Gypsy den, where it stinks like urine and cheap cigarettes. Look at me standing naked in the middle of my room, in a basin, rubbing my dark skin with a sponge. Look at my skinny chest, covered in a tangle of white hairs, my sex down to my knees, veiny and wrinkled like a horse's, my crooked legs. Yet here dwells a man, a true man, who grits his teeth and smiles in the face of life's horrors, who won't let himself be beaten, who clings like a mangy burr to the piece of earth where he found himself. I am I, Eftene, inside a ragged work coat of living matter."

But for my colleagues in the teachers' lounge, the shop teacher was no spirit, no Gentleman Jim, but a probable thief, a smelly, lazy Gypsy. "Another one of those who chose their profession with their head and work with their feet, like gym teachers. While we, idiots teaching Romanian and math, we walked right into it and now we're in over our heads. And serves us right; you get what you pay for. I mean I could give the kids a ball and tell them: 'Go play, I'm the teacher so I'm going to drink a coffee.' Or make them pound out things that I can sell and pocket the cash, like our Eftene, who laughs all the way home at us when he sees our mounds of homework . . . When it comes to money, the pay is the same but we go blind grading papers, actually theirs is more than ours, because they get all kinds of bonuses, the poor guys . . ." But when Spirescu mentioned Eftene's name, there wasn't any doubt: he stole the ring, who knows when, maybe the secretary was gone for a second, went to the bathroom, and bam! The ring disappeared into the Gypsy's pocket . . .

"Jeana, go and tell Eftene to come here for a moment, since it's been so long that people've forgotten what his mug looks like," Gionea, the physics teacher, told one of the janitors, after which everyone sat silently around the table with dark shadows on our faces, like a sinister tribunal.

The snow fell furiously, at a slant, against the pitch-black windows, so the whole room seemed to be flying toward the sky. The silence was so great in the frozen room that when someone set a cup down on its saucer, it sounded like a gunshot and everyone jumped.

Mrs. Rădulescu opened her mouth as soon as the shop teacher was in the door:

"Close the door behind you, Jeana, and don't let me catch you listening. Go to the office, you haven't watered that asparagus in who knows how long, all the spears are hanging down . . ."

Then, turning toward the shop teacher, she continued in a different tone.

"Mr. . . . Eftene . . ." she cleared her throat. "Mr. Eftene, look, don't be scared, no one's going to do anything to you . . ."

"Don't worry, we'll settle it among ourselves, scratch my back . . ." intervened Gionea, stony as a gorgon.

"Look, we all know full well that you took something from the desk in the office . . . You were seen . . ."

"Sure, a cup of tea, and I was going to bring it back just now, as I was leaving," Eftene said, without losing his composure, although in his eyes you could already read not the suspicion but the certainty that he was again in some kind of shit. It wasn't the first trouble he'd had in his life, not the first time he'd had to pay for a dish someone else broke. He was just trying to figure out what was up, before it was too late. He knew that everything was already against him, that in the eyes of these people he had been born a crook the same way he had gotten his dark body at birth. It made no difference how hard he worked, even when he was starving to death, he didn't touch even the end of a thread, it didn't do him any good; it made no difference that he tried his whole life to be twice as honest as the people around him, something always pulled him back, something pushed him into the swamp every time, no matter what. He had gotten used to it, he was resigned to the way people looked at him, the way a hunchback doesn't worry, after a while, about his curved spine, or a blind person doesn't complain about his fate. What more could he have done? He kept his distance from the other teachers, he didn't act like their equal, although he knew he was smarter than most of them; he even spent his breaks in his den of sawdust and filings. He knew, though, he had known from the start, that something ugly would happen here, as always. Starting in first grade, they put him in the back of the room, they found lice on his head, the kids kept away from him, they called him monkey or darkie, the teachers smacked his neck and pulled his hair more often, and for less reason, than they did other kids'. Eftene had had to learn early on the art of talking through his teeth, and that's what he did now, when the school faculty, the "didactic cadavers," as his big mouth would often say, enjoyed acting out the scene like they were in a movie with trials and guilty parties, lawyers for the defense and the plaintiffs, jurors who couldn't decide.

"Cup, what cup? . . . You know full well. Someone saw you, you should know, someone saw you take Mrs. Rădulescu's ring from the desk in the office."

Gionea (everyone, the children and the teachers, called her "Gionea," without "Mrs.," without anyone remembering her first name) could have been a state prosecutor. She was made of ice, and the children were more scared of her than of anyone else. When she entered the classroom, there was a terrifying silence and a smell like a cemetery. Gionea sat at her desk without moving for the entire period, like a statue. She didn't blink, didn't turn her head. She spoke calmly, sharply, she never needed to raise her voice, or scream like crazy the way the other teachers did. When she called students to the board, they panicked, as though they were facing a poisonous reptile, even though they knew their material by heart. Not one muscle moved on Gionea's face when she gave them grades, which descended like a guilty verdict onto the back of the children's necks: four, three, two, four, three. But they weren't as scared of failing grades as they were of being turned to stone, the monstrous gravity of her gaze, the lack of any smile, of any relaxation in the constant mechanism of terror. The other physics teacher giggled like a tickled kid when he gave twos and threes, and the students didn't care about those grades at all. But with Gionea, you trembled with holy fear even when you got a seven, the highest, almost legendary, grade she ever gave, and that only three or four times in her life, since, as she told her colleagues in the teachers' lounge, "Tens are for God, nines are for the teacher, and eights are for the student who not only knows the material perfectly but also studies further outside of school. Any student who comes from the end of Colentina should know that the highest grade for them is a seven, and they will never see it . . ." And on that winter evening, Gionea had the shop teacher in her sights, her green eyes almost colorless, frozen, in the most pallid face possible.

"Mr. Eftene," she said, "we don't want to make this a big deal. We don't even want to keep talking. We are all going to go to our homes, it's late, and you, when you want to, when your own conscience tells you to, you will go to doamna profesoră Rădulescu and return her ring. And that will be the end of it. No one will know. We won't speak to the militia, because we are all colleagues and we want to maintain the school's reputation. You shouldn't feel embarrassed, a moment of weakness can come to anyone, we're all just people . . ."

This was fairly elevated. The shop teacher would contritely bring back what he had stolen and they wouldn't have to contact the authorities, they would all seem understanding, human. If you thought about it, a guilty thief could be useful for the cohesion of the collective: each person would see him tiptoe through the world, pressing himself against the wall when others pass, his knees sagging; everyone could feel themselves this wrongdoer's savior, his benefactor, and the act of charity wouldn't cost them a cent. Every teacher, those at the table and the small group next to the frozen heater under the windowsill, strove to project an attitude of understanding, so that the poor man, caught with his hand in the cookie jar, wouldn't feel bad, since, after all, who were they to judge?

Eftene's yellow teeth chewed on his tobacco-colored mustache. His wrinkled face, always an unhealthy color, seemed more pallid than ever. He looked quickly from one person to the next, let his head hang down, thought for a moment, suddenly wrinkled like a fig and diminished in his eternal blue shop coat, and then, making a decision, he said:

"Okay, I'll bring it. I'll bring it back right now." And he walked out of the lounge, closing the door softly behind him.

Great joy and relief among the teachers.

"Mrs. Gionea, you are wonderful, nothing can withstand you," raved Spirescu, who congratulated himself, with a thought, for his intuition. "Do you all see the power of words, even on uneducated people?"

"On them especially . . . We, people like us, what do we care about a word or two . . ."

"Mrs. Rădulescu, go easy on him . . . Who the hell cares about this Gypsy? Do him a favor, he's definitely going to bring it, and he won't forget what he went through today, for as long as he lives . . ."

"I don't know," she sighed, still standing and obviously struggling inside. "I don't know, it was theft, I still think the militia should . . . I'm thinking that if we, of all people, who beat socialist ethics and behavior into the kids' heads, if we close our eyes to such a thing . . . It's not right, dear colleagues: no matter what you say, I'm going to file a complaint."

"But we promised, we told him that it would stay among us, otherwise he wouldn't bring the ring back . . . Catch the thief, take out his eyes . . . It would be better, I'd say, to leave things as they are. Don't you remember what happened two years ago, with Maftei's husband? That was actually proven, he had a heap of money in his briefcase, on payday, caught on a hidden camera . . . And what did they do to him? Fined him three months' salary. And we wore the mark on our foreheads, they said we were a school of thieves . . ."

The argument began. Some took the side of the history teacher and wanted to put Eftene into the hands of the militia, others agreed with Gheară, who had just been speaking. They shouted loudly across the table, no one could understand a word, so no one noticed when Eftene was back, with the janitor, her hands on her hips, behind him. They noticed him only when he came to the table and hit it once, his palm on the red cloth, so hard the cups and spoons jumped. Then everyone was silent. There was no sound but the snowflakes falling against the window. The teachers, and even the bizarre Montenegrin characters in the paintings, all fixed their eyes on the shop teacher.

"The ring . . . to give you the ring," he said with a tired voice, as though it wasn't coming out of his mouth but running from his yellow eyes, suddenly as old as the start of time.

Everything happened so quickly that no one could stop it. Everyone just jumped up, knocking chairs over, Florabela fainted, the tangle of shadows and lights was impossible to sort out.

Eftene, in a single movement, had reached into the large, torn pocket of his work coat, taken out an old, black hammer, and whacked his mouth. He grabbed his gold tooth and, howling like an animal, yanked it out by the roots. Then, his mouth full of blood, and blood running down his chin and neck, he held it out over the table, triumphantly, the way an alchemist would show the speck of gold he found in his crucible of melted lead. Then, with demented strength, he threw it at Mrs. Rădulescu's face. It rolled from the spot of vivid blood on her ample chest onto the table, almost as large and heavy and shining as her legendary ring, but with two extensions of bloody ivory.

Eftene turned his back and walked out, leaving drops and puddles of blood on the carpet, and the teachers, many with blood-splattered faces and clothes, went to the coatrack, wrapped themselves in hats, coats, and scarves, and rushed outside like they were escaping a blazing fire. Through the window, I saw them scatter into the snowy streets, crazed, trying to forget their participation in this nightmare.

I was left alone in the dark room, among the portraits shining on the walls. I picked the tooth up from the table, looked at it closely, then tossed it, like a die, onto the red cloth. It shone there, in the middle of the shadowy chamber, in the shadowy school, in the world where we all walked blindly, waiting for a sign or miracle. I left it in the middle of the table with the painful sensation that I had been given a sign, one which, like all the others, I was not able to interpret.

Of course, Mrs. Rădulescu found her ring the next day, forgotten in the letter box in the office, and everything went back to normal. The first child's busted head appeared in the neighborhood clinic only a few days later, a sweet, golden-blonde girl. The cut needed no fewer than four stitches.

19

It was eight in the evening when I reached my boat-shaped house, hidden among the gusts and snowdrifts. In the empty lot in front, the old refrigerators and car tires and furless animal carcasses were buried in snow, and the low sky was just as white as the air and ground. I was hustled into the house by a sudden wind, and I heaved the wrought iron door shut behind me. I was so out of sorts from the snowstorm, the hours I had spent in the cold knocking on people's doors, and the travesty of Eftene's trial that, for the first time, I got lost in my own home. I never really knew how many rooms, hallways, staircases, and corridors it had, and often, on my way to the bedroom, I ended up in dens or bathrooms that were not only completely foreign to me, as though one of the walls of my house had disappeared and another house had been grafted onto it, but also from another time, another space, and another memory, with odd, glistening pieces of furniture, with walnut grandfather clocks and candelabra with copper branches; but now, the dark house, with snow falling heavily against its windows, seemed infinite. I only found my bedroom the next morning, exhausted by dozens of kilometers of corridors, by the mechanical operation of thousands of light switches, by the desperate repetition of opening hundreds of doors, hoping every time to see, finally, my rumpled bed in the center of this mandala of corridors, the way you might peel away hundreds of rose petals to find, in its scented center, the tender organs of an androgynous sexuality.

I reached into the nightstand for the Tic-Tac box where I kept my baby teeth. I got into bed, still dressed, and I pressed the button for levitation. Suspended between the bed and ceiling, my bones suddenly loose within my body and my limbs floating leisurely in the stuffy air, I was suddenly overtaken by a terrible weariness, an irrepressible need to sleep and to dream. I was rocked by the mild currents of air that crept under the windows and door from the storm outside, I was calmed by the tame howl of the winds. I had been longing for this moment of privacy, because—like the pit of a plum that cannot be torn from the orange flesh invading its body—I felt I was in the center of an enormous world I could not understand. I poured the twenty-odd white, shiny bones in my palm; they looked more like pearls or bits of coral, and in a way that is what they were: shells, flakes of mother-of-pearl produced by my gums in a distant life, that once made two rows in my mouth, constantly smoothed by my own tongue, crushing crackers and apples, revealed in my smiles at my parents, my twin brother, my neighbors on Silistra and later Floreasca. They had budded in the bones of my jaw and broken through my pink gums, making them itch and hurt, growing crystals within my soft and suffering flesh. And then I got rid of them to make room for other teeth that would torture me endlessly my entire life. I rubbed them against my palm, the sweet granules, in a sleepy reverie, and then I let them go, to float in the air like a weightless astronaut. My teeth scattered slowly above me in an arch, making strange constellations in the room's penumbra. I fell asleep still dressed, in the flickering lights of my former teeth, like flashes from the fountain of my body's depths of time.

I have often wondered, what if I—along with the bits of thread that tied my navel, the photos that preserve my effigy in silver nitrate, my pigtails from when I was a child, and my teeth that either came out on their own or at the end of a thread tied to the doorknob of a door slammed mercilessly shut by my father—had kept a vertebra from when I was a child, or one of my fingers, or my mother, the way she was then, or a cloud from the sky over our street . . . It wouldn't have been any more incredible or bizarre, it wouldn't have created a more intolerable incursion of the past in the present. My teeth, my pigtails, my old pictures, these are strange phantoms spilling out of the crypt of memory, incarnate, hardened memories, shining, concrete. Not evidence of your youth's reality, or the body in which your being once lived as a child, but evidence of the unreal nature of time itself, of the coexistence and interpenetration of ages, eras, bodies, within the unanimous hallucination of the mind and world. I could have kept, in the morgue of my nightstand drawer, hundreds of billions of creatures with my name, each one a second younger than the previous; I could have visited this enormous edifice, looking each one in the eyes, listening to their thoughts, dreaming their dreams, myself being the last of them and leaving behind another me, like an insect who escapes the shell that is precisely its shape, every second, ever younger, ever farther away . . . They would be the perfect equivalents of my baby teeth, once a part of me, now objects in the universe, the boundless universe, the universe without rhyme or reason.

I dreamed—or remembered from an immemorial past, since in the dream state you can access the brain you had as a child, like an enchanted castle in the center of your mind, disaffected, ruined, and covered in cobwebs, transformed into a sanatorium or a rabbit hutch but keeping its regal architecture and preserving, above all, in the center of its knotted corridors, the forbidden chamber, the place you always wanted to escape into, because you can escape nowhere but inward—in that night of levitation, in the soft buzzing of the solenoid under the floor and the whistle of the storm outside, about the frightening mausoleum of pain that was, for me, throughout my childhood and adolescence, the Maşina de Pâine Clinic. I recalled its gray, heavy construction, the massive cornices of its roof, the grimy windows under enormous arches, glittering like eyes of evil. The entire area around it, the old brick factories on whose blind walls giant letters spelled NO SMOKING and LONG LIVE THE ROMANIAN COMMUNIST PARTY, the entry passages through the colossal walls, the vast courtyards closed in by concrete fences, cypress trees leaning over them, that barrenness that came from beyond the world itself, the sadness of piaţas where tramlines crossed, that place bordered by Str. Doamna

Ghica and Teiul Doamnei and Maica Domnului like the minuscule eyes that form a triangle on a spider's forehead . . . All that silence and stillness around the gray building made it an awful and mysterious locale, the place of barbarous rituals and incomprehensible tortures. Adolescents in distant tribes are made to drink poison and throw it back up again, their skin is perforated and they are left to hang from hooks or branches piercing the skin of their backs, their arms are cut and their chests are burnt, they are tattooed over every part of their skin, until they carry the signs of their initiation for the rest of their life, one whose meaning, if you asked them, is totally obscure. I have these kinds of scars, too, sometimes I think my cerebral husk was so often pierced, removed, branded, and rent that now it looks like an old battle flag, torn and pierced by lances and lead from harquebuses. What purpose could that much physical and psychological torture have served? How were the corrosive acids of adrenaline allowed to dissolve my internal organs, just from hearing the name "Mașina de Pâine"? I went to the eye doctor there, I waited in line, on uniform benches made of the worst brown plastic, in a long line of cross-eyed boys and girls wearing glasses or a patch over one eye taped on with pink bandages, they put my head in a mechanical device and I was forced to look through steel-bound lenses at plates with bugs and letters from unknown alphabets. I waited in line in the mornings, fasting, for them to draw blood, ready to faint right in the waiting room, and then I was called in and I had to see my veins rise in relief over my thin arm, perfectly visible under my skin, red and blue, after the rubber band, an ordinary piece of tubing, was brutally tied around my arm. Then the nickel syringe, its components clinking, came toward my arm, and the ice-cold alcohol pad wiped my veins, and the thick needle entered one of them and began to suck, and the thick, foamy blood, my blood, something I should never see, traveled into the glass cylinder . . . My eyes wide with fear, I watched the doctor remove the needle from the syringe and leave it hanging there, in the vein, and then she put another tube into its mouth and my blood, in short bursts, filled it slowly . . . Then it filled another tube, then a third . . . A muscular nurse with a mustache wrung my arm like a wet shirt to get a few more drops of my life's sap. I was in their lair, I was in the depths of the spider's thick web, there where the spider was hidden, two black legs just poking out. Then they took out the needle and untied the band. I would walk out of there pale as death, with the alcohol pad pressed against the wound. In a few hours, that part of my skin would be purple, like a dead body, and yellow dots would remind me, weeks later, of this sordid calvary.

"Don't worry about it. Something as small as that won't kill you. It'll be gone before you're married," my mother would say to me, and after a while, she would find another occasion to take me to Mașina de Pâine, carrying urine and fecal samples in medical jars wrapped in paper, and with a box of Springtime chocolate in her purse, for the doctor. The building appeared enormous from the outside, but inside it was much larger. You were always walking up monumental staircases, you'd pass through vast hallways, elegant in spite of the ordinary white tiles lining the walls like a public toilet. In contrast to the grandeur of the general layout, the spaces for the offices and waiting rooms were stingy and narrow, poorly lit and stuffy. The plastic benches stank, the tile floors were never clean, cockroaches scurried wherever they wanted. It was full of people, especially the elderly, deformed, hunched, with wrinkled, edentulous faces, just as green in the face as the paint on the walls. To reach the place where you would be tortured, you had to squeeze between them. Their masochism amazed me: they came alone, on their own initiative, to subject themselves to the most severe agonies. They took revenge on their own old, powerless bodies, they pierced them and trepanned them, they surrendered themselves into the hands of their torturers. They constantly yelled at people trying to cut in line, as though they were in such a hurry they'd die of impatience before they got to the abattoir. I, on the contrary, if my mother hadn't been there with me, would have let everyone go in front of me, and then night would have fallen and I, alone on my chair in the suddenly empty corridor, would have seen the doctor come out of her office, not in her starched white coat but in a normal dress, and then like a prostitute at dawn locking up the room where she sat behind a shop window, she would have shut the office and left without so much as a glance at me. And I would have been alone inside the giant organism of the building, free to explore its rooms and corridors, suddenly liberated from my fear and helplessness . . .

I went there for lung X-rays, since the double pneumonia in my first year of life had left me, it seemed, with a weak chest, a condition that within a few years would have me in preventative care at Voila. I waited in the room or in the corridor among all kinds of men, young and old, undressed to the waist, with hairy or with womanly chests, bony or their guts overflowing their belts, black as coal or red as boiled lobsters, and when my time came I entered the mysterious, dark hall, where a large and odd device loomed, with thick glass plates and screens that slid along leather straps. The doctor placed me between the freezing plates. My skin erupted in goose bumps, my back and chest were squeezed by the cold plates that the doctor, turning a lever, brought closer and closer together, until I was crushed between them like an anatomical specimen on a microscope slide. "Don't breathe!" said the person in white, who had already slipped out of the room only to reappear, through a kind of teleportation, in the next room, full of medical instruments with dials and ebony buttons. There was a buzz from no particular source that lasted for an eternity. I was writhing there, between the panes of glass, trying to hold my breath. Someone was looking inside my lungs through my now transparent flesh, I could feel their gaze in the fourth dimension, one that could see heaps of money inside safes, one that could penetrate, like the angel Peter freed, into prisons with bars as thick as your hand and could examine the formation of stones in your kidneys. I felt the weight of that gaze as it understood me not only wholly, from within and without and in all directions at once, but also as an animal stretched out in time, beginning with the egg fertilized in my mother's uterus and ending with my last breath on my deathbed, understanding in a glance not only the shape of my body but also my fate. After an eternity I was allowed to breathe again, and the doctor ratcheted back the plates where I had been pressed. I felt so free that I could almost fly, because breath is nothing more than the beating of our wings through the godly azure of life.

While I had to have my blood drawn at dawn, before I ate, and while I could visit the doctor whenever, anytime outside of blessed Sunday, I could only go to the dentist in the middle of the night. No one knew why the dentists here worked the night shift, alongside the doctors on call and the solitary pharmacist, who didn't open his door but only, his eyes puffy with sleep, pushed your medicines toward you through a little opening. My trip to the torture chamber always began at Dinamo stadium, one tram stop from our block. During my whole childhood, the stadium was the most difficult place to enter and our most coveted place to play. I had never been to a soccer game; a few years later would I accompany my father, to lose myself with him in the sea of men shouting in chorus, to watch with fear and fascination their red, manic, bestial faces, to hear their obscene words never uttered at home, and to walk back in a crowd, relieved that I had escaped with my life from this inexplicable assembly of warriors. Many of the kids from my block would climb the stadium fence and wander for hours among the tennis courts, through the gyms, under old trees, gathering chestnuts with their spiny covering, cracked and dry and stuck to the shiny chestnut; we would chatter and brag, our hearts moved by the loneliness of the huge athletic complex. Our adventure would usually end poorly; a porter would sneak up from behind, grab us by the ears, and lead us, like rabbits, to the nearest gate, where he would give us a kick in the pants and throw us out. Still, every week, we would go back to see the athletes training, the tennis balls flying soft and heavy through the air, the goalie throwing himself after the ball on the soccer field, and more than everything else, the cyclists spinning down the long lanes on their bicycles as light and fragile as paperclips.

I never rode a bike, none of my friends from the back of the block had—or ever dreamed of having—something so expensive and precious. Balancing on the two wheels with glittering spokes seemed to me like a kind of levitation, an impossible trick for an ordinary person. What I really wanted, when I played in the Circus Park, jumping from one bench to another, was not to have my own bike but just for a rich kid to move to our block, a kid with a bike. Maybe he would let us ride it once in a while . . . What if I had climbed on the saddle and pedaled down the alley? How could I have kept myself in the air on the thin bars of metal?

One morning I left the house for the stadium, because the evening before, as my parents and I passed that empty, distant place on the way to see a movie at the Volga, I had read on a poster that there would be tryouts the following day for various sports, for children ages seven and up. Maybe one of the sports would be cycling. Even if I didn't pass the test, at least I would get to ride a bike, pedal a few meters, it would be a dream . . . My mother didn't say one way or the other, she just put my best clothes on me the next day, the ones I wore into town or to visit my aunt. All gussied up, my hair tamed with a little walnut oil, I went to the stadium entrance, where, to my joy, there were dozens of kids, all boys, older and younger than me, including a crowd of Gypsies my mother had told me to stay away from because they stole and had lice. I was the only one dressed up, the others were in play clothes, stained T-shirts and torn pants, with cheap tennis shoes on their feet. I waited among them, awkwardly, for an hour, thinking of nothing but the moment when I would get on the saddle, start pedaling, and, miraculously, I would stay up on the bike, gliding along as if by magic. I had never wanted anything so much. I imagined it would be yellow and black, like the wasps that I drowned in the honey jar in the kitchen while my mother fried potatoes in the burning skillet. With a generator on the back, with a light and a bell. The generator had to be there, because it added to the miracle of floating on the bicycle a second miracle: transforming movement into light, in a way I did not understand, but which filled me with joy. Who said there were no miracles on Earth?

Finally, someone came to open the gate and we all entered the complex. We kicked our feet through mounds of rotting leaves; it was autumn and cold, and it looked like rain. The unshaven man led us from the entrance to one of the training fields and threw us a ball. I was on a soccer field for the first time in my life. I didn't know the rules, I had no idea what to do. We divided ourselves into two teams and began to play, crowding without a purpose, running and clustering around the dirty, wet leather ball; the field was nothing but mud, thick mud up to your ankles, that swallowed my good shoes completely. I ran around, giddy, with the other kids, for more than an hour, during which time I never touched the ball. The others always got there first, I was always shoved away and I slipped in the mud, until it was everywhere—on my hair, my face, my clothes. The dirty water squished in my shoes. I ran and I cried, it started to rain, but I kept hoping that after this miserable game the tryouts would start and I would get to ride that wonderful bike. I came home mud-stained and crushed, with bruised legs and a torn pocket, because after the game the unshaven guy had picked three kids and sent everyone else home—there hadn't been anything else. I sat in the hot bathwater and cried for my bike, which I had dreamed of all morning and so clearly that it seemed real.

I had to wait until the next summer to get on a bike: one day on vacation when I was impossibly happy, yet it remains in my memory as one of the saddest days I have ever experienced. My mother and I had taken the ferry to the other shore and now we were walking through Herăstrău Park, hand in hand, down the endless paths among ornamental shrubs, looking at the reflection of Casa Scânteii in the lake. For me the press building was the most majestic in the world. The open areas had shiny-headed peacocks, flowing in waves of color with every movement, suddenly unfurling their tails of shining eyes, the enormous semicircle of metallic colors spread to either side of their bodies. Behind the apartment block, where we hung out in the long days of summer, we never saw the sky, but here, in Herăstrău, there was a fantastic azure dome under which we walked, two minuscule mites in an unthinkable and incomprehensible world. We walked toward the Ferris wheel that we saw on the horizon, turning slowly alongside the wild castle of Casa Scânteii. Along the way, we passed booths selling sweets and drinks, cotton candy vendors constantly twisting their sticks in the nickeled tubs, stands where you shot at moving figures . . . In the middle of an empty sandy lot, in the middle of nowhere, I suddenly saw a bicycle. It was a vision, sudden and dazzling, and my heart stopped. The bike was standing, held by a bar attached to a central pole. Beside it, a sign said that for a few lei, anyone could ride it. I ran over, pulling my mother along behind me. The attendant, who wore the shabbiest of purple uniforms and worked the merry-go-round with its chipped and scratched horses, took our money and, finally, I could get on the saddle. The bar was a few meters long and allowed the bike to move in a circle around the pole like a tethered horse. It was wonderful, I couldn't fall over, and I was pedaling, finally, like in my dreams! "Twenty times," the attendant said, and so I went around counting up to twenty, and then I wanted to go again, and we paid for another twenty times, but the third time the man's cirrhotic face said to my mother, "He can go as long as he likes, no one else is going to come at this time of the day." So I rotated around endlessly, beneath the skies slowly turning pink, one rotation after another, and another, and another, until it was dark; I protested whenever my mother came to stop me, pushing her away with my foot, galloping farther along the narrow circle where I was levitating in joy, one meter above the earth, feeling (in an irony of fate we all know too well!) freer than ever . . .

At the end of many hours, my mother had to pull me from the bicycle, since it was dark and we were alone in the emptiness of the silent Herăstrău.

The peacocks had gone up into the trees and, from time to time, they cried out in rending voices. Today I have often seen myself, as I drift off to sleep, the way I was in the depths of that evening: a kid revolving endlessly on a heavy, ordinary bike, in the sinister emptiness of the large park. What's more: I have never had a bike of my own, not as a child, not later, not today.

I often began my journey in Dinamo stadium, in the middle of the large soccer field surrounded by curving rows of empty benches. Across the star-filled dome overhead, the installation of night spread its spider legs. I was alone in the giant valley of the stadium, and the entire sky collapsed over me. I walked over the darkened lawn like a minuscule tick under the wing of a dead crow, I went toward the screen where in the summer they showed movies, and then I began to climb the steps between the numbered benches. I got to the top, to the lip of the stadium, then under the same sky dotted with stars, I left through one of the entry tunnels, through the piles of dead leaves. I came to the foot of one of the four light posts, and I looked up toward the end of the enormous skeleton, where the unilluminated spotlights hung in the night like heavy clusters of fruit. I walked a long way, until I was out of the athletic complex, and I continued down Ştefan cel Mare in the dark of the night. Once every great while, luminous, empty trolleybuses passed down the cross streets. I often took one through the spectral city, completely unknown to me, with its illuminated buildings as translucent as sugar cubes, with palaces full of statues and decorations, with artesian fountains in deserted pieţas. You wouldn't see even a single person, as you dozed in your seat in the empty bus. Only facades, shop windows, billboards, dark streets, unknown parks. I got off at the end, long after we had left the city, in a vacant lot. Strange industrial constructions glowed in the distance.

I walked down the boulevard and saw no cars. I passed the newsstand where, when I was a child, I would buy every issue from the series *Science-Fantasy Stories* and *The Adventure Club*, I passed the grocery, the fruit and vegetable store, the bread distribution point across the road, and the B. P. Hasdeu Library, where I got my books. The road was still narrow—only years later, when I was in high school, would they expand it—and along it came rows of lumberyards, scrapyards, and repair centers for stockings, with an ugly fat woman dressed in red fussing over a hose behind a minuscule window. I knew every one of the square paving stones, every building, every bar and store on the street that was now taking me to the dentist; it was like a long vein through my body that brought blood toward my lungs. In the middle of the street, the streetlights had a horizontal bar where the tram power lines were attached, forming a long line of crosses that arched over the street, and on every cross you could clearly see a man in his death throes, naked except for a cloth around his hips, bleeding in the pallid neon lights. I knew them, each man; I had often spoken with them. The children from behind the block, Vova, Lumpă, Mimi, Mațaganul, Mona, Lucian, Mentardy, Iolanda, and all the others, would often gather at the feet of one of the men, looking in fear at the terrible wound made by the spike through his feet, and ask him everything under the sun. With his head hanging on his chest and regarding us with puffy eyes running with tears, the martyr spoke to us of his distant homeland and about the awful guilt for which he was being punished. When a tram passed, the passengers crowded inside looked at him indifferently, as though at a statue of painted wood that dripped blood.

I passed the militia headquarters, attached to which was my parents' block, with its eight stairways and entryways buttressed by two thick concrete columns, with the furniture store and television repair center; I passed the Circus, the block with Restaurant Hora, and I passed the endless fence of Colentina Hospital. I entered the empty grounds of the hospital and wandered a while among its various wings in the oddest shapes and colors: buildings in the shapes of blimps, battleships, pillboxes, bunkers, warehouses, hangars, mosques, bordellos, factories, anything you could or could not imagine. I passed the clinic on Str. Doctor Grozovici, where the nurse with no nose was assailed by clients with bouquets of flowers, I went in front of the Melodia cinema, the most modern one in the area, I crossed Str. Lizeanu, and I was there. At night, the clinic looked like an enormous sludge of pitch blocking the sky's glittering dust of stars.

The interior was empty. I climbed the monumental staircase that contrasted so oddly with the disrepair of the Nile-green walls and the cheap tiles. I continued until I reached the waiting room in the attic, just under the roof. That was where the dentists worked. From time to time, the entire clinic would rattle when a tram passed down the street, past Resurrection Cemetery.

At the top, huffing from the endless stairs, I found myself suddenly in a hallway sunken in shadow. The hall was vast, and along its walls were the same benches covered in brown melamine you found in every public building at that time. There were always three or four patients sitting there, unmoving, staring resignedly ahead. All the light in the windowless hall came from the four doors with painted transoms: the dentists' offices. Through the old and peeling yellow paint, a cloudy glow, impossibly sad, mixed indiscriminately with the mysterious sounds that resounded through the doors: isolated clinks, the whir of a drill, a cough, a jet of water into a glass.

I sat on the bench for most of the night, as still as all the others in the room, staring emptily ahead of me and jumping whenever one of the four doors opened. The light was too weak to read by. There was nothing to do but collapse inside yourself and try to ward off any thought of what was to come. In fact, you were waiting for some frightening and providential event, for an earthquake to destroy the building, for your heart to stop, or for the end of the world to come—anything just so long as you wouldn't have to go in there. In the end, though, the door opened for you, as well: first the doorway yielded a patient with crazed eyes, a bloody wad of gauze between his teeth, and then after him, as though shoving away the patient who dashed quickly down the stairs, the doctor, with hairy hands and his name crudely sewn on his shirt pocket in yellow thread. "Next," he said, looking not at those on the bench, but straight ahead, like he was blind. I was next.

Why were there were four doors, when they all led to the same office, where, like four elephants sat next to each other in a circus ring, four massive, unforgiving dental chairs awaited—each one made of a heavy metal—matte white, complicated constructions with fearful tools? Why did each one need its own giant panel of multiple light bulbs looming overhead? The cables, hoses, and braids of steel that exited dozens of orifices in the chairs' massive trunks looked like a tangle of snakes, an obscure charade, but many of them led to polished metal ends hanging above you, attached to drills, chisels, pliers, all apparently from the same soft metal, yellowed with use. On the tray in front of the patient, there were odd syringes with crooked pistons and rings for the finger, with needles pointing not straight but sideways, there were dental pliers, spatulas, and mirrors with their handles made from the same nickeled metal.

In the chairs you'd always see an old woman, a child, a bald man, their heads tilted back against the round rests, their eyes clenched shut, and their red mouths open wide as though screaming; inside were tooth stumps, damp from rigid tongues, with black bits like mold, or crude dentures the color of vomit hooked onto other teeth with wire. The room had a sinister smell, the dentist smell that clings to your clothes for weeks, more persistent and horrible than the stink of cheap tobacco after a night at the bar. The doctors leaned over the mouths and those tight eyelids, working like insects feeding their larvae. The rest of the office sank into darkness, because the light from the panels was insoluble, it fell through the air like a jet of frozen water, only reaching the martyred faces with bloody mouths.

I took my seat, with death in my heart, in the free chair, which suddenly bound my wrist with a rubber cuff. My throat was held by a steel band, so tightly I couldn't lift my head from the headrest. The light blinded me, and was just as bright when I closed my eyes. I was an innocent, velvet butterfly with feathered antennae and plush white wings, immaculate, bound inside the dense horror of a spider's web. I was the eternal victim, powerless, dissolved in his own fear, awaiting the intolerable. However still I kept myself, however I controlled my breath, the beast would find me in the end, with its unerring senses. And the doctor finally emerged from his dark corner and I found myself suddenly under his power, under his expressionless eyes, in his hairy arms that had already begun to manipulate my body, looking for its points of vulnerability.

The universe turned rock-solid and extended endlessly in all directions. In all the dense, dull-colored night of being, there was only one irregularity, one small imperfection: the minuscule cell, without doors or windows, only big enough for the victim and the executioner. There could be no escape, the stone of night was infinite, it was you and him, you paralyzed on your torture chair, he all-powerful, dominant, without pity and without humanity, put in motion by the neurotransmitters of his frozen fury. In the end you became just one, clenched together like a man and woman in coupling, you were an assemblage, a complicity of screams and horror. The torture would never pause and never end, because, as I always realized as soon as the cold clamps of the dental chair trapped my arms, legs, and throat, leaving my body helpless, I was in hell, in that version made for me and me alone, my own personal devil here in this world only to pull out my teeth, which would grow back a billion times over, only to be pulled out again and again, the thread of living nerve hanging from a porcelain crown. A frozen sweat covered me as the doctor prepared the vials and needles and tools, clinking on the tray. I was then forced to unclench my jaw, to open the purple entrance of my crucified body. From this point on, the doctor had access not only to my pitiful teeth, already packed with crude lead fillings, the fossils of a childhood spent in terror, but also my larynx, my vocal cords, my trachea, and my lungs, my heart, and my intestines. From this point on, he could insert his hand and arm, up to the elbow, into my body, he could grab hold of its depths and turn me inside out, like a glove, leaving my organs hanging in their sacs of bloody fat, my heart, kidneys, liver, the networks of my nerves and veins.

Next came, inevitably, the pain. He worked on my teeth and gums without anesthetic, directly on the nerves exposed once he drilled through the protective enamel. After the first time they gave me shots in my gums, I would have preferred not to be anesthetized, so awful was the sensation of venom diffusing into my flesh from the thick needle, like for horses, that was used back then, over and over for dozens of patients, the same way they vaccinated the entire school with a single needle. It's no wonder, I often think, that I am packed to the gills with anomalies, hallucinations, and insanity—the only real wonder is my survival.

The pain came with the first tap of the little spatula against the diseased tooth, and then it grew, as though the room were slowly filling with water. In the end, I was breathing pain. I was no longer a human being, I no longer thought or felt. I only experienced the anticipation of pain, then the intensity of billions of volts of pure pain, the shock that hit my teeth, making me recoil against the headrest, until its round cushions almost entered my brain. I pushed myself so hard against the dental chair that later they had to peel me off its back. My mouth filled with saliva and blood, sucked up endlessly by a hooked tube that would catch on the veins under my tongue. And my teeth, the shells secreted by my gums like a snail secretes his shell, like coral builds its reefs, like a child's bones knit together in its mother's womb, they were open caskets of white tile presenting the filaments of nerves, the braids of pain. My nerves were deadened with arsenic, they were cut with routers attached to the canopy of lights over the dental chair, I screamed for hours on end looking up at the dentist with my eyes dilated in fear, he bent over me, a few centimeters away, enlarged as though under a magnifying glass, red-faced with effort. It would not end, this would continue forever. The drill and turbine whirred ceaselessly, sculpting my teeth into unreal shapes, but above all this noise, even above my screams, I could hear, clearly, under my feet, from the metal, white-yellow trunk of the dental chair, a quiet, constant gurgling, like the mechanical sucking of a newborn on the breast, the pleasant absorption of a vital substance. That had to be what a leech feels, in its voracious unconsciousness, the waves of warm blood inundating its stomach, or the same ecstasy that aphids must feel on plants, as they receive through their long proboscides the thick, sweet sap of the flowers they cling to with their miniature claws. Whenever I escaped the grip of the dental chair, reeling, my face wet with tears, I immediately noticed that where the four thrones of pain were held by enormous bolts, the floor was not flat as it should have been, but the tiles bulged with long, swollen branches, like roots rippling the ground around old trees. They all began from the massive metal trunk, and they all throbbed softly. But maybe it was a hallucination caused by clenching my eyes shut for so long, maybe my eyeballs, red with suffering, could only see a deformed space . . .

I left with my mouth full of dressings soaked in a horrible-tasting substance. I went down the monumental staircase and left the desolate mausoleum. The dawn blued the cold streets around Bucur Obor piața. The first trams rolled by, just emerging from the depot, empty, clattering like beasts knocking together. Street cleaners stood beside the dumpsters, taking drags on their cigarettes and rubbing their hands together in the cold. I walked through the fog, among the blocks, without knowing who I was or where I lived, but I still managed to find Ştefan cel Mare in the end. I came home insane with suffering throughout my brain, because the anesthetic had begun to wear off. Then I waited, in front of my room's panoramic window, contemplating the perfectly spherical sun made of molten metal that appeared between the blocks, for the time to come for me to leave for school.

20

"The master of dreams, the great Issachar, sat in front of the mirror, his spine against its surface, his head hanging far back, sunk deep into the mirror. Then Hermana appeared, master of the twilight, and she melted into Issachar's chest, until she completely disappeared." I have often wondered about the source of my aversion to the novel, why I would have looked down on myself if I had written novels, "books about," endless stories, why it is I hate Scheherazade and all her children who labor to produce narrations so we can learn morals or wile our lazy hours. Why I never wanted to write from pleasure or for pleasure. Why I don't want to draw monumental gates, or even little cat doors, on the walls of literature. Why I define myself by my illnesses and insanities, not through my books. Why I am so resentful that I was kicked out of literature. This fragment from Kafka answers all. You will not find sentences like this one in any book, because not even Kafka dared to transform them into the tiny ear bones of any narrative. They were left in the obscure pages of his journal, destined for the flames, pages that did not delectate and did not instruct, pages that did not exist but were more meaningful than all those that have ever existed. You don't need a thousand pages for a psychodrama, just five lines about Issachar and Hermana. No novel ever gave us a path; all of them, absolutely all of them sink back into the useless void of literature. The world is full of the millions of novels that elide the only sense that writing ever had: to understand yourself to the very end, up to the only chamber in the mind's labyrinth you are not permitted to enter. The only texts that should ever be read are the unartistic and unliterary ones, bitter and incomprehensible books that their authors were crazy to write, but which flowed from their dementia, sadness, and despair like springs of holy water. Issachar. Hermana. Le Horla. Malte. And hundreds of faceless voices whose every page is written with the only word that matters: me. Never him, never her, never you. Me, the section through time of the impossible fourth person.

If my poem, *The Fall*, had been well received by the Workshop of the Moon that distant November, today I would have maybe ten books with my name on the cover, novels and poems and essays and academic texts, I might be in textbooks and invited to book fairs in distant Nordic countries. I would have been swept up in celebrity. I would have won the world in the only way possible: through the loss, step by step, of my own soul. Weaving my sails from narrative cobweb, knitting my poems from gilding and tinfoil, acting out dramas that never happened; I would have forgotten that my skin is my body's heaviest organ, heavier than the brain or liver, and that the only, only respectable place to write is on your own skin, that no books are possible except those bound in your skin, with living pages full of nerves, full of Golgi corpuscles and hair roots and sweat glands and tunnels teeming with mites. I would have forgotten the raw material from which clear drops of suffering were wrung, like liquid gold flowing from a lumbar puncture, the material from which Maldoror was created. I would have forgotten that a book, in order to mean something, must appear at a certain perspective. I would have written immanent, aesthetically autonomous books, which the reader would have looked at the way a cat looks at a finger pointing to the ball of yarn on the floor. But a book should be a sign, should tell you to "go over there" or "stop" or "fly" or "disembowel yourself." A book should demand an answer. If it doesn't—if your gaze ends on its ingenious, inventive, tender, wise, joyful, and wonderful surface instead of pointing you in the direction this book *shows*—then you have read a literary work and you have missed, once again, the meaning of any human effort: to escape from this world. Novels hold you here, they keep you warm and cozy, they put glittering ribbons on the circus horse. But when, for God's sake, will you read a *real* book?

At the Last Judgment, one will come and say, "Lord, I wrote *War and Peace*." Another will say, "Lord, I wrote *The Magic Mountain*, where the world depends on the sacrifice of a child." Another will say, "Lord, I wrote over eighty novels and story collections." Another will say, "Lord, I received a large international prize." Another will say, "I wrote *Finnegans Wake*, and only for You, since no one else can read it." And another: "Lord, look at *One Hundred Years of Solitude*. A better book was never written." They will come in droves, each holding his heaps of books, with sales figures and quotes from critics and press clippings, like the church founders depicted in the naos with miniature edifices in their hands. They will all be outlined in rainbows and energy, all their faces will shine like the sun. And the Lord will say to them, "Yes, of course, I read all of them, even before they were written. You gave people hours of enjoyment, you led them to meditation and reverie. You painted the most amazing *trompe l'oeil*, the most baroque, most ornamented, most massive portals on the smooth, yellow bone of the interior of the forehead. But which of these portals ever actually opened? Which of these allowed the eyelid of the forehead to lift from the brain's eye? Which of these allowed the brain to actually see?" Over to one side, humble in their rags, will be: Kafka and Judge Schreber, Isidore Ducasse and Swift and Sabato, and Darger and Rezzori, along with another thousand anonymous writers, the authors of torn, burnt, frozen diaries, buried in the rush of time . . . They will have empty hands, but letters scribbled across their palms: "The master of dreams, the great Issachar . . ." After them will come millions of writers who only wrote with tears, with blood, with Substance P, with urine and adrenaline and dopamine and epinephrine, directly onto their organs with ulcers of fear, on their skin, excoriated with ecstasy. Each of them will carry their own skin, covered with writing, from which the Lord, gathering them together between the cover of birth and the cover of death, will create the great book of human suffering.

I would like this text to be that kind of a page, one of the billions of human skins covered by infected, suppurating letters, bound in the book of the horror of living. Anonymous like all the others. Because my anomalies, however unusual they are, do not overshadow the tragic anomaly of the spirit dressed in flesh. And the one thing I want you to read on my skin, you, who will never read it, is a single cry, repeated page after page: "Leave! Run away! Remember you are not from here!" But I am not writing for someone to read me, I am writing to try to understand what is happening to me, what labyrinth I am in, whose test I am subject to, and how I can answer to get out whole. Writing about my past and my anomalies and my translucid life, which reveals a motionless architecture, I try to make out the rules of this game, to distinguish the signs, to put them together and to figure out where they are pointing, so I can go in that direction. No book has any meaning if it is not a Gospel. A prisoner on death row could have his cell lined with bookshelves, all wonderful books, but what he actually needs is an escape plan. You can't escape if you don't believe you can escape from a cell with infinitely thick walls, without doors and without windows. The convict in the cartoon can escape by moving perpendicular to the page of the book, toward me, who is reading it in another dimension.

I have read thousands of books but never found one that was a landscape as opposed to a map. Every page of theirs is flat, but life itself is not. Why would I, a three-dimensional creature, take as a guide the two dimensions of an ordinary text? Where will I find the cubical page where reality is modeled? Where is the hypercubic book whose covers gather the hundreds of cubes of its pages? Only then, through the tunnel of cubes, can we escape from the suffocating cell, or at least breathe the air of another world. If I could breathe the clouds and streets and trams, the trees and women, like the pure air of a much denser world . . .

Today, of course, is Sunday; I am not teaching. Last night I read Kafka until one in the morning, stopping at the fragment with Issachar and Hermana. I couldn't go any farther. I don't think a truer thing has ever been written in the world. Master of dreams, master of twilight. Issachar losing himself in the mirror, Hermana melting into Issachar's chest like it was another mirror, infesting his flesh and blood with melancholy. I placed the book facedown on the bed and walked to the mirror. I stared at the mirror for the rest of night. From the start, I realized I should be naked, like Issachar, like Hermana. I quickly removed my clothes and was shocked to see that in the mirror, I was a woman. I had golden hair that lit up the entire bedroom, I had slightly saggy, pear-shaped breasts. In the room I was Issachar, in the mirror I was Hermana, my sister hidden by the all-too-powerful light of reality. "That's why," I said to myself, looking into the eyes of the woman with my features, wrapped in the spiderweb of her hair, "that's why the master of dreams sank his head so deeply into the mirror: there he could see Hermana, who had melted into his chest." Because Hermana is always on the other side of the mirror, she *is*, in fact, the other side, the parallel world in which Issachar is a woman.

I pressed my hands to hers, my chest to her breasts, my lips to her lips. And then she melted into my chest, where I feel her even now, like an overwhelming emotion.

I don't believe in books—I believe in pages, in phrases, in lines. There are some, in some books, like in the coded text a general receives on the battlefield: only some of the words mean anything, surrounded by meaningless blather. The general places his cardboard stencil over the letter and reads only the words that appear in the cutout spaces. That's how we should read the three-dimensional text of existence. But who gives you the stencil, who tells you the real words, who sifts the diamonds out of the slag? Which wire will you cut in the bomb in front of you, ticking as though it were your own heart, the red one or the blue one? When everything is urgent, when there is no time, when you are under pressure, you make mistakes, even if you have the stencil. When you don't have it, when you rely on the intuition of the blind, on the vigilance of the deaf, everything becomes unimaginably complicated, hopeless, and absurd. I will die before I unravel the enigma, I tell myself every day of my life. I have filled the drawer of my nightstand with things I thought might help reveal a stencil: my baby teeth, the thread from my navel, my diary pages, fragments from my readings hand-copied onto scraps of paper: "Master of dreams, the great Issachar . . ." In another drawer, the drawer of my mind, I have ancient memories, hallucinations, and imaginations, also chosen by who knows what stencil, whose rationale I cannot understand. How will I put them all back together? What do they want, what are they supposed to say? Are they pieces from a puzzle? Are they pieces from the same puzzle, or from dozens of games with no connection to each other? What do they want me to find? What do they want me to say? I don't know, I only know that my instinctual searching pushes toward something, tells me something, shows me something, the way you scratch where you itch and you look for food if you are hungry. Nothing else matters.

You can think of the world as an enigma, as a labyrinth, as a question that imperiously demands an answer. Or like a puzzle box full of mixed-up pieces. You are forever damned if you lived happily, if you were a billionaire, a great actor or great scholar or great writer, if you won prizes and received extended standing ovations in gilded theater halls. You are saved if you are a beggar at one end of a bridge who solved the enigma, gave the answer, found the exit. You shook the puzzle pieces in your hands, you let them fall, faceup or facedown, into the box. If they were just squares with fragments of images on them, you would never know they were parts of a puzzle. But their shapes, the indentations and excrescences on their sides that permit their combination, show they are part of a system, that they were cut apart and scattered intentionally, in order for a mind and fingers to put them back together. It is not a collection of absurdly framed photos, as the world so often seems. This piece connects to the next, nothing happens by chance, everything has to be remade through reverse engineering. But can I fit the fragment with Issachar and Hermana to one of my baby teeth? They both have invaginations and protrusions along their edges, they are obviously pieces of a puzzle. But are they from the same puzzle, part of the same image? Be careful here, be careful: in this box there may be pieces from more than one. You can see from the pictures on the back. Some of the pieces have green backs with white spades, others are orange with blue dots. They first have to be sorted into piles according to their backs. Each pile is another world, another image, and incompatible with the others. Only now can you choose your pieces, your world, your books, your mind, or your fate. Only now can you look at the chopped-up images on the shiny side of the cardboard. Only now can the game and story begin. Where does each piece go? Will you ever be able to complete the entire picture? And what will it show? What frightening face, what disturbing scene? You are broken into pieces and scattered across an enormous, empty world. How will you put yourself back together? Where does each of your organs go, each plant, and each sun of your world? How does your moon match your liver, your dream from last night match your memory of your first days at Voila?

From time to time, one of the puzzle pieces is completely black. This is inevitable. You just have to pray it won't be in your brain or on your retina. In fact, I have written this entire, useless fragment to cover a black piece. There was something else that happened at the Mașina de Pâine Clinic. An event that I have not yet decided to tell (myself). *I know* what it was, at least in part, I know in fact what *I think* it was. But what terrifies me is what it *possibly* was; I cannot imagine or describe it yet. I don't want to mystify anything: I remember everything, although it could be a false memory, but I cannot write about it here or now. I have never promised to be completely truthful. No one ever has. I've found other black pieces in my mind. I have often wondered whether the game, test, life, doesn't come down in the end to this, the illumination of these pieces at the end of all our searching. I don't dare approach them, not yet. They are inoperable tumors hidden in the depths of the mind. I may be writing to illuminate them, or to be swallowed up by them. Maybe in one hundred, maybe in five hundred pages, the way you'd say maybe in ten years or fifty years, in the unknown and unforeseeable future of this book that is writing itself, and that doesn't resemble anything so much as a life that lives by itself, with its unsoundable future, maybe then I will find within me the strength and courage to clear these dark pieces up or to throw everything down the toilet like those kidney stones removed long ago that I got tired of keeping in a jar.

21

Because I had a visitor last night, for the first time since I began this notebook (the second notebook, in fact, of my writings), I thought it might be time to transcribe, as I have wanted to do from the start, the diary fragments that relate to my nocturnal or phantasmatic or hallucinatory life—it is more real, however, than reality—fragments which I chose a few good months ago. It's just that the presence last night shook me deeply and left me somnolent, distracted, and frightened at the same time, because being chosen is never an easy fate on this earth. I had been sleeping for at least two hours, I had had some of my normal dreams, about trains and empty stations where I lose my luggage and wait forever, about silent bedrooms in orphanages, when suddenly I woke up and, as I opened my eyes, I saw him. As usual, he sat on the edge of my bed, staring at me. He was a visitor—like a relative who comes to the hospital when you're sick and bursts into the room, greets the other ill people in bed in their pajamas and robes, and drops a bag on the nightstand, with some yogurt, juice, and soup in cellophane-topped jars. Then he sits on the edge of your bed and stares at you. You chat for half an hour, and then, as though a bell has gone off, he gets up and leaves as though he had never been there, leaving you to gaze into the eyes of a paralyzed patient across the way. This time it was a young man with a heavy, thick jaw, slightly dilated eyes, and ears that stuck out from his head. He looked at me intensely, like all the others did, the children and women and adults and the elderly, as though they wanted to remember me for forever. As usual, I broke out in a cold sweat. I could not move, not because I was paralyzed or lacking will, but because the thought of the smallest movement scared me more than the image of someone, in the depths of night in my bedroom, staring at me. I have never gotten used to these visits. Even now, as I write about them, I feel the same cold chills. There have been maybe twenty, maybe more, over the past few years. I could draw a picture of each one, down to the smallest details. And yet every time felt like it was the first.

The young man seemed, like all the others, somehow lit from within, since in spite of the darkness, all his features were as clear as if in daylight. The colors of his clothes—unusual garments, though at the moment I can't think how—were bright and unaltered by our strange nocturnal blindness that keeps us from noticing the colors of the stars; and retroactively, they provoke the same fascination I felt as a child for the foil wrappers around chocolate figurines, with their glittering colors and strange shapes; I would run my nail over the foil to make it perfectly smooth, flat, and thin as paper.

I stayed, therefore, as I was: on my stomach with my face turned to one side, the blanket only covering my legs, the complete silence ringing in my ears. I looked obliquely at the silent one sitting on the edge of my bed, who smiled barely perceptibly and never took his eyes off of mine. How long had he been there? Had he been staring for an hour or only a few minutes? He was not a ghost but a real, corporeal being, with thousands of details and, I would say, his own personality and psychology. Even though, like all the others, he didn't make the smallest movement, he was no frozen image, no photograph: he was clearly breathing, he was alive. And intolerably, in the most private and secure place I could imagine: my own bed in my own bedroom, in my house, with its doors well locked. I told myself many times, during the ravished mornings after a visitor, that it was only a hallucination, an image from a dream that stayed on my retina for a few seconds, but I have never been able to believe it. Not only because no dream is ever so detailed—like a camera lucida in which every strand of hair was clear in all the graceful geometry of its curves and every texture (of the skin, shirt, jewelry) is felt as though by unseen fingers—but also because they are all human beings who stand next to my bed and look at me. But more importantly because *I know*, beyond a doubt, because the mechanism of my mind that is responsible for the distinction between real and unreal gives, every time, a verdict with no right to appeal: he is true, he is here, in reality.

Without trying to touch me and without saying a word, the young man stayed next to me a good ten seconds longer, lit by his interior radiance, then he stopped being there. As usual, I stayed awake, unmoving, my eyes open, completely afraid, for a period of time I cannot measure, after which I fell back asleep and dreamed, returning to my tribulations in empty stations and restaurants, conversations with women as pale as insects, clambering over lichen-covered ruins.

I wasted my morning with a pointless walk through the cold and empty house, with a cup of coffee in my hand, unable to gather my thoughts. I saw snow falling outside, all the windows half-covered with lacy frost, I blew clouds onto their glass and watched the moisture crystallize into a Jugendstil hoariness; I walked down completely unheated corridors where the leaves of my plants were frozen to the glass and showed, through their transparent stalks, the sap undulating in their woody, vegetable ducts. I remembered, looking at their life without life, the day I mistakenly entered the biology laboratory.

As usual, I was looking for my classroom, on the upper story. I was walking down the Nile-green hallway, past classrooms with their doors closed. The period had begun some time ago, and there wasn't a soul in the hallway. I passed the bathrooms and rounded the corner toward the end of the hall, where, since there were no windows, everything was dark. I passed, in the semishadow, a group of children lined up to receive on their tongues a cube of sugar laced with a pink drop of vaccine, I greeted the nurse, who smiled at me with her brightly painted lips, and I came to the end where I thought I would find my students. There was no reason to remember where the rooms were, because they changed every day. I followed a kind of instinct, maybe I had learned to detect, subliminally, the smell of my students, since I usually found the room within a quarter hour of the period beginning. At the end of the dark corridor were three doors. I opened the first one and immediately stepped back: it was the physics lab where Gionea, motionless, with her arms crossed, reigned from the teacher's desk over thirty deaf-mutes, their eyes round in terror. Vis-à-vis was the dentist's office, now closed. I entered the third door, which proved, to my disappointment (since I would have to run down the corridors to catch at least the end of the Romanian period), to be another lab, the biology lab, filled with plants and aquaria. The teacher had not yet shown up, she was probably next door, where they kept the microscopes and frogs. The children were at their tables, and in front of each one was a large jar full of water. A gauze pad was tightly bound at the mouth of each jar with a rubber band. On each pad was a crinkled bean from which phylliform roots sprouted, extending and branching like spider legs, into the water in the jar, while a yellow, damp shoot raised its pale throat in between the two cotyledons. Each boy and girl had their hands pressed against the round jar, as though they were trying to warm the water inside. Their eyes were trained on the chalkboard, and all waited feverishly for the teacher, to show her the vegetable embryo, the way pregnant women wait in line in front of the obstetrics and gynecology office. The children were supposed to have grown the plant at home on their windowsill from the crusty seed, the jar's ever cloudier water was supposed to have filled with filaments, the stalks and sickly leaves should have spread, avid for light, across the window, until one day this whole commedia of a life doomed from the start would end: their mothers would flush the putrid water down the toilet, along with the parody of living life and the black, rotten gauze pad. As yet, however, the laboratory was flooded with light and the jars shone, projecting flashing moons onto the walls and the children's strange faces. And suddenly I saw, from the corner of my eye, the horror: at the back of the room, beside the door I had just opened, was the red-haired girl whose right eye was covered by a gauze patch. She also held a jar between her hands, she also stared intensely ahead with her remaining eye, but her plant was much larger, fleshier, and more elastic than the others, as it lay on the damp pad of white fabric, because not all of its filaments twisted into the water that gave no nutrition. A long, graceful, yellow stalk climbed toward the girl's face and penetrated the gauze, held by pink bandages over her eye, drawing a dark red liquid from the depths of her eye socket and transporting it through the transparent root to the embryo pulsating on its thin fabric bed. The water in the jar was tinted, darker and darker toward its lenticular bottom, by an evanescent blood diffused among the tangle of roots. At the very bottom, a layer of pure blood as thin as a fingernail had settled, unaltered, the triumph of the most vibrant colors permitted to our eyes. The vision lasted just a moment, because I slammed the door in fear and ran, the register under my arm, down the empty hallways. When

I was out of breath, I opened the first door and recognized my students, who were waiting for me, talking loudly and running about.

I left for school without eating, since I usually eat dinner at the mechanic's, which is cheap enough, and the food, while always the same, isn't so bad. The long break is twenty minutes but the teachers take at least a half hour—even though the shop is only a few meters from the schoolyard, it's just time enough to inhale a few marinated meatballs, soup with dumplings, or a rubbery, yellow schnitzel. A few children from the upper classes eat there every day, alongside the mechanics in their grimy overalls. Today I went with Gheară and Goia, and we sat at a plastic table to one side, overlooking a few cars on jacks in the incredibly dirty shop that lay in apocalyptic disorder: tire rims, tires, jacks, hoses, and batteries scattered everywhere, all equally greasy and so black you couldn't say what color they had originally been. The main worker, the shop boss, was an older man, well groomed, always in a suit and gold-rimmed glasses. He never touched anything, he seemed fresh out of the box. Around the neighborhood they said he was terribly rich, that he even loaned money at shameless rates of interest. When it came to the seventh- and eighth-grade girls, however, he was no different than any mechanic: his eyes ran all over them. It's true that the girls behaved completely differently at the mechanic's: three or four at a table, they talked loudly and laughed, they stretched and pushed out their breasts, then shot back a "you wish!" when the apprentice mechanics made comments. When they got up from the tables, holding their trays, they walked in their old and broken shoes as though they were stilettos, moving their hips with a verve incredible to us, the teachers, who knew the girls only as insipid blank faces sitting on a bench.

Ever since I had explored the old factory with him and had that hallucination in the water tower, where his body stretched out like a giant snake and twisted along the entire spiraling staircase in the heart of the tower, I never felt as comfortable around Goia. Of course, we saw each other in the lounge and crossed paths, registers under our arms, in the hallways, but neither one of us dared to look the other in the eyes, because then we would have understood that we both knew, that we were both afraid to begin a conversation, that if on the inside we had decided it was all a dream or a strange vision, all it would take was a look for us to give up on that childish consolation. We both knew everything had been real—everything is always real. I wouldn't have been able to bear eating with Goia today, so it was lucky that Gheară had appeared, tubby and jovial, with his comb-over. I like Gheară, as I have said, even if he takes part in the mandatory masquerade of *Montage*. He is a happy boy, living without a care, who had dreamed of being a comedian, telling jokes on a small stage in a packed bar. You don't even notice, through his constant giggling, how many indiscretions and gaffes come out of his mouth, but I suppose that's his charm, that's why his colleagues love him so. He imitates Borcescu, for example, so perfectly that everyone jumps up at the sound of the croaking they all know so well: "What's all this? What do we have here, pull your socks up! The bell rang five minutes ago, what are you still doing here, comrades?" "Come on, Nicu, you scared us to death," someone mumbles, then laughs along with everyone else, in relief. "So Nicu, tell us, what's your wife like in bed?" When I first heard one of the female teachers ask this question, I must have blushed, but then I learned it was just one of the usual lounge rituals; not a week went by without Gheară doing his best bit. The comedian wouldn't leave the teacher waiting for long: he threw himself onto his back on the long table in the middle of the lounge, on top of the open notebooks and registers, and he would start to writhe in pleasure, rubbing his imaginary breasts, his eyes rolled back into his head: "Uh! Ah! Mmmm! Faster, faster darling! Uh . . . aaah!" until, after a supreme spasm, he flopped onto the table with a moronic smile across his face. Then he jumped up and awaited his applause, but if it didn't come, Gheară wasn't angry. Everyone abused him. He was the school's go-to for everything. "Nicu, won't you go across the street and get me a soda?" "Nicu, won't you take my class for me this Saturday?" "Mr. Gheară, we need someone for guard duty next week, okay?" Nicu Gheară didn't know how to say no. With the same amiable smile, he took care of everyone's issues, he taught the extra choir and *Montage* classes, he showed the boys how to break down a rifle during drill practice, but the story he told us at the mechanic's today outdid them all. "You're not going to believe me," he said with his mouth full, "but I did it with Steluța." "With Mrs. Dudescu? Are you serious?" "For real, but don't tell anyone." A few months ago, Steluța, whom Gheară had flirted with for ages, called him one Sunday to come to her house and help move some furniture. "But where is Mr. Dudescu?" he asked, his heart full. "Eh, my husband's busy. Can you help me?" And Gheară went over. Her husband, much older and a little deaf, was in the living room at his desk, his eyes in a book. He was writing something in a notebook, also making note on scraps of paper . . . Nicu greeted him, but he seemed not to notice. "Leave him alone, didn't I tell you he was busy?" said the teacher, as she handed him the vacuum cleaner. "You mean you cleaned up with Steluța?" "Yes, yes, I did . . . And the next week the same, and the next, until last Sunday. Vacuuming, dusting, cleaning the windows . . . But it was worth it in the end, I know what I got . . . Last Sunday, my brothers, I did it with her. She's hot, let me tell you. A little on the big side, but it works . . ." "And her husband?" "Didn't even notice. He was at his desk, holding his papers, I was in the bedroom, holding Steluța." "He really didn't know anything was going on? What if he'd walked in on you?" Gheară laughed like he'd been tickled. "That guy, I went over and stuck my hand right in front of his face, it's like he's blind. While he's scribbling away, pro patria mori—he can't see, can't hear, he's on a different planet. I have no idea what he's doing, but he's in all the way. Like I was in Steluța, she was hot to trot . . ." "Bravo, Nicu," Goia said out of the side of his mouth. I had also heard that her husband was some kind of nut, but at least he didn't hit her, like her first husband.

I wouldn't have had the strength to write Gheară's story down, at this moment, in this diary, if it hadn't cheered me up a little after last night's terrible encounter. It's dark again and snowing furiously against the window of my room, illuminated by the dim streetlight across the way. Before I started this session, I reread the diary I started on September 17, 1973, at the age of seventeen. When I started to transcribe what I thought were the most significant fragments, I often hesitated: *everything* seemed worthy of copying, even if it would have made my text a thousand pages long. In the end I took a few passages that, as it seems to me now, say something, although I still don't know what; they push the story of my anomalies toward something.

The first note I am copying down is dated June 16, 1974. I had just turned eighteen, and I was living with my parents on Ştefan cel Mare. My room faced the street—it was a fairly large bedroom with an immense panoramic window in three sections, through which I could see Bucharest like an unending flood of houses mixed with the crowns of trees, blind walls, glinting windows, enigmatic buildings in silhouette, all beneath an overwhelming sky, higher and more curved than any I had ever seen. The daylight was teeming with multicolored clouds, which, through their flowing, abstruse architecture with pilasters and colonnades and basilicas and cenotaphs, created a second city above, just as labyrinthine as the one below but endlessly shifting and sliding along the crystal bell of the sky. At night, my window filled with stars. When I turned out the light to sleep, after I had spent the majority of the day lying in bed and reading, the sight of them petrified me. I don't know if my siderophobia (or whatever the name is for the terror I felt at the sight of a star-filled sky) has a place in the picturesque, rebarbative jungle of fears with strange, long, and sinuous Greek names, but ever since I was a child, I have felt a dizzying horror of being under the stars. When I was just a few years old, my mother and I were going to visit her sister in a faraway part of the city that we crossed by tram through the tunnels of yellow, cracked plaster facades of the streets. On the facades, between the dirty windows, were plaster statues, women with naked breasts and scornful smiles, pink angels with their noses broken off, granite gorgons with heads full of snakes, atlantes whose taut muscles held the entryway arches and balcony pillars. I stared wide-eyed at this decrepit populace, covered in lichen like eczema on the peeling paint of their skin, with an arm busted down to a rusty stump . . . I remember my sense of discomfort on the entire trip, my need to clasp my mother's floral dress, to see her face, to assure myself that she would not disappear and leave me in that world of fear and stillness. But my diffuse fear during the day was nothing in comparison to what awaited me at night, when we returned after I had been playing in my aunt's house all evening, peering through every drawer and book in the bookcases and endlessly pedaling her sewing machine, whose clinking, mechanical cadences fascinated me. As we exited her brick house, the last one in the city before the fields began, the stars overwhelmed us. I always tried not to look at them, I would keep my eyes on my aunt's silhouette, her squirrel-like shape waving at us from the pink light of the door frame. The unplastered brick walls had absorbed all the rays of the sun and left a total darkness. Along the street—no bulb was on. Above—worlds of stars, legions of stars, peoples of stars with their idols, gods, and stories, starry maps of all the unreachable places . . .

I walked hand in hand with my mother under the oriental rug of stars, spread to the limits of sight and beyond. A gigantic hand filtered a luminous flour through its fingers, scattering it in Mandelbrotian patterns over the pitch-black sky. As I breathed in the cold night air, inhaling the smells of roses and petunias, I felt like I pulled the stellar dust into my lungs. Here and there, out of the flour rose pieces of quartz, sugar cubes, finely ground splinters that gleamed with all their might. The eye would not stop itself from tracing the barely visible lines between them, such that the sidereal machinery quickly formed axles with cams, gears, levers, tiny silver springs, under the mute ticking that followed our movement toward the tram stop. I held my mother's hand tighter and tighter, but I felt that she was afraid as well, not of dogs or muggers, but of the starry silence, the hypnotic stillness of the stars above us. If billions of spiders with their legs spread, some barely visible, others as big as your fist, had descended above us, each hanging from its shiny thread, we would not have been as scared. Eventually, we hurried more and more, until we were running with all our might, yelling under the torrential downpour of the stars. At the empty tram stop we embraced, trembling, me with my head pressed to her stomach, feeling (I can still feel it!) the rough texture of her velveteen dress. An hour passed before we saw the tram's dim headlight in the distance, arriving with a terrible sound, rocking along the rails. "Lord, we thank you," my mother said as always, and we gratefully climbed the steps into the polished wooden interior, as reassuring as our own home. I always had the feeling that if we had arrived at the stop even a minute later, the stars would have simply absorbed us into their empire, an empire capable of freezing the blood in our veins.

The greatest number of my most disquieting memories happened there, in the room that was never completely dark, because the streetlights, each cross-shaped pole with its crucified Christ, cast luminous stripes of various nuances and textures across the ceiling, and the trams and cars that passed down the narrow street at night also drew green fans over the walls and ceiling. Today, I would be too frightened to sleep either there or in the back room, toward the flour mill; throughout my adolescence, I would dream there of bombers and strange ships floating in front of my window.

Here is the note from June 16:

So I won't forget.

Last night I woke at three thirty, when I thought I heard my parents. I didn't even open my eyes. I fell asleep again. I don't know what I dreamed, but afterward, while I was still asleep, something happened that has made me crazy.

I don't know if it was suddenly or slowly, but my ears began to ring so intensely that I "saw" somehow, inside—at the limits of sight, sound, and touch—my cranium overcome by fantastical trepidations, painful, burning, unbearable chills, all yoked together by a yellow, fiery light and paroxysmal spasming. I had two fits, one after another, during which I remained completely aware, as though I were awake. I know in the second one there was something mystical; or it was provoked by something mystical and terrifying, beyond words and the senses. I dreamed that I was awake, that I could make no movement, that I tried to scream and could only whisper. At the time, I did not doubt that I was awake. I was able to scream, twice, "Help!" Then I saw my mother in the front room, all gray and blue. I only remember telling her I might have meningitis.

Then I actually woke up, more shocked than scared, sad but less agitated than I'd expect. I lay there for a bit with my eyes open, thinking that I definitely needed a psychiatrist. I had an oddly clear sense of the time that had passed from the first time I woke until the dream I had. Then I went to the bathroom, I don't know why, and I looked in the mirror. I looked strange, scornful, a little hungover. My hair and my skin, in a way, trembled. I recalled the dream and kept thinking about it. I cut my fingernails, all except for the fourth one on the right, which I left uncut, I don't know why. I know that I opened, semiconsciously, the metal top to a bottle of rubbing alcohol and I threw it into the water in the sink. My ears rang the entire time. Always that ravenous fear, controlled by itself, not by me.

I went back toward my room, but I stopped in the living room, where I saw something that, curiously, I knew beforehand: my parents gone, the beds unmade, and the gray hour of four thirty floating in the room. A pink stripe on the wall made me look at the window, where the liquid, purple sun had risen.

Still in a trance, I climbed into my bed but I didn't dare fall asleep. I read, and that's how my parents found me when they returned. My mother gave me a glass of milk and told me to go back to bed. I slept until eleven thirty, and I had other dreams.

Headaches, ringing ears, all day. Now at night, I can barely get up the courage to go to bed.

I read this text several times over, the only one in my first notebook, lost among reading notes—Rousseau's *Confessions,* Thomas Mann's *Doctor Faustus,* Anatole France's *Thaïs*—poems, tribulations in love, prose sketches about angels and monsters, and I attempt to remember the thin, lunatic adolescent I was then. I can imagine how disturbed I must have been by my experience that June night, the first of its kind, to be followed by so many other strange nights. If I didn't understand anything of what was happening to me, if my nights as an odd, lonely boy became more painful over time, when my dreams no longer at all resembled what I thought dreams were, if they became more visions or prophecies, I began to acquire a kind of scientific interest in what was happening to me, and to gather facts and witnesses that seemed to be leading somewhere. Little by little, I began to feel a kind of strange and masochistic pride, to feel I had been chosen, for who knows what mystical or magical operation, or theological or scientific or poetic operation, I was not at all sure; it remained only a feeling, strong and irrepressible, that I had been chosen, that something coherent, something incomprehensible, was happening to me. I don't know what guinea pigs feel like, when they are repeatedly placed inside plexiglass labyrinths with constantly changing and more and more complicated paths, where the bit of cheese is always harder to find, while someone is injecting them with cloudy substances, attaching electrodes to their skin . . . I don't know whether, aside from the painful sensations and absurd situations, and hunger, and running down white, curving, antiseptic corridors, the thought ever takes root in the little ganglions in their heads that what is happening is unnatural, that the accumulation of implausible facts, amazing coincidences, unexpected grasps from huge hands that lift them from their feces-filled cages, can only mean they were chosen by an intelligence foreign to their own, such that they cannot even perceive it as intelligence but just as a series of manipulations and atrocious sufferings. The unbearable vibrations and the sharp, siren-like sounds would be accompanied, in my dreams to come, by a yellow fire, like a flow of liquid gold that dissolves my brain.

I will note here other fragments from the following months, following years, up to today, up to last night. They are facts and sensations of various kinds, spread like bullet holes over a paper target, but my feeling, which I find impossible to contradict, was always that the target has always been the same, that everything is connected and coexists on a level of the world I can barely begin to intuit. Many things repeat, identically or in subtly different ways, connecting to dreams that I haven't noted here, but which form the eternal background for the others: my train stations, my unknown cities, my houses, my empty movie theaters. I won't write the date down unless it seems significant, but I will try to put them in the context of my memories and to unify them, provisionally, as lies within my powers, through the illumination of certain subterranean connections.

> *Last night I woke up at, I think, four in the morning, or earlier, when that particular fog was floating in my room. I had just dreamed, as has happened once before, that I saw a chandelier, an ordinary one like ours, with two or three arms and white shades, but instead of hanging from the ceiling it was sticking out horizontally, as though attached to a wall. I had the impression that it was somewhere outside of my gaze and I could only see it from the corner of my eye, forcing my ocular muscles to their breaking point. I made desperate efforts to turn my head toward the chandelier, but I could turn neither my head nor neck. It was as though I was only that peripheral and painful gaze, the pain of gazing, which eventually became the need to wake. I was saying that I had dreamed the same thing a long time ago, but framed differently: it was a kind of analytical cubist tableau, a kind of sculpture, a group of objects divided by a mirror: a chair, a piece of bark, and, fantastically, the same horizontal chandelier, all animated by my inability to bring them into the center of my gaze, twisting my eyes back into my head and moaning with pain and despair. Then waking, in the full morning light.*

I read, many years after these adolescent experiences, about sleep paralysis: when you wake up but your muscles are still inert, as they were during your dreams, so everything stays there, in the palace of your skull, so our limbs won't carry us through reality according to the labyrinthine story they heard from the brain. But these two or three awakenings of this type, that never repeated, left me with a completely other type of memory. I see even now the chandelier with the horizontal stem, I see it sliding slowly toward me, with the white lights at the ends of its arms, I can feel the fear I felt at the time, amplified by my immobility and deracination. I felt, in fact, like an insect caught in a spider's web, already paralyzed by its venom, who sees the black, fat beast approaching on its monstrous legs. I have always felt that sleep and dreams contain something disturbing, because they abandon you to the one who slowly penetrates your house, climbs the stairs toward your bedroom, and approaches your bed, while you are lying in the penumbra, unconscious and defenseless, wandering through a distant world.

A few months later, I wrote:

> *A dream of levitation. Nighttime, leaving myself on the balcony, flying in long leaps over the yard at Moara, amazingly precise details, such that it was reality, feeling my stomach drop exactly the way it does when sledding.*

I was referring to Moara Dâmbovița, which for a long time was the most enormous construction I had ever seen: it was just behind my parent's apartment block, a brick flour mill seven or eight stories tall, with enormous pediments dominating the flour-covered roof, and countless windows, barred and likewise covered in flour. Clouds would break across the triangular peaks that held round windows, like cathedral rosettes, and at dusk, when the bricks glowed like rubies, the entire construction exhaled a tragic grandeur that amazed me. There, at night, in the space between our block and Moara, bordered on one side by the Pioneer Bread Factory and some militia buildings on the other, things took place that shook me, things I cannot believe were only dreams. The window in the back room, where I seldom slept and only in the afternoons, looked out onto this vast space. Through the windows of our kitchen and the balcony door, you saw Moara, its electric sifters churning away in a low rumble. Once, one miller, seeing me jump the fence with a friend and timidly sneak up to the colossal building, crossing the vast courtyard where a few ancient trucks remained, called out to us and asked if we wanted to see inside. We were overawed as we entered its endless industrial halls, the air full of flour, and the floor, and the windows; the flour collected on the enormous sieves like snowdrifts, we climbed endless stairways toward other floors, with other halls and other millers with their hair dusted with flour, with another cloudy light settling on them from the windows, and then even higher, down long dark corridors, and then into other rooms of equipment, and in the end we saw our apartment block in a way we never had: from above, through a pediment's round window, four or five meters in diameter. Beyond the block we saw the city, wall after wall, to the end of sight.

Only later did I make the connection between my dreams of levitation, so ordinary yet so magical, and the fact that, usually at the start of a trimester, the school nurse put atropine drops in our eyes, to dilate them for examination. We would have to skip the next period because we could not read. Our hands looked small, red, and far away, like a bud at the end of a branch. Then we went back to the office, laughing and talking nonsense, because the nurse in our high school was well known. All the teachers, it seemed, had paid her a visit, had parted her athletic legs on the examination table and rubbed her generous breasts overflowing the corset she wore under her white lab coat. Even many of the students, at least a fair number from the twelfth grade, bragged they had done it with her. She taught sexual education, leading one class with the girls, one with the boys. We had never heard anyone talk like that. She stood in front of us, with her red-dyed hair and a cheeky smile on her lips, calmly enouncing words like *testicles, penis, vagina, masturbation,* while we—fifteen boys in scratchy uniforms, fighting the terrible erections caused by the forbidden words—we would have eaten her alive, there on the desk, one after the other, the way we had heard about in stories about "women like that." But the nurse didn't seem bothered by the ever-increasing tension, on the contrary, she seemed to act more provocatively as the class went on. She put the teacher's chair beside the desk, then she sat there and crossed her impressive thighs, wrapped in nylon hose. Leaning toward us, so we could see her breasts better, she spoke impassibly about condoms and birth control pills, until, red-faced, we could barely wait for the end of the period to run to the bathroom stalls and relieve ourselves, at last, onto the filthy toilet lids and walls covered with dirty graffiti . . .

After the eye examination, I always dreamed I could fly. Sometimes I only floated, riding a kind of half-inflated balloon a meter above the ground, down vesperal park paths, new to me but somehow very familiar, turning around the park's central pond that shimmered with all its might in the sunset. I would always find, in the depths of the darkness, an open, vast, starlit space, and there I always found the same rectangular basin full of black water. Other times, I flew over fields in the glistening dawn, rising and falling through the transparent air, sometimes landing in wheat fields, other times losing myself in the thick clouds. I felt the blue air whistle past my ears, my hair fluttered in the currents, everything was true, and my chest burst with happiness. In the Moara courtyard and in the space behind the block, I flew differently: I usually made great leaps, ever higher, like ever-deeper arches of a viaduct, and each rise toward the stars felt insane and dizzy. My highest jumps cleared the brick chimney of the bread factory—when we were children, one of us, the youngest and most timid, would climb it and stand on top, his arms out to the sides like a cross, to prove he wasn't a coward—I surpassed Moara's giant pediments . . . I have never been in a plane, and I don't think it is given to me in life. But the way I look down over the panorama of fields and roads and rivers and cloud-obliterated cities, lashed by rain or shining like precious stones in the triumphant sun, cannot be other, I have told myself dozens of times, than that which is truly seen at the height of hundreds and thousands of meters. In my flights I never flew above this realm. I often passed over nonexistent cities somewhere in our world, with excessively, baroquely ornamented yellow edifices, with frenzied crowds on wide boulevards, with the heavy traffic of odd vehicles, some of them also floating in the air, completely unknown on Earth. But there will be more to come about flying and floating.

A few days later:

Last night, levitation over Bucharest, with an absolutely natural feeling of flight.

Then on July 5, 1976, I recorded this, terrified:

A nightmare I've had several times recently: I am in my room, it's dark, everything as real as though I were in bed with my eyes open. The violet, star-filled sky in the window. Suddenly, I hear a piercing, oscillating noise, it grows louder and louder until I'm going mad, until a terror seems to burst my skull to pieces. I am thrown from my bed by an immaterial force, with my sheets and blankets and everything, and I am slammed against the wardrobe. I walk around the dark house for a while, every piece of furniture is in its place, then I go back to bed; only then do I wake, faceup, with an extremely acute awareness of everything that happened. The sensation is pure and simple that I actually walked through the house while dreaming.

And two weeks later:

Recording last night, another attack of pavor nocturnus. Precisely the same story. I woke (as always, after a false awakening) faceup, in a hieratic pose, like I was dead.

I have never slept in more than one position. I go to bed and wake up the same way: on my stomach, head to the right, sunk into my pillow, my entire body, including my head, covered with blankets, with just a small hole to breathe. I only wake up on my back, with my arms crossed over my chest, after these nightmares. How could I ever forget the sensation of being suddenly grabbed by the feet, pulled from the bed, and thrown to the floor, then slammed into the opposite wall? As though your last memory would be you lying there, apparently dreaming, in any case calm and flaccid, as though waiting with vague curiosity for something to occur. And then the band of darkness, the abyssal void of memory, then the senseless wandering through empty rooms, then another blank, then waking posed like a cadaver on a catafalque, then fear . . .

I'll also record some utterly strange dreams, an invasion of monstrous creatures, dwarfs with enormous heads . . .

This dream repeated more and more frequently. As we lived next to the State Circus, I often saw the dwarfs who worked there, walking alone or together down Aleea Circului or shopping in the local stores. "Don't stare," my mother would say quickly, "or they'll feel bad, the poor things . . ." But I couldn't help myself. How strange they were! Heads like large people, without anything unusual, maybe a little more curved in the forehead, otherwise people like anyone else, but their heads were connected directly, without a neck, to scrawny children's bodies with crooked legs and short arms, and often with six or seven fingers on each hand . . . Why did they visit my adolescent dreams, why would I wake up to find them in my room when I offered them my mind in my sleep, vulnerable, without any shell or carapace, like a hedgehog who falls into the water and exposes his soft stomach to the fox's mercy?

Out of all my dreams over the next year, I have selected some that seemed (but what right do I have to make selections?) stranger and more typical for the world that deepens, like a wax seal, in my sleep:

> *. . . and on the same topic, I dreamed last night, for the first time in several months, that I could move objects by concentrating on them. And like last time, the dream was extraordinarily realistic, I was sure I was awake, without a doubt. I was happy to have discovered such a fascinating power: telekinesis . . .*

I've had this dream dozens of times, in different variations, and I think that it's one of the most pleasant I have experienced. Rarely do I feel prouder of myself or happier. It's always the same: I look at an object, usually not that large, about the size of a tennis ball, and I concentrate all my strength somewhere between my eyes, as though I could create a void powerful enough to absorb things, like a vacuum cleaner. I don't have to think of anything in particular—just like, if I want to move my finger, I don't have to say, "move!" I just do it, as though the command and execution were one process. And then the ball of paper, or the cup, or whatever, *it comes*, in a series of jumps, toward me. The concentration isn't painful, but strong and quiet, as though the space between my eyes held the mustard seed of belief without doubt, enough to command the mountain to jump into the sea.

I also recorded a small fragment that wasn't a dream but something I wrote, in a kind of trance, one evening after Irina had left, leaving me exhausted and naked on the bed where she had whispered her dark fantasies into my ear in the pitch black. But I don't want to think about them now. I turned on the light and went to my desk, I sat there naked on the chair and wrote these lines on a piece of paper, then put it in a notebook of student homework that happened to be on the desk. The next day I returned the homework assignments to the sixth-grade class, and only then, the following afternoon, did I remember the paper. I ran from the school, despairing as though I had suffered a terrible loss, to the Bazavans', home of the ill-kempt student who had received his grade along with that fated piece of paper. I found them all at home, the lame old man and his four boys, and I didn't have any patience to talk about children and grades with the old working man who was raising his boys all alone. With the paper recovered I ran off, and only then, in the tram, did I read it, because I couldn't remember what it had been about. It left me confused, holding the paper in my hand. For the rest of the evening, I thought how wonderful it would have been if my lost notebook of stories, the one I could only read in my dreams, would suddenly appear on my desk . . .

> *When I dream, a girl leaps from her bed, goes to the window, and, her cheek pressed to the glass, watches the sun set over the pink and yellow houses. She turns toward the bloodred bedroom and curls up again under her damp sheet.*
>
> *Something, when I dream, approaches my paralyzed body, it takes my head in its hands and bites it, like a piece of translucid fruit. I open my eyes, but I don't dare move. I jump from the bed and run to the window. The sky is all stars.*

And on March 11, the same year:

> *I am talking to someone, when suddenly I sense a danger in the air. Everyone is running toward an underground passage. A nuclear bunker. I barely make it there and throw myself to the floor, because I feel two powerful explosions, along with the fear of everyone in the shelter. When I raise my head, I am on dirt, and in the distance, in the night, there are clumps of black trees. "Look, a double sunrise! Triple!" people say. I*

look and see it's true—two and then five or six clear, red suns, rising like any other morning. One of them is coming toward us. It is a transparent sphere holding five child-faced dwarfs.

Even before I had ever heard about nuclear bombs, when I was nine or ten I think, I had dreams that repeated identically: I was always in a large clothing store—at the time the city only had a few, named Victoria, Eagle of the Sea, and Bucharest. I would go up crystal elevators to a different floor each time, one full of racks of dresses, suits, jackets, shirts, all flowery and sparkling. There were narrow places to walk among them, like a maze where you could easily get lost. The elevator would carry me slowly toward ever-higher levels, all arranged around a central void, toward which escalators rose—I surely had never seen these and I didn't know they existed in reality, I took them for one of the wonders of my mind—I saw everything through the shining glass walls, when suddenly, through the store windows, I would see a great explosion, like a red mushroom, in the distance near the city center. Everyone would run like madmen, I also would descend quickly and run out of the store, down the streets, while the purple mushroom behind us grew larger and larger, almost reaching us.

Last night, after an ordinary erotic dream, another followed, in which I seemed to repeat the dream I talked about in "Chimera." It filled me with the holy terror of a prophecy fulfilled. This fear suddenly grew, jetting toward infinity, along with that unbearable, yellow-gold whistling in my head. Of course, I woke facing up. I don't know what these can be, these terrors greater than anything.

And on the same day:

All night I dream about strange boats. They always appear above Moara Dâmbovița.

I don't have the strength to comment now on these fragments. It's almost four in the morning, anyway, and I have to be at school at eight. I will return to transcribing from this diary later, I hope with a somewhat clearer mind. Now,

I can only confirm the feeling that there is something there, that the dreams I have chosen, out of the hundreds recorded in these dusty, deteriorating notebooks, actually chose themselves and they require all my attention. I have always wondered whether everyone's interior life is as exhaustingly complicated as mine, if everyone is placed, like a white mouse, in the middle of their labyrinthine mind, through which they have to find a path, just one, the true one, while all the others lead to traps with no escape.

22

The school has three math teachers. Mrs. Băjenaru, a pale, wilting woman with thin lips who would go unnoticed if it were not for her eyelid ptosis, which gives the poor woman a completely implausible air of craftiness. The other, Florabela, is on the contrary, a firecracker: large, ruddy, full of life, gold, and freckled, she is the school's absolute goddess. Even those teachers who go green with envy at the sight of youth love her like their own daughter, because she is kind and generous, and the school, as melancholy as it is, trembles with the constant sound of her earrings and laughter. Also from her hysterical screams during her classes. Rarely has anyone ever yelled louder at the children, rarely have the children ever cared less. In front of the children, Florabela dances with lightning in her hands, large and curvy like an Indian goddess, her furors a kind of decoration, like her bloodred mouth on her heavily made-up face, her ponytail that spreads through the olive air of the classroom like the long tentacles of poisonous jellyfish. Florabela throws lines of fractions, numerators, and parentheses onto the chalkboard then whips around triumphantly toward the thirty gnomes and dwarfs, and louder than her stature suggests, she opens her mouth and yells—sharply and intensely, and in her yelling they see her perfect teeth, her tonsils, and her uvula, as though she were a diva on the Scala stage, frozen in her splendor as she hits her highest note. The kids draw their heads down into their shoulders, but they smile: this superb woman manipulates the current of an obscure desire, the clinking of her large, circle earrings stimulates their pituitaries and gonads all the more as she inhibits the taxonomic function of their right hemispheres. Behind the always elegant and sophisticated dresses that Florabela changes like hankies, the black chalkboard fills with numbers, but it could just as well stay black and clean to the end, because the teacher is so intense that she projects a luminous void that erases the signs and shapes. The children don't learn even a drop of math, but they learn from her: the girls strive to be like their giant, freckled teacher with a big mouth, the boys will look for lovers a head taller than they are and dream of the red fire of an inaccessible pubis.

No man thinks of getting close to her. She inspires fear with her basketball-player height and her Kriemhild screams. In comparison to her, the men seem reedy and weak, and that must also be true in bed with such an inferno. Watching Florabela walk down the hall during breaks, passing by the children who make an unholy noise, I can't think of anything but the bronze feet of La Vénus d'Ille climbing creaking stairs toward the nuptial chamber where two poor mortals live their last moments of happiness. You cannot desire this type of female, you can only resignedly inhale the pheromones that flow from her like an amber light, and continue on with your measly little life cupped in your hands like the male mantis who knows he cannot escape alive from the arms crossed in prayer of the statuesque, enigmatic female.

And then, finally, there is Goia, whom I have become close with in recent years, because, although he is withdrawn and awkward, maybe due to his mutilated face or his severe social anxiety, he has a contagious passion for the discipline he teaches. Many times, after school or during the summer, when we come to supervise the children cleaning the rooms and hallways, washing the windows, and painting, we sit on the school steps and talk. He has a low, almost inaudible voice, a monotone that would put you to sleep if not for the almost maniacal passion with which he speaks about the only topic that ever interests him: mathematics. As a child, he made friends with numbers, not other children. Every number had a shape, taste, smell, texture, and personality. Every one matched with others according to subterranean affinities that Goia did not know how to explain to me, but which I felt clearly, the way you feel air pressure or gravity. Later, he became friends with mathematicians, he knew each of their lives in detail, the history of mathematics flowed out of him easily, with its tens of thousands of influences, interrelations, ideas forgotten for centuries and rediscovered, errors and revelations, impasses and orgasmic releases, with a grandeur equal to nothing except the birth of the universe or the evolution of species. He has told me about his favorite mathematicians: Galois, Cantor, Abel, or Gödel, about the enigmatic Bourbaki, about Fermat's theory and the mathematics of nonlinear equations, about René Thom and Mandelbrot, the fractals and bands of Möbius, writing and drawing on the ever-browner air with his fingers, each about twenty centimeters long, figures in two or three dimensions, as well as paradoxical and impossible figures you could not visualize unless you were familiar with fourth-dimensional maneuvers. Goia loaned me the first book on topology I ever read (skipping the lines of equations and wringing out the intense poetry of the geometry of rubber from the apparently dry pages) and from him I also learned details—coincidences that startled me and rebuked the indifferent, aleatory nature of life—about George Boole and his astounding family, which included, of course, the first writer who made me drench a book's pages with my tears, Ethel Lilian Voynich. Their story has remained deep in my memory.

It appears that George Boole was the first prodigious individual in his family, which would later be just as rich in amazing minds as the gifted genealogical tree that included Bach. But who can say whether people of modest origins who don't receive brilliant educations, like Boole, Newton, Tesla, Einstein, or da Vinci, don't have—among their tens of thousands of ancestors, who knows when, at the root of their miraculous ramifications—someone like Bezalel, whom the Lord transformed in the blink of an eye from an ordinary Jew into an inventor capable of building the tabernacle? Tesla's mother, a simple Croatian housewife, could tie three knots in an eyelash and invented pepper grinders out of nothing, with complicated wooden levers, with networks of gears, with thick thread as a drive shaft. Boole's environment promised nothing intellectual. His father had repaired his Lincoln neighbors' thrashed-out shoes. The man who would change the shape of logic and mathematics had a mediocre education, limited to small business schools. Despite all of this (and, I think, it would have been the same if he had been a shepherd), he found the books that so excited his mind, always oriented toward abstract thought like a compass needle toward north, that if they hadn't existed his mind would have written them itself: *Celestial Mechanics* by Laplace and *Analytical Mechanics* by Lagrange. Following the line of thought discovered there, Boole developed, over the following decades, symbolic methods that turned logic into a branch of mathematics (if not the reverse) and laid the foundations for modern higher algebra. Boolean algebra, developed in the second half of the nineteenth century, opened the way for all mathematics of the following century, through Boole's formalization of the operations of mathematic language. In *An Investigation of the Laws of Thought on Which Are Founded the Mathematical Theories of Logic and Probabilities,* Boole revolutionized logic so radically that it took decades for his work to be understood. Frege and Wittgenstein would not have existed without *The Laws of Thought,* which this person of little schooling, this prodigious autodidact, like Newton, explained with such rigor.

A year after the publication of this crucial text, at the age of thirty-nine, Boole married a woman just as gifted in her own way: Mary Everest. Her uncle was Colonel George Everest, who had coordinated The Great Trigonometrical Survey of India north of Nepal and gave his name to the highest mountain on the planet. Mary was twenty-three when she married Boole, and she lived with him for ten years until he died of pneumonia after a speech he delivered, drenched to the skin by a torrential rain. During this time, she gave birth to five girls. Each of the Boole sisters was remarkable in her area, like their mother, an autodidact mathematician and librarian at Queen's College, London, where she had moved after the death of her spouse.

Mary Boole, an anodyne figure in a Victorian bonnet, as she appears in the history of mathematics that Goia later loaned me, was an eccentric, in fact an enthusiastic, woman full of life and sensuality, since nothing deceives or perverts the image of a person as much as a photo or an engraving. The Booles must have loved each other frequently and passionately, seeing as every two years, with geometrical regularity, a girl was born to them. It is difficult to imagine them in bed—not just Boole, but any of the illustrious men of the nineteenth century, with their grave, patriarchal airs, their bizarrely combed beards and mustaches, their eyes fixed on continual and unabated progress. How would they caress their women, what gestures of love would they respond to in the bedroom where they cast off, along with their clothes, the absurdities of honor and power that corseted them? Or did they keep them on even in bed, the way they never took off their nightshirts? Did the blushing objections of their life's companion, her almost virginal embarrassment, the violation of feminine delicacy by a bearded brute somehow give a grotesque charm to sex in that age? Sex may have been demonic, yet it somehow took place in secret, in the middle of the night, in shame and guilt. Pregnant women were hidden because the growing womb was proof of fornication, of appetite, of the fact that only a few months ago the mother of the family—who, night after night, read moralizing stories to everyone around the hearth, who was inseparable from her sewing hoop, where she stitched naïve images of butterflies and flowers, who never missed a Sunday service—had lain with her legs spread obscenely under a man, had let herself be penetrated by his disgusting phallus and even, horror of horrors, had enjoyed it . . . But this could not have been true of the Boole family, because, surely, not even the horrible Victorian period could have produced only Pharisees. The fact is that Mrs. Boole remained, even after her husband's death, a sensualist, sublimating her impulses into a tangle of capriciously textured writings, like a blanket woven from dozens of scraps with different patterns. She invented a mathematics of the sewing hoop, which helped young women understand advanced geometrical ideas by sewing curves on cloth and by constructing sophisticated figures in different colored threads, she wrote *Philosophy and Fun of Algebra,* in which she attempted to express the emotions and subjectivity of experience in abstract symbols. She feminized the aridness of her husband's world and brought it among the winged fairies, no more than a fingerspan in height, that had invaded the epoch. She lived as a widow for fifteen years, during which time she raised her girls in the liberal-fantasist-spiritualist spirit that would (through a providential cross-grafting) bear the most exotic kinds of fruit.

I didn't want to write anything here about the Boole family, about the ways they made math and love. It's not even justified by the fact that their youngest daughter would become a revolutionary, an atheist, and a celebrated author in the Soviet Union, by the fact that her novel was the first book that evoked a response from me. But without this story, from an era both absurd and obscure (and yet charming in its mechanical naïveté), I couldn't come to these pages' highest stakes, their enigma and the world's. Because, even a few years ago, when I spoke to Goia for the first time, on the sun-heated steps in front of the school, I could intuit that something in the story of George

Boole (or in the story of Ethel Lilian Voynich, or in their confluence) was taking shape, something I had been searching for for a long time, the way that, when you recover from a powerful concussion, the image in front of your eyes becomes clear only little by little. Over the course of these years, I have seen how my stories—which began in the sixth grade, when I read, without knowing what I was reading, *The Gadfly*—collect, out of everywhere, more and more colored threads, like on Mary Boole's sewing hoop, all united in an ample, slow, soft curve, which leads asymptotically and inevitably toward the absolute. Every new thread has increased my wonder and stirred even greater expectations. Night after night, levitating over my bed with open books floating around me like in a spaceship, I read about Boole, Lewis Carroll, Edwin Abbott, and everything about this subject I could find, feeling that I was slowly approaching something or someone who as yet, frustratingly, stayed hidden. If there are signs, if in the next cell an impossible neighbor (because on the other side of the wall are just the cliffs and sea) starts to tap, to give you an escape plan, with crescents, gears, triangles, and crosses, if life is a test of perspicacity or, what might be one and the same, of personality (draw a tree; draw a person; put these drawings in the order they occurred; interpret the multicolored butterflies spread over the page), they must appear from where you least expect it, heteroclite and allusive above all, making you doubt not them but yourself, making you blush before your own paranoia and making you try to forget it, to return to the pervasive conspiracy of normality. But the tapping on the wall won't let you sleep, and the privation of sleep leads to hallucinations and insanity, and in the end, inevitably, to the illusion that you hear tapping on the wall. And all this until the metronome stops, and you have yet to give an answer. No one plays this game of their own will. You don't choose it, you are chosen by it. You don't look for it, you are the one it looks for.

I have gone farther along this strand of the cobweb whose ends were handed to me by chance, following them with my finger to where they connect, node after node, as when, in childhood, I would tie dozens of threads over the doorknobs with many complicated knots so my mother would not have another child. I studied every node, as though under a shining magnifying glass, following how the different colors and textures and thicknesses curled around each other, hoping that they would be the letters of an unknown alphabet, because my search depended on the first question—are they or are they not signs?—but the response didn't need to be the denouement. Because it would have been (and still is) terrifying to understand that, yes, there are signs for me everywhere, that they are crying out to be deciphered, but that my mind, the ganglion protected by a bony skull, is not able to connect them into something coherent, let alone into a tunnel or an escape. I have not lived in vain, I tell myself in every moment of my life, because I didn't become an author, because I am a lowly Romanian teacher, because I don't have a family, or a fortune, or a purpose in the world, or because I live and will die among ruins, in the saddest city on the face of the earth. It is rather because I have asked a question and not found the answer, because I have asked and was not given, I have knocked and it has not opened, I have searched and have not found. This is the failure that frightens me.

23

I was five years and three months old when, one damp and foggy autumn, we moved to the apartment block on Ştefan cel Mare. I had grown and needed to exchange my shell for a larger one, just as the skull that housed the tender grapefruit of my brain had grown to fit my memories and desires. I remember how the eight-story block lay on its side, in a thick fog, like a beached whale, its skin just as gray, with just as many scars from ancient confrontations. The deafeningly loud trams careened by, made of ordinary metal with polished wood interiors and movable steps that snapped suddenly back up, often catching the feet of careless passengers. My father took me several times to the Tram Museum, housed in a decommissioned depot somewhere in Predoleanu, where I saw on a shelf a line of feet cut off at the ankle, still wearing high heels or men's loafers or children's sandals, from those unlucky people who were caught in the carnivorous steps. I also saw fingers, some wearing rings, severed by the tram's equally inhumane folding doors, designed to crush those who threw themselves into the crowded cars at the last moment. How many times, as a child, did I not hear a terrible howl somewhere near the tram's front door, how many times did I not see through the window a woman cry and howl on the snowdrift while she clutched her bloody hand to her chest? The trams were usually so crowded that my face would be crushed against the butts and hips of the big people around me, however much my mother tried to protect me, as she pushed with all her might to give me a little room to breathe. When the tram came, the people at the stop trampled each other, they clutched the door handles like they were drowning, they pushed like animals. The tram would desperately ring its bell, sparks would spray from the wires, the driver could barely shift his brass handle, pressed as he was beneath the crowd, and in the end the tin contraption would heave forward, its windows rattling, people hanging from the doors and bumpers, like a bumblebee overwhelmed by parasites.

And behind the block was Moara Dâmbovița, the brick monster that stuck its pediments into the sky and made a constant racket, more deafening than the trams. There, in a three-room apartment on the fifth floor, I lived most of my childhood, and all of my phantasmagoric and schizophrenic adolescence, feeling a loneliness like no other creature on Earth ever had. Since that first autumn, I remember nothing but the frozen fog extending everywhere through empty, gray space. Our building was isolated among giant empty lots. At that time, there was no Aleea Circului, no blocks on the other side of the street, and even our building still had scaffolding on the front. It was autumn 1961. One year earlier, in the middle of nowhere, they built the State Circus—an improbable flying saucer that touched down beside the infamous garbage heap called Tonola. In those first days I walked all around it holding my mother's hand, hugged by the fog, unable to hold our eyes on the undulating cupola and prismatic windows of this building that would become so important in my life, because the screaming and nervous world of the circus, with the colored gels of its lights and sequined riding costumes and spots of living fire on the panthers' fur as they leapt through hoops of flame, remained always in my memory like a circular world, a coin without connection to the conspiratory misery of reality. I cried in the stands when I saw the triumphant horse rider, her breasts bare and her hair dyed a million different colors, a Semiramis of illusion, a mayfly of eternity, circling the ring before the faces of the livid and impersonal spectators who stared at her like giant insects. I also saw the flea circus and watched the unbelievable writhing of the Snake Man. The performers' trailers were behind the circus, and there lived the children who went to the same school where, after two years of walking along that same foggy path with my mother, I would also start the first grade. I had classmates who, in the evenings at the circus, juggled colored balls or flaming torches, who stole the clown's harmonica and hid it in a box wrapped in red crepe paper, who were launched from a seesaw into the arms of their older brother, who sat on the shoulders of their father, sitting in turn on the herculean shoulders of their grandfather with a forked mustache. But in class, they were like all the others, dressed in polka-dot shorts and a ribbon around their neck, like clowns without joy.

When I think of my first years at school, that's what comes to mind: three lines of small, sad clowns, sitting on ink-stained benches, themselves covered in ink up to their eyes from the bent nibs on their pens and the inkwells that always tipped over on the rickety tables, in the sinister classrooms where I studied. Even like this, the impregnation with blue liquid didn't seem to completely satisfy the educators, because we were taken to the nurse, where, at the slightest sign of a cold, they rubbed our throat (and our tongues, and our lips, and the pimples on our faces) with a blue menthol, exactly the same color as the ink, such that, covered with stains both inside and out, shaved to our scalps if they'd found lice, we ended up looking like Makarenko's students, guided by the famous dictum: "You don't know? We will teach you. You can't? We will help. You don't want to? We will force you." We didn't want to, not at all, so our teacher, a hunched-over old woman, always holding cardboard bunnies and carrots, forced us every day to walk out ashamed of ourselves. I only have a few memories of those first years at school:

At eight in the morning it is still dark, and outside the classroom window is a thick, slanted snowfall. The teacher is reading from a book, but I haven't been paying attention: I look out the window, and suddenly I have the feeling that the room is flying at a slant, upward, at great speed through the black air, past glittering, motionless snowflakes.

Also, in the dark of winter, the ceiling lights are lit. The classroom shimmers in their yellow light. I look at the other kids through my plastic ruler: I see them surrounded by thick, puffy rainbows of shifting colors.

I cut fruits and vegetables out of a shiny, multicolored paper, odd-smelling, like fresh ink. Then I take Pelican-brand glue and stick shapes together: cucumbers, tomatoes, grapes, apples, pears, and oranges, on a white, fibrous tablet of drawing paper.

I am writing on the chalkboard and, without my wanting to, the letters move upward, toward the far right corner of the board. Soon, I will have to hold the chalk over my head, then I will have to rise on the tips of my toes, and in the end I'll have to stretch as far as I can, until my bones pop, to be able to continue the line of words. The chalk falls from my hand before I can finish the line.

During the break, on a dirty and rickety bench, I unwrap the packet my mother makes for me every day: two slices of bread with cheese and salami and a bunch of large, wet grapes in a plastic bag. I eat the grapes outside in the yard, where dozens of kids run around like crazy. I sit in the only corner where the sun doesn't reach, and eat the entire bunch, grape after grape, watching the commotion of kids at recess.

I do not exist, I have no personality, I do not know who I am. When the teacher with the cardboard rabbits comes in, many of the kids give her a hug, they pat her and caress her. I don't, I am cold and distant. In fact, I don't even notice her, just as I don't notice the other kids, just as I don't look at myself in the mirror (when I did so two years later for the first time, I didn't recognize myself). I live in a world of colored outlines, strange smells. I am not even attached to my own parents, I don't hug them or kiss them. "You're going to miss out on a lot if you are so *unfriendly*," my exhausted mother tells me whenever she wants to show me affection and I push her arms away indifferently.

We are at recess (in my memory, elementary school seems to have been a recess that went on forever), I am sitting quietly on my bench while the other kids, in their shirts and polka-dot headscarves, are jumping over the benches and throwing erasers at each other, when I feel something above my head. I look up and see a blue sphere, larger than those ceiling lights that hang from stems. It isn't right above my head: it is a little toward the window, but it's coming closer. Its surface is smooth, but it isn't made of glass or plastic. It's not a balloon. Its surface is featureless, but it is the color, a pale yet powerful blue, that suddenly moves me—as was no surprise: all colors made deep impressions on me, from the color of chocolates to the fleshy hues of hyacinths. I have trouble painting or drawing, because the red, yellow, green, and brown on the paper fill me with wonder: they shout and burn, they penetrate the depths of my consciousness. The sphere descends slowly, it seems made of air, it seems to have been delicately painted upon the stale air of the classroom. No one else sees it. I look at the other kids, I even point it out to Mihaela, the best in the class; the pale blue falls onto my raised face, I feel the color on my nose, cheeks, and lips. Then it's gone.

I am cut out of all I see, of all I experience, as though an unskilled portrait photographer had not focused on the face but on the background. But that's not it. The fact is, I am the background, I am everything around me, while my shape is the cutout. In my box of treasures, I have a picture from the third grade: we are all on our benches, with checkered uniforms and red Pioneer ties on our necks. We all have our hands behind our backs. The teacher is at the back of the room, resting her hand on my bench. I am in the last row, even though I am the shortest kid in the room. "I mean, if we've never given her flowers or chocolates," my mother says, who on principle never gives anything and, although she is religious, never goes to church because her husband is a communist true believer. Because I am so little and dark-skinned, in shadowy pictures I am just a featureless brown dot. For four years, I was the third best student out of thirty boys and girls, and I never made a friend.

I don't remember anything else, in the same sense that I don't remember how I worked porous calcium to build the line of vertebrae hidden in the flesh of my spine.

In the third grade, they discovered I had an embarrassing disease. It was in the spring, the second trimester. The room was full of light when the nurse came in holding her nickeled box. The other kids turned pale because they knew a vaccination was coming. We were vaccinated from time to time, that is, we were given shots. Afterward, the arm or leg they stuck would ache terribly. This didn't stop the kids from hitting each other mercilessly on the vaccination spot, and then running through the room with stiff legs, as though they were in the metal braces that polio patients used. Other times, the nurse would scratch a few lines across the shot's blister, with a needle heated in fire. Most people had, on their left shoulder, a kind of brand on their skin, as though they belonged to someone. You could see it plainly on the arms of the neighbors smoking in their undershirts on their balconies, on our mothers when they took off their flowered housedresses to take a bath. This kind of vaccine was the most feared, many kids fainted when they got it, because the needle, heated in the spirit lamp, was a semitransparent orange, it wasn't metal anymore, it was made just out of diabolic, pure suffering from another world. When it touched the already inflamed skin, the damp surface would crackle, smoke came up, and it smelled like pork frying in a pan. There were also easy vaccinations, on a sugar cube: a pipette dropped a sticky pink substance onto the compacted crystals; we stood in line, and in front of the nurse, we stuck out our tongues and received that dessert that melted, like candy, in our mouths. In the bleak poverty of that time, we were starved for candy. We looked at the shops that sold jelly beans, Little Dwarf chocolates, Neapolitan wafers, or bonbons, all of them crumbling, stale, and clumped together like geological amalgams, they seemed untouchable paradises, because in response to any request you raised toward the gods who walked the streets with you, with their faces cut out against the sky, you heard only the eternal, "I don't have any money, sweetie, how am I supposed to buy you something?" or "Wait until your father gets paid . . ." We would die of happiness when we looked in our mother's purses, as we did whenever she came back from the market, and found a glucose tablet, or a box of one of the disgusting substitute treats, pink or blue granulated calcium, which I would gnaw on to sate my body's despair for the sugars that it needed to shape—out of bad food, infested water, milk diluted to a blue color, bread with bran husks and mouse excrement, pasta as old as the earth—its anemic form, battered by every wind.

On that morning in March they gave us the PPD tuberculosis test for the first time. Those that had been held back the previous year knew all about it, they'd had it already, no big deal. Yes they stuck you, but the needle was small as a bee stinger, and it went just under the skin. It didn't hurt that much, and it didn't swell up. You waited in line with your sleeve rolled up, they rubbed you with alcohol, then they injected a watery liquid under your skin: you could even see the little blister of liquid rise when the nurse pushed the piston. Then she would put the wad of blueish gauze over the skin and needle, pull the syringe back, and leave you pressing the gauze over the injection. In the evening, a weird redness developed around the dot left by the needle on the skin of your arm, at first pale and no bigger than a five-bani coin. It itched a little, you almost didn't notice. You went to bed with the little sting on your arm, hoping that the next day there'd be nothing, but in the morning you woke up with a big red mark, the size of a one-leu coin, and by evening it was like a saucer, and rigid and shiny. Or at least that's how I woke up, one morning that will be hard for me to forget. The spot was itching even before I was completely awake, it itched in my dreams. But when I opened my eyes and I looked at the inside of my upper arm, I couldn't believe it: it was like a wax seal over my white skin, like a stigmata on a former criminal, a mark of shame and guilt. I couldn't stand to look at it for more than a few moments. At school, the kids gathered around me when the nurse came to measure our spots with a plastic ruler. For most of the kids, the sign was almost invisible, it was at most a reddish vapor, a few scarlet granules around the sting. For a few it was about a centimeter across. The nurse placed the cold ruler over the burning red disk on my skin and recorded, with a grave face, something in her notebook. Then she spoke with the teacher, who was cutting out and coloring bunnies at her desk, and then the two of them came to my bench. I was overwhelmed by the dozens of heads bent over me, sitting at the dirty desk with my sleeve rolled up. The monstrous spot on my arm was throbbing, and soon its flames seemed to extend into an allover blush, because I had turned red from head to toe, I felt even the whites of my eyes turn purple in shame, I wanted to run and hide in the first rathole I could find. But the crowd of kids with their heads stuck together, with mocking, evil eyes, with mouths gaping in wonder and hilarity, surrounded me like a foam of faces. It was in fact an infinite sea of kids, above, below, everywhere, there was no escape. This inferno lasted until the bell sounded and class was over.

The two women walked away down the hall, leaving me in the hands of the other kids. I tried to pull my sleeve back down over the infamous spot, but the kids grabbed me and yanked it back up, yelling the name that I would hear for years afterward: "TB-boy!" I tried to run, but this just incited the swarm. They caught me, crowded me into the corner of the classroom, tore the sleeve off of my shirt, they held out my arm with the spot, while others held my legs and the other arm. They were hanging over me, girls and boys, avid to see, again and again, the stigmata of my difference from them, of the strangeness they tried to erase from the face of the earth. I was infected with tuberculosis, a pathetic, infectious person, an outcast whom it was their duty to remove from the room. A girl gathered her strength and smacked me as hard as she could on the spot, a boy that had previously been friendly ground the heel of his shoe into it. I screamed and twisted under the heap of them, almost suffocating, until the bell rang and the gray-haired teacher came in, with the register under her arm. The kids got off of me and went to their benches, red from exertion and their eyes shining, but I stayed in the corner in a ball, my face matted with tears, for the entire period, because the teacher didn't have the heart to try to comfort me. She left me to lie there, with the torn sleeve beside me, my arm against my chest, as though I didn't exist or I had been sent to the corner for who knows what fault.

The PPD was, in the first years of school, a constant torture. They did it again after a week, just for me, out of all the kids. The next day I didn't go to school. I went down Aleea Circului, among the already planted chestnuts, with my arm throbbing and itching worse than the first time. I was TB-boy, millions of bugs were in my blood, like underground moles. I was full of worms and cockroaches and spiders and locusts and lice and snails, they were all running through my veins, rending my lungs, devouring me from within. At home, my mother held me in her arms and cursed her guilt, because she remembered that, in her desperation to not lose me after Victor disappeared, she had given me milk she bought from a neighbor at the end of the street, when we lived on Silistra. He had a cow, he took it out to graze through the ponds covered with algae and through the brambles in the fields. The cow had tuberculosis for sure, but—what can you do. That's how things were. The milk in the store was three-quarters water. The powdered milk at the day care had bugs in it, and it was so old that sometimes you had to break it up with a chisel. People were poor. At their wedding my parents didn't even get a spoon, what a world! "But don't worry, sweetie, we'll go to the clinic, we'll talk with Doctor Vlădescu, she knows what's what, we'll see what we need to do. This isn't how people die. If this was how people died, just like that, all you'd see was dead people everywhere. Don't worry, it'll be over before you're married, without a doubt." But at the clinic, while my mother waited outside the office on the vinyl bench, I was bored and read the posters on the walls, the ones with "Dangers of Venereal Diseases," and "A Bite—the Microbial Transmission Vector," and "How to

Wash Vegetables Effectively," etc. I found one about tuberculosis, where it said, "If well taken care of, the sick person can live a long time with this disease, even twenty years." I pondered this point. So my life would last about that long: twenty-eight years. It didn't seem so catastrophic, there was a bunch of time until then, but in comparison to people who reached a hundred . . . Even my parents had already lived longer, and they didn't have terrifying living creatures in their blood.

The doctor invited us in and, as always, I lay down, my bare back on the cold rubber pad. She listened to me a long time with the even colder stethoscope. She looked at my ragged file, written with different colored pencils in a hand that no one could read. She weighed me, measured my height on the white scale, whose sliding weights fascinated me so. "My boy," she said, "why don't you eat? Aren't you embarrassed that your ribs poke out of our skin? Look, your stomach goes right back to your spine . . ." "If you only knew how I struggle with him, doamna doctor! I don't know what to make, he turns up his nose at everything: not that, not that . . . What in God's name should I make him, anything and everything with a cherry on top? I never thought I'd have such a picky kid." "Fish oil, one spoonful a day, it will work wonders, you'll see. As for being picky, don't give him anything for two or three days: he'll wolf down crab apples! Don't try to please him so much. A child should eat whatever there is, and thank God there's something on the table. Give him something to eat, and if he doesn't try any after five minutes, put it back in the pot, and that's all the food he gets for the day. He doesn't get to do whatever he wants. Did you hear, my boy? You've become more desperate than class struggle, but we'll get you back on your feet . . ." We left the clinic with a prescription, they stuck a vitamin B complex in me, they forced me to swallow the spoonful of fish oil that made my stomach turn over—but the PPD, first every two months, then every four, showed no change. I didn't go to school for the rest of the trimester, I told my parents I would throw myself under a tram if they made me go back. The teacher visited us at home, some party comrades also came to speak to my parents: the child cannot be left uneducated. But when I heard them talk about school, I would run into my room and cram myself into the cabinet, among the blankets and pillows that smelled faintly of sweat. In vain they promised the other kids wouldn't treat me badly anymore, that they would treat me like a normal kid, in vain they tried to pull me back into the room where I had been martyred. When my father, with his face as fierce as those of Soviet soldiers in the movies, decided one evening to lay down the law, and he took his belt off and whipped me up and down, I didn't sleep the entire night. Later, when the pinochle game was over and they were asleep on the foldout bed in the living room, I got dressed in silence and, walking past them in the blue light, I went toward the front door. My bottom and back smarted as though the red PPD dot had spread over my entire body, covering me with its turpitude. Before leaving, I glanced at them: they were sleeping on their backs, pale in the blue penumbra, like two statues, a king and queen lying on their sarcophagi in a crypt at the bottom of the world. What did I have to do with these people? Why was I living in the same house with them? Why did I have to listen to them? Why did they have limitless power over me? "Damn you, kid, I made you, I'll take you out!" my titanic father would shout, lifting the belt for the tenth time, letting it fall over my back and thighs. I turned the key in the door and went out slowly onto the fifth-floor landing.

It was dark and silent but for the distant, continual buzzing of the mill, which made our block vibrate hour after hour every day but Sunday. The elevator hadn't been working for a few days, so I walked down the stairs, holding the railing. Some landings had a weak bulb burning over an apartment's peephole. By this light, as weak as a candle's, you could see the other three doors and the pipes that ran down the wall. The landings were huge and extremely far from each other. In the quiet of the night, in the still, obsidian air, they seemed like a column of successive crypts, an endless vertical cemetery. At first I counted the floors, but soon a terrible fear made me forget not just the place where I was but myself entirely. I ran huffing and yelping down the stairs, I tripped on the steps; instead of the exit on the ground floor, I found more and more landings, with strange doors, with unknown names on metal plates, with yellowed, anemic plants. Cockroaches, of course, swarmed everywhere, in their translucent chitin shells: they climbed over the door handles and crawled over the floor tiles. My teacher once showed us a moth that had landed on the sunny class window: "Children," she had said, "insects are living beings, like us. Their bodies have all the same things as ours: flesh, blood, soft organs . . . But their bodies are covered with a hard, almost transparent substance, like our fingernails." Then, in the classroom, while the other kids examined the plastic sticks, I was paralyzed by the thought that I could have been born completely coated by a large, gray fingernail, the product of my own body, the way my nails grew on my hands and feet. "Here, take off your socks so I can trim them, I bet you've grown hooves it's been so long." And my mother would cut shapes from my toes' strange crowns: lunar crescents, thin scythes, cow horns . . . I would play with them, I would test their elasticity and transparence, I would wonder how they had been parts of my little body. "Look how long and thick they are, we'll chop them up and put them in the stew . . ." The thought that I could have been bolted inside plates of nail armor, that anywhere I touched, face or body, I would have felt the shiny, continuous nail with odd folds and orifices, made me press the heels of my hands against my eyes and try to push away the sinister chimera, the way I did when I imagined chewing paper or my father's razor splitting open my eye.

But now wasn't the moment for these kinds of thoughts. The building seemed infinite. I had already been climbing down the stairs for hours and still the landings did not end. Terrified, I tried to go back up more than once, but there was no point: my parents' door had totally disappeared. I was lost, maybe I wasn't even in the world anymore, but somewhere else, in a different kind of place. I couldn't hear the mill buzzing or the cars that sometimes broke the silence on Ştefan cel Mare. A new fear came over me: had I passed the ground floor and gone somewhere underground? Filled with the terror of this thought and covered in cold sweat, I stopped and, rising up on my toes as far as possible, like I did when I wrote on the board at school, I tried to open one of the little windows—the ones that let a little light into the stairway on every other landing, next to the reeking trash chutes. By day, the windows showed the enormous mill, but now its dark walls were barely visible. I turned the handle and suddenly smelled the strong scent of dirt. I tried to reach my hand out of the window and I touched dirt, sticky dirt—the entire window was blocked by dirt. I ran up two floors, then two more: but it was just the same. My hands felt slimy, I had to wipe them on myself, getting dirt all over my shirt.

I had lost any sense of direction. Since it was much easier to go down the stairs than to climb them, I rushed, suddenly, in a fit of despair, down dozens of floors. These floors were not the same as before, with four doors each now they extended into ever-longer corridors, into the body of the building, making angles and twists, going up and down at random. Some of the doors were monumental, carved in stone and gigantic like an Arc de Triomphe. Others were so small you would have had to bend far over to enter them. The shadows turned olive-colored, solemn and freezing cold. I don't know how many times I stopped, racked with sadness and exhaustion, in those endless hallways. I don't know how many times I curled up like a dog on one of the welcome mats, for minutes or for hours, listening to the hollow tapping of cockroaches examining the tile floor with their antennae. I would get up and continue on, trying to get someplace. The space decayed the more I descended, the rot and mold crept up the walls, wearing the surface away, showing the spongy concrete panels the block was made from. Pale spiders stuck their legs out of their dusty, dirty webs. The floor was more and more cracked, entire pieces of tile began to disappear, until I found myself walking through mud up to my ankles in a clay tunnel that slanted downward toward an end obscured by darkness. Where the apartment doors had been before, were now hideous voids, open realms of swollen and mold-covered debris stuck out from the former thresholds, pouring out beyond them like folds of dirty intestines. In the former apartments the furniture was broken and moldy, the mirrors were chipped, the bathtubs petrified. Soon, the doorways became narrower, then they disappeared altogether. I walked downhill through the conglomeration of all the earth's systems, through an oily, peristaltic intestine, along damp walls where an intense and confused life appeared: grubs wallowing in cells full of cilia, red globules gathering in vessels full of varices, but everything was so pallid, ghostly, washed-out, that it seemed more like I was passing high relief carvings on the tunnel's organic kaolin. I descended for years on end, entire lifetimes, trying to make out the messages that flashed on the walls, when suddenly the tunnel expanded and I entered the caverns. I will never be able to express their peerless grandeur. It was an entire karstic system carved into the soft, semitransparent rock. The successive cathedrals were immeasurably high, and stalactites flowed down in the shapes of people, gods, and embryos, one flowing into the next, illuminating the gigantic, melancholic space around them. I walked like a mite beneath the overwhelming emptiness, I passed through constricted passages that shredded my skin, and then I emerged into even vaster spaces, where a multicolored network of rivulets housed newts with pink skin and human hands. Many of the stalactites, thick as twenty oaks, were scattered with holes where yellow larvae with disgusting claws and hairs pushed out their blind heads. Here and there, in that tangle of underground intestines, in an olive atmosphere, large, naked women, larva-like in their pallor and consistency, were bathing, alone or in groups of three or four, some in basins of water up to their thighs, others up to the waist. They didn't seem like independent, human creatures, but more like fruits of the earth, mushrooms or pale green truffles. They watched me with their deep eyes, where the dark green of shadow suddenly concentrated and peeled away, showing irises as limpid as emeralds. Drops of water from their wading swelled on their young breasts—unexpectedly small and tender on their fat, larval bodies.

I remember the swollen red and blue hoses that ran under the floor's soft glass, making it look like the damp area under the tongue. I remember the hands of the newts spread toward me in imploring gestures. I cannot forget the yellow gazes of the embryos sculpted in icicles hanging from the ceilings, with their unformed foreheads, their cerebral ganglions visible through their flesh. The channels between the caverns also began slowly to swell, and in the end more of them united into larger channels, with incomparably more ample rings. I explored until they met, suddenly along with many others, in a trachea that seemed carved into the pink rock of a distant planet. The animal that breathed through this tunnel, kilometers in diameter, must have been deeply asleep. The tunnel vibrated with the beating of a distant heart. The current of air, in inhalation and exhalation, rustled my hair like a quiet breeze. I walked along the damp, elastic membrane until, at the end of entire eons, I reached the place where the divinity of the language opened the operculum full of gills. Glued one to the next like imaginary, somnolent labia, the strings of a harp larger than the mind surrounded me, pressing me hard against the glassy hyoid bone. I stayed there forever, listening to the roar of a captive intelligence formed from mucus, membrane, and muscle, as it protested, in harmonies and disharmonies, melodious and rending, its ancillary condition.

The next day, however, I woke up in my bed, full of purple marks on my buttocks and legs. To my surprise, my father hadn't gone to work, even though it was not a Sunday. He sat at the table wearing the expression I had long wished I could see on him: guilt. Before I was out of bed, he knocked on my door and then my mother, Dr. Vlădescu, and he came into my room, where I was lying among the sheets, in pajamas wrinkled and sweaty like a dishrag. "My boy," my father said after they had all stood quietly for a moment, "in the fall you're not going back to the school down the street. You're going to go somewhere else, to the preventorium at Voila . . ." "It's a very pretty place, in the mountains, where you can get better," the doctor said, looking at me with pity. "You'll stay there the whole time, study there, with lots of children . . . From time to time your parents will come visit, they'll bring you good things, toys even, isn't that right?" She looked with forced happiness at my mother. But my mother could not respond, because she had burst into tears. Then the doctor left, handing my parents the paperwork, and my mother brought me a cup of hot cocoa. They stayed with me the whole day. We went to the café, but even when I was eating a Lotus cake that cost five lei—a fortune for my parents and for most of the parents in the block, such that none of the children knew what it tasted like—I couldn't think of anything except the fact that there, underneath our block, under our world, there were phantasmagoric caverns from another world, full of disturbing creatures. My mind was invaded by the whispers and terrible voices—rough, murmuring, and complaining—of men, women, castrati, cherubim, and nameless beasts that I had heard there, in the cenotaph of language, with my ear pressed against the great hyoid bone. I heard terrible things, things that it was not given to people to hear, and then they commanded me, with the voice-will I knew from the circular hall, to not tell anyone about them, ever.

24

Before I go further transcribing the pages from my diary, I thought I would set down here, in this kind of a diary, an odd discussion I had this morning in the teachers' lounge with Irina, who hasn't visited me for a long time. I was there for all of third period, which was skipped in favor of wastepaper collection, sitting at the window beside the radiator, looking at people swaddled in their thick coats, at the old factory and the water tower, the whitish sky above. In the somber aquarium-like atmosphere of the lounge, Irina always appeared like a slow-moving, pale, chloroid fish; her face had two intensely colored spots—ostentatious warnings to the cosmos not to devour her by mistake—her unreal blue eyes.

We spoke about children first, about the power of half of the population to give birth, about the terrible responsibility of bringing other people into our hell. About their inhumanity and foreignness, about the fact that they are a different species, not different from us in degree, but structurally, the way a larva is different from the adult insect. About our instinctive fear of children and the antiseptic isolation they impose through taboos and barriers. "It is fitting to receive a child into your house like a foreign wayfarer and to raise him in honesty and dignity," she quotes to me from the Vedanta. "Doesn't it clearly follow that your son is not precisely human? That you have to honor him with awe and fear, like a sacred object camped in your house? But the sacred has never meant anything other than the foreign and incomprehensible. Maybe the mind and senses of children are connected to another reality, the one from which they appeared among us, through the only tunnels that run between worlds and dimensions: uteruses . . ." The bell would ring in a few minutes, and we would go back into the rooms where thirty foreigners with disproportionately large heads and giant eyes were waiting to examine us, to manipulate us expertly, to study our anatomy in detail, our psychology, ethology, the way experts handle white rats . . .

After she stared off into the distance for a while, Irina suddenly turned to me:

"As long as we're talking about children, answer me this riddle. Not a riddle, really, more like a fable (I found it in a commentary on *The First and Last Freedom*). You know, these stories that are meant to provoke you, like a personality test, you just have to answer honestly . . . For example, this one: if you knew that you could push a button and someone would die in another hemisphere, someone you have never seen, and at the same moment you would receive a fortune, would you do it?"

"Ah, I know these stories, there's even a novel based on one: would you murder and rob an old pawnbroker, a no-good, evil person, a human louse, if you could use her money to become a benefactor of humanity? But there's always a catch: there's nothing more dangerous than letting a parable become reality. An intelligent and creative person like Raskolnikov did this, just to understand later that he had deceived himself terribly, because he didn't know himself at all . . ."

"At least he answered honestly, like no one in a thousand."

"Precisely because he didn't. If he had been honest with himself, he could not have killed her. But he didn't have the courage to be a nobody. Irina, the horror of the book is this: that a person on the street could commit murder out of a dumb lack of self-knowledge. Because he didn't understand and couldn't withstand the value of anonymity. Okay, what's the next test you have for me?"

"What would you do if you could save one thing only from a burning building, and you had to choose between a famous painting and a newborn child?"

I looked out the window, thinking about the Grand Inquisitor, the one for whom bread was more important than the words that came from the Lord's mouth. The ruined factory was visible through the fog, enclosed in its enigma. I felt the warm radiator through the fabric of my pants; its hot air fogged up the top part of the window: millions of glassy dots, like the eyes on a spider's forehead, their shining curvature refracting the olive interior of the lounge with the two of us at the window, the table covered by a scarlet fabric, and the portraits on the walls.

"Hey," she whispered to me gently, moving her face closer to mine, "I asked you a question. Answer me, now: What would you do? Which one would you save?"

It was not a rhetorical question, and judging by her intense stare, it wasn't a parlor game. I had always thought you couldn't talk about things that reveal yourself. Not face-to-face with the other person. That is why I write instead of talk. When you're face-to-face, eye-to-eye with someone close to you, as though your face were actually poured into his and your eyes were enclosed by his, like in a spherical box, only then do you feel the insurmountable wall between your minds ("What does blue look like to you?", "How can I feel your toothache?"). That's why people used books to say important things, because a book assumes an absence, on one side or the other: while it is being written, the reader is missing. While it is being read, the writer is missing. The disgust and abjection that come from putting the judge face-to-face with the condemned thus disappear.

"I would save the child," I said slowly, after a long silence, still staring out the window, as though I were speaking to the desolate scene behind the school. Irina looked at me with increased attention and disbelief.

"You would save the child . . . Even if the picture were a Rembrandt or a Vermeer? Even if it were a triptych by Bosch? Even if it were an irreplaceable and unforgettable da Vinci? Even if it defined humanity? Even if letting it burn would disfigure the face of humanity with an irreparable scar?"

I didn't know where she was leading me, and I didn't want to have this conversation, but there seemed much more to Irina now than I had realized, more than the physics teacher who didn't believe in matter or atomic structure, and more than the lover lost in excited fantasies. There was something at stake in what she was asking me, she really needed my response, I couldn't wriggle out of this test—my test, her test, or ours.

"Imagine if no one ever saw a painting like *Lady with an Ermine* again, or *Woman Holding a Balance* or the palaces of Monsù Desiderio . . ."

"I would save the child," I interrupted her without looking at her.

Now Irina seemed like a doll with yellowed skin, filled with an intense blue liquid that you could only see in her eyes. Clearly, her body had a core of melted azure, a slow-moving lava, a dense milkiness like the inside of a pupa where the worm had completely melted so that a winged creature could be born from the cream of its liquefied body, one with eyes of fire and a turgid stomach and fragile black legs with strange articulations . . . I didn't think about what I had to say to her, or why I had to say anything. I was waiting for her skin to burst along her spine, to fall in strips to the floor and for the entire lounge to fill with a light of dreams and nostalgia, as though instead of the Macedonian scholars and writers, the walls would display *The Girl with the Pearl Earring* and *View of Delft* and *The Man with the Golden Helmet* and *Venus with a Mirror* and *King Asa of Judah Destroying the Idols* and *Portrait of Ginevra Benci*, and in front of me would stand, interrogating me with a majesty that had no need of my answers, and filling the lounge with its unfurled azure wings, an archangel carved in transparent ivory, through whose flesh I could see veins and internal organs.

"I would choose the child," I repeated, just as slowly and impersonally.

"Why?"

"Maybe because the only way to hang a child on the wall is to crucify him."

Irina paused to gather herself. It was clear now that she would not give up her dry skin and unwashed hair, falling in blond waves over the collar of her coat.

"But what if you knew," she added, watching her cards like a card sharp, "that it was going to be autistic, that it would never look anyone in the eyes, that it would spend its life looking at the wheels of cars, or at geese, at the way light fell on the floor, or just out the window or Lord knows what else? If you knew that people, for that child, would always be things, just scenery?"

"The child," I said, looking at the abandoned factory.

"What if you knew that the infant who was crying in the flames would one day be Adolf Hitler? Or Pol Pot? Or Stalin? What if you knew it would be a monster, a serial killer that would bring an endless, stupid, absurd suffering to those around it? What if it would become Messalina and wallow in abjection like a pig or Medea and chop up her children's bones and throw them in the sea? What would you save from a burning house, if you could only take one thing from that inferno? *Mona Lisa* or Hitler? *Adoration of the Magi* or Pol Pot? What would you do? Tell me now! Don't hesitate, your first thought is the most honest in stories like these!"

"Irina," I said, still looking out the window, "if someone told me that child was going to be Hitler, I would know in that moment that I am being deceived and tested. That I'm being tested by the one who once said, 'If thou be the Son of God, cast thyself down from the top of the temple, and angels will bear thee up.' I would be even more sure to choose the child, Irina. Because a child doesn't have only one future, he has billions of creodes ahead of him. Any pebble he steps on, any blade of grass he looks at is the switch that can change the track his life is riding on. Every moment of his life is a fork in the road. No infant is destined to order the slaughter of the innocents. In another future, he might be the one who saves them. In another, maybe the one to paint Herod's slaughter. Before us is an endless branching of worlds, but without the child at the start, none of them exist."

Before the geography teacher—the very discreet Ionescu—came in the lounge and went straight to deposit her register in the cupboard, Irina had grabbed my hand and squeezed it tightly. Evening settled over the ruins outside. She let go, of course, right away, but we didn't leave the window, we stayed there, shoulder to shoulder, like an impossible couple, until the lounge filled with noisy people, multiplying themselves like ghosts on double-exposed film. Only we two were concrete, drowned in brilliant light from outside, as though we were not just a couple standing with our backs to people, but we were joined by a child, the one from the parable, the one saved from the flames instead of all the icons of the world, and which, through our care and love, would never become the murderer, torturer, executioner, scoundrel, or demon in the story.

I will continue to record, without the exact date and without context, although they might sometimes be relevant, the fragments from my diary that have always given me pause for thought. If this text is insane and misguided, I do feel relieved in the end that it contains truths, that its core occurred in *this* reality, and that at least this core means something, the way symmetrical seeds are the truth hidden deep in the vegetable flesh of an apple.

I have had dreams, one of which was horrible, impossible to describe, impossible to remember, the Rimbaudian horror of H-hour, and another with a terrifying fall through emptiness (naturally, I woke faceup with a stiff neck and the hair on top of my head standing up).

Last night, another "microepileptic seizure" (?) horrifically intense. At its peak, I screamed in my sleep. It happened two more times, one after the other. The same ringing in my ears, intensifying until it was unbearable, the same yellow explosion of fear. Everything followed by the usual sequence of events: I dream that I'm awake, I go to the living room, I look for my mother.

Restless sleep. Could it be "nonconvulsive Morpheic epilepsy?" And in this case, is the focus point somewhere in the top of the head? Or possibly it is only an anomaly of blood circulation in the scalp (this would explain the ringing in my ears and the pressure on my head that wakes me, the sensation of congestion, a cold or fever perhaps).

I read Moody's La vie après la vie. *Charmingly naïve, unscientific, but that's just what gives it a primitive sense of veracity. In any case, the dream that leaves me awake on my back has clear resemblances to the "scenes" of the dead returning to life: ringing, overwhelming light with something divine about it, violent rushing, shooting out of yourself in the perfectly realistic scenery of your room, then walking around the house in a "spiritual body." Is it possible that something is happening in these moments, that I am "dying" for a few seconds? Or is it all a seizure? An exception to Moody's descriptions, in the case of my "funeral" dream, is the infinite terror that encompasses me in those moments, rather than the beatitude the book describes. Additionally, I have never seen my body sleeping in my bed, as though I have never turned back.*

Even more so, now I would say that I remember very well that after I was pulled from my bed and, still wrapped in my sheets, thrown on the floor so hard that my head and shoulder hit the opposite wall, I lay on the floor with no thoughts or energy but, although my room was dark, I clearly saw that there was no one in my bed. At the end of my disoriented sleepwalking through the entire house, I didn't go back to bed, or better said: I don't remember going back. Pure and simple, I woke there, face up and hands on my chest, as though I had been placed on the mattress by a stranger who didn't know how I slept.

Horrible dreams, with large flying machines gliding between the block and the mill, with other mixed colors, blue and pale yellow.

Three nights ago, I had my "epileptic" dream again. This time I was looking down a dark metro tunnel or a car underpass. I was looking, I think, at the outline of a human in front of me, barely visible in the dark. Someone outside of myself commented: "Can you imagine how good this person's vision must be, to go through the tunnel at his speed?" And suddenly I was moving at that speed. Faster and faster, until it frightened me. The walls fled madly past. I hurtled forward at thousands of meters per second, inside of a scream that grew constantly louder. An unbearable light began to burn my brain. A feeling of the supernatural tore me to shreds. The end of the world had come. I screamed twice, as loud as I could, "It's exploding! It's exploding!" and the entire universe exploded inside my skull like a mushroom cloud, but a million times faster and more intense.

And yet, right away, so you can see how my memory plays tricks on me and how everything disappears, fragment by fragment, like a sugar cube melting in coffee, I have selected a fragment in which I remember exactly what I had written only one page before, the dramatic return to my own body. Only here am I aware of the ambiguity and irrelevance of the distinction between dreams and reality, and I understand that the series of "dreams" of this kind could not have been either one of these states, but a third, which I could call, as it has been called so many times, "charm," "magic," "enchantment," if it hadn't been so frightening to remember. A dark charm, a black and destructive magic, a detour through a world for which your brain was not created, one that requires another type of mind and other sensory organs:

After three months—last night I reexperienced the "epileptic" dream in completely foreign circumstances. The same stages—unbearable ringing, fear infinitely increasing, the sensation that I am thrown to the end of the bed. But what was new and horrifying was my acute awareness that I was dreaming, and my desperate attempts to wake myself. I saw my entire room sunk in darkness, I felt how my shoulder hit the wardrobe, and then the most amazing thing happened: as usual, I went toward the living room to look for my mother, but there, on the narrow bed, was only my sleeping father. I found my mother in the other room, sleeping alone. I "came to" and tried to slap myself, to move around and to wake myself up. My body would not listen. After a long time, I actually woke up. In the morning I discovered that my mother really hadn't been sleeping next to my father, but in the other room! The only possible conclusion is that I have been leaving my body during the past five or six years of nightmares. When I woke, my neck was cold as ice.

And unexpectedly, much earlier than I remembered, the first "visitor." The end of May, 1980, when I was almost twenty-three. I was visited constantly from then on, at irregular intervals, but without any interruption of this flow of strangers into my bedroom, wherever I slept or at whatever hour of the day or night.

Last night, something bizarre happened: I opened my eyes and, in my room, next to my bed and looking at me, there was a young man, perhaps a teenager. I immediately thought that this was not possible, and then the young man unraveled in the air. I closed my eyes and fell back asleep.

Next, a "dream" that I remember clearly, in details that will never be erased from my mind, perhaps the most "real" one I have ever had:

A terrible nightmare last night. Some children appeared in my window (on the fifth floor!). Eventually they entered my dark room. One was small, purple, sensuous, androgynous . . . I fought them, almost dead with horror.

I don't know if I should connect this one to other dreams, which for me are fragments, the way a piece of shrapnel fragments into hundreds of shards, the way that abyssal caves explode when unearthed, in a story that could be the unseen side of my life. I don't remember if I have ever written about the dream with "mama," for example, probably not, and I don't think I even could, but I should wait for this ragged material to speak for itself, before I give it the shape that it half took on in my mind.

One April evening I had the following hallucination. If I ever were to write "a great novel," it would probably be in the wake of these panoramas of a much greater grandeur than I could describe in any less than a thousand pages:

Last night I had one of the most extraordinary dreams of those I have ever been given. I have to try to express the inexpressible. The first thing I am aware of is that I was speaking to a princess of the New World, who had come to Europe for me. I don't remember what she looked like, and, in any case, she was not part of the actual dream. "You will see new worlds, completely different from what you have seen before now." And an overwhelming image did appear, of the night breaking into dawn. There were about a dozen semicircular, pinkish-orange moons illuminating the fantastic scene we looked down on from above. It was the vast outline of a continent, toward the center of which numerous lights took the shape of cities, with all kinds of minuscule architectural details. On the ocean shore there were ports from which hundreds of ships with illuminated portholes suddenly set out onto the water, casting phosphorescent green and orange reflections. It was like I was watching a movie and admiring the charming delicacy of the images. The "screen" of the landscape became circular, surrounding me with the image of mountains with stylized trees, with Renaissance cities full of columns and capitals, each one drawn in detail. There were city halls, temples, and cathedrals, all yellow or gray. I was in the center of this diorama, beside a pool of black water, looking at the magisterial church in front of me. Suddenly the bells seemed to ring, and I knew that a holy service was happening. A mystical shiver ran through me and I brought my hands together, kneeling beside the edge of the pool. First, a child in white vestments emerged from the church with a smiling, clean face. I took his hand, and my mind filled with gratitude. Then, from the same church, an adult with gentle features came out, also smiling, also in white vestments. He was carrying a few lit candles, shining through a glass jar. I began to cry, "I, oh Lord, never lit a candle." And then, thinking of my uneasiness, I shouted, "Forgive me! Forgive me!" And he smiled, and he forgave me.

Many years have passed since this dream, and writing it down surprised me because I hadn't remembered the last part. Yes, I was in the central square of a medieval city, there was a pool that seemed to be extraordinarily important, but when the dream began, on either side of it were two young, blond people in white clothes. That is how they appear in my memory. They looked at me and seemed to smile ironically, not cruelly, but the way you would act toward a child. "You have been forgiven," they told me. When I woke, I was moved and happy, because at the time I was suffering from a cyst on my right testicle that could have been cancer. After this dream, the cyst decreased and although it is still there, it doesn't bother me anymore.

> *Last night, another dream: I am in a tram full of crippled people, women and children with wounds and terrible ulcerations. I get out quickly and go home. Here I realize that my lips have come off. I am holding them in my hand. They bend like rubber and stay in the shape of a mouth. I put them back on in the bathroom mirror, but they fall off again and a face full of fear looks back at me, with tiny, pale lips that bleed and with only wounds for eyes. I feel I am paralyzed; I break into tears and cry for my mother.*

It is a terrible period, infected by a nocturnal life that overflows the borders of sleep, that comes into my mind on the street and at home, and during classes at school, making me turn toward the chalkboard and rub my eyes with the same demented strength with which I claw my nails against the heel of my hand, just to crush the horror and hell of these nocturnal visions. But the visions do not stop. For a few years, they have stalked and attacked me in all their monstrous details, not corporeal like dreams are, not like nightmares, but like another realty. Rarely have I felt more powerless in front of "the horrors of my own mind," as I thought they were at the time, opting perhaps for the most anodyne explanation. Was it because I was teaching at the school at the end of Colentina that there were so many children in my dreams? So aggressive, so manipulative and powerful? Perhaps I was so scared of them because, in my subconscious, I was actually terrified by the crowd of them, by my helplessness surrounded by thirty gray larvae, ready to devour me at the slightest sign of weakness? I'll continue with these diary fragments, but I don't know if I'll keep commenting on them as I have. I reexperience them myself, I am disturbed and perplexed: what does this opened capsule of my life want to say? What has been kept, deformed by the pressure of these nocturnal fabrics, by this sinister sheet wound around my body, from the message of a strange and pitiless world, denatured by folds, by circumvolutions, by the bones of my face, by my thoracic cavity? Who appears in the aleatory and disturbing stains of this Shroud of Turin?

I dreamed all night about flight machines gliding over the mill yard, very close to my block.

I dreamed that I wake in my dark room, and that I leave my bed full of terror, I go to the window, I move the blinds aside and see, projected onto the night outside, a child resting his elbows on the sill, staring at me with round eyes.

. . . A series of terrible dreams last night. From a number of cadavers spread over the floor, a yellow mist (in fact, a wave of unreal images) rose and took the shape of horrible, linen-yellow children, hideous abortions, with huge heads and deformed limbs. The fear grew infinitely. I opened my eyes and found myself sleeping on my back, my neck immobile.

Last night—a nightmare. Suffocation, drowning. I was at the bottom of a body of water and realized that I had to get to the surface to breathe. The climb transformed into a painful struggle to wake up. I climbed toward consciousness, I knew I was asleep and I had to wake. Next, the feeling I was tossing in bed, in between the sheets and blankets, hastily, endlessly. The conscious effort to wake was terrible.

Then, about two months later:

After yesterday, when I had nothing but complicated hallucinations (in the tram, at school, everywhere) of being abused, run into, tortured, last night I had the following dream: I was in a tram, only myself and the driver. A thick fog began to envelop the tram. I could barely see even the outlines of old, ornamented houses as we moved through the city. Suddenly, the tram picked up speed. Faster and faster, until the outside blurred into a tunnel. The speed was enormous, unreal, incalculable.

But a fantastic dream from last night has brought a bit of reality to the exhausted fiction of my life over the last few days. As I was out walking, I suddenly noticed an odd, large building. I entered. The door was white—a hospital door. In the first room I saw just a few people peering into microscopes. This confirmed my impression that I was inside a clinic. I opened another door and came to a long, white hall with nickel-plated devices in the corners and some operating tables. On the tables—various human parts: hands and legs flayed, covered in blood. In the corners, in chairs and attached to strange devices—diseased people with open incisions. "I don't want to look," I said to myself. I opened another door after I walked down the hall, and—here, this scene was the most overwhelming. How can I describe it? The hall wasn't white anymore, but darkened by an olive air. The only things in the hall were some dark green-gray forms that writhed on the floor. They were women giving birth—it was a maternity ward. But why were they all green-purple, and why were they wrapped in pleated sheets of the same color that seemed to be part of their bodies? They looked like twisting, Plasticine, green-purple larvae, their green-purple hair flailing about heavily and covering their faces. I helped one of them give birth, using that organic, cadaveric "sheet" and wringing it out like a wet rag. She was relieved, even though no child appeared, and she became gray and immobile, like a statue on an Etruscan sarcophagus. All of this disturbed me deeply.

Perfectly authentic telekinesis last night. I concentrated hard, frowning, and the objects moved in any direction my will pushed them.

Here we have the round room where I woke after "the operation"; that distant day when my mother carried me to the hospital, through the snow, reappears after a quarter century, in a dream . . .

. . . coherent, and perfectly clear. I retain only the image of a hemispheric hall. Its glass walls extended into a dome, but cream-colored curtains covered them almost completely. The cupola and the floor rotated slowly, the cupola with visible speed, the floor extremely slowly. The room was about seventy meters in diameter. I was with dozens of others seated on curved benches along the wall. A girl, maybe fourteen years old with beautiful bare breasts (she was half-naked), rested her head on my shoulder. Then

everyone lined up at these windows or counters in the wall. When I got to the front I saw, on the other side of the window on a long table, an enormous fish with its eyes wide open.

I remember this dream well, especially the "fish"; it was actually hard to describe, a creature set in a kind of tube, the same cream color as the walls and curtains. It was five or six meters long and while I don't know why, and while a number of descriptions come to mind for this melancholic beluga, I would rather leave it in a vagueness befitting its presence.

A horrible dream last night. I was inside a kind of museum. The entire dream came down to an intense, desperate monologue from me about death, delivered imperiously, coercively, with my full throat, with my eyes dilated, with acrid, cold sweat. "Lord, half my life is gone, the end will come unimaginably quickly, in a few moments it will all be over." I was sobbing yellow tears, in the vertebrae of my spine I felt the eternity throughout which I would be nothing, forever. But there is no word to express the pain and sudden feeling of finis I was experiencing. On a high but rickety white stage were an old woman and an old man, she was fat, he was shaped like a bonhomous patriarch, with his head attached directly to his torso. They called me over and examined me with a radioactive device. "So we can check you for tumors"—the old man said with a laugh, unraveling into multiple old men and snapping back together. I didn't want this in any way, I ran back toward the undefined objects in the museum. I was sure that if I climbed onto the stage, I would know how close to death I was. It was very hard to wake up; until I started writing, I felt like my brain was wrapped in cotton.

And after a few days, another visitor, also earlier than I ever remembered:

I don't want to forget an odd vision I had last night. I had fallen asleep after a series of scares (furniture knocking together, suspicious sounds at the front door and on the balcony), when, maybe a sound but more likely an intuition, a sudden interior disturbance made me open my eyes. In the half-dark of the room, beside the bed, I clearly saw, for a good many seconds, the image of a creature looking at me. His face was dark and slightly pointed at the chin, he had high cheeks and shiny hair pulled back in a ponytail. I sat up, frightened, and held out my hand toward him. Only then did he disappear.

A dream recorded on a scrap of paper, July 26:

A dream that felt "extraordinary," after a series of nights of perfectly realistic aesthetics. First, I was in a noble family's salon. We were speaking of our fascination for starry skies, then I noticed that through the salon's tall, narrow windows, which were made of crystal, I could see the enormous moon was flat, like a geological map. I found myself transported to the middle of a field, under stars glittering red and yellow in unknown constellations. I went into the salon's back room, and there I found a young man out of Salinger, maybe he was ill, in any case blasé and intelligent and insipid, who showed me I don't know how many glass cases displaying an amazing collection of motors and other miniature devices, including solenoids made of fine copper wire, wrapped thousands of times, spiral next to spiral, on a torus-shaped frame. In front of it, and recently built, was an indeterminate object of complex structure: nickeled stems, gears, cylinders, all set between two plates like a clockwork. The unusual part of the dream began here and is very difficult to express. Suddenly it began to thunder and lightning in a frightening way. Through the window, on the right, the sky had turned dark as blacktop. I was at the window in my parents' back room ("the little room"), and I saw Moara Dâmbovița through the window. Then a cloud descended, shaped with an unreal precision, and covered, quickly and slowly at the same time, all that could be seen in the window. It was exceptionally dense, almost like rubber, but still made of mist, frozen and superconcentrated. Thousands of hallucinatory layers settled one onto the next. The entire earth underneath was a single dappled and rippling cloud. The clouds descended, the sky and the air descended, in ever thinner and flatter layers. Vast brick constructions remained in the bitter void—clear, arid, inhuman. The buildings had lost all color, the brick of the mill turned an ash color mottled with lichen. Along with the sky and colors, the feeling of reality had also disappeared. Everything was strange, distant, inconsonant with my senses. Stunned, I walked in fear and fascination through an unmade city, through the pale simulacra of streets and buildings.

And on the same note, just a few nights later:

Last night I dreamed that the Circus Lake turned to a dense gelatin and rose into the air like an enormous gray lens. It left a perfectly dry pit behind.

It was December 3 of the same year. On December 8, I married Ştefana at the Sector 2 People's Council on Str. Olari, outside it was minus twenty degrees, with a sad, fairy-tale snowfall. I remember us afterward walking down Moşilor between blocks that looked like pieces of dirty cardboard, the street was almost empty, lined with huge piles of snow. Her arms were full of flowers, she could literally barely hold the enormous multicolored bouquets, and her head was bare, her hair filled with glittering, perfectly dried, hexagonal snowflakes. We were walking in the middle of the street on the dirty snow, between the empty shop windows. The very few cars drove around us, buses passed with silver gas cans on their roofs, the tram rails were invisible beneath the snow. A tram came up behind us, out of the foggy depths of the city. We heard it and turned around. Motionless, we faced it, snow on our hair, our eyelashes, our frozen hands. In the white light of Moşilor, my bride's flowers glowed so strongly that the snowflakes evaporated before they landed. The tram stopped, the driver's face, like a fetus in a jar, broke into a wide smile, the doors opened, and we climbed in, applauded by the half-asleep housewives and retirees. We rode a long way, to the end of Colentina, standing, embracing; we got off at the turnaround beside the water tower and walked into the school's neighborhood, where her parents lived. If someone had said to me then—when we stopped outside the gate to the house and kissed for fifteen minutes in the thick snow, crushing the flowers between us, feeling the perfumed breath from dozens of mouths, red with yellow strands, azure with lace loops, pale white-green with transparent pistils—that in only fifteen months, within a single night, that little girl with eyebrows a bit more slanted than they should be would be switched out for someone else, who looked the same down to the last mole and last eyelash, who spoke the same and moved the same and yet was different, foreign and threatening, I could not have believed it, just as it is hard for me to believe now.

25

I did go to the morgue, as I had promised Caty, not a month but more than a semester later, because I had rushed home every night, in the eternal tram 21, eager to continue my manuscript. In a way, it has become reality for me, the world where I breathe and think, ever since I have become picky, like a fussy child, before the plates of existence my life offers. Two nights ago, I came through the door cold and impatient to copy out other inexplicable and haunting fragments, new clippings to graft onto the brain of an ever more improbable reader, but then as usual I wandered about without turning on the lights, through the large, echoing house, never the same house as the one I remember, until I found myself again in the little entry hall, in front of the front door through whose window came the gold and blood clots of the sunset. The silence had never been more total, the silence of those deaf from birth and of the world in which the ear had never appeared, than in these pauses, these interstices where no one lived, these places locked within their shadow and enigma. Here, you are not living in the world but in a photograph with pale hues and frozen shadows.

This time, however, someone was knocking. I could spy, deformed through the bulging glass between the volutes of wrought iron, the image of a woman who could be none other than Irina, my only friend from School 86. I opened the door before she could ring the doorbell, and we walked through the rooms together, through the studies, the painting studios, the corridors with yellow glass windows, the libraries lined with books, and kitchens full of heteroclite objects, until we reached the bedroom, where, as always, Irina embraced me without disturbing the silence—but this time it brought frustration, because I was feeling a more textual than sexual fervor and, furthermore, I was so intrigued by the image of the girl with multicolored nails that I wasn't at all tempted to exchange an evening of lonely meditation for a simple sexual embrace. It was so strange how the same woman's body could sometimes seem so sexual to your hormone-soaked mind, while at other times, when the golden liquid didn't bathe your mind and senses, she became just as inert, as neuter, and as detached as a lamp forgotten on the nightstand or an umbrella in the dark of a closet. Although she was naked and wanted love very much, for me in that moment Irina was not a woman but a person acting strangely, incomprehensibly. A brain injury can leave us unable to perceive an entire spatial area—everything to our left for example—leaving it always empty, like the abyss that precedes our birth. Or we can go so blind that we can no longer imagine seeing. But these things don't usually happen in our lives, and never more than once. But the on and off of our sexuality, just as complete and just as astounding, happens frequently and we don't give it a thought. When Irina pulled me onto the bed, when she pushed the button on the wall and we rose to float gently a meter over the sheets, where, in the delicate shadow, she began to passionately caress me, the problem was not my limp sex, but the fact that I could not remember that something called sexuality existed. However, I still got undressed and we still embraced through force of habit, and her bony body turned, as usual, until our faces were in front of each other's sex. What happiness this is—when your erotic madness takes its place within you! Sometimes it seems like you don't need anything else: seeing in detail the other's sexual flower—her flower of folded flesh, the bewitching ambiguity of is ugliness, drops of dew on her thick petals, her notched, scarlet depths, the little star of her anus between her spread buttocks of ivory skin, everything dissolved in the liquid gold of pleasure, there underneath, where the cistern of gold of your vitality resides, your core of incandescent lava . . . But at this moment I looked at her vulva with a kind of indifference, the way you look at a painting on the wall in your own room that you know so well you don't even notice it. Everything was good, I was relaxed, I had forgotten the manuscript, but I couldn't be anything but very distant, sensing the futile contact of the lips and fingers of the woman I floated beside, inside a silent cloth of images. I had somehow turned back into a child, the happy darkness of love hadn't yet tumefied my mind still enclosed in its chastity. I tenderly caressed the skin of my girlfriend next to me, the way I would pass my fingers over the silky vellum of a brand-new notebook. The catlike torus of the solenoid under the floor filled the bedroom with a kind of mechanical, elastic tension, like a tram vibrating as it crosses a boulevard of unknown buildings.

When she turned toward me again, Irina was smiling. She actually started to laugh: "Let's try something else," she said, and, naturally, I knew what was coming. Always, no matter how passionate or fulfilling or uninhibited our sex had been, and no matter how long it had lasted or how exhausted we were after being whipped in the face by the wet, elastic strands of the other person's hair, in order to feel completely released, Irina needed the absolute darkness in which she played games that frightened, fascinated, and excited me, ever since our meetings began. And now we turned over, floating gently above the bed's crumpled sheets, we turned off the light and stretched out under the blanket, our naked bodies next to each other, she with her head on my shoulder, barely noticeable in the deep dark, I with my arm along her pillow and looking at the ceiling without wanting to see, because my eyes, open or shut, were useless in that moment, the same way they are no good for caves in the depths of the earth.

I descended along her shifting, raspy, melopoetic voice into the vast bolgia, and dungeons and oubliettes of pure sex, detached from any humanity, to such depths where rationality was a hyperdistant constellation, so high and so impersonal that in the end it entirely dissolved. Soon, we no longer had names or identities or brains or hearts, everything had been left behind, like lovers passionately and slowly undressing and leaving their clothes scattered from the front door to the bed. As fervent as a copper statue heated in a kiln, burning my ear with the torrid summer breeze of her gasping and whistling breath, Irina told me about orgies a waking mind could not imagine, about frenetic couplings, about piles of men's and women's bodies exhausting every possibility of our apparently so limited sexes, about penetrations and caresses that stirred an ecstasy utterly beyond what you can feel in your impoverished, conscious life. About willing executioners and voluntary victims, who moan in languor and burning sweat under horrible, maddening tortures. She spoke to me about the terrible pleasure of being wholly in another's power, bound and crucified like a sexual specimen, about penetrations in which the woman moved like an Indian divinity, in which fingernails left bloody tattoos on the skin. In the utter darkness, unburdened by the other's gaze to remind us who we were, Irina told me about the overwhelming need to be regarded as a simple object of pleasure, about the need to twist together on the sheets with another woman, about wandering the streets at night in search of one-night stands. Void, blasphemy, degradation, but through them and beyond them, a destructive and radiant pleasure, like a black fire that never goes out. You were deep, deep, deep inside yourself, there where the shape of the sexes is only a symbol for another world and another life, where your body has escaped the chain, where it is free, in a monstrous and dangerous splendor. As she continued her stories, always changing, always exceeding anything you could imagine ever experiencing in life as given to people on Earth, the voice of the unseen woman next to me was interrupted more and more, as it sank into moans and gasps. The air passed through her lungs and blood, irrigated her hyperexcited pelvis, and flooded over my cheeks like a gust from an open oven.

At first, I had resisted her craving to lead me there, the hypnosis of her monotone voice, I had been scandalized and disturbed by this side of her, something I never could have imagined. I stopped her the moment her stories broke the limits of domestic, ritual sex as it existed in my mind before I met her. Then, however, I accepted it, I took her hand, and like two explorers, naked and shining in the dark of underground caverns, I followed her farther and farther down the mazelike path, always in descent, until one evening we both melted into the transparent flowing metal of the earth's core. Beside her, by means of the mental voyage within a world of unlimited pleasure without space or time, the infernal paradise and celestial hell, I suddenly had an orgasm glorious beyond compare, like the sudden aperture in my skull of a miscreant and sublime inflorescence. I knew there was no true I, no will, no rationality, no skin, and no internal organs, that beyond their illusion was a world shaped from pleasure, pure pleasure, like a blinding explosion beyond which there is not even nothing. That was how our hours of love always ended, in a crazed embrace in total darkness, all the more violent the longer we had lain still, leaving only the odd plant of a voice that was no longer Irina's but her womb's, growing between us, twisting its fresh tendrils around us. And after the ivory Jordan flooded the holy land, we woke, turned on the light, dressed without looking at each other, and Irina left, to my relief, because I could hardly wait to return to my dark and lonely life. I often said to myself, "Again, I escaped," as though the physics teacher were one of those insects whose females, after mating, meticulously devour the male.

Thus it happened that the night before last, when the Mina Minovici adventure was so fresh in my mind, I could not bring myself to describe it, and yesterday I was too upset by the story of the girl with the multicolored nails to write it down. However much the pressure of daily events steals me away from what I should be recording here, I am trying to maintain a certain order in my account, because every living organism is symmetrical and develops asymptotically from the few sediments that cast a shadow over the pole of the initial egg.

❋

Mina Minovici's dark, haunting eyes stare at me from his *Treatise on Forensic Medicine*; they are in no way different from those of the hanged, shot, buried, burned, defenestrated, and poisoned people who populate the pages of this book, which I consider as important as the Bible. After I bought it from the Sadoveanu Bookstore and leafed through it the first time, I felt ill, just as I had a few years earlier when a treatise on skin disease passed through my hands (and left them covered in a rash)—a book full of photographs of backs, thighs, and inguinal zones covered in exuberant and unreal flora: pustules, eczemas, excoriations, carbuncles, explosive hives, and lichenous scabs over engorged, ashy epiderma. The iller I became, both physically and psychically, the more these readings fascinated me. Diseases, parasites, deformities, the ruins of the most noble temple on the luminous face of the world: the blessed human body.

His family came from Tetovo, from Serbian Macedonia. They had driven their donkeys and sheep, from the depths of time, through the dizzying scent of Balkan roses, then, after making a heap of money, they went up toward the mouth of the Danube and settled as merchants in Walachia. His father handed down to him and to his other eight children his deep pessimism. He was, for his entire life, a very religious man. In Brăila, he was one of the trustees of the church on the outskirts of Cuțitari, a new church, splendidly painted in hues of purple and sapphire, that glistened like a jewel in the manure and muck of that side of town. Its oddity, not at all foreign to Minovici père, was that in the depiction of the final judgment, which covered the entire west wall of the church, no one was being saved. No one stood in the flock of sheep, to the right of the Father. Rather, the wayward goats, with their stiff necks, filled the left sode with feminine bodies, a little too pink and too voluptuous, and green-black masculine bodies with prominent ribs, crowding toward the river of boiling blood, pushed by devils with pitchforks and ridiculous chin-beards. Mina, a boy seven years of age, would never forget the moment this wall, on which the detail painter had worked in secret, was unveiled. Just like the rest of the faithful people, many of them thieves and whores, he was deeply disturbed, not as much by the terrible fate of the crowd of sinners, but by the emptiness of heaven, by the desolation of the angels, by the tears of Christ shed over salvation's inadequacy for a broken people, for the twisted wood of humankind that nothing could straighten. Likewise, his mind was marked forever by the morning Terente was brought in, the infamous bandit and rapist, king of the marshes, two months dead, his body mummified in the swampy air, pecked by birds and sprouting grass, carted into town surrounded by police, as though he were just as fearful in death as he had been alive. They tossed him down in front of the mayor's house, in the square where the bust of an unknown, mustached person lorded over a fountain, and they stripped him bare, in sight of the entire city, because the citizens of Brăila wanted to confirm a legend immediately: the bandit's manhood, the length of which bore a red ink tattoo of a long and flowery obscenity, was, they said, the longest any living person had ever seen. If he were buried facedown, the market people grinned, it would reach the dusty outback in Australia . . . Mina, his hand held closely by an older brother (who would later become a liberal politician) in the press of the crowd, had a good view of the bandit's stiff, blood-covered pants as they were sliced apart, and he heard the crowd as one say "Ah!" when Terente's sex, truly enormous, descending along his thigh and past his knee, was revealed in its brown, veiny monstrosity, complete with the infamous inscription. After a few days and before he was buried, without a priest or a cross, like a rabid dog, his third leg was cut off and preserved in formaldehyde. Over the years, it became one of the morgue's most admired specimens, under the care of its founder, who would later give the institution his name.

After his father's death, Mina moved to Bucharest, and then, at the end of the nineteenth century, to Paris, where he studied forensic medicine and the young science of thanatology. His first academic publication was "Sudden Death Following Blows to the Abdomen and Larynx," a short, illustrated study that gained some attention. Monumental works followed, such as *The Medical-Forensic Study of Cadaver Alkaloids, Rot from the Medical-Forensic and Hygienic Perspective, Regarding Female Criminality in Romania*, and the classic *Complete Treatise of Forensic Medicine*, in two volumes. Mina Minovici was, additionally, a taxidermist and a specialist in embalming whose services were called on after the death of many crowned heads of Europe.

In 1892, he founded in Bucharest (and built according to his own plan, assisted by the French architect Jean-Baptiste Leroux) one of the first institutes of forensic medicine in the world—also the largest and most modern. It was a colossal construction, with an enormous stone cupola like an eye open toward the sky, surrounded on its flat, circular rim by twelve statues depicting the soul's dark sides: Sadness, Despair, Fear, Nostalgia, Bitterness, Mania, Revulsion, Melancholy, Nausea, Horror, Grief, and Resignation. They were all made from blackened bronze, three times the size of human beings, and they were all women with bland clothes and coal faces. Their bare arms were vibrant and full of convulsive force, unimaginably expressive in their frozen gesticulation. Their hands ended in claws raised blasphemously toward the sky, they seemed like articulate legs of an exorbitantly designed mite. At the apex of the cupola, a pedestal levitated half a meter above the shiny stone (so low that no one noticed that the grand, heavy statue didn't touch its plinth at any point); here was the thirteenth statue, Damnation, four times taller and more massive than the others, lifting its face directly toward the zenith, its mouth gaping in a mute, terrible, eternal howl. Since none of the birds that filled the city, the ravens and crows that Bucharest was known for, ever came near the sinister cupola on Splaiul Unirii, many supposed that the mouth howling under the dusty sky actually emitted screams inaudible to the human ear. The morgue, with its levitating statue—there's no need even for me to tell myself—was set on a node of energy similar to the one on which my house was built on Maica Domnului. As I always suspected—and confirmed a few days ago—there is a solenoid under the cupola, similar to the one under my bedroom, but of course much larger and more powerful.

Aside from the large cupola, which housed a dissection hall with eighty tables and cold storage lockers, the morgue also contained lecture halls, libraries, a popular museum, and outbuildings where no one ever entered, with the exception of the director and a few of the morgue workers. The most fascinating place was (and still is) the museum, one of the few places I visit from time to time. Because there, there is something to see. Alongside Terente's penis, the *Mona Lisa* of this morbid Louvre, his skull and broken jaw are exhibited; while in other showcases, you find malformed skeletons, mummified and stuffed bodies, jars with twins conjoined at the skull, children mutilated to be made into beggars, thick vials with teratological specimens, from hydrocephalic fetuses to headless newborns (the strangest must be the one without eyes, with a smooth forehead down to its lips), adolescents with two sexes, androgynes with conical breasts and purple penises, a uterus sliced open to reveal the infant that seemed to threaten you with its fist . . . You can see, alongside countless other effigies of human unhappiness, dwarfs and hunchbacks, people burnt and disfigured in war, and some of the most heteroclite objects: the ropes that hanged various murderers, atrocious instruments of torture, rubber dolls with O-shaped mouths and folded arms, the underwear of celebrated prostitutes, all that the black melancholy of the human mind can produce, the world's dark and eternally hidden face. Organs devoured by cancer, stomachs still holding strychnine, bloody hymens, and extrauterine pregnancies complete this museum of horrors and pains, the counterweight to all the pinacothecas, concert halls, libraries, and academies on the sunlit side of the world.

Mina Minovici had collected the morgue exhibits over the course of forty years, and they had often provoked nausea and vomit from the visitors. More interesting than the gallery of monsters in the museum is what happened in the examination rooms and in the laboratories of pathological anatomy. For decades, the head of this section had been Mina's brother Nicolae, the seventh child of the family from Brăila, and its black sheep. He had the same dark eyes as his older brother, the same taste for cemeteries, cypresses, and hell, the same melancholic madness, but trained toward the brilliant domain of the arts. As a small child, those who research his life have said, he was attracted to the abstract art of tattoo. The knife wielders and fisherman that filled the Danube city during his childhood had on their vigorous, skinny bodies, from their foreheads to their feet and from their lips to their testicles, the crude decoration of countless drawings over their skin—a true chronicle, simultaneously primitive, grotesque, hilarious, and terrifying, of their conquests, their loves, their desires, their illegal activities, their fears, and their ecstasies. There were pierced hearts, snakes with green and blue scales, women with enormous breasts and oligophrenic faces, icons with divine, triangular eyes, saints with halos, bowlegged women with obscenely bright red vulvas. There were tally marks for stabbings, names written with crooked and uneven letters as though scribed by a seven-year-old, there were lacy patterns, there were Greek friezes, brazen, crude phrases, moons, gears, stars, and crosses . . . When at age thirteen he had followed his older brother to one of the picturesque bordellos on the banks of the great river, spread between fisheries and market stalls where fish with white and pink bellies still writhed, Nicolae could contemplate the even more exuberant tattoos of the whores, more delicate and more provocative than those of the men. Around areolae sporting nipples as big as blackberries, around their vulvae and navels, even, on one Tatar woman, a ring of tiny letters around her mouth, the strumpets presented charming flora and fauna. Butterflies, peonies with spread petals, jewels and bracelets, names accompanied by passionate declarations, knives with flowing blood, crowns of thorns, entire icons of the Mother of God and Holy Infant painted on the stomach, Gospel passages on each buttock—all carved, with atrocious pains, into the epidermis by fishermen-artists, all to the child's delight and amazement, such that his entire life he could never feel close to a woman with immaculate skin.

When he began his studies at the School of Fine Arts in Bucharest in 1888, Nicolae bought a kinetograph, a simple plywood box with two lenses mounted on polished copper tubes, and he returned to his fabled Brăila. The result was four hundred photographs of naked men and women, tattooed from top to bottom, and an ethnographic study entitled *Tattoos of the Danube Area,* enthusiastically received by specialists. On the same occasion, he signed contracts with dozens of people from Brăila who, for quite the meager sum, agreed that after their death and before their burial they would give Nicolae their skin. And so it is that even today in the morgue museum there are five or six of these tattooed skins, stuffed with dried seaweed by the institute's skilled taxidermists and mounted with glass eyes, like the animals of the other museum founded in that epoque, Grigore Antipa's natural science museum. The vast project, however, was quickly abandoned, since, before finishing his degree, Nicolae Minovici discovered his true passion.

During his painting classes, among the young apprentices in large, comfortable smocks stained with oil paints, naked and indifferent models posed for various allegories, taking the forms of fauns, nymphs, shepherdesses, or mermaids, because each of the beginning painters dreamed that one day he would receive his big commission: to paint the stage of an art institute, or at least one of the boyar houses, the walls of a building that housed a minister, or, why not, some salon in the royal palace at Sinaia . . . The male models were usually porters at the college or some gardener from the area, and the women—unimportant young women, stenographers at the courts or instructors who rounded out their income with this work. Some were available, for pleasure or for money, and they often slept with the students who already knew, in any case, every fold of their bodies. Others were chaste and honorable, respected by the boys that penciled the cardboard on their easels as though the women were their own sisters. One of the girls who posed naked—surrounded by dozens of young men with forked mustaches and curled hair, who tried to not stare at their hairy pubises, because art was something divine, far from vulgar temptation—fell in love with Nicolae, the young man with melancholic eyes who looked at her coolly, judging her proportions with his thumb. Coolness and melancholy, they said at the time, often make a young man irresistible. Women sense depth and drama in those gazes and try to save the man from himself, from his afflictions of women, drink, or cards. But Nicolae had nothing to offer modest women, those slumland seamstresses with milk-white skin. He walked with the model a few evenings through the spectral city, he invited her over just to show his collection of photographs of tattooed people, and he let her leave untouched, watching out the window as she climbed, sobbing, into the horse-drawn tram at the stop in front of his four-story building. Then he took out his drawing of her posed as the Little Mermaid, and as the room turned darker brown, he began to draw, on her shoulders and arms, braids of images and lace in ink. Then he colored the drawing with an ivory emulsion.

After a few months of suffering, the girl hanged herself, following the custom of unhappy girls from the slums, differing even in their deaths from their sisters who stayed behind in the country, who, once their stomachs rose up to their mouths, threw themselves down a well. The fine arts student went to see her, still hanging from the ceiling girder in her room with geraniums in the window. The room smelled of basil and cleanliness. A bowl of water threw a trembling light onto the walls. The indifferent patrolman smoked, sitting on the bed, a hand's width away from the girl's pointed, bare feet. His chief had ordered that nothing be touched until he arrived. The girl hung from the rope, with her face purple and her neck broken. Her blue dress seemed made of porcelain in the clear light coming through the window. Her milky white arms and legs seemed more beautiful dead than alive. Her nails on her hands and feet had a special transparence, as though illuminated from within. Nicolae looked at her with his entire clan's fascination for sinister and funereal scenes. She seemed, at this moment, unspeakably beautiful. This was a girl he could have loved, not the one who once moved, ate, and drank; this large doll, from whom revolting and worm-ridden life had withdrawn, was exciting for Nicolae, irresistible in her angelic serenity. If it had been possible, Nicolae would have cut the rope with a knife, taken the young suicide in his arms, and lain her across her bed that smelled powerfully of lavender. He would have covered her with a sheet and tucked thousands of pleats over her stony body, and he would have lain next to her, staring along with her at the ceiling and beams. She would have been his departed beloved, his bruised icon, beside whom he would have stayed for eternity in the vast crypt of the world, he would have grown old there, gazing now and then at the charming, black trace of the noose on her martyred neck, he would have died beside her and they would have decayed together, holding hands, on the bed that was now a boneyard, would have crumbled like plaster in their own vestments, and in the end there would be left only two skeletons in a heap of rags, he and his dead lover, he and his undying love.

He looked at the tumescent face and saw, as she rotated infinitesimally in the air filled with glittering dust, a mystical voluptuousness, an all-knowing smile, an abstract sensuality. It was the smile of the Buddha, the lowered eyelids of those who knew, the ataraxia of those who understood that the eye impeded sight like two fleshly plugs and that only the blooming eye under the skull actually saw. What did this unschooled girl perceive, this girl who understood nothing of life, in her last frightened moments of agony? What had imprinted her face, the color of indigo poppies, with lines you only see on the faces of saints painted in churches, of martyrs for the faith, and of scholars and illuminators of sacred texts? Crazy ideas came to Nicolae's mind: to go to the morgue and steal her eyeballs, to detach her retinas, to spread them out like chocolate wrappers with his fingernail, and to look at them through a microscope. What would he have seen, printed on the stamp-sized papers with a black mark in the middle, what visions that humans had yet to have? He remembered the testimonies of those who had hanged themselves and been saved at the last minute: they all spoke of the unexpected orgasm they felt after the jolt of falling into emptiness. They all said it was tens of times more powerful than the supreme spasm of mating, and those who inhaled ether or injected morphine described the incomparable pleasure, surpassing even drugs, of those moments hanging in the noose, their sex erect and pumping thin jets of hot sperm. Not the hypothetical images that the agony of passage to another world left on the retina—this was not his path. Nicolae suddenly knew what he must do with his life.

He left the room of the hanging a changed man. Starting the next day, he no longer went to the studio but instead went directly to his brother, to become his disciple and close collaborator in the science of thanatology. Over the next two decades, Nicolae Minovici would conduct experiments on himself with ever more sophisticated techniques of controlled strangulation, as part of the research arm of the Institute of Forensic Medicine. At first, he created a simple autoasphyxiation device: a mattress, a pulley attached to the ceiling, a rope that was yanked by the researcher himself, lying on the mattress with the noose around his neck. The brutal interruption of respiration by closing the larynx produced a few seconds of fainting, after which the hand holding the rope became inert and slackened its grip. Nicolae precisely recorded every phase of the fainting: the wave of purple that fell over eyes, then the wave of darkness, the electric flashes and clouded light that preceded the descent into unconsciousness.

Because the grand hallucinations he imagined, and which he secretly yearned for beyond simple scientific interest, were slow to come, he moved to a new stage of his experimentation, in which an assistant would raise him into the air, by pulling on the free end of the rope. It took him a few years to be able to withstand the agony for twenty-five seconds, without touching the ground with his feet, an act which made him a world champion of controlled strangulation, a record unequaled even today. The photographs made to authenticate the study show him hanging from the noose, his body immobile and face serene, his forked mustache, ever thicker as the scholar grew older, adding a note of grotesque farcicality.

Nicolae Minovici hanged himself hundreds of times over two decades in the strange depths of the morgue, but only in the last five of those years did he reach Nirvana. Only then did he publish his principal work, *A Study of Strangulation by Hanging*. From those last years came the many drawings—of incontrovertible talent, the same that had driven the younger him toward the arts—which the thanatalogue made of his visions in the ever-longer periods of asphyxiation. They were images from the threshold of death, they were the mystical and luxuriant sculptures created in the ivory gate between worlds.

My friend the painter Emil G. (whom I don't want to involve in this text any more than this) once showed me, during our adolescence on Ştefan cel Mare, in his breezy house on Str. Galaţi covered in ivy and resounding with cooing doves, some copies of Minovici's drawings, a complete portfolio he had obtained through obscure means. He left me to enjoy them in the living room while he occupied himself in the bedroom with the vulgar and voluptuous Anca, a high school classmate who until that moment had sat at her desk with her legs crossed, letting us see her thick thighs and, when she changed position, her underpants. Hopelessly excited, virgin kid that I was, frightened by girls and by my own sexuality, as I would remain for many years afterward, I untied and opened the grimy portfolio and, becoming more and more absorbed, I perused the thanatologue's drawings.

They were tattoos. The piece of paper was a soft, docile skin made to suffer atrocities. They were incisions made with a reddened needle, immediately filled by black powder. Each drawing looked like a scar from an operation or the floral stamp of a terrible burn. Because, only after he passed through the phase of mechanically blocking the larynx through crude compression, the stage in which, beyond all the burning waves of purple and pitch and the terrible howl in his ears, nothing but nonbeing showed, and arrived at actual hanging, which involved a shock to the cervical vertebrae and the marrow channel of the spine by raising the body from the earth in an ironic levitation, did the visions appear. It was not asphyxiation, not the tightening noose around the throat, not the protrusion of the eyeballs from their sockets, not the purpling of the face and tongue that delivered the mystical apparition of a world impossible to unveil, but an awful aggression against the cerebral centers, the marble and ivory temples where dwelled the gods of another reality. They induced nocturnal dreams, they generated—with their Christ faces and elephant trunks and annihilating Krishna arms and prostitute lips—the hypercubes and superspheres and four-dimensional labyrinths that found their insertion point in the vast and barbarous empire of cerebral structures, that found their portal to transmit hallucinations and visions, the experiences beyond our skin and beyond the skin that covers constellations. These portals were the goal of all searching in the world, of all those who believed in the dictum, "ask and you shall receive, search and you shall find, knock and it will be opened unto you," of all those who knew, like Novalis, that the true path leads inward. These pores in the dense skin of reality produced orgasm and ecstasy, trembling before poetry and music, schizophrenic excess, and the delicate brutality of revelation. Under the weight of a body lifted by the noose, through the pulley, by the assistant of the one subjecting himself to a voluntary hanging, the cervical vertebrae began to slowly pop, like cracking your knuckles, as the spinal cord stretched. Minovici had learned to remain, however, on the side of the living: if he had been allowed to fall even just a half meter into the void (like actual suicides, who kicked their own chair out from under their feet), his neck would have snapped, and the spinal cord, with its billions of braided neuronal snakes, would have suddenly broken, instantly killing the man in the noose. There, between worlds, in a bardo state, was the zone where Nicolae's visions blossomed.

They were tattoos on the passive faces of the paper sheets. There were unreal choruses of saints, their halos crushed together like grapes on a vine, like beads of caviar. There were crosses flying through the sky like flocks of birds, pointed and ready to pierce the transparent cornea of an eye that housed a brain. There was a naked man with dozens of erections, the way that ancient terracotta sculptures of women had dozens and hundreds of breasts. There was a geometrical figure so intricate that it seemed to rise from the page like an iceberg. There was a swarm of insects, a rustling of buccal mechanisms, articulating legs and furry stomachs, and each insect had a human face, drawn as by a child or a cave man. There were rivers wrapped in rivers wrapped in rivers, rings of water with totemic fish that hurtled toward the viewer. There were bunches of ovules in a woman's transparent womb. There was God, with a triangular halo, face to face with a disproportionately large louse who seemed to offer him something on a tray. There were jewels maniacally arranged in tight rows. There were splendid drawings of unknown plants, unknown yet familiar, the way a poppy would seem if poppies had never existed, and which I recognized later in the Voynich manuscript. There were syringes with needles stuck between the vertebrae of recumbent patients. There were flashing rays of light that seemed to come from far away and which, once they reached the viewer, became celestial messengers with faces carved in coral. There was the sacred gate between the thighs of all women, ornamented with exuberant tattoos on tumescent labia. There were multitudes of people, multitudes of mimes, multitudes of cherubim, multitudes of roaring pyres, multitudes of cities, mountains, and valleys, heavens and stars, dodecahedrons and icosahedrons, piled into drawings, which, along with Anca's moans and the glassy chirps of birds and the green shadow of the ivy, I contemplated, one after another. I did not understand the gold and amber clay of these frighteningly primitivist images. I didn't know where to look at the tens of thousands of faces on worms, lilacs, and mites in Minovici's illuminations, drawn immediately after every resuscitation. It took me some time to learn the technique, because at the start I didn't notice the resemblance between the drawings I discarded onto the table as I went through them and the so-called autostereograms, very fashionable during the seventies—that afternoon was in the autumn of 1973—rhythmic designs, abstract, rainbow-colored postcards, where at first you can't see anything. Once you relax the eye muscles, however, such that you are not focused on anything, your dream sight superimposes the right eye over the left, and suddenly, through a wonderful magic, you see a deep and brilliant world where creatures and objects appear in relief, things you had not been able to perceive until then. Could Nicolae Minovici's visions have been a kind of autostereogram? For a quarter hour after this thought came to me, I forced my eyes to lose focus, until the pain became unbearable. The images slid but I couldn't make them superimpose, and the blinding worlds did not appear. Anca growled unreproducible words, louder than the clearly audible squeaking of the bed.

I went to the window. The ghosts of the drawings persisted on my retinas and now were projected over the late-summer sky: tattoos. With the somber sensitivity of an adolescent, the most unhappy of human avatars, I suddenly understood the entire world as an enormous riddle. One word was missing, just one, but this absence caused everything to be lost, because enigmas, mazes, jigsaw puzzles, cryptograms were nothing but questions, worlds left incomplete in the absence of an answer. This was what we were all looking for: the answer, the answer that was the truth. For a long time I simply stood at the window, without looking at anything, listening to the dozens of voices inside me. One of the threads would disappear and return, until it presented itself as a strange image: what if our cerebral hemispheres were eyeballs? What if their specialization, so well known (the left—reason, mathematics, speech, "masculine"; the right—intuition, space, emotion, art, "feminine"), were the equivalent of the difference between the viewing angles of two eyes? What if our thoughts and, certainly, our egos were born from the convergence of these two types of cognition? Focusing them would itself keep us from reading reality, from understanding its encoded message. Wouldn't we need—when we regarded every enigma—to let both hemispheres gaze inattentively, like in a dream, making the two faces of the world change position slightly, until they superimposed? Wasn't everything somehow right in front of our eyes, like in the autostereogram I held between my fingers, but our habits, learned from our predecessors, kept us from seeing the message in their depths?

I went back to the table with the drawings scattered all over it. I looked at them all at once, as they lay at random, superimposed and turned over, at every angle. My mind was a void, completely fascinated, as though by itself. The tattoo-covered surface of the table seemed to rise gently, like when you throw a scarf onto the bed and it catches a passing bubble of air. Anca moaned deeply, agonistically, many times in the adjacent room, and suddenly I saw.

26

So, I reached the morgue at 11:00 PM. A chill had arrived, along with that special darkness only possible in large cities when the streetlights all quit at once. This was probably how it felt in a war, when mandatory blackouts turned out public illumination and put mattresses against the window. There was no war in Bucharest, and yet everything was in the most desolate state of ruin. At every step you saw half-collapsed houses, their windows shattered, trees growing through their roofs from who knows what wind-borne seed. Everywhere, blind brick walls radiated the heat they had accumulated during the day, attracting moths the size of two hands, with brilliant red eyes. Among the crumbling walls of an old house's second story, people still lived; they ate a miserable supper by the light of stars and candles. The gusty sky was obliterated by pitch-black roofs. When a tram passed on its way back to the depot, the houses along the street visibly shook. How did these houses not collapse into heaps of rubble, how did they stay standing, year after year? No one would have been bothered by another fallen house, as part of the curse of overall ruin, the way no one cleared away the shattered and rusted carcasses of old cars becoming one with the asphalt. Because all the houses were connected by communicating tunnels and secret doors, you could spend your entire life wandering from one to the next like in an endless coral reef. You would never find anyone interested enough to stop you. The few inhabitants would look at you without surprise while you walked through the hallways and rooms, while you tore a page from an abandoned calendar, while you opened a drawer to find an old pair of glistening glasses and the cold metal of a thimble . . .

In front of the monumental edifice, crowned by funereal statues in slightly paler outlines against the black sky, the Picketists were already waiting, with their improvised signs hanging down for now. They were speaking quietly in small groups pressed close together, like at Easter before the priest comes out with the light. They were dressed in black, and the women covered their hair with tulle scarves. The signs were crude, made in haste from plywood and coated cardboard, the kind used to pack furniture. There must have been seventy or eighty people carefully clustered within the impenetrable shadow of the building and cupola, probably ready to scatter if an especially zealous patrolman passed by. But the militia officers—parasitical, potbellied, and corrupt as they were—instinctively avoided dubious places. They weren't looking for complications.

I found a place for myself in the crowd, next to some people I didn't know. The energy crisis had an unexpected benefit: a modernly illuminated Bucharest would lack its most beautiful feature: the stars. By their light I saw a few familiar faces, colleagues from the school at the end of Colentina. I knew that Caty would be there, attractive even in black, even with her scarf on her head. Goia, also, wouldn't miss it, or at least so I thought at the time. But what was the beautiful Florabela, who seemed to clink with gold even when she left her bracelets at home, doing in this dark crowd? Looking at her from a distance, people must have thought that one of the statues on the temple cornice that enveloped us in its shadow, perhaps Sadness or Resignation, had come down to the people to fill them with amazement. There was also the school's drunken porter, who night after night begged the UFOs to take him, and the geography teacher, whom I have not had the chance to write about—a small and silent being with a large, rose-colored wart between her eyebrows that made her resemble a woman from one of the Indian soap operas that everyone watched and wet their handkerchiefs with tears over. They all chatted about this and that, like in the teachers' lounge, but their minds were elsewhere. The porter's sign was written in crooked letters, like obscenities on concrete fences, and it read: "DOWN WITH CANCER." Caty yammered on, as was her wont, while the others were forced to listen. It seemed there was a woman from the school neighborhood who wanted to do one of the algae treatments, to purge toxins from her organism, so she had asked her daughter's homeroom teacher to give her a few bits of algae in a jar with water. So, you know, she took the jar home and kept it on her sill for a few days, in the sun. To her delight, the slimy creatures, white like little scratches, multiplied considerably and clouded the water with their droppings, until the liquid in the jar was as dense and milky as . . . (here Caty lowered her voice, giggling). She steeled herself and drank the liquid down, but you see, sweetie, no one ever told her not to drink the algae. And wouldn't you know it, next time of the month she doesn't get her period . . . Her husband never touched her—they already had four kids and slept apart. She goes to the doctor to see what's up, and: she's pregnant. "Sweetie, it's true, it's Angelescu's mother from group D in the fifth grade . . ." "And what's she going to do?" a woman asks, but there's no more time for talking, because the crowd is stirring and the signs are going up. "Virgil's here," Caty tells me, and then she turns around, fanatically and ecstatically gazing toward a shape that approaches the great shadow where we all are, only to melt, after a few steps, into it.

I looked curiously at the man who walked awkwardly through the Picketists, a man without aura or charisma. I was surprised to see everyone's hands reach out to touch him, as though he were a healing Christ, and everyone's eyes were on his lips, waiting to see them speak a revelation. Virgil seemed more like a tired engineer working in a provincial factory—pale, a little hunched over, carelessly dressed in whatever he had at hand. His hair made deep coves at the temples, where it had turned gray. His several-day stubble also had many white flecks that glinted in a ray of light. He walked through the crowd, looking at one person or another, stopping and saying something, but his mind seemed elsewhere. Or more probably, it seemed that he was not there of his own volition, that for him it was an obligation to be among the Picketists this evening.

Virgil continued until he came to the heavy entryway, as massive as a safe door, with high relief sculptures of skeletons walking paths that led to nowhere, desperate people trying to emerge from the frame of the ebony-black door, offering their screaming faces toward the walls and holding out their hands and fingers perpendicular to the door, as though they wanted to escape the two-dimensional hell where they were trapped. Virgil stood there—among those blackened bronze hands, like those of drowning people, grasping toward us, the Picketists—with the same weary regard of someone overworked or an insomniac. Caty took me by the arm and yanked hard enough to tear it off. The Picketists lifted their signs in silence and shuffled around, as though they wanted the sole viewer, Virgil, to read them first, the way small students, when asked a question, raise their hands and wave them frenetically in front of the teacher. I read their unified protest again: "Down with Death!", "Down with Rotting!", "Don't Bury Consciences in the Dirt!", "Shame on Epilepsy!", "Stop Murder!", "NO to Crushing!", "NO to Being Buried Alive!", "Suffering is a Sin!", "We Don't Want to Perish!", and many others that cataloged the swarms of diseases, fears, and horrors located in human flesh and which we accepted as our fate on Earth, resigned like the slaves had been to their enslavement when everyone around them considered it natural and inevitable. "Down with Accidents!", "Let's Skip Spinal Fractures!", "NO to Agony!", "NO to Eternal Disappearance!", "Down with Unhappiness!", "Enough with Trigeminal Neuralgia!", "Stop the Massacre!" Caty shook her old sign with "Down with Age!", and the little geography teacher held a piece of paper in front of her chest, reading only, "Help!" Above us and above the building's funereal cupola rose the giant, flowing statue of Damnation, concealing a quarter of the stars in the sky and making us, far below its enormous feet, appear to be a procession of mites, barely visible in the night that veiled the city. The quiet humming of the great solenoid in the cupola and the faraway sound of a tram going back to the depot were the only noises that disturbed the otherwise total quiet. It's like I'm inside an ear with tinnitus, I thought. The black hands that came out of the door stretched hopelessly toward us, while we, the living and the whole, in the volumes of our bodies, were the unreachable and incomprehensible gods of a flat, unescapable hell.

Before speaking, the man in front of us opened the bag he had been carrying on his shoulder and removed a stack of papers, typed and mimeographed on who knows what clandestine machine. He handed them to the first person next to him and waited, appearing ever more tired and hopeless, for the papers to be passed among the Picketists. When one reached me, I saw three texts written one after the next, separated by asterisks. The first and the last seemed to be poems. There wasn't enough light for us to read them, so we all folded them into our pockets, bags, or purses to read at home. Since I have it in front of me, now as I am writing, I can copy it here, although I can hardly wait to finish telling the insane story of what happened at the Institute of Forensic Medicine.

Here is the first poem, without a title or author's name. When I read it the first time, I had a vague and somewhat unpleasant feeling, like when someone you don't know introduces himself with your own name, which also happens to be his. It has always seemed problematic to me that there are multiple people with my name in the world, as though out of nowhere I might run into creatures who resembled me in every way. Moreover, I have always felt that only I had the right to say, "I," that "I" was not a pronoun but a proper name, my name. Its use by someone else seemed absurd, a usurpation, as though I was in a dream where all the characters had your face and your voice.

i look at a rigid photograph taken before 1900
all these people are dead. still this is also a life
in chemical glory; in place of an angel
i touch the emulsified layer not with my eyes
and not the tip of my finger, but with the dimension
i have to my advantage: i live and think
i can feel, i can speak. i touch my fingers and then the glass
of water on the table. i look at the newspaper: "the situation in beirut
is tense again. determent force helicopters . . ."
and then emptiness. historical emptiness.
there fall incendiary bombs, here i touch the glass
and i can say my name. i see for a second
a section through the larynx from an anatomy book
in a black world. they, who have lived
or not, little do they care. like they lived
maximally through the moment
they were sliced in two by a train, everything filmed
in slow motion. i see the sweat
frozen in enormous droplets on their necks, flowing down
toward what? while the train unleashes an entire discourse
of terror. paralysis
in a pressurized cabin, a landing
toward death. and everything discolored and sepia
until it goes dark.

—

i am like iron in comparison. the glass
likewise trembles at the touch of my hand.
little do they care. they look straight in your eyes
like revolutionaries up against the wall
facing an execution squad. chemical glory.
and you, from the center of your flesh, you cast a glance like a coin
into the center of their loneliness.

And now, having read this anonymous poem for perhaps the tenth time, I tremble, I actually, physically tremble in the piloerector muscles on my arms and neck, and I feel a frozen spot on my spinal cord, as I did as a child when I encountered the story of the woman who disappeared from the middle of the snow-filled yard and when I read about the prisoner who escaped with the help of taps on the wall from outside, dozens of meters over the rocky shore of the sea. I feel the same trembling of unconscious fear as I do when the visitors appear, the same violent tremor that shakes both the bed and myself. I don't collect only my baby teeth, photos from childhood ("all of these people are dead"), and other fossils from my personal Precambrian period—braids, pieces of rotted thread from my navel—I also collect fears, ever more of them, ever more varied, of different colors and textures, like stones polished on the shores of flowing waters. I examine my fears in the light, one after the next: translucid, opaque, with brittle mineral deposits: a conglomeration of disparate fears.

The following text was from Herodotus (*Histories*, 7, 44–45, as written in the note under the quote):

> When Xerxes had come to the midst of Abydos, he desired to see the whole of his army; and this he could do, for a lofty seat of white stone had been set up for him on a hill there with that intent, built by the people of Abydos at the king's command. There Xerxes sat, and looked down on the sea-shore, viewing his army and his fleet; and as he viewed them he was fain to see the ships contend in a race. They did so, and the Phoenicians of Sidon won it; and Xerxes was pleased with the race, and with his armament.

But when he saw the whole Hellespont hidden by his ships, and all the shores and plains of Abydos thronged with men, Xerxes first declared himself happy, and presently he fell a-weeping.

Perceiving that, his uncle Artabanus, who in the beginning had spoken his mind freely and counseled Xerxes not to march against Hellas––Artabanus, I say, marking how Xerxes wept, questioned him and said, "What a distance is there, O king, between your acts of this present and a little while ago! Then you declared your happiness, and now you weep." "Ay verily," said Xerxes; "for I was moved to compassion, when I considered the shortness of all human life, seeing that of all this multitude of men not on will be alive a hundred years hence." "In our life," Artabanus answered, "we have deeper sorrows to bear than that. For short as our lives are, there is no man here or elsewhere so fortunate, that he shall not be constrained, ay many a time and not once only, to wish himself dead rather than alive. Misfortunes so fall upon us and sicknesses so trouble us, that they make life to seem long for all its shortness.

The pages ended with a real poem, powerful and musical like a scream of despair and a hymn to the whole of humanity. At the bottom, Virgil had written the name of the poet: Dylan Thomas. I want to read more from him, because he is obviously one of the very few who actually know what they are talking about:

Do not go gentle into that good night,
Old age should burn and rave at close of day;
Rage, rage against the dying of the light.

Though wise men at their end know dark is right,
Because their words had forked no lightning they
Do not go gentle into that good night.

Good men, the last wave by, crying how bright
Their frail deeds might have danced in a green bay,
Rage, rage against the dying of the light.

Wild men who caught and sang the sun in flight,
And learn, too late, they grieved it on its way,
Do not go gentle into that good night.

Grave men, near death, who see with blinding sight
Blind eyes could blaze like meteors and be gay,
Rage, rage against the dying of the light.

And you, my father, there on the sad height,
Curse, bless, me now with your fierce tears, I pray.
Do not go gentle into that good night.
Rage, rage against the dying of the light.

"Why do we live?" Virgil began, speaking as though to himself, but with an almost brutal musicality in the quiet of the night. "How can we exist? Who allowed this scandal, this injustice? This horror, this abomination? What monstrous imagination wrapped consciousness in flesh? What sadistic and saturnine spirit permitted consciousness to suffer like this, permitted the spirit to scream in torture? Why did we climb down into this swamp, into this jungle, into these flames full of hate and anger? Who kicked us out of our higher home? Who locked us inside bodies, who tied us with our own nerves and arteries? Who forced us to have bones and gristle, sphincters and glands, skin and intestines? What are we doing inside this filthy, soft machine? Who blindfolded our eyes with our own eyes, who plugged our ears with our own ears? Who approved pain, and who approved feelings? What do we have to do with the clusters of cells that are our body? With the material that flows through our body like through a tube of agonistic flesh? What are we doing here? What is this game? Why are we drowning in acids that eat our thoughts away? Protest, protest against consciousness buried in flesh!

"Why do we hurt, why do we writhe, why are we drawn and quartered by blades and poison darts? Why is our heart pulled from our chest, why are we bound to the torture chair with black hoods over our heads? Why do we break out in hives at the slightest breeze? Why do we get sores at the touch of dandelion fluff? Why do we scream in pain at the agony of our lives, and why is fear the greatest and most difficult pain of all? Fear of loss, of disappearance, of leaving your shell behind, of pain and of pleasure, of life and of dreams, of sex and of thought, but especially of the spider the size of one hundred universes who weaves the illusion in which we reside. Why was fear allowed, why do we drink fear in our daily cup of spider venom? Why is fear the substance of the world in which we live? Protest fear, rage against the manure that darkens our clarity!

"Minuscule within our own nothingness, micelles on a speck of dust in the infinite. We must protest the disappearance of consciences! It is diabolic, it is intolerable that a spirit should die. It is beyond the limits of evil that a creature should understand its own fate. It is crude, barbarous, and pointless to bring a spirit into the world after an infinite night, just to cast it out again, after a nanosecond of chaotic life, back into another, endless night. It is sadistic to give it, ahead of time, full knowledge of the fate that awaits it. It is abominable to murder billion after billion, generation after generation, saints, criminals, geniuses, heroes, whores, researchers, toilers of the earth, poets, philosophers, penniless doctors, torturers, executioners and victims together, evil and good together: this work of serial murder is melancholic and desolating. Our world will be extinguished, the universe will rot along with all the other billions of universes, and being and nonbeing will last as long as eternity, like a bad dream, like an infinite spiderweb. And we, the pearls of the world, its crystals that ought to shine eternally, we will never exist again, ever, however much time passes and however many disasters occur in this hell that is the physical world, in the infinite dungeon of the night. Protest, protest against the snuffing of the light!

"Cry the tears of Xerxes, rage, rage against the dying of the light! Come out of your eternal petrification in photographic emulsion. Writhe, slap your faces, and wake from this horror. Picket evil places, the morgues and cancer wards, leper colonies, concentration camps, wards for the burned and crushed, throw your manifestos from the peaks of the tallest buildings, refuse aging and disease, defy death! Never in the history of mankind, that is, in the history of slaughterhouses, has anyone protested the way you do. So desperate and so heroic. Never has human dignity evinced a more moving glory. Raise your signs as high as you can, shake them against putrefaction and against oblivion!"

After he fell silent, he looked at us for a while with the same eyes, those of a completely depleted man, and then he turned slowly toward the grand door from which the bronze hands jutted out with their fingers spasmodically extended toward us. And he wove his fingers together with those of the high relief creatures mourning among tombs and cypresses, and the door began to open.

A long, deep corridor gaped in front of us, lined in an incandescent metal. And we all entered into the morgue's intestines, following Virgil, who walked silently a few steps in front of us. I thought about the Gospels, I thought about salvation. Could such a cruel executioner of generations exist? I thought about Kafka: salvation exists, just not for me. I thought about Kierkegaard: if I were the only one condemned to the eternal sufferings of Hell and all others were saved, I would still, from the depths of the flames, raise a hymn in praise of Holiness. Could he have put his finger on a red-hot stove, even if only for a minute? Did he know what it meant to burn eternally, without hope, millennium after millennium, eon after eon? Caty trembled, holding my arm while we trudged down the seemingly endless corridor. On either side were sordid showcases of torture instruments, unidentifiable and repulsive, so old they seemed covered in a kind of salt. They had probably violated, for decades on end, the soft and helpless machine of the human body, which preserved to the end something of the delicacy and honesty of babies, a fact which made aging and death even more hideous.

Dragging our meager signs along, we came upon the dead. At the end of the corridor was a hall with dozens of zinc tables on which green cadavers of men, women, and children lay, all naked, all on their backs, staring up at the ceiling with clear eyes. The air smelled sweet, like at a wake. The unbelievable complexity of those bodies—their hierarchies of levels and holons: systems and apparatuses, organs, tissues, cells, molecules, atoms, pheromones, given life by the whirlpool of energy that once passed through them, raising them up with its irresistible breath—was not able to save them. It didn't matter if these bodies had lived fifty years of fifty billion. Now, they were not alive, now they were inert pieces of clay that derisively pretended to be flesh and life. From now on, they would never be, however many eternities would come and go. Although the sight was funereal, you could not but marvel, with a dark smile, at the ridiculous amount of material that had been mobilized to ignite, like two pieces of sandstone knocked together, the unimportant spark of life.

At the far end of the hall (along whose walls were not windows but white metal cabinets with glass doors, like in all clinics, showing instruments of medicine and, probably, embalming, with beaks, claws, and barbs, with unusual joints and bolts like the mandibles of predatory insects), there was another door, unremarkable-looking, above which was a number plate. The plate had been painted over at some point and was now unreadable. You couldn't have guessed that beyond this hospital door was anything besides another corridor lined with doors or another hall. Virgil stopped in front of the door, turned toward us, seemed to want to say something, but decided against it. He had the pale and tense face of someone in pain. He turned his back to us again and opened the door. One after the other, we entered the great hall.

It was circular and boundless. Nothing it contained was human-sized. The columns along its continuous wall, which held up the arched ceiling, were absurdly, unreasonably thick. And yet, in comparison to the giant dimensions of the hall, they seemed long and graceful, shining in their polished, flaked porphyry curvature. The floor was mirror-polished, and in the middle sat the room's only object: a gigantic dental chair, maybe twenty meters tall, with scarlet vinyl cushions. It was yellow-white, massive, an amazing, incomprehensible object from another civilization, frozen in silence and bathed in a cone of milky light. It was covered in fluted hoses and canvas hoses and metallic hoses, it glittered with nickeled accessories, levers, and hooks from which hung drills, mills, and alligator clips to hold X-rays. The table in front of the chair, emerging from the trunk held to the floor by enormous bolts, was much too high for us to see what was on it. Our heads barely surpassed the height of the footrest, two metallic grilles on mobile joints stuck into the device's massive base.

From the circular base to the edges of the hall, visible under the semitranslucid tiles of the floor, spread a ramified network of hoses, knotty handfuls of veins through which gurgled a liquid the density of honey. Everywhere under our feet this circulatory system was visible, with vesicles the thickness of a hand branching out endlessly, until it became a fabric of capillaries no thicker than strands of hair. I immediately thought of the thousands of pale hairs on the bean-plant roots growing through those gauze pads, crowded in the children's cloudy jars of water, in biology class. We walked over them now, fascinated by the colossal dental chair under the ceiling, made for who knows what species of giant. It looked like the throne of an evil god, come down to the earth to pass it across the blade of its sword.

It is difficult for me, not just to write, but to remember what happened next. Because the monstrous vision that followed has seared my brain. I haven't slept the two nights since, for fear that I would dream about our guide's terrible end, and that the jets of blood that I tried to wash off of my pants would spread over my body and over all of those who saw the abomination, that they would fill our bedrooms with a scarlet swamp, would flow out through the windows, down the gray streets of Bucharest, and into every house and impregnate the lakes, parks, and metro, until the blood would rise dozens of meters, like the Sargasso Sea covering the pillars of an ancient Atlantis . . .

Virgil walked to the metal throne, separating himself from us. He went into the narrow space between the footrests where, as we only now saw, there was a panel of twelve buttons, each the shape of a half sphere, set in four rows. The buttons were the color of marbles, the kind children clink in their hands, polished and variegated. The engineer touched the round buttons gently with his fingers in a certain order that was probably a code, the buttons made quiet sounds that oscillated on different tones. Then all around the hall, a kind of paneling we hadn't noticed lifted to expose what the circular walls had enclosed: the solenoid, a torus shape one and a half meters high, covered in row after row of intricately braided copper wires, tightly packed together, crossed with thick cables. The bobbin ran the entire circumference of the room and gave the impression of a strange perfection. It looked like the pigtails braided into wheels on the head of a young girl from Leonardo's notebooks. Virgil looked around and seemed satisfied, so he fluttered his fingers again over the twelve knobs, touching them in a different order than the first time. This created a brief melody, and suddenly the dome of the building began to open briskly, like a camera shutter or a flower blossom filmed in stop-motion, in a sliding, spiral movement, until its petals descended all the way, melting into the room's circular wall.

Now the night gaped wide above us. A cold, vertical wind made us shiver. Caty held on to my arm with both hands, pressing her head against my chest.

Above the dental chair in the center of the room, amid the solenoid's pervasive, pulsating hum, the black plinth levitated, blacker than the night, beneath the building's highest statue: Damnation. The folds of its clothes, although made of blackened bronze, seemed to flutter over the world. Virgil moved away from the chair for a few moments, to see better the great woman floating over the morgue. Then he went back between the footrests and his back shielded the panel from our view. From the little jagged sounds we understood he was inputting another code, touching the buttons with his fingertips. Suddenly, the continuous buzzing, like from an electrical plant, of the bobbin changed: the pitch dropped a few tones, and as the sound became more grave, the statue began to descend slowly, with its flowing hair and robes, toward the ground. We all ran toward the walls, where no door was to be found. In the chaos, we dropped our little signs and slogans to the floor. We pressed ourselves against the circular wall, but however much we did, it didn't look like there would be enough room for the giant statue.

Before her enormous bare feet touched the bare floor, the statue—now as alive and slow-moving as soft glass and black as anthracite—sat on the dental chair, which creaked under her weight. The folds of her toga settled, slowly folding together under a gravitational pull they hadn't felt before. Calm and straight on her metal throne, illuminated by the light bulbs above that deepened her eye sockets and accentuated her pursed lips, casually scornful like the moai on Easter Island, the woman placed her arms on the chair's armrests and her feet on the two foot cushions. She looked straight ahead like an empress, like a goddess whom the horrors of life in this world could not touch, because she was not from here, nor from now, but from the golden dawn of myths and icons, their eternal dawn. The solenoid's buzzing had stopped completely.

Virgil moved a few steps back to see the statue, in a foreshortened angle no artist had created. He, perhaps reaching half the height of her thigh, was the only one of us who confronted her, who dared to stand dangerously close to the vibration of her obsidian flesh. He tilted his head back to look at her face, framed by the thousands of twisted vipers of her hair falling to her shoulders, and he lost his balance for a moment, like a child who looks up at an immeasurable height to see his mother's face. But he collected himself and, without taking his eyes off the face of the mute idol, he feverishly felt through his pockets, from which he took the paper, copied and recopied by who knows what clandestine mimeograph, the same one he had given us. He didn't even look at it, he only felt across it with his fingers and let it fall to the ground, where it softly mated, like two fluttering butterflies, with its mirror image. He seemed to want to read in front of the statue the three litanies of mourning and fear, but he decided not to, who knows why, and now he gathered his strength to speak without a text. His face was so pale you could see the bones of his cranium beneath his transparent skin. His lips moved for a few moments before we could hear the first sounds. At the same time, his trembling fingers began to feel for the buttons and holes of his ragged clothes. While he spoke, Virgil peeled off his clothes, tossing them onto the crystalline floor around him, until he was naked, crooked, greenish, with thick hair on his shoulders and buttocks, with the tendons of his knees, the bones of his pelvis, and his ribs visible through his unusually saggy skin. His cervical vertebrae groaned from the effort of looking up. He was speaking to her, to her face and eyes staring straight ahead; he would have liked to meet her gaze, as always happened when two minds transfer a thought between them, becoming one alone. But the air, the cold night air, descended undisturbed from the stars, impartially, a vertical wind that froze our exposed heads. A distant horn or barking dog reminded us we were still inserted in the world, in the life we led.

"I bring you the offering of my body," Virgil began. "It is a splendid construction. It is an unimaginably complicated mechanism, begun from an egg that cracked and transformed into two, then into four, then into eight, then into sixteen isolated worlds still amazingly interconnected. Look at the result of eighty divisions, look at me formed from billions of universes. Don't they shine like a Shiva with billions of arms? Before knowing I was the owner of this body, I assembled its organs with a precision beyond imagination, such that every organic sheet and every piece of fascia is irrigated by blood, nourished by air, innervated by nerves, and animated by hormones. I have built my own skeleton the way no architect in the world could do, I have planned my intestines like an interior labyrinth, I have assembled by myself, with endless patience, the purinic and pyramidical bases of my genetic mechanism. I ingest alimentary substances and eliminate feces, urine, sweat, and sperm, and all these substances are holy. The water of my body is holy, the blood and lymph are holy, my spit is holy. I have shaped my kidneys more aesthetically than any statue, I have made my heart beat like a metronome measuring the time left to answer a great question. Look at my jaw, with the alveoli of teeth and molars, with tiny holes for nerves to pass through, and with veins and arteries: it is perfect. Look how the eight bones combine to form the cupola of my skull—it is unrivaled. Look at my lacrimal bone and the hyoid bone, look at the skin, look at the spinal cord. I bring before you my holy and genial body, with its organs, systems, and apparatuses that I have combined, organized, and hierarchized; I have done this, the one who lives inside his skull like a tank driver inside his steel mammoth, even though I do not know how I did it, and even though I couldn't do it again, I could not even shape, out of calcium and wind, the shameful and holy bone of the coccyx.

"I bring before you my brain, the most paradoxical object in the universe, because it contains this universe and the other 10,500 universes that work together inside the body of the creature where we live. The mandala of mandalas, the rose of roses, the thought of thoughts. I would like to disassemble the bones of my skull so you could see it sitting there, soft and heavy, on the multicolored butterfly wings of the sphenoid bone. I bring before you this soft hyperarchitecture, this godly mollusk. Only through this frontal bone is the brilliance of the other side of reality visible. So you could see how through the eyes and only through the eyes does the light penetrate. My skull is an eyelid over the eye with which we see the logical field, the same way the eye projects the visual field in front of itself. Receive the offering of my brain, the unique and splendid pearl from the shell of the world.

"What else can I sacrifice to you? My memory? I offer you all the moments that make up my life, which has passed in a moment. Take a bite of my brain, like it was a juicy apple, and you will know its texture and flavor. I adorn your feet, oh terrifying one, with the field of tulips taller than me that I saw in my grandparents' yard when I was two, and which I never forgot. The snail I put on a leaf in the forest, and then watched, for an hour, as it gnawed the green edge with the gray drapery of its lips. The icy cold sheets of my college dormitory. The pale nipple I sucked of the first girl I undressed. The day I left the house wearing one black sandal and one brown, and I only noticed when I was in line at the cheese shop. The panic at the nuclear reactor in Măgurele when the gauges in the control room went nuts. A fleeting shade of blond. The clink of a fork (where?). The dream where I'm walking down the street wearing a shirt, but nothing on the lower half of my body. The cigarette we shared, first one of us, then the other, lying across the mattress, Sanda and me. Countless other moments, decanted there in the impenetrable thicket of the synapses. Look at them all, raise each one in front of your eyes, so you can laugh and cry at the rending comedy that was my life.

"I come before you with all my parents' knowledge, with all my books and my inventions and my poems and my tables, my mathematics and my physics, with all my power to comprehend. I come with my music and my architecture, with my astronomy and my history. I come with my cohort of saints and the enlightened people who have shaped my inner being. I come with Hermes Trismegistus and Bezalel, with Hemon and Lao Tzu, with Jesus and Plato, with Herodotus and Homer, with Pythagoras and Dante, with Sappho and Sei Shōnagon. I come with Shakespeare and Tycho Brahe, with Michelangelo and da Vinci, with Newton and Volta. I come with Bach and Mozart, with Rembrandt and Vermeer, with Milton and with Darwin and with Gauss and with Dostoevsky. With Caspar David Friedrich, with Monsù Desiderio. With Eminescu. With Kafka, Wittgenstein, Freud, Proust, and Rilke, with Einstein, Tesla, Maxwell, Frege, and Cantor, with Joyce and Canetti and Virginia Woolf, with Planck and Feynman, with de Chirico, Max Ernst, and Frida Kahlo, with Faulkner, Ezra Pound, Carl Orff, Abel, Hubble, with Lennon and Bourbaki, with Chaplin and Murnau, with Tarkovsky and with Fellini. With thousands of other geniuses who shaped, misshaped, and shaped our minds again. They are all here, in my skin, in my skull, in the enormous span of my wings. I come before you with the entire inheritance of civilizations, with the entire peacock's tail of cultures, with the five thousand languages and hundreds of thousands of races of my species. I offer you a speck of dust from the world we carpet-bomb with our wonders!

"Is it enough for you? Will you ever have enough? Will you ever be sated? Will you ever take your shadow away from our lives?"

The black glass statue had lowered its gaze toward the one speaking in a grave tone and with controlled gestures at her feet. It was a neutral gaze, lacking either rage or goodwill. While Virgil listed the names of "saints and the enlightened people" of humanity, she began to rise from her sinister throne and the skirts of her toga, the creaking plates of soft metal, hung straight. She kept her gaze on the more and more broken speech of the one who stepped backward as she rose, because, standing, the statue's head reached the sky. Hypnotized, we could not take our eyes from "her pure nails on high displaying their onyx."

And suddenly the Picketists against the circular wall were screaming their lungs out, with their hair on end and their hands at their temples. I did not turn my head away, because suddenly I knew what would happen. I wanted to see everything to the end, to be a witness to wretchedness and catastrophe. The giant woman raised her foot and stomped on Virgil, crushing him against the floor. A yellow and red sap jetted out from under her foot, spraying disgusting liquids over a large area, over the floor and our clothes. All around me, people were fleeing chaotically in desperation, zigzagging in every direction along the walls. We saw the goddess rise slowly and heavily into the air, with Virgil's guts and crushed brain stuck to her sole. The room stank of fear and feces. After the statue rose past the round walls, the cupola reversed its earlier turning, lifting its petals toward the apex of the dome. Once it closed completely, the statue remained above it, unmoving, levitating a half meter above the roof surrounded by the other twelve figures along the circumference of the cupola, as when we saw it from outside. Only then did the exit reappear, directly across from my group, so we had to escape along the base of the giant dental chair and past the hideous remains of the one we had followed. Blinded by horror and terror, I don't know how we fled the chamber, then the corridor lined with display cases, how we found the exit and in the end the bus station.

It was long past midnight. We waited for over an hour and no bus came. The city was cool and empty. The stars were burning madly above the identical apartment buildings that stank from a block away, from the poison of their cockroaches and heaps of trash. I walked home, barked at by dogs and asked, from time to time, for my ID by bored patrolmen. A sinister city, enormous, uninhabited. A necropolis, waiting for the arrival of a cosmic body to shave it off the face of the earth. A necropolis, polluting the earth with its workers' blocks, ruined already from the moment they were designed. I walked down the middle of boulevards with no traffic, passing through identical neighborhoods, past unlit stores and hospitals with no patients and places where an out-of-tune violin sounded. I got home at the break of day and fell asleep in my clothes. I remember the last thing I did before sinking into a heavy, black sleep: I saw again, under my eyelids, down to the smallest detail, clearly and luminously, the person who had brought a slip of paper from home, written in black marker in large letters: "Help!". "Help!" I shouted, too, with all my being, sinking my face into my pillow, loud enough to break my larynx, as though I were cornered in my own house by an unknown murderer, "Help! Help! Help! Help!"

27

My life runs along a single axis: home and school, the way those who have a fractured spine are pasted into a plaster corset. Day after day I take the tram from either Teiul Doamnei or Doamna Ghica (one of my few moments of choice) and I bury myself in my book, reading on my feet, pressed on every side by people who smell bad, some like salami, others urine, others sheep wool. After a few dozen pages from *Maldoror* or *Gaspard de la nuit*, I'm at the end of the line. The rusty water tower rises over the vast landscape: abandoned factories with broken windows, lumberyards, newsstands with sodas and sweets. A few martyred prune trees between the tramlines. All the soot of the world has turned them black. Their leaves are dry, bumpy, and few, like the leaves inside a teabag. A prune is a miracle in this world of dirt and grime, but soon it also turns dirty. I see children going to school with their school bags: "Good day, comrade," they say as they pass, wide-eyed, their heads shaved almost down to the scalp. The girls have charming little beads in their hair, held with dirty elastics. They walk two or three abreast, telling each other all kinds of stories and laughing. Amazing and frightening like fairies, like gnomes at the bottom of the forest. The tiny population I have to face, day after day.

I turn right at Dimitrie Herescu, I pass the repair shop and arrive at the school. From the office comes the smell of Nechezol, the "coffee mixture" we all drink. A mixture of what with what? No one dares to imagine: tree bark, acorns, roots—these are just some of the possibilities. Better than nothing, at least it warms you up. In the lounge is the same greenish light that fills the halls. I enter, I try to do an about-face, but Agripina has already seen me, I can't escape. She is the other Romanian teacher, there are only three on our team, and the third, in fact, doesn't matter, she is a complete imbecile who is always bugging the other teachers with awkward questions about sex ("My dear, pardon me for asking, but . . . what do you do when you get really hot? Do you ever do it in the butt? I mean . . . is that normal? My husband says . . ."). The two of us are the actual Romanian faculty, Agripina and me. I am better at literature, she at grammar, she always says, but in her heart she thinks she is "an elite teacher," the best in the school, if not the best in the sector.

"What are we *creating,* dom profesor?" she asks whenever she sees me, because I once made the mistake of telling her I wrote poetry, just as I can't pass Borcescu without hearing him whistle through the giant gap of his missing teeth: "Young man, don't ever get married! Do you know what being married is like? Do you?" etc., etc. Agripina looks like a widow, probably a brunette beauty in her day, she has the energy to move mountains, and she doesn't wait for me to answer before she babbles on: "These little bastards! Cattle with shirts on! They learn nothing, nothing, nothing! I always tell them: Hey, I came in on the turnip truck and lifted myself up to where I am now, with no help from anyone! And now I'm the best teacher in the sector! The bumpkins in this neighborhood never dreamed they'd get a teacher like me! Dom profesor, last Saturday I was at the sector faculty meeting (you were absent, probably you were at home *creating* . . .), and we were talking about pronominal adjectives, when this cow from School 24 read a paper saying there is no interrogative adjective, can you imagine? I sent her back to the manual. With these kinds of teachers, no wonder the kids come out like they do . . . What am I doing here, dom profesor? Or you, for that matter? These kids won't learn anything, look at this, their test grades. Calalb: two! Jugănilă: three! Even Ilinca, dom profesor, who I sent to the sector Olympiad: look, Ilinca, six! Six in Romanian! She didn't study the characterization of Moș Dănilă! How can this be, dom profesor? You have to imagine the comments I put on their papers . . ."

Agripina is a nut, and the children are as afraid of her as they are Gionea. She has one method for teaching literature: she dictates "literary commentaries," ten to twelve pages long, crazy things she takes from pedagogical journals, and she makes the children learn them by heart, word by word. Woe betides the child who doesn't turn on like a faucet when put in front of the class: the register rains down on their heads, their hair gets yanked, and Agripina's knuckles leave bruises and knots as big as an apple: "You bovines! How long am I going to waste my time on you?" she shouts at the frightened children, standing wide-eyed up against the wall. "What can I do? How can I pull you in? That's what they tell us at the inspectorate, Lord knows, we have to pull you in . . . to show you the beauty of literature . . . What can I do? Do you want me to jump on the desk and do a striptease? Is that how you learn? Because I've tried everything else . . ."

Vulgar, gossipy, full of herself, coming in like a storm and shouting until her voice is gone, Agripina isn't a bad person. Often she makes us laugh until we cry, making fun of herself as much as everyone else. They all know, the old hands at School 86, that she had an active youth, one to which Principal Borcescu is not completely foreign, because they have both been at the school at the end of Colentina for thirty years. They say that the bastard tried his moves on Agripina, with the car and leaving her on the road, but he regretted it for the rest of his life, because under the uncontrollable fists of the then young woman, a worthy representative of the Young Workers Union, both Borcescu's head and the Fiat suffered terribly . . .

"Especially that goat in the eighth grade! At this moment—with the entrance exams coming, when they know how hard it is to get into a good school, that there are only fifteen places at Nursing and eighteen at Business—this is the moment they choose to start with hair dye, makeup, perfume; they look like the girls downtown, forgive me, dom profesor, but they do! Their hormones are on fire, dom profesor! Look at them with bare legs, dresses hiked up to their butts, these darling little ladies . . . they grin and look away when they see one of these mechanics next door, little squirts . . . What do you want to be, you lazy beasts? Barstool ballerinas? Intercontinental Hotel sluts? I tell them to study, to read, don't pluck your eyebrows and spray Bulgarian rose perfume, that stuff reeks. Where's their common sense? At their age, we were working construction at Bumbești-Livezeni, wherever they needed people. The instructor came and told us, 'The best toilet water is soap and water.'

These dirty girls don't even know what shame is, if you ask them about their modesty, about their common sense, they look at you like cattle . . ."

Agripina has put herself in charge of the girls' moral education. "She would have made a good prison guard at Târgşor," Florabela once whispered to me. At the start of every class, she makes the girls stand up, to check how long their dresses are: they're supposed to be a hand's width below the knees (and the hand of the "black widow" is remarkably wide and slappy, probably because she came in on the turnip truck). If it isn't so, the girl is sent right home. Their hair has to be in braids. Bangs are prohibited, "You're no Mireille Mathieu." Heaven forbid they should forget their headbands. It's the end of the world if a girl leaves hers at home.

Agripina lives with a very popular character in our school, simply named The Writer. "I won't be here tomorrow, I'm going to the doctor, The Writer will come instead," she tells the principal sometimes, and the next day we actually find ourselves in the lounge with a writer in the full sense of the word, more a writer than Dostoevsky, Kafka, and Thomas Mann put together. If there were a casting call and a thousand people tried out for the role of the novelist in a movie, Agripina's friend would receive, without much to-do, the jury's congratulations. He is about fifty, tall and presentable, dressed much more elegantly than the school's neighborhood has ever seen. He has gentle and intelligent eyes, long hair brushed back, but not like a hippie, no strand out of place, and a melodious and measured voice. A cream or scarlet ascot, something we've only seen in movies, is never absent, nor are any of the mannerisms by which even the simplest hairdresser would recognize a painter, musician, or a poet in their romanticized television biographies. His good manners toward the teachers raises him in their eyes, because, do we even need to say it? Agripina's friend exhibits a courtly manner with women regardless of their age or looks. When The Writer appeared in the lounge, everything became meaningful and celebratory, the poor housewives, dressed up as teachers, felt that not all was lost, and even the Albanian characters in the moldy paintings seemed overcome with admiration. The children were the happiest of all, because they had escaped another day of terror. The word "bovine" was foreign to the vocabulary of this "handsome man," as my female colleagues said, melting, and his impeccably manicured fingers would never touch anything as dirty as the thick black hair of the neighborhood children. Of course, with this noble personage smelling, discreetly, of cologne, the way the children's fathers never smell, even on Sunday visits with family, the students don't learn a thing, but they emerge transfigured after class because The Writer has told them, in minute detail, about the novel he has been writing for three decades, and which he revises and revises, without ever finishing. He has not published any part of it, in fact he has never published anything, ever, yet there has never been an author more encompassed by sympathy and understanding: in the stairs of the block where he lives, at the grocery and the tobacconist's, at the seltzer shop and the fruit and vegetable shop (because, since he stays at home, while Agripina works for both of them, The Writer does all the shopping, pays the bills, buys the newspapers, and does all the cooking), he is met everywhere with the greatest and most sincere respect. He is the pride of the central neighborhood, near Orizont, where they live. To his credit, he receives everyone's respect with a modest smile, like a crowned head waving to the crowds in front of the royal palace. He has lived his entire life this way, and now, at his age, he feels fulfilled and reconciled to his own fate, like a prophet surrounded by the love and veneration of his disciples. He once gave me, as a fellow writer, a chapter from his Novel, typed on good-quality, bright white paper. The protagonist was, by coincidence, also a writer, a superior being, the center of attention for all the other characters. No woman could resist him, but all his loves were fleeting. In fact, his comfortable life was steeped in melancholy. He had had only one true love, in the dawn of his youth, a delicate, innocent child. Her name was Roza, and she had been the mystical rose of the writer's life. All his life, after Roza's death—she poisoned herself when the writer left her, the result of a complicated and tragic misunderstanding—he went, as they say, from flower to flower, looking for Roza in an unending chain of women. One had Roza's eyes, another her lips, another her voice, another the flower-petal delicacy of her skin . . . In the end, he remade his lost love from the sum of these moments, but—disappointment—the woman who had all of Roza's characteristics was not Roza. The whole had been more than the sum of its parts. Toward the end of the novel, named *Love's Women in Passing,* the writer met a scientist who had spent two decades perfecting a time machine . . . No, Roza was not completely lost . . .

"And there you go, dom profesor. That's how things are in our school. A whorehouse, not a school, that's what we'll be, and we're already a cesspool. Have you seen Zgârbacea, in 7-D? You ever looked at her hands? Fingernails as red as the Party! And have you seen how she moves her little butt! I'd be surprised if she didn't end up a slut like her mother, that lab worker, they keep her on at Sanepid just to get their jollies with her . . ."

I can never get rid of Agripina before she fills my head with her inanity. She rides me like a horse, she is large, dark, and dominating; I can't interrupt the manic current of her words. Her hair whips against my face when she turns her head, the way the mare's tails would hit me when I was a child next to my father on the cart bench. Her coal-black eyes, like those of a feisty peasant, peg me to the spot. If no one else comes into the lounge, I'm lost. But this time I somehow find the power to excuse myself (and in any case, the bell rang a few minutes ago), and I escape to the registers, grab one, and almost run down the hall, while I hear her shouting behind me: "Cattle with shirts on, dom profesor! We're not going to make people out of them!"

I am upset, because the story about the seventh-graders with painted nails reminded me of something. Nails, colored nails. Once, at my aunt's in Dudești-Cioplea, in the garden, my cousin Aura made long fake nails from the wrinkly, pointed petals of mallows and zinnia. Then she would threaten me with them, spreading out her fingers like a witch. With this image in my mind, with Aura's fluttering, multicolored fingers illuminating the school's Nile-green walls, I wander down thousands of halls that lead to nowhere. It must be the largest school in the world, with dozens of wings and floors, all steeped in shadow. I hear voices, bangs, shouts from behind every door. Florabela's sharp voice that would raise the dead from the dirt, the deep, muffled voice of Goia, the solfeggios of Mrs. Bernini. Clinking test tubes, crashing Bunsen burners, the beastly whine of dental drills. After years of teaching, I still can only find my class by chance, after opening a host of other classrooms. Each time, thirty children turn quickly toward me. Their eyes, in the shining classroom light, burn into my body. I close the door excusing myself, and it's dark again, darker than before. I come across a child who's been kicked out of class, waiting petulantly in front of the room leaning against the radiator. Some halls have water all over the floor, just washed by the janitor;

others, in distant areas, dozens of kilometers from the lounge and main office, have dirt on the floor, six inches deep.

Sometimes I come to places the children and teachers rarely go, in the foul-smelling basement with its petrified feces and rat skeletons, with large, spoked spiderwebs across the corridors. Once I opened one of the strange doors numbered with irrational and imaginary numbers to find the heart-rending sight of a desolate classroom, abandoned, with the benches turned over and the blackboard chipped, with rude drawings on the lichen-encrusted walls. One of these drawings depicted lice, tapeworms, mites, and flukeworms. I dragged my feet through dirt full of tips of colored pencils, plastic cuttings, broken rulers, pages marked up in red ink. Out of the student desks I pulled crumbling wads of gum, wrapped sandwiches green with mold, a forgotten pen, a moth-eaten hat. I went to the teacher's desk and sat on the paint-splotched, rickety chair. I opened the register and began to call roll, making flakes of plaster rain over the room with the vibrations of my voice. The emptiness spread from me to the end of the world. Spiders showed their thick legs in the cracks in the walls. Full of the dandruff of flaking plaster, feeling a moth running over my skin and between my shoulder blades, I stood up and left quickly, not wanting to discover, under the benches, who knows what mummified child, wrapped in thick cobwebs, beneath a quivering layer of pitch-black arachnids.

At the beginning of this week, I taught group 8-C. Circumstantial complements of purpose and circumstantial complements of cause. Easily confused. The poor students learned them by heart, the examples and questions and all, but they can't apply anything they know. It's no wonder. You see them stand in line all day for fish or cheese, crushed by a mob pushing them forward since there's never enough for everyone. You see them in the evening sitting in line, summer or winter, in front of the propane distribution point with their ancient carts, their rusty tanks lying on the ground like metal pigs. The full tanks won't come until dawn and there won't be enough of them, either. Many homes don't have electricity or plumbing. How the children are able to do their homework, late at night by the light of a spirit lamp, after they've finished all their difficult chores, you're better off not asking. What can the stupid things they hear at school mean to them (morphology and syntax, algebra and trigonometry)? What connection do they have with their lives? Just one: reciting by heart, flatly, "literary commentaries" and solving math problems are their ritual prayers, their invocations and incantations, all ways they implore the incomprehensible gods of the school with one single message: Don't hit me! Don't slap my hand with the pointer! Don't make me stand against the wall with my hands up for an entire hour! Don't make my nose and mouth bleed with the back of your hand! Don't call my parents in for a meeting! Forgive me, at least this time, look, I know the incantation that will tame you, I know the magic formula: For the circumstantial complement of purpose the question is: "For what purpose?" For the one with cause: "From what cause?" Is it enough? Has the glint of cruelty vanished from your eyes?

I listen distractedly to many of these kinds of recitations. They aren't that feverous, but I am a tolerant god. I don't make thunder or lightning. Thus, many of the believers get caught up in their chores and forget to pray to me. I call Valeria up to the board, the chubby girl, brown-haired and sweaty, who sits by the window. Whenever I glance at her, I remember the awkward situation in which, a year ago, the janitor found us: I was tutoring her, sitting on the same bench in the dark room. We both started violently when the door opened. We hadn't realized how dark it had become. But people from the neighborhood could have thought something else. Now, Valeria was writing on the blackboard, and suddenly in the room there was nothing but her hand holding the chalk, as though everything else was covered in fog. I noticed that her nails were painted, something that would not have been unusual, many of the eighth-grade girls painted their nails quickly in the bathroom before classes with the more permissive teachers, then afterward, also in the bathroom, they cleaned them off with acetone before classes with the strict ones. Valeria, however, had painted every nail on her right hand a different color, like Aura on a different occasion, but what amazed me and turned me pale was the fact that her five fingers were the colors of the concrete rings at the base of the mechanisms in the old factory, the same order and exactly the same shade: dirty pink, dark blue, scarlet, sienna orange, bright and light-filled yellow. Sunlight flooded through the window and her nails gleamed like glass shells, casting little colored dots against the Nile-green walls. I sent her back to her seat, I taught, mechanically, the next lesson, and when the bell rang I told

Valeria to come with me. She turned completely red, to the whites of her eyes, and followed me resignedly. We stopped at a barred window that looked out onto the athletics field. The girl looked directly into my eyes, perspiring and more worried than she had ever been, even when the janitor had walked in on us. I told her to show me her nails, but she kept her hands down with her fingers tucked into her fist. "What's all this?" I asked her, frowning. "Show me, please, your fingernails." Her lips were trembling. She looked like a creature who was sure her time had come. Slowly, she bent her elbow and raised her fist to the light of the window. Then, even more slowly, she opened her hand.

Her hand looked like a flower opening almost imperceptibly slowly. The flesh of her fingers and hand were transparent in the rays of the sun, revealing, like an X-ray, the thin phalanges on whose tips grew, like shoots, the colored nails: they themselves, like the metacarpals that held them, like the carpals in the heel of her hand, were the color of her nails, but paler and more diffuse. The radius and cubitus appeared, under the thicker tissue, blond and blue in color, and toward the elbow the illusory radiograph disappeared. It was like the girl's whole skeleton, as multicolored as butterfly wings, had produced the fluorescence of her nails at her right hand's extremity, the secret code that also appeared at the old factory. "What's this? What's all this?" I asked her again. Valeria, apparently at a loss, looked at her fingernails, and suddenly her legs went out from under her: she fell onto the dirty tile of the hallway, in the midst of the children running around insensibly. Her kneecaps, as she lay on the floor in the sordid sundress in which all the girls were corseted, looked a little like the glistening flesh of oranges.

There was suddenly a multitude of uniforms and curious faces around us, the children helped their classmate up and took her to the nurse, then the bell rang and the hall emptied. I went to the lounge and, feeling very upset, I looked out the window toward the old factory, which gleamed dementedly on the horizon against the bloodred background of twilight.

What was this world? In what petrified and strange insanity was I given to live? Would I survive long enough to find the answer? To find the exit? Would I ever understand, from the core of my loneliness, this otherworldly apparatus that was my life? And suddenly, in the concrete, empty teachers' lounge—with its large table covered with red cloth, with its cabinet for the registers, with its mold-stained paintings—I was enveloped in a fear that I had never felt before, even in my most terrifying dreams; not of death, not of suffering, not of terrible diseases, not of the sun going dark, but fear at the thought that I will never understand, that my life was not long enough and my mind not good enough to understand. That I had been given many signs and I didn't know how to read them. That like everyone else I will rot in vain, in my sins and stupidity and ignorance, while the dense, intricate, overwhelming riddle of the world will continue on, clear as though it were in your hand, as natural as breathing, as simple as love, and it will flow into the void, pristine and unsolved.

28

The vision of the creature looking at me, from a few months ago, came again last night. I had fallen asleep when something made me open my eyes. I saw him for just three or four seconds, then he disappeared. I was left in the dark bedroom, and inside me was a strange, warm fear that didn't hurt. He was sitting beside the bed, to the right of my gaze, and he was looking at me. He was a man this time, with a long face, with gray, thin hair combed close against his temples. He wore an undefined white garment.

I continue to transcribe, here, the underlined parts of my diary and only now, after marking them with crude, thick pen strokes, do they appear for what they have always been: the spinal column of a long manuscript, of torn notebooks, and already yellowed writing, already bleeding from one page to the next like bad tattoos whose lines unravel in the sweat of the martyred flesh. Each fragment is a vertebra in the spinal column of fear, and at the top, supported by the obscene mechanism of the axis driven into the atlas, is the bone cupola where I was born and which has no exit. I climb inside it, I scamper across its porous bones, I cling to the spinous process and the transverse process, I press my ear to the blade of the vertebral curve and listen: the marrow flows inside with a roar, like a waterfall. Above is the great neural basin, I am a water tower that feeds fear to the distant neighborhood of my body.

What I am writing down now happened at the beach, and it is perhaps my most powerful memory connected to the visitors—the one I cannot doubt, just as I cannot doubt, in this moment, that I am not dreaming, that I am awake in the real world, writing in a notebook with a real pen. The first summer after we were married, Ştefana and I vacationed for a week at Mangalia. The sea that year was full of dead jellyfish. On the shore, heaps of rotting seaweed. We lie the whole day on our towels with an arm over our eyes so the sun would not blind us. The seagulls fought over the trash that covered the sand. Yet we were happy: we had made it to the beach. Back in the room, we would shower together, make love on a bed with dubious sheets, and go for walks in the evening in our best clothes, bought at Bucur Obor. The whole week we ate nothing but roast chicken at places by the beach. The sea was at its friendliest in the evenings. We liked to watch it at twilight, when the last swimmers moved along the last, brilliant strip of sunlight. It pulls at my heart when I think of Ştefana: her adorable figure in a swimsuit as she came out of the sea and toward me with her hair full of water and icy drops landed on my legs. On the second or third night, something alarming and inexplicable happened:

> *On the night between July 14 and 15 I woke suddenly, probably there had been some sound, and I clearly saw in the frame of the door (or more precisely in the little hallway) a tall and hefty man, forty-five or fifty years old, coming slowly into the room. I yelled, "What's going on?" but I didn't lift my head from the pillow. I felt paralyzed. Ştefana answered from the other side of the room, coming inside from the balcony. Then I realized that the room was completely dark and the person in the hall had disappeared. Ştefana went to check if there was anyone. Although the door to the room was unlocked, there was no one there.*

What was Ştefana doing out on the balcony at three in the morning? At the time, I didn't even think about it, but afterward, more and more often—especially after someone else took her place, as happened later—her presence on the balcony, under the stars, came to seem more important than the man's convincing appearance in the hallway light.

A dream last night: in the front room on Ştefan cel Mare. A feminine presence and I notice that where my bed used to be is instead a rectangle of loose earth. "What in God's name?" we asked ourselves, as I began to dig with an old shovel. Little by little they appeared: two frightening, decomposing, reeking, green cadavers. Small and curled up, the carcasses of two children. "Now what will we do? We can't stay here in this stink." We looked at them and the smell made our stomachs turn.

I don't know why I marked this fragment. Perhaps I felt that, like with others, it was part of the network of dreams that has driven me so powerfully, ever since I reread my notebooks.

After many years, last night I returned to my series of dreams about museums. I entered a dark museum lit only by a soft glow from the objects on the walls and in the display cases. The sole exception was a large panel in the first room that depicted the earth in the most beautiful green and electric blue, covered with white arrows pointing to odd, oval paths. In the other rooms, everywhere, were maps. Of continents, countries, even the human body, the interior organs, famous painters, all crossed by a network of numbered rectangles.

And another dream, which I'm writing down not because I feel it means something, but just because I like it:

A vision of a man with a shaved head, horribly sweaty. His entire head was a river of water. At a certain moment, he stuck his index finger into his mouth, seemingly to pick at his teeth. But I was amazed to see that the finger pushed out the skin on the nape of his neck and rubbed and cleaned his vertebrae. One side of the man's neck turned transparent as glass, and you could see the finger passing between the vertebrae and the skin. Then his face and scalp began to peel off, until, from under the skin and muscle, his skull appeared.

After two weeks in which I had not recorded much of anything of note (something about what I was reading at the time, *Cold Stars* by Guido Piovene, and some of the eccentricities of my ambiguous relations with Ştefana—hanging from the balcony, the cold shower, etc.—and, yes, two or three lines about the disturbing similarity between da Vinci, Newton, and Tesla, because I had just read from Vasari), I find in my diary some other writings in the wake of those from the sea. I remember that in the thick of that summer I was scared and sad—I felt that something was happening. I think that the episode from Mangalia made me truly pay attention to what happened to me. Then I began to look for dreams and notes about the visitors in my diary. Then I understood the breadth and seriousness of my anomalies.

> *Last night I was looking at my hands in the dark. All my knuckles were violently colored, fluorescent: crimson, emerald, azure, extremely intense. Otherwise, my hands were white and pale against the brown background.*
>
> *A fissure in the walls of my psyche? Again, a few nights before, when I was ready to fall asleep, I saw next to me, watching me, a kind of transparent phantom, green, condensing into the form of a girl, twelve or thirteen years old. She disappeared after a few moments.*

And on August 17:

> *Last night I woke in the middle of the night. I saw phosphorescent lights in the doorway, like at the sea last month. There were two men. One was very tall, and the other one's head came up to his shoulder. They were watching me. Their clothes were Nile-green and scarlet. I saw them perfectly clearly against the black background of the room.*

And a few days later:

> *In the dream, I had, instead of my upper teeth, a black metal bar. Only the incisors seemed somehow stuck to it. I grinned at the mirror and from behind my lips the metal bar appeared, hideous, the two side teeth like*

stones on top, and I wondered how in God's name my teeth had ended up in this state. What in God's name could have happened to my jaw?

I also dreamed I was visited by a great Angel.

I have thought a lot about this last line. I don't remember anything, not a single image, in connection to it. I am intrigued as well by the fact that I capitalized it. I don't often do so. I don't know what was going on with the Angel, the great Angel that visited me that night. As for the dentures, I had had other dreams, and I would have many more, about the hallucination of my strangely deformed face in the mirror, monstrous, incomprehensible, and unrecognizable. I have often wondered if it wasn't in fact an obscure memory, deformed by the undulating waters of dream, of an unreal and malign face that I had seen at some time in real life (if reality exists). In any case, these also made a series, like my "epileptoid" dreams and the string of "visitors" beside my bed, clotting so many strange nights.

One of the most hallucinatory dreams from the last few years. I woke up on my back, with all the skin on my head tensed—my scalp felt as thick as a pachyderm's skin and my blood was pulsing strongly in my neck. I was in an enormous pit full of green smoke. I searched desperately for an exit. The dirt walls, over ten meters high, were unclimbable. Walking through the green fog, stirred by the violent light from above, I saw two ladders leading up and crossing in an X in the deep pit. The light fell on them dramatically, like in Piranesi's prisons. I climbed one of them halfway and there I froze: at the end of it, two cleaning women had appeared, looking at me with frighteningly cretinous faces. Scared, I asked them if I could climb up there, and one of them answered me in an unintelligible, lisping babble. Suddenly I understood: they were demons. And then everywhere, on all the ladders and planks, terrible creatures began to teem, hideous, decomposing, I saw them in the finest of detail. They came out everywhere and grinned at me stupidly.

It was a grin I would see again, later, in some of my most overwhelming nocturnal experiences, and in the *most* terrible of them—I don't know if I can bear to write about it here, because I can't stand the memory.

Halfway through autumn:

(. . .) And then I realized I was holding my head in my hands like a ball, detached from my body, and I was plunging it into water. My hair was shaved, and yellow insects swarmed over the scalp. "But how can I see my own head?" I wondered, thinking that my eyes were still there, in the oddly shaped ball. Then I remembered that I had had a brain operation, and what I was holding was only on the top half of my head—the part with the cranial cavity and brain. I lifted it carefully and put it on like a hat, above my face. I pressed my skull down to stick the two parts together, but a gap remained. I looked in the mirror: the gap was right above my eyebrows, a finger-width high. I started to panic at the thought that the two parts of my head would never join back together. I left the top of my skull to rest on my neck and face by its own weight, and I began to touch my face. When I pulled my chin, my jaw came off in my hand: a dry bone, brown in color, shaped like a U. I tried to put it back, but I heard a loud pop from behind: the top of my head had fallen off onto the cement and shattered. My brain was like an ashy gelatin spread over the floor. "I'm a dead man," I said to myself, and I woke up.

And the same night, toward morning, lying in bed with my eyes open watching the whitening dawn, I thought of something that seemed like a key, but when I jumped out of bed to write it down in the notebook that lay open on the table, most of it faded away. Still, I was left with what I am copying here, like the bone of an unknown animal:

Sometimes my skull seems as fragile as an eggshell, and my hands light and white, like a child's.

At that time I was reading the little, black Bible I had been given on the street, by a woman with weary, resigned eyes (she had a beat-up bag full of Bibles, but—I followed her a little while—she only gave them away in the most hidden places, in apartment block entryways or hallways, or on empty streets) and I remember what a powerful impression the Bible scenes made, in which transcendent beings came into our humble reality and grappled with ordinary mortals, mutilating and transforming them forever. Jacob struck on the thigh by the angel he fought with for an entire night, and limping later, proud and calm, as though the terrible blow was a golden source of his glory and light; Moses was just about to be killed by the Lord, who had appeared at night in his tent, under the cold stars of the desert, when Zipporah, his wife, cut their son's foreskin with a stone knife and touched the godly feet of the poor man, saying, "You are my blood husband"; Saul, a head taller than all other people, was transformed by the same Jehovah who later regretted that he had chosen him and sent the unworthy kingdom an evil spirit to torture it terribly, proof of how frightening divine choice is; and finally Bezalel, whom the Lord gave a spirit of invention and craft and mastery of all trades. In this period, my nocturnal hallucinations and dreams alternated with novelties from the Old Testament, the book to end all books, the book which—after the hundreds and thousands of texts I had read up until then with great pleasure: poems, novels, stories, essays, and literary studies—showed me, and everyone else, that it was possible to speak the truth, to lay the truth out over pages as thin as the discarded skins of vipers. That little book with thousands of transparent pages, with its twin columns of tiny type, with its numbers and footnotes, with the maps of Judea at the end, seemed as valuable to me as the tablets of Moses, where, it was said, the writing was not carved but floated one finger-width above the stone's polished surface: written by the finger of God, floating in the air, glittering a holographic blue, casting a gentle light just like the face of the prophet who, on the mountain, neither ate nor slept for forty days. That's what literature must be, in order to mean anything: an act of levitation over the page, a pneumatic text without any point of contact with the material world. I knew that I would never write anything that could burrow into the page, buried within its ditches and tunnels like semantic mites, the way all storytellers wrote, all the authors of books "about something." I knew that you shouldn't really write anything but Bibles, anything but Gospels. And that the most miserable fate on Earth belongs to him who used his own mind and his own voice to utter words that had never been dictated to him, had not been placed in his mouth: the false prophets of all literature.

Last night I read for hours and only fell asleep at five in the morning. I dreamed that (it's so difficult to explain) there appeared in my room . . . a kind of living doll, a dwarf with a gangly body, dressed in black, dark and pale in the face, with a large head, obviously made of flesh and alive, but somehow a caricature . . . He moved strangely, disoriented, but so concretely and alive—I touched him, I saw him looking toward me, moving . . . I wondered if I wasn't dreaming, but it didn't seem possible, everything was clearly true. "You can't dream like this, in such detail," I told myself.

And from here, unleashed stream of apparitions for a few weeks in a row. My days passed in a blasé confusion, as though nothing made any sense; my nights had "a holy charm" woven of fear and curiosity and the feeling that soon something decisive would happen to me, that I was being somehow manipulated (how, I didn't know and didn't dare imagine: a struggle like Jacob's? something crazier, holier in both senses of the word?), that I had been chosen for shame or for honor, or for something far beyond either one.

And the next night I suddenly opened my eyes in the middle of a dream and I saw, I really saw, a "visitor," one of those that have appeared to me in the last three years (but never before). This time it was a young woman. She had very blond hair, high cheekbones, and blue eyes. She stood next to my bed and looked at me. She wore green clothes. I saw her clearly for a few seconds, then she disappeared. I didn't even have time to be afraid. I was able to invoke the spirits of the dead in my dream the night before last. As proof, a dead young man came into my room. Also, I was able to push, without touching them, coffee cups, spoons, a glass of water across the table. With an effort of will, I poured the water out of the cup: the transparent, glassy liquid ran slowly, in an odd waterfall, and the empty glass rolled and exploded into shards on the floor.

Quick as a flash, my head is being severed with a very thin blade. For a few seconds I don't understand, then the blood reddens my neck. I put my hands against my temples and find myself holding my own head yet staying lucid, and the last image that forms in my brain is the fountain of blood spraying from my carotid arteries.

A new ghost, the most real one up to now, paid me a courtesy visit last night. It seems the seals have recently developed serious cracks. I opened my eyes suddenly in the middle of a dream, and I was horrified to see, one step away: outlined against the black door of the seltzer shop, an old, hunchbacked woman with an impossibly expressive face under a conical hat, wearing a brick-scarlet dress. I was flooded with an inexpressible terror; covered in an icy sweat. The old woman looked at me for a few seconds, then she melted into the black air. I tried to calm down, to tell myself it was just a hallucination, but my heart was beating violently, and a strange shiver, like I had never felt before, encompassed my pelvis and thighs. There was a full, brilliant moon, and I could not fall back asleep for a long time.

*Last night (*after another week, while autumn leaned toward winter and the nights became short hibernations within my blanket's heat, lying beside a more and more estranged Ştefana*), for a few moments, I felt extremely strange. I was afraid. Something was coming. Not a thing, rather it seemed like a whole other reality was pressing against some border in my dark room. I hesitated a moment, trying to decide whether to leave myself in the sway of fascination or to run. In the end, I rejected the feeling of a foreign presence in the room.*

Ah, last night, opening my eyes, I saw a hand held out toward me, a Rembrandtian hand with delicate fingers. I couldn't see whose it was because of the sheet over my head. Whoever it was, they pulled the hand back slowly, delicately, and I saw nothing beyond the dark space of the room.

November 12, the same year, I wrote nothing but this:

Evil images in my dreams, about which I don't want to write anything (last night).

But I know all too well what horror I lived through that night when I argued, for the millionth time, with Ştefana and I left her on the street late at night, swearing at all that was holy. It was around Teiul Doamnei, in total emptiness. I didn't look back, I didn't care that I had left her by herself on the unlit street, beside some cars. I just walked off toward Obor, and from there down the immense arc of Ştefan cel Mare. I remember the smell of rancid fat that came from the Stela soap factory, then the arcade of reinforced concrete outside the Melodia movie theater, the paperlike buildings (ships, tanks, citadels, nuclear bunkers, molehills, honeycombs, lighthouses, tenements, all yellow, scarlet, and dirty pink) in front of Colentina Hospital. I finally arrived at my parents', I complained to them, for the tenth time, that my wife wasn't the same, that we couldn't communicate, and the three of us looked at each other like we were watching an absurd television program, on a Russian television whose screen was the size of a postcard, and then I went to bed in the little room, on the mill side. And there I had that dream that cannot be put on paper, the one that even now makes my hair stand on end, "the evil dream" that destroyed a week of my nocturnal life, which even now I am not prepared to reveal (to reveal *to myself*, to recall it to *my mind*, because I know it like the ten-word summary of a manuscript that cannot actually be summarized). Maybe later, maybe after many other chapters, maybe in another organ of my manuscript will I allow it to open, in all its fascinating abjection, the flower of pus that stained, then, my skull from inside. I am skipping over, as I did then, a night in my sublunary life in order to further my list of anomalies.

What follows had happened to me before, in more bearable ways, a few years earlier:

> *I was in my bedroom when it happened. Suddenly an unseen force grabbed my feet and threw me with irresistible violence from the bed toward the door. It didn't feel like a dream. I was awake, horrified, and overwhelmed by that power. The walls and doors came toward me; I was yanked wildly down the hall and through the rooms; an infinite horror grew within me. I stopped suddenly in front of a large mirror, where I saw my head wrapped in something black. Only then did I wake up, on my back, with my head crushing the pillow.*

December 30:

> *In a dream I wanted very much to move objects by force of will. In a state of euphoria, I focused my powers on a glass and it hopped and scooched quickly toward me. This gave me enormous satisfaction.*
>
> *Last night a frightening dream, in black and white, with violent, expressionist contrasts between dark and light. All I remember is the final image: the bestial face of a cadaver emerging from the darkness toward me. "It's death," I say and am paralyzed with fear. And death comes and literally takes me. I woke up on my back, with my neck stiff and damp from adrenaline.*
>
> *I'm only noting that last night, for the first time in a long time, my "fit" returned—either mystical or epileptic, or both at once. I saw a large white light—it seemed to be inside my skull, behind my eyeballs. I remember that, in the paroxysms of the fit, when I was completely dissolved into the light and in a way inside an annihilating orgasm, I screamed as loud as I could. God appeared. In the morning, in the mirror, I had unnatural eyes, frighteningly sad without being, in fact, actually sad, just detached, indifferent to all that existed.*

And in February, I was in an exultant and angry mood, reading Urzidil's recollections about Kafka and recording strange sensations in my diary, strange as though I had taken drugs (*I had the feeling I was much taller, that I was looking at the room from somewhere above, as though I had grown a half meter . . . and in all this time my head feels a bit like a balloon, it is completely addled, and in my chest and stomach a feeling of dizzy happiness . . .*). I often dreamed about the image I saw, in my childhood and adolescence, through the triple window of my room on Ştefan cel Mare: Bucharest spread under the stars to the edge of sight, but lit up a way it never was in real life, as though it had been illuminated by my eyes looking out of the shadow, my light brown eyes like two lakes in a pale, thin face, lighting up the city that, in turn, lit their transparent irises.

Heavy snow over Bucharest, the air dark, and, in the house, the smell of coffee, mandarins, and chocolate. My head thick with a kind of nostalgic grouchiness and recent dreams. One is the clone of a night that has to do with an event a few years ago: I am in my room on Ştefan cel Mare and I see the city laid out before me. It is night, the houses are pale and above them is a fabulously starry sky. Suddenly, a shooting star changes its arc toward the earth and falls like lightning somewhere in the center of the city with a powerful explosion. And then it is day, there is a yellow light over the houses, I am standing at the wide, slightly foggy window and I cannot believe that the block across the street is gone, the one which, when I was seventeen, stole Bucharest away from me. "But I'm not dreaming," I tell myself, absolutely sure of reality. My mind was completely clear and I could perceive every object, as though awake.

I'll close with February 28, the record of a pure fear, immaterial, like a color, an endogenous fear diffused through the gelatin of my brain like a chemical droplet that spreads through the billions of filaments and interstices to the bony boundaries, that passes through the pores of the cranium and surrounds it with a black halo. I was always afraid, I have always received not objects but the reality behind them, reality itself, with a paradoxical horror: Why am I here? Why does my mind, like a loom, weave the world? What does all this mean? Why can't my hand pass through walls or the hard surface of the table? Who locked me inside this demented fabric of quarks and electrons and photons? Why do I have organs and tissues like cockroaches and worms? What do I have to do with my fingers, my house, my stars, my parents, my skin? Why don't I remember the time before I was born? Why can't I remember the future? I have always been scared by the enormous world in which I am buried, such that, in the end, I cannot help but think that reality is just pure fear, frozen fear. I live in fear, I breathe fear, I swallow fear, I will be buried in fear. I transmit my fear from generation to generation, just as I received it from my parents and grandparents.

There is an image that often comes to my mind, one I didn't make up but that was imposed on me somehow, I don't know when or how, but which returns from time to time to torture me, the way you sometimes have the vision of a knife coming toward your eyeball or of a millipede crawling in your mouth: you clench your eyes, you throw up your hands in defense, you try to escape the painful image, while it seems to have a life of its own, independent of your psychology:

I live between two infinitely thick glass plates that extend to infinity. I find myself on the surface of one, with the other far above my head like a flat, shining sky spreading out to the edges of my visual field. However far I go, everything is the same. There is no one around me, there is nothing. It doesn't matter whether I walk forward or stay in place. But as time passes I realize that the space between the plates is decreasing extremely slowly: implacably, the plates are coming closer together. For the first few years (or the first few centuries, or the first few millennia, none of it matters), I am not too worried: I have such a long time ahead of me that it seems equal to eternity. But however long it may be, it is not an eternity.

The plate approaches and suddenly I realize that, after a long, quiet life, my "sky" is only a few meters above me; soon I can touch it on tiptoe. Not even then—although I can already see the atrocious and inevitable end—am I completely overwhelmed with fear. I just become more mobile, I spread out my senses farther around me: maybe I will find an imperfection, a hollow in the flat walls where I can shelter my fragile body even after the slow, predictable collision. I even imagine the ceiling may stop its imperceptible slide. How should I know what law governs it? But the ceiling keeps coming down.

I find myself running farther and farther over the flat, gleaming surface, but everything, everywhere, is completely smooth, and the plate above me is always falling. I can't fool myself: it is already touching my hair, suddenly risen in fear, on the top of my head. Yes, only when I am directly touched do I start to know, because you can't read anything unless it is written on your own skin.

Hours pass, years, or eternities until you understand you can no longer stand up straight, you have to lean far over to move through the tunnel that extends in every direction. Then you can only crawl on your hands and knees. Then you are squirming on your stomach, with the soft, patient, almost maternal pressure of the ceiling on your spine. Then you can't move at all. From now on, your story is the completely local story of each bone being crushed, slowly and implacably, of each organ being burst, of mixed puddles of your corporeal liquids extending across the glass floor. Everything happens more slowly than can be described, with moments of resistance and moments of spontaneous surrender.

You don't know (because for eternities your life has been a continuous howl, like in the depths of the depths of the inferno) when the fragile structure of your constitution is destroyed, when you are no longer anything but a large, sticky stain between two infinite blocks of glass, but you can be sure that their approach has not ended, that it will continue until the gap between them becomes less than a millimeter, then less than a micrometer. If you are still somewhere in this monstrous universe you will hear every cell of your former body pop, then every molecule crumble with tiny snaps. You will be witness to the minuscule clicks of crushed atoms, then of the nuclei, of the individual quarks, of the bricks of space along the Planck scale. The material stain will extend over the unimaginable surface of space now almost nil between the metaphysical walls, it will become the size of a galaxy or a universe, but it will remain a meaningless event in the infinite crevasse.

In the end, any space, any stain, any presence will disappear and the world will reduce to an infinite, unified block, reconciled within its enigma by a gentle atrocity . . .

And last night, in absolute darkness, the curtains completely shut, I felt a terror fall over me without warning and without reason, a demented terror, like the one I felt when I saw the last "visitor." As before, my whole body began to shake under my blanket. My abdominal muscles, especially, vibrated terribly. I was slowly becoming a medium, which alarmed me and at the same time filled me with pride. I feel chosen again, even if only for disaster and insanity. I feel that I am not alone, that if you are chosen, you can be sure that somewhere there is at least a single being: the one who chooses you.

PART THREE

29

IN AUTUMN 1965, I LEFT FOR VOILA, THE PREVENTORIUM in the Bucegi mountains for tubercular children. I was nine years old, and had I believed anything about the world, it would have been that it is formed from a few nuclei, residing more likely in my mind than in an impossible concept of reality. Each was accompanied by a different feeling, the way you would perceive a different color or a different smell, a different state of my body: in a certain way, I sensed the local reality of our house, with one area of the boundless city where the park and Aleea Circului were located, and Ştefan cel Mare, the bread center, and the grocery across the street, the B. P. Hasdeu Library and the newsstand on Tunari. Within this perimeter, itself surrounded by fear and emptiness, each edifice was either a temple or a mausoleum: the apartment block, cafeteria, militia station, library, and school were not made of bricks and mortar but a psychic substance, the sweet and shiny stones of emotions. By the same token, in a completely different way did I remember the ancient houses where I once lived: Floreasca, Silistra, all painted in different colors of my affects and populated with different phantoms: the group of four- and five-year-olds in the yard of the U-shaped house, whom the motor lifted up the wall of the neighboring house, up to the high window, where they could see inside the ghostly space; the bell jar over the Floreasca neighborhood, where it was always spring, the store at the end of the street where we asked for "a loaf of bread, and don't forget the change." There was also my aunt's house on the edge of town, under the hallucinatory clouds, always the same, as though the purple walls, porch, and crooked tower had been stretched, along with the abstruse architecture of the clouds, into a strange and static picture. Within the frame of the same tableau, with their clothes reflecting the clouds, with their deformed faces, with their dangerous, troll-like airs, my godfather, the illiterate carpenter who always smelled like hide glue, his wife who was twice his size, with breasts that appeared naked no matter how many blouses and sweaters covered them, and their child, Marian, with his underwear over his pants and his jam-smeared face. In between these perfect globes, enclosed inside their sensations of different colors and tastes, the connections were more mystical and less understandable: there were trams, there were buses, there were even trains. But, as neither time nor space meant anything to me, embryonic buds of my future conscience, I didn't imagine these places at any distance from each other, I didn't put them in a line or in an architectural perspective: they were five or six colored beads in a bowl made from my cranial bones, knocking together and clinking, casting sparks of pure emotion onto the kaolin walls. Yes, they were emotions before they were drawings, and drawings before they were realities, because the idea of reality—the most fantastical creation of the human mind—was formed only then, in those years.

Even today, I don't know how I got to Voila. What I remember is something different, from before the bus left. It's morning and we have already said goodbye to our parents. We are sitting in green swings with four seats, two facing two, in a yard outside a building. I am alone on my swing, which is not moving. Beside me is a pathetic, cardboard suitcase; my things must be inside, all tagged by my mother with my initials, sewn crudely, in haste, with black thread. The buses are late, so I take out a book and begin to read. The page I read then, before leaving for Voila, is one of the most important of my life. With that page I began, in fact, to truly read. I can see so well that I can make out on the slightly yellowed, scented page, the minuscule bits of blue or pink lint between the ink letters, as brutal as though they had peeled off the page and were floating above it. But soon I don't see the letters or the page, or the swing, or the park. My world disappears and, like in the coiled stills of dreams, another world suddenly shows itself, another visual and mental space, into which I dissolve, with solemn wonder.

There it is evening. There is a holy and limpid water, under a moon that floats like a golden apple in the sky. There is an old king who, his head resting among pillows, allows a narrow, black boat to carry him over the water. There are colossal landscapes, giant buildings lining the shores. Pyramids raise their blinding metal peaks toward the vaporous sky. Hanging gardens are mirrored in the Nile, the sacred river, with their infinite terraces. A dome rises from an island, its height and grandeur refuse to fit into words: the king, as he floats along the incommensurable walls, looks like a black beetle, lost in the void. Under the dome, supported by pillars, there is a great hall with windows all around. The minuscule king passes over the marble platform of the mirror-polished floor, as he passes each window he pulls the long curtains down, in foamy waves of pink fabric, over the vesperal scene. The hall fills with pink darkness. From the breast of his robe, the king removes a vial carved from a single amethyst and pours three drops into a brilliant, carnelian chalice. In the rosy darkness of the circular hall, the water takes on colors: gold, pink, then deep blue, like the sky. And then something else happens, something disturbing and strange: the entire floor transforms into a mirror, the arc of the dome extends into the depths, and the king stands in the center, resting his feet on the soles of another king's feet, the one hanging down into the mirror. What was above was also below, but different, a different degree of presence, brilliance, and magic.

The pharaoh then walks into the night, toward the great pyramid, a tetrahedron of pitch outlined against the sky. He descends into its stone intestines under the colossal edifice's triangular eye. Within the belly of the labyrinth there is a grotto of a size never before imagined, lit by an enormous torch. At the bottom of the grotto is a transparent lake; on the lake—an island with golden sand; on the island—two crystal shrines. Within one is a dead woman; the king goes inside the other, lies down, and closes his world-weary eyes, so he and the woman may take the form, there in the depths, of two statues made of dust and dreams, Mother and Father, present in the quick of our mind, of everyone's mind.

I read, in the green swing, that first page from a large, white book, and I was left unable to believe, not that someone could write it, but that I was capable of receiving it, of deciphering it, that I was able to transpose it from another mind's logic into the logic of my own, to dress the fine, symmetrical joints of the supple-boned skeleton of the text with the incarnation of my own life, of my own memories. Who constructed that Memphis, that Nile charged with the reflections of the stars, those megalithic and bizarre palaces? A long-dead person had grafted a slice of his brain onto mine. The world of Egypt appeared, like a phantom, at the confluence of our minds. The author was the reader, the reader was the author, like two ends of a bridge where hallucinations circulate. I was in him, and he, although long dead, lived in me.

That morning, I remember, while reading the book I had chosen at random, I was afraid. I didn't understand half of the words, but I had seen another world for the first time, beyond the black letters, my surroundings, and myself. I had been there, in Memphis; I had seen everything; I added, without trams, buses, or trains, another colored sphere to the others that clinked together, without a hierarchy, inside my skull. After the first two pages of fascination and absorption, my hair stood up on my arms and I had to close the book.

I arrived at Voila along with autumn, quickly, as though the torrid summer, with its red-hot walls and tramlines, with its black, desiccated tree leaves, had existed only over Bucharest. Voila was another world. Heavy gray clouds, promising rain, hung down a few feet above the large rectangular buildings that housed the dorms, cafeteria, and the round tower of the infirmary. The entire complex was surrounded by forest and smelled green and fresh, like a forest without end. After we got out of the buses, dazed by the aggressive novelty of the concrete surfaces, of the windows reflecting our pale faces, the melancholic peaks of the trees rising over the buildings, we were taken, each with his suitcase, to the dorms. We put our suitcase on one of the thirty white, hospital-style, metal beds in the dorm room. The beds were connected to each other, such that I was smiling, probably, at the boy who would sleep next to me, and he was probably returning a somber and suspicious gaze from under his eyebrows. The beds were all the same: a starched pillow with two blue initials awkwardly sewn into the cover, a starched sheet, an ironed blue blanket with sparse fibers, and the band of another sheet around its foot. Everything was so strange, so bare in its repetition: thirty beds all the same. The room was so large and austere, the lamps on the ceiling hung so still from their stems, that it must have been a long time before any of us uttered a word. We sat there on our beds, thirty children staring at the floor. We all looked identical, like the beds, like the lockers along the wall with the double door, like the curtains along the other wall, the one with the windows, and in a way we were identical, because we were all children born for asphalt, in the endless field of ruins that was our city, the only world we knew. We had been raised in minuscule apartments in workers' blocks, had played, as long as we could remember, on asphalt and on sewer pipes and gas pipes and dumpsters reeking of trash behind each block. Now our familiar gods, Mother and Father, had let go of our hands and turned into ghostly memories.

I remember my poor and impersonal bed, smelling vaguely of vinegar, with sheets torn in places from frequent washing. I would sleep a few hundred nights wrapped in the blue blanket that did not keep the cold off, I would hear the other children turning in their sleep, and I would often open my eyes, frightened by the light of the moon that broke through the large windows in the wall my head pointed toward as I slept. A young instructor with curly hair and an animal appearance—emaciated cheeks, bristly mustache above his mouth, lips clenched in a constant snarl—told us to stand up and let us know who was in charge around there. He called roll and assigned us each a locker. There we left our clothes and suitcases, shoes and sneakers, after which we were allowed to leave the dorm room, by the long hallway outside it.

The hall was wide and had a tile floor, at the other end of it opened the washroom doors. What a strange feeling I had when we passed them! I had never seen anything like it. First, the washroom was the most foreign and hostile place I could ever imagine. Even when it was full of children, it seemed cold, silent, and solitary. It was all nickel and tile. Tile tubs for washing feet, sinks with mirrors one beside the next, showers in stalls without doors, toilet stalls with doors. The walls were covered in a white, shiny tile from bottom to top, like in the clinics where I had been with my mother, and everything was glacial, unmoving, and frighteningly quiet. In the evening when you went to the bathroom, you had to go through the washroom, and you didn't know if you should go around the wall of metal-legged washbasins to the right or to the left, if the room with the toilets was before the one with the sinks, if somehow the antiseptic symmetry of the washroom had suddenly inverted and now south was north and east was west... When I was first in front of the sink, ready to wash my face, I stared at the faucets, frozen in their definitive form. As I looked at myself in the shiny metal, my shape, naked to the waist, slid over the metal spigot, a snaking rosy color. For a year, this was the only way I was able to see a reflection of myself, because the actual mirrors were too high for us. The sink, however, came about up to my chin.

Outside this room you could see the stairway to the second floor, where the girls' dorm was. They arrived the same day, a little later, in other buses, and we saw them going upstairs with their suitcases, kids like us but with long hair, with cherries over their ears, and with different clothes: calico dresses, skirts and blouses of stiff cloth, many made at home by their mothers on the same table where they poured cocoa to roll out the Easter cozonac, the one that became the sewing table, full of yellow ribbons, numbered with centimeters and with metal clips at the edges, large scissors, and paper patterns out of *Femeia* magazine. And the ever-present thimble, the little object that entertained me so, just like the broken bit of a magnet full of needles and pins. Slow and pale like they were being deported, the girls with damp eyelashes climbed to a place that, like women's public toilets in the city, would be forever inaccessible to us. A powerful and dizzying taboo, as strong as the temptation, protected the second story and, although nothing prevented us from going up the stairs toward those fantastical places, for a long time the idea never crossed our minds.

After we left our belongings in the lockers, putting our pajamas, with their giraffes, elephants, and frog designs, on the bed, we were taken to the instructor—named Comrade Nistor—in the mess hall in the next building. Giant trees along the path smelled strongly of the forest. It seemed like it would rain. Far away, over the treetops, you could see the mountain peaks. Everything was so different from my world, I felt like I had landed in another universe, where things had other shapes and appearances. When we entered the mess hall—a vast, white rectangle, full of four-top tables—we were smacked by the nauseating smell of cafeteria food, the food that would torture me, more than anything else, until the end of my time at Voila. It made my stomach turn over the first time I ate it, and after a period of subjugation to the torturous food, I couldn't enter that hall without running to the toilet to throw up, my empty stomach producing an acrid, greenish liquid. Then I would sit at the table, pale and resigned, knowing all too well what was next.

In the Voila preventorium, children had to eat everything. There was no more inflexible rule. Everything that was on the plate had to be eaten, no matter how disgusting or how difficult to swallow it might be. If you didn't finish during mealtime, you were taken, your plate and all, to the infirmary, where you were left with your plate in front of you until nightfall, supervised by the nurses. You vomited, you started over, you vomited again, you ate another spoonful . . . During this process you were goaded along with a smack on the back of your neck.

I sat at the table, feeling nauseous, beside Traian, the one who had chosen the bed attached to mine. He was still glaring at me from under his eyebrows. He was massive, with a blond crew cut, and he seemed older than the rest of the kids. His eyes were very blue, set widely apart, full of tears. As he ate, some tears dropped onto the chopped meat and into the soup he constantly stirred with his spoon. I was also having trouble eating: I had always been a picky eater, I never liked anything; at school I would even throw the lunches my mother made down the elevator shaft. But unlike Traian and the others, I didn't miss my parents; not the entire time I was at Voila. It was as though they had never existed. They had been, I realized for the first time, transparent and ghostly parts of my life, and so they would remain. Things were good when I was around them: they served me as believers serve a tiny god. But when they were absent, I didn't feel bad. I liked to explore the world alone, in spite of my fear of strange places. And at Voila everything was so new and so vast that the past, engrammed in my memory, faded and became inaccessible: I was completely oriented toward the future, toward the surprises that awaited me. This is why I didn't have, like other kids did, any personality of my own: I was the space in which they moved, I was the visual field that completed them. I was wholly consumed in looking at them, at them and the surrounding places. I didn't even know what I looked like, what my voice sounded like. A nine-year-old kid, lost among others like him.

Even though I didn't clean my plate, they didn't take me to the infirmary the first day. They took us back to the dorm, where we waited for the doctor's first visit. He arrived, a gentle man in a white coat, accompanied by the assistant he later married. They first checked us for lice and nits, and, of course, a few of us had them and were immediately sent for a "zero cut." I also had had the "little babies," as my mother called them, but we had gotten rid of them quickly: a kerosene wash and then the metal comb with fine, sharp teeth that scraped my scalp. "Look at the little babies," she would show me in satisfaction, the little yellow seeds caught in the metal teeth. They were the capsules where the worms that would become lice were visible as black, pulsing points. Then they stripped us to the waist, looking over our skin for hives. Whoever had a rash found themselves with a blue menthol mark, negligently brushed on, the same brush for all the kids. The doctor had a lot of hair on his fingers, but well-trimmed nails and a delicate touch. He always smelled fresh, like cologne. His stethoscope, with its pink rubber tubes and cold, nickeled end, fascinated us like an object from another civilization. A superior creature used it to palpate, who knows for what purpose, the bodies that housed, under their velvety skin, soft, complicated organs that throbbed, extended, and retreated like living animals in a subterranean lair.

They distributed our medicine, after consulting slips in thick, overused envelopes, like those a fat, bored woman would give to my mother when we went to the clinic. I would get hydrazide, little yellow pills that looked like lice eggs, eight a day, every evening. I would always take them all at once, with a little water, in the washroom, hurrying back to catch the beginning of the bedtime story. Strangely, I didn't feel ill or weak, even though the smell of the cafeteria food made me sick every day, because of the soups and stews, the soft and insipid chicken meat, the gizzards and livers that I would have died before eating.

Next, we went out into the drizzle in the preventorium yard. Comrade Nistor showed us the buildings, some were new and modern, made of reinforced concrete, with wide windows, not that appropriate for the wild landscape around us, but others, especially the castle of the infirmary with its beautiful tower, seemed ancient, black with damp, and made of lichen-covered stones. The paths rose and fell, turned strangely around the buildings, lost themselves among the black trees that crowded around everywhere, their branches bouncing with their woody cones. In the end, all the paths seemed to disappear into the deep and dark forest that surrounded the complex. Along the large buildings there were wooden barracks scattered here and there, some we would later learn housed the cooks, teachers, janitors, and gardeners, and others were little tailor or carpentry shops. Where would we study, though? There was no school to be seen, and the guide was so dour and emanated such ill will that no one dared to ask. I was in the third grade, and my mother had put a few necessary things in my suitcase: notebooks for composition and for math, a wooden pencil case, a triangle, a few Chinese pencils with erasers . . . Maybe we wouldn't have to do school, since we were all so sick? I glanced at the kids around me: they all seemed tough and, in spite of having said goodbye to their parents, more and more energetic and curious. It was ridiculous to think they could have tuberculosis . . .

We went back to our dorm, now as dark and strange as an old picture. Comrade Nistor had turned on the lights, and we went to our beds and pulled the sheets down to sleep. How stiff and strange the sheets were! They were stiff from so much scrubbing, but my eyes, so clear then, could see the minuscule knots in their surface, flat and rough like sandpaper. What an unusual texture the blanket had! I would pull long, white threads out of the fraying edges. They looked like they were made from pressed plant stalks, dyed violet. Through the holes in the sheet, you could see the dark mattress, apparently moldy, and we saw what it was on the last day of every trimester, when we undid the beds and heaped the sheets together on the floor: on each iron bed was a kind of marine animal—slimy, yellow-black, ancient—that had waited patiently on its back, enduring the tossing and turning of who knew how many children . . . But on departure day, with our bags packed and the dormitory empty, it seemed so sad; even today it appears in my dreams, connected to my constant theme of trains and unknown, empty stations.

The pillow, where I cried on so many moon-filled nights, was flat, shapeless, lacking the corners and folds mine had at home. A reddish goose feather, with some quills underdeveloped and others expanded into an immaterial puff, poked out of the white fabric, which was softer and shinier than the sheets. We all lay on the beds, we looked at each other with sympathy. The instructor was still telling us things in a harsh and rigid tone: rules for behavior, punishments . . . How we should organize our lockers—the line of tall, narrow cabinets attached one to the next on the wall across from the large windows—how we should act with the caretakers and the cleaning ladies . . . After lights-out at nine o'clock, the dorm door would close and no child was allowed in the halls. But most of us didn't listen. Everything was too new, too much at once. In the past, when I had encountered unknown worlds, I had at least had my parents as a constant, as a strong thread on which to string the ashen pearls. Now I was alone, I had to figure out for myself what was good and what was bad, which gods wanted good and which wanted ill. Comrade Nistor would be one of the most abject, but only a tiny demon, without consequence or importance. Other tiny demons would reveal themselves that first evening, when three caretakers burst into the dorm, banging the doors against the walls. "Enough! Everyone in your bed and don't get up! I don't want to hear a thing!" They looked like the bread and milk clerks, like the ticket-takers in the trams, fat and impersonal women, the ones who, no one knew why, populated all the clothes stores on Lipscani and butcher shops in Obor. That evening they raced from one bed to the next to trim our nails with large, oiled iron scissors: they cut them to the quick, with hostility, indifferent to screams or the pulling away of wounded fingers. As soon as they finished with one of us, they lurched like vultures to the next kid, they caught him between the sacks of their breasts and bellies and giant thighs and pulled their nails off without pity, until they finished with us all. "Now get in the bath! Get undressed and walk single file to the washroom!"

I had never seen other children without their clothes. At home I knew how shameful it was for someone to see your bare bottom. For a long time, I wouldn't even let my mother come in while I was in the bath. And now, twenty boys, most of them so skinny their ribs showed, got in line—trying their best to not touch each other, and especially to not look at each other—in front of the dormitory door. The ceiling floated far above us, its four lamps hanging from their stems. I was very embarrassed, I felt like a little animal in a herd; I had been abandoned in a place where I had vanished into a group of small, naked bodies, dreading the next unforeseeable trial. Shivering and naked, we walked down the cold hallway, our feet sticking to the tile, and we found ourselves inside a mist and sudden heat. All the showers were running in the washroom, making round, white puffs of steam that spread through the whole room, clouding the mirrors, their matte surface streaked with long drips. We were forced under the scalding jets that shot out of tight nozzles, and in a few minutes we were as red as boiled lobsters. His shirt soaked with mist, the instructor paced through the room where the steam suffocated our squeals, and his gaze shot through anyone not under the jet of boiling water. Soon, I couldn't even see the boy sharing my shower. So I was completely surprised when a hand grabbed my arm and yanked me out of the stall, onto the flooded and slippery floor. It was one of the caretakers who, with amazing speed, was rubbing a rough, soapy sponge all over me. "Hand up!" she said impersonally and fast, like a soft machine. "Now the other!" With surprising energy, her hand moved over my fire-red body, pulling my hair, rubbing my face with the same wiry sponge she scraped over my chest, back, and stomach. Through her blouse you could see the scarlet circles on her breasts, her dark navel, the hams of her hips . . . She twisted and wrung me out like a rag. "Bend over!" And then I felt the sponge going over my bottom, between my buttocks, then over my wiener and nuts, and I knew how shameful it was to show them to anyone, let alone let someone touch them. I tried to keep my legs together, but the massive woman easily pushed them apart, with insectoid disinterest. When it was over, she shoved me back under the shower and moved on to the next child. We went into the washroom pale and came out red; we went back to our beds to put on new, velveteen pajamas, brought from home, and climbed under the sheet. "Whoever needs the toilet should go now, because I don't want to catch you in the hall before morning," squawked the instructor while he put on a dry shirt. After all this was over, the light went out and we were left in a complete and profound darkness.

The next day, the light was even more brilliant than ever, the cold light of autumn. The hard edges of the beds and the gleaming stems of the ceiling lights blinded me. The other children sat up in bed and moaned, looking around at each other. It was the day we changed realms and landscape, when we saw something we didn't think we would ever see: the forest. After breakfast we were led, single file, into the forest. And the forest was endless, deep and mysterious, black and green, full of empty spaces, almost screaming in its silence. I had lived my entire life on asphalt, like a roly-poly that had run its dozens of legs for eternity over the same bulging, blind wall, scarred by ancient fires. All I had seen up to that point was ruined city houses, newsstands, groceries, and tramlines. Now, in the blinding morning, we left the wooden castle of the infirmary behind and walked into the forest.

I didn't know what to do with so much green light, with so many thousands of green hues, transparent, opaque, shading into yellow and rust, pulsing and throbbing under the archways of giant trees. I didn't know how to think about this glittering world of smells, chirping birds, black and damp bark so rough it hurt my eyes, soft, elastic earth full of plant shoots and covered with leaves in various states of decay. In the low branches were great wheels of spiderwebs, shining in their almost perfect polyhedrons, swelling with each breeze, their rigid architecture holding the large raisin of the animal in its center. Everywhere trees lay fallen, with gaping holes, with meaty white mushrooms growing in their rotting interiors, dripping, melting into each other. Stumps anchored by solid roots, like poorly capped, blackened molars, teemed with ladybugs. The humid and dark air would burst into unbearable flames when the sunrays pieced the leaves, drawing trembling puddles on the ground. Even the children's faces showed the same texture, and their clothes and their bare arms, as though they had grown here since they came into the world, set within this world of shimmer and darkness, one with it, like the pattern in the carpet.

We scattered into the forest—as we would later do hundreds of times, especially on Sundays, going so deep into the forest that you could hear nothing but muted shouts from a distant group. I never found the end of the forest. It was like it extended all the way to the edge of the world, in every direction, surrounding the preventorium in its core. There were no paths, no landmarks, the forest was the same everywhere: dead leaves scattered on the ground, large rocks we would turn over to find nests of red ants with larvae bigger than they were, black trunks that supported flexible and graceful canopies, where birds we never saw cast other canopies, made of their calls, over us. In groups of three or four boys, armed with wet sticks and bark belts, we ranged all over the world of transparencies and rot, calling each other over to see a huge millipede hanging by its claws in the air from a fragment of a tree trunk, a wild arum with red and green bubbles on its phallic stem—a sign that a lot of tomatoes and peppers would grow that year—crescent-shaped mushrooms, undulating and yellow-green like bile, that we tried to break with our fingers. We ran through the transparent gnats that followed us everywhere, we came to streams where we drank the icy water even on the first day, even though it was teeming with pale insects, their abdomens caught in mottled armor, we clambered up rises and down into ravines, always in damp shadow, smelling like sweet, wet earth and sap, and smelling bitter, at the same time, of tannins, of the secretions of half-crushed beetles, of wilted flowers with disgusting details.

I liked it best when I would end up alone. I would try, every time they let us go in the forest, to walk as far as I could in a single direction, until around me there was only the humming silence of the forest. It felt even quieter when a sudden buzz, as violent as if it were a metal propeller, spun past my ear; when an unknown bird spoke a few notes, followed by a green silence. I would stop and stand there. If I cupped my hands, the air would sit in them like a dense water, full of algae. The air flashed and darkened with the branches' every shifting, casting a thick, rosy gold tinge onto the fallen trunks. I was in the bowels of the forest, in the deepest, most hidden place, dissolved within its gastric juices.

How I savored every detail of my new world! I lay on my stomach, on the wet leaves, mixed with the earth. I would hold a single leaf in front of my eyes: it was unique, different from all the others, and before I came, no one had noticed it, not even it had noticed itself, not even God. It was what it was: shiny yellow, pointed, scarlet on the edges, with visible veins, with insect stings hemmed with circles of a certain brown, peanut color, light and joyful. The petiole was still intact, made with a certain grace and ending in a porous area where it had separated from the twig. The leaf was torn in one place, the tissue detached along the veins, and on the back it was more matte, more orange, and more affected by the damp than on the front. Under it, over it, around it, there were thousands and tens of thousands of other mottled leaves, each one different, but all touched by decay: some were just the skeleton in a kind of brown fluff, others were broken in the middle and ragged toward the edges. From the middle of some leaves, a shiny green shoot sprang up, rising avidly toward the sun, with a cluster of curled leaves on its tip.

I would investigate a rotting tree trunk, breaking off pieces of its spongy wood. What huge and unsettling holes gaped under its roots! Spiders as big as rats could come out of there. In the trunk's fibrous flesh, in its rings and points, I found brightly colored, elastic pupae, perceptibly throbbing with something only then being formed. I found beetles with green, metallic plating, and worms as hard as wire, curled in spirals. I watched the bestial worlds there for an eternity, I leaned my face toward them, I breathed the smell of earth from the feet of crickets and the rings of centipedes. Blind and belabored red ants, who built their slanted sawdust piles against the trunks, glittered everywhere. From time to time the silence became so great that you could hear the wooden thunk that antennae made when two ants met and mutely conversed. But it would soon be broken by a bird's trill, arching high overhead, like the green canopies of the trees.

If I had let myself lie on the earth, among the hundreds of shoots and little plants, each one different from the next, each one shaped in a different way by time and weather, if I had let my inert body be overtaken by sun and shadow, if I had let a poisonous bush's clusters of red and black berries arch above me, nothing would have distinguished me from the world of the forest. I could have died there, I would have quickly turned into dead wood, with my interior juices hardened, with my eyes covered in cobwebs and my skin cracked, a host for insects, a fertile soil for mushrooms, my carcass more and more decomposed, worn smooth by the wind and by loneliness. It would have rained and snowed on me, and in the spring, there would be some bones and rags spread around, under the grass, growing bells with violet cups and brown saplings. I would have belonged, at last, to a world; I would have been one with it, one with its humid, green air, with its carpet of transparent leaves, with its sweet and bitter smells. I would have died and been reborn there, in a complete lack of consciousness, knowledge, or doubt, only a model in the endless tapestry of the forest.

A distant whistle, foreign to the echoes below the canopy of branches, called us back, after a few hours of running and reverie in the place I would love best for the rest of my life: the forest. It was the referee's whistle that Comrade Nistor wore around his neck. I stood up from my bed of rotted leaves and hurried toward the sound. Through the trees I saw the other children, in groups, usually girls with girls and boys with boys, all hurrying to the meeting point. Over time, I came to know them, to make friends with some, to keep away from others. I have a few photos from those years, where I can name almost all of them without any hesitation, Bolbo and Prioteasa, Nica and Goran, Iudita and Horia, the boy with glasses that told us, for a year, every night before bed, the most amazing stories. I have these photos, old and cracked and stained with who knows what, among my meager treasures, in the same pile as my braids, baby teeth, papers and receipts, many other photos, and a few objects that would seem to almost anyone completely heteroclite and mysterious, but which for me are as ordinary as a fork and knife, as shirt buttons. My museum, my memorial house.

We gathered in front of the infirmary, the last outpost of the human world, jabbed into the ribs of the forest, half-surrounded by it, and, in a way, one with it, because the little castle, with its octagonal tower and dirty yellow walls, had beams all over its outside, exposed, crossed, blackened like the trees in the background. In a line, in pairs holding hands, we were led down the paved paths between the pavilions, toward the gate where yesterday we had arrived in the buses. The day was brilliant, one of those autumn days when the air burns with cold light, or more like limpid water that could flood everything. At the entrance there was a booth with an open window. We lined up in front and received, from one of the fat women who seemed to be teeming everywhere, a round pastry with half a walnut stuck on top. "It looks like a brain," one child said, and I smiled, because that was just what it looked like. About the size of a bird's brain, I imagined. Then we crossed the street toward an identical gate that opened in a long wall of prefabricated cement panels. Above it rose the forest-covered mountains. A few pine trees were visible through the wire gate at the schoolyard entrance.

On the other side of the street there was an apple orchard, and in the middle of the orchard was a school. I would see the apple trees—where I would sit so often, sprawled among them in waist-high grass—in all their avatars, rotating through the seasons: now they were green, green to their core, green in the depths of their stems with wooden networks of vessels gurgling with green sap, green in the ever-changing hues of their leaves, and in the evanescent flesh of their fruits that dislocated with a pop at our bite, whose weight pulled the branches down toward the earth. For my entire time at Voila, my real nourishment was almost nothing but apples and hydrazide, since I vomited all of the cafeteria food. Later I saw dried, black apples in snowdrifts, as though drawn by children on wavy sketch paper. In the spring, I saw them full of pink flowers, with five crepe paper petals and, in the middle, stamens like the horns of snails. In the summer I could eat the fruit's amber stickiness that had only a faint taste, before we were sent home on our homogeneous asphalt, behind our blocks carbonized with the passage of time, only to find the trees the next fall loaded with the sweetest apples I could imagine, and so juicy that after you bit into them you saw the cold and crystalline juice running down their flesh. Among the hundreds and thousands of apple trees that attracted all the winged insects of the world—wasps and ichneumonids, firm and whirring dragonflies, butterflies of countless species identical to those I colored in art class—were the cottages for the doll-like first-graders, short buildings with pointy roofs housing two classrooms back-to-back, each with a porch and entrance and windows like a house in the country. The classrooms were tiny and dark, because the apple branches filtered out all wavelengths of light besides a homogeneous green; there were rows of ancient benches, rotten and spongy like the fallen tree trunks in the forest. A wooden chalkboard on a three-legged stand, a type we didn't think existed outside of the drawings in children's books, stood in the corner. Its tray always had a rag that stank of vinegar alongside a few broken pieces of chalk half-wrapped in red paper. Everything was narrow and ink-stained, on the walls were posters with unknown animals, with numbered arrows pointing to exotic organs, and the teacher's desk was so rickety that more than once it collapsed into a heap of planks in the middle of a lesson. There, in the third-grade cottage, is where I studied that entire year, classes in the morning, and in the afternoon, after the obligatory hour of sleep, we went back to do homework, supervised by a young, ugly, and bored monitor, who constantly walked up and down the rows and gave our necks unexpected, sharp smacks, without our ever knowing what we had done wrong.

I would live for almost two years in that artificial world, as far from real life as Castorp's magic mountain, taking eight hydrazide pills, as small and yellow as the seeds of silkworms, each evening, tortured all night by an uncontrollable, agonizing need to pee, vomiting the stews and boiled meats in the mess hall, and writing my essays, slowly and meticulously, with a wooden pen. If Traian hadn't been there, I would never have known what really went on in the fake preventorium with its fake tubercular children, and my untroubled memories would have combined with all the other memories from which the horror of my life is woven, without my knowing how to spot the fissures between them. I was this close to being fooled by the paradise at Voila, to being suffocated by its mountains and forest and drugged by the smell of its apple blossoms, because I lacked a vantage point from which the crooked perspective lines would straighten and the demonic game it played with my mind would appear in the evidence of its nightmare.

30

I seldom see the lower school teachers, except for Steluța, who is practically my neighbor on a street parallel to Maica Domnului. Sometimes we happen to take the same bus or tram to school, if we have a meeting in the morning or if we are going to collect litter or chestnuts. In fact, this is when I see the other lower school teachers, too. Their world is even smaller than ours. They are the poor women at their desks eternally crocheting macrame, when they are not cutting out cardboard rabbits and carrots to teach the children to count. They almost never come out of their classrooms; they stay inside, surrounded by their little subordinates, like ant queens, chubby and indolent, while workers clean their joints. There is an entire fauna, which, albeit dominated by the housewives wearing beehives and dresses made from unnameable material, the poor women worn down at home and at work, nevertheless contains some exemplary eccentrics. Mrs. Mototolescu and Călătorescu (real names, "squeezed" and "traveled"!) are twins: they always teach parallel classes, one next door to the other, always visiting each other, at school and (so we heard) at home, too. Never would you see either of them alone in her room. At any moment during class time, if you opened the doors, you would find one room where the children were alone, trained to sit still, and the other room with two teachers endlessly chattering away. They have been scolded in meetings countless times, but they can't do anything about it: neither one—however much they try, like people who have smoked all their lives trying to quit—can endure more than a few minutes of separation from the other. Mrs. Spânu is a woman-man, tall, broad-shouldered, her hair cut short, with a military gait. Her chalk, when she puts it to the board, screeches worse than any other teacher's. You have to believe she does it on purpose. When you come in from Dimitrie Herescu, you hear the unbearable screeching even before you pass the auto mechanic's. The children from her group often end up in the nurse's office with thin lines of blood running from their delicate cochleas.

The real problem cases in the lower school are two other teachers. One is a slumland beauty, a wasp-waisted Madonna with a heart-shaped mouth. Her catlike green eyes regard you languorously through fluttering eyelashes. Her double chin invokes a kind of oriental voluptuousness, likewise her unusually abundant breasts, where gold chains hold throbbing crosses. Gheară, who, for all his fear of his wife, would plow blindly into the harem that is any teachers' lounge, often told us, too often in fact, about the time he went home with "the venomous hyena," how he put up with her fastidious fussing for a few hours, fighting for every centimeter of unveiled skin, until the barricades suddenly dropped and he found himself violated with a terrifying ferocity by the owner of the juiciest exotic fruit he had ever seen between a woman's legs: "My boy, I never even imagined something like that, a woman just sopping wet: that bale of hair between her legs so drenched and the juices running down her thighs to her knees . . . When you entered her you didn't feel a thing, like you were in a cave . . ." After that he couldn't get rid of her. He found himself anonymously reported to his wife, to the Party, to the Securitate. He was told that he had been distributing manifestos, that he wanted to replace Borcescu at 86, that he was the driver in a hit-and-run. He had never regretted more getting involved with a woman. Higena's specialty was lying and manipulation. The children in her class became experts in this, the sole subject their teacher taught them. They broke into little groups that hated each other and took revenge in turns. They came to the school a half hour early to write obscenities on each other's benches. They approached her desk one after another to whisper what people said about her at home, what radio stations their parents listened to, what boy liked what girl, and what they did in the toilet or in the little room beneath the stairs. Sitting at her desk, graceful as a praying mantis with a triangular head and extended abdomen, Higena tsk-tsked: "People can be so bad . . ." In the lounge people left a space around her, because whenever she caught someone with her merciless, spiky legs, she held him tight and began to devour him down to the last crumb. Whichever teacher was cornered would learn who was talking bad about him, who was trying to cut his pay, how the other teacher in his area was undercutting him, what the school's intelligence officer had said about him. Then she would complain how persecuted and undermined she was herself, how the children lied to her, the parents insulted her, and the other teachers belittled her. At many meetings, Higena was criticized for her destructive attitude toward the collective. "Comrade . . . Floroiu, please don't be so—my dear Higena—so mean, or you'll never get married," Borcescu would mutter, having had her some time ago, so they said, also at her house, also under the gaze of ten or so porcelain dolls with sponge dresses lined along the back of her bedstead. And he enjoyed the same consequences as Gheară. He was lucky that those in charge of the school had come to know her like the back of their hand, and her denouncements usually didn't get any farther than the first trash can.

The other, a decrepit old lady with her gray hair pulled back in a tight bun, who smelled of urine and booze, was the school's train wreck, the famous Comrade Zarzăre. With her breasts and stomach sagging like a Neolithic Venus, always hungover, with straggly whiskers and the smile of a cunning whore on her face, Zarzăre was, still, a teacher, and every four years she produced an animal menagerie of a class that not even the best teachers in the school could deal with. Whenever I was on morning duty and stuck my head in the door, I found her slumped on her desk, her room a filthy and indescribable chaos. The children raced around, spat on each other, and swore, kicking dust up to the ceiling. They toyed with her body, lifted up her dress, dyed her gray hair with ink, wrote dirty things on her neck . . . Everyone knew that Madame Zarzăre was not just the Pena Corcodușa of the neighborhood, forever reeking and three sheets to the wind, but also the zaftig Rașelica Nachmansohn. She lived with a young man, good-looking by neighborhood standards, and the other teachers were sure they knew what magic charms kept him close to the hag. Agripina would often tell me indignantly: "You know what that disgusting woman does, dom profesor, when she's at home? *Urgies*, dom profesor! Full-on urgies with two or three men, tell me there's a woman, too, and I won't be surprised. When she was young she worked Crucea de Piatră, and in forty-eight or forty-nine, when the communists came and closed the whorehouses, what were they supposed to do with the whores? They made them teachers. Some of them were stuck in the factories, but if they knew how to write they were sent to the schools to give the children a good upbringing. I'd hate to tell you, dom profesor, you're young and don't know what the world is like, how many whores there are among our schoolteachers, even the schools downtown. They had connections, they knew people . . . My husband, the writer, he told me that a lot of our classic authors would visit Crucea de Piatră. You want to tell me they didn't have a favorite, a girl who knew how to please them? Do you think they didn't read her what they had written, didn't teach her poems, and a bunch of other things? Don't be surprised that someone like Zarzăre ends up knocking thirty kids dead and refusing thousands more in the next thirty or forty years before she retires . . . And to think, dom profesor, that I, a lot poorer and in worse shape than those girls, I raised myself alone, up from the sticks, I worked the hydraulic press, I put the coating on wire bobbins, and at night I studied to become a teacher, I mean come on . . . I wasted my youth on that, dom profesor, just so this heifer, this bovine can waste my time now . . ."

No one could get rid of Higena or Zarzăre, however much the teachers' councils or district inspectors tried. Everyone had to have a job. The other teachers resigned themselves and waited for the years to pass until those two retired. Each produced students like themselves, year after year, graduation after graduation. You came to appreciate the other teachers' mediocrity, because at least with them, no one got maimed.

I wouldn't go into such detail about these women, hidden all day like gnomes in their classrooms and huddling together during staff meetings to knit, if all the crazy fads that shook the school didn't start with them: the jars of algae and spoonfuls of oil and Cico enemas and the book *Rosaries*—no one knows who wrote it, but everyone read its story about an old woman who fell in love with a blind man, the only one who couldn't see what a state she was in, it made you cry your eyes out—and the card readings done with playing cards with pictures of famous soccer players, and stamps from Madagascar, Qatar, and San Marino, and guppies and hamsters that had the bad habit of dying after a week, "and I tried everything, I tore up fresh newspaper every day, I gave them lettuce and shaved carrots, like it was my own child, dear, it ate better than I did," and all the other crazy things that, once the fad had passed and something else appeared, they were the first to laugh and ask themselves how they could have been so silly.

Now there is a new fad, the multicolored cubes that rattle and twist in everyone's hands, during class and in the hall and in the lounge, trying to make at least one side all the same color. They're cheap, they sell them at Obor, and they break easily: a couple of twists and the plastic pieces all fall out. In the gray-green of the lounge, the cubes, twisting and rattling in livid palms, are like lay miracles, like modest flowers in a field that glow enchantingly under the low, oppressive skies.

The poor women lost what little of their minds they had left on these plastic cubes, each one dirty and sticky from so much manipulation. Once a week, someone triumphantly brought in a cube with two sides done: all nine squares, on one side and the other, all the same color. Yes, but there were still the other four offensive faces, insolently mottled, and this drove them crazy. Some of them, after pulling their hair out in desperation, threw the cube on the ground and shattered it, and they swore they wouldn't waste their minds on the stupid things anymore. The janitors patiently cleaned up the multicolored shards, shaking their heads at the teachers' lunacy. As did, seemingly, the Kalmyk personages on the walls, who kibitzed sympathetically around the table covered with red cloth, where groups of four or five full-grown women (but also Spirescu and Gheară for a few days) furiously twisted the cubes that cast dim reflections on the walls and ceiling.

❂

Because I imagined that the new hysteria running through the school had a logical-mathematical basis underneath the exuberant colors of its plastic surfaces, I asked Goia if the famous cube had been scientifically studied, and if there were an algorithm that generated the monocolor arrangement of all six sides. "Of course," he wheezed, a full head taller than me, even when we sat on the steps in front of the school entrance, as was our habit during breaks or on the holidays when we had to come to school, just after it began to warm up in the springtime. Neither one of us smoked, we only went outside to see the azure skies over the neighborhood, as though cut out of old photographs, other times, and other gazes, those from the depths of our childhood. Our hair moved in the still-cold breeze. We might spend an hour looking at the ordinary people in cheap sweaters and proletarian caps who passed carrying two or three dirty bags, at women with vulgar, printed dresses, at a patrolman or priest walking with all the dignity of their uniform, looking neither left nor right. Goia was the epitome of gentleness and of gravity. I never saw him laugh. His face must have been hidden, like in Salinger, by a mask of poppy petals, so people could talk with him without falling over, their hearts bursting with pity and terror. His voice emerged, full of ash, from a larynx with burnt vocal cords. If you asked him a personal question—where he lived, if he lived with his parents, what he did at home, how he did with women—he would shut up, not to make a point, but just as though he hadn't heard or understood what you said. Any objective question he would answer straight out of the book, especially things connected with his field, mathematics. But even here his passion was steady, like his wheezing voice that came from deep inside him. An immaterial and almost inhuman oracle would answer, a source of knowledge that beckoned something that already existed within you (from the moment you asked the question), because any question knew in fact its answer, being the absence in the precise shape of the question in the mind of the one who asked. Goia didn't answer you, he reminded you of the answer with the careless gentleness of a mother explaining to her child for the tenth time how to tie his shoes. "Of course," he said. "Rubik's cube was a complicated mathematical object, based on a great deal of theory. It was part of the field of topology, the magical part of geometry, and even though it's become a toy you can buy at Obor for ten lei, it has noble origins. Its inventor created many of these logical toys, but only the cube enjoyed an incredible commercial success that made everyone in the deal rich, except him. What Rubik invented, in fact, was the mechanism that connected the cubes and turned on multiple planes. Because the principle, *primum movens* of the colored cubes, came from one of the most fascinating mental experiments of the whole history of mathematics (possibly of all of human thought), and it involved many of the most brilliant names, the most mysterious and controversial characters in the history of mathematical logic, the equivalent of Lewis Carroll in literature. Both of them," Goia told me calmly, "tried to go through the looking glass."

In a way, they were masters of the most noble art, the one toward which all other arts strive, the great art of escape. Because it's clear that Alice, following the ever more complicated messages that came from another world (crescents, gears, crosses, and asterisks, I say to myself as I listen), found, in the vision of the hare or through the waters of the mirror, that for which we all search from the moment we are born: an exit from the world's sinister prison. Just as strange as the author of Alice, as Poe, as Darger, as Nabokov, as so many other illuminated monsters for whom girls had butterfly wings and scholarly minds, embodying the burning and concupiscent angel of temptation, the character from Goia's story would captivate me like one of the most important pieces of the impossible jigsaw puzzle I was facing, the one with the king's eye and a third of a crown. I didn't connect it right away with the old story of the book I read in the sixth grade, unable to stop myself from crying. Only when I was home again, levitating above my bed, naked and free of the pressure of the earth that crushed us in its embrace, did I understand the delicate structure of the skeleton in all of its articulations: nothing had happened by accident. It had been no accident that I had experienced my first emotional outburst, so violent I would never forget it, reading *The Gadfly* by Ethel Lilian Voynich, and no accident that the author had been one of the daughters of the founder of logical mathematics, George Boole, and not at all an accident, it was now so clear to me, that Goia had revealed to me the existence of Charles Howard Hinton. Few characters, real or imaginary, have the resonance of this name, which came to represent the Searcher, the demented disease of the dream of escape. I was surprised, without yet understanding (as the line of coincidences did not stop here) that, according to Goia, Hinton had been the husband of Mary Ellen Boole, one of Ethel's sisters, and had had an overwhelming influence over the entire family of the great mathematician, even causing one of the other sisters to never marry and spend her life constructing fragile, multicolored polyhedrons out of cardboard in four virtual dimensions, to illustrate Hinton's theories.

The name of him who invented the term "tesseract" (which I had used in poems without knowing the source, just that Dalí's Jesus had been hanged not from a cross but a three-dimensional illustration of a quadradimensional cube) was not completely foreign to me, and I spent a few days searching for it, going through my books until I found it in the place I had, in fact, first expected, in "Tlön, Uqbar, Orbis Tertius" by Borges. Even so, it was difficult to find the name I looked for feverishly, as though it were hidden from my eyes in the labyrinth of Borgesian language. But, in the end, I located this passage charged with mystifying erudition: "In March of 1941, a handwritten letter from Gunnar Erfjord was discovered in a book by Hinton that had belonged to Herbert Ashe. The envelope was postmarked Ouro Preto; the mystery of Tlön was fully elucidated by the letter. It confirmed Martinez Estrada's hypothesis: The splendid story had begun sometime in the early seventeenth century, one night in Lucerne or London. A secret benevolent society (which numbered among its members Dalgarno and, later, George Berkeley) was born; its mission: to invent a country." Hinton was, therefore, a landmark name on the path toward Tlön, the planet soon to be invented, preceded by a compass made of trembling blue gelatin that would become the basis of the world.

Hinton was born a century before me, in an English family famous (or, better said, "infamous") for their libertinage. The father preached polygamy and called himself "a savior Jesus for women." The young man studied at Oxford and taught mathematics at Rutland. He was, at the time—a few days later, seeing my fascination for Hinton's works, Goia brought me a large book on the history of mathematics, where I found facts about Hinton and a blurry sepia photograph showing him in a family group, alongside an ugly woman and four children—a young man with a Raskolnikovian make, a blond beard and pale eyes, his expression containing something of a quiet fanaticism, a serene aggressivity. With impeccable manners, contrasting the mad vigor in his gaze, he must have impressed the oldest daughter of the even then celebrated George Boole, taking her as his wife in 1880, having four children with her. But this did not stop him from following, in a short time, in the footsteps of his polygamous father. Because, in spite of his real attachment to Mary Ellen and, we can say, to the entire Boole clan, after only three years Charles married again, in secret and under the assumed name of John Weldon, to a second woman, with whom he had twins. The scandal broke shortly, Hinton was sent to prison and fired from his teaching position, but this incident did not destroy his relationship with his first wife and her family. Charles and Mary left for Japan, then the United States, until all the traces of the ugly scandal had been wiped from peoples' minds.

The Hinton family had a hard time in America, the two held modest jobs in various cities, they lost all their money and were enveloped in despair. One of the most limpid minds in the history of mathematics, and just as great a writer, accepted inferior positions at universities and scientific institutions scattered across the American territory. A single unexpected and picturesque invention promised to put an end to the Hinton family's financial tribulations, but the mathematician didn't live long enough to enjoy its fruits: while he was an instructor at Princeton, he patented a machine that pitched baseballs to help the university team practice. It was a steel tube with rubber lining that used gunpowder to propel the balls precisely, at different angles and speeds. A cerebral hemorrhage put an end to the bizarre life of the explorer of the fourth dimension, just after he turned fifty-four.

We are all gastropods, soft, sticky creatures pulling ourselves along the earth from which we came and leaving a trail of silvery drool behind. But the snail, a worm that eternally slides along the horizon, lifts into the air, from its soft bivalve back, the geometrical wonder of its spiral shell, seemingly unrelated to the body that produced it in fear and loneliness. We secrete our shell in the sweat and mucous of our skin, in the transparent, scaly flesh of the foot we use to drag ourselves along. Through an alchemical transmutation, our drool turns to ivory and the spasms of our flesh into an undisturbed stillness. We curl around our central pilaster of rose-colored kaolin, we add, in our desperate drive to persist, spiral after spiral, each one wider, asymptotic, and translucid, until the miracle comes to pass: the revolting worm—existing in the life it lives, fermenting in its sins, irrigated by hormones and blood and sperm and lymph—rots and dies, leaving behind the ceramic filigree of its shell, a triumph of symmetry, the deathless icon in the platonic world of the mind. We all secrete, as we live, poems and pictures, ideas and hope, glistening palaces of music and faith, shells which begin by protecting our soft abdomen but after our disappearance live in the golden air of pure forms. Geometry always appears out of the amorphous, serenity out of pain and torture, just as dry tears leave behind the most wondrous crystals of salt.

Hinton's tortured life, his sufferings and lusts, his bizarreries, the perverse beauty in his pale eyes so similar to Rimbaud's, produced the ivory curve of an abstruse work, a logarithmic spiral like those that, after only three or four rotations around the central point, exceed the page, after another ten they exceed the planet we live on, because after another twenty, the universe will not be able to contain its advancing madness. Hinton's work was not, in its totality, more than a metaphysical lever able to propel you rapidly, counterintuitively and magically, toward the edges of the world, in order to go beyond them. You put a speck of grain on the first square of a chessboard, two on the next, four on the next, eight on the next. On the sixty-fourth, the square would hold the entire harvest of the earth. You fold a piece of paper once, twice, three times . . . With the fiftieth fold you get to the moon. Let mitosis double the number of cells coming from the initial egg: we have your entire human body after only eighty divisions. Hinton used his mind in the same way to understand the unintelligible, to record, like the poet whose eyes he had, the inexpressible. Through analogy and telescoping, he spent his life in an attempt to surpass the intuitive forms of three-dimensional space, the only forms where our mind feels at home, because it was shaped by them and has their form; to compel a three-dimensional brain, focused on the volumes of our world, to let its hemispheres diverge; to contemplate, aimlessly and dreamily, until the familiar forms melted and, suddenly, like an epiphany, opened a portal onto the fantastic dimension immediately above our own, a dimension until then accessible only to saints and to the enlightened. Breaking through the prison of these three dimensions through the use of mathematical reasoning equals, in fact (or doubles, as proof that in the end, all the paths of knowledge converge on an incandescent point, mystical-poetical-logical-mathematical), ecstasy, divine infection, the blinding state of satori.

The world of four dimensions is, to our three-dimensional world, what ours is to the world of two dimensions and, as follows, what the bidimensional world is to the world of one dimension. Here is Hinton's lever, his mental mechanism with which, making much more effort than we can imagine, we can intuit a space otherwise forbidden to our thought. The point generates the line, the line generates the plane, the plane generates the volume—what space will a moving volume generate? Through what can it move if it is taken out of the three-dimensional world? As the point is a part of the line and the line a part of the plane and the plane a part of the volume, already containing it as a potential of their structure, the volume already presupposes a world with an extra dimension, one in which it already participates and which it can generate through a certain type of movement. We can visualize it: we can enjoy its sudden revelation through a thought exercise. We imagine a transposition among parallel worlds—each with one dimension more than the previous—of some simple geometrical objects. If we smoothly transpose a cube from our world toward a bidimensional plane, it will be perceived by the presumptive inhabitants as a square. If it continues toward a world of a single dimension (a long thread floating within a plane that floats within a volume), the filiform inhabitants of this world will perceive only the apparition on their thread of a line segment. Finally, everything is infinitely compressed into the dimensionless world of the point.

For us, those who live in three spatial dimensions (now we know that there are many more kinds of dimensions, and that one of them is time), the inhabitants of the plane seem incredibly simple. We can look directly into their brains, we can see inside their houses—as they don't have walls facing us—we can steal valuables from their vaults. They are like characters we created: we know their future because we also invented their past. We are their gods, we can appear suddenly among them, like ghostly projections, and we frighten them. If a sphere passed through their membrane, they would see at first a point that grew into a larger and larger circle, then ever smaller. The final point would disappear, inexplicably, from their sky. If, for fun, we poked a fork through their world, they would first see only four points, then four circles, then all the circles would combine into a curve, one that widens and narrows over time until it perishes in a final point. We may imagine their world as an uninterrupted surface that surrounds our world, and onto which our world is projected, like onto a screen.

People set within a flat world cannot imagine a third dimension. A prisoner inside a cell made of four lines will remain there forever, never noticing that he could escape by moving perpendicular to the plane, by taking flight, pure and simple, up through the nonexistent wall facing the third dimension. That wall only exists in his mind and in his habits, the habits of right, left, forward, and backward, but not of up or down. Nothing would be easier than to help a prisoner escape, if you have, in comparison to him, an extra dimension: you simply take him between your fingers and lift him up, perpendicular to his world, into a space he cannot imagine. Those around him will only see him miraculously disappear: his footsteps in the snow will stop suddenly, in the middle of the front yard . . .

We can imagine (if not truly grasp) a world that has, in comparison to our own, an extra dimension. Each object in this world would have four dimensions, like the space in which it is set. Our world could be imagined as a three-dimensional membrane surrounding and reflecting a world of four dimensions. If a hypersphere passed through our world, we would first see a point in the sky, then a small sphere that grew to its maximal width, then diminished slowly to the dimension of a point, only to disappear without a trace before our wondering eyes. If a four-dimensional fork passed through the membrane, we would see four spheres appear out of the blue—the three-dimensional projection of the tines—soon combining into a flattened, three-dimensional ellipsis, one which suddenly ends, which disappears, as a final point. In just the same way, the inhabitants of a world of four dimensions could send us three-dimensional projections whenever they desired. They would appear to be ordinary human beings, and we would never suspect their fantastic bodies and minds, their amazing powers. But they would be able to work miracles, they would heal the sick—since they would have direct access to each organ without needing to open our bodies—they would raise the dead, they would suddenly appear and disappear. Their nature, as it appeared to us, would be only a shadow of their actual nature, cast upon a screen. For them, our world would have no walls or chains. If we could grasp the extra dimension, if we could imagine other directions beside left and right, forward and back, up and down, we would realize that no one can hold us in the prison of our world, that one of its giant walls is unoccupied, unwalled, because the jailers are betting we will stay blind to the open door.

A line segment is limited by two points. A square is limited by four lines. A cube is limited by six surfaces. In the same way, a four-dimensional hypercube would be an object, counterintuitively for us, limited by eight cubes. This is the object Hinton named a tesseract. The tesseract's projection in our world is the cube, just as the projection of the cube onto the two-dimensional membrane is the square, and the projection of this object into the world of a single dimension is the line segment. In school we learned to make a cube out of a hopscotch pattern of six boxes cut from a sheet of paper. The sides of the hopscotch are turned, inside the extra dimension of our space, glued together, and there in our hand, fragile and wonderful, is a paper cube. The equivalent of the tesseract made in our world is thus easy to visualize: it is a hopscotch pattern analogous to the paper one, but made of cubes. But it is incredibly difficult to imagine how to assemble the hypercube from the cross of cubes, where

Dalí imagined Jesus crucified, or, better said, his human icon projected into our world from his inconceivable quadradimensional body. Because you need to rotate the projected cube in a way we do not comprehend—"hyper-up" or "ultra-down"—just as we do not perceive infrared or ultraviolet; our ear cannot hear ultrasounds, the same way that a psychopath can feel no pity.

The tesseract, the major creation of Hinton's thought, described for the first time in *A New Era of Thought* in 1888, is the mystical mandala of his world and the key he saw looking at the quartz padlock of the fourth dimension, the home of the angels, as well as the demons, of our mind. What's strange is that I had used the word in a poem, ten years earlier, when I still believed in literature, not the way you believe it will snow that evening, but the way you believe there is life after death. I wrote then, in a kind of trance:

if you were a number, but you are *not* a number
if you had veins, but you do *not* have veins
if every droplet of your sobs were a planet
or a sun, or a universe.
you are a gnomon, a chestnut shell, the other side of the mirror
some chick's lipsticked mouth
or Jordan. *wrong*.
because all these are words, and words do not enter the flesh
or concrete or grapefruit. and even taking them as images
would be wrong, because it would not be a dot, but a sphere
a cube, not a tesseract. and if space-time
is the plasticine you played with when you were little
what will describe your bones, your glands, your internal organs?

if you were a brain, but you are *not* a brain
if you were me, but you are *not* me
not death, not existence. it is a mistake to think of you, because you,
like tachyons, start from the place
my thought stops.
light seems crude to me: little golden boulders
running down your face like sand; the galaxy seems hideous to me

like a thread of pollen in your eyebrow. i myself, a drop of fat
sizzling for a moment on the stove, trying to know you.

maybe the world can be described
fold over fold, like the statues at tanagra; maybe the theory
of catastrophes, maybe *cantor arepo*
but i, curled up like a mouse inside your splendor
a Crystal Palace for the people, mouth gaping like a nimrod
among your barrels of jewels—
what will describe my wrinkles?

if you sweated, but you do *not* sweat
if you existed, but you do *not* exist
if you made a world with millions of seasons, with ten thousand
dimensions
and you destroyed it with fire and ice . . .
dear phantom, show yourself! speak to me, i see you want to!
but your words would be people or branches of a peach tree
and your silences are rocks.
i read you best in a fuchsia petal
in the lilac veins of my cat's ear
in the icy memory of another time. because you
are all i love and all i hate and all
i don't care about; if i were female
your bones would have formed in my stomach; so, i feel you throbbing
and moving inside my skull; i feel you looking
through my eyes and touching with my fingers and swallowing
with my esophagus.
sat within me like a charioteer
you pull levers, you push buttons
and i move and smile, laugh and dream
at your command, by your pity . . . maybe you
take me apart the way a child takes a machine apart
to see the springs and flywheels and gears . . . busted,

with the paint taken away, *what* will describe
nothing, my nothing?

if you were a fog of stars
if you were a textile of worlds . . .

The tesseract, or hypercube, is the trace left by a cube that moves through a fourth dimension, perpendicular to our world, the same way a square sliding through the third dimension generates a cube. It is a totally abstract and counterintuitive geometrical figure, a cube with sixteen corners, thirty-two sides, twenty-four faces, and a hypervolume bordered by eight volumes. We cannot visualize this kind of an object by means of our senses and reason alone, because those are the tools a three-dimensional world created so that an amalgamation of soft organs might survive. We are worms hanging from our horizontal branch: to release ourselves from it, perpendicularly, toward an inconceivable "up," we must be, in the blink of an eye, changed. We must grow wings. A tesseract is an object of contemplation and meditation, a vehicle toward the lofty goals for which our mind—born of our much too concrete brain, too sticky, too soft, cracking under its own weight—is searching, feverishly, longingly, forever. A poet dreams at the incandescent peak of the pyramid of knowledge, where geometry and poetry become happily one. The tesseract is above even this point, because it is, in comparison with the immortal platonic polyhedrons, what they are to the cardboard or paper polyhedrons in the world of the senses.

The hypercube, the luminous levitating object of the fourth dimension, was not the end, but the departure point for Hinton's intense meditations. Because, starting from this image, Charles Howard Hinton began to imagine practical modalities by which anyone, with patience and practice, could visualize a tesseract, thus entering the fourth dimension. In *On the Education of the Imagination* he describes a system of cubes with colored sides, a kit he perfected over the years and completed in his work *The Fourth Dimension*, published in 1904. His one-inch cubes were painted in fifteen different colors, with some left unpainted. In total, the tesseract visualization kit had eighty-one cubes. They could be arranged in such a way that they formed larger cubes, each with a side made of three or four Hinton cubes. The fourth-dimension visualization technique was complicated, but in its essence it involved the simultaneous visualization of all the cubes' interior colors, such that the mind would enter the great multicolored cube, seeing its hidden depths just as clearly as its surfaces, grasping the whole of it at the same time, exactly as it would be seen by an inhabitant of the fourth dimension. After a monumental and exhausting practice, in which novices memorized the colors first two at a time along one edge, then four, and then eight, the mental barriers suddenly fell and—in an amazing miracle—the tesseract appeared in the middle of the brain, like a portal to a higher world of an inexpressible grandeur. The visions provoked by hashish, the brilliant mosaics that appear before practicants of mescaline, the annihilating orgasm within the epileptic skull, the magical wonder of lovers of autostereograms when out of the tangle of lines and colors the hidden symbol appears, tridimensional, glittering like crystal, the Zen Buddhist's satori when he understands, after years of pain and torture, that the koan holds no contradiction and his mind is as free as a bird, the pure laughter of a two-year-old, and all the other joys our existence allows are only weak approximations of the overwhelming relief of the shattering of the prisons of the brain and thorax that his followers experienced, by their own testimony, when they were once again in a state to give it, having seen the tesseract.

Hinton's kit was sold at the beginning of the century, and it had some success in occult circles, where, following in the footsteps of theosophists and anthroposophists, as well as vulgar spiritists, many had long tried to find the fourth dimension. The box of colored cubes was sent mail-order to those who, on hearing about Hinton's experiments, could not wait to try for themselves. It was the era of renewed interest in the ancient wisdom of humanity, the search for the mythical Agartha, or the nightmarish Shambala, the era of spirits conjured by grotesque mediums, of walking specters drooling from the corner of their mouths or spurting ectoplasm from their fontanelles like blue cigar smoke, the age of moving tables and fingers selecting letters on a board to piece together messages from the beyond. All these were the exuviae of an era that passed from steam technology to electricity, meant so people would not forget that technology and magic are two sides of the same medallion, that in their primitive-sophisticated minds the miracle of technology was always counterbalanced by the technology of miracles.

The sale of Hinton's kit was soon halted, because psychiatric hospitals were filling up with more and more practicants of the colored cubes. There were dozens, perhaps hundreds of cases of women and men discovered in their rooms with a lap full of cubes and on the table an unfinished great cube they stared at vacantly, without seeing it, within a cataleptic state from which they never returned. Others reached ecstasy in the bathtub, the front lawn, at dinner, or while reading the newspaper, or even while sleeping, because like the continual prayers of the hesychasts, manipulation of the cubes and visualization of their interior faces became a continuous, automatic activity in the minds of these searchers for the absolute. The cubes appeared in front of their eyes at every moment, whatever they were doing, and their agitated manipulation continued within their dreams. Those to whom—after months or years of work with the cubes—the tesseract appeared might become inhabitants of the world above, but here, in our world, nothing remained of them but a prostrated carcass, exiled to a white-walled sanatorium.

The mania for the multicolored cube, whose late and inoffensive echo (in the same way that the once all-powerful myths can be found in children's fairy tales) is the Rubik's cube, which all my colleagues, from the janitors to the teachers, at School 86 continuously twist and turn, soon encompassed the entire Boole family, but it only truly conquered—perhaps along with the blue eyes and purposefully mussed blond hair of the man who became the mystical-sexual center of the logical-mathematical clan—Alicia, the third Boole daughter. The most vapid of the sisters, who up to her meeting with Hinton had confined herself to awkward embroideries and sentimental romances, suddenly discovered her incredible talent for visualizing quadradimensional objects. She had no problem seeing the colored innards of a cube made of twenty-seven Hinton cubes (is the blood in our arteries red, where no one sees it?). The tesseract that appeared to her suddenly, one golden afternoon, in the middle of her mind, did not impress her very much, in spite of its thirty-two edges of glittering quartz. Alicia, who had been gently initiated by her bother-in-law into the sweet ritual, had far surpassed her master. The hypercube soon bored her. Clearly, our world is not reducible to cubes. She quickly realized that the tesseract could cross the three-dimensional membrane of our world in multiple ways. Only rarely would it enter perpendicularly, such that its three-dimensional shape would be a cube. It could enter at a tilt, leading with a corner or edge, along continuously varying angles. Furthermore, it could also rotate while passing through the membrane. Thus in our world, it could generate an endless number of three-dimensional polyhedrons, the acute or obtuse shadows cast by the tesseract over the surface of our world. Even furthermore, Alicia, a true Alice in Wonderland, began to imagine a long line of quadradimensional polygons that she named polytopes. It seems that, in addition, she was not much older than the fictional Alice when she let Charles, carefully and skillfully, lead her fingers across the voluptuous volumes and surfaces with which he had worked his entire life. Polytopes were bodies from the fourth dimension that cast shadows onto our ordinary world in the form of polyhedrons: tetrahedra, octahedra, icosahedra, dodecahedra. She soon reduced the number of regular polytopes to six, which were bordered, in the four-dimensional world, by five, sixteen, or six hundred tetrahedra, eight cubes, twenty-four octahedra and, respectively, one hundred twenty dodecahedra. She visualized them all in the wondrous depths of their depths, and then she set to work. For the rest of her life, Alicia Boole built and hand-painted incredible cardboard objects in space, representing median, three-dimensional sections of polytopes. They were enormous gemstones of a rare beauty, faceted jewels, brilliant geometrical forms more fascinating than the tropical butterflies in their family insect collections. Violet, pink, purple, and saffron throbbed over their faces, they spread their colors into each other, they changed places and shapes, amazing those who looked at them. Most people only saw colored balls, but Alicia had the gift—coming out of nowhere, as the young Victorian woman had not received any education—of falling into a trance before the shapes and seeing in them true objects from the true reality of a world with two extra directions, ultra-up and infra-down, a talent equal to that which someone blind from birth would need to see colors.

Out of these desperate attempts of a visionary mind to express the inexpressible, to perceive the imperceptible, and to intuit the unintuitable emerged, in the end, Rubik's toy, at a distance of seven decades from Hinton's experiments. Mrs. Diaconu, the fulsome and always jovial Russian teacher, twisted the cube between her fingers under her desk even during tests, without the faintest idea that the plastic mechanism, which obstinately strove to remain in its most natural state of coloristic chaos, had once been one of the most successful tools for attaining the absolute that the human mind had ever been able to conceive. Struggling against the specter of insanity and the limits of our pitiful, flesh-wrapped consciousness, Hinton and his disciples had found, perhaps, the path toward the superior world, floating above our own like the Platonic Isles of the Blessed that raise their brow above the ocean of air in which we are all set.

But it was impossible that a mind like Hinton's or Alicia's would not realize that, far from being the highest goal and Ultima Thule of their mental efforts, reaching the fourth dimension was only an insignificant beginning, the first turn of an asymptotic spiral around the central point, the first move in an infinite ascension up a stairway where each step is two times higher than the previous. Because neither the pleasure of contemplating the mystical tesseract (which the spiritualists soon employed to conjure the dead and to locate buried treasure), nor the splendor of the polytopes, nor the escape, albeit virtual, through walls open toward the superior (and yet forever hidden to our gaze) dimension could avoid the fact that, in the same way the point generates the line, and the line the plane, and the plane the volume, and the volume the hypervolume bordered by volumes of the fourth dimension, we could conceive of a world in five dimensions, generated by a hypervolume in movement. The world of four dimensions would be, for this even higher new world, a four-dimensional membrane surrounding a sphere of five dimensions. And this new world would, in turn, be the screen onto which shadows of the six-dimensional world were cast, and each world would be grander, more intense, and *truer* than the one before, not proportionally so, but madly, asymptotically—something neither the mind nor the gaze could comprehend.

Perhaps it was this infinite progression—this concentration of light within light, this mystical rose with a rose in its core, with a rose in its core, with a rose in its core, ever more concentrated and more perfumed rose mandalas—that Kafka was thinking of in his great parable at the center of his writing: each guardian in the infinite succession of doors of the law is more and more powerful. Humans only face the first one, Klamm, Godot, but he is the most insignificant God in an endless line, in which each guardian of the gate is twice as powerful as the previous. How powerful must the tenth one be? And the 1,010th? When the poor human, waiting in the antechamber of the infinite, dies, the last sound he hears is the simultaneous slam of the infinite number of doors that separate him from the truth, each twice as grand as the one before. These are the doors that Hans and Amalia hear, that the subterranean monster hides behind. They are the heartbeats, each twice as strong as the one before, that accompany the most amazing scene a human mind ever imagined and put on paper: "The master of dreams, the great Issachar, sat in front of the mirror, his spine against its surface, his head hanging far back, deeply sunk into the mirror. Then Hermana appeared, master of the twilight, and she melted into Issachar's chest, until she completely disappeared."

Could the same infinite progression be taking place inside my mind (the inconvulsive Morpheic epilepsy of the left parietal lobe?) when, at night, a soft whistling in my ear amplifies like a siren, increases in magnitude, becomes a deafening scream that quickly generates an intense yellow color, and the sound-color invades my skull with its golden scream and shatters it into fragments in an infinite terror, in ever more amplified wreaths of ecstasy and despair, into insanity and beyond insanity, leaping from spiral of fire to spiral of fire, a superconcentrated, ultraconcentrated, hyperconcentrated fire, to the place where words to describe it do not exist, neither does a place or time to encompass it . . . Maybe in these moments, in that tunnel of horrors, in that rifled tube, red with the friction of the bullet of my brain, I am hurtling toward the truth beyond the truth beyond the truth beyond the truth of our world. That one beyond which there is no progress, or truth, or mind, or being, or godliness. I won't be surprised if after one of these nights, I am left in a state of abulia and stupefied dreaming. I will only be surprised if I survive it.

In the end, I bought myself a Rubik's cube from the newsstand outside school. But, after I threw away the cheap cellophane packaging, I didn't change the uniform faces. I left it as it was, already solved from the start, complete on its surface, but I could not stop myself from envisioning the tragic disorder of the faces hidden in its depths, the twisted innards in the center, which no one would ever see. In the same way that no one will see the color of the blood in my veins, of my bones, liver, or spleen or intestines. Even I don't know, lonesome inhabitant of my flesh that I am. I only know I have internal organs and only because someone, from a higher-up world, can see them in all their shapes, colors, and details, as though they were drawn on my skin. For that sacred being, in the terrible sense of the word, all the Rubik's cubes, in whatever chaotic state they may be, are solved and complete, just as they were at the beginning and as they ever shall be.

31

I've thought often about the fat women scattered like bizarre ganglions along the lymphatic pathways of my life. Massive, almost perfectly round in their work coats; affable, asexual, and ageless; I have found them everywhere, from the depths of childhood up to today. They were the clerks at the bread distribution center and all the groceries in the neighborhoods where I lived with my parents, they were the women who darned socks behind a glass window next to the ironware shop on Str. Lizeanu, which we passed, before it was closed in the fifties, on our way toward the wonderous Little Red Riding Hood toy store, located at Obor in a subterranean bunker four stories deep. They were all the nurses and medical assistants that came toward me at night when the light suddenly came on, with primitive syringes, bubbling with penicillin and streptomycin, filling the room with an unbearable smell of mold. They were the rubicund, naked women, with red nipples and rings of fat on their stomachs, who populated the three throats of the tunnel that ran from behind the office door in the militia station and, through a complicated network, communicated with the maw under the apartment block on Ştefan cel Mare. Identical, with barely sketched features, as though the baroque girth under their skins spoke of its own accord, with their sexes enclosed between elephantine legs, they swam in tubs and cisterns in green, undulating water, they slid through convoluted tubes, they shook their red, yellow, and orange locks under the heavy, symmetrical, and incomprehensible suns of a strange zodiac. They were the ticket-takers mumbling in the trams, overflowing their seats behind veneer counters, who sold you tickets for shining coins, fifteen bani, twenty-five bani, or forty bani, while you also mumbled, holding your father's giant hand, snow-covered and muffled as you were with your scarf tied over your mouth and nose during those endless winters. They were the cleaning ladies at Voila, who scrubbed us in the bath with rough sponges until our skin was red. They were my jovial colleagues in the teachers' lounge, the sinister librarian-jailer, or the blind woman with a paper icon on her chest, begging outside the neighborhood church. They are scattered more or less evenly through my entire world, like bits of food that await me here and there in the laboratory maze where I live, like signposts along my tangled route toward the exit. I cannot imagine them at a kitchen table, in a bed, or surrounded by their own children, but only there, at their posts, where they seem to appear out of the void, without passing through childhood and adolescence. They were large, round sacks, with the same barely sketched features of those who dwelled on the Asian steppes. Even their oversized breasts were completely neutral, white, and placid, as though they were humps on a camel, not in the least attractive. The cooks, collectors, nurses, barbers, and darners were as sexless as the cabinets, cash registers, and pots for boiling syringes that surrounded them.

At Voila, their reign of terror began at dusk, when we came back to our dorms after supper. Comrade Nistor went back to his hole, and we were left in the hands of the women who took care of us. Their sharp, commanding voices grabbed us like brutal hands and shoved us under boiling showers, then stuck us in blue pajamas, all with identical, awkward drawings of zebras and giraffes, the same as on our Chinese pencils. From the moment they turned out the lights at nine, no one, for any reason, was allowed in the hall. The door stayed closed all night, and the caretakers patrolled the tiled hall.

At the start, everything seemed bearable. I made friends: Traian, Bolbo, and Prioteasa, also Mihuț, the son of a man my father worked with at the newspaper. Once the women left the dormitory, we would get out of bed and climb onto one of the wide windowsills that ran the length of the room. Then we pulled the drapes shut around us, ensconcing ourselves in the most private place in the world. Outside the windows the moon shone, its light magnified by the glass. By its light we could see the black, endless forest. We also saw our blue faces, ready to listen to a new story. The sill was warmed by the heater underneath, so we soon entered a kind of trance in which Traian's voice appeared, visible in the dark air like a length of thin wire, drawing strange objects among us.

Bolbo was fat as a bear and had a dark face, he never fought with the other kids, probably because he could have broken their necks. Prioteasa was pale, with a white blaze right above his forehead. He seemed older than the rest of us, as though something had happened that had made him wise before his time. Mihuț was much closer to me than the others; he shared my bench at school, as well behaved as the girls, his black eyes constantly pleading for protection. I don't know why, but I loved the kids at Voila more than all the others I ever knew. I still have a picture of us, in our terrible uniforms, the fabric that came already rotted from the factory, together in the apple orchard. I can remember a few faces: Sica, Iudita, Mihaela. I can name most of the boys, as though we said goodbye yesterday. Comrade Nistor, with his bestial, Nazi face, is standing in the middle, and we are on the grass under the apple branches, transparent in the sun, dark in the shadow, smiling dumbly toward our future ghosts. I see myself, too, somewhere in the second row, smiling sadly, my chin on my hand. As always, I tremble: seeing myself, in mirrors or photographs, has always felt sinister to me, as paradoxical as a sword that cuts itself. I am sure that for the better part of my childhood, if I accidentally saw myself in the mirror, the broken one with worn silver my mother kept on a nail, I didn't recognize myself, or, better put, I didn't recognize that it was me. Maybe it was because I didn't yet exist, and my reflection was as indifferent to me as the rest of the room, with cabinets, afghans, and pots of geraniums, sunk below the virtual waters of the shard of glass. A strange prosopagnosia accompanied me in those first years, when I was supposed to pass through the mirror stage and didn't. I delayed, perhaps from a suicidal drive, this revelation until one day at Voila when all the boys, after the torture of a forced nap, went to the large washroom, a solemn temple of white tile. I will never forget that moment: the giant hall echoed with the shouts of pajama-clad children, and one of them—the same as any other, connected beyond the frontiers of our skin and mind, through ineffable channels, to all the rest of them, in an emotional and acephalous tangle, a madrepore of arms and feet and navels and teeth—was me, just as impersonal and as servile as a pawn on the chessboard of our mind. I was brushing my teeth or splashing water on my face or smiling at something another kid said, when Bolbo began to shout in his broken voice, "Hey, horsey, come here and let me give you some sugar!" Crețu, who had failed two grades, appeared immediately, and Bolbo climbed onto his back. During our breaks in the school day, we went out of our classrooms into the wide yard behind the school, and we fought each other two at a time, riding another kid or being ridden, pulling and pushing until one of the red-faced, panting, laughing contraptions collapsed into the ant- and centipede-filled grass. It was dangerous to make a horse in the washroom—the rider might hit himself on one of the tubs or sinks, he might land on his head on the floor . . . We all knew that in a few moments the caretakers would rush in, screaming, snapping their wet rags at us. Still, we all put horses and riders together and started to fight. I was on Horia's back, he was the smartest of us—of course aside from Traian. He was the one who, every night before bed, told us a story from *The Paul Street Boys*, so beautifully and fluently that if the light hadn't been out, you would have thought he was reading straight from a book. We lined up by the sinks, in front of the row of mirrors, hung too high for us to see ourselves while we were at the sink. Suddenly, I saw myself in the mirror, for the first time in my life I saw and recognized myself, with horror, like in autoscopic dreams, as though without my knowledge a mad scientist had cloned me and, without warning, put my doppelganger in front of me. It only lasted a moment, but it was a moment of unique and violent brilliance. That was the moment I saw myself, surrounded by a golden fluid that made the rest of the world seem dark: a little, brown-haired girl, darker than the other kids, and thin, much thinner than anyone. Eyes so black they looked violet, surrounded by circles most kids didn't have. A long, pale neck, two clavicles bulging under the skin, above the stiff, open collar of my printed pajamas. A little body, light as paper, a child that was me and yet had its own age and its own world, a special and strange world, there, behind the glass wall. Never had identity and difference, fire and ice, woman and man, dream and reality, helf and helvol ever created such a haunting, disquieting couple . . . I looked at him, and through him I saw myself as though with an eye that could see itself, as though a system could completely describe itself from within, as though you could determine suddenly, precisely, the position and speed of a particle, as though one of your hands could draw the other, and the other, emerging from the page, could draw the first, as though mirrors and paternity were not only abominations, but also had a meaning beyond symmetry and reflection, a meaning that only through an incomparable act of concentration could you ever access.

Now, I remember only the surprise and disappointment of seeing myself in the mirror. I was completely different than I had thought. I forgot about the battle, I climbed off the kid's back and walked away from the children. I wandered a long time, thorough the tangled corridors that always led to the same antiseptic rooms, with urinals, stalls, foot-washing stations, all of them made for adults, not me; I ended up in distant and empty places, the way I pictured Antarctica, and, finally, I sat down on the edge of a tiled basin, holding my face in my hands. I existed: I, too, was in the world. And it wasn't just that I existed, but I was and I would always be a double being, a being in search of his other half. I had a twin in every mirror, as though each were a glass cylinder where my clone lay in a vegetative state, to be galvanically reanimated whenever I stood in front. I was only whole when standing eye to eye with myself, as if I were the unseen one, although I was myself, and he the one seen, although he was not myself, and we were conjoined twins who shared a common organ: sight. Sight connected us, flowed from one of us to the other, as imperceptible as the illusory outlines of a Klein bottle. In just the same way, I had a twin enclosed in every photograph, inside a cell in the foundation of memory . . .

At night, in the warm space between the window and drapes, illuminated by the stars and moon, heavy with sleep but intent on staying awake as long as we could, we talked about everything that we didn't hear during the day, about what they didn't tell us in school, because it didn't have to do with nature, language, history, or geography. The world was mysterious. A small and intimate world existed, like primitive peoples who huddled around the fire in their caves, dancing their shadows across the wall: this was our world, the children's, it belonged to those people always in someone else's care, always handled and managed, but more than that, always lied to by those from the other world, who tolerated our presence at the border of that world, like barbarians at the limits of an enormous and shimmering empire. Those beings were almost twice as tall as us and had much larger minds. If they were left in the middle of the city, they knew how to get home. They could use money. They lived in pairs, similar yet different, and together, through a kind of mystery that reached us only in degraded and useless forms, these pairs had made us, the small and helpless, the same way, probably, that they had built everything that existed in the world: houses, cars, planes, gardens, even the Voila preventorium. Yes, the big people were gods, our gods. We could not understand how, but someday, we would end up like them. The flower in the middle of our minds was still just a bud, but it would grow and open little by little until, someday, in that obscure place called the future, it would sparkle in the airy plenitude of its petals. Every brain would adhere, through billions of transparent, sticky threads, to the immortal, inaccessible space of logic, whose mundane name was God. And we could become, each of us, one of the eyes through which God contemplates his world. Now we saw as though through a glass, darkly, but then face-to-face. Now we knew in part, but then shall we know even as we shall be known . . .

The big people's world was founded on two jealously guarded myths. They all knew these secrets, but no one wanted to share them with us, the small people. First, the mystery of those two personal gods, mother and father, mating in the middle of the night. It was a taboo locked under dozens of padlocks. Many of us had seen things we should not have seen, knew things we should not have known. Even now, behind the drapes, when we lined up the bits of twisted and caricatured knowledge, as frightening as stone idols, that had come our way, our hair stood up on our arms: we were guilty, we would pay for our obscene theft through who knows what terrible punishment. Yes, Bolbo had seen, one night, his parents strangely wrestling, huffing and making the bed creak. You couldn't ask your parents about this, there was no way to find out *what* and *how* and *why* it happened. You were not allowed to expose certain parts of your body or to talk about them. Why could you show everyone your hands, even your stomach, but not the little worm underneath your stomach, between your legs? And why did our coevals, the girls, not have anything there, just a hole, as we had heard? Yes, that's right, said Mihuț, they just have a crack. Anyway, we all used our sexes to pee, boys standing up, girls squatting, as we had sometimes seen in the forest, when they hid like ostriches behind a tree. But the big people also used them for something else. And that was where children came out. Yes, nine months later, we had heard about this, too.

We knew, and not just from what we saw in the forest, that girls were made differently than we were. Once, the four of us took the chance, during the evening showers, to go upstairs where the girls' dormitory was. We simply hid in our lockers until the fat women had driven the other boys, naked as devils, into the washroom, and then we snuck into the hall, still in our pajamas. The stairway was wide and grand. There was no physical barrier to keep us from going upstairs, but the obstacle in our minds had the weight and inertia of the door to an armored safe. It wasn't allowed, you couldn't, you shouldn't. The farther we climbed the stairs, in a nervous little cluster led by Traian, who was always the metaphysical head of bad behavior, the more the damp air smelled like soap, like in our own washroom. But the soap was scented, expensive, like what my mother kept in the wardrobe, behind the clothes, not the eternal Cheia soap the caretakers used on us. The air seemed to turn pink . . . We turned back a few times, but in the end, our hearts thumping from confronting a horrifying prohibition, we reached the upper level and, on the last steps, we froze at the sight of the corridor's fantastic tableau.

Their hall, lined with dorm room doors, was much larger than ours. The other end was lost completely in steam and fog. The doors were all wide open, and there seemed to be hundreds of them, not just four, like we had. The smell was powerful, dizzying. It rose, along with the dense vapors and soap bubbles, from hundreds of pink bathtubs, the kind usually used for infants, and around them the girls were standing, dozens and hundreds, their blond and chestnut hair held back with colored plastic balls on white elastics. They squatted or knelt down and happily washed small lacy clothes in the foaming tubs. They were all completely undressed, and their small bodies were like ours, but lighter and more graceful. They were like large dolls, with shiny nylon hair and rigid, awkward limbs. The girls filled the whole space, as far as our eyes could see, and the air was full of happy cries and smells. Looking at them from the head of the stairs, we understood how different they were from us, how strange they would remain to us, how their enormous clan was unified and indestructible. The border between the sexes, apparently so troubled and illusory, was just as inflexible as that between the species, except the border wasn't in the body, but in the mind. There was an impassable chasm, not just between the big people and us, but also between us and the girls.

We were enclosed in multiple strangely intersecting cells in the world's single prison.

Suddenly, the girl closest to us turned her head, and her lips opened in wonder. She stood up quickly, and in the next moment they were all standing, their hair spread on their shoulders and their skin wet with soapy foam. Water spilled out of the tubs, covering the tile floor, and wide bands of suds flowed toward us, already running over the first step. We stared, fascinated by the bodies with boys' nipples, with a fine line between their legs, until a sudden terror made our hair stand up. Under the amazed eyes of the unmoving girls, who were still holding their lace things between their fingers, we fled down the stairs; when we got to the hallway, we smacked with all our might into one of the caretakers, whose immense body rippled with the force of impact. Others immediately appeared beside her. All four of us were pulled by our ears into the empty dorm room, where thirty iron beds lay unmade and stuck together in pairs, under the light of the large ceiling globes. The next day we were called into the yard immediately after singing the song that began all our meetings, "The Republic, the Grand Hearth." They gave us a lecture as vehement as it was abstract, of which no one understood a thing, then they sent us off with a "shame on you!"

We didn't need to know what our parents did at night, after they sent us to bed, nor through what rupture in the smooth surface of reality did children penetrate the world. Our beginnings, all of ours, were veiled in sacred enigma. A winged, stone gargoyle, with its finger on its lips, sealed the origins of our seed. A monster just as impenetrable, with its wings unfurled along flexible bat bones, obscured our end. Between these two figures of silence, our life extended in an eternal moment. We would be always the same, eternity after eternity. We would never become big people, because nothing ever changed. Mommy and Daddy had always been adults, our grandparents were old, not as a result of aging but because that was their essence, as it was the essence of wolves to be wolves and not people. Everything was given, once and forever, every house and tree and flower had existed from the world's beginning and would exist, without end. Each day was the same as the next. Our bodies were the same: we had been born residents of the preventorium, we only remembered flashes of what had been before, so vague that we mixed them up with dreams we'd had that afternoon. If it were not for the two mysteries, if we hadn't had Traian, we would have never stopped indulging in the grand illusion of immortality, the air the fragile lungs of children breathe. Coupling and death, however, told another story, one we didn't yet need to know, but which reached our ears along hundreds of illegitimate, obscure paths.

There, in the warm womb behind the drapes, looking at the moon and stars multiplied in the double window, we talked about all of this until we were almost crazy with excitement and frustration. What was sex? What was death? What sinister connection lay between them? We argued over the details—things did not connect, there were important pieces missing from our jigsaw puzzle. The first myth was surrounded by filth, referred to by curse words and nasty songs. And yet, we had to imagine our most venerated gods, our purest, the only ones who fed us and took care of us, doing, in the dark, like criminals, this dirty thing we'd seen written on all the walls and benches in the school. I sensed I couldn't bear this image, that I couldn't imagine my parents having genitals, or that at night, or in the afternoon when they sent me out to play, they got in bed and mated, their tumescent sexes interpenetrating . . . "But they do," Traian said, "and this is how kids are made, because the big people mate, this is why. Then they grow, they become big people, they mate, they make kids, and then they die. This has been going on here, on Earth, for millions of years. Billions of people have died just because they mated. This is punished by death. You were saying that the big people are like gods to us, but it's not true, *we* are the gods. Our minds are closer to holiness than theirs. They fall into godliness when they mate, then they get old, shrivel up, hunch over, their teeth fall out, their hair falls out, they get terrible diseases, and they all die. Yes, they know more than we do: they know what awaits them in the future. They are more afraid than we are. They are more resigned, more hopeless. They don't tell us the truth, not about birth, not about death, because we aren't supposed to see them for what they are: shadows passing across the earth. They guard the secret piously so we don't find out that *we* are the gods, that our mind is crystalline, while theirs reeks of mud and fear." Traian was one year older than us, a feisty boy with blue eyes, who always walked as though he were asleep. He never seemed to pay attention to what was around him, in class he was always looking out the window at the apple trees that seemed to stretch their heavy branches toward us, and if he got called on, he kept quiet, smiling and looking out the window. He would stand up, slowly, like a sleepwalker. But the teachers were used to him and didn't pay his daydreaming any mind.

When we talked about death, we got even more uneasy. People died, we knew that, but we didn't understand it. Anyway, we were nine, there was a long time before we were seventy or eighty, so we could just as easily think we would live forever. Still, old people died and young people died, from terrible diseases like cancer, even kids died sometimes. We knew kids, classmates, who had been run over by trams when they didn't pay attention crossing the street. Others had fallen from a building onto the asphalt. I had seen a friend of mine's brother, after he threw himself from the top of the apartment block: he was lying in his own blood, behind the block, surrounded by a bunch of people. After you died, you never existed again. You didn't hear, you didn't see, you didn't feel anything. It was like you were asleep and not dreaming, but you didn't have a body (it rotted in the dirt), and you never woke up. Not after a thousand years, not after a million years. When you talked about death, everything was absolute: all people died, without exception. And you died forever. At the thought that we would not exist, we felt an animalistic fear. We just couldn't disappear, pure and simple! We were the outlines of children sewn, with colored thread, into a vast needlepoint: where would we disappear to? We couldn't perish except along with the entire fabric. We were a sketch, a gesture across the cloth of existence, connected to it through billions of little threads. In a curious way, it could be said that we secreted it and wove it, as hardworking as those spiders in the forest that wove enormous webs. We wove reality, we *were* reality. And outside of that there was nothing. Therefore, our death would have had to be the unimaginable end of existence.

"But that's not how it is," Traian told us one night. "Death is not the end of life. After we die, there's a long journey ahead of us. It feels like we are traveling down a long road, very twisty and very dark, all at night. There are no stars in the sky, in fact we don't know if there even is a sky. There is just a road that stretches ahead, where we walk in silence. From time to time, our road crosses another, where another person who has just died is also walking. And then another. Because each road only has one soul. We only meet and look at each other at the crossroads, and how we look scares us. Because we don't look like people anymore, we are different. Some of the dead, after pausing at the intersection to look at each other, continue down their path. Others decide to trade fates, and then, after they embrace mournfully, each walks down the other's road. Because after you die, you know what's waiting for you. You wander for thousands of years on roads that cross forever, sometimes you must stay in this giant node surrounded by the night, to eternally meet dead people, all with the same inhuman face, all silent and worried. I have seen this kind of people in my dreams, they have pale faces, big eyes like flies, narrow lips. They have thin necks and discandied arms. They glide down their roads, looking at them is scary . . ."

Once he had gotten this far with his story, we were all too scared to wait for the rest. We jumped off the sill and stumbled through the dark to our beds. What a strange sight, the dark dormitory! How the other kids were all asleep on their backs, like the statues carved into sarcophagi . . . And the light fixtures on the ceiling looked like spheres levitating in the dark air, without a stem to hang from. We threw ourselves into our sheets, but not before we hung our blankets over the bedstead, to protect us from the moon. We had heard about sleepwalkers, we knew they were led out onto the roofs by the moon's mysterious power.

My bed smelled like pee. They all did, actually. Because after lights-out at nine, we weren't allowed to leave the dorm room, for any reason. The halls and washroom were haunted by the cleaning ladies, with their enormous breasts and bottoms, with their cheeks so swollen in their mongoloid faces there was no room for their eyes. If one of us, insane with the need to urinate, dared open the door, he heard a bestial bellowing from the other side that woke all of us up. How many nights did I suffer, lying on my sheets, my knees to my mouth, my bladder ready to burst, trying to fall asleep to forget the terrible need to urinate! How many times did I poke my head into the clear light of the hall, hoping the women were somewhere on the girl's floor, or the stairs . . . But every time I went back to my white, iron bed, feeling I would let go at any moment. In the end I clenched my eyelids shut, and, consumed with a terrible shame, I put the pillow between my legs and soaked it with liquid, trembling so much my teeth chattered. Then I would throw it under the bed and, relieved, I would sink, my eyelashes wet with tears, into a heavy sleep from which I would awaken only when the morning horn sounded. We all peed in our beds, there was no escape. Our sheets were changed once a week, when they washed them, along with our clothes with our names stitched awkwardly into them, no one seemed surprised by the large yellow stains on our sheets and pillowcases, or by the smell of urine that permeated the dormitory.

But the following nights, in spite of our fear, or perhaps precisely in order to feel its strange pleasure again, we made Traian tell us more from the story of the dead, which we all believed, because we knew that Traian was not a child like us but one who knew the sinister secrets of the big people. We gathered again in the warm, protected spaces behind the floral drapes, in our pajamas printed with giraffes, elephants, and pigs, we tilted our shiny heads, with their short, student haircuts, toward the light of the moon, which day by day became more intense, at the cusp of the harvest, and we listened avidly to the strangest story, the one that neither our grandparents nor our parents had dared tell us, the one that we didn't learn, alongside history, geography, and mathematics, at school. "Okay, I'll tell you," said Traian, "but first look at this." And under our collected heads (Bolbo, Prioteasa, and me), he raised his closed fist. Then he opened his hand. We started back, instinctively, because Traian was holding, visible in the tiniest details under the clear light of the moon, a large, living insect, a mole cricket with giant legs for digging, with a strong, hairy thorax. Under its short wings we could see its swollen stomach, brown and ringed, continuously throbbing. He held it up to our eyes. "Isn't it beautiful? I found it behind the pavilion, after supper. I'm keeping it in a jar in my locker." Each of us touched it, timidly, with our fingers. We had never seen such a large insect, so energetic, so clearly dangerous. But Traian allowed it to rub its legs lazily, his hand lying open like a livid flower. "It will be our secret. We'll keep him and feed him, and no one can know. If Comrade Nistor finds out, he'll throw it away . . ." Traian climbed down from the sill and came back a few minutes later, without the cricket. Then he continued telling us what happens after we die.

"Our life on Earth," he whispered—not to avoid waking the kids still sleeping in their beds, because they were sleeping deeply and happily, but because you could only talk about the beyond in a whisper. "Our life here is only a preparation for death. It's like a riddle, like a hard and complicated problem to solve. Someone arranged the world where we live in order to test us, someone scattered signs and allusions, transmitted hidden messages in all kinds of things, the same way that, orienteering in the woods, you have to find the notes in the hollow trees and the symbols painted on the bark.

Everything is connected, everything is glaringly different from the banal scenery of houses and streets and fields where we play, the schools where we study. From time to time, we hear someone say something that doesn't fit with everything else, as though it comes not from outside you, but from the depths of your mind. Who among us hasn't heard, at least once, in the middle of the night, someone call our name? Who hasn't found something that was different from all the others, something they don't know what to do with, and hidden it in a tin in a drawer? Who hasn't been left with their mouth gaping when something happens that can't happen: you find a bleached cow's skull in the grass, with its rippling molars, with the bone so porous it looks like it would crumble between your fingers, you look at it all over, you follow a ladybug climbing across the bone and going up a nasal passage, and suddenly you look up toward the endless and raging sky to see a cloud exactly in the shape of the skull you're holding in your hands, with its eye sockets, with its blunt forehead, with its purple horns, one of them broken off halfway . . . Life is a game, like Sorry! or Piticot. You have to learn the rules and navigate the paths through bad things and good, past the nice faces and the bloodthirsty glares. This game teaches you everything you need to know to make it down the long and hard path waiting for you after death. Nothing happens by chance—for example, the fact that we are all here, now, to talk about this. We have to remember everything, because we are going to need all the keys and all the pieces of the picture, jumbled up in life, but clear and shining after death. Those who don't understand, those who live for no reason, without connecting the signs scattered everywhere, those content to eat, drink, and be merry, those who run after money, pleasure, or fame will get completely lost and fall prey to fire, ice, giant insects, spiders, and centipedes, or they will be locked forever inside a room with infinitely thick walls, where there is nothing to do. But the others, the searchers, they will know where to go and how to answer.

"After the tangled paths where they wander for thousands of years," Traian continued, "the strange creatures into which we transform after death come to a series of monsters, and each asks one question. You may answer with a word, or an object you hold out to them, or a knife stuck into the monster's heart, or by entering its mouth of crooked teeth and walking out the other end, or by shuffling a deck of cards and finding the one it asks for on the first try. Anything might be the answer, but you may only draw from what you have learned by yourself, with your mind, in your unique life. Each of us has our own path, with our own monsters. Only the desperate, those who were fed up with life and found not signs but disappointments, they exchange fates and find themselves in front of someone else's monster, whose question is ten times harder than their own. And if you don't know the answer, the giant creature—who could be an inexistent animal or a mechanism with shining silver wheels or a wide river full of flowering islands or an angel with a chrysolite saber or a butterfly bigger than a vulture that drives its proboscis between your eyebrows—locks you in its hell, one of the numberless hells that there are. And if you do know the answer, you pass, and after millions of years, you reach the next monster."

"How many are there?" Prioteasa asked. "For some people, they are innumerable," said Traian. "For others, just one, or not even one. You never know. But after you finish with them, a gigantic cavern opens in the walls of night. Gods larger than your mind spread their wings along its walls. And in the middle of the cavern, stretched along soft, shining, translucent slabs of rock, your mother is sleeping; she looks giant, her body seems to fill the entire cave. Your mother could be a moth or a lizard or a lioness. She could be a woman with black or pinkish skin. She could even be a transparent larva, with hooks continuously writhing in the front of her mouth. But from the first moment you see her, you feel a limitless love that binds the two of you together. Under the long eyes of the gods that surround the cave, you approach the large female; after many days of walking across the soft, sonorous slabs, you reach her body and you begin to climb her, until you slip into her womb, where you curl up, happy, in a gentle light, like at the beginning of the world . . ."

"And then you're born again?" "Yes. You are born again and again. This is the greatest defeat. Because your mother is nothing more than the last in the line of monsters. She is the last question, the last trap. Being born again and again and again is not the escape. When you see your mother sleeping in that deep cave, you are overwhelmed with a thirst for life, a limitless longing and love. These things cloud your mind and you fall prey to the most terrible monster, whose hell has no escape. You're led back into the world again, a failure, and again you are shown the signs. This shouldn't happen."

From time to time, clouds covered the moon and stars, then released them again, seemingly brighter than before, to cut our dreaming faces out of the dark. The distant forest hummed, the air was full of divinities that extended their transparent lips toward the snails of our ears, whispering their hoarse and guttural commands in an unknown language. They were everywhere, they implored, moaned, and shouted, they spoke to us intensely, intensely like being punched, but we didn't have the matching sensory organs. We would have needed the delicate plumage of a moth's face, the forked tongue of ophidians, the lateral line of fish, the organ with which spiders understand everything that happens in the world, that is, their glittering webs. The malign or beneficent creatures were everywhere around us, they observed us and guided our movements and meandering thoughts, they desperately tried to contact us, but our skin did not see them and our retinas did not hear. Even then, while I was under the strange power of Traian's voice, the one who knew what would happen after death, I understood that life is fear and nothing else, that fear is the substance of our adventures in the world. It is the blind man's fear of anyone who may approach slowly, holding an instrument of destruction or just with his all-crushing arms, the deaf man's fear at night of not having an eye open in the back of your neck, the fear of sleeping, yes, especially the fear of sleeping. How defenseless was our body's castle of flesh and skin! Why could we not see the diseases that approached them, penetrated them, and occupied our organs? Why didn't we have a sensory organ for suicide and insanity? And above all, why hadn't our body evolved, over millions of years, an eye to see clearly into the future? Why did we stumble forward in the dark and fog, among predatory insects and nameless beasts?

Traian's steady and convincing voice dug an eye into the rock face of our foreheads; we could now see brilliant images of the world beyond where we would wander, the livid paths, the creatures with human shapes, their compound eyes, hideous noses, mouths with tight, dry lips; then the endless line of monsters, each one different, each one asking another question; then the stone cavity where our mother slept. It was past midnight before we climbed down, our hair standing up on our heads and arms, and went to our beds in the fantastical silence of the dormitory. A single stripe of light was visible below the door. I got under the blanket that I knew was blue, but which now had no color or shape, just a rough texture, partially covered by the coolness and rigidity of the starched sheet. I lay in bed, on my back, listening to the breathing of the boy next to me, without knowing if I'd closed my eyelids or not—it was just as dark either way—paralyzed with fear at the thought that in the end I would fall asleep and feel under my feet the pallid, endless, twisting path leading deep into the night.

32

I undo the fly of my pajama bottoms and, in a type of devotion, slightly bent over the porcelain receptacle, at the bottom of which the water lies motionless, I look at my offering—the sometimes creek-clear, sometimes yellow jet that emerges, twisting like a liquid drill, from my body. Because I haven't emptied my bladder in a long time, I feel the usual reflexive pains in the veins of my forearms. At other times, when the pressure is greater and the need to evacuate is more imperious, I suffer unbearable pains in my back, as though my kidneys are going to melt and flow through my urinary canal like a river carrying stones and sand downhill. Always, when it comes time to make my daily prayer before the porcelain altar, to entrust its stomach with an elixir given to me, one that irrigated my tissues, that took away my interior debris, and which contained traces of sperm (a liquid as sacred as blood), lymph, iron, and melancholy from my body and mind, I contemplate the turbine jet, without any thoughts or any worries, be they practical, ethical, philosophical, or mystical: my "I," in these moments, disappears. I become a simple place of crossing, a stone around which flows water that belongs not to the stone but to the world at large, much larger than itself: the yellow water has dug into the heart of the mountain, twisted through its karstic system, it rose and fell in the depths of its groundwater aquifers, received the dead bodies of transparent spiders from its walls, and it sprayed into the light, throwing itself forward in foamy waterfalls. It would later follow the path through the city sewer system, the filthy catacombs filled with rats, condoms, and scraps of dirty rags, then into the sinisterly polluted streams, into the rivers with catfish and sturgeons, and finally into the sea. My devotion to the water that runs from me and through the world would be no less intense if I urinated blood, cerebrospinal fluid, or saliva. I would look, slightly bent over, without thoughts and without an I, at the fountain coming out of me, waiting for the minute to pass in which I was not, still feeling the delicate skin on my fingers, irrigated by burning veins. I would like to contemplate for a moment more the bright yellow water at the bottom of the porcelain bowl, I would like to smell the air that rises from it, and then, just as empty of self, I would let it flow into the ground, taking with it the organic material from my body, to scatter into the body of the world.

Then I go back to my room, in my house, in my unique life. I wander among pieces of furniture, I open drawers, I look at the dozens of things that have gathered, the way a harsh wind heaps the snow into corners and along fences; they have begun to tell stories together. Because, yes, beauty is always the chance encounter of an umbrella and a sewing machine on an operating table. My baby teeth. My old photographs, with the cracked emulsion over the faces and dresses and suits and bare child's thighs. The bits of thread from my navel, the manuscript of *The Fall*, my diary. For entire nights, to the limit of sight, in the brown remanent light—coming not from the window but from things, from the musty, Nile-green air, from the dusty surfaces—I have dallied like a ghost over my treasures. The silence and stillness, in this kind of evening with a pink canvas in the window, were so deep that I often felt I was in one of my old photos and I could have pushed my finger through the crack that slanted across my face, neck, and stomach. But the largest and quietest object in my room, growing constantly, perhaps asymptomatically, while the others stay the same or even shrink, corroded by time and nostalgia, is my manuscript, the one where I am now adding, look, the phrase, "the one where I am now adding, look . . ." Many autumns have passed over its notebooks, many winters, springs, and summers. It has glowed in the blinding light of July and rustled in the cold and glinting light of December. The crystal dome which the stars adorn has turned hundreds of times around it, and a strange chimera has cast its shadow over it, hours on end, tens and hundreds of times, its hair and cheeks lit by the sun or paled by the twilight.

I like my desperate gesture of writing here, and the more desperate it is, the more senseless, the more anonymous, the more stuck in the mud of centuries and millennia, of galaxies and metagalaxies it is, the more I like it. Because I make the absurd gesture, without motivation and without consequences, without history and without psychology, of writing a manuscript, I feel privileged, as though I am one of the few beings given the chance to ransom their lives. When I think now of what I could have been—and perhaps still am in another world, perhaps separated from ours by a single, impenetrable film—one of thousands of writers, a literary unskilled laborer, caught in the cobweb of egos and cabals of the literary world, with enough pride to commit the abominable gesture of signing his name to his superficialities, of giving his unjustifiable blessing so that his manuscript, transformed into impersonal tomes, should be accessible to foreign eyes (the way professionals strip in peep shows and doctors regard the ashy-brown substance inside a trepanned skull), I tremble, as though at the thought of murder, of incest. So many times I remember the yellow faces from that time, that October 1977, when, for the first and last time, I read to someone from my writings. There are hundreds of nights in which, syllable by syllable, I have recollected the sound of *The Fall* read in the room where the Workshop of the Moon was held, one full-moon night, then the silence that followed, then the commentaries. The most important night of my life. In the complicated spiderweb of railway tracks, there occasionally are movable sections which, before the trains pass, change the line, with a simple and sometimes barely observable slide from one divergent track to the next. Every moment in our life is this kind of a switch; we are at every moment at a switch point, and we have the illusion that we are choosing one of the two ways ahead, with all the ethical, psychological, or religious dimensions of our choices. But, in fact, the path is the one that leads us, the maze of rails makes every decision for us, constructing us along the way, a real and virtual anatomical model, from which we hang with our organs eviscerated, like pigeons and rats in natural science museums. The path, on which—as it chooses for us each moment, with each breath, heartbeat, secretion of insulin, thought, love, eclipse, and orgasm—we advance dreamlike through the spiderweb of life, solidifies and becomes history, that is to say memory, while all the possible but unrealized other paths, the enormous reservoir of our virtualities, all our billions of lookalikes (those who, moment by moment, turned left when we turned right), form, on the skeleton of reality, on our time-solidified bone structure, the hyaline organs that we see in mirrors and dreams, the ghosts with our face, the puffy, abstract pleroma, curving around us like a dandelion sphere. For the divine eye that looks at us from above, I am not my life—the accidental, zigzagging path through the giant maze, the line that leads from the periphery to the center—for it, I am the labyrinth itself, because there is one for each of us, constructed unconsciously by our own selves, as the snail secretes his calcinated shell, as we secrete, without knowing in what way, our brain and vertebrae.

But, among the billions of switches, there are some that are crucial, at first indiscernible from all the others, but which send you violently and irreversibly away from your initial course. If I stand up from my chair in this moment, go look out the window, and then come back to my desk and write again, the change will be, almost always, infinitesimal, a drop in the ocean of possibilities. But if, looking out the window, I am a witness to murder, or if, rising quickly, a terrible pain pierces my heart and I fall to the floor in the agony of cardiac arrest—the one I will become in only half an hour will be radically other than the one before, who never imagined, the way we never imagine, this crisis and change. This is how we move ahead, or this is how we are borne through our personal maze, defoliating, moment by moment, into thousands and thousands of kagemushas, most of them almost identical to us, while others are strange, even monstrous. But their sum is me, the sum of their virtual lives.

That was the crucial switch point of my life, in that miserable classroom, under those unforgiving eyes. That is when I cracked in two, feeling the split like a saber blow to the top of my head, like a spinal fracture. Two creatures were born in that workshop, under the eyes of the great critic and the participants, who noticed nothing because they, and the room, and the Methuselian university, and the looming moon also cracked, in a series of mitotic events, until two worlds, virtual twins until that evening, like transparent, conjoined fetuses, advanced in two separate directions that would never meet again. Along one of them, which for me is the real one, the one that matches my life and memories, the audience scorned my poem and I, mocked and lost, gave up literature forever. I became, painfully aware, a failure, one of the many; I became a humble, anonymous, interchangeable Romanian teacher in a world made of ash. But in that decisive moment, the other also appeared, the writer, the success, who over the course of decades would write poems and novels from our common substance, from the trunk of those twenty-two years in which we were one. If our joint poem, *The Fall*, had been successful, if, after we, the two of us in duet, read its happy-unhappy syllables and the hair on the audience's arms had stood up in emotion, if there had been a sacred silence, if, after a break of stupefied-admiring comments, the students and critic had come back to their places and begun to show their surprise and enthusiasm for our unfinished poem, if the critic's final verdict had been more filled with faith and hope than any he had ever given, then another starved child with a sparse mustache, but with a completely different look in his eyes, would have been born there, on the spot, fleeing his defeated shadow. He would have been someone else, from the start, and he would have felt the interior of his body bubbling like champagne, his ribs would have come undone and his mind would have exploded on his lonely journey back home. No drug could make him so high, higher than the buildings on Magheru, higher than the full moon. That night, he wouldn't have been able to sleep for happiness, reciting his poem over and over, until, toward morning, he would have decided to write others, much better ones, in the months and years to come.

But, just as any of life's successes hides a failure, and any failure camouflages a success, perhaps two hands are always needed to write a text that isn't just for fun, consolation, or self-hypnosis. One writes hunched over the manuscript, shadowing and dominating it with his authority; the other, the tenebrous, widowed, disconsolate, anonymous person found within the manuscript, below the page that the first one writes, fills it from underneath with his own signs, he scatters images throughout, curled up under the platform, like Michelangelo on his high wooden scaffold, the paint dripping into his eyes and on his face, depicting strange characters on the chapel's interior. Perhaps there is only this thin skin between him and me, between glory and shame, perhaps it is straight and smooth, without dips and rises: I sustain him, I support the tip of his pen with the tip of my pen. We write frenetically, at the same time, the same text, but mirrored: read in reverse, his paradise becomes my hell, his sun is my night, his butterfly is my obsidian spider.

Because I am not a writer, I have the unsoundable privilege to write my manuscript from within, surrounded by it on all sides, deaf and blind to anything that might distract from my penal labor. I have no readers, I don't need to sign books. Here, in the belly of the manuscript, wandering through its tangled intestines, listening to its strange rumbling, I feel my freedom; I also feel freedom's obligatory companion: insanity.

But tonight, I won't write anything, because I am overwhelmed with melancholy. Because it is a spring night, with a green-yellow sky, and I am a man alone, with no purpose in the world. As has happened so often, from my adolescence to today, I cannot endure this isolation. I have to get out, without even the illusion that I will encounter people. Yes, I will meet creatures with their faces turned away from me, going toward places I cannot go. I will go out to breathe a less stuffy, more emotional air, more charged with the images and colors of my world. I will go out into Colentina, and after winding through the workers' apartment blocks, I will head down, through the warm evening, toward Obor, in the inverse direction to my school. The sky above the large piața will be a dome of vast, complex, low-hanging clouds sunlit in different degrees, coloring with their light and completeness the faces of those who wait at the tram stops, those who cross the streets. I will take a tram, I will go four stops down Ştefan cel Mare, passing Colentina Hospital, then the clinic on Grozovici, and finally my parents' building. I will get off at the end of the line, at the tram depot. I always get off there. The tram tracks that run in a large curve along Ştefan cel Mare abruptly bend before Piața Victoriei and take a small street lined with old, merchant-style houses ornamented with yellowed stucco, with daft, tin cupolas on top, all of them old, sepia, worn by time and weather. The depot is at the end of the street. Since it is not yet time for the trams to return, I walk, balancing on one rail, in the sinister silence of the evening. An old Gypsy woman sits on her heels at a house's entrance. She looks at me in confusion: no one goes there, only the trams shake the houses that have no light or water, these bizarre ruins. I will continue down my rail, toward the depot building, with its triangular pediment with a round, glassless window in the middle. The building is brick, and at the corners it has strange stone gargoyles. The entrance is much larger than the trams need to pass. The rails, at a certain moment in front of the vast entrance, trifurcate, so the returning trams will rest at night in the hall in three rows. But now, in this ever-darkening evening, pink as only the evenings you remember from your early childhood can be, the interior of the hall is empty, with the exception of a single service car, without a chassis, in a pile in the corner at the end of the right-hand line. Frightened, I will walk toward the giant entrance, like a hero from long ago who means to knock down the castle walls. I will be a black, minuscule dot on its threshold, and there I will be suddenly overwhelmed by the absurdity and uselessness of my life. With my aloneness treading the world's aloneness, I will enter the vast mausoleum, stepping through puddles of burnt oil and tripping over rusty, twisted, dust-covered parts of metal. The building seems like a cathedral where someone, from who knows what caprice of a saturnine mind, parked their trams. The sides of the building have large windows, and a dim yet present light filters through the ceiling onto metal rafters, among which, blackened but still translucid, there is a window with a green, twisted wire screen. The hall is much larger inside than you could imagine, such that it takes me a few good minutes before I come to the service car at the end, whose windows and single headlight gleam red as blood in the penumbra. I will reach it, without encountering a porter, or repairman, or locksmith. No one, it seems, has ever set foot here. The car is an ancient model, a cabin that only suggests the front part of a tram, while behind it is a meager, seatless space. It ends with a small trailer where a crane raises, strangely resembling a gallows. How many times, when I was a child and waited with my parents in empty tram stations at the edge of town, was I not disappointed by one of these kinds of service cars that would rumble up the line, instead of the tram we were expecting!

As always, I will climb into the car, I will sit on the broken driver's seat, dirty yellow foam poking through dozens of holes, I will move the old, tarnished copper levers, I will look at my distorted face in one of the large domes. I will stay there for hours, driving my tram through an imaginary city. Only when I hear, past midnight, the noise of the first tram coming back down the line to the depot will I be shaken from my reverie, I will sneak out of the car and along the wall to the exit. Then I will walk home, and this will take up most of the new morning.

33

Except I didn't go anywhere the evening before last, because, while I was writing the last line, barely able to read the letters of the manuscript, Irina came over. Melancholy is also exciting, but in a different way than the stringent drunkenness of sex. When I opened the door, I didn't perceive a woman in the shape before me—even though we hadn't made love for more than two weeks—but a chlorotic sister, another version of myself. In the vast and empty city under the dome of my skull, the tram still glided along its rails toward nowhere. And so, we didn't go directly to the bedroom, as usual, to levitate naked and mate like a strange monogram over the unmade bed, rather I brought her to one of the infinitely numerous rooms of my boat-shaped house. Descending through twisted corridors lined with doors, with paintings you could see nothing in, with desiccated plants from times immemorial, my surprise each time I opened one of the doors was always complete: each room was new, never seen before, glittering in its stillness like a photograph: no speck of dust, no sign of use, the tablecloths perfect, the knickknacks gleaming dully on the shelves. I entered, with Irina, a very tall room where all the furniture was painted red. We sat at the table, in front of a window where the last rays of the evening sun fell, and we looked at each other. In the light that seemed to transubstantiate, hesitatingly, into dark, Irina's face became thinner, her hair grayer, and her famous blue eyes were now almost dark, like her austere lips.

"Did you hear the porter disappeared?" she asks me, looking in my eyes significantly."

"The porter?"

"Ispas, the porter at the school, the old guy, dirty, drunk . . ."

"Oh, Ispas. Right, I haven't seen him for a few days, I think, since Monday or maybe last week. Usually no one pays attention to him, he sits there, between the entry doors, on his chair, but I did wonder why he hadn't shown up. What do you mean he disappeared? Maybe he's just drunk. He looks jaundiced, like he has liver problems . . ."

"That's what everyone thought, but yesterday Borcescu came into the lounge with the militia. He called everyone who was left at the school at five o'clock and questioned us about Ispas—what was with him, where he lived, if he had a wife and kids. No one knew anything. Just a poor man kept on out of pity. During the long break he'd open a newspaper, peel a boiled egg, take a bite of salami . . . No one ever caught him taking a swig at school, but he surely did, because he stank of țuica enough to make the kids dizzy. He must have had a bottle hidden somewhere, maybe behind the door for the fire hose, or some other door only he knew about. We heard he slept wherever he could, in a stairwell, maybe in the bushes in the summer . . ."

"And for this Borcescu called the militia."

"Yes, he's not as dumb as he seems. You can say he's gaga, that he can't remember what he had for lunch, and he always says to me, even if he's already seen me ten times that day, 'Irinucă, Irinucă, where are your little goats?' But that bastard knows everything that's going on at school, he sticks his powdered nose in everywhere. Not that he cares, he's just working on us for the Securitate, I mean really, I think his office is a snake pit of microphones. I bet he noticed the first day the man was missing, but he waited a week to call the militia. It's because Ispas won't let the kids come in if their hair's not cut, and to Borcescu's sick mind, long hair is a crime lèse-majesté—as if the school would crumble if a boy came in with his hair uncut or a girl without her headband. He called the militia, saying he didn't know where to find him, they checked the address he had on his ID, somewhere on Saint Gheorghe, but he hadn't lived there for a long time. Who knows how, but they found out he had been sleeping for about a year somewhere on Avrig, in a stairwell, like a dog. Actually not on the stairs but in the basement, where the furnace is. He had a mattress there. The janitors, who are a bunch of drunks, let him bed there. But not even they had seen him during the time he's been missing. It's like the earth swallowed him up. Since they didn't have anything better to do, the patrolmen, in their well-known wisdom, hauled the janitors in, but they didn't need a poke before they told everything, the same that the rest of us know: that he got pig-drunk every night and told them that one day he wouldn't come sleep there anymore. That he would be taken up in the sky, in a ship from another world, that this was his fate. That it was prophesied to him in a riddle when he was a kid. This is what he told everyone, with that greasy smile of his, he told the school janitors and the kids, and they laughed at him and made him say it again. He laughed, too, at the silly things they thought about him, but he wouldn't give up, no one could get the idea out of his head that he, the last man on Earth, would be the one who was raised to the heavens. He'd rub his unshaven cheeks and stick to his guns, 'Laugh all you want, but I'm going to look down on you from above and you're going to look like a bunch of bugs. They're going to take me before the year is up.'"

"Iakab says people saw him on his knees, near the field past where the streets come together, his face turned toward the sky, yelling, 'I'm all set! I'm ready! Take me now, right now!'"

"Yeah, everyone saw him, with his bag falling apart in his arms. Who knows what trash heap he'd found it in. But this is the part that you'll be interested in."

The painted furniture in the room had turned black. Irina, across the table with her hand in mine, was only an abstract silhouette, a voice with something around it, a nymph, like the unimaginable faces of the cherubim must have appeared, as they stood face-to-face at the ends of the ark, covering the lid's gilded wood with their wings. But her voice, now when the darkness filled the room, seemed to come from in between us, to be born there, between our faces, while the two of us were only impassive shadows, in stillness.

The janitors saw him for the last time on Saturday evening, by the trembling light of a spirit lamp. He said some things that they remembered, in spite of the bad vodka they had been drinking until it came out their eyes, because it seemed as though they had heard it somewhere before: "In a little while, you won't see me anymore," the drunkard had whispered, breaking his baguette in two, in the basement smell of caulk and kerosene, "and then, after a year, you'll see me again." "Take us with you!" they had said, with a laugh, but still intimidated by the porter's fixed stare. "No, where I am going, you can't come." For a moment the janitors had been worried that Ispas, who had raised a finger with an infected nail as he said these words, had either gone completely crazy or was going to kill himself. But Ispas had crawled onto his mattress and fallen asleep in his clothes, as he usually did, until morning, when the janitors, arriving at work, found him still asleep with a hand across his eyes.

But he didn't come back that evening. They waited for him and he didn't come. They didn't think much of it, they were only letting him sleep there because they felt sorry for him. Maybe he'd found something better, or maybe he'd been hit by a car or something, anyway he didn't have any family of his own, and no one even knew why he cast a shadow on the earth. They leaned the mattress up against the wall and that was it. Now they had more space to play craps. But after the porter didn't come to the school for a few more days, the militia listed him as missing and patrols started to look for him. People from the neighborhood around school found out, they began to ask around . . .

And, while the teachers sat in the poorly lit lounge at the table with red, ink-stained fabric, the patrolman produced a bulging briefcase, made of worn, flaking leather, that smelled of oakum, grease, and prune țuica. He undid the latches and poured the contents out in front of them, as though throwing them in their faces: Look what kind of a bastard you kept in your school, in this neighborhood I'm responsible for.

"Where did they find the briefcase?"

"The Bazavan boys, in the eighth grade, they found it in a field, on the other side of the train line. You know what the boys around here are like, they were there to dig for spiders."

"Yes, they tie a ball of pitch on a thread and put it down holes in the field. I've seen it happen. After they get enough of them, they put two spiders to fight inside an old fish can that they heat up over a candle."

"Huh, can you imagine . . . This briefcase was standing up in the middle of the field. It had rained and the earth was black and soft. The kids saw impressions in the mud, footprints leading toward the case, and they followed them. They were shocked when the footprints suddenly disappeared: the rest of the field was as smooth as the palm of your hand, as far as you could see, all the way to the trees. They didn't touch the case, because they had heard the militia was looking for the porter. They knew from their Party youth magazines that if you found something on the road, a wallet say, you were supposed to take it to the militia and you'd be a hero, everyone would sing your praises and at school they'd put you on the honor board. So they ran straight to the station.

The patrolmen drove one of their off-road buggies to the end of the neighborhood. On the other side of the train tracks was a farm. They saw the footprints: a straight line of them, from an adult man's shoe, and on the side, irregular prints from the kids going out and coming back. And so it was, the first set of footprints broke off in the place where, all by itself, inexplicably in the middle of the muddy field, the briefcase stood. It looked like whoever had brought it there had been swallowed up by the earth itself."

"Irina, this reminds me of something I read about a long time ago, when I was a kid. But the footprints were in the snow, and it was a Russian story, set somewhere in Siberia . . ."

I was shaking. One of the stories that had made me tremble as a child, all through the night with the blanket over my head, imagining the horror that had happened to the peasant's wife that morning in the divine snow, had seeped into the world and seemed determined to harass me.

"Then maybe I shouldn't tell you what the Bazavans said at the station. But this could be a hallucination or just something they made up to make the story more horrible. They said, both the brothers, that when they got to the briefcase, they heard, from the sky above their heads, a kind of bawling, a desperate screaming, that sounded like the porter. They thought they could hear him 'like he was on the fifth floor of a block,' so twenty-five or so meters up. If it wasn't for the shouts and wailing, like someone who fell in a trap, maybe they would have taken the briefcase without giving a thought to those footprints that never came back. It was morning, a clear blue sky with no clouds, the air dusty. Nothing looked unusual, the cries simply hung in the air. The boys scrammed."

The patrolman had stopped talking, the teachers looked at him unmoved, the Latvian, Estonian, and Lithuanian personages in the mold-stained paintings regarded everyone over their shoulders. The case lay on its side, in the middle of the table, and all the dirty things around it made it look like a miniature trash pit. There were bits of dry bread, half a green salami, crinkling Eugenia wrappers stained with cream, an almost empty oil bottle with a corncob stopper and a strong smell of țuica, crumpled sheets of paper, a cloudy bottle with pills (antacids, the poor bastard probably suffered from an untreated ulcer), and a wooden cube with its sides painted, probably from a set of kids' building blocks. There was also a naked doll, as big as your hand, made out of soft rubber, with shiny copper hair coming out of visible holes on her skull. Maybe Ispas, maybe someone else, had drawn on her body with a pen, making breasts and a triangle of hair between her legs. In the alcoholic's sick mind, the doll must have served a sublime-obscene purpose, maybe it was his secret fiancée and partner in disgusting rituals.

It wasn't the doll, though, that was a problem for the officer, who over the course of his life had confiscated, and kept in his house to feast his eyes on in secret, crates of pornographic photos and towers of magazines that socialist ethics and aesthetics condemned. Nor did the enigma of the porter's sudden disappearance seem worthy of serious investigation by the organs of public safety. It happened, people disappeared, the Securitate knew what it was doing, and it wasn't the militia's job to go peeping over the fence. No, the real problem was sects and insects, the neighborhood's most irritating problem, and which, with their weak forces, the three or four officers could not eradicate no matter what they did. Again and again the damned Picketists appeared in their reports, with their signs, with their bugs in their hands, the whole shebang. The patrolman was counting on the schoolteachers to hear from the children which parents were making nighttime visits to the cemeteries, the morgues, the cancer wards, and other sinister places like these, who was inciting them, what hidden goals they had. In what ways they were preparing to undermine the order of the state. The officer now had proof that Ispas was a member of the sect. His briefcase had contained a piece of paper, a poem they had found on others who were now sitting in the deepest level of the prison, maybe a manifesto or their secret code. On another piece was written, "DEATH TO DEATH!" a slogan well known to the organs of order. There was no clearer proof.

Having come to this point in her story, Irina—all I could see were her eyes faintly shining in the dark—looked at me again, with the same intensity as at the start, apparently waiting for something from me. I wasn't in the mood to tell her anything about the Picketists or my terrifying night at the morgue. It was enough that the gigantic obsidian statue haunted my dreams; I didn't want it to step into Irina's nightmares as well. The dome of her brain seemed better suited to house another god, one that would gaze from time to time through her blue eyes, the way children look through the mysterious attic skylights.

"What could it be?" I whispered, smiling, in the phrase my mother would invariably use to end all her morning stories, and there was no morning when she didn't dress me in the multicolored lights and shadows of her fantastic interior scenes.

Then I stood to turn on the light, and a chandelier I had never seen before returned the red lacquer to the furniture and the metaphysical stillness to the room.

"Exactly, what could it be?" laughed Irina, once again the bright and exalted physics teacher, secret follower of the anthroposophists, spiritualists, mediums, exorcists, of anyone who denied reality and that our terrestrial life had meaning. "And what do you think it could be?"

Then I noticed that she was holding a scrap of yellow-brown wrapping paper in her left hand, torn from a larger piece. She had probably been holding it the entire time that her right hand held mine.

"I swiped it in the lounge, while the officer was stuffing the doll and old food back into the briefcase. The Eugenia wrappers and other papers were on the table, including this . . . The officer probably thought it was a scrap of newspaper."

I took the piece of paper and looked at in the light. Now it's in my diary, pressed between its pages like a rare flower. The message, written on the torn scrap with chemical pencil, probably wet on his tongue, was a number scrawled on the top part, and underneath, in tiny letters, a text. The number was—is—in two parts, separated by a space slightly larger than the others: 7129 6105195. Below there were four lines from a nonsense text. I am carefully transcribing each letter:

polairy oair olpcheey ykaiin olpchedy opchedaiin dairody
ysheod ykeeedy keshed quodaiin oteodair or chkar otaiin
dshedy qoedaiin ytoiin okair quotol dol okoldy qokedi opked
olkeeol orchsey qokeedy chdor olar ol keeol chedaiin

The text seemed broken off, since at the bottom edge of the page there were some points that seemed to be the upper tails of another line of letters. The irregular tear separated them from those on the scrap. Since the moment I said goodnight to Irina, I have read and reread the four lines dozens of times. They didn't sound like any language I know, not at all. If the words had any meaning, it must be something in code: a secret writing that someone has to know how to decipher. In contrast, the number did mean something to me, I thought I had seen the first part somewhere before. But I had seen it as though in a dream, it felt like a fact from another kind of reality. Seven-one-two-nine—I said it over and over in my mind, fascinated, recalling countless images that could be associated with the number. It was as though I had forgotten a very familiar name and, try as I might, I couldn't remember it. Tortured by this mental block, I tried in the end to drive it out of my mind. The woman in front of me ceased to be a cherubim of mist over the ebony ark, she was once again a body, in flesh and bone, tempting and tender in her slender helplessness. Embracing, we left the space of mystery where we had been talking. We moved down the hallways, rubbing along the walls, our lips pulling at each other's lips, our hands desperate to feel flesh and skin. The path we had followed for an hour to the room took us only a few seconds of sexual fever to retrace. The bedroom door rushed toward us with a frightening speed, we passed through it as though shattering it to pieces and suddenly we were across the bed, mixing with each other in an incomprehensible mandala, one trying to pass through the other like Dante's prisoners in the circle of thieves, melting into each other like Plasticine and emerging, in the other part of the bed, me in Irina's body and Irina in mine, after I had curled up inside her uterus and she had floated inside my skull in the golden air of orgasm. When we came back to this world, we were both half-undressed, the damp sheets stuck to us, sinking into the mattress with our inert bodies subject to gravity. We had forgotten to rise into the air, we had forgotten to sink into the demonic labyrinth of fantasies and ecstatically abject words. We lay there separated, peeled apart from each other, the way all lovers lie after their embraces, enclosed within themselves, because the sword between Tristan and Isolde is not the sign of chastity but fulfillment, the satiety that always returns you to your aloneness. In between a woman and a man released from the mystery of coupling, two swords always appear, one she places, the other he, such that two skins, two bodies, and two brains always separate us from the one we love. Only in this state of weariness and self-forgetting did I remember: on the latch on the tower, in my own house, there was a numerical lock whose code, as the former owner had once whispered to me, was 7129. It was a great mystery, he had suggested, I should never write it down or tell anyone.

We got up, arranged our clothes without looking at each other, and then we left the bedroom slowly, burning with the fear that we had left reality. Because, in all of my labyrinthine, infinite house, only the bedroom was concrete, with solid textures over which the papillary peaks of my fingers vibrated and slid, with sounds and colors braided differently than in hallucinations, narrations, and dreams, but more importantly, interlocking with that validation mechanism found under every perception, the one that says: Yes, go ahead, the ice is firm, it will hold, you are in your world, where red is true, cool is good, light is beautiful, everything is the way you learned and confirmed over and over, in your deepest and darkest childhood. There, in my bedroom, if we pulled the paper, it tore; if we turned on the water, it always flowed toward the ground; if I smiled, the woman in front of me returned my smile. Only there did the statistic certainty, the always changing quantum state, the always clear, unbroken, and quiet mustiness tell me, in the voice of a guardian angel: Be not afraid, you are within reality, where nothing sudden and terrible can happen. As soon as I walked through the door, my belief in this world stared to waver, creodes started to multiply, the infinite rooms, each one different from the others, to whir around like so many possibilities, probabilities, hybrid creatures adjoining "if" and "maybe."

We left by the old ladder next to the wardrobe that, as we passed, reflected us briefly in its weary undulations. We climbed up, opened the hatch, and found ourselves beneath a giant, windy autumn sky that had fallen suddenly and unexpectedly over the city. Standing on the grand terrace that extended across the roof, with our clothes and hair fluttering like flags in the gusts that drove rain clouds northward, we started to laugh like children released from the cage they shared with a terrible monster. We were on the prow of the ship, it seemed to slide under cloud-swept skies and over the waves of houses and vegetation of the picturesque and ruined neighborhood. For a little while, caught up in the ecstasy of autumn's arrival, we pretended to be statues: Irina embodied Pusilanimity, I strove to contort my body into a representation of Venustraphobia, then we spun, just spun around in the whirling air, both of us wrapped in Irina's hair, in my gazes, in the sleeves and flaps of our open coats. The dust got in our eyes, in our hair, but the feelings of happiness and freedom grew inside our ribs that housed a small god of illumination. "You know what?" she shouted in my ear while we held out our hands like dervishes, spinning in the whirling air, "I'd choose the child, too!" At first I didn't understand what she was saying, but then, more by looking in her eyes than by hearing her, I remembered and responded, laughing, "Even if it would be Hitler?" "Even if he were the actual Antichrist!" Ten meters from us, the tower rose. Its round, porthole-like window was now opaque, because it had nothing to reflect but the windy evening around it. "I would save him from the flames and I would let the masterpiece be consumed. We would raise him together, and you know we wouldn't end up with a jerk, or a dictator, or a demon. We would shape his fate, we would put his karma on the right track, we would make him worthy of us and try to be worthy of him." "Or her," I said, "it could be a little girl." "Sure, it could be a girl. All the more so! I would dress her like a doll, in those sundresses and skirts, I'd tie ribbons in her hair, put it in braids around her head . . ." Listening to her, I thought about the eternal power of parables, and how they overflowed into the world. But my world wasn't here, it was over there, between quartz walls, housed in the shell of wind of everlasting analogies . . .

We walked toward the swollen tower glowing white in the night; I ascended the stairway that wound around the building ahead of Irina and we reached the platform outside the door. No one could have known at that moment that the door was scarlet: in this light it looked like pitch. On the spongy wood, where insects with voracious claws had dug their paths, we could see the rectangle of rusty metal, with its four digits shining weakly in the night. I moved the tumblers to make the combination, the same one found in the porter's briefcase, because I had finally remembered where I had heard it before, how I knew it so well . . . "Unbelievable—it's the same," Irina whispered, "how can that be? Such a coincidence?" The tumblers released the door with a click, and we stepped into compacted darkness. It was like we had found a portal to nonbeing.

Just as it happened the first time I went into the tower, as soon as we closed the door we were left without a world and without bodies. It wasn't just that our eyes couldn't see: our ears were blind, our fingertips blind, our nostrils blind, we were dressed in a skin as blind as the cornea of a blind person. The bottoms of our feet did not perceive the pressure of the catwalk where we were standing, our hands felt around us without touching anything, because they didn't touch themselves. The giant hands of the homunculus hanging from our brain had dropped us. He remained, with his tumescent tongue sticking out between his thick lips, with his body as thin as a thread, but with a strangler's hands, like a statue of Pataikos under the dome of our skull, more alone and more foreign and more helpless than ever. Before, we moved our fingers only when he moved them, we talked only when he opened his tattooed lips. Like a tank driver in his steel turret, he sent our bodies where he wanted, on caterpillar tracks made of Ouroboros snakes, and our body's cannon spit seed at his command. Now the tank driver was blind, lost in the limitless dark, and he couldn't feel his own body, his arms, his face . . . We stood in the darkness, disconnected from ourselves, incapable of closing our eyes; we tasted, without taste buds, the deep black of death, in comparison to which our deepest nights were explosions of blinding light. This time, I knew where to find the old, brittle button made of ebony, and without touching it, as though through an effort of pure will, we pushed it together.

What we perceived in that moment was not light: two arrows struck our eyeballs. We struggled to pull them out of the mud of vitreous liquid and blood. We would have liked to pull our eyelids down to our feet, to dress the sensitive retina of our skin with the peplum of our eyelids, so we would not be devoured by the fire of light bathing our body. We stood, Irina and I, for many minutes with our hands over our eyes, looking through them, until we began to breathe the light, our interior pressure equalizing with that inside the tower. Only then did we dare to open our eyes.

The dental chair was there, on the polished glass floor of the chamber, below our feet, shining white-yellow under its great dome of lights. We climbed down the metal ladder until we found ourselves in the minuscule examination room. The old, outdated metal chair took up almost all the space. On its right side was a tray, and on the wall above it was a white cabinet, as you find in these types of places. I had opened it once a long time ago, to play with the strange, impossible, metallic instruments with hooks, pincers, jaws, incomprehensible appendages, handles you couldn't grasp (they weren't made for human hands with five fingers), blades so sharp they sliced the eye that looked at them . . . Irina ran her fingers across the headrest's light brown plastic. This chair was the last thing she would have expected. Her surprise was so great that she didn't ask me anything. My finger turned a small metal switch and a violent cone of light came out of the cupola over the chair. I pressed a button on the console and one of the drills, hanging from above like a metal spider leg, began to whir. The dental chair was completely functional, untouched by the passage of time, as though in that circular well, the ages did not age.

Irina, curious and amused, sat down in the chair and was bathed in a light that wrapped her like a bridal veil; her hand wandered among the instruments on the tray, marveling at their loud clink when she put them back or turned them over; she turned on the water and filled a glass, she touched the back of her hand to the saliva sucker, with its disgusting metallic extension shaped like a hook.

I sat on the stool beside her and pushed the pedals that lowered the chair and reclined the backrest. I took the metal drill out of its orifice, and the reptile with shining scales now whirred in my hand. I made a threatening face and leaned over, with the end of the drill almost invisible in its wild rotation, toward the pale face of a woman who was not amused by my joke. Because it wasn't a joke. We were here in the bottom of the earth, in a bolgia without escape, with infinitely thick walls. We would play here, for eternity, reiterating again and again this game of endless, hopeless torture, the most terrifying game of all the hells. I was, here in the cylindrical oubliette, victim and executioner wedded in the instrument of their suffering. Here, living, healthy teeth could be blasted away in shards, blood could flow all over your tongue, gums, and lips, and drip across your tortured body onto the floor. As the enamel and core were destroyed, within the air of smoke and bestial screams, your teeth would grow back, ready to suffer again and again and again and again, without rest, without time, without place, just pure pain imposed by the beast above you, that could not be corrupted, swayed, or convinced . . . In the end, Irina got up from the chair, laughing nervously, but I stopped her, because I noticed something strange happening with the floor under our feet. "Sit back down, just for a second," I said to her, but it was like the chair was threatening. A quiver went through her body. In the end she did sit, put her arms on the armrests, and let her head fall between the two leather disks of the headrest. Then I saw again, on the glass of the floor, that which I had seen at the start, something like an intersection of shadows. Now it became clearer: from the thick trunk of the dental chair, a kind of vein or almost living root extended into the floor, like the one you can see through the skin on your forearm, and the thick tubes branched out into other, smaller tubes, into tendrils and fans and transparent filaments, fluttering slowly as though in a gelatinous liquid, like the tentacles of an enormous jellyfish. I turned out the lights so we could see, she sitting back up again, me cheek to cheek with her, the palpitating, phosphorescent network under the soft glass of the floor, avid for food. I say "soft" because the thickest roots made the surface bulge, they snaked along like swollen hoses, with a constant, peristaltic motion. What did the subterranean animal want, this coelenterate hanging from the metallic foot, with all its pedals and sockets, of the dental chair? If Irina got up from the chair, the floor slowly turned opaque, the swellings flattened out, and the floor was silent and ordinary. As soon as she sat down again, the subterranean spectacle restarted: the mouths and tentacles and stinging filaments resumed their longing, their imperious rustling, their motions of sucking and pumping . . . Amused, I took one of the needles from the tray and pushed it gently against her cheek, motioning for her to sit quietly in the arms of the chair. The moment I penetrated the derma, stimulating one of the thousands of free nerve endings, I saw a simultaneous change under the floor: the organic threads and cables branching in the depths turned purple and began to absorb the living jet of pain with the avidity of a starving person who sees a bowl of food. I pierced Irina's lip, she yelped, and the frenzy underneath grew even greater. There were intestines that took up the horrifying food and drove it farther along, beyond the walls, down transparent, throbbing channels. There was no longer any doubt: we were inside an alveolus that absorbed algic energy, that transformed pain into impulses that, who knows where, who knows how, fed monstrous creatures. We had given a spoonful of food to an animal starving for the incandescent substance of pain, while others, perhaps, before I purchased the house, had stuffed it with chunks, shanks, buckets of living, desperate pain.

We turned the lights on again, we stood up, and in a short time the space within the great cylinder was the same as before, as though the digestive system underneath were only a bizarre illusion. Right in front of the one who would have sat in the chair, in the curved wall of the tower, was the round window that sometimes glinted so powerfully in the twilight. I had never been able to open the cap, held on the left by a thick hinge and on the other side by a combination lock, this time made up of a host of numbers, each written on little, metal cubes. It would have been pointless to try combinations at random.

"You know, I was wondering . . . If the first number on Ispas's paper opened the tower, maybe the other one works here?"

We could only try. I turned the tumblers, getting old grease on my fingers, to 6105195. I immediately heard the mechanism throw back the bolt. I pushed the cap aside until it banged against the wall, and we looked through the little porthole. The sight surprised us and frightened us, because it was not of this earth.

On the other side of the curved glass was light. It wasn't morning or afternoon or evening, it was another kind of light, constant, unvarying, powerful, and transparent, flowing from nothing over the things that, as though from a great height, we saw spread out past the horizon. We saw forms, rough textures, bits of grain heaped together, flakes of a substance like horn. Fields dotted with orifices, pools of another substance, cloudy and shiny. Porosity, milkiness, translucidity alternated, gathered, and dispersed in this world over which our language cannot extend, just as you can't mold a rubber mat to a woman's hips and breasts. The vision was overwhelming; the objects we saw—outside of geometry and all that was familiar—rose and fell and grew tiny toward an unclear horizon, beyond which you saw, through the fog, pale colors churning in place of a sky. The only constant was the crystalline light, with lens flares and doubled edges here and there, that veiled everything like a tranquil and deep sea.

Through this scene, in a melancholy impossible to put into words, passed processions of beings, herds of creatures that sometimes looked like elephants—but with spiders' legs, like those from Dalí's *The Temptation of Saint Anthony*—and other times like cattle who had been given bestial masks, and other times like insects from an evolutionary branch that disappeared long ago. They could barely pull themselves along on their legs articulated like the fingers of a hand, their deformed bodies covered with a soft cuirass sprouting thin curls of hair. Each protuberance, each coarseness, each mole and hair were clearly visible like under a raking light. Their faces, dominated by horns and mandibles, were blind. They felt their way along a path of fibers and braids with their sensitive bristles, always in contact with the back of the creature before them.

Thousands of creatures following the path, the blind led by the blind, toward who knows what distant region; they seemed to be mourning, like family members dressed in black in a line behind the hearse. And also like them, they had to let time pass between each of their movements, between the steps they took together. There were many of these herds, under our eyes, moving in different directions, the farthest away visible only as lines of ants among mountains of trash.

Directly under the porthole, shuffling slowly like lobsters in a crate, a procession of these massive beings passed by, wavering on their thin legs. We could now see, from our vantage (a lens or a porthole or an unknown device—whatever our window corresponded to in that world, housed in one of the nameless objects in the vast scene?), their physiological details: the peristalsis of their internal organs, visible through their translucid shells; the eggs clustered in the females' wombs, from where some, with the same exasperating slowness, slid out, falling on porous rock; the bead of feces that came out, in a curl, to adorn, with a strange, spiral grain, a glassy surface. But the most terribly violent thing was that, in the convoy of prisoners traveling toward a distant country, each one ate the other, alive. I saw them feed: a mandible slowly sheared off a dried piece of material, or a granule of earth, even a spiral of their own feces. But occasionally a vivid elephant drove its tusks into the back of the beast in front, it pierced the pleats and folds of the outer layer and extracted the fragile organs from its belly. The victim did not seem alarmed; on the contrary, we saw its steps slow down, until it halted, lying on its stomach as though to make its devourer's work that much easier. Multiple creatures feasted on its body, without a struggle, as calm as a wake, and when there was nothing left of the cadaver but its claws, they all set off again, speeding up a little to catch up with the others, the blind, hunchbacked, and frighteningly sad. Almost immediately, another one, in another part of the convoy, pierced the stomach of the one ahead of it, and everything started over, without end. Sometimes, a cow with articulated legs clambered onto the back of another and drove a fist-shaped organ into its flesh. There was no female organ, the wound could be made anywhere. The tip of the fist just needed to reach the abdominal cavity and pour out its fluorescent milks, directly over the translucent shells of the eggs. Once the eggs were deposited onto scraps of earth, babies emerged, identical to their parents, and the just-hatched joined the ranks of those who proceeded through their tactile and olfactory world.

The light of this world painted a hue of honey over our faces. We stayed until morning and observed the habits of the beings who populated it. From time to time, one of them would raise its blind face until it was right in front of ours, as though it felt it was being watched, and it moved its buccal palps back and forth for an extended period, as though it wanted to speak. These tragic, inexpressive faces, frozen in their abject masks, pulled at our hearts. We could not help but wonder why life would take shapes of such unbearable sadness. Why had these creatures been born? What meaning existed in their eternal procession through a world that no one knew about, that no one cared about?

Overwhelmed with exhaustion, we finally closed the porthole and scrambled the lock's tumblers. We went back into the house, and I walked Irina to the door. Through the door's Jugendstil floral designs, the light of day poured in.

34

I don't want to start talking about Vaschide, or, if I'm honest, about the Voynich manuscript—although I have not been able to refrain from a few allusions—until I finish recording the significant dreams from my diary, those I have chosen out of a thousand, not for their plot and character, but for the pure emotion from which they are woven, because, yes, Vaschide, dreams are emotions, not landscapes or stories.

On January 18, two years ago, I wrote:

A strange mole has grown on my skin and somehow pierced it, creating a complicated configuration. I go to the hospital and get one Dr. Funda, who talks a lot about the need to resect the formation. He places me in a device that, with unusual scalpels, resects all three protuberances on my back.

The truth is my skin is covered with moles. All shapes, sizes, and colors: bright as mushrooms, black and wrinkled, transparent with a drop of blood, bits hanging from a filament like poorly sewn buttons, or rough lichen crusting over my skin. At night, sometimes, when I don't have anything else to think about, I mentally stretch my flayed skin, like a map, across the wall next to my bed, and I look at the moles scattered up and down, imagining they are letters in an odd code. What could be written on my skin, I wonder. The moles appeared, stealthily, over time, they have taken control of the blank page of my skin, the vellum that wraps around me, as though, with unusual protraction, someone were writing an illegible text across my body. Like a cabalist, in sleepless nights, I strive to find correlations, to decode the code, to decrypt the encryption, to decloak the cloak that surrounds me.

And a summary, from the twelfth of the same month, of my nocturnal life:

In any case, it seems another stage of my oneiric life is behind me, following the "essential dream" (from age sixteen to twenty-four) and "the visitors" (age twenty-four to twenty-eight, but still active, as we say of a volcano that could erupt at any time): the period of dreams about my childhood houses, with desperate attempts to reconstitute/reconstruct my literally immemorial past (twenty-eight to thirty-one). Everything here is much more complicated, because as I connect these large areas together, there are other virtual whirlpools—unreal-panoramic dreams, maybe the most wonderful imaginable: the one from when I was twenty-seven, with the sea and the hills covered with temples and pagodas, the one with the enormous coast of Africa, the one with the red castle and the view of the gulf, the one with the Straits of Magellan . . . Also those with mountain climbing and towers, with magic flights (but these ended at age twenty), with baroque and polymorphic sex scenes. All of these are scattered throughout my childhood and up to today, like many, many others, intersecting, repeating, and collaborating, forming an infinitely richer texture than my diurnal life, as though the carpet of my life were placed on the floor, by mistake or perversity, upside down, exposing the ugly knots and hiding the splendor of the multicolored pattern.

February 14:

. . . now I was on a soft, sticky bed, and I was a woman, surrounded by beings who said that a god would come fertilize me, and I awaited his arrival in a state of languor and abandon. Pale pink rubber tubes pumped a kind of milk into the mattress, like a wet batting, and I was already pregnant, and one of those beings came toward me with a syringe: "This is to start your contractions" . . . I woke up tangled in other thoughts, other dreams . . .

My femininity is nothing new or surprising for me. I have always felt that my hidden sister—manifest in me via the strange imagination of my mother, who dressed me, until I was four, in girl's clothes (until the vision of the circular room with an operating table in the middle, under bare, raw stars)—was still inside me, a shrunken conjoined twin but not dead, there in my mind, in a space from which I have heard continual whispers, pleadings, sighs. An oppressed discourse, thin and pure, lives permanently inside me, lacking the resonating chamber of an Adam's apple, as though within my being, the sun of masculinity blocked the feminine moon, but her phantom still floats in the luminous evening sky. What a relief for me to be feminine! How much do I owe to the ambiguity of my mind! I have always believed in a deep causal connection between Tiresias's androgyny and his ability to see the future. You cannot truly see the temporal being of your body except through two eyes: a man's and a woman's, simultaneously, the way that both sexes are necessary to give birth to the temporal navigator that is the newborn. But that was not all there was to the dream above. In dreams, all characters are interchangeable. Essentially, it was about a miraculous fertilization and birth. I participated in that scene, I may have seen it, and the dream mechanism, game to destroy mythical images, assigned me the role of mother, perhaps because of my femininity. Sometimes I feel the extreme power of the subterranean connection between all the dreams I record, their powerful hesitancy, their limpid babbling toward a unifying meaning.

Four months later, in a series that I remember better, because it is closer and closer to the date when I am writing:

> *Two nights ago—an "essential" dream, but it didn't go all the way. I think I have developed defense mechanisms against interior aggressions, because for some time now, this happens: I wake up, before the critical moment, before I enter the insane tunnel (perhaps an actual tunnel of insanity or of something else, something much more terrifying). I was in a kind of fortified city, at night under the stars, in a magical atmosphere of intense expectation. There were the starry skies, glittering like diamonds, that appear in so many of my dreams: overwhelming skies, not at all natural, skies from other worlds. I looked up, waiting for something to happen there, for someone to arrive. When I knew it would happen, however, when I knew that it was imminent (the stars had changed in an inexplicable way), I fled down the empty streets of the city, past yellow walls, in and out of buildings that were just as silent as the streets, until I reached an area of daylight. It was, I realize only now, stairway 1 from my block, but different than in reality, it had a strange setting. I was on the bridge over the pit, facing the walled-over entrance. I was waiting there, unmoving, trapped, held by magic. And suddenly, from around the corner, a golden air sprang toward me, a river of living light, trembling, glittering with the thousands of tiny particles it carried. They had come, it seemed, they were here, their light flowed toward me, soon it would encircle and transform me. I watched without moving, with an ecstatic enchantment but also with fear, as the intense golden avalanche full of butterflies advanced implacably toward me. When it reached the foot of the bridge, I awoke, with an effort of will I still remember. Naturally, I was sleeping on my back and the back of my head (which, if I press on it, seems so fragile I can almost touch my brain) was swollen and had a feeling of pressure. In fact, even now as I write, I feel the same thing, there, on that vulnerable area of my cranium: a kind of pressing heat spreading toward my neck.*

I have touched that place many times, beyond the hair and skin on my head. There, my cranium is almost artificially smooth, as though someone had applied a large, heavy stamp. The area that swells after these kinds of dreams is round, the size of a large coin, in fact it feels like there is a disk inside my skin. I feel it there, I can shift it around, but in the moments after I wake it is burning and irritated like an incandescent lens.

Here is a grotesque demon:

> *I turned my head and looked at the inspector. He had a massive head, his hair in a crew cut. Somewhere his cranium had a melancholic deformation. He was heavy and slow-moving overall, like an animal without any natural enemies. On his upper lip were two bumps that, when his head hung against his chest, transformed his mouth into a slightly elongated muzzle.*

Connected to all of this, the next dream, from May of last year:

> *Two nights ago, after two or more paralyzing attacks of fear, I had a dream in which I was in the middle of a room whose large windows gave onto a star-filled sky, and suddenly I began to feel strange, as though I were filled with an aggressive, acidic light, with an irresistible revelation. My exaltation grew into a paroxysm. I fell backward, pierced by rays that came from all sides, and I immediately awoke. I was sleeping on one side, not on my back. My scalp did not feel numb or burning, but it did seem slightly swollen. Not as a cause, but as a consequence of the dream, I told myself, and perhaps this dream of dissolving into an epileptoid sun produced my physical sensations, and not the opposite, as I had believed.*

June 11, 1988:

> *I saw the corneas of a condemned man being burned, slowly, with two powerful magnifying glasses, each focused on a single point, one on each eyeball.*

In place of a commentary on my oneiric situation, I record the fragment that follows and which, I believe, shows a progressive clarification, slow but sure, of the thoughts all of this stirred up in me:

> *I thought about that dream, about that world, about the two young men that couldn't have been anything but heralds. About my crises, about the light with "something mystical" in the center, as I wrote at the time. About the way I woke up safe on the shore when I was about to drown in the Sabar. About the two-meter fall onto my back at Voila. I think I am beginning to make something of all this, as though I have been wrapped in fog up until now. I am searching—at least this much I do sincerely, if I have nothing else to offer. My life opens, it can proceed, even if the great gate of literature, the only one I ever knew, was never accessible. Today, however, it looks like a cat door at the bottom of the real door.*

Yes, my manuscript goes beyond literature, because my manuscript is true. Its arrow does fly over the mark. But today, I don't care if the game is to hit the center of the concentric rings. I don't care about aesthetic laurels. I refuse to run the cat-door gauntlet.

> *In the dream, my tongue was cut into hunks of meat. I didn't feel a thing, because I was anesthetized, lying on an operating table. They kept cutting, deeper toward my throat, until they could see, in the incision, severed veins with no blood inside. The evil was in the larynx, and they could not get in without this operation. "Will my vocal cords be removed?" I asked. "No," they answered, after a moment of hesitation.*

> *A frightening dream from the very start of last night. A woman had an incurable disease, probably a brain tumor, that distended her face into a manic grin. Animal teeth poked out, her eyes bulged, an aggressive suffering covered a face that should have belonged to someone gentle and sad. An X-ray showed the white bones of her cranium and the tumor behind her ear, a more intensely colored mark, as though white smoke had collected there. But it was a double X-ray— now I saw that there wasn't*

one cranium but two, and her son had the same disease, with the same symptoms. He was also screaming mutely, and he was also grinning, like his mother. And suddenly I was in a hospital, in a kind of cell, behind bars. I wasn't a patient, but somehow a visitor. An oligophrenic dwarf brought me, one after another, unseeable horrors: children's cadavers, infected and rotting flesh, trepanned crania, and he showed them to me with a kind of oafish sadism, grinning with pleasure at my disgust. One after another: stainless steel trays full of fetuses, aquaria of broken bones, desiccated monsters, all carried in the arms of the same dwarf. "I don't want to look," I told him, "I've seen enough." I was nauseous and disgusted. Then I saw him coming with a kind of walrus made of blue gelatin, flowering with mold, and he sat on my bench with it in his arms. That long form revolted me more than all the horrors up to then. "Move over," I said, because the muzzle of the rotten walrus was almost touching me. But the dwarf only smiled more lecherously. Then I stood up and dropped some notebooks which (I now realize) were in my lap. "I'm here to study, not for you to make fun of!" And I stormed out of the cell. I woke up shaken by this dream. My room was hostile and dark, and my head hurt more than ever.

I don't yet have the strength to digress, here, as has long been needed, to talk about the grins, about the inhuman mouth twist that I am calling a "grin" only because I don't have another word for that obvious imitation of the human smile which—not in dreams alone, absolutely not only there—I have seen in key moments and which stayed with me as though cauterized on my meninges. I can't now, but at some point I will gather my powers to describe a scene without which all of these currents of dreams are pointless, are suspended in the air. For the moment, I'll just write down one of my secondary memories, maybe one along the same trajectory, but attenuated somehow in comparison to the terrible, real scene. Not even this encounter have I recorded in my diary, out of fear, or superstition.

It happened many years ago, I was still sleeping in my room on Ştefan cel Mare, with my head toward the large triple window. At the end of the bed was the massive, yellowed wardrobe, and between it and the bed was about a meter of free space across the floor. That is where I saw it. It was not a dream, or at least I cannot believe it was. I opened my eyes in the middle of the night, feeling completely awake, the room around me apparently normal, with bands of light occasionally running along the walls, from the headlights of cars passing on the street five floors below. And I saw it there, in the narrow space in front of the wardrobe that was just as real. I don't know why I thought it was my aunt, my mother's sister, although the fragile and green-hued creature was clearly a dwarf, only a little more than a meter tall. It stood there, looked at me, and grinned. Its mouth was clenched into a line that may have been intended as goodwill but was nothing but grotesque. We looked at each other without moving for about a minute, until the fear made me turn over suddenly and pull the blanket over my head. I have no further memory, aside from that terrible fear.

On May 16 I recorded the following:

> *Last night I opened my eyes and saw, clearly outlined against the dark drapes, a man beside my bed, looking at me thoughtfully. He was young, about thirty, wearing a light blue suit. His face was long, his eyes (maybe blue on a dark face) intelligent, and he seemed compassionate. His hair was very strange: parted down the center, light brown turning into white, it fell in small curls to his shoulders like a lawyer's wig, like wigs in Molière. Because of his distance from me, he was (it seemed) much smaller than my old acquaintances, which increased my sense of reality. I saw him for a good seven or eight seconds. My darkness continued, the ever-clearer division between my mind and my life. What will bring the slow, twisted progression of the bullet called the future into the hard wall of my cranium?*

I still ask myself this today, although today I don't see everything as darkness, only a baffling flutter of light and shadow in the corridors of a convoluted maze. The period last spring and summer, when there was a crowd of "visits," did me completely in. The gallery of nocturnal guests never ended. I read books on neurology, psychiatry, phantomatics, mysticism, and metaphysics to try to understand, but it didn't have anything to do with knowledge, instead it was fear, a tightening of the heart, a melting in the solar plexus. Why was I visited? I couldn't understand. I looked for similar cases in psychiatric books, but I didn't find any. Yes, kaleidoscopic hallucinations, reading and stealing thoughts, taking control of the will, imperious voices driving you to do abominable things. But not real people, living and concrete in the smallest detail, who watch you, who sit on your bed in the middle of the night.

There were two. One, though, was completely eclipsed by the other. I only really saw the one leaning over my bed, looking at me carefully. He was bald, tall, I think half-naked or wearing a skin-colored T-shirt. I am sure he did not come from the dream I was having when I suddenly opened my eyes, because that dream I remember: there were no people in it, just landscapes of violently contrasting colors, with large dots of a red that the word "red" cannot describe: a soft red, things sculpted in soft red. As a result, as always, my visitors are not the afterimage of a dream, a remnant still on the retina or in my consciousness when I open my eyes. They are always people, women and men, usually dressed in a normal way, clearly visible, even in the dark. I can describe or draw them all with satisfactory precision. They are human-sized, they are concrete, there, beside me. When I suddenly open my eyes, I surprise them, in fact, because they rush to melt into the dark, leaving trembling and fear in their place.

But at the beginning of this year, in a period of rain during a warm winter, I was attacked again, like the first time, when I was grabbed by the ankles and thrown against the opposite wall. My actual bed, in the house in the shape of a boat, is considerably higher than in the one on Ştefan cel Mare, so I felt the final blow even more powerfully:

I was sleeping on my stomach, with my face to the right, when I clearly heard a small spark in a corner of the room. I sat up in alarm and suddenly felt myself grabbed by an unseen force and pulled through the air toward the ceiling, through the dark bedroom, then toward the door clearly visible in the wall. I felt the exact point where the force was being applied on my chest, and I remembered other dreams in which I was pulled from my bed in the same way. When I got to the door, I knew I was dreaming and with an incredible effort I woke myself up. I opened my eyes and I was left in the state of confusion that usually follows this kind of dream. I shivered in horror for a long time, and when the little spark came again, in exactly the same place in the corner of the room, all the physiology of fear wrapped around me like sticky threads.

The glass cupola, the one from my memory of the hospital, the one from so many dreams scattered through the years, returned to my nocturnal world a few weeks ago, when I dreamed I was in a kind of hospital, and I had a child, a son that I, in this world, never had. Perhaps that's why, even in my dream, he was lost:

I was in a building in the shape of a cupola, with a hall that spiraled along the inside up to its apex, crossing multiple floors. I carried my son in my arms, or somehow under my armpit, as I ascended the slight incline. I was, I believed, inside a hospital, and on both sides of the hall there were white doors, like hospital rooms have. I was looking at the gray, barred windows, when I realized I had lost my boy! All I had under my arm was a kind of domed metal lid, inside which, I knew now, the child had been. Desperately I turned around to look for him. Where could he be? As I descended, each floor became darker. In one of the rooms behind a door in the wall, there were many children who looked at me with interest. "Dad!" one of them shouted. I found my son and was too happy to notice how strange he looked. The seven- or eight-year-old embracing me was dressed like a girl and had a brutally deformed cranium. Down one side, from his forehead to his neck, there was a bony ridge a few centimeters high, and on the other side a round swelling the size of a tight fist. "Ah, here are the speech and understanding centers," I said to myself. "You can already see how intelligent he will be . . ." And so it was, the boy spoke with a strange voice, in a manner far above the aptitude of a child . . .

And the last dreams, from the last month, the last dark seeds within the apple of my manuscript. I am happy I've managed this, that at least this stage of the churning sea of my interior life gives its deposition for the enigma. If I had just one moment of pure, inhuman lucidity, of Kantian, of Cantorian mental clarity, then I could begin to perceive, out of the amorphousness and redundancy of my dreams, a model that is not itself the enigma but which leads toward it, like a path that forms under the feet of the person walking. But I know that it would likely be the last image permitted to my mind's eyes before they melted, a clear slush of ice in a heated pot. I will delay the revelation until the last moment and perhaps even longer, the way I would endlessly delay giving someone dear to me an explanation, the kind that nothing could follow but separation.

> *I have had dreams that did not frighten but fascinated, disgusted, or even amused me a little. In the first, I was holding a rough, spiral shell from a large underwater snail. I thought it would be the perfect shape for a spaceship. "Yes, but for that," I said to myself, "we'll need to clean off these bits of pink meat . . ." And I began to carve spirals of fatty matter off the shell. And suddenly I was carving my own skull, holding my cranium and peeling its skin, then opening it and with my fingers pulling out the damp brain . . . The second dream followed the first, near dawn. A girl, as delicate as a baby, completely naked, but not erotically so, with thin, white skin. She had no head. Moreover, her neck and back were peeled away to reveal her muscles and bones. Her head, still alive, was on another body, resting on that neck only through the mechanical pressure of gravity. I, over the course of a single night, was supposed to transplant this head onto the real body of my beloved. But I could clearly see that I wasn't up to the task: "You should know that I won't be able to connect all the veins, nerves, muscles . . . it's too complicated," I shouted to the head that sat quietly on its provisional body, like a statue on a pedestal.*

And the last one, from a few days ago, a feeling much more attenuated in written form than the actual desolation in the dream, which I can still feel in this moment:

> *I am sleeping alone and scared of the dark, I twitch and wake up several times a night. I am dreaming of the end of the world, furious waves*

breaking against the railing of our balcony on Ştefan cel Mare (yes, on the fifth floor!), a solemn ship appears above the flour mill, blocking out the empty sky, like in so many old dreams. It emits an extension of energy, like a pseudopod, toward the shining window, behind which I am waiting, alone.

Yes, this is what I am, this is what I have been as long as I've known myself: a solitary person, waiting behind a window. Here, in the cardboard box of my manuscript, I have dumped a heap of jigsaw puzzle pieces, each one in itself incomprehensible, each one falling faceup or facedown onto the others, scattering across the vast field of play. Out of these pieces, the long fingers of the logic of dreams could—through meticulous maneuvers of combination, rotation, positioning, augmentation, and diminution, centralization and lateralization, highlighting and blurring—arrive at a partially coherent picture, at least coherent for me, while for everyone else it would remain absurd, because there are both intelligible and unintelligible coherences, just as there are comprehensible and incomprehensible absurdities. You can understand the intelligible, and this is calm; you can understand the unintelligible, and this is power, you can not understand the intelligible, and this is terror; you can not understand the unintelligible, and this is enlightenment. As in the deepest darkness, you can no longer tell if your eyes are open or closed, sometimes I feel that in the midst of my life's fears and tremors, I do not know on which side of my brain I am.

35

Every evening in the washroom, in the commotion and confusion of the other naked kids spraying water on each other or running across the wet tiles, I took my eight hydrazide pills, with the same horror and repulsion with which I would have swallowed eight silkworm seeds. They were so small, dry, and yellow that sometimes they disappeared in the trenches of the lines in my palm, losing themselves among the folds of transparent skin that drew the lines of life, luck, heart, and head. I had to stretch my palm out, spread like a flower with five petals, to find them, to pick them up with my tongue, where they stuck immediately, and to swallow them with a little water. We all imagined that they were, in fact, insect eggs. My friends Bolbo, Prioteasa, and Mihuț each received different pills, each named with different nonsense pairings of syllables, just as strange as my "hydrazide." Bolbo's were as large and round as birds' eggs, most of them green as grass, but some the color of amethysts. Prioteasa took transparent crystals, as clear as water. Mihuț didn't take any pills, but on Tuesdays and Thursdays the doctor took him and brought him back to the dorm two hours later (while we suffered through the afternoon nap); he never wanted to tell us where the doctor took him or what he did, but when he came back to the dorm he would sit on the edge of his iron bed and stare into space, and the smile we all loved would only return to his lips that evening, when the boy, the smallest and most delicate of us, would be himself again. In contrast, they simply drugged Traian. He also took eight pills, also in the evening, also in front of the much too high porcelain sink. I imagine he could only see the top of his head and forehead, maybe his eyes, in the mirror installed at adult height. The nurse, one of the fat women in whose care I was, but who only appeared in the evening with her little cart packed full of meds, would place eight pills into his hand, in a strange way, in a kind of ritual, each pill a different color, some oval, others spherical, some immaculately scarlet, pistachio, or azure, others stamped with letters or unknown signs. I was the first to notice that Traian didn't take them, because, since my bed was beside his, I followed him everywhere, especially since he was so smart, so unusual, so mature compared to the rest of us, the other kids. In the evenings we washed at neighboring sinks in the porcelain row that ran the entire wall. On one of the very first nights, I noticed that Traian—with an eye on the cleaning ladies who supervised us while we took the medicine—only pretended to swallow the pills, dropping them like a con artist down his sleeve, where he had undone the seam on his cuff. After lights-out that same night, I asked him why he did that. Wasn't the medicine good for us? All of us at Voila were sick, we had tuberculosis germs, our parents had said so, the doctors at the clinic did, too. Our parents were paying for us to be here a year, two, as long as necessary for the evil to be taken out of us. They were making great sacrifices for our good... If Traian threw out his pills, he would go home even sicker than before, he would die young and all his family would be crying around him, while he lay there, inert and cold, on the dining room table.

"Yes, what my parents won't do for my good," Traian mimicked me, barely visible in the weak light that came from beyond the drapes. "They'd even eat fried chicken . . ." Then he was silent, face up on his bed, but not asleep, I saw his shining eyes staring at the light hanging on its stem from the ceiling high above us. Although all our beds had the headboard toward the window, for fear the moon would make us sleepwalk, as we got used to the dark more details became visible: the kids sleeping on their beds in three rows, attached in pairs, the row of lockers along the wall at our feet, the stripe of light from under the door. The room smelled of pee and kid sweat, but honestly it didn't smell bad. It was like you were in a stable or a barn, where the manure didn't smell like a toilet but like the country, the village, like animal warmth and intimacy.

Then Traian turned toward me: "I know you won't tell anyone that I don't take the pills. If you do, it's going to be bad, very, very bad. And another thing: stop believing what the big people tell you. You don't know your daddy, but I do. And I know there are a lot like him. Nothing they say is true or good for us. I don't know why they sent us here, to Voila, but it wasn't to make us better. Maybe our moms believed their lies, but I doubt it. But them, the dads . . . they know exactly what they're doing. They work hand in hand with the doctors." He whispered these words with a frown, practically with tears in his eyes. I was scared, not by the meaningless, unreasonable things I heard, but by the way that they came out of Traian, who was talking more to the ceiling than to me. It was hard to fall asleep that night. I thought about my father, who was a stranger to me. I wondered what I knew about him. He was the man in the house, the one who brought home money. He only came in the evening, a little before we ate. He read *Sport*, he ate and watched a little television on our black-and-white set, and he slept in the same bed as my mother. What did he do with the rest of his day? Where did he get the money we lived on? I didn't know, it wasn't any of my business. My parents visited Voila maybe twice, both times on a Sunday. They were in long raincoats tied at the waist. My father's hair was combed back, black as a crow, and he was holding a folder under his arm; my mother was wearing a printed headscarf. As always, they seemed like a pair of statues, inseparable and united, heroically detached from the gray background of autumn days. But who they were, those two, between whom I appeared in old, wilted photos with cracked coatings, the three of us in front of Casa Scânteii, the three of us in the forest at Băneasa, the three of us outside my aunt's house in Dudești-Cioplea, this I didn't know then and I don't know now, except with the same blurry subjectivity with which we "know" anything in this world.

We woke up early in the mornings and, after we went to the cafeteria for our eternal bread with butter and jam that turned our stomach for the rest of the day, and after we drank the butterscotch tea that, strangely, we liked enough to ask for seconds, we were taken outside to line up on the path. We left, with Comrade Nistor or Comrade Cucu marching like a sergeant beside us, toward the main gate on the road, passing under enormous pines and beside damp buildings, then we crossed the street and went in the other gate, into the apple orchard in the middle of which the school buildings were. We walked through trees loaded with pink flowers, or little green apples, or with black, bare branches, depending on the season, but always with the same porcelain clouds above and hundreds of apples underfoot on the long, soft grass, often rising, in the depths of June, up to our waists. We went into our classroom, the third, attached to the back of the fourth, and we sat on the ancient, time-blackened benches, as though the Voila preventorium were hundreds of years old. On each desk, made from a kind of pressed sawdust, was a round hole for the inkpot, always flooded with ink, mixed with ugly drawings of princesses and tanks and guns. The room smelled like petrosin, the kerosene cleaner country houses often used on their floors. The classroom was kept dark by the apple branches filling the window, and in the springtime, they grew far inside. Often, one of the kids sitting in the row by the window would be told to stand in the corner, because he had pushed his face into the leaves and bitten one of the acrid, musty fruits without even picking it from the branch. There, in the troll-house classroom, with its chalkboard in the corner on three legs, we spent our mornings laughing, making saltshakers and boats out of paper, responding to questions about history and Romanian, kicking the girls to get an eraser (Chinese, perfumed) that had fallen under her bench. It wasn't a real school: in fact, there in the orchard, nothing seemed real. The instructors glided in front of our eyes, shining like glass fish in the display shelf of the dining room when a ray of light hit them, and if you looked closely, you could see directly through them, to the posters on the walls and the writing on the board. Only we, the boys and girls, had real bodies, complete, three-dimensional. Everything else around us was just a sketch, everything was a nostalgic watercolor or a design made with the tongue poking through the lips, the way we painted in art class: castles and snow-heavy pines, and a few birds like tilted number threes against the smoky sky. During class, we didn't do anything more than tap the Chinese pencils, with a picture of a giraffe printed along their lengths; or draw a tank, right under the teacher's nose, with the Papagal pencil whose tip had four colors; or, especially, wait for Sunday, the literally endless day when they let us go (we were driven, better said) into the forest. During the breaks, we would rush out the narrow door and run around behind the huts, where, behind the three lines of flowering apple trees, the plant-filled valley began, where we would disappear completely. There we would play for the whole break, "girls with girls and boys with boys"; we played in bunches of tall grass, making nests that held us tightly; there I learned, one shining April morning, when the wind blew the pink petals of the apple trees through the grass, about the fantastical masquerade in which we lived, and where, if, through who knows what mistake, Traian hadn't existed, we would have been happy to live, not just for the two years we would be forced to spend at Voila "to get better," but for our entire lives. In a way, our lives stopped there, there was only the present, a photograph of us all under the apple-filled branches, but in which everything was charmed because it was concrete and palpable: Iudita's soft, iridescent chestnut hair, each strand free and flexible in the spring wind, Mihuț's oval cheek with golden fuzz, the texture of the starched shirts, the uniform, the cheap shoes, always torn and busted. Each person's unusual figure, contrasting so clearly with the anatomy of the trees, grass, and clouds; the green apple trees, all the same, like atoms and waves in the sea. We sat between tall tufts of grass, the way at night we sat behind the drapes on the windowsill, but here we didn't talk about mating and death; we inhaled the sap that evaporated from the blades of grass, from the earth full of worms and roots, and we watched the ragged sky thrown over our nests of trampled grass. The clouds unraveled like cigarette smoke, but more slowly and hypnotically, only to gather their strength for another imperceptible and endless movement. Sometimes, Traian, hidden from the teacher's eyes, brought the jar where he kept his mole cricket. There, hidden in the grass, he would let it out, and the brown insect, larger than our palm and covered in spikes and rough plates, would start to dig tunnels in the soft earth with its mole legs in front of monstrous mandibles. We would leave it there, and during our math classes it would hunt beetle pupae and worms full of bloody veins, and we would put it back during the next break, when on hearing Traian's voice, it would climb out of its hole and let itself be picked up and put back in the jar. We were not that impressed by this dressage demonstration, because we already thought the blond, heavy boy in our class was capable of any magic trick. We were likewise unimpressed when, during a break one afternoon, when we climbed far up the peak of the hill where we could see the entire spread of the orchard in its splendor and perfumed mist, Traian whispered to Bolbo, Prioteasa, and me that Comrade Nistor was not a person, but an automaton. We all laughed, because the director of our dorm, with his Hitler mustache and the dumb brutality of his punishments (so many times, during those impossible afternoon naps when no child actually slept, but we had to lie in our beds with eyes closed, we would get an unexpected, heavy smack on the neck, followed by, "The hell is wrong with you, child? Why're you moving your legs so much? Do you have worms?"), did look like a marionette; but no, Traian insisted, Comrade Nistor was a robot, he had seen for himself, one night when he couldn't sleep—because the pills made you sleep, it was one of their effects—and he would show us, too, whenever we wanted. But we needed to not take our pills for a few days ahead of time, to flush them down the toilet, instead.

Bolbo and Prioteasa kept laughing, and I realized they wouldn't do it, they were scared. The cleaning ladies kept their eyes on us, but Bolbo and Prioteasa weren't scared of the women, they were convinced they had tuberculosis and they would die before they were twenty, as we'd been told, if they didn't eat everything at every meal and if they didn't take their pills. Traian's stories had shaken me, they made me wonder, for the first time, if there wasn't a veil over my eyes, if everything I had believed without a thought from the big people, like from infallible oracles, was just deception and illusion. I knew now that we were locked in our world, that we were lied to about birth and death, about diseases and agonies, that the adults used their superior mental powers to cast a web of glittering ghosts over us, "for our own good," the way they lied to us about Father Frost, who came every year to bring us a bag of moldy oranges and pale, inedible chocolate. I was ready to believe the kid in the bed next to mine, and—even though the very thought of mutiny grabbed my stomach like a claw—I decided I wouldn't take the hydrazide for a week. That night I flushed them, as Traian advised, down the toilet, without stopping to think, trembling at the thought that somewhere in the rusty pipes where the water flowed, pale larvae would come out of the minuscule seeds and feed on the slime, would grow, would swarm through the maze of elbows and tubes, would attach themselves to the pipes, changing into pistachio-colored pupae, and from the shell of their chrysalises horrible butterflies would emerge, pale as death, thick and blind, clambering toward the light . . .

It was halfway through May, the apple flowers had fallen, and among the soft, green-gray leaves, among which irregular pieces of the sky glinted like sapphires, I saw how the future apples were already taking their curved shapes on their petioles, little green balls with white points, with a half-dried stamen at one end still full of pollen, and its sepals already black. The grass at the edge of the orchard wafted green, its color mixed with mists and lazy clouds, in an imperceptible advance toward nowhere. Day after day, my mind became clearer and my sensory organs spread open, like avid tentacles, over the surface of my skin, like eyes on my fingers, my lips, my eye sockets, the cliffs of my temples, my tongue, and my nostrils, they shed the horny scales that had covered them and began, like on the first day outside the womb, to see. I stopped taking the pills on Tuesday, and by Sunday after breakfast, when we all ran down the thousands of forest paths where we were left as always to wander completely free for the six hours until dinner, I was clear of the venom, like a glass of glittering water, cold and pure, with a dense swamp at the bottom, like a layer of slime, the settled slurry that had infested the liquid. My bones turned more easily in their joints, the world's colors were brighter, the words came more easily from my lips and were better placed in the transparent matrices of syntax, almost visible in the perfumed air of the endless forest.

I ran more freely than ever on the elastic earth, I jumped over fallen trunks bristling with mushrooms and ladybugs on their pitch legs, I scratched my shins on saplings, and my muddy sneakers crushed the arum lilies that showed it would be a good year for tomatoes. All the earth was covered with dozens of kinds of plants, woven together, spreading their flowers as high as they could, in violets and pinks and blues, as though there were proud of themselves, and under every flat stone, with the underneath part black and wet, you found the tight spiral of a centipede, or a hive full of pupae, like white, transparent jellybeans. I ran under the colossal dome of the trees where birdcalls glittered, I flickered between shadow and light, between the burning spots of sun and the somber, cool shadows. As always, but with a much purer air in the interior trees that ramified inside each lung, I kept away from the others, because I was not, and would never be, anything more than a solitary child; and I sunk into the forest, walking straight ahead for an hour, in a single direction, between the irregular, abrasive, wounded tree trunks, between logs of rotted wood, between bellflowers vibrating in clearings in the wind, between enormous white spiderwebs, swelling with each breeze, caught between the trees and saplings, elastic and durable, with the horrible animal that wove them right in the center.

The amazing monotony diversified, exhilarating boredom of homogeneous green into a thousand different hues; they drove me farther and farther along, until I suddenly found myself in the total aloneness I was longing for, the one before people appeared on Earth, the place of untrodden places, the only one worthy to leave your bones to whiten, because among all the orifices of your porous vertebrae, and among your pulverized ribs, and from your eyes as though on the butterfly wings of your iliac bones, only here will they rise, only in the silent deep of the forest, only on the bed of yellow and brown leaves, the crumbled and rotten stalks of grass; and minuscule trees will grow and dislocate your skeleton, will make it one with the mottled core of the forest. Far beyond the border where the weak and wind-scattered voices of children were audible, I began to hear another sound, all the more powerful in the active silence, the popping, chirping, whirring silence of the green sanctuary: the continual flow, the hurried rippling of a spring. It was still far away, I went around sun-puddled thickets and clearings with blackened branches fragile as graphite fallen on the earth, in order to reach it at the end of a twisting path. The rippling and whispering became stronger, but sometimes the bird trills arching overhead or the wasps darting past my ears drowned it out. In the end, through the bent grass, I spied a spot of melted glass, its shards burning in the sun. Its long run, that lost itself among the tree trunks, was blocked here and there by rough, round stones, constantly splashed by the currents of water, constantly dried by the sun. Here was the center, you couldn't go any farther. Here, in the forest's aloneness and quiet and timelessness (here, only the water ran), in the forest's amniotic scent, I knelt beside the spring and bent over it, casting a shadow over the icy waters. In one place, away from the stones and branches that dipped into the water, the surface was smooth, and if you put your hands on either side of your face, you could see blind olm salamanders, with their childlike hands, who lived at the bottom of the water, and the constantly moving tails of slippery pollywogs. And above this disturbing image, in a green different from the sap-filled air, my face was superimposed, trembling slightly on the always flowing surface, my little, unimportant face, very white in the deep shadow, with something spectral and sad in its brown eyes, as though they did not belong to it, like holes in the place of eyes in a porcelain mask. And yet it was for those empty eyes, through which the bottom of the water was seen, that I came, they were what I wanted to see, and more than that—I wanted to absorb them, along with my entire child's face, to find, in the end, my lost brother. I leaned in farther, and my lips touched the icy lips of the mirrored child, and, with my eyelids squeezed shut, I swallowed his pure, cold substance, feeling I could remove him from his reliquary and take his place in eternity.

This time, drinking the spring water drove off the last traces of my mental fog. I felt ready, although I didn't know for what; I was waiting, for the first time in my life, for the veil to be torn. There, beside the spring, in that world that had nothing to do with the crumbling blind walls, yellowed plaster, block stairwells, and red-hot tram rails of the ruined city where I lived, I remembered a glinting winter in which, carried by my mother, with my cheek pressed against hers and looking back over her shoulder, I understood for the first time in my life that we were going the wrong way. No, this was not the way to Doru's, Mama was wrong, she was walking through unknown palaces, under the skies of other worlds. Every person we passed, as we continued among the snowdrifts, looked at us with bestial eyes. From every window, frightening beings glared at us. But the most frightening of all was my mother, the goddess who had betrayed me and whose neck my hands held tightly, as though I wanted us to be a single being once again. First she had expelled me from her warm, amber womb, and now I felt the terrible contractions of my loss of faith in her. I remember the most inexplicable place in the abstruse city of my memory, the circular hall where I woke, that same day, on a bed under the stars. I had already, in the nine years I had lived at the time, dreamed of that hall several times, and the unseen doctor's voice still resounded, imperative and brutal, in my ears. What did these dreams tell me, who was I really when I was not the utterly normal child on the fifth floor of the block on Ştefan cel Mare? The forest turned around me without moving, like a circular photograph in the middle of which you stood. What if I never went back to the preventorium, or to the world? What if I kept going straight as far as I could go? But there was no "straight," because I had already reached the target's narrowest circle. From there all you can do is go back, and that's what I did. Suddenly, subliminally, I started to hear the echoes of the other kids' voices, and then I saw them, armed with sticks and girded with bark, running down the thousands of forest paths. Traian was alone, with one knee on the earth at the foot of a giant tree, with the veins of roots spread like black tentacles all around him. He was looking, through the ferns full of brown spores, at a bustling group of bugs. He stood up when I came over, he looked at me with his gray-blue eyes and said, "Stay awake tonight."

After the bedtime rituals, the instructor turned out the light and closed the double doors that cut off our dormitory from the cosmos. We knew he didn't sleep somewhere far from us but on the same hall, because when a child ran to the WC, crazed with the need to pee, if the fat women didn't grab him by the ear right away and pull him back to his bed, often with his pajama pants drenched to his skin, Comrade Nistor would appear from somewhere, dressed not for sleep but in the same vest and white shirt as always, even the tie around his neck, as though he had fallen asleep in his clothes, to corral the child, with an attitude of absolute hate and cruelty. He took the kid under his arm and threw him into the bed without a word, giving him a terrible smack on the neck. Then he left, and the dormitory sank back into darkness.

I could tell Traian's eyes were open and staring at the ceiling. For more than an hour, the kids all squirmed and chatted: the pills' soporific effect didn't kick in until midnight. Prioteasa, his white spot of hair shining dimly in the dark, came to our bed so we could go to the sill, as usual, but this time Traian said he wanted to sleep. I also looked at the ceiling. In ever-larger circles, the darkness grew diluted, the stripe of light from under the door became a blinding blade, enough to outline the kids' faces and the transparent fingers of their hands. One by one, the other kids fell asleep. They were on their backs, identical, like sculptures in translucid amber. I soon lost any orientation in space, I didn't know if my bed had its head or foot toward the door, the entire dormitory seemed like a minuscule box, like an insect collection, with strange pale butterflies, held on their layer of batting, floating in the limitless night. I wasn't from here anymore, from the common dream, but I didn't enter my interior dream, either. I was in limbo, where you still live in the world, but without the reality-validating mechanism, as though you were walking on ice without hearing that voice that constantly whispers: Yes, keep going, the ice is solid, everything is okay, it will hold, nothing monstrous or illogical can happen. How could I believe in the fiction of reality without this judgment, without the commission that approves and stamps things, that attests and takes responsibility for every texture of every wall and every tablecloth, for every hue and vibration of the voice, for all the vestibular systems, for ice and heat, for love and hate? In dreams, the reality validation committee rises from their bottomless chairs, they go to eat and have a smoke, leaving us, amazed and unable to believe it, on uncertified ice, where we are overwhelmed by emotion and euphoria and horror and the charm of a world without the psychical bureaucracy of the real. Then I felt Traian's hand on mine, and we slowly sat up. We walked among the iron beds, barely visible in the dark, where children breathed gently, almost in unison, and we moved toward the wall where the lockers were, in the center of which was the door. Traian took me to the corner, in front of the first tall, narrow locker. I knew that this locker didn't belong to any of us. He opened the door and, instead of seeing just a locker, as deep as we could reach, with shelves to hold our clothes, I entered, after my friend, into another space, a small room lit by a lamp attached to a brick wall. The room smelled stale, crumbled mortar had fallen from the bricks, and the holes in the walls were plastered with thick, gray cobwebs. Comrade Nistor was lying there, on an iron bed like ours, the only furniture in the room. When I saw him

I froze, but Traian smiled serenely: "I've been here many times," he said, not even whispering, as though the fearsome young man that drilled us every day was deaf, or deeply asleep. He walked over the bed, grabbed Nistor's chin, and turned his head back and forth a few times. "You see, he can't do anything . . ." He lifted up an eyelid and revealed the eyeball's yellowish cornea. "Because look at what I found," and he scooched Nistor's left pant leg up to show the hairy skin above his sock. The light was weak and pinkish, but I saw clearly there, tattooed on the skin, a square, with seven or eight numbers, crosses, crescents, and gears, written in an unsteady, childlike hand. Traian gently pressed one of the signs, and, to my horror, Comrade Nistor got up and stood beside his bed, looking sternly ahead. "Don't worry, he won't hurt you," the boy shouted to me, but I couldn't stop myself. Horrified, I ran back out the narrow opening, dashed to my bed, and curled up under the blanket, trembling with fear.

Traian came over almost right away, he pulled the sheet from my head and told me we could go talk on the sill. I was still trembling when I got up and climbed onto the marble slab behind the drapes. Outside was the same moon, thin this time and tilted over the peaks of the forest. "I saw the same tattoo on the cleaning ladies, even on the doctor's arm, high up, where we all have our vaccine marks. One time the stethoscope got caught on the sleeve of his lab coat and I saw. They are all the same, all the same story. Don't be afraid, you haven't seen anything all that frightening yet. I'm telling you, we have to get out of here as soon as possible, or something bad will happen to us. Or maybe it's already happened, and then we can't do anything about it . . . Wait a little more, try not to fall asleep, because usually it happens at this time of night."

"What happens?" I asked, thinking that maybe I was dreaming, although I was there, with Traian, in the light of the moon, and the slab under us was warm, and everything could be touched, smelled, and seen without the possibility of doubt.

"I don't know, we have to wait for the sound."

"What sound?"

Traian pulled the curtain back a little and the thirty metal beds appeared in the penumbra, in their orderly lines, stuck together in pairs as though made for a population of conjoined twins. "Wait," he said. The kids' breathing was continuously audible, like a tired song, evanescent, even ghostly visible in the night, as though the dorm were very cold. We sat there at least an hour, without my knowing what to think, but I sensed that something would estrange me even more from the mental place, exposed to all the karmic winds, that I called the world.

And then I heard the sound. A clear, pure clink that dissolved quickly into the darkness. Immediately after it stopped, like a lightning bolt after which the night is even darker, I saw one of the beds begin to sink, slowly, as though it were on the platform of a large, silent elevator. I thought I was seeing things, but I looked at Traian and he nodded: "Every night, or almost every night, one of us is taken." The bed, with the child asleep in its sheets, descended under the floor, without the slightest sound, and when the boy's body was completely below, the floor closed above him, leaving an unexplained interruption in the regular series of beds. I could not believe my eyes. The dorm was still silent and sunk in darkness, the children moaned softly in their sleep, they turned onto one side or another, in their blue pajamas printed with giraffes, hippos, and elephants, but one of them had been stolen from the world, had sunk into the womb of the earth, still alive, without anyone noticing or being afraid. What was Voila? Why were we there? I was suddenly so scared that I began to shake and my teeth chattered like a cornered dog. The hair on my arms, lifted by minuscule pilo-erector fibers, gave me the sensation of a space full of electricity, tension, plenitude, and bottomless fear. Had I also sunk, while asleep, on the moving floor? Had I been taken by those transparent hands and by those eyes that only show themselves in nightmares? Had I been manipulated by them the way wasps rub the necks of spiders they pull from their webs, to find the vulnerable ganglions? Had they paralyzed me with an injection in my brain stem, in that area called *locus coeruleus*? Had I woken suddenly, completely unable to move, in a hall with white walls, in the blinding intensity of lights over dozens of operating tables? Had I been blinded by the monstrous, metal instruments displayed on the walls—metal crabs, metal lobsters, hooks, needles, and lances with handles not made for human hands? Had I seen disfigured faces leaning over me? Had I heard secret words, terrible words that no one should ever hear? Traian held me tight around the shoulders, trembling himself from my own shaking.

"Have they taken me, too?" I managed to whisper, through my teeth.

"No, not that I saw, it's okay . . . Maybe they didn't . . ."

But my dreams told me something else. I had felt (I clearly remembered one of the dreams I had at Voila) that I was descending toward the center of the earth, I had the feeling of going down to the depths. No, I couldn't doubt it, I had been there, my body open and inert in the powerfully lit hall.

That's when I decided to run away. I couldn't stay at Voila another moment. "I'm coming, too," Traian whispered, and we got off the sill and went to the lockers. We got dressed in the dark, we put the rest of our clothes in the little suitcases we had brought when we came. Traian took his jar, with the giant mole cricket propped against its glass wall. We tied our sheets into a rope and knotted it to the window handle. We escaped through the window, landing in the grass behind the pavilion, dropping from a bit of a height since the sheets didn't reach all the way down. We jumped down in silence and took the dark street toward town, up and down hills of wild and whistling forests.

No car passed, there were no lights. The crickets chirped as loud as they could. We walked toward home all night. At dawn, we hid for a while in a switch house beside the railroad, then we kept moving. They didn't catch us until Ploiești.

36

Aside from Mangalia, where I went with Ştefana for a few days, Voila is the most distant place I have ever visited, and it will, I do not doubt, always be so. I have heard that there are places even farther away, at school they showed me an atlas with colored spots labeled China, Africa, Argentina, New Zealand; they told me I was living on a sphere mostly covered by water. The universe they described was fantastic and chaotic, with the stars above my head as the closest neighbors of our terrestrial world. I know about galaxies and quasars, but I cannot help thinking that when I was a small child or when I went to school, they could have told me anything, they could have talked about Rogaviria and Lezotixia, about the infrared rivers of Zoroclasia, the zirconium cliffs of Nbirinia. They could have taught me a different mathematics or none at all, they could have asked me to memorize entire literatures invented just for me, and chemical phenomena impossible to replicate. So little of what I learned from my parents and at school has had any connection to my daily life. How could I know a place like Malibu existed, when I've never been there and I've never met anyone who's been there? How can we give the name of "reality" to that which we directly perceive—the things around us, with their topography that we intuit through our eyes, ears, fingertips, and tongue—and also to those rumors about places, cities, and stars we will never see? But how can I really know that the things right in front of me, the hairy surface of the back of my hands, my hornlike fingernails, the cup of coffee on the table, really exist? *What* is reality? What visceral and metaphysical mechanism converts the objective into the subjective? I have often thought we are mistaken when we regard reality as a simple, basic given, when it is in fact the most twisted of creatures, the most stratified, most packed with organs, glues, tubes, fats, and cartilage possible to imagine. The animal in which we live, the annelid worm with flesh made of the infinite dust of stars.

I live inside my skull, my world extends as far as its porous, yellow walls, and it consists, almost entirely, of a floating Bucharest, carved in there like the temples chiseled into the pink cliffs at Petra. Stuck like a fibroma to my meninges, at the far edge of my left temporal lobe, is Voila. The rest is ghostly speculation, the science of reflection and refraction through translucid media. My world is Bucharest, the saddest city on the face of the earth, but at the same time, the only true one. In contrast to all the other cities I've been told exist—although it is absurd to believe in Beirut, where you'll never go—Bucharest is the product of a gigantic mind; it appeared all at once, the result of a single person's attempt to produce the only city that can say something about humanity. Like Saint Petersburg and Brasília, Bucharest has no history, it only mimics history. The legendary architect of the city pondered the best way for an urban agglomeration to reflect, most truly and most deeply, humanity's terrible fate, the grand tragedy and everlasting disappointment of our tribe. The constructor of Bucharest planned it all as it appears today, with every building, every empty lot, every interior, every twilight reflection in the circular windows in the middle of the timeworn pediments. His genius was to build a city already in ruin, the only city where people should live. A city of blind walls with bulging bricks barely held in by rusty iron bolts, of daft plaster ornamentation, of antediluvian trams, of bug-eaten doorframes and decomposing window frames, of unearthed paving stones, of sad courtyards with forgotten, unwatered oleanders placed on a timeworn stair. Of transoms with broken glass, of identical schools with walls all painted dirty yellow, of chipped statues, of rusted cupolas over destroyed palaces downtown. A city of department stores with ancient elevators and racks of outdated clothes, of tailors where no one goes, of barbers with broken hair dryers. A city of museums with stuffed cadavers that look at you with a single glass eye, of seltzer shops with a large, blue wheel that knocks a silver piston, of movie houses with crumbling ceilings that fall with predictable regularity onto the audience. A city of dusty poplar trees, the saddest trees in the world, that fill the streets year after year with heaps of their dandelion fuzz. A city of unplastered houses, of storefronts with scarlet cupolas full of wasp hives. Of neighborhoods with clotheslines between houses and idiots sitting on fences . . .

The architect planned every detail of the ancient furniture in each house, the green buffets in the kitchens, the beds with sunken mattresses, the Doina and Felicia bookstores that offer everything but books, the display cases with glass fish, dolls with sponge dresses, the ancient Singer sewing machines. He left doors and access halls, access tunnels and access points between all the buildings. He gave an odd preponderance to places even more sinister than the typical neighborhoods: cemeteries with their baroque, extravagant crypts, sometimes vaster than the houses where the deceased had lived, the central morgue and the dozens of funeral homes in the peripheries, each one with coffins, hearses, and paper flower wreathes in their windows, miserable hospitals, true medieval lazarettos, full of the most hideous examples of merciless disease, of skin diseases and of all the stunted and infirm human mechanisms, churches with sweaty saints under their sunbaked, metal steeples, jails pouring sad songs, lice, and unnatural loves onto the edges of town . . . The architect worked long and diligently on the shapes of the clouds in dusty skies, porcelain globes in continual travel, and the unique, typically Bucharest way in which the twilight sets them on fire, into which they sink slowly, evening after evening, into a sea of melted, twilight amber. The skies over Bucharest, high and narrow like the center steeple of the churches hidden between lindens and plane trees, always painted the same, in artistic detail, with the most unexpected allegorical images.

Bucharest is not a city but a state of the spirit, a deep sigh, a pathetic and pointless cry. It is like old people who are nothing more than walking wounds, clots of nostalgia, like dry blood on scraped skin.

As a bonus for the conurbation of ruined palaces, the nostalgic center around which rotates the armada of workers' apartment buildings, brick factories, locomotive depots, and water towers, the architect thought to bury, here and there in the foundations of certain buildings, among the ruined basements, immemorial skeletons, cables, and sewer points, in the most unexpected areas of the city—solenoids that created beautiful levitation effects. There were five: one in the center, above which rose the giant building of the morgue. The others were scattered along the edge of town, maintaining a hidden connection with the central solenoid, the way coins touch when you make a flower on the table's shiny surface. Above them rose heteroclite buildings, so the secret would be discovered slowly (or never) by their inhabitants, who, distractedly pushing a button they hadn't noticed before, would one day find themselves floating between the floor and ceiling, in a state of grace and relief, not just corporeal relief but throughout their being, as though a hand made of delicate light had picked them up between its fingers and held them in its palm, in front of its unearthly eyes. Or they would have been amazed not at themselves, but at the entire building, the detestable tackiness of a merchant-style house, decorated like a wedding cake, as it pulled itself from its footings and floated smoothly above its hideous foundations, rocking gently in the wind like a pig-bladder balloon, its inhabitant standing at the window, waving goodbye to the gobsmacked crowd on the street. Or, at the edge of Ferentarilor, at Fontanelă, at Vaschide's famous, though abandoned, hall of dreams, they would have run away like headless chickens when they saw, above the cranium-shaped dome (with the bones clearly outlined in zigzagging sutures), their dreams from the night before rising and levitating in the air. It is hard for me to understand how I, the one who by definition does not matter, happened to receive, in this life, my mystical bobbin, in the focal point of which, more than a meter above my bed, I deploy my personal constellation—my poor little baby teeth—and inscribe the always fluttering and changing and otherwise knotted mandala of my embraces with Irina. I know that it was not just for this, for two regressions into paradise, that I've been given this gift, and I have not lost the hope I will learn what the solenoids in the city's energetic points are actually for. So far, I am content to enjoy the delicate spot in my bedroom, unlike anything else in the world. When Irina and I turn toward each other's stomachs, feeding there like lotus eaters with our eyes half-closed, letting the waves of pleasure flow slowly, like thick honey, between us, floating with each other's hips held tightly between our hands, forming a ring of melted gold, a knot of arms and thighs of melted gold glowing in the dark room, I feel so good that the rest of the world becomes nothing but wind and dreams; I feel that escape—our lives' only goal—is near, is at the door, is here. But after we both explode, conquered by the imperious, throbbing orgasm, which, if it lasted more than a few minutes, would certainly kill us, we retreat behind our skins, just as unknowing and as scared as we have been since we came into the world.

However fleeting, moments of physical love are still, for me, like those gold points on armor and those decorations on the pupils of characters in chiaroscuro paintings, that glint all the more strongly when the rest is sunk in shadow. Aside from them, and aside from my constant search, of which they are essential parts, my life is nothing more, for, look, almost ten years now, than the tram rails where I glide in the morning toward the end of Colentina, and on which I return home in the evening. My life as a shuttle, my life as a piston, my linear life between the pitiful poles of my planet: home–school. School–home. There, in that distant, industrial place, stained with oil and diesel, where even the sky smells like hydrocarbons, where the poor apple trees inside the curled termination of the rails are painted pitch black, there, ten tram stops away, after the building warehouses and tire shops, is my life's public space: as soon as I get off the tram, I encounter students going toward the school, other teachers, already bored, parents walking their little kids home after class. I recognize the landmarks: the water tower, the pipe factory, the abandoned factory. The juice stands. I turn toward school down the street with its country-style houses, with kites stuck in the telegraph wires, I pass the auto shop, and here I am at school. Day after day, summer and winter, in torrential rains and in the unbearable heat of Bucharest summers. The idiot perched on the fence next door, with two wool hats on, one over the other, grins at me with his unnaturally fat lips: welcome. I go in the main door and find myself suddenly in my personal hell, where the penalty is eternity. The teachers' lounge, the registers, the other teachers talking about last night's TV shows, the green heaters, the paintings stained with mold. Irina, whom I don't look at, because here we are the Romanian teacher and the physics teacher. Spirescu. Gheară, who shakes my hand and, without ado, tells me a joke about Transylvanians. The incredibly strident sound of the bell. Each of us takes his register under his arm and walks into the hall and up the stairs. The glacial aloneness and the shadow swallow us whole.

Today, the school is in a state, as even I can tell: the porter's disappearance has thrown everyone for a loop. Each teacher comes in with a new detail they heard in class, where the children seem to do nothing but dress up Ispas's story, to pack it with details that sometimes seem more like jokes. The desperate cries from the air were supposedly heard over the entire neighborhood four days in a row, especially around midnight, waking people from their sleep covered with cold sweat. Then the yells, the begging, promises to God and all the saints, groans like someone being beaten and screams like someone flayed alive, these decreased, these calmed down, turning, little by little, into lifeless babbling and moaning, like someone caught in a collapsed mine, dying of thirst and hunger; and then on the sixth day there was quiet again over the black field with its spider holes in fresh furrows. When the martyred cries were at their height, they said a fire truck raced to the field, spinning its wheels until they were half-sunk in the mud, and they lifted up a long ladder toward the sky, with a man in uniform at the top, helmet on his head and, just in case, an axe held optimistically in his hands. The children told Florabela, seeing she was more impressionable and desperate for sensational details, that there in the sky, the fireman ran into an invisible sphere, a few meters in diameter, whose skin was elastic to the touch. Inside he could hear Ispas screaming. Amazed that he couldn't see anything else where his fingers encountered resistance, the fireman chopped at it with his axe, but that turned out to be a bad idea, because the tool was yanked from his hand and thrown to the ground, just as he would have been, with a broken neck, if at the last second he hadn't grabbed one of the rungs of the aluminum ladder . . . Of course there were even wilder stories, from even hotter heads: angels showed themselves, circles of light and comets with people sitting cross-legged in the middle, reminiscent of the icons that many of them had on their walls in the old houses in the neighborhood; even that the sky opened over the field to reveal a sphere of black, scaly glass, which rose through the gold and purple air, only to perish in the eternal glory of God. In other versions, Ispas, buck naked and without a sphere, rose into the sky along a ray shining from the clouds. At least that is what a few older people swore they saw, at six in the morning, waiting in line at the propane station next to the field at the end of the neighborhood. The teachers forgot their recipes and panaceas and did nothing but blather about the porter, scaring each other and making their own contributions to the story. The general conclusion was, "You know, dear, Mr. Ispas always had that feeling, maybe he wasn't as nuts as we all thought. Maybe a flying saucer really did take him. We might not be the smartest people in the universe." This was followed by endless philosophizing about the shape of the cosmos, the billions of worlds that must be inhabited, the miracle at Fátima, and who knows what documentary on the Tele-encyclopedia that proved, scientifically, that . . . The janitors were also involved, sitting elbow to elbow with the teachers in the lounge, as was their habit, until they thought of themselves as faculty, and even the Ukrainians were blathering about Ispas from the oil portraits along the walls.

Thus, maybe for the first time in my life, I was happy to hear the bell ring. I took my register and went upstairs, looking for the fifth-grade B group, or D or F or who knows which, always farther away and foggier, and, in the end, more dubious than Ultima Thule. As I traveled the endless and mazelike path lined with closed doors, I waved to the nurse putting a piece of sugar with a drop of pink, gluey vaccine onto the tongue of each child in a line in front of her, and she responded politely, smiling and sending the boy who put the sugar in his mouth back to the end of the line. Behind the doors, as usual, came the sounds of the menagerie: screeching, confused clamor, and snarls, as though animals of unknown species, examples of a flamboyant exobiology, were held there with ten layers of chains. Somewhere at the edge of the school I finally happened upon my classroom, marked on the door with a letter from a forgotten alphabet and filled with thirty boys and girls, who stood up when I entered. I realized again how scared I was of them, how difficult it was to have dozens of brown eyes concentrated, like the sticky beads of a unique, carnivorous plant, on my body in its cheap street clothes. Such was every class, a sundew plant with sixty brown spheres that caught you and didn't let you go before you were turned into a gray skeleton, empty of the thick juice of your cerebral substance. I didn't feel at all like teaching ordinary substantives and adjectives, or how to pull the main ideas out of *The Grandfather*. I gave them something to do, and, sitting at my desk with my head in my hands, I started to think about my story, the one I build, layer by layer, out of gears, infinitesimal screws, and watchwork springs, without being able to understand either how the mechanism functions or what meaning it has, as though I were below the dial where the clock hours were written, living like a mite on a speck of dust, lost between colossal wheels and springs, stuck in the fine oil on their surfaces. I perceive the metal pieces moving like heavy planets, but I cannot see the gigantic numbers or the clock hands that shift imperceptibly under the sapphire sky of the lid. They are on the other side of the world. Even if I suddenly rose, through some miracle, from my tangle of weights, wheels, and pinions, even if I emerged onto the surface over the dial, I still wouldn't be able to understand that I lived inside a mechanism that measured time.

I can give a deposition on my first memories, about the brother missing from them, about the moment in which my mother left me in the unlocatable hospital where I woke on an operating table, under the stars. I can talk about my incomprehensible feeling of predestination. About doctors and dentists who tortured me throughout my childhood. About the book I literally bathed in tears when I was twelve, even though I understood absolutely nothing from it: *The Gadfly* by Ethel Lilian Voynich. About the way I rediscovered the novel with Carbonari and Freudian conflicts much later, in the Department of Letters library. About how amazed I was when Goia told me the story of the Boole family and the mathematician's five prodigious daughters, about the chaos that the amoral, young genius, a friend of Lewis Carroll, produced in this family, unraveling its logico-mathematic geometry, exploding its Victorian principles, and infusing their thoughts with the telescopic insanity of the fourth dimension: worlds within worlds, in the depths and heights arranged in an asymptotic spiral of grandeur that the poor ganglion imprisoned in our skulls cannot comprehend. How can you not think that the series *Gadfly*–Boole–Hinton is a sign, a model trajectory, a map for your great escape plan? And how can you ascribe to chance the fact that Ethel eventually married the one found, after a rocambolesque, six-century adventure, by the manuscript that today bears his name: the incomprehensible, monstrous Voynich manuscript? And why are the manuscript's fat women—naked, with their pink nipples and curly hair, bathing in communicating bathtubs in a bizarre system of pipes—identical to those in Bucharest's underground passages, on the trajectory of the Floreasca militia station–the block on Ştefan cel Mare–the Maşina de Pâine Clinic? And why, again, are Nicolae Minovici's visions, from his controlled auto-hangings, performed over the course of decades in one of the wings of the morgue (scientific ardor? morose hedonism?) so similar to the cabalistic circles painted on the pages of the Voynich manuscript?

A second mnesic fiber leads me even farther away, without letting me realize where, without being able to understand, as yet, how it intertwines with, how it intersects, how it alternately attracts and repulses, like the poles of a magnet, the first. At Voila, thanks to Traian, I found out that my body, as may have happened before, was subjected, in a subterranean clinic, to a manipulation about which I remember nothing, but which my dreams later would reveal in their frightening field of images. I dare to connect my nightmares and visitors, and the elliptical phenomena that accompany them, or perhaps generate them, to the trajectory of hospital–Maşina de Pâine–Voila, without pretending that I've cleared up even one unimportant corner of this giant jigsaw puzzle. My hope in fitting this corner's pieces together is connected to what I've found out recently about the tamer of dreams, Nicolae Vaschide—but this is not the time for him.

And then there is the surface of my life, the trajectory house–school, that certainty through the bars of which comes the muted snarl of the beast. The banality of the world and of my being, both of which have their origin in the little bang: that night at the workshop when *The Fall* fell. The great critic's verdict, with no right to appeal, that made me sink inside the manuscript I otherwise would have written from above, with the tip of my pen resting on the inverse, Leonardo-esque, cabalistic writing of him who (here, in this very moment) soils, with ink splattering into his eyes, a risible Sistine Chapel. My world, since then, is the one we all experience: a world of ruins and dictators, a world of fear, hunger, idiocy, and cold. I have always wondered, before complaining about my fate as an anonymous Romanian teacher in the saddest city on Earth: would the celebrated writer, whose *Fall* would have been the beginning of his rise, had a solenoid built into the foundations of his house? Could he have levitated, if his pockets were loaded with glory? Would he have learned, as he led his life of receptions, colloquia, and tours, about the Picketists, and if he had, would he have joined them? Would the scales of public adulation have fallen from his eyes to let him see Virgil crushed like a cockroach under the foot of the giant goddess? But do writers ever see anything? Do they ever open the doors painted on the infinitely thick wall of their cells where they serve their death sentence?

During that terrible night at the Workshop of the Moon, not only did the course of my life bifurcate like a tree with two enormous branches, each in turn endlessly bifurcating into thousands of branches that cover the entire realm of the real, but the world also split, in a cosmic mitosis, a universal fissure that produced two realities, infinitesimally different at the start, then stranger and stranger to each other as time went on. I don't know what his world looks like, even though it's possible we are only separated by an infinitely thin membrane. Maybe there, the dictatorship fell long ago, maybe a comet already annihilated everything, leaving cold stars and astral dust behind. Maybe afterward, paradise came to Earth. Maybe, in the world of the distant and celebrated writer who bears my name, no one ever heard of School 86, even though it exists, as far off as the Marquesas and Hyades, with its useless, motley crew of instructors, moving like mites in their dermic underground. Whatever the situation, he keeps writing, keeps tattooing the skin of his books, weaving beautiful and useless things together, atrocious and useless things, enigmatic and useless things, for those who admire him, the way they admire someone who juggles ten plates at once, or someone who lifts barbells weighing hundreds of kilos, or someone with really big breasts. Like all music, painting, thought, prayer, and judgment in his world, his books remain inside, they are inoffensive and decorative, they make the prison more palatable, the mattress softer, the pot cleaner, the guard more human, the axe sharper and heavier.

At times, I think maybe something does link me, maybe even moment by moment, like electrons in nonlocal connection, to my dissimilar twin, and at these times, I think these rickety bridges are dreams. Maybe we meet there, maybe there are nights when he also opens his eyes suddenly to look into the eyes of a visitor, at the same time as I do, on the other side of the membrane; maybe he also feels sad and lost, for days on end, after an epileptic dream in which his skull shatters, exploded by a whirlwind of gold. Or it may be that, along with his other world, he is given other dreams, just as false and contemptible, in which he wins international prizes, he has the adulation of women who line up outside his bedroom, and he looks down from his pedestal, having become a statue of himself, one that lords over a clean, cultured, aseptic city, a Brasília on the Dâmbovița . . . *Enfin,* I sometimes think that, by digging my escape tunnel for decades on end, throwing behind me, like a metaphysical mole, cubic meters of earth, I will finally reach, like an unhappy and hirsute Abbé Faria, not a godly exterior space under infinite skies, but his cell, just as suffocating, just as infested with the smell of spoiled cabbage, as claustrophobic, and as buried in the core of the giant fortress as my own. There won't be anything we can do, other than hug and cry, and then rot, two skeletons embracing in decomposed rags, like the dried fly husks and legs in spiderwebs. All the difference between success and failure, life and art, edifices and ruins, light and dark—annihilated by exterminating time, time that takes no prisoners.

The bell makes me jump. The children leap to their feet and, without waiting for my permission, they run off in every direction, banging on the desks, scribbling on the board, leaning far out the window, and invading the hall. I am borne by their wave, carried on their shoulders, feetfirst, like a dead man leaving the chapel. I am thrown into the hallway, with the register and all. The laziest and fattest girl in the class picks up the register and hands it to me, while I sit up awkwardly, my shirt hanging out of my pants. On her small and puffy shoulder, as speckled as a quince, I glimpse her registration number, inscribed on her skin forever by a tattoo needle. It is an imaginary number, the square root of a negative. She straightens my shirtfront and sleeves gently, then she disappears into the collective play. I go downstairs to the lounge, arriving after many years, at the end of countless peregrinations.

37

Nicolae Vaschide dreamed a lot, more than anyone who has ever lived; he dreamed deliberately and methodically, but never did he dream of the line of women, ever more beautiful—each one twice as beautiful as her mother—that would spring from him, almost without a mother, and then would emerge, almost without a father, one from the next until the last in that line, eighty years after the death of her great-grandfather, came to shine in all of her pagan exuberance. His great-granddaughter, Florabela, was a true, freckled Venus d'Ille: a red mane down to her hips, a heavy gait, breasts whose nipples were impossible to hide as they jutted out, chilled and excited, piercing even the elegant suits she wore in winter, the thick thighs of an autochthonous deity, dozens of gold and chrysolite bracelets clinking on both arms and a delicate necklace measuring her steps, heavy eyeliner, a red purse with *Salammbô* in tatters from reading in the tram, and high staccato notes in her voice, happily imperceptible to our adult ears, but which made threads of blood flow from the student's tympana, knocked moths out of the sky, and confused the flight of bats. In spite of the sexuality that radiated from her like a multicolored halo, our mathematics colleague was inaccessible and pure in the niche of her pink-ivory nautilus. Florabela was completely single, maybe because it was impossible to imagine a man who would suit her, able to withstand the avid embraces of her arms and legs. Wherever she appeared, covered in gold and freckles, whether in the eternal tram 21 that carried us to the end of the line, or in the Andronache forest, where we took the children to collect acorns for the pharmaceutical industry, or in the halls of the school, Florabela burned everything for dozens of meters around her to a crisp, she was left the only full-color creature in a cemetery of ash, an iridescent, immense tropical butterfly with greens flowing into purple and back into green, with velvety brown eyes, standing at the peak of a sand dune that extended for millions of kilometers. It was as though her great-grandfather, the enigmatic Vaschide, had filtered his last dream through a system of female lenses placed at equal distances in time, until it reached the limit of beauty that human eyes and minds could endure.

After showing us, one afternoon, photos of her mother and then her grandmother, the only child of a scholar of dreams, Irina and I suddenly looked at each other, across the kitschy photo album—lotuses and Chinese carp with transparent tails—and we started to laugh at the same thought. "I hope you never have a daughter," Irina said to her, "spare a thought for the poor men . . ." And even the poor women, I added in my mind; since each of Vaschide's descendants was twice as beautiful as the previous, a sensual tsunami twice as violent as Florabela would have razed everything from the face of the earth. Florabela was the limit of tolerable beauty, more would have been terrifying, as scandalous and as inconceivable as the fourth dimension.

During this time of lack and deprivation, we don't visit each other that often. People don't have anything to offer for food or entertainment. Most people live in workers' matchboxes, with thin walls of uninsulated, prefabricated concrete, where you melt from heat in the summer and die of cold in the winter. The teachers socialize in the lounge, and more often than not, it's more than enough. Few become good enough friends to visit each other at home, and parties are out of the question. All the restaurants are nothing more than seedy bars, with nothing to eat, and to drink they have, at best, an acrid, watery juice they call beer, with bits of dill floating inside. In any case, they are too expensive for our pathetic salaries. Of course, Gheară spends most Sundays with Steluța, "I'm beating her rugs," in the presence (and with the blessing?) of her husband, who is not of this earth. And of course, Mototolescu and Călătorescu are inseparable, rumored to share the same apartment and maybe the same bed. "*Honi soit qui mal y pense*," Spirescu says casually, "who the hell cares, maybe they like to sleep in each other's arms because it keeps them warm on winter nights." And everyone laughs to themselves, because once at a camp, some kids found the two teachers, all on their lonesome, in the same bed (even though the room had two), lying head to toe, covered in sweat and wearing troubled faces. But who believes what kids say? As for the rest of us, we are alone, or at least very discreet, as is everyone, in every institution, in the miserable age we live in.

This is why we had been taken by surprise, Irina and I, when our math colleague invited us over, one evening after school, "to chat a little over a glass of vișinata." We all left the school together, in a green-yellow twilight the color of snake venom. To get to the tram station a little more easily, we took the path behind the school along the abandoned factory, now dressed in autumn and melancholy, outlined against the limpid color of the evening. The building was silent and grand, closed within itself. Ready to fly off their ancient stone cornices, plaster angels full of pathos leaned toward the sky casting shadows from their broken wings, where an iron stem poked out, onto the windows as round as the eyes in triangular groups on spiders' foreheads. A stucco angel, its cloaks dripping plaster flakes, was able to break away from the wall from time to time to circle over the neighborhood like a bat and to return to the factory pediment, becoming still again in the ever-bloodier stripe of twilight. Our feet were muddy when we came to the intersection and waited for the tram to turn around; it was sitting on the other side, beyond the group of blackened apple trees. Around us—a limitless loneliness: the pipe factory somewhere distant, toward the bridge, the water tower with its large white cistern on top, and Şoseaua Boulevard, straight as an arrow, narrowing toward the horizon, with its miserable line of tire shops, bread centers, and cobblers. No sign of life, as though we had been lifted by the hand of an enormous creature and placed on the thick cardboard of a city model, without a history, a reality, or a destiny. After a long time, the tram slowly began to make the half circle toward us. We got in where the two cars met and sat on the hard plastic chairs. Florabela in a tram was like something from Magritte: the chair creaked under her silk-wrapped behind; the road, seen through the window, multiplied the rings of her large, gold hoops, so heavy they visibly pulled her earlobes toward the lower part of her powdered and powerful jaw. Her mouth, always excessively lipsticked, intincted everything in the homogeneous color of rotten cherry; when she laughed it went out to her ears, Homeric you would have called her if she were a man; her excited bacchante laughter, which always showed not just the gap between her teeth, not just her catlike tongue, but her tonsils and uvula, shattered the tempered glass windows. An Indian goddess with six arms in a tram that should have been sent to the ITB cemetery long ago, a goddess sparkling in mudras in this functional and lowly space, a source of life and of death, without life and immortal, among the rattling sheets of metal and the windows held in dirty rubber gaskets, and the handles that swung and knocked against the roof...

After fourteen stations to take us past Obor, we went down a completely ruined Calea Moşilor, like a line of yellow, broken, and rotting teeth; we crossed the boulevard and came out, through the same apocalyptic ruins, toward Saint Gheorghe, at the other end of the line. I seldom came to the center. When we got out of the tram, I saw the moon over the department store called Osprey's. What hallucinatory memories, from my childhood, did I have of this store! The way the crystal elevator lifted us through the five floors full of clothes, dresses, and frightening mannequins . . . How I would cling to my mother's hand, in that unfamiliar smell of fabric and waxed parquet, until my hand was drenched in sweat . . . The center was full of these kinds of buildings, they looked like they were made of paper, glowing inside in ghostly illumination; it was another face of the city which, at my age of three or four, must have seemed endless. There were statues in every piaţa, colossal people made of stone or bronze, but still transparent and ghostly, because what made them this way was the dim and fluttering streetlights under threatening stars. And now I had the same feeling of unfamiliarity, of dream, of untruth in the center, when it is night and the wind blows, and the bright trolleybuses rumble down empty streets . . .

Florabela lived alone in a studio, on the second floor of a small, very old apartment block. Her mother had lived there, and her grandmother, because it was the apartment where, when he returned from Paris and settled in the Dâmboviţean city, Vaschide had moved his workshop. One full wall, covered with old photographs in rectangular and oval frames, was dedicated to him, or, better said, because there were always little oriental candles lit before them, it formed an altar to the master of dreams. On the floor in front of this evocative wall were silver candlesticks, vases with dried-out flowers, tall heaps of yellowed books ready to topple over whenever a tram passed under the windows. The photos, which Irina and I studied for a long time before we sat down, showed the dream researcher always in the company of a girl with ribbons in her hair, she was either in his arms or on his knees, or when they were both standing, they held hands, and here you were amazed by the difference in their heights: the man seemed endlessly tall, with his head bent slightly to avoid the ceiling, while his daughter lifted her face barely above his knees and held her hand as high as she could to grasp his acromegalic hands. An atmosphere out of Poe, strange and melancholy, floated in each of the photographs: a sepia world, a terrarium of frozen creatures, smiling toward you crookedly from the midst of their loneliness.

Florabela's great-grandfather, Ortansa's grandfather and Alesia's father, had actually been unusually tall. But beyond the fact that, when he strolled down Calea Victoriei, or in Paris on Rue Saint-Denis, where for many years he kept his dream-making workshop in an upstairs chamber, among those rented to the hundreds of whores who held the walls up outside, he rose above every other person by a head, he gave the impression of a constant, vertical lift, of flying through himself, as though through his ogival, gothic, tubular bones, first to his pelvic girdle, to acquire a burst of energy, and then to reach, like elevators in a tall building, the shoulders, clavicle, and shoulder blades, and in the end to stop in the cupola of his cranium, a sizzling champagne flowed, whose bubbles ascended higher and higher, threatening to lift the oneiric scholar a few centimeters above the sidewalk where he stepped. He was not just tall: he ascended, moment by moment, through his own body, until, like a steeple, he completed his vertical form. He looked the same in every picture: dark-faced, with knit eyebrows above the brilliant and unusually sad eyes of those destined to die of phthisis, a high forehead, strong contours at the temples, a straight nose, and attractive, sensual lips, perhaps out of place in the overall austerity of his face. The line of girls that started from him, each one twice as wonderful as her mother, inherited the feminine mouth of the master of dreams.

He was born, according to Florabela and confirmed in my subsequent, desultory investigations (I wasted a few afternoons in the National Library looking for his famous book, *Sleep and Dreams*, published in 1911, from whose preface I gathered a few uncertain and disputable dates), in Buzău in 1875, during a windstorm that crowned one of the harshest winters anyone had known; a white, luminous winter had for a time entirely erased the miserable city, one about which you can only say that you have nothing to say about it. A few houses, a few storerooms, a few empty lots—and above, a hopeless yellow sky. The child took a long time to start talking, such that his father, the cheesemonger State Vaschide, had no greater ambitions than to tie an apron on him when he grew up and keep him as a shop boy, destined to spend his life fetching hunks of telemea from the barrel and slicing them, thinner or thicker as the client desired. All the more so because, at the age of four, once Nicu began to repeat a few words, his family would have preferred that he had stayed completely mute. The child spoke a mixed-up "gibberish," and said different things than his older brothers and sisters, as though the world he saw was not the same as theirs. His mother, Eufrosina, for example, was told that the night before she had woven a sweater "out of pig guts." His sister, Fevronia, had given birth to a second sun that rose from her womb into the sky "like a balloon filled with helium from the fair." State himself was said to have sliced up a large piece of cheese while it cried, imploring him to not kill it, and it bled onto his apron and over the floor, making an enormous lake that flooded the city. And there were more and more crazy things, until, too embarrassed to send him to school, his parents hid him in their house on Strada Carol until Nicu was ten. Constantly wet with whey up to his elbows, he helped out in the store, under the floor where they lived. But soon, while State and Eufrosina continued to hear, every morning, in spite of Nicu losing many arguments and battles, news of their nocturnal adventures (they were said to have grown wings made of pearl and risen, like a pair of fat sparrows, to the roof of the house, where they sat between two plaster angels, gossiping and laughing with them and watching the empty street, or Nicu said they grabbed him and kneaded him and patted him like dough, giving him four hands and four feet and eyes at the ends of two snail stalks, or he said they stood together behind the stall with barrels of cheese, and they laughed and all their teeth were made of gold, and their oldest son, Honoriu, had his silhouette on a butcher's poster hanging from the wall, divided into numbered areas, smiling with all his gold teeth), customers began to notice something else: Nicu knew how to write, using the chemical pencil he kept behind his ear, and he could read the newspapers in which he wrapped the cheese better than any other child his age, that he was unusually smart and knew a lot of things. He had begun to collect the almanacs printed on the backs of calendars, and books of adventure stories . . . The child devoured everything in print. One day, his father pulled him out of the outhouse at the end of the yard, after Nicu had forgotten to come back. He was holding a book without a cover, whose yellowed pages were nothing but tables of logarithms; State was so shocked, he crossed himself and forgot to take off his belt. "Nicky, do you understand these numbers?" he asked, holding the child delicately by the ear. "No, but I like to read them." "Where did you find it?" "In the field . . ." In an empty lot beside the city trash pit, he found pieces of books, licentious pamphlets, pages torn out of treatises on zoology or architecture. He brought them all back to the room he shared with his brothers and put them in his crate, the only space that was completely and exclusively his. He read by candlelight long past midnight, and the orthogonal projections of the buildings, the anatomy of the buccal parts of insects, the giant breasts of women tossing their hair back and moaning in pleasure, the lines of enigmatic signs in books on symbolic logic, the scenes from stories and novels without a beginning or without pages in the middle got mixed up in his mind like a chernozem made of thousands of dissimilar fibers, and once he closed his eyes, this heteroclite humus fed his nocturnal visions, which he would—when he awoke amazed, enchanted, or shaken the next day—recount to his parents and whoever else wanted, or didn't want, to hear.

In the end, they put him directly into the fourth grade, after the teachers, seeing his test scores, crossed themselves like they were in church. It was true, the child didn't know any of the things kids his age were taught at school. But he read and wrote without mistakes and could talk for hours on end—he, once a mute—about anything you could think of. In the sixth and seventh grades, his classmates (simple, scatterbrained kids, their coats worn through at the elbows) found themselves presented with large sheets of paper torn from a notebook, a little wet, a little dirty, a little stinking of mold, but covered with panels of drawings. They were cartoons, in which one and the same person went on infinite adventures, from the Stone Age to the near future, the bottom of the ocean to the Amazon jungle, fighting snakes and giant spiders, brontosauruses, pirates, and mad scientists. They were all imagined, drawn, colored, and decorated with speech balloons full of words coming out of the characters' mouths by this same Nicu Vaschide, the tall loner in the back of the room. For months, the children had no greater joy than passing the colored pages around. They regarded the author with a kind of sacred horror, meant to isolate him even more, to make his dark halo gleam even brighter. After he stopped producing his illustrated stories, a new surprise came from the silent boy, who usually didn't bother with kids' games and their constantly changing friendships. It was a newspaper, a real newspaper, entirely written by Nicu, a newspaper about them, their classroom, their everyday life, but which, although it made nothing up, saw things differently, like under a powerful magnifying glass, such that the children were amazed by the fondness and resignation and melancholy and laughter and sadness that, now they realized, had always accompanied, like the shadows of clouds over the city, their day-to-day and hour-to-hour activities. The newspaper, a single copy of which appeared each day, was read by all, in a specified order arrived at after many punches and pullings of hair. The paper appeared like clockwork until the end of eighth grade. Many girls, full of admiration for their special classmate, tried to win his affection, but he rejected them, the way that he seemed to reject, elastically, like a magnet with like poles, everything around him. But the really exciting moment came in physics class, when he was called to the board, alongside many others, to work on optics: reflection, refraction, angles of incidence, the spoon that looks broken in a cup of tea . . . The young, green-eyed, and very intelligent teacher, who not long afterward would disappear from the school, asked Nicu how an image forms in the eye. Nicu, to the children's amazement, but surely also to the teacher's, asked in turn, "With regard to optics or anatomy?" "Both," the teacher shot back, amused. And Nicu began to explain sight: the structure of the ocular globe, the iris, pupil, and retina, the inverted image received by rods and cones and transformed into electrical impulses, the nerves and optic chiasma, thalamic projections, and then the visual centers of the occipital lobes. He added everything he knew about light rays, about the way the soft, crystalline lens focused them and projected them onto the retina, even about the blind spot that we all have and all ignore—but how many metaphysical, emotional, mystical, and karmic blind spots does our fantastical body of flesh and thought contain?—in the area named macula lutea . . . He spoke in detail, as though reading from a book, for more than half an hour, during which time not a breath was heard from the rows of students. No teacher had ever spoken to the children this way. When Nicu fell quiet, the young man at the desk remained still for a while, he started to say something then changed his mind, he looked out the window, where his green eyes were intensified by the green of the mulberry leaves beating against the glass, and then he picked the register up and walked out, without a word.

From that moment, Vaschide became a school legend, as he would later be at Saint Sava High School in the center of Bucharest, his parents' new place of residence. Unexpectedly, one of Eufrosina's uncles had died, leaving her, as his sole living heir, a pair of houses of a noble and generous ugliness (neoclassical constructions, yellow like dead teeth) in a Bucharest neighborhood packed with these kinds of merchant-style houses, with colored glass in their transoms and courtyards with statues or fountains in the center. The young man was enthusiastically admitted to the most storied high school of the age, on the basis of his maximal grades in every subject (with only the gym score acquired dishonestly, in exchange for a wheel of cheese each trimester) he had taken at his school in Buzău. At Saint Sava, Vaschide revealed his full self, spread out like a peacock's tail, the plethora of loneliness and oddness that would accompany him always, until his sad disappearance in 1907.

Grandmother Alesia, who became a nun three years after giving birth to Ortansa—conceived with an unknown man or with none, through who knows what parthenogenesis, the same way Ortansa gave birth to Florabela—told the story many times, when her granddaughter visited the hermitage: her grandfather had been, as an adolescent, one of the most famous Bucharest eccentrics, alongside Chimiță, Sânge-Rece, Bărbucică, or the onanist Ibric, but different from them, because his extravagance had to do more with the decadence and dandyism at the time flowering in the West than with Bucharest's apocalyptic slum life, and it anticipated the affected bizarreries of the surrealists. Like Baudelaire, who had died murmuring "*nom, crénom*" more than two decades before, the young Vaschide often appeared, at school and in public, with his eyebrows shaved and replaced by green or blue stripes of paint. Once he caused the dignified ladies on Calea Victoriei to faint when he strolled down the street with a pointed rod inserted through both cheeks and emerald lizards dangling from the ends. He shaved his head and decorated it with tattoos that precisely delineated the meandering sutures of his cranial bones, each numbered and carefully shaded: the frontal bone, the ethmoid, sphenoid, parietal, temporal, and the occipital. The bones at the base of the cranium were only suggested, through ingenious foreshortenings. Later, when the adolescent dream was reabsorbed and Vaschide became an honorable scholar, his hair grown out over his cranial tattoos like a jungle covering the ancient temples of a vanished civilization, he claimed that he had had his skull tattooed while imprisoned at Văcărești, where a master of the art (a counterfeiter steeped in evil) had followed an anatomical diagram torn from a book on osteology. What no one saw and what no one yet knew, because Vaschide had descended deep into a schizophrenic solitude, more so even than at elementary school, was that the skull tattoo extended down his spine: each vertebra was masterfully drawn and numbered with arrows that pointed to the spinal ridges. In a kind of flourish, the five lumbar vertebrae, drawn on the dry skin of the small of the young man's back at age seventeen, were colored in: the ring-shaped bones, with their prongs and spongy cores, were, from top to bottom: dirty pink, dark blue, scarlet, ocher-orange, and luminous yellow. Vaschide never knew why the convict had overstepped both his instructions and the anatomical diagram. Vaschide had simply discovered the colored vertebrae at home, after the torture of the tattooing was over, sitting with his back to one mirror hanging on the wardrobe door, while looking at himself in another that he held in his hand. But this combination of colors threw him into an ecstatic pleasure, as though he saw this aura radiating from his body like a rainbow in five magic hues. "It's fine," he said to himself, as though he suddenly understood it must be this way; then, he leaned his head backward until, like a swimmer, his cranium entered the waters of the mirror up to his ears, then his entire face, keeping his eyes wide open, with his feminine lips and his chin, until Vaschide melted (for a minute that to him seemed like centuries on end) into the empire of dreams.

His thoughts, until then unsettled and cold like crystal vials, now burst open, the way a lily bud bursts, arching and turning in a brilliant efflorescence: they were the floral tableaux of Dutch masters, they were the plethora of blue and metallic green of a peacock's tail, they were the dry lace of frost, they were the vulva's anatomy of skins and cat mouths, they were the feathery and vesicant black explosion of unhappiness in love. They were all the landscapes of the world, they were the flutter of light over every gulf, they were the quiet cruelty of all beasts with striped fur, they were a wedding dress sewn out of all cities, they were an enormous underground basin filled with every tear ever shed. They were the inside-out human, the human glove with its internal organs displayed, the human Christmas tree with its ornaments of lymphatic ganglions, intestines, glands, and bones, with the tinsel of veins and arteries, while within, the constellations, sun, and moon burned with all their might. Vaschide's skull no longer belonged to the cosmos. It was suddenly full, like the chalice of the Holy Grail, with the hyaline hashish of dreams. When he pulled his head, still full of hallucinatory gelatin, back out of the mirror, the young man truly comprehended the path to the interior, like a mining tunnel that extracts astounding crystal mine flowers from the dark. He scorned the superficial extravagances of his life up to then. He let his hair grow over the tattoo, he dressed in clothes befitting a studious young man, and he forgot, until the autumn of that year, his old mannerisms, which many had connected to hebephrenia.

You could sow the world with dreams, because the world itself was a dream. The end of the century, however, in the most modern clinics in Vienna and Paris (even though none of them had managed to completely leave Gall, Lombroso, or Mesmer behind), brought a resurrection in the investigation of the human mind. A half century before, the Romantics had discovered the lost realm of dreams and childhood. Achim and Bettina von Arnim, Jean Paul, Hoffmann, Chamisso, Nerval . . . Poe . . . They often wrote too affectedly and poorly, but they knew how to capture, like a flame rising from wet wood, the grand light of dreams. Freed from parable, taxonomy, and explication. Heterotopic and paralyzing. In their footsteps, Nietzsche, Kierkegaard, and Dostoevsky dug deeper, against the grain of the inept progressivism of their age, to unveil the abyss of the mind, unsoundable like karst complexes: the shame, embarrassment, hopelessness, animal fear, hate, cupidity, and evil that lie within us, the perverted will that deforms the crystal palace of thought. Poets passed the baton of the search for the deep ego to philosophers, who in turn handed it over to clinicians. Charcot and Freud were the new prophets, and the young scholar Nicolae Vaschide entered, bit by bit, reading books that cited other books, into the depths of psychology and the study of human life's more enigmatic aspects: sleep and dreams. He studied philosophy and literature for a few years in Bucharest. During this time, he grew closer to the hallucinatory city, doubtless the saddest in the world, that sea of bizarre roofs and chipped plaster figures, of blind walls and skylights; and with money from the cheese shop at home, where his parents couldn't contain their pride at having a university student, he rented and later purchased the studio where we now sat with Florabela, listening to her stories. From that moment, his world became the desolate space of Saint Gheorghe, the end of the line where the trams turned around a church that quaked with every carful of passengers, making the halos of the saints painted on the pronaos audibly vibrate, like large, prismatic soap bubbles. In the evening, when the air turned dusty red, when passing people's shadows looked like shades from the inferno, the young man walked by himself, for hours on end, to the Colței Tower and back, toward the Cantacuzino Hospital, not infrequently crossing the old city, the center of the rose of chipped plaster, a tangle of streets and houses that emptied out completely at the hour of vespers. Then he went home and began his workday, which for him was the night. Soon, he left philological concerns behind, including the study of philosophy, to take dreams as his only object of inquiry.

If dreams had never been, we would never have known we have a soul. The concrete, tangible, real world would have been all there was—the only dream permitted to us; and because it was the only one, it would have been incapable of recognizing itself as a dream. We doubt the world because we dream. We perceive it as it is—a sinister prison for minds—only because, when we close our eyes at night, we always wake up on the other side of our eyelids. It is like the way traveling opens your eyes and mind, it is like a bird's high flight, where it sees far-off realms. Your village is not the only one in the world and not the navel of the world. Dreams are maps, where the widespread territories of our interior lives appear. They are worlds with one more dimension than the diurnal, and many more than our brains, which cross new landscapes without being able to understand them. Even from his seat at the university, where he studied Schopenhauer and Nietzsche and read Nerval, Barbey d'Aurevilly, and Baudelaire, Nicolae Vaschide understood the mechanism of dreams in all its shining detail, the way Tesla visualized his alternating current motors piece by piece, in the air in front of his eyes.

Night by night, we fall sleep and dream. We sink into our visions' cistern of melted gold. Like pearl divers, we cannot stay in these places for a long time: the need to breathe and the pressure on our tympana force us, periodically, to the surface. Four times a night we descend into the deep waters of our mind, we stay there a time and then, almost suffocating, we work our way up to the surface. In the morning we open our hands to reveal, glimmering among the lines of our palms, the frosty pearls for which we put our lives in danger: small fragments of our interior caliphate. Although we go there every night, most of the time we come back empty-handed. We are left amazed and unhappy, because we *know* we descended, we *remember* how our knife opened the oyster valves, but the pearls were scattered along the way, as though they had been nothing but unusually dense clouds, or abyssal fish who exploded from their own interior pressure.

Among the pearls we manage to keep, the so-called dreams (as though we said, holding out one fish scale: here is a fish, and, pointing to a hyoid bone: here is a man), not all are of the same quality: the texture and color, the size and softness to the touch vary so much—and our state of enchantment and magic is so different—that even in times when dreams were accessories for parables and stories, and set in long tables beside unambiguous explications ("if you dream of urinating eastward, you will become king"), they carefully taxonomized the night into so many oneiric insect collections. For Calcidius (whom Vaschide read via an edition of that man's *Timaeus* translation containing more footnotes than text), a philosopher in the fourth century after Christ, there are three types of dreams. The first come from our two souls: one inferior, sublunar, and one above the moon. Our ordinary soul produces *somnium* or *phantasma,* dreams produced by exterior impressions or the mnesic remains of previous days. These are insignificant, only a distant rumor of the world filtered through the walls of our closed eyelids. The superior soul produces enigmatic dreams, mazes where the mind loses its way: *visum, oneiros*. These also do not have lofty meanings, they are only bloodthirsty sphinxes. The second category of dreams contains those sent by angels or demons: *admonitio* or *chrematismos.* These are dreams that obsess you, revelations promised but not yet concretized, like a word on the tip of your tongue. Few people have these dreams, but those who have experienced them cannot forget them: you meet beings dear to you, who died long ago, or you encounter frightening spiders who scour the underground of your mind and wrap you in silk. Ecstasy and nightmare, sometimes combined in dreams of agonic coupling, in which sexes search for and endlessly penetrate each other, releasing vice's aura of amoral pleasure, they are the punishments/recompense we receive with our lips swollen in pleasure or with teeth unveiled in scream, from the angels of intersynaptic space. This second type of dream also doesn't reveal anything about you, about your true avatar.

Revelation, the kind you receive only a few times in your life, the essential dream, truer than reality and the only tunnel that opens in the walls of time, a tunnel through which you might escape, is only conveyed by the third type of dream, the supreme dream, the dream of escape. It comes from another dimension, and it bears the name *orama*. It is the clear, unambiguous dream, because the enigma, converted into a hyperenigma, reveals the soul with hallucinatory clarity, without shadow, like a crystal pyramid in the center of our mind. *Orama* is the escape plan you receive in your cell through taps on a wall dozens of meters above the sea. Clear in front of you, if still strange and unusable, like a typewritten page for an illiterate person, like lines of equations for a layperson. You see everything clearly, every letter with its serifs, each number with its absurdity, but *what* is written there? And how does what is written there connect to your fate? You receive vital instructions in an unknown language or in a code imperceptible to your senses, but you know that there is the code and there the response, and you strive to decrypt them. *Orama* is the whispering voice, without vocal cords or phonic trajectory, that calls you by name in the middle of the night. It is what you whisper to yourself, you, who know much more, who know in fact everything, to yourself, who does not know he knows. Vaschide left the University of Bucharest without completing his degree, to begin a safari that would last his entire life: hunting the supreme dream, *orama*.

In order to experience it lucidly, to manipulate your own mind and, more importantly, to escape the fantastical adventure safe and sound, you had to live in a city of dreams. Bucharest, with its rending ruins, pediments, chipped statues, and streetlights with broken glass, could not take you any farther than *chrematismos*. In one of the last days he spent at the University of Bucharest, Vaschide had the chance to meet his idol, Alfred Binet, whose treatise on applied psychology he had read, with great emotion, from cover to cover. Binet was giving an elegant speech in the lecture hall of the Letters and Philosophy Department, on the very new school of human intelligence measurement, both normal and pathological, that carried his name, along with his collaborator, Simon's. At the end of his talk, Binet—who looked like he was cut out of the photos of scholars of the age, all sideburns, waxed mustaches, and a lorgnette, now glinting in one lens, now the other—invited volunteers to take his test. Vaschide raised his hand first, then spent a half hour in strenuous effort, alongside fifteen other students, on a strange form, one that seemed more like a collection of cryptographic codes than an intelligence test. Once they finished, the celebrated scholar himself collected the papers and retreated into a small side room. He returned after a few minutes, so pale that the decorative hairstyle of his lips and cheeks shone even brighter in its hazel curls. *Qui est Monsieur Nicolas Vaschide?* he asked in a trembling voice. *C'est moi*, the young man stood, surprised. *Venez*. Face-to-face at the little table in the side room, Binet revealed, looking Vaschide in the eyes, that he had seen in his completely unusual answers the signs of an oneiromancer. One of exceptional talent. While the scholar perorated in exclamations and superlatives, showing him in various places on the questionnaire how the young man had exploded the usual expectations for a normal intelligence, breaking through the parameters toward something no longer connected to understanding or to rationality, but to a kind of levitation of the mind above itself, Vaschide could already see Paris, the only place on Earth where you could reach *orama*. And truly, Binet, enthusiastically grabbing the student by both his hands, explained that he would award him a Hilel grant to work with him in Paris for two years at the Physiological Psychology Laboratory within the École des Hautes Études in the Sorbonne. The very next summer, 1895, Vaschide moved to Rue Saint-Denis. Wandering the long Parisian boulevards, between rows of haunting five-story buildings shadowed by gigantic, pale plane trees, he experienced a completely different kind of loneliness in those sunny days than he had been accustomed to feel. He was so alone that his body did not cast a shadow. He only visited Binet—once every few days, and for never less than six or seven hours. They wrote together, in a kind of communion of ideas, a few papers so strange that they were never presented to the scientific community: "La logique morbide," "Les hallucinations télépathiques," and, above all, the terrible "Essai sur la psycho-physiologie des monstres humains." Binet introduced him, that autumn (after having expounded, in front of a grave jury with masked faces, on the young Romanian's great talent for dreaming), to the obscure fraternity of Oneiromancers, only a few years old, which included important people from various domains who wished to become explorers in the realm of dreams. The model for the society was the famous group of poets the Hydropathes, founded a decade earlier, whose members had included Jules Laforgue, Charles Cros, Rollinat, and other Symbolist funambulists.

The young scholar's trial by fire was the same as for every initiate: Under the foundations of the Sorbonne, there was a compartment occupied almost entirely by a single basin of tepid water. The one being tested would have to sleep inside the basin, standing up, with his feet against the cistern's bottom and only his head, from the nostrils up, above the water. Around him, floating on the placid surface, five oneiromancers would lay their bodies like daisy petals, their heads as close as possible to the head of the central dreamer. They would all be naked and all asleep, drifting slightly on top of the rocking liquid in the deep darkness. The next morning, all six of them would write down their dreams from the preceding night. The candidate was admitted if at least half of their dreams were the same: their commonality signaled the dreamer's talent and his power to transmit his oneiric experience. Nicolae, who to those foreigners was known as Nicolas, agreed to be the center and stalk of this aquatic flower. Of course, he found it hard to fall asleep standing up, aided only by his total sensory deprivation. The five, who entered the chamber one by one, in the dark, did not know each other. Soon, perhaps as a result of long experience, they all fell asleep. There was, at first, only the sound of their breathing, filtered through the beards and mustaches found on all the personages of that time; eventually not even that sound was heard. Vaschide visualized his brain, as though the rest of his body had dissolved into the water, and around him he saw five other brains, open like lotus petals in the middle of the pool. He closed his eyes and fell asleep; thus, he did not see the bands of golden light, timid and retractable like the horns of a snail, that extended from his mind toward the surrounding minds, shining in the night like the tips of a crown. No one saw them, in fact, because the domed chamber had been hermetically sealed from the outside.

The next morning, all the oneiromancers, upon separate questioning, recounted the same dream. Vaschide became the preeminent member of the group, which included about two hundred men from all levels of society. As a result of the deep-rooted chauvinism of that time, women, considered to be hybrids of children and adults, were not admitted. This was a shame, because the Romanian scholar believed more in the feminine soul of oneiric states and wanted to experiment with women, as many women and as many kinds of women as possible. His catastrophic fall from grace in the oneiromancer group and his return to Bucharest came, more than anything, as a result of this *hybris*.

And more than anything because of Chloe. With her first words of introduction to those she did not know, Florabela never forgot to allude to the French blood that ran in her veins. The more familiar she became with someone, the more that person was given the honor of details about her great-grandmother Chloe, about her fiery red locks like Botticelli's Venus, about the constellations of freckles that covered every little part of her body, about her fabulous appetite for food, about her affair with a marquis, and her tragic death, a precursor of Isadora Duncan's: at an aeronautical festival, her mane of hair became tangled in the wicker basket of a hot-air balloon, which picked her up and bore her through the clouds, watched by the spectators' terrified eyes, without the navigator having the slightest idea what ballast he was carrying. The balloon rose into the stratosphere, and on landing, Chloe's body shattered into translucid, frost-covered splinters like an enormous, frozen doll.

But at the time that Nicolae was pursuing his experiments in his Parisian cell, the red-haired woman was only one of the hundreds of prostitutes who held up the walls in the area around the Saint-Denis gate, girls of every nation, color, and specialization, from nymphs of antic marble to hideous dwarfs, from (sometimes literally) impenetrable Chinese and Javanese women to grotesquely painted old ladies, the skin around their throats hanging like a turkey's caruncles, from fake women of double utility to angelic teenagers with short skirts and ribbons in their hair that a loving mother brushed. Through the churning crowd of perfumes, bared breasts, and somber men feeling up the goods before purchase by the urine-like light of the streetlamps, the dream researcher passed in search of the perfect prey, a sexual but also psychic prey, because (an amazing, counterintuitive, and in any case scandalous fact) each whore—even the most infested and downtrodden, who never opened her mouth without screaming obscenities, and who accepted seven or eight men's liquids, night after night, all her orifices reddened and tumescent from use and abuse—possessed beneath her skull a brain indistinguishable from Volta's, or that of Flammarion, Immanuel Kant, or Leibniz, and through it she had access to logical space, to the crystal sphere of fixed stars, to the knowledge of good and evil only possessed by the archangels. Up from their flesh chafed by males and females, full of bruises and excoriations, up from their green cadavers, in the unhealthy light of gas lamps, up from the hell of their urogenital space, a thin stem ascended through the vertebral tube, to open under the cupola of their cranium, as the purest, most diaphanous, most virginal, and most fragile dandelion globe: the mystic circle of the mind. Vaschide did not find the minds of thinkers, mathematicians, or scholars interesting; he preferred rather those of ruined women, of the daughters of pleasure, because diamonds are best revealed when placed against black felt and paradise when lit by the flames of hell.

Every night, he chose a woman; every night, together with her, they sampled a new form of pleasure. Although the possibilities of mating our bodies seem stereotypical and meager, pleasure jets in a thousand different ways through the mind's inexhaustible thirst for bliss. Sex between the thighs, sex between the buttocks, and in the warm, damp mouth, its tongue more erotic than labia, are only the readily cartographed foundation of the edifice of carnal love. But the center of pleasure is in the brain, and this is where the dark and burning mole maze begins, as Irina revealed to me through the stories she would whisper in my ear, raspy and gasping, while our hands touched our obscene and delicate sexes, sometimes our own, sometimes the other's; and as revealed to Vaschide, eighty years earlier, by the hundreds of women who passed through his bed during his Parisian sojourn. He learned that there is an intelligence of the sex, just as amazing as that of the brain; that just as the brain overflows with desire, sex radiates divine wisdom. The most desired and sought-after street women were not the great beauties, many of whom were frigid, but the scholars of pleasure, the thinkers of passion, the poets of bliss. More than any of them, Chloe had an irreducible and miraculous genius for sexual mating. She didn't do anything special, different, or perverse, she was, rather, well behaved and timid in bed, like a warm, good wife. So why were the men worn out at dawn, why did they need the rest of the day to recover? Why did they look for her, with glassy eyes, every night thereafter? Why did one sonnet leave you cold, while another, written by a great poet, following the same rules of prosody, and also using words, shake you to your depths?

Vaschide regarded sex as a portal leading to the true palace that was the brain, as though the vaginal tunnel, like all others, led to the depths within this crystal palace. His night, with an unknown woman lying in bed with him, only began after the wrestling and penetration had ended, when quiet fell over the room, barely disturbed by the restless noises from the streets. Then the two animals who had wildly and tenderly melded together closed their eyes, and at almost the same time, they lost the world. For two years, Vaschide fell asleep holding hands with a strange woman, weaving his fingers with hers as though she were a sweetheart fiancée he had known since childhood.

He slept and dreamed. He dreamed their dreams—as though he had rolled a banknote into a tube and snorted lines of cocaine—each one a different hue, consistency, and texture, like the thirty colored pencils in a child's kit. The dreams Kyrgyz, Hottentot, Uruguayan, and Arab women dreamed. The dreams of lesbians and of brilliant students who practiced prostitution for pleasure and perversity. The dreams of cabaret singers, of Gypsy beggars, of fifteen-year-olds and gray-haired women who embraced more sweetly than nubile girls. Each woman constituted in her daily life her own climate, a world as ripe and juicy as a fig, with her sisters and lovers and children and parents and money and things. But each was herself only in her dreams. There, no man reached, there they lived alone with their deep privacy, the pleasure of those who, in lazy afternoons, naked and sprawled across their beds, gave themselves, alone and with eyes closed, pleasure. Nicolae let himself be enveloped, night after night, in the golden plaits of their visions, in a golden web of spider thread, connected to their captive mind, connected to their insatiable mind. In this way, he created, among the brains with which he came into contact, an underground city, an ant or termite hill with spherical chambers linked through long, airy tunnels. In the center was his skull, as the master of dreams, around which ran hundreds of dreaming crania. He wandered through his great castle for nights on end, reaching distant spheres, like caves filled with precious stones; he visited them one by one, each frightening bordello and each ecstatic torture chamber. He explored, like a wine taster, the *somnium* dream as well as the *phantasma, visum,* and *oneiros,* but he spent the longest time in those sent by evil angels and benign demons: *admonitio* and *chrematismos.* The creature, tall and strange, wrapped in his robe, glided like the ancient king Tlá through the subterranean labyrinth of his nocturnal life. He opened doors that all gave onto circular rooms, he ascended and descended stairs in gigantic, marble dungeons, he enjoyed all the goods of his oneiric temple. Only one of the rooms was he not permitted to enter, because he knew that there, closed inside a cask with steel staves and bound in chains as thick as his hand, a frightening monster awaited him. Because there is no castle without a forbidden room, there where dwells the most unbearable object in the cosmos: the truth.

For two years, Vaschide experimented happily, in his monastic cell, with sexual pleasures and dreams, so closely related as they were. But until he met Chloe, he could fulfill neither his experiments nor his destiny. Many times he cursed the day (November 19) when he met her, but more often he gave thanks to heaven, because through her he reached the supreme dream, *orama.* The woman seemed at first ordinary to him, like all the others, aside from her special, red-haired smell, which surprised him and made him prefer her over all the other whores holding up the wall. Chloe was as massive as a brass statue, as her daughter and granddaughter and great-granddaughter would also be. When she lay down on the bed, the boards under the mattress moaned, and the tall and melancholic man felt his power ebb away. He lay next to her and embraced her like all the others, but his sex remained as soft and small as a worm, and no mental effort, no wild image, no touch from his hand or the woman's was able to wake it. He kept to kissing her, wrapped in the wire locks of the first woman to ever leave him powerless, and thus, with their lips combined and their long eyelashes interlaced, they both fell asleep, she melting into his chest, he lowering his head, far behind him, into the mirror of dreams.

In her dream, which became his during the year they slept every night beside each other, they held hands and walked across an enormous, circular room, vaster than outer space, more encompassing than the mind. The room had a dome above, at a dizzying height, and their bare feet (the two of them were completely naked) padded, barely audibly, against translucent stone tiles. Behind them, outlined in chalk, their glowing footprints were slowly reabsorbed into the squares of two colors, like a chessboard. In the gigantic space of the hall there were people scattered about, small as a population of mirmicoides, people of every type, women and men, old and young, who, as still as statues, all faced the same direction. It was the same direction they were moving in, toward the hall's sacred center. Yet as the embracing couple passed them, the people regarded the pair with an enigmatic expression, a shadowy smile, as though the revelation waiting for them in the center could still be avoided. But Chloe and Nicolae continued, attracted like moths to a flame, through the crowd that increased in number as they approached the target. The air, too, seemed to thicken, to gain a consistency, the muted whistle and alkaline taste of a storm wind. Their advance, over the course of hundreds of dreams spent under that dome, larger than the dome of heaven, encountering herds of people in strange clothes from bygone eras, clawing their way through the crowds of immobile bodies, knocking them over in the end, as the crowd became denser. Over the course of the many dreams that melted into a single one, that became so haunting and concrete that Vaschide instantly forgot, that evening on meeting Chloe, all he had done during the day—the shopping, reading, and studying, working in the lab, walking down Rue Mouffetard and Rue Morgue—as though his daily life were a disappointing line of necrotic dreams. Chloe's stomach began to expand, slowly, as though a magic fruit were growing inside. Although he had never been able to penetrate her, Nicolae had somehow inseminated her, because the large naked redhead became, with each night that passed, heavier, more luminous, her stomach fuller, her gait more rocking, the impressions of her feet on the cool tile became wider and traced in a misty dew that quickly evaporated. When, after almost three hundred nights of progress through the circular hall, of struggle with the center-pointing crowd, the two of them broke into the front row of visitors, Chloe's time had come.

In the center of the hall was a hospital bed with a white metal frame. On top of a sheet tucked firmly under the mattress was a brown, rubber mat, covering three-quarters of the bed. A child of about five years was lying with his head on the pillow on this bed much too large for him. He was not asleep. He looked at his fingers from time to time, he looked around him, he played with the buttons on his pajamas printed with zebras and elephants. He didn't seem to see the people who had halted some twenty meters from the bed, as though around him there were a boundary no one could cross. Vaschide, at least, felt this through all his body. The air beyond the unseen circle turned even denser, it transformed into a suffocating gelatin, and it cried out inaudibly like a bat or a cetacean in the depths of the sea. It repulsed you elastically like the identical pole of a magnet. Hundreds, thousands of gazes passed through it, however, from all sides, the barrier invested the central stage with an unbearable tension.

In the last dream, toward spring, the circle of spectators had been unexpectedly broken by a naked, pregnant woman, who, abruptly separating from her tall and saturnine husband, walked through the empty space and came to the bed. The child saw her immediately, and, betraying no surprise, he sat up on the brown mat. The woman sat next to him, on the edge of the bed, looking intensely, with motherly love, into his black, dreaming eyes. There on the bed, a girl emerged from her stomach, clean and pink, with her eyes open like a living doll, and she rose into the air above them, tethered only by her umbilical cord, like a balloon filled with gas lighter than air. Vaschide looked around himself in amazement and saw the immense crowd give a shout of victory and utter happiness, their eyes full of tears. The girl levitated, moving her gentle limbs in the amber space like an infant in the ocean, swimming without being taught, like a supple and agile seal. The boy grabbed the cord connected between the mother's thighs, where no drop of blood flowed, and he moved the girl like a kite, raising and lowering her over the heads of the crowd. Finally, he leaned down and he cut the cord, with shining teeth sharper than you would have thought, revealing, like in a piece of insulated cable, the two arteries and single vein, whose ends poked out of the wet skin wrapper. Then he released the girl; she rose and rose toward the apex of the dome, until she melted into the amber mist of the heights. The totemic woman and the child embraced, pressing their cheeks together and looking up at the girl, and then, when she was no longer visible, they stayed like that for a time, like a statue of maternity or perhaps like a Pietà, covered in the snowfall of thousands of blue, green, and brown gazes, until Vaschide decided to cross into that living space of quiet moaning, the psychic space of obsessions and phobias, to take his woman home. He threw himself toward the hospital bed in the middle of the hall, as though he was leaping from an airplane without a parachute and without hope of reaching the ground unharmed. The musty, dense air scraped against his skin, it rippled against his ribs, it fluttered behind him like the palpitating plates of a stegosaurus, his gaze was ground against his cornea and turned back inside his ocular globes, blotting his retinas. But the man pushed forward through the emotional current, as though he was confronting a depression, as though he dared defy hallucinations without the help of medication, like jumping from one trapeze to another without a net, twisting and tumbling virtuosically in the air. When he reached them, he desperately clasped the metal frame near the child's feet, like a drowning man, and he tried to embrace Chloe around her waist. But the red-haired woman had emptied herself of her own substance, as though, like insects, the baby had occupied her entire body and emerged through a longitudinal split in Chloe's skin, pushing her head out of the woman's head, her body from her body, her legs from her legs, her arms from her arms, leaving behind her a nude exuvia, a lifeless simulacrum, a translucid shell meant to be shredded and scattered in the wind. Chloe was now as motionless and empty inside as a sex doll. And yet only now, much too late, her image powerfully excited the man, who finally, finally, felt his sex erect, stronger and harder and more rigid than ever. Since this had never been possible around Chloe, and as he knew already that an erection always accompanies a dream, whatever its content, Nicolae knew that he was in the other realm, and he decided that it was time to wake up. He leaned on the bed frame and gently kissed the inflatable doll, and under the wondering-enchanted eyes of the boy, he slapped himself in the face, he hit his head against the frame, he threw himself to the floor and writhed, rolling around and hitting himself without mercy, until he finally opened his eyes, at dawn, in his apartment on Rue Saint-Denis. Chloe was not beside him, and she would never be again.

Vaschide did not attempt to find her: literally, the woman had gone out of his mind. He also abandoned his dream experiments—the geometrical location where sex allies with the brain, taking the heart off the chessboard—because he had been in the grotto where the siren swam. He felt he had reached the deepest room in his interior palace and had contemplated his own truth in the face of the girl who rose toward the sky. After this unexpected and unhoped-for daughter, produced by the milks of his dream, Vaschide wandered, utterly ruined, for the rest of the time he was given to live. He stayed another year in Paris, alone and completely dedicated to his scientific works. He had learned, and he demonstrated in eighty papers written in fear, that dreams were not images but overwhelming emotions; that ungoverned emotions, without a face, often without a name, dress themselves in the mantle of visual space, in scenes and characters, in order to dance their nuptial dances: hideous, charming, perverse, and, in the end, murderous dances. Thus the heart, having been banished from the center of the world, in between the sex and brain, and thrown into the garbage like a worn-out romantic rag, returned to the psychodrama as its true motor, hidden under the chessboard, a powerful magnet that pulled the iron filings into bent, tensioned lines of force.

But what was important was the daughter. Before he found her, he had already given her a name: Alesia. First, he searched for her in the Paris orphanages, where nuns took care of hundreds of futureless girls, shepherding them like herds of aphids. Next, he tried to find her in the parks, where groundskeepers pushed large bins down the paths. Soon the gendarmes were called on the maniacal man, tall, thin, and shadowy, who peered into every pram and approached the benches where, in full view of the world, corpulent nannies fed infants from their breasts. He was arrested, interrogated, and released. The oneiromancers—who already considered him a dissident because femininity and dream, so closely intertwined in the mind of the Romanian scholar, were heresy for them—became, once they heard about the arrest, overtly hostile to Vaschide. His grant renewal was refused and any chance of being hired in a clinic in France became so slim as to disappear. After four years in Paris, the most fruitful of his life, the master of dreams was forced to return to his country. He corresponded with Binet until the end of his short life, concluded brusquely and bizarrely in 1907, at the age of thirty-two. The fruit of these close collaborations was the Buzău scholar's essential works: *Essay on the Psychology of the Hands*, *The Psychology of Attention*, and, above all, *Sleep and Dreams*, the cathedral of his citadel, which made him, after Freud's *The Interpretation of Dreams*, published a decade before, a renowned pioneer in oneiric cartography.

Back in Bucharest, Vaschide opened his eyes to the unique architecture of this city that could not exist in reality. He became excited by the correspondences between the ruins of the city and those that populated his own dreams. He was fascinated by the broken windows of its industrial halls, the beguiling stucco ornaments hanging off its cornices, and balconies like a maimed people lifting their stumps in protest toward the sky; he was astonished by the blind walls: rising the houses' full height, barely held together by planks and rusty metal cross bracing. He developed the habit of wandering through the city, melting under the summer heat, of crisscrossing the outskirts, toward which noisy horses pulled the trams, to discover the sad ornamentation of the periphery: a pitch-black water tower standing against the twilight, an old factory worn down to the bone by clouds that penetrated its intestines, a seltzer shop that packed glass bottles with a yellow, sulfurous, and amnesiac gas. He realized he could enter any house, and, moreover, he could go from house to house through more or less negligently disguised doors and tunnels. Bucharest was a plaster sponge, a coral reef, a place unlike any other on this earth.

Every evening he came home with another image in his mind, just as in Paris he had come home with a woman. His memory captured: yellow, bony dogs sneaking around trash heaps, pigeons with human eyes, the sun glinting on the tramlines, gusts of hot wind lifting and scattering leaves, the despair in the eyes of humble clerks he ran into on empty streets. Countless times, walking the streets of distant neighborhoods, he asked himself if he were actually awake, and, above all, what it could mean to be awake in such a city.

One afternoon there was a sun-shower, and afterward a rainbow, barely noticeable and yet brilliant, arched over the south end of the city. Vaschide walked directly toward it. If he sometimes lost it behind a house with falling plaster, he found it again at the end of a sonorous and empty street. When he finally arrived under the seven-colored Conestoga, the master of dreams saw, without surprise, that the curve of painted air bent over an unusual hill, covered with grass the heat of summer had browned. The rainbow was like a halo emanating from an enlightened mind, like a diadem of shining opals on the forehead of an antic beauty. Vaschide was in Ferentari, a neighborhood populated by gangs and clans in constant conflict. Every man, Gypsy or Romanian, carried a knife at his waist, its foot-long blade glinting in the sun. The women let their braids hang over the balustrades of their plant-filled balconies. They bore naked infants, as animal as the puppies in their houses, on their breasts.

The green hill at the end of the group of houses could have been a water basin or even the arched roof of a large cottage. Or only a mound of dirt the wind had heaped over a demolished house or a few bones. Vaschide knew, however, that it was a skull. He had seen it his first night at the Sorbonne, when he floated, naked and vertical, in the subterranean cistern, with only his cranium above the water. That night he had had a dream which, through obscure channels, and outside of any interference that human knowledge could explain, he transmitted entirely, down to the smallest details, to the five oneiromancers floating on their backs around him. In the dream, he walked through a large, ruined city. At one end of it rose a hill surrounded by a rainbow. In the dream, Vaschide approached the great grass dome and climbed to the top, entering the colored air of the surrounding halo. From there he called to people, workers with unusual tools in their hands, who came from all sides and began to excavate the hill, removing about a half meter of earth, still wet from that day's rain. Shortly, a skull was revealed, a pale swelling of polished bone. It looked like the unearthed carapace of a fossilized turtle, but along its curved expanse the suture lines between the bones were clearly visible. The frontal, temporal, parietal, and occipital bones were numbered, like the crania studied in laboratories and used for teaching. The powerful arcades at the base of the enormous skull showed that the cranium was male. Vaschide had been able to measure it in the dream, climbing from the occiput to the pommel. It was fifteen steps to the top, the place named fontanelle, and another fifteen to the forehead that dropped like a bone wall. He turned back to the top of the head, under the splendid rainbow, and there he heard the whistling. It was a kind of continuous mechanical whirring, and it was getting louder. It came from somewhere below, louder and louder. Soon it was imposing and monstrous like the roar of a great waterfall, pulsing more feverishly, like a voice that orders you to throw yourself into the abyss. Nicolae melted into this howl, this current of terror that picked him up, twisting him like a tornado, and soon the man was also shouting, but not just with his larynx, tongue, and teeth, his mouth wide open and trained at the sky, but with every organ of his body dissolved in fear and screaming. "Help!" he tried to shout, melted into the liquid gold that rose from the great fontanelle toward the already bloody sky, but he could only manage to whimper this word, as he woke to feel the dark, cold water.

And now, in the real Bucharest, over which the page of the century had recently turned, the scholar heard the dull sound beneath the earth again. As though a large, heavy animal were snarling there, nested in for a long sleep. The entire hill was vibrating from this as yet gentle whirring, powerful enough to shake two or three minuscule parachutes off the dandelions on the hill, which took flight toward the run-down neighborhood. Even the rainbow was vibrating enough to blur its colored bands. Vaschide climbed back down the hill and went home, but he returned the following night with a shovel, and on the opposite side from the darkened houses, he began to excavate the base of the hill. It took two full nights of digging under Ursa Major and Cassiopeia, limpid among the thousands of stars, to reach the eye socket. Dogs howled, lifting only their heads from their beds, yellow dogs with human eyes, dogs of the city—you saw them everywhere, pawing through the trash, crushed under cart wheels and tossed to the side of the road, or begging beside restaurant tables. The right eye socket was sunk deep into the earth and teemed with worms. The scholar freed it from the ground completely, and toward the dawn of the second night, he took shelter in its cavity, where, had he been a little shorter, he could have stood up. The bone was smooth and soft to the touch. Underneath, between the two sockets, there was the half-revealed vomer bone. The mandibula would be under the earth, and, like the vertebrae of the neck and the entire gigantic skeleton that extended a few dozen meters toward the depths of the planet, would never be unearthed. But Vaschide already saw the entire skeleton in his mind's eye and already knew that around the cervical vertebrae was a woven necklace of the purest copper: a torus-shaped solenoid, the source of the vibrations and dull noises audible from without. There, sat within the egg-shaped cavity of the orbital bone, the scholar hesitated. He weighed for a few minutes the advantages of penetrating the cranium immediately against those of a preparatory excavation. The temptation was great, but he controlled his compulsions. For two weeks, under the pretext of an archaeological investigation, the man strove, just as he had in the dream below the Sorbonne, to remove the half meter of earth that covered the cranium. The neighborhood workers, railwaymen, and thieves helped him, baited by Vaschide's promise of Technicolor dreams, the like of which no one from their families had ever had. "The person buried here lived in the time of giants," he told them. "Everything they wanted, they received in their dreams." It didn't take long before the numbered cranium in Ferentari, under the name of "Vaschide's Hall," became a city playground, surrounded by a fair with slides and shooting galleries, Gypsies with crystal balls, and strongmen breaking chains with their teeth. Bad țuica and new and old wine flowed like water in the surrounding bars. In a ring a few meters wide around the skull, there were beds, simple beds, brought from the hospices and lazarettos, full of bedbugs and covered in dubious sheets, but which sold for exorbitant prices to those who wanted to spend a night there, under the stars, near the enormous head. It absorbed their dreams, who knows how, and paraded them across the night sky in pastels, in raw, faded, or obscene colors, or just in sepia, or in black and white, as though in the top of the skull, on the fontanelle, there were a projection lens like those used in the lonely lighthouses on shoreline cliffs. Gape-mouthed crowds watched the panorama on the sky, licking their lips at the cursed dreams, shuddering at the nightmares, and falling in love with landscapes from the world of fairy tales.

But Vaschide himself, the duly documented owner of the land where the wonder sat, was not tempted by the strange cinema. He walked around the skull each night, tripping over drunks lying across the ground, trying to steel himself for the great penetration. In the end, he made up his mind. One Sunday night, while the fair was deeply asleep, he stole into the eye socket with a chisel and a lamp, and he began to crack the bone where a gap, a handspan wide, had always been, where the optic nerve entered the cranium. After two hours of sustained work, he reached light. First an intense, shining point, then a kind of fireball, and finally, after more hammer blows against the beveled chisel, an entrance filled with flame as bright as the sun at the height of the sky, through which the dreamer entered, his heart thumping against his chest.

Although it burned, the light was cold. It filled the large cavity where once slept a brain that must have weighed as much as an elephant. Now the walls were bare and smooth, yet bore some traces of the former cerebral lobes. It looked like a large, long hall, with a yellow dome and flattened floor. Vaschide, peering through his clenched eyes, needed some time before he saw colors and details inside the large cranium. Soon, the light, or the frozen fire, didn't seem as strong, and with greater and greater surprise, he began to perceive what seemed at first to be a mound rising in the center of the bone floor. He saw that the sphenoid bone, in the middle of the cranial base, was colored like a tropical butterfly, while all the rest of the bone was pale. The great wings of the sphenoid were electric blue, the small wings were an emerald green which, from a different angle, morphed into violet. The body of the butterfly, perhaps four meters long, was dark scarlet, as much as was visible under the girl's body. And the dorsal fringe, the scaphoid and pterygoid fossae, as well as the hamulus and rostrum, were a pale, sad yellow, almost the color of the inside of an orange peel. No more wonderful butterfly ever spread its wings under the glass of an insect collection. But the fantastic sphenoid did not fly: its fate, like that of Atlas, was to hold the sphere of the world on its back, that sphere that held everything: our incomprehensible brain, with its Gödelian drama.

Curled up along the spine of the great butterfly was a naked girl, about four years old. The light was so powerful that her body appeared semitransparent, as though chiseled from marble. Through her skin and interior flesh, her delicate bones and her intestinal peristalsis were visible. The girl was asleep and, curled up in this way, she was, without a doubt, the most beautiful creature in the world. She could be no one other than Alesia. Vaschide approached and looked at her, moving a few locks of red hair to one side. He was happy to see the girl looked like him. He wrapped her in a butterfly wing and carried her toward the orbital gap. He passed into the other realm, careful not to wake her. He wandered with her in his arms until he found himself at the station for the horse-drawn trams, which didn't start running until five in the morning. He rode to the end of the line at Saint Gheorghe, and he carried her up the stairs to his one-room apartment. There, he took care of Alesia for all of the six years still remaining in his life.

From then on, the regulars of the vast empty lot at Saint Gheorghe, with its church, horse-drawn trams, and group of already ruined houses, were treated to the daily spectacle of a very tall man, dressed in black, with austere features and intense eyes, who walked the streets hand in hand with a little girl. She was dressed like a fairy, with ribbons in her soft, silky hair, with delicate crêpe de Chine dresses and lacquered boots on her feet. If he seemed to come from a black-and-white photograph, she was from a hand-painted photo, distant and sad. The girl's supreme beauty lit up the horrible, sunken world around her.

Vaschide was happy, for the first time in his strange life. The girl loved him, spent a lot of her time at home sitting on his lap, the two of them tall and straight like statues of Abraham Lincoln. At night they dreamed together, temple to temple, tapping their dreams toward each other the way you might blow soap bubbles. He saved her from atrocious circumstances, she put crowns on his head. Many times the scholar closed his eyes and prayed, "Lord, please make these moments last forever! I don't need anything else in life. Make it so nothing changes, so that every day is the same as today, with every shadow, every cloud, and every one of Alesia's giggles the same, over and over . . ." But one night, in the middle of a dream where a tiger tore out his throat, he started to spit blood. The line of blood that ran over the pillow from the corner of his mouth was shaped like a long finger, pointing at the girl. He moved to a lazaretto on Saint Vineri, where Alesia, who would turn six that autumn, slept in the next bed. Vaschide's neighbor on the other side was a hunchback. He left the hospital after three weeks, with the recommendation that he travel. Hand in hand with the girl, riding trains and stagecoaches and ox-drawn carts, they crisscrossed that Italy of rosy marble. They walked under domes with allegorical frescoes, they toured Tuscan villas, they regarded the transparency of the sea beside Capri. Then they embarked in a large ship that sailed for weeks to Valparaiso and they disembarked on the enigmatic South American earth. Later they reached the Orient, at Petra, with its basilicas carved into pink cliffs. They returned to Europe after two years, and the continent seemed foreign. In all this time, while the girl grew, innocent and illiterate but unbearably beautiful, Vaschide continued to write studies about the mechanisms of sleep and dreams. He felt more and more exhausted, weariness became his only god, to whom he bowed, ever more deeply, each day that passed. Returning to Bucharest (back to the same one-room apartment, which they now realized was terribly meager, they barely had room to move past each other), the ill man and the little miss resumed their daily walks.

On October 4, 1907, Vaschide disappeared from the world, fallen into the chasm of his last dream. Alesia woke up alone, for the first time since she had fallen asleep on the great sphenoid bone. She knew what had happened, however, because her father's final dream had been, like all the others, received by her sensors, as delicate as the bushy antennae of the butterflies of the night.

The pheromones of the dream had opened a fantastical and grand landscape in her mind. It was a cavern larger than could be described, dug into yellow rock. The mouths of three tunnels opened here, like trachea. Their height must have been hundreds of meters. Her father, as minuscule as a termite, walked over the floor of the cavern, constantly looking at the three mouths that invaginated, organically, into the rock face.

He stopped in front of them, as insignificant as a speck of dust; he hesitated, and in the end he chose the left-hand passage. He walked for many lifetimes, always descending, while it became darker and darker, until a desolate dusk erased everything. Far away in front of him, monstrous shadows were visible. The black mite was moving toward those unforgiving idols, stepping almost imperceptibly through the great tunnel. With an effort of will, Alesia moved toward him, she was able to turn the axis of the dream and to see his face up close. Vaschide was crying. The girl saw his face deformed by his tears. And he seemed to see her and to smile through the tears, like a sun-shower. Then he melted into the dense amber of that ending.

The police searched for the scholar for months, but his disappearance remained, as it does today, a mystery. His parents, the stalwart State and Eufrosina, now gray-haired and resigned, held a kind of memorial service at Buzău, without a priest but with the mayor and every last notable person in the city. The red-haired girl immediately transformed the sorry provincial market town into a city of lights, as though everything were lit up by the color of her hair. She stayed there, raised by her grandparents, until, without the father ever being known, she gave birth to Ortansa. And Ortansa became a young woman twice as splendid as her mother. Time passed as fast as a hurricane.

And now, Irina and I were speaking quietly, over coffee and cookies, with Florabela, the one twice as ravishing as Ortansa. Vaschide's story shed light in an unusual way on my own searching, it gave my own nocturnal lives meaning and substance. We left after a few hours, with the image of the shrine still in our minds: a wall with dozens of photos of a very tall, very grave man, one who would seem like a stranger wherever he was, hand in hand with a girl. When we reached the front of the block, Florabela shouted a goodbye down to us from her open window, and it was as though a fantastically decorated Astarte was waving from the height of two stories. In an unspoken understanding, we didn't go back toward the tramline, but in an oblique direction toward the distant Ferentari. We changed buses several times in the deep, starry night that lay over Bucharest, and, in the end, we found the place. It was no longer at the edge of the city. Beyond the hill, hundreds of workers' blocks had been constructed, pathetic chicken coops inhabited by poor and unhappy people. And they were designed as ruins, with their reeking trash chutes, shriveled facades, and crooked, rusty balconies amplifying the city's hideousness. Surrounded by blocks with numbered entrances and beat-up Dacias parked wherever, the skull of the giant buried vertically in the earth had been covered with dirt and grass again. We climbed to the top, under the autumn constellations, and we sat down on the crest, from where the dreams of those sleeping around it had once been projected onto the sky. We stayed there, Irina and I, equally alone, equally without destiny, waiting for our lives to end. The great escape seemed to us, in those moments, a dream like any other. After a long time, we stood up to catch the last tram, and after an exasperatingly long series of stops and changes, we reached my house, embracing not from passion but from cold. We went to bed and fell asleep immediately, hoping we would never wake up.

38

Of all the ultrabanal stories of my life, none scared me as much as my marriage. Maybe because it is the only one that didn't have to exist, that had nothing to do with my plans for my life. I never wanted to get married, and yet I was impelled toward marriage by a force that always felt strange and hostile. "Young man"—Borcescu's nasal voice was always in my ear, even at the People's Council on Olari, one minus-twenty-degree morning, when the registrar, wearing the flag across her chest, told us that the state protected the family—"Young man, you know what it's like to be married? I'll tell you, because I know from experience: it's worse than being hanged! Not *much* worse, but a little . . ." But the principal was wrong, as I would discover in the fifteen months I lived with Ştefana, when I learned just how much worse than being hanged a marriage could be. As yet, on that December day with snow-covered streets, I adored the girl next to me, in her thin, lilac-pink two-piece suit, with heaps of flowers in her arms. When we came home, we scattered them in dozens of jars and waterglasses through the whole house, and for a few months the number of rooms in our boat-shaped house remained constant (exactly four), as though the flowers (we constantly bought more to replace those that wilted) were strong, flexible anchors that kept reality from going mad. Ştefana was short and a little chubby, energetic and attentive, the very picture of "a good girl": there was nothing out of the ordinary about her, she behaved correctly, she was always there, she filled the space where her body fluttered, moment to moment, like a flickering movie. She filled time in the same way: it started to flow normally for me, as it never had before, like the heartbeats of a tender, luminous creature. Evenings full of dreams and confessions followed in the minuscule kitchen over a glass of mulled wine, holding hands, looking each other in the eyes and telling each other stories we never dreamed we would ever tell, while outside a somber fog collected, and finally it was so dark we couldn't see anything but the gleaming of our eyes and the faceted glasses, sitting empty on the table. Then we went to bed, and the bed suddenly felt so good, it fit our bodies so well, the sheets sank so predictably beneath us, providing coolness and warmth at the same time . . . We made love in the simplest position, and this is why I don't really remember her body. It was the luminous banality of sex with someone who feels dear to you but whom you don't love passionately; it was as though we weren't having sex, weren't making love, just embracing, the way two good friends do when they meet again. Never, in my later erotic fantasies, did I excite myself by thinking of my nights with Ştefana—but I didn't regret them. We held each other, and it was for me deeply satisfying. The fact that, however long we spent tenderly embracing in bed, she never had an orgasm wasn't dissatisfying to me: penetration was no more important, in the happy part of our relationship, than interlacing our fingers or caressing a cheek, as two people do while facing the world together. We were together: this was the essence of my marriage, during the first three of four months. We left the house together each morning, we took trams in opposite directions: she toward downtown, I toward the end of Colentina. I came home earlier than she did and made us something to eat. Sundays we went to the piața at Obor, to argue with the farmers over a half kilo of plums or onions, and we came home with snowflakes in our hair. We smiled a lot, in fact we smiled so much at the start that a smile became my natural face: I was surprised to find myself smiling at the clerks at the bakery and the ticket-takers on the tram, and at every child in my classes. In the evenings, when I was reading at one end of the living room and she at the other, I would write her little notes and fold them into airplanes: I sent them through the air to land on her lap or at her feet or to bump into her, like a confused bird or a lazy bee, or to fly past her face, as a soft and wry surprise. She would unfold the plane and read the note, then smile and go back to reading . . . During this time, I abandoned all my searching: I had found it. The world existed, because she did. She radiated certainty; calm and benign intentions flowed from her like from a mountain spring. I was not in love, I was in something else, something deeper: I knew. I knew her. She was like a tabletop that could be nothing other than hard and shiny. She was like sleep: she could do nothing but arrive. She was there where I expected her to be, like the floor, like the air. Sometimes, when I came back from teaching, I took the 21 to Saint Gheorghe and got off at the end of the line, then went toward Universitate and came to her bookstore. I found her there, among books and clients, and when she saw me, her face gave off a smile like the blinding flash on a camera. I would stay with her until six, there among the shelves that rose to the ceiling, then we would go home together, on the tram again, I turned in my chair toward her behind me, quietly chatting the whole ride.

It wasn't just our house that lost its dimensions and transparency and hum, like a stopped propeller reveals its simple, unmoving structure: three shoulder blades welded together. My school also reabsorbed its virtualities, it solidified into a banal educational institution populated by children and teachers, generating its own meaning, moment by moment; a stupid and deceitful institution, yes, but not disturbing, as it had seemed to me before. Its reality—registers, grades, calling kids to the board, grabbing them by the hair, standing them up, their notebooks filled with calculations and formulas, lice in braids held with hair ties, packets of food that stained the white, paper textbook covers with oil—hardened into a clear form that left no room for crumbs, goo, or any kind of mess. Things were not in process anymore, and they didn't overstep the razor-sharp limit of words: the classroom was the classroom, blackboards were blackboards, windows were windows. Living was so simple. I went home inside a tram made of metal and glass, under clouds of steam, in a city of limestone, leaves, and wind. I had a smile on my face, the only immaterial, though precisely outlined, thing: as life is a certain disposition of the body, and as the sound of the Platonic lyre is, in its harmony, a certain disposition of the parts of the lyre, the smile only appears when everything is the way it should be. Happiness burns and transmutes with petrifying speed into its inverse, or maybe it is only an unstable amalgam of happiness-unhappiness; and joy, the luminous state of the soul, is the true substance from which reality is made. Nothing concrete and true can exist without it, just as sight does not exist separately from light.

I often looked at her from very close up, I would take her chin in my fingers and gently turn her head to see it from all angles. I was so pleased that she was concrete and real, like a cat, and not like a creature on the street or in my dreams. I touched her hair and I was filled with wonder at how it was wiry and soft at the same time, and that each strand, if you slid your fingers along it, had tiny irregularities and knots, like willow shoots or reeds. I would separate her lips with my index finger, and she would bite me slowly, docile and smiling, and then I would pass my finger over the little prongs of her teeth. I undressed her sometimes in front of the mirror, without feeling any kind of erotic pleasure, just amazed and happy that I was touching her warm skin, that I was sharing the house with this three-dimensional nude, with this being who carried her buttocks and navel and breasts and clavicles through the house, allowing me to touch them whenever I liked, to feel and forget and to feel anew her textures, dampness, aromas, harshness. We did the laundry together, with the antediluvian machine, I grating the cadaver-like cakes of soap, she mixing the bubbling soup of sheets and shirts and underpants and socks with a piece of wood, then we rinsed them in the blue water in the tub. We listened to music on the (also ancient) radio/record player, and sometimes we would put on an ebony disk of jazz, and we would sit together on the couch, hand in hand, moving our heads to the rhythm, looking out the window. This was life, forever unmoving under a shared smile, like photos under their transparent glaze, and life couldn't be any different, because if it were different, its name would have to change.

One morning, a sharp ray of springtime light woke me, penetrating like a blinding razor through the slats of the shutter. It was Sunday, and we woke up late on Sundays, after ten, and we only really woke up in the afternoon. I looked at the alarm clock: it was a bit before seven, it had been the first ray of light that fell over Maica Domnului, dampening my boat-shaped house in the frozen light of morning. Ştefana was not in the bed next to me, maybe she was in the bathroom. But after ten minutes she hadn't come back. I got out of bed and walked hesitatingly toward the kitchen. I saw her there and did not recognize her.

She stood at the window in a harsh light that eroded her outline and set her hair aflame. She looked out the window, completely immobile, her arms crossed. She was dressed, even though we never, on our only free day, got out of our pajamas before we ate. Still, like in a dream, I didn't realize at first that there was something unusual and strange in this lonely image of her without me and almost without the world around her, the way she was standing, unmoving, looking out of the window. Until then we had been a double body, floating in a shared, universal smile, and now, facing the world, she was grave and immobile. "Morning," I said, and she whipped around, and again I didn't recognize her. "What the hell, what's going on?" a voice rose, just for a moment, and almost inaudible, within me. It was Ştefana's face, it was her neck, her shoulders, even her eyes, but it wasn't her. This irrational, absurd feeling impacted me powerfully when I looked at her, the old smile frozen on her lips, but I pushed it away. So what if this face I knew so well had fallen under a shadow from another world? It wasn't even sadness on her face, it wasn't aching or longing. It wasn't boredom, grogginess, fury, disappointment, disgust. It was something that I couldn't make out, that had never appeared before, and that changed her into another person. I couldn't have identified a particular detail, no clearly changed feature, but for a few moments, it was so clear that Ştefana wasn't herself that I was simply frightened and the hairs on my arms stood up. We looked at each other for a few moments without moving, like two creatures from different worlds who suddenly find themselves face-to-face, then we parted, and reality reformed around us.

It was nothing: an accident I'd already forgotten, an almost invisible crack in the clear glass of our common life. For a few weeks we went out again, holding hands, walking through spring scenes, we were part of the crowd at antiques fairs, we took a quiet getaway that made us feel light as feathers. We made love, at dusk, just as calmly and predictably as before. I enjoyed her warm and docile body so much that often I would hold back my orgasm, and we separated like two tired friends, lying next to each other on our backs in the window's blood-colored light. It was like going to work, like eating together: without ecstasy, contractions, or moans, but with the feeling that reality was more complete, the way you always feel when you do what you're supposed to. We had completed the hour reserved for making love, the way the lamp on the nightstand fulfills its shape in time and space. Then we got up slowly, so as not to disturb the other, it seemed; we took showers and put on our pajamas, and stayed that way all evening. Each time, after the hour of making love, I wrote a poem to her, but nothing publishable; just some words, sometimes just one, sometimes not even one, sometimes just a drawing on a half sheet torn from a notebook. She would read them and smile, like she did the paper airplanes. I would find them later in the bottom drawer of the nightstand on her side of the bed, transformed through skillful, origami-like folds into twenty or so paper demons that expanded and stuck their horns out when you blew in one end. They were all inflated, they all had black, huge faces drawn on them, like bees. They were crisscrossed with my sorry little improvised poems. I lined up the light and fragile demons on the windowsill, and there they still are today; I am looking at them now, while I'm writing: in the day they swallow the light, at night they spread it around them, polyhedral and transparent, like poppy petals in an arrangement of dry flowers.

But the almost invisible crack in the glass of water was not an optical illusion. It was there and it grew, in infinitesimal pops, revealing an irregular green down the fissuring glass. I will never forget the moment when, returning home from school through a miserable snowy rain in the most depressing of Aprils, I found her lying, curled up on the floor, in total darkness. I turned the light on and suddenly there she was, lying still on the mostly red Persian rug, like a large, dense fetus arranged on the placenta that fed it and bathed it in is folds. She lay there, as though she were paralyzed; only her one black eye, like a wounded animal, looked at me sideways, in a way I had never been looked at before by a human being. I spoke to her and she didn't answer, I turned her face up and she stayed inert, looking at me like a fox caught in a trap. I picked her up and put her on the bed. She tried to say something, but her tense throat only made these weak gurgles, and I was scared. I wanted to run to the clinic, to call a doctor, but her hand, which had been inert until that moment, clasped my wrist. She came back to herself slowly, over the course of about half an hour. She stood up without saying anything, she went into the bathroom, for a time that to me seemed endless, after which she went to the kitchen, where she sat looking out the window with her arms crossed. For the rest of the night we couldn't talk. I asked her to say something, to tell me what was going on, to explain what had happened and what we should do. Her face, which I knew so well, was now motionless, in profile at the window, as though it weren't a human face where interior shadows and lights played, the most expressive and attractive segment of our body, but an inert object, like a vase or an impersonal sculpture with white, empty eyes. After another half an hour, the psychic mist descended over the features of her face, which became, through a joint effort, Ştefana. She was herself again, without any memory of what had happened ("I must have been a little sick"), and without being able to understand the terror I went through. We sat and ate, then went to bed.

The normal periods of our shared life, as spring glided toward summer, were interrupted more and more often by dark bands, each one wider than the previous, more dramatic, more incomprehensible. Ştefana's body and life became a battlefield: something would grab her and whisk her away, like an eagle sticking its claws into her thorax. She began to miss work, and soon she didn't go at all. I would find her at home, sometimes quietly reading in the bed, without being able to explain the dark black mark on the wall, under which, scattered across the floor, were the remains of the flowerpot that had once been sitting nicely on the sill: shards, clods of dirt, crushed stalks and leaves, violet petals scattered everywhere. Who, if not her, could have thrown the pot at the wall with extraordinary fury, even if she wouldn't answer my questions, or did but with something evasive.

What was going on with the woman I lived with? Was she losing her mind? Was she entering a deep depression? Since she ignored me completely, I once dared, when she was lying in bed facing me, to say, "Ştefana, look at me, it's me, your friend. If you don't love me anymore, just tell me—at least then I'll know what's going on." She started to laugh, in a laugh that wasn't hers; it was cynical and raspy like a drunk's. "Is that what you're so fucking worried about?" she said, looking at me from the corner of her eye, a mean eye with something crazy inside, an unbearable eye.

It was harder and harder for her to emerge from these states; they didn't last an hour anymore, but days in a row. When she was doing well, I was happy and hopeful. But I always hoped the incomprehensible episode that had just ended would be the last. We went to a psychiatrist, an old, bored man at Hospital 9, but Ştefana never took the pills prescribed her by that slothful state employee. She threw them down the toilet, on a regular basis, as though they belonged there in the porcelain bowl, and they had their intended effect by dissolving into the underground sewers, curing the world of its endless insanity, and thereby illuminating Ştefana's tortured spirit.

One night I heard screams from somewhere in the house, somewhere nearby. I sat up: she wasn't next to me. I ran to the hall, but the screams were coming from the bathroom. Now I heard the shower. I turned on the light and tried to open the bathroom door, shouting at Ştefana, but the door was locked. She was screaming as loud as she could inside, echoing off the walls of the bathroom. "Open it, open the door!" I shouted, but since the screams didn't stop, I threw my shoulder against the pressboard panel, which eventually gave way.

She was in the bathtub, in the dark, her sopping wet pajamas stuck to her body. The water came up to her hips. She was holding the showerhead, spouting icy water, directly over her head. The water ran through her hair and over her shoulders and breasts, until it flowed into the equally icy water in the tub. She was screaming with her eyes closed, with bunches of hair covering her face, she was purple with cold and shaking like I had never seen anyone shake. Her clattering teeth sounded like clinking glasses. I don't know how I got her out of there, how I hauled her, water coursing off her clothes, to the bed, how I wrapped her in the winter quilt to warm her up. She lay there until morning, like an almost dead dove, alone with her agony, with her incomprehensible struggle.

But the next day she was fine and completely uninterested in what had happened. I could count on a few quiet days. I could enjoy the concreteness of my wife, her anatomy and physiology, the texture of her skin, the tension of her muscles, the atmosphere of familiarity and quiet that covered everything around her. I never tired of touching her, even if only with my sight, even if only with my hearing. I was amazed she had fingers, I would trace her knuckles with my fingers, slide across her nails, feel the vibrations of her fingerprints. I would touch the red, crinkly hair, held in a warm mist, under her arms, I would pull her ring up her finger to see the disintegrating skin beneath it that never saw the sun. This was what marriage meant to me: the happiness of having a second body, different than yours and therefore endlessly fascinating, and having a second spirit, serene, normal, quiet, with a smile that made you smile, without knowing it did and without intending to. When night came and the sheet folds made violent shadows in angles and crescents across the bed, we knelt on the mattress, facing each other, we undressed, and then I liked to put my hands on the damp under her breasts, to feel the pattern of her ribs, in the chiaroscuro of the blue evening light, to touch the hollow of her navel and her flat stomach, her buttocks, above which, on her curved back, rose a double column of muscles in relief under her skin. I liked to lay her onto her back and part her legs to see her dark flower, her petals dipped in tannin, damp and wrinkled, which I parted with my fingers, to let my gaze dive into her purple interior: the round orifice with jagged edges that gaped toward the walls of her peristaltic vagina. I gently pushed her buttocks apart to enjoy the reclusive star between them, rough to the touch and just as innocent as the sleepy flower in front. My palms would trace down her smooth, soft, and warm legs, I would caress her knees and all their little mobile stones, I would cup the muscles below them, her ankles and arched feet, then I would feel every toe, each bumpy nail, and the crusts and excrescences of their yellow calluses. I enjoyed Ştefana the way I enjoyed sunny days, starry nights, the grand illusion where we lived in our blessed sphere.

We entered into summer, the overwhelming Bucharest summer that instantly desiccates the city like a thermonuclear explosion. The scorching sun of July and August was enough to set the buildings on fire, to melt the flesh of the plaster angels on the roofs, to make the windowpanes run like curtains of water within their irregular frames. People lost so much weight so suddenly that you'd think summer was a communal cancer that sucked out their interior energy. Trees, alders and black locusts, cast the shadows of their branches onto blind walls pierced here and there by an asymmetrical window. The asphalt softened and smelled unexpectedly sweet; you wanted to lie down in its thick pool and pull its hallucinatory aroma of grease into your nostrils.

In the evenings, Ştefana and I would go out to a little, anonymous bar squeezed in between crumbling walls. Above us, the rosy sky was so melancholic, so transparent, so silky, that it looked like the belly of an enormous sea creature as it traversed the irregularities of a vast, deep ocean. The pints of beer on the rustic table became more luminous as the evening went on and the sky turned scarlet. In the end, the beers were the only lights on our faces. In the interior courtyard that fit our shoulders tightly like a too-small jacket, the black, warm wind wrapped us in a kind of creole sadness, as though it came from very old memories. "I've lived this evening before," Ştefana told me, while the waiter polished the metal ashtray until it gleamed like an unidentified, enigmatic object. It was like we were inside a photo, we were the shadows cast on an emulsion, on a layer of silver nitrate that outlined my wife's lips and hair, each minuscule link of the necklace on her neck, the ivory of her buttons, the pleats of her plaid skirt . . . We were on vacation, and I wanted summer to keep exhaling, forever without end, its blistering halitosis over the city. Most of the time the bar wouldn't kick us out until, in the small space between the buildings, among the cornices and horns, the stars came out, multiplying slowly, like transparent lilies in the water of the sea. We were at the bottom of an ocean of fantasy, it pressed its millions of tons of water and fish and algae and marine monsters and fishing boats, so heavy upon our meager bodies that we had to oppose it, from within and at the same pressure, with the bitter waters of nostalgia. Long past midnight, we paid with some crumpled bills and a rain of loose change spinning like tops on the table; we stood up stiffly and left hand in hand, squeezing through the sole entryway of an apartment block plastered in black, in the chaotic womb of the city. A tram whistled past, its rails shining in the light of a moon so close that it looked like it was rolling down parallel tracks. There was no sign of anyone else, not on the streets nor in the lit windows covered with pink cloth, whose enigma had intrigued me since childhood. How happy I was, holding hands with her, as we lost ourselves in the twisting streets! We wouldn't always make it home: when we got tired and the stars became our personal enemies, we would go into a building at random, the one with the most absurd high relief carvings—plaster satyrs and bacchantes, basalt gargoyles, silica trolls, and imps, all clustered under the window frames and guarding the ogive gates—and because all the doors in the city were unlocked, we went from room to room with the most unexpected decors. We would always find a bed wherever we went, to lie across it, still in our clothes, and to sleep until morning.

During the summer we were almost inseparable, like symbolically conjoined twins, with a shared heart that beat for the both of us. Yet her crises became more frequent and more dramatic. I would find her on the ground, in the hall, in the bathroom, once in the empty lot in front of the house, another time in the tower's dental chair, laid out almost horizontal, with bruises on her face, contorted impossibly like a fakir, or other times, conscious but obtuse and vulgar. I found her in a puddle of vomit after she had swallowed who knows what. I called an ambulance five or six times in September alone, and I followed her iron gurney, sinister green in color, into the hospital full of roaches, its walls blotched with smashed mosquitoes. I kept watch over her in rooms with twenty other patients, where she was the youngest, I looked at her sweaty hair, stuck to her cranium, and her eyes evacuated with suffering. I once found her hanging from the windowsill, hanging by her fingers, seven stories up and screaming that if anyone came near her she would let go. In the end she spent six weeks at Hospital 9, taking an antipsychotic medication. After spending September and half of October like this, Ştefana came out of the hospital transformed.

Not changed for the better, but changed into a different person. She didn't have crises anymore and her appearance, habits, and mannerisms were unaltered. As usual—and to my great amazement, because everything had been a constant torture, with oases of calm that made the next storm more dramatic—she never spoke about what happened, as though it all had taken place in a parallel life. But it wasn't just that. Ştefana had been one of my body's interior organs. I felt her there, even when I wasn't thinking about her. We lived together, wrapped in the same atmosphere, the same painting, the same myth, like Theseus and the Minotaur, Leda and the swan, Haman and Esther. Her figure overlapped with mine, like two wet watercolor brushes that made trees bloom in each other's colors. I brought her with me wherever I went; whatever I did she was part of its cause, aim, and significance. All this disappeared the minute I brought her home in a rickety taxi. She was still herself, but the version she must have been before we met. She could have been any woman off the street. She could have been anyone. Never, not when I found her in the icy shower, not when I pulled her out of the puddle of vomit, not when I grabbed her hands and screamed like a madman lifting her thirty meters above the traffic was I ever as frightened as I was that first half hour she was home. Everything was the same and everything was completely changed. The statue that had once been painted the color of flesh, whose hair was brown and whose eyes were blue, was now a white, marble doll, white to the whites of her eyes, in the silence and constant whisper of museum-like air. The atmosphere of tenderness and memories that once made us laugh were gone. We were individual bodies from different realities, only apparently coplanar, the way that the stars of Orion are of different depths in space and only happen to create the outline of the mythical hunter. We were married and shared the same house purely by chance. Not after an hour, not after a day, not in the three months that followed—the deepest hell of my life—did I get used to it. Ştefana had disappeared and was replaced by someone not just foreign but, in a way—I felt it much more clearly than I could say—foreign to this world. I had read somewhere about undercover agents on missions to foreign countries with false identities who managed to integrate themselves perfectly into the new world—they had an ordinary job, they traveled and had children, they drank beers with friends on Sundays—but all the while they were someone else, and their will was not inside them but somewhere else, hundreds or thousands of kilometers away, the way that bodies without souls walk among us, while their souls—as Dante said—already reside in the somber edifice of Hell. I couldn't prove it, I couldn't talk about it to anyone, but there was someone else inside Ştefana now. The identical was different, even hostile.

I was afraid of her now, much more afraid than I had been during her crises. She was calm, she smiled, cooked, ironed, and shopped; we made love in the evening and read next to each other, but I knew she was stalking me, hunting me, transmitting my every move to a distant place. Whenever we were together, I was as tense as I was at the dentist, worried she would know I knew, and I tried as hard as I could to act naturally, to not give her any reason for suspicion.

We went out at night, in the rain, in long raincoats and with a worn-out umbrella over our heads; I must have looked as pale as death. The city itself around us had changed, because every love is another reality. Now I was living in a city without love, a frightening termite colony, a perfect prison with no escape. The delicate dandelion puff of desire and nostalgia that had once dressed our Bucharest evenings was now despair and void: how could you live with a stranger? How could you cohabitate with a doppelganger, with a kagemusha of the person you once loved? Who would understand if you told them your wife, although she hadn't changed at all, had become an evil spy who betrayed you, moment by moment, for who knows what terrible power, for who knows what purpose? The impossible situation in which I found myself increased my loneliness exponentially.

One night I opened my eyes and saw her in the semidark: she was sitting on the edge of our bed, looking at me. Who knows how long she had been sitting there, like the visitors I had written about in my diary. More so than in any of those visits, the reaction of my body—while my mind was in a prone refusal to understand—was devastating: I started to tremble so hard I shook the bed, and all the hair on my body stood up at once. I pulled myself from the bed with the sheet and all, and I ran out of the room. I sat on the floor in the hall, with my back stuck against the cold wall, until I could breathe normally again. I went to the window: a full moon. This blue light was what let me see everything so well. I stayed there at least an hour, until I went back to the bedroom and got into bed. Ştefana was sleeping on her side, breathing gently. In the morning we drank coffee together, without talking about what had happened. The way I looked at her was like an amnesiac being told: This is your wife, you've been married for years; but he sees, from across the kitchen table, a strange woman staring him in the eyes, a bad actress who smiles with obscene familiarity and whom, however hard he racks his memory, he cannot identify at all, or find the shadow of a feeling that would connect them. From that night on I started to suffer insomnia. For four or five nights I couldn't close my eyes, as though I were sharing a jail cell with a murderer or I was forced to sleep in a tiger's cage. I was shaken by the thought that if I fell asleep for even ten minutes, I would be utterly under the power of the terrible being with whom I shared the room and bed. After four nights of no sleep and tense expectation I surrendered. I couldn't bear it anymore, the masquerade had to end.

"Ştefana, I need to tell you something," I said one night, before we went to bed. I felt guilty and troubled, as though it were real, even though it was only a dumb ploy. I had been trying to think how I could separate from her without giving myself away. But I never would have thought it could be so hard. Ştefana looked at me with passing curiosity, putting her book on the nightstand. Shadows and light flickered across her face, the way a mountain landscape turns light and dark as the clouds run above, alternately revealing and obscuring the sun. Ten times a minute she was herself, then she became someone else, as though the problem were not in her but in me, in my mental mechanisms, as though I had lost the ability to recognize her emotionally, to feel she was my wife, the one who had walked through the snow with her arms full of flowers, the one with whom I would go out on summer nights to a patio bar, under scented stars gathered in the small square gap between rooftops. Sometimes I recognized her so clearly, without any doubt, that I wanted to take her cheeks in my hands and embrace her then, because in the next moment she would become foreign again, a threat to my life. "Look . . . I've met . . . there's someone else." Ştefana didn't react right away. For the first few minutes, she didn't even seem to understand. We were lying in bed next to each other, with only our faces turned. Her eyes were transparent, as though empty of thought. There was an innervating quiet in the room, difficult to bear.

"Who? Irina?" she answered quietly.

"Yes . . ." Before then, I had hardly ever paid the physics teacher any attention, and, as far as I could recall, I had never talked to Ştefana about her. But when I was trying, in my torturous, sleepless nights, to come up with some pretext to end my impossible marriage and I decided to invent a lover, I couldn't actually think of anyone but Irina. I was defending myself from a woman empty of reality by using a woman who didn't yet have a reality, I was fighting a ghost with a ghost in an insane game beyond my control. The fact that, without any hesitation, Ştefana knew who I was thinking of confirmed my longstanding suspicions and halted the palpitation over her face. A homogeneous cloud, unbroken by any ray of doubt, darkened her features. Suddenly she lifted herself onto her elbow and moved her face close to mine. She dominated me with her eyes, pitch black in the shadows.

"You don't have to worry about anything as far as I'm concerned," she said. "And as long as we're talking about it—I have someone else, too." The whole scene took place as though in dense time, much more slowly than the time that had run up to then with the indifference of water from a faucet. Each word, separated by minutes of silence, materialized between us with the gleam and roughness of objects that were as concrete as they were unintelligible.

"What did you say?" I asked her, amazed, looking at her impassive face bent over mine. I hadn't expected this and couldn't believe it. How could she have someone else? Ştefana had been, since she came home from the hospital, almost always at home, except for the two or three times we went out to Tei Lake, to take a turn around it and come back. How was she meeting another man? The idea was totally foreign to me, and yet it hit me with a completely unexpected force. I was stunned. I had always thought she was my feminine double, my image in the mirror of sex. This was why I could never love her passionately, but only like a sister, a possibility that was blocked inside me but manifested, miraculously, in the vast dream of reality. Even after her metamorphosis into an identical yet completely different being, the idea that she could have her own sexuality, that she could enter someone else's life, maybe precisely that of the person controlling her gestures and words at a distance—this seemed crazy to me, absurd.

"I meant what I said. I have someone, I have a . . . lover. The question is, what do we do now?"

"Who is it?" I asked.

"You don't know him. Anyway there's no point in talking about it."

We were both quiet for a few minutes, looking at the ceiling. Then she did something amazing. With the same clear eyes, she started to read again. She was reading normally, breathing quietly, while I, without even daring to move, stared at the ceiling in the semidark of the room, as though I were paralyzed, wrapped in the elastic threads of a spiderweb.

Suddenly I couldn't stand the insanity and horror of the situation. A wave of hate flooded over me, and I lost control. I jumped up and grabbed her by the shoulders, and I began to shake her and scream madly: "Who are you? Who are you?" I was sitting across her hips, I saw fragments of her face, strands of her hair, flashes of her decomposed and recomposed eyes, unreal in the light of the reading lamp, I hit her shoulders, I pulled her up and slammed her back against the mattress. She was as soft as a rubber doll, she didn't try to defend herself, I could have strangled her or hit her face until she was senseless. Something protected me that night, something stopped me from going where that tsunami of despair, fear, and incomprehensibility pushed me. I collapsed beside her and began to sob, balled up on the mattress, which seemed more sunken than ever. After a long time I got up and went to the bathroom. In the mirror over the sink, my face looked disfigured. I just couldn't anymore. For months I had been beating my head and fists against an impassive wall. In fact, it was hitting me, it was cutting me, it was flaying me, it was breaking my skull and fracturing my bones. There was nothing else to do. Ştefana had turned to stone and become another wall of my prison.

One morning I left for school as usual, but it was Saturday and I wasn't going to teach; instead, I was going to a high school in Iancului for pedagogical activities, where everything that went on at these so called "counseling sessions" was so stupid that I would skip them as often as I could. I hid behind a heap of snow that had been plowed onto a car, leaving only a wheel exposed, the result of the big, wet snowflakes that had been falling since the first of December. I stayed there, the snow falling on me, feeling cold, for over and hour, until I had forgotten what I was waiting for or why I was there. Maica Domnului, with its empty lots and strange houses, was quieter than ever. The road was invisible under the snow. The old carcasses of Fram refrigerators and the scraps of caterpillar treads on the land in front of my house were now just white heaps with blue shadows. The snow fell at a slant, constantly, calm and silent over my boat-shaped house, whose front door, made of art nouveau wrought iron, was now under my surveillance. My eyes were drooping with exhaustion when I finally saw her leave.

She was wearing her blue hat and a scarf I knew well, and her hair blew wherever the wind and snow wanted. She crossed that blindingly white world and turned down Maica Domnului. She was walking strangely, a little stiffly, without paying attention to the other people on the street. She pulled her chin down into her scarf and let the glittering little stars cover her hair. She seemed so beautiful to me at that moment, I wanted to run up and put my arm around her shoulder. It had been so good between us, those first months! But now I had to know who she was seeing, what was really going on with her.

After a few streets she turned left. She dove into a small neighborhood where I had seldom been, more ruins than anything, with a few walls still standing, and then she popped out onto Colentina. That street was also completely snowed over. Cars passed one per minute, a service tram spread salt on the rails. The workers' blocks, ten or twelve stories tall, emerged from waves of snow like a cetacean's gray spines, full of wounds from the harpoons of time and neglect. A homogeneous, dirty-pink twilight blanketed the neighborhood's desolation. Ştefana crossed the street and continued on the opposite sidewalk, toward Doamna Ghica. I walked behind her with my hands in my coat pockets, without trying to hide, because she never looked behind her and I sensed she wasn't going to. Not a year but a lifetime had passed since we had walked together down the same street, a few kilometers farther toward downtown, dressed too lightly, she with her arms full of flowers, in the middle of the road with even more snow than now, and the tram stopped between stations to let us on, and the passengers clapping their frozen hands, laughing and happy for us, in spite of the general unhappiness. Now she was walking, as though pulled by a thread, to meet her lover, or her superior officer, or God knows who. Then, she turned right, onto Silistra, the street where I was born! Silistra 46, the U-shaped house full of a motley and happy group of people. However many times I went there, my heart beat so fast I thought I would suffocate. Silistra wasn't a real street, it was part of the funambulate world under the dome of my cranium. When I turned the corner, something rose up inside me, and I found myself suddenly face-to-face with my own forehead, whose bone had turned clear enough for me to see the melancholy alley, with its tarred telegraph poles, with kites caught in their lines, with the brick, unplastered houses, with kids sitting on the steps to play cards or button-soccer. I passed through the permissive gelatin of my frontal bone and continued down to the end of the street, where the field began. There, at the end, when I wasn't more than two, I dropped a golden bell into a little pond, a bell I got from who knows who, and I looked for it, crying and pawing through the water with little my hands, without ever finding it.

Ştefana now turned decidedly down Silistra, passing the grocery, the building with, who knows why, a giant blue ibrik painted on it; the courtyard with grapevine trellises, topped with green, red, and blue mirrored balls, that collected icons of the street and nearby houses; the house with a little tower that always fascinated me . . . She came to the rented house where my parents once lived, in the room with a cement floor, but she didn't stop at its door. I did, with frost on my eyelashes and tears in my eyes: empty, it was all empty there. The windows were covered with newspapers, the broken shutters were knocking in the wind. An ancient car was on bricks in the yard, covered in snow. Dry geraniums in rotting pots beside the doors. No one in the windows, no one in the yard. An abandoned bunker in an ancient battlefield. It was a fold of space, of time, or of the manuscript page that contains them, the brane of the universe folded itself over, the bane of its own existence, maybe, and I now found myself on the other side of a curl longer than a quarter century. It was like it was and also not like it was; it felt like a déjà vu, in which not the image, ah Vaschide, but the emotion floods over you, overwhelms you. It was like an afternoon daydream or a dream at night, a dream with houses taking shape in the intense magic of recognition. "Yes, that's how it was! Yes, I was there!" You say to yourself, frozen in your suffering and nostalgia, looking at the edifice sculpted from the substance of your cerebellum, bathed in the storms of your endorphins.

I also immediately recognized the neighboring house's blind wall, more ruined and more timeworn than I remembered. Two places buckled so much that the brick wall had to be propped up with huge, rust-covered girders. The snowdrifts were the height of a person, and the whiteness snagged on the bricks' irregularities. The street side of the house was painted a melancholy green, with a few steps up to a scarlet door and a few windows covered with drapes of the same color. As a child, I had once peered into the depths of the house, from the street, when someone opened the door. I had felt I was doing something impermissible, shameful: the front hall looked like flesh, like red, palpitating flesh, as though a creature were living in the calcium shell of the house.

That, to my amazement, was the door Ştefana entered, unlocking it with a large, iron key. She disappeared into the house, leaving the door wide open, as though she knew I was following her and wanted to invite me in. My heart had never beat so fast. I didn't know what to do, I was just as afraid of the house as I had been as a child, the snow was falling against the ground in whispers, I was in unreality, in the unreal. Only fear truly existed, like a field that united and gave weight to a parallel world's evanescence. I went in. The house at first seemed completely empty, icy, it smelled like winter and cold. No one had lived there for a long time. I walked down the tunnel of the entry hall wrapped in blood-colored tapestry, I climbed the wooden staircase to the second story. A dry oleander, almost black, with a small, deafening pop dropped its black petals as I passed. The doors to the four rooms were wide open, and each space was empty, frozen, with pale traces on the walls where once there had been furniture and pictures. Through the cracked windows came the blinding light of snow, making the brown floors gleam. At the end of the hall was a bathroom, and, beside it, a steep staircase led to the attic. I climbed it slowly. My visual field throbbed along with my heart. I huffed, making clouds in the air like a dragon, swirls and twists that disappeared into the glassy air. I paused a while at the top of the stairs, in front of the door painted dark scarlet, like a scab. I put my ear to its cold, damp wood: no sound came from the other side, as though there were no room there, just the fullness of space, many meters thick. I put my hand on the knob, so cold my whole body shivered. I pushed and, without a sound, I opened the door.

The room was empty like the others, but the air was sweltering. It blew from the middle of summer through the narrow window where, with her elbows propped on the sill, Ştefana stood with her back toward me. The snowflakes in her hair had melted because of the hot wind coming from the window, like out of an oven. The intense, melted gold light corroded her outline, it made her hair glow like coals. I crept toward her. The melted snow on her coat ran to the floor into a puddle of gold. The glory of the azure sky came in through the little window, with clouds spread uniformly into the distance. And against this background were visible, almost cheek to cheek with Ştefana, but on the other side of the window frame, the heads of multiple children. Small, snotty slum kids, girls and boys in their playclothes stained and torn to bits. They clutched each other, yelling in fear and surprise. Ştefana looked at one in particular, the dirtiest and poorest, with a pointed face and large, heavy black eyes, now even wider with fear. From the corner, at an angle, with the so-familiar profile of my wife only two steps away but without her giving any sign that she saw or noticed me, I stared at them avidly. Ştefana was not smiling, her face only showed that insect-like impersonality that in recent months had so exasperated me. But all the intensity of her predatory gaze was fixed on the pale boy . . . I couldn't doubt it, it was me, the me I was then, the one from the U-shaped house, crowned with his mother's love and armed with the smell of oleanders from the ancient courtyard of my childhood. They were looking each other in the eyes, she had picked him out from the others, who all melted away, transparent, into the landscape with flowing July clouds, until only the two of them were left, like two pieces in a strange game, like a coupling mechanism ready to click, closing over who knows what mystery, opening who knows what portal. The boy's body suddenly relaxed, his face didn't show fear anymore but a sleepiness, his eyes half-closed, when she cupped her one hand in her other, offering them palms up to him, on the windowsill. The child hesitated, but not for long, and soon his little hand was resting on Ştefana's. The pure nails of her fingers, "*Ses purs ongles très haut dédiant leur onyx,*" closed slowly over his hand, until it could not be seen. They remained like that, an indecipherable figure, while I retreated, backward, toward the door, feeling more relaxed and, in a hideous way, happy. I had felt the woman's hand close over my own. Contact had been made.

39

Three winters have passed since then, and I started writing just as long ago, here in the notebooks of my manuscript. I stack them on my desk and look at them sitting there politely and silently, in the bright light of snow from my window. The first is covered in a white and blue floral cloth. I have read it so many times, I almost know it by heart. Lice, fear, school ID numbers, dreams. The outer eye closes and the inner eye opens. The abandoned factory, with its bizarre machinery. Irina. The second notebook is bigger, massive, wire-bound, with a shiny red cover. Even looking at its edges you can see, like the intestines of creatures crushed between the pages, the pen lines, their psychic trajectory, the quantum flux of the white pages that gives birth to them all. The morgue, dreams, the Picketists, the gold ring, teeth knocked out, spitting on the icon in the atheist club. Tesseract. Voila. And the last notebook, with a black and blue cover, at the moment three-quarters full, the only one that still has immaculate pages, as enigmatic as faceless gods. I always knew that writing was a palimpsest, scraping away at a page that already contains everything, a revelation of signs and curls brought to light for the first time, the way as children we turn big rocks over to see, in the wet impression left in the dirt, the panic of disturbed ants, fleeing with white larvae in their mandibles, the lazy unraveling of wiry centipedes, the dazed flight of a translucent spider. The subterranean murmur of white sheets, their avidity for all stories, all the glory and all the shame and all the thought and all the inferno on Earth. Yesterday I finished, writing "contact had been made" (without knowing what that meant and without worrying that I didn't know, satisfied by the sensation that the painful story of my marriage must end precisely this way) on the left-hand page, which sits much higher than the blank one I am facing at the moment; the stack of more than a hundred pages already written, fanned out by the pressure of the pen tip and weighed down by its blue paste, dangerous and dizzying to smell, overwhelms the modest heap of smooth, white pages remaining on the right side to be filled in the future, I don't know when, as yet, or with what, parallel to the life over which they unfold. I have just one inkling: I feel this is the last notebook, that the story will end in the moment that there is no room to write a letter more, the way the greatest of the tattooed, over the course of their lives, cover their entire skin, to the last square centimeter, the one between the eyebrows, where by convention you always tattoo the triangular eye that looks inward, and then retreat somewhere to die, leaving their skin to a museum. Already the right-hand page is half-tattooed, and the shadow of my arm darkens the lower part, as pure and prudish as smooth snow, untrodden by human feet. Many times, after I've written in the evening until dark fell and the air inside turned the dirty yellow of a gas lamp, I've closed the stiff cover of the last notebook and placed it on the other two, and on top of the shiny cover, I've made a flower out of some three-lei coins and a one-leu: the big one in the middle and five small ones around it, touching each other like petals. The slanting light from the window throws the ridges on the edges of the coins into relief, as well as the numbers, letters, the emblems on their silver faces. I've looked at them until it is completely dark and they are the only glimmers in the melancholy room, and I've tried to figure out (to remember?) *what this means*, as though I were searching for a word on the tip of my tongue. Then I take a curved, black magnet, chipped at one end—the one I found at the Electrospooling Cooperative factory, whose fence I jumped so often as a kid—and I move it toward the coin flower resting on my notebooks' strange Baalbek. I've always felt surprise and happiness at the snap, the miracle of their clinking together to the black stone, their clinging to each other, their chain in which the coins, now vertical, undulate in the glints and sudden shadows of the twilight. I pull them, I separate them forcefully from each other, feeling their shared invisible tension, their mystical solidarity. I have always regarded magnetism with the eyes of a child, just as I have always been amazed that we can see through glass (but not through walls or metals) and that mirrors repeat reality endlessly, doubling the volume of the world . . .

The third notebook, as yet only half filled, discovered, exposed: Voila. Traian. The master of dreams, Vaschide. Ştefana and her strange estrangement. Characters, places, figures engaged in a ballet as fascinating and incomprehensible as the manifest dream that congeals, like the skin on the surface of milk, over that which it hides and reveals: the beauty of the abyss and the bestial beauty of the latent dream. You wake up groggy, it's still dark outside, you reach for your clock, when a mixture of pre-images and not-yet-emotions flashes through your mind, things you don't grasp or see, you don't even really feel, but which are there, like a dagger in the middle of your mind, a sensation of déjà vu that knocks you to the floor, like the smell of burnt hair or the patina taste that epileptics sense before they collapse: yes, yes, there was something, I experienced something, it was . . . magic, impossible to explain . . . You remember with your fingers, your tongue; the walls where lichen blooms. Yes, I was there, how strange, I was in that world . . . you're left motionless; like a spider in its web, you try to attract another message, another flash from the deep. And at once you see, and suddenly you feel: a fragment of your parallel life becomes palpable, concrete, like any other object in your world. It is an icon, a photograph, a film; but the constellation of faces and rooms and words that comes from that distant world does not explain the nervousness, like falling in love, the grief, like at a wake, that leaves you paralyzed in your bed as the day begins to shine through your window. "What could it be?" my mother would wonder aloud whenever she recounted a dream, and she remembered all of them, keeping them in the infallible insect collection of her memory, in her unwritten book of poems, worthy of Pliny and Lautréamont. What could it be? you wonder as well, in your craven syllogisms, automatically thinking, the way a mantis makes a nest without looking back, of an interpretation; unpacking the warm, newborn dream, its organs and apparatuses, its gears, crosses, asterisks, and crescents, so that, through an inept and inefficient process of reverse engineering, you may reconstruct a meaning, an alphabet, a language. You wave the photographic paper through the revealing bath, but the revealer cannot reveal the revelation; on the contrary, it hides it on its back, the reverse which introduces insanity into the world, losing the world from which the terrible and sacred message comes. Every dream is a message, a call, a portal, a wormhole, a multidimensional object that as you interpret, you mystify and squander. You are used to books you can read placidly, eating a sandwich, during the break in the teachers' lounge, or in the tram on your way home; to illusory doors painted on the walls of all the paintings in all the galleries of the world; to your head rocking to the beat of all songs. But you're deaf, blind, and mute to the desperate call from their core. Dreams are escape plans, like music, metaphysics, and spherical geometry. Everything that speaks to us in the world says the same thing: get out of here! Leave! This is not your home! Every dream asks you a serious question. You won't understand if you interpret, you'll only understand if you answer. Whenever you are called in the middle of the night, by name, don't hesitate: answer, "Here I am, Lord!"

I don't try to understand, I proceed with the story of my anomalies. Philosophers have hitherto only interpreted the world in various ways—I sometimes tell myself, parodying the famous phrase that has spilled so much blood—the point is to escape it. A sort of vision I had a few nights ago seemed, at least to my desperate mind, to show if not a method, at least a distant, final light, like the one you can see at the center of a crystal maze, so close, but still separated from you by kilometers of corridors. The parabola's transparency, like the transparency of glass walls, the irony of the horn gate of true dream, sent by gods, which you still will never understand. I'll write here, the same way I have written down my dreams, transparent and yet obscure (the more limpid they are, the more indecipherable they become), the little story that occurred to me:

I once possessed a vast kingdom, I might say the sun never set upon it. Its geography was grand and varied, its riches—endless. To protect my property, I built a circular wall, as flexible as a membrane yet almost impenetrable. My enemies were equal to my wealth, and they had surrounded me since the start of time, but the wall's circumference was so unimaginably great that nowhere along its length could they concentrate enough of their forces to break through. This state of affairs lasted a long time, today I regard it as my golden age, my era of otiose indolence.

The day came when I was informed that, along a small section of the wall built in a distant province, the number of enemies, who knows for what reason, had grown a little greater than in other parts. Not enough to penetrate the wall, but still, a worrisome development. I decided to make a cut through the wall and slide the two ends over each other, so that at least one part would be doubly thick. It was a precaution my subjects criticized at the time because the portion in question was not even one-thousandth of the circumference, and the doubled section was almost unnoticeable. Still, however small the covered surface, doubling the wall affected my borders as a whole: my kingdom narrowed. I had lost a sliver, infinitesimal, perhaps the thickness of a hair, but still it was a loss of territory, and that hadn't happened for centuries. My precaution, hasty as it may have been, had other effects, some quite paradoxical. Seeing the wall doubled, my enemies decided not to attack there and moved toward the border of their province, joining with those who were already fighting my guards.

I was thus forced to pull the interior end of the wall over a little more, increasing the arc of the circle that was doubled. For a few years, this strategy succeeded against the increasing attacks, but at the price of new constrictions of my kingdom. Losing hope, my enemies in that area moved again toward more marginal provinces, which led, on my part, to a new rotation of the interior wall along the one outside. Soon, a quarter and then a half of the circumference—tighter and tighter—of the exterior wall were doubled by the interior wall, and my patrimony dramatically decreased. In concentric bands outside the wall, I lost district after district, mines of precious metals, forests of noble wood; villages and fields were captured by my enemies, cities and markets once full of happiness. After decades of tireless battle and fear of the always increasing attacks, I came to double the entire circumference of the wall; I found myself much poorer than I had been, though still a noble, an important castellan in our realms. My entire dominion was now protected by a double wall, but my enemies had likewise gained in strength, and now they attacked all along a much shorter wall than they had initially confronted. In this way, my situation, instead of getting better, became all the more difficult, because my resources had decreased and the war required more and more money.

Yet I had no choice when, in one of the border regions, my enemy began, for who knows what reason, to attack even more decidedly than in other parts. I was forced to pull on the inner end of the wall again, tripling the total thickness—at first along a modest portion, then over an ever greater expanse. I covered more and more of the frontier with this triple wall: a quarter, a half, three quarters, and in the end, the entire border. My remaining domain, after these new reductions in circumference and surface area, was no greater than the land where I was born: the castle and a few villages around it, a tin mine, a water mill, a hillside dotted with herds of sheep. All that my sword had conquered, from the days of my youth, was now forever in the hands of my enemies. But the more my possessions were lost to the sands of time, the more numerous my adversaries became, although their total number did not grow, all along my wall. Their surge was now so large that it seemed they weren't fighting for my riches, but just out of spite for me and my stubborn resistance.

Soon, my wall was quadrupled, then quintupled; soon I lost the mine and the mill and the villages, one by one, and the hill with my flocks, until, when the wall was six layers thick, like a snake coiled around a gasping stag, I realized the inside part of the wall pressed right against the wall of my own castle, hugging it with the ivory skin of its elastic band.

If the wall took a few days to sextuple, the septupling took only a few hours. Under the constriction of the defensive wall, the castle ramparts, once thought invincible, crumbled, and I could then see, with horror and fright, that the exterior wall, just as thick as it was crowded with enemies, had shrunk so much it only held the walls of the throne room where I lay captive, unable to escape. My enemies were now so close that I could hear, on the other side of what had become a twentyfold wall, their bestial cries, I could sense their frustration when they couldn't swing their weapons in such a crowd, and they were forced to bite and claw their way toward the besieged wall.

It only took a few minutes before I grabbed the interior part of the wall, and I pulled it toward my own body, pressing it against it, as this much was all I had left in the world. My terror, pain, and despair had no boundaries when the border of my skin yielded and the circular wall, now one hundred and one thousandfold, invaded my internal organs. My enemies conquered, one by one, in ever quicker succession, my heart, liver, and guts, the vertebrae of my spine, the same way they had made themselves, over the preceding decades, masters of my vast kingdom. Now the wall wrapped around itself with lightning speed, encompassing my cranium and crushing it to splinters, surrounding my brain and advancing toward its incandescent center. My enemies now fought for my sensory areas, for my motor areas, they conquered, finger by finger, the deformed homunculus projected onto my cerebral hemispheres, they breached my memories and reason, they enslaved my visual and logical fields, in their assault against a wall that now had tens of millions of coils and continuously whipped around itself, like an unforgiving tapeworm, to encompass, in the center of the center of my mind, the pea of my pineal gland, which wise people claim is the seat of the soul.

And look at me now, after only one millionth of a second, reduced to that which I truly am, to that which I always was: the pearl in the center of the dizzying spiral of the mind. Living here, dying here, without time, without properties, without enemies, the same way that I, while living, always died.

It's not that bad, I tell myself, rereading my little parable. Maybe there's a chance, even now, so many years after the workshop that split my life in two, for me to get back, maybe I could slip back under the skin of the Other, of him who is traveling across the earth and signing autographs and writing brilliant books on another world, under other skies. Just the thought of it makes me want to throw up. Just the thought that I would take the painting from the burning house and not the living child, as tongues of fire roast his skin, elicits an unbearable self-hatred. This is what all writers do, all the philosophers, musicians, and painters in this world, this is what circus magicians and flea trainers do: they save the masterpiece and let the child burn. What I am writing here, evening after evening, in my house in the center of my city, of my universe, of my world, is an anti-book, the forever obscure work of an anti-author. I am no one and I will stay that way, I am alone and there's no cure for being alone: but I don't lie to anyone, painting doors that will never open on the walls of this Piranesian world. I could take my story to a newspaper. It could appear in a Sunday literature supplement. I could write more and publish a small, hundred-page book. Even Kafka, even Rotluft, even Fyoritos did this. I could go into the teachers' lounge one day with my freshly published book, I could show it off, with well-played modesty, to Florabela, Goia, Mrs. Gionea, and Mrs. Uzun, I could approach the drawing teacher, Spirescu, and ask him, ingenuously, what he thought of the cover (he, the great specialist . . .), and I would hear "Congratulations, dom profesor" everywhere, even from the green paintings that line the room, even from the janitors, even from students' ink-stained lips. That's how it would start. It could still start. The nightmare of my transformation, after a night of restless sleep, into the Other.

PART FOUR

40

OUR SCHOOL LOOKS BETTER IN THE SPRING. INSIDE, of course, it's just as dark, with its endless hallways, with its floors that seem to multiply above- and belowground, but at least when you're walking up in the morning, the school seems bathed in frozen, luminous water, as though you were sixteen and for the first time you saw things not with your eyes but directly with your interior being. Even the walls' lumpy, dirty yellow appears to glimmer, like inside a camera lucida, even the shadows of the leafless walnut trees look like strange neurons, braided together and swaying in the excited morning breeze.

The women I work with put on makeup and dress their hair differently in the spring. They complain less about female illnesses and arthritis. They get more excited by the eternal, ever-changing fads: after the period of oil under the tongue, of slimy algae in jars, of love-in-idleness root, of Rubik's cubes, of insects held in your hand for ten minutes a day (two years ago or so, after the insanity of the Picketists had rocked the whole neighborhood, there was no clerk, plumber, carpenter, teacher, or beggar who didn't keep a grasshopper at home, or a praying mantis, a metallic green beetle, a roly-poly, a stag beetle, a dung beetle, or, in a taxonomical confusion, a spider, centipede, a tick, or a silkworm moth, just so people would take them for members of the sect that fought obstinately against death, pain, and agony), now came the flurry of cheap cameras, toys almost, that appeared this winter. They are little black boxes without a lens, where you put film in, look through the glass viewfinder, and push the button. The light goes through a needle-point orifice in the cap that would cover the target, if one were to exist. When the pictures are developed, you're in for a terrible surprise, because photos made with this primitive device come out something more than abstract: the halo of blinding light that surrounds the faces and makes the landscapes unreal is nothing but nostalgia, the way you see things and faces in dreams or your oldest memories. Portraits, especially, look like ectoplasm dissolved in light. The people look like pale larvae preserved in formaldehyde, sitting in thick cylinders from natural history museums. All the teachers have made photo albums, they spend their breaks together in the lounge, showing each other what look like pictures of a distant planet.

Last Thursday, Borcescu called a meeting. We all gathered, the elementary and high school teachers, in the classroom next to the lounge. I sat on the first bench beside the window, and Gheară sat beside me, with his dumb jokes that still manage to cheer you up. Many of the elementary teachers were crocheting or knitting, others read or chatted in a whisper. Above the teacher's desk, a portrait of the Comrade gleamed, the "one-eared" version with the flashy, metallic necktie. He smiled out of the corner of his mouth, as though trying not to laugh at whatever joke he just heard. On the wall across from the windows were the inevitable posters of cows, pigs, and "literary geography," that is, a map of the country with pictures of writers pinned to their birthplaces. In the back, above the coat hooks covered with raincoats and hats, there were two Albanian personages who probably couldn't fit in the lounge and, between them, the national crest.

A strange, lazy happiness, probably caused by the intense azure of the April skies that inundated the classroom as though it were a light-filled aquarium, energized my colleagues, especially the women teachers who never shut their mouths. "Yesterday we had a *Fasching*, dear, we dressed him like a knight, did the boy up. My husband drove the Volkswagen to the Pioneers Palace. I can't tell you how amazing his costume was, rented from the National Theater, it was splendorous. Rooster feathers, real chain mail, dear, and a Crusader's cloak! It cost, if you can imagine, eight hundred lei! Yes, dear, eight hundred for a single day! I mean, girls, is it made of gold? I paid it, my boy only gets one *Fasching* with all the other kids from the ministry, but, eh, what can you do, you know as well as I do what it's like to have a kid. My Tony . . ." Caty never notices whether anyone is listening to her, and she doesn't notice the other teachers bitterly rolling their eyes. She is sitting on a bench, wrapped in her overly elegant dress, like an exotic butterfly among moths, turning her glistening eyes toward one person or another, just as tempting as she was that time in the office when she innocently showed me, one by one, the underpants she had gotten "shipped in." Whenever I saw her, I remembered that terrible night with the Picketists, the circular room and the gigantic statue of Damnation that crushed Virgil under its foot like a bug, a Virgil that had guided no one through the immanent inferno of our world. Many of the Picketists had been arrested by the militia and Securitate after that night, since there had clearly been a homicide, but the movement seemed—still seems—unstoppable. Virgil, of course, has become a kind of martyr, photos of him, copied and recopied beyond recognition, have flooded the city; you find them in every house. Many of the old pilgrims now walk a mystical path through the buildings downtown, always choosing the rooms where his picture sits framed on a desk, on a wall, stuck in the corner of a mirror in the bathroom, or even torn up and thrown in the trash, the way you might go through a maze by always turning left.

Ispas's story stirred the whole business up again, as it had last spring when he disappeared, when his screaming—they say—could be heard for days above the field at the edge of the city, frightening people walking the swampy ruts beyond the train tracks, and as it had last autumn, when the porter, forgotten about by almost everyone, was suddenly found, alive and intact, lying on the ground in a construction site three blocks from school, drunk out of his mind and very confused. An extraordinary buzz went through the neighborhood. The farce with holding an insect abruptly disappeared, because the Ispas plot had thickened: once he sobered up, the porter had gone to the militia and put his name to a story that would freeze the blood in your veins, and which utterly transformed the great sect of the Picketists. Ispas's declaration circulates, it seems, like Virgil's photograph, copied and recopied by hand, but with such secrecy that I have not yet had the chance to read it—not that I'm itching to do so. The fact is that since the porter's return, herds of people, all dressed in black, have started gathering again, like when Virgil was around, gathering at the most sinister places in the city, living the double life that so amazed me in Caty's case. You shouldn't have let yourself be fooled by the geography teacher's frivolity and languorous shapeliness and poppy-shaped mouth: the moon had a dark side, disfigured by fear and disappointment. Even without the exhausted figure of Virgil—the dead hero had proven more powerful and more active than he had been in life—the Picketists have regrouped, and an apocalyptic chill floats in the air, one I have felt on my own skin for weeks.

Illnesses, the dentist, children and grandchildren, Saturday night TV—my fellow teachers don't have that many things to talk about in the lounge or before meetings. Each one regards herself as the master of her "specialty": they have divvied up the world and each keeps a piece in her pocket. The music teacher, usually as delicate and ornamental as a statuette that's been polished too often, and just as silent, abruptly awakens when Mozart or Tchaikovsky comes up: her eyes start to shine, her round bracelets clink together, and she produces details about concerti, overtures, symphonies (or piquant anecdotes from the lives of musicians) like she was opening a chest of pearls, as pedantic and useless as Mrs. Bernini herself. Nothing true and nothing, not even her dumbest thought, is ever her own. At the slightest mention of a character from Dostoevsky, the Russian teacher, who fittingly is a true commissar, jumps up like she touched something hot; the children think she's the devil: she smacks their hands with a length of silver-cored cable. More than one has ended up with sprained fingers or fractured bones in their palms. "Yes . . . Dostoevsky . . . Fyodor Mikhailovich Dostoevsky. He was a great Russian writer who showed love and compassion for the peasant. But he had his own ideological limitations. You know, comrade profesor, whatever you may say, he is no comparison to the great Tolstoy, whose works encompass all of humanity." And then Tolstoy this and Tolstoy that, like a broken record whenever she sees me, such that now I'd rather have Borcescu's "Marriage is worse than being hanged." Mrs. Rădulescu, of course, is the master of history. Say a word about Mihai Viteazul (or even the high school named for him), and she leaps up like a robot: "Fifteen fifty-eight to sixteen oh one." Did you say you're going to see your parents on Ştefan cel Mare? The same voice, in the impersonal tone of a phone operator giving the time: "Fourteen fifty-seven to fifteen oh four." Beside dates (ascension to and descension from the throne) she knew what she called "causes." What started the Napoleonic Wars? Why did Spartacus's gladiators rebel? Why was the steam engine invented? Why is there an eclipse? Why do fleas jump on the sheets? What knocks over glasses on the table? With a superior smile, Mrs. Rădulescu gives the same response to every question: because of man's exploitation of man. "Dig a little, comrade profesor, into any philosophical idea, 'idealism' or 'metaphysics,' and you will always find the same thing: class interest, the haves defending their privilege against the poor and dispossessed of this world." For decades on end, my colleagues have repeated laws, theories, dates, explanations, poems, quotes, "the best of what has been said and written by humanity," and they attack the children the next day if they can't repeat back what they heard, by heart, word for word, even when it doesn't have any connection to their lives at all—and because of that, the children forget everything as fast as they can. Every student at 86 must have, under the translucid cupola of his little cranium, a landscape just as ruined as the world around him, as the school itself, the old factory, the mechanic's, and the pipe factory. By the time all that has been said and written over the centuries gets to him, it has turned to rubble, chipped bricks, rusty and bent pipes, the broken shutters of a Babel fallen into disrepair.

At the teacher's desk sit Principal Borcescu—whose vitiligo has advanced over the years such that it is painful to look at him: his entire face is full of dark, red spots, and the thick layer of foundation he uses only makes it more obvious and vivid, such that now, from the front of the room, a hypnotic lizard stares at us with two large yellow teeth coming out of his Aztec god face—and Comrade Băjenaru, the Party secretary, a pale, wilting woman with ptosis of the eyelids, a math teacher through who knows what odd twist of fate, because her mind doesn't seem capable of more than her annual cucumber pickling. To be fair, the pickles are crispy and well seasoned, and she brings us a plate at the end of every autumn. The conversations slowly stop, and soon there are no sounds but the quiet clicks of knitting needles. The meeting starts in the most desperate boredom, always the same, with Borcescu mouthing Party directives, quotes from the Comrade, truisms about teaching, ethics, and etiquette in our socialist society, and so on for an hour; if you don't crochet you feel like climbing the walls. Isn't the world a terrible place anyway? Don't we already live for a moment on a speck of dust in eternity? Aren't we going mad, packed like hams into our soft sacks of gristle and bones? Don't we endure, day by day and hour by hour, the thought that we are getting older, that our teeth are falling out, that we are going to contract awful diseases and nightmarish infirmities, that we were going to suffer and then disappear and never give the world shape and meaning? Do we need another tyrant? Or imbeciles who preach from the desk without believing one iota of what they say, the same way they don't believe in classical poetry or mathematical theorems, or the laws of physics, or in atoms, or in gods, or in class struggle, who would preach about anything in the same tone, just as long as they got their afternoon nap, their *only* god and friend?

Then he moves on to the agenda, which only has one point, our top issue for the last several years, in comparison to which the educational program has become a kind of atavistic appendage: collecting bottles, jars, and scrap paper. Each child must bring fifteen kilograms per month of paper and one hundred kilos of empty bottles and jars, all well washed, ready to reenter production. The homeroom teachers are responsible for fulfilling the plan. Each one has to call a meeting with the parents, one evening after they come home from their jobs, and to work them over, with the greatest resolve, regarding their patriotic duty to recycle trash, thus contributing, according to the powers of each student, to the good of the nation. No whining is allowed, such as, where in God's name should the poor parents get hold of fifteen kilos of paper, or a hundred bottles and jars, per month? The teacher has to cut short anyone who complains that they have two or three children in school. You can't bargain with the law. That is the quantity set per child, so that is what they have to bring. If they don't, the child could be expelled from school, after, of course, preliminary punishments such as pulling their hair, hitting their palms with a three-sided ruler, pulling down their pants in front of the class, giving bad behavior grades, or holding them back a year.

I knew the terror that was to follow, since the same thing happens every year. Desperate children raided the stores, stole packaging, stripped the newsstands of their newspapers. The parents bought scrap paper from the collection centers or they bribed the porters at printshops. Bands of students attacked other schools' storerooms and stole their precious jars, which traveled to one school after another. Every school posted special guards to their libraries, since they didn't want to be cleaned out: books were dismembered and put in the scrap pile. Children would ride their ancient bikes for kilometers to the trash heaps on the edge of town, and they would pick through them, looking for moldy newspapers and chipped bottles among the dead animals and excrement fermenting below enormous skies. Corruption and bribery reached unimaginable levels. Two out of three paper factories produced only scrap for the schools. Breweries, oil processors, and jelly factories sold their bottles and jars empty, because they were worth much more than the contents. On collection day, at our school, you saw lines of panting children hunched under giant bundles, like Himalayan sherpas, slipping and falling in a deafening noise of broken glass, their fingers cut by the cords around enormous packets of yellowed newspapers. Everything was put in an unused classroom (one of the far-off ones, numbered with imaginary, transfinite numbers), after which the homeroom teachers recorded what each child brought. Those that didn't satisfy their load suffered terrible consequences. Many students who couldn't meet their quota ran away from home and didn't come to school anymore; some actually tried to hang themselves. The room quickly filled up to the ceiling. The stacks of magazines, many meters tall, constantly fell on top of people bringing in more, the bottles smashed against each other until they were nothing but brown, green, or water-clear shards, and these were ground down to the sand from which they came. The process moved to a second room, which also filled up to the ceiling. The scrap paper blocked the hallways, it extended farther and farther into the space of the school, it filled entire floors, it blocked up the furnace in the basement, it took over the attic and the annexes. At first, they left narrow pathways through the heaps of paper, so you could get to the labs, the nurse, the dentist, the office, and the lounge. But after a few days these were also full. We stopped teaching; one teacher would report to guard the cabinet of registers, which were likely to be stolen and thrown in with the scrap. When the school was so packed there wasn't room for a pin, the students left their burdens outside by the walls, they clambered up the old bags to put their own as high as possible. Like the fellahin of the pyramids, they built ramps to roll their bales of paper and raffia sacks of bottles and jars, and soon nothing of the school was visible beneath the giant mound of scrap. Then, long lines of dump trucks came, loaded everything up, and left for an unknown location. After another week of this, we could retake the school.

"Esteemed colleagues," Borcescu continues, spitting between his two remaining yellow teeth, curved like boar tusks, "I draw your attention to the fact that it is a Party duty, priority zero, yes, zero, comrades. We also have, we have . . ." The principal is confused for a few moments, staring into space. He looks through his papers, but doesn't find . . . "What else do we have, Comrade Băjenaru?" The jaundiced woman beside him startles awake, as though from a long dream, "Well . . . ah, there was the cork . . ." "Yes! Yes, the corks, the Romanian economy needs corks, comrades . . . we know how to drink, no problem, but we're not quite as good at collecting corks. One hundred corks per child per month, end of discussion. No matter the cost! If they refuse, write them notes home, comrades!" the principal added, grinning with great enjoyment, to which a few elementary teachers showed their teeth in servility. "Ummm, if you'll allow me," Comrade Băjenaru consults some crumpled documents from past years, "there's also the acorns." "Yes, also the acorns, ladies and misses, do you hear? That is . . . in autumn, not now, but still we should keep it in mind with all due seriousness."

In autumn, we looked for acorns on the edge of town, in the Andronache forest, and if we couldn't find any (since there was a competing school in the area) we walked, with all the children in a flock behind us, down the side of the road to the town of Voluntari and beyond, almost to Afumați. There was a beautiful little oak glen there, where we dove in, filling our canvas sacks with smooth acorns, green and brown with reddish hats, mixed among dead leaves. Last year I was in Irina's group, and while the children scampered among the damp tree trunks, we walked deeper to the heart of the forest. There, we suddenly saw something as unexpected as it was beautiful. At the start it was just a flutter of colors: scarlet, azure, pale green, and here and there trembling patches of gold. When the trees thinned out, we found ourselves in front of an abandoned chapel, with a broken roof and crooked walls, but still standing, its walls painted from top to bottom in saints and prophets with heads surrounded by halos, showing scenes from the Gospels, and a naïve Last Judgment on the eastern wall. A small ceiling with a rusted cross crowned the sloping ruin of amber light and autumn shadows. We piously entered the chamber, which was just as charmingly decorated with ancient stories of the resurrection: Lazarus, Talitha, the Roman centurion. Someone had come to Earth to wake the dead. There was a dirt floor and, to one side, a niche with a wooden statue, so swollen by damp and mold you couldn't tell who it was. Our discovery made us as happy as children. We pretended we lived there, together, that it was our house, that every day we breathed in the colors of the walls, that we walked out of our hermitage and into the forest to get water, to gather wood . . .

As usual, the meeting ends with a slap on the wrist, almost literally, for the gym teacher, Uzun, who is always doing something wrong. For her classes, she throws the kids a ball and disappears, hiding herself somewhere for a cigarette and a coffee, and she doesn't come out until the end of class. "And this little slut calls herself a teacher, as though she worked like the rest of us, hunched over our stacks of homework, grading until we can't see straight . . . she gets the same salary as we do, even more, because she gets some kind of danger pay, since, my Lord, how you can hurt yourself in the gym . . . And she hates us, she hates us like the dirty Gypsy she is, not that I have anything against other races, but there's no other way to say it." Uzun was not worried. She knew her role very well: she stood up modestly, with her eyes on the ground and a little smile in the corner of her mouth, she let the principal chew her out, then with her hands in the pockets of her track suit, she performed self-criticism and promised to turn herself around, to everyone's great satisfaction. She was completely aware of her importance as the school's black sheep.

After the meeting, the teachers gathered their skeins of wool and we dispersed throughout the school. The bottle and jar collection had begun last Friday, first in the corners of the classrooms, with twine-bound heaps of old newspaper. In a few hours, the piles of newspapers along the walls grew taller than the children and interrupted classes as they banged onto the floor. I went toward 6-G, with the register under my arm, wondering how far we had gotten last class, if we were doing grammar or literature, when out of the corner of my eye, I saw something shiny in a dark corner of the upstairs hallway. There was something in the corner opposite the eternal line of children waiting for their vaccine sugar cubes. The dark hall—lit only, clearly and precisely, by the large windows on one side, such that the columns of light, like in Piranesi's carceral paintings, fell at a slant and blinded you—had bizarre irregularities here and there, like giant goose droppings on the chessboard floor. If you looked at them more carefully, they were heaps of chipped and broken bottles and jars next to a box with a class's name on it. These carcinomas had been planted everywhere and threated to destroy the fragile, useless, absurd organism of the school.

In one of these heaps of green and brown shards that intensified drops of light in their reflective concavities, I noticed a blue palpitation. It reminded me of a poem, and I suddenly had a vision of a peacock's metallic blue throat: under the heap of fragmented images a peacock was buried, maybe still alive, waiting for me to free it, to pull it out from under the bottles of oil and jars of jam, to pet its delicate wings, to touch its pink lids rising to cover its eyes, to see it unfold its unreal tail, making it glow in squares of molten gold on the stone tiles and to melt the colored eyes of its feathers into the penumbra. There I would stay—unmoving, for an eternity, in my suit with the register under my arm—facing the peacock as it turned, slowly, its tail spread and undulating, pushed hemispherically forward, toward the cardinal directions, consumed in turn by flames and shadows, dissolving its tail inside itself into an emerald and minium sphere, with the crowned head of the imperial bird in its core.

The intense blue flashing in the corner of the hall was, however, something even more wonderful than the vision of the great peacock, something that did not negate the vision but drove it to its hallucinatory, miraculous extreme. It wasn't a peacock's neck, but, as I saw when I came closer, it was an unexpectedly delicate, ultramarine glass stem emerging from the chips and bottle caps. It looked like the fragile tendril of a plant just emerging from its seed, filmed in slow motion, because I could see it rising slowly, trembling, pushing its leaves into the air along the still, transparent neck of the stalk. I squatted beside the pile of bottles and jars, and I touched the blue stem piously. I felt a chill in my fingers: the object did not seem a part of this world. I pulled it out, and soon I stood up holding a vase that I tried to describe to myself, there on the spot, and failed. The blue amphora, translucid in the light, was not an amphora, or any other kind of vase known or possible in our world. It was, in fact, ineffable and indescribable.

I held it very carefully, in the windows' slanting, violent spring light, a delicate fruit of trembling glass, a kind of large, translucent pear, whose narrow part rose like a throat, then curved and reentered the rounder part of the pear, without touching it, only to then emerge from the lower, wider part, evaginating toward the surface. The soft structure, curved and intricate, of this object was impossible to understand. You could follow the stem of ultramarine glass with your eyes, centimeter by centimeter, and you still wouldn't understand how it reentered the glass without touching its curve, like the handle of a pitcher that in an unknown way became the pitcher itself. In our world, this kind of object seemed to be at best an optical illusion. Because the neck of the amphora could not turn back on itself unless it were rotated within a fourth dimension, along a direction our brain could not think or visualize except by analogy, and then return to the three dimensions of our space and the bottle's. In planar, two-dimensional space, you can never put your right glove on top of your left. To do so, you have to rotate one of your gloves in three-dimensional space, lifting it from the plane and putting it back down again on top of the other glove. That was what the vase was like, which a student had brought in for bottle and jar collection, and which, if I hadn't spotted and saved it, would have been melted in some glass factory, and this artifact from another world would have been lost: its neck rose, not upward but in a direction without a name, it went into that other universe like a plant rising under asphalt, making it buckle, and then it returned, miraculously, to our world.

> "Look at it, encompassed in the sole light
> The sky grafts onto the earth"

I murmured these lines from Arghezi, holding the warm, polished object against my chest, the one that now, as I write, I see in all its impossibility, glinting in the shadow on my desk, casting its blue tongues onto my manuscript. And as though my whispers, in the air frozen for centuries in the school's second story, had the power to raise the dead and shatter the circle of iterative eternities, I suddenly noticed a movement in the other corner of the hall: from that distant point a column of creatures marched toward me through the alternating dark and dissolving light: it was the nurse with her line of children.

It took them a few minutes to reach me, to surround me, to stick out their long, thin tongues toward the body of the blue bird: dwarfs with large heads, with insect-like eyes, with skin blue-gray in the deep shadow. The nurse seemed to float above them, with her syringe of pink, almost pasty liquid, in her left hand. The same liquid dribbled from a corner of her mouth, as though, from peckishness, she had taken a couple of swigs on the syringe in between squirts onto the children's cubes. It wasn't easy to escape their circle.

They crowded against me and squeezed me with their small, bony bodies, they grabbed the neck of the vase and yanked at it with greater force than I could have imagined. "Give it back," they all murmured in monotone, "give it back, it's ours, this is our class's pile." The nurse stabbed my chest with the syringe, as though this were some sinister weapon; luckily the needle was short and blunt, not made to penetrate skin. I had to wrestle with the amphora until I pulled it from their outstretched hands.

I went to the school again on Saturday, after spending the whole afternoon doing nothing but staring at the blue amphora in the luminous darkness of my study. The light that entered its curved, ultramarine pipes coursed through an unreal circuit, like blood through a heart where the delicate aortic arch emerges, and just like in a heart, the luminous liquid seemed to depart, to irrigate a distant, invisible realm, and return thicker, more oxygenated, more loaded with nutrients, as though the pear-shaped vase spread a wing in another dimension and there it threshed in an auroral, psychic world, a medium just as different from our world as the immense ocean is to the islands it bathes. Or perhaps it fanned out into a baleen, like cetaceans have to filter the teeming, transparent krill, and in fact sometimes it seemed that bizarre little animals, like scarlet or saffron sparks, danced in the rotating light, and I forced myself, examining the shiny neck very closely, to see their constantly moving antennae and legs. The object seemed to be alive, and by way of an unusual tunneling effect, it emanated an azure aura. At one point I took it into the bedroom and placed it on the bed, among the folds of the crumpled satin sheet. It sat there, at a tilt, like an enormous jewel or a large bug with metallic blue elytra. I pushed the button and the vase began to rise slowly, turning lazily along its vertical axis, until it was levitating a meter above the bed. It reflected the window in its stomach and, when twilight fell, the painful and sad twilight of springtime, the undulating red of the sky over the mercantile houses across the lot blended with the intense blue of the glass into a hue of delicate violet, the kind you see on butterfly wings and fresh violet petals. The palpitating Grail looked, more than ever, like a heart.

I went from classroom to classroom, I showed all the children the vase, and finally some kids remembered who had brought the blue pear to school for bottle and jar collection. She came from 8-C, one of mine. It had been

Valeria who brought it, along with some ordinary bottles, the girl who had come to school with the fingernails on her right hand painted the same colors as the mechanisms in the abandoned factory. After she had fainted in the hallway when I asked her to show me her fingernails, other teachers had intervened, Florabela first of all, her homeroom teacher, furious that the little snot had dared to come to school with her nails painted, but it soon turned out that the girl was not to blame. Her mother—a clerk at the neighborhood grocery—had told Florabela, very frightened, that just a few days after the girl had had her first period, her fingernails began to turn different colors, along with the bones of her preadolescent body, which now showed up in intense colors even on black-and-white X-rays. The bones of her pelvis, for example, had turned an enchanting strawberry pink: a pink butterfly, ready to take off! As a result, far from an object of decoration, the girl's nails were the cause of her shame and pain, and she tried to keep them as hidden as possible, as though they were leprosy . . .

Valeria wasn't at school that Saturday, so after school, around four, I walked the neighborhood's long, straight streets toward Str. Puiandrului, where she lived. I passed the grocery, the propane center, and a seltzer shop I had never seen before. The neighborhood, in the clear light of late afternoon, looked like an evacuated village. I was greeted by some of the few people I passed: my students' parents. Little by little, after so many animal checks and child censuses, after the registrations at the start of each school year, I had come to know the place pretty well. I especially liked the kites hanging over the streets, caught in the electrical and telephone wires, the smell of slop from the ditches, the mercilessly pruned cypress trees beside the road, the opaline skies out of de Chirico. The kind of quiet you only found there, on these gravel streets crossing always at right angles and continuing as far as you could see. On the other side were the rail tracks, and after that—country land, black and swampy, all the way to the horizon, under an enormous sky. I live in such a strange world: it might not be reality, it might be a stage set built just for me, one that will disappear as soon as I stop perceiving it. How often have I thought I could whip around and catch the stuttering stagehands knocking the backdrops together, see the single wall of the propped-up buildings fall over, or catch the moment when all perceptions dissolve into the void of death!

I might be the last person on Earth, the maze I am in might be generated, moment by moment, just for me; my consciousness might be the projection of a much vaster mind, one I contemplate without being able to understand it, the way a cat regards its giant master. Can a mind accept, once it imagines totality and eternity, the fact that it is not eternal nor all-encompassing? Can I accept the fact that to contemplate the universe, this life has given me the mind of a cat, crab, or worm? Can I *know* that the universe is comprehensible, but accept that it is not given to me to understand it?

I walk a long time, for endless hours, down continuously crossing streets. I turn right, then left, down a street parallel to the first, and everything is the same, the same country houses, the same decrepit fences, the same faces: bitter, worn, and sad. Only the light changes from one moment to the next: evening is falling. The strip of yellow light on the horizon, that seems almost to smell of lamp gas, soon turns to blood. Shining blood paints the trees and the roofs and walls of the houses. People on the street no longer trail dark shadows, but thin ribbons of blood that clot and dry into a homogeneous scarlet. Everything turns into the rough, painful granularity of a scab. Inside the houses, lights came on. The scarlet darkens, minute by minute, as the streets become emptier. The only luminous patches are the kites in the electric wires, their dragon tails hanging almost to the ground. I travel half the hemisphere, I come to the world's dark side, where, finally, I find Puiandrului, the last street in the neighborhood. Beyond it, just the rail line and the night. A few streetlights cast a dim glow.

I know the girl's house from the census. The Olaru family: he's a worker at the pipe factory, she's a grocery clerk. They have three children, two grown boys and, at a distance of more than ten years, Valeria. I look at my watch: almost nine. I realize suddenly the absurdity of the situation: what is a teacher, not even her homeroom teacher, doing at a female student's house at this hour? I stand for a few minutes in front of the gate, looking at the blue flickers on the window—they're watching television. What should I do? I suddenly notice, above me in the dark sky, millions of stars. My old fear of stars overwhelms me, I feel like I'm suffocating, as though I were at the bottom of a deep pool and the stars were the glimmering waves above. I would not have gone into the Olarus' house that Saturday evening, I would have turned back through the maze of gravel streets, if I hadn't needed shelter, if I hadn't needed to get out from under the stars. I almost ran across the yard to put my finger on the doorbell.

Valeria opens the door, then closes it quickly behind her, standing on the threshold under the sky dusted with stellar flour. "Good evening," she says. "My parents aren't home." "Where are they this time of night?" "One of my cousins is getting married." She is looking up at me guardedly. She is wearing a fairly old and shabby track suit, like every other kid in this neighborhood when they're at home. I don't know what to tell her, I can't feel anything but the panic, I need to run somewhere, a hole in the ground, anywhere but directly under the sky. Almost at random, I take the blue amphora out of my bag—it's practically black at that moment, but still it reflects, like a pitch slurry, the points of light around us—and I hold it out to her. The magic urn, impossible for our world, is now throbbing, imperceptibly, between us. The girl glances at it, then turns her white face and shining eyes back toward me. "Please come in," she says.

I enter, and everything is just the way it is in any other house in the neighborhood: flowerpots blocking the light in the windows, paintings and needlepoints of kittens in baskets, a display case for knickknacks and the indispensable glass fish, a sewing machine in a corner, a black-and-white television running with the sound turned off. Men and women in formal dress sing and dance on a street behind the narrow, domed screen. A wide stripe rises up over the images from time to time. We sit at the dining table, in the light of the screen. Much later I realized Valeria should have turned the light on. We sit face-to-face, the glass vase between us, on a tablecloth covered with a large macramé doily. I look at her: with her back to the screen, her face, framed by curly red hair, seems a little chubby, dark, and sad. I don't feel the need to say anything, even though I walked so long to get there, to the end of the earth. I just feel very uncomfortable, as I had that evening long ago when I was tutoring her for the Olympiad, when the room turned dark and the janitor found us on the same bench, bent over a notebook with barely visible letters. But the girl, outlined against the shining screen, suddenly and calmly begins to talk to me, as though she has been waiting to explain something, and her story, too, seems to palpitate like the blue light on the walls of the modest room in a house on the edge of town. I imagine the weight of the stars on the roof barely able to bear them, bowing and cracking under the stellar pressure.

"I grew up here, in this neighborhood, playing with the girls on my street. In the summer we would put down a tablecloth and play dolls. As we got older, we started to be drawn toward the train line; we would climb the levee of oily rocks it was built on and balance on the shiny rails that curved in the distance, as if they circled the whole city. The boys our age would put beer caps on the rails: the train wheels turned them into a metal circle as smooth as paper. Our parents told us not to play on the rails, that it was dangerous, but we knew when the trains came. So we would climb up without any worries and then climb down the same heap of pointy stones, covered with burnt oil, to the other side where the endless field began. It's just black earth, hard and dry sometimes, swampy other times, covered in snow in the winter. That's where we played for years, in our dirty dresses, all our childhood games: I Lost My Handkerchief, I See a Prince A-Riding, The Sassafras Girl . . . The boys would fly kites they made out of paper and plywood, painted with watercolors and decorated with long tails of knotted ribbons. Late in autumn, when the earth was covered in frost, we would look for the holes where the strong, gargantuan spiders lived. We would fish them out with bits of pitch tied to the end of a thread. We were very scared of them. The boys made them fight in an empty can they put over a flame.

"I don't know what summer it was when I found the place. But I wasn't in school yet. Mama had just bought me a yellow dress, so yellow it hurt your eyes. I went out to show it to my friends, but none of them were home, even though the weather was nice, very bright, and the wind smelled like spring. So I had to play alone. I twirled and danced in the middle of the street, in the cool of the morning, until I was dizzy; I threw my doll in the air and sometimes even caught it—its head was broken already—I skipped through an old hopscotch, but in the end I got bored and decided to go back inside. But just then a cloud moved and revealed the face of the sun, and the railway shone like gold. There was only one house, from where we are now, between us and the tracks. At the time, I was little and I'd never climbed up on the tracks. The freight and passenger cars still scared me, they were as loud as the end of the world. Even at night they would whizz by, thirty meters from our house, and make the walls shake. But that morning I was lonely, and the tracks were shining like lines of fire, so I walked over to them, step by step, sure that when the moment came I wouldn't have the guts. And yet the temptation proved more powerful than my fear: I started to climb the stones, I slipped, I started to climb again. I was crazy with joy when I got to the top, even though my new dress was covered in oil from the rocks. The oil didn't come out in the wash, so my yellow dress only lived a single day.

"I balanced on one rail for the first time. If you touched it, it was hot and vibrated gently. I walked quite a way, to the corner of the street parallel to ours, then I came back quickly. I climbed down the other side, into the field. Thistles with woolly tops grew in the rocks, and weeds with blue flowers. Now I couldn't see my house, as though I was in a story and had crossed over to another realm. I suddenly felt like a child alone in a world without end.

"I had only crossed the tracks a few moments ago when I heard, coming from the right, the sound of a large, heavy train lazily approaching. Soon, from my valley, I saw the giant locomotive, then dozens and dozens of rusty cars, tarred cisterns, platforms with large bundles wrapped in tarps. The train slowed down and stopped there, its wheels screeching. I was cut off from my world, I couldn't go back home! I started to cry, but no one heard me. The engine, somewhere far away, made beast-like sounds, bursts of pressurized steam, and terrible siren screams. Then, with my face in my hands, I ran off into the field, toward the horizon.

"That's how I found the spot. It was on the other side of a little rise, in the middle of some trees, so you couldn't see it from the neighborhood. You had to go a few steps in there, after you crossed more than a hundred meters of field, to see the perfectly round little island, covered with poppies and other plants and hundreds and thousands of multicolored butterflies. I stopped there, amazed, sopping with sweat after my run, tears flowing over my cheeks and chin. From there to the horizon, nothing else but the same black farmland, full of spider holes. I walked down to the flowering oasis, and I stood there in flowers up to my chest. Bugs climbed up their stalks, beetles in green and blue metallic armors. The sun was now directly over my head, and nothing cast a shadow. In the midst of this island of vegetation, bit by bit I calmed down, as though the poppies, with their mouths, sucked the toxins of panic from my body. I sat on the ground among the flowers, and their red, crinkly crowns closed over my head. I fell asleep. I had been left alone in the world, inside an immense and fantastical place.

"After a long time, the piercing train whistle woke me up. The freight had begun to move, and soon it wasn't blocking my way home. I ran back all the way, I crossed the tracks, and I felt like I woke up, as though I had been dreaming.

"After that, I often went to the place I had discovered; I told no one about it. I went in summer, autumn, winter, and spring. Even when it was raining and the mud was up to my ankles, I would put on rubber boots and trudge over to my spot, where I found the poppies, depending on the season, either budding, flowering, wilting, or one with the earth. Even in the winter winds, wrapped up so much you could only see my eyes, I would go there at least twice a week. And how could you not go, when the spot sent you presents? Soon I started to call it The Island of Gifts. It didn't happen often, or on a regular basis. About once a month. But I don't think that the moon over the endless field was ever round—first like a slice of lemon, then like a fingernail, then like a half face, and then round again—without me getting a gift from my enchanted piece of earth. Come, I want to show them to you."

Valeria stood and took me to her room. There she lit a lamp with childish decorations that projected over the walls and ceiling. A little bed, a wardrobe, a table with notebooks and textbooks. Two or three broken toys. She went to the wardrobe, whose doors had a key with knitted tassels. When she opened the door, hundreds of brightly colored objects suddenly poured out onto the floor. At first I thought they were balls, but when I picked one up I understood. The object was as light as paper, it was in fact made of a kind of thin cardboard. It looked like a brightly colored polyhedron (each side was a different color), but just as in the case of the little "amphora" I found among the bottles and jars, there was something strange about it; it looked impossible, incomplete, the way the photograph of a polyhedron in our space would look, with an extra dimension where the back of the object in the picture was hidden. And the bizarre shape I held in my fingers, although three-dimensional, seemed to have a back, an inaccessible hidden place. The polyhedron was only a three-dimensional section of a fantastical four-dimensional object. My mind flashed to Hinton, the lord of the fourth dimension, and his psychic experiments with colored cubes, his tesseract (which was also one of the cardboard shapes scattered over the room's cheap Persian rug). I thought about the stormy sexual history of the Boole family, the five genius sisters, one of whom had dedicated herself to making the Hintonian insanities concrete, creating the most unusual sections of the fourth dimension, unspeakably beautiful mathematical sculptures which she displayed, on mahogany shelves, under the name of polytopes. They were all there, on the rug in Valeria's room, burying our feet up to the ankles in fragile and multicolored pieces of origami.

"I found them in the center of the spot, every once in a while," the girl dreamer continued, "I took them home and, hour after hour, I would look at them from every angle, then I put them away in the wardrobe with my other precious things. Sometimes I would find a little pieces of glass, like the one I mixed up with my dad's beer bottles and gave the school by mistake. Inside those I would put ants: I would catch one of the big red ones and let it go in the opening at the bottom of the pear. I watched it through the transparent walls, as it was walked along the pipe that twists inexplicably and bizarrely in the body of the pear, but without ever touching it; I saw the ant disappear and, after a long time, reappear in a different color: the most vivid blue, yellow, pink, or violet. If I put it back with the other ants, they attacked it with an extraordinary ferocity, they dismembered it and took the remains as far away as they could. So I would keep them in jars from the doctor, until they died.

"The 'gifts' started to appear two years ago, which is also when my fingernails started to turn different colors. I think I was in the wrong place at the wrong time. One time, on a November evening, I went across the tracks because it had been almost a month and I hadn't found any gifts. At the time, I thought I couldn't live without the joy I got from finding the little things among the poppies. It had gotten dark early and the sky was filled with dark clouds. An icy wind was blowing, as though it could scatter the few stars that had appeared near the horizon where the sky was still clear. I climbed up the tracks and saw the spot in all its autumnal sadness: nothing but wilted stems lying on the ground. The crowns of flowers, the butterflies, the insects had all disappeared long ago. No cube, no multicolored ball. The wind ruffled my hair and dress as though they were drapes. I was getting ready to go home, when

I felt, above my head, the light changing. I looked up and I saw a dark cloud, like a raincloud, hanging in the air, but its inside was glowing. Something soft and transparent, like a large soap bubble, was coming down through the dark fog, emitting a blue light. When it came out of the cloud, still descending, I saw it better: the surface was like silk, but more immaterial. It was a whiff, a gentleness, a chimera that slowly descended with an aura around it: it was the most beautiful thing I have ever seen. It was somehow alive, it looked like one of the animalcules we studied in biology—the ones that emit gelatinous legs, that don't have a precise shape—but giant and undulating against the dark sky. It stopped at the height of a small apartment block. There was, in its flesh as immaterial as air, a kind of agitation. A soft, trembling leg stretched toward the ground and deposited something like an insect egg sliding down a transparent ovipositor, it was one of the little paper things I had been waiting for so desperately. The soft column then retracted, and the soap bubble began to rise, until it disappeared back into the layer of clouds.

"I think I wasn't supposed to see that. Anyway, I went home just horrified, feeling really ashamed and really guilty. I never went back to my spot. Winter came, and the weather was really bad. I had a lot to study for school, chores to do at home. The next spring I grew a lot, the neighbors said I 'became a little lady.' Only two springs later did I dare to go back across the shining tracks. Then I found, in the sprouts of grass, the blue vase. It was full of dirt, you could barely see it. It had probably been there a long time, waiting for me. I took it home and washed it well. The water that went through its curved pipes came out colored and thick, like gelatins in the shape of a raspberry or slices of orange that my mom buys me sometimes. The rains came right after that, the mud was up to your knees, and that was when I heard about our school's porter, who disappeared in the field. I went, like everyone else, to see his footprints, the ones that stopped suddenly in the middle of the field. I was shocked when I saw they stopped right in my spot—but now it looked burnt, like a leprous scab over the earth. Nothing ever grew there again."

I helped her pick up the cardboard polyhedrons and put them back in the wardrobe, then I said goodbye and left. It must have been two in the morning. The stars were shining like crazy all over the sky, and along the whole street there were hardly more than one or two dim streetlights. I walked through the night, down Colentina, for two hours, completely alone, mad with the muted whirring of the stars. It was as though each one were a spider that could fall on me at any moment, along a transparent thread, with its legs spread, and inject its venom into my body. I could be flooded with billions of them, a swarm of articulating legs like I'd never seen. I turned onto Maica Domnului as though it were a familiar port with calm waters, and soon I was asleep in my clothes, across the bed, in my boat-shaped house, the shell of my strange life.

41

I saw crosses, flocks of crosses scrawled in red ink
circling in the stormy sky.
I saw cities, thousands of kilometers underneath
attacked by transparent bombers
inseminated with the germs of fire, death, and desperation.
I saw nautiluses with each compartment teeming with human hordes
navigating the flesh of all oceans at once.
I saw ivory tapeworms in humanity's intestines
emerald ticks sucking the vitreous fluid from its eyeballs.
I saw whole armies of skeletons, shielding themselves
with coffin lids in a landscape of fire and brimstone.
I saw the gods of death and love
trading places in rolling allegorical processions,
coupling with cadavers and hacking the bodies
of lovely women to pieces.
I saw fear devouring our cranium.

I saw people spitting on icons in metaphysical schools
expectorated truths from broken lungs
the people's executioners crowned with mint and gentian violets.
A saw rams with billions of horns impaled
in the spider holes of all the stars.
I saw the bestial faces of the exterminating devil's children.

I saw all 10,500 parallel universes at once. They are the living cells
of a body of stars. They form the vertebrae
livers and guts of an unknown god.
I saw gods, flocks of gods on their knees
before him, before her
before its billions of sexes
while the flocks of blood crosses spun around them.
I saw the empires of mites fighting over pillow feathers.

I saw hell, in all its wealth
and grace and atrocity.
I saw the letter M scalpeled into everyone's palms.
I saw the skies opened and the sky's intestines
falling down on top of us.
I saw morality going insane, intelligence babbling
fire soaking, night screaming
moon moaning, horses barking
with their snake legs amputated.
I saw the earth covered with ten meters of flies
the galaxy suffocated under cubic parsecs of stag beetles.
I saw flocks of crosses taking plants and animals away into the sky.

I saw icons with their lips cut out.
I saw crania surrounding a wise man's head.
I saw, I felt, I foretold, and I prophesied the destruction
that will come, that had come, that has come. The filaments
of the Lord that control our thoughts.
The black breasts of melancholy.
The black udders of the female archangels.
The black tattoos of white pages.
The white eyes of black faces.
The black tendrils, the black tendrils of death!
Life as the spectacle of death!
Death as the spectacle of death!

Being as the finger ring of nonbeing!
Nonbeing as the finger ring of insanity!
I saw All, o Lord
all in a moment
in the eye of a needle
in the geometrical point
in the ardor of my leechlike brain.
In the serotonin of quasars
in the poems of monsters in the abyss.
I saw fear devour our minds.

And today, when I remember the black epiphany of Nicolae Minovici's designs, I feel like my mind is exploding. I wouldn't look at them again for anything in the world, the wretched placards that he said were only the shadows of shadows, in comparison to what he had actually seen during his sessions of controlled hanging. When I was able to see them for real at Emil's (while Anca screamed orgasmically from the next room), allowing my two cerebral hemispheres to extend, diverge, and perceive a different mental field than the one our mind permits, formed by hunger, cold, the drives to mate and to kill, I felt that I was also hanging from a beam, I felt the noose constricting around my trachea and my tongue, swollen, purple, bloated, and hanging grotesquely from my mouth, and demonic and angelic visions were parading before my bulging eyes, with the white outside and the iris inside, looking directly into my brain, fascinated by the depths of our interior palace. I often wondered why all of us, within the marble palace of the mind, have a forbidden room—perhaps one alone, shared by the entire human species. Why, in hypnagogic moments, when we are lying in bed between two worlds, incompletely free from the dream of reality and incompletely captured by the reality of dreams, do frightening monsters and visions of hell rise from this room? Fangs, gaping jaws, eyes injected with hate, giant crab claws and venomous scorpion tails, devils and dragons and terrible beasts flood our incendiary visual field, hordes coming from the depths of forests and the cores of stars and the ends of the earth, in order to tear our mind to pieces. We have the inferno inside us, we also have paradise; we have the horn gate, we also have the ivory gate; we have to choose between many exits, between numberless exits, because the scarlet doors are unnumbered, going down thousands of floors, in the hypogenic edifice of our mind. But for someone searching for the true exit, the one that leads beyond the skull and the edges of the universe, outside the cranial box of three dimensions, all the doors with melting locks are only drawn on the walls, are all traps, illusions, and tricks that aren't worth your time. You will find true signs extremely seldom, signs that show you a true path toward a suddenly blinding exit, with a new earth and a new sky, the one for which our restless souls have always searched. The larva that lived for years in its hole in the earth, gnawing on roots and tubers, one day emerges into the sun, spreading multicolored wings under a glorious, undefiled blue dome.

But the unbearable moments of ecstasy and destruction I experienced while looking at Minovici's drawings—so painful I felt like I was being tattooed with a burning needle across my entire skin, even the delicate skin of my internal organs—briefly reminded me of other drawings, from another region of the world, that had given me the same sense of enigma, of an exit from this world of ours. When I was writing the call slip, in the reading room of the Letters library, for *The Gadfly* by Ethel Lilian Voynich, I saw out of the corner of my eye, attached to the metal bar in the drawer labeled VL–VU, other cards for the name "Voynich." I didn't pay much attention at the time, because I was in such a hurry to get a copy of *The Gadfly*, but something remained in my mind, because suddenly the Boole–Hinton–Lilian Voynich line, with its coincidences and its painful insertion into my own life, seemed to me worthy of research, and I wanted to learn as much as possible. Only this, or this in convergence with other continents of my curiosity, could lead to the sole meaning of my life on Earth: the completion of the jigsaw, the cartography of the labyrinth, the end, salvation, escape.

So I returned, after several years, to that transatlantic steamer made of books, in the room with an undefined number of floors lined with books, to reopen one of the many drawers of the massive wooden catalog and to search among its cards. I found *The Gadfly* in five or six editions, a biography of the author translated from German (first published by Volk und Welt Verlag in GDR, 1972), another author named Voynich who lived a century before the Boole daughters and had no connection with her family, and, in the end, a card on which was written, simply, "The Voynich Manuscript," without any details. Even odder, the card was handwritten in minuscule letters, like a medieval miniature. The words were barely legible. It made me think of the entire Bible written on a matchstick or the Tao Te Ching carved into a grain of rice, which I read about in who knows what collection of facts. Not even then did I understand that card; I left the library still pondering, and I remember that I went into a coffee shop on Magheru. I ordered a piece of cake and a soda, sat at a table, and after I finished I left without paying, so deep was I in thought. The waitress ran after me and chewed me out, so loudly that people stopped to watch the show. I didn't mind: I knew I had to go back, that I had to know more about this manuscript. There had to be a sign that I had missed. I went back into the giant hall, I called a librarian over, I showed her the card, and she looked at it blankly and asked if this was a joke. It obviously wasn't one of their cards. Without exerting herself with other ideas, the woman—who had a round and hypothyroid face—simply yanked the card off the drawer's metal bar, tore it in half and threw it into the trash. I grabbed the pieces as soon as she turned her back.

I reassembled the pieces at home, and that's when I noticed the line of ink on the back. It was in the lower right corner, barely visible. But in the powerful light of my lamp, and under my philatelist magnifying glass, I was able to decipher its secret. It wasn't actually a continuous line, but a series of dots that, magnified by four, proved to be numbers. There were six numbers, in pairs, like a telephone number.

I am a shy person, I'll do anything to avoid talking to strangers. At the teller windows where I pay my gas and light bills, I feel completely lost. The plumbers and painters I have to call to my house from time to time intimidate me, as if they were scholars or professors. So it took me a few days before I went, with my heart in my throat, to Tei Lake, the closest phone booth. There was always a nervous line of people listening to and commenting on the phone conversations or arguing among themselves. When my turn finally game, I dropped in a coin and dialed, but before anyone answered I panicked and hung up. I walked around for a quarter hour, I looked at the poor, dusty shop windows (this shabby city, the worst on the planet), then I got in line again. I wasn't sorry. It seemed to me that the effort I was making showed how much was—or might be—at stake.

I heard the line ring and someone answered. A tired, parchment-like voice, an older man, perhaps. "Good evening," I said and stopped talking. I hadn't thought out what I would say, how to introduce myself. "Good evening," he responded, then waited for me to speak. "I'm calling you about . . . I found your number at the library, the Letters library . . . it's about the Voynich manuscript." It's strange how hard my heart was beating. The old man didn't respond for a few good moments. "Where are you calling from?" I told him, and he gave me an address at the end of Pantelimon. He would be expecting me in about two hours. Then he hung up without any niceties.

I took three trams to get there. Şoseaua Pantelimon is endless. On both sides, like a continuous wall, like a reservoir dam—workers' apartment blocks, with the plaster falling off, narrow rusty balconies, and trash dumpsters beside them where insects swarmed and a filthy substance fermented in the sun. When evening came, the trams looked like transparent, solid honey. The passengers seem like insects immortalized in their block of amber. Along the street, on the blocks' first story, I counted about twenty dentist offices. The people here seemed to have teeth as ruined as the buildings where they lived, one on top of the other, in heaps separated by paper-thin walls. When someone flushed their toilet, the whole block heard it. Everyone knew what everyone else ate for dinner, everyone had their ear against the wall to listen to a husband mounted on his wife, making her moan in the middle of the night. But the man I had talked to on the phone didn't live in a block. I got off at the last stop, in front of the Titan theater, in absolute darkness. The stop itself was in a field, just past the last line of houses. The movie theater, whose name I had read in the papers, since my mother ran her finger down the list of theaters when she wanted to see where *Scaramouche* was playing or *Treasure of the Silver Lake,* was an ancient building, covered in rococo stucco, with a bizarre metal cupola and a chipped pink angel, apparently flayed of its flesh, on the top. The house I was looking for was a long walk away.

Who knows how, but at the end of the neighborhood, a clump of old houses had been forgotten by the excavators and bulldozers that had demolished the others. They were mercantile houses, more than a century old, hideous, kitschy, most of them abandoned in an advanced state of ruin. Some were full of vegetation and lichen, other yards had plaster statues staring toward the stars with blind eyes. Many of the windows were missing their panes; they were simply holes in the wall where you could see the empty, desolate rooms. In two or three houses there was light shining through a tacked-up pink or orange cloth. I wandered for a long time down the alleyways lit by a single dim bulb hanging from the top of a tilted lamppost, until I came to the pink house, pink like the first moments of twilight, with a wide facade with chipped and worn plaster. The walls' rose color was clearly visible in the light of the wrought iron lanterns, shaped like dragon heads, over the entryway, only to darken at the edges into a melancholic gray. The door was dark scarlet like a scab over a wound. An elderly man opened the door, with gray hair and brown eyes, dressed in a gray suit so worn out I assumed it must be his only one. With a curious expression, he held out his hand: "Palamar." Inside, we passed through somber rooms decorated in an old style, without anything to strike your eye, but which showed signs of a former prosperity: oil paintings with their varnish intact, silver trays on the coffee table, nicely bound books in the bookcases. A stale, olive air, like a museum; an active, tense quiet, foretelling something that had probably never taken place. We arrived in an office with sculpted wood furniture, whose entire left wall was covered by a large metal cabinet. The pearly gray of the cabinet, which stretched from the floor to the room's high ceiling, contrasted strangely and unpleasantly with the room's old-fashioned appearance. We sat face-to-face on either side of the massive, lion-foot desk, whose surface was full of books and handwritten papers and spiral notebooks, all in heaps about to fall over.

"I wonder when you will recognize me," he said slowly, as though he needed to protect his voice, then he fell silent, looking at me steadily, like a portrait in a gallery that demanded study. The desk lamp lit the depths of his eyes, a limpid and weary brown. The gray hair, combed back over his head against his skull, did remind me of someone. I imagined the search mechanisms in my mind, the articulating arms that open and close dozens of thousands of files at once in the pulsating darkness of the brain, the circuits of comparison and validation, the negatives fired through all the fibers of the mnesic networks, the way photographers fill large baskets of wire with curled ribbons of celluloid. Without my knowing how, my mind searched, it flailed through epochs and scenes and faces and gestures and attitudes. Each being we remember is like a statue in a public piața where long spatial, temporal, and psychic boulevards intersect. I invoked from the Hades of memory a name and a cup of steaming blood, as bait and promise. We should be frightened of the ghosts who live within our abyss, feeding on us, riding the hypothalamus, baring their furious fangs to their tonsils. To recall a figure in memory is to conjure a dead person, to see him rise from the earth with a skull face, with dark, sad eyes, to remind you of your own zombified life in the memory of someone else. Then I suddenly remembered, recovering not a face but an emotional climate, from where I knew the person in front of me.

I am twelve years old, still living a larval life in my parent's house on Ştefan cel Mare. My life is arranged along the streets, from Lizeanu on the left, until the faraway Volga theater on the other side of the intersection with Dorobanți. The rest is lost in fog and nonbeing, as though I were living on a speck of earth that had somehow been spared the catastrophe that destroyed everything else, a speck floating in space with tram tracks down the middle, with buildings on both sides, with three or four cars that pass slowly once a minute (Pobedas and Wartburgs with peeling paint), with an inexplicable trolley that crosses from a lateral street and disappears enigmatically into the void full of constellations, with the grocery, cafeteria, fruit and vegetable stand, and bread center, with the point where they distribute ice on Tunari, where people pick up their translucid blocks, streaming water, in raffia sacks, and especially the three great places of interest for me, and about which I dream quite often. The banal tobacco store on the corner was not banal for me at the time, it was fascinating, vested in twilight. I pushed its heavy, almost impossible door open, and I entered a fantastical space, like from another world, that reeked of tobacco. Everything was tightly packed, like in a car; you barely had room to turn around among the racks of postcards, packs of cheap Carpați and Rarău cigarettes, the mysterious boxes of condoms, the books I looked at avidly, the fresh newspapers smelling of celluloid and printer's ink. It was always twilight in the tobacconist's. Behind the counter was a fat woman in a work jacket, sister of the ticket-taker in the tram, the woman who repaired nylons, and the nurse, her face shiny and swollen like a lymphatic ganglion, with the Asian features I also encountered in the caretakers at Voila. She didn't seem to have her own life, or any kind of psychology, just the minimal physiology of a parasite, a vegetable, a sack of fat and eggs pressed against the walls behind the counter. On the opposite corner of the street, which led toward an impossible and exceptionally faraway Floreasca, was a round newsstand with a small opening where you saw, among the racks of publications, another twin of the saleswoman from across the street. Each Thursday, the *Science-Fantasy Stories* and *Adventure Club* pamphlets came out, and I would get up at dawn to buy them. Finally, the last place where I provisioned myself with books was the neighborhood library, on the first floor of the block across the street, the farthest place I had ever been under my own power. It was so far away that the block, with its groceries and library, seemed, like the street, like the summer clouds above, chiseled in crystal that threw off sparks and rainbows. I would borrow books from this neighborhood library about twice a month.

That's where I knew Palamar from: he was the librarian! That ashen man, as quiet as death, with soft gestures, with inaudible footsteps on the floor of the room where you entered, where you saw nothing but him sitting at a desk, reading. I went there dozens of times, and I always found him reading. He would silently receive the books I had borrowed in previous weeks and gesture toward the door to the right of the entrance. In fact there was no door. You went directly into the second room, no larger than an ordinary room in a workers' block, but with shelves of books on every wall. I would while away there for hours. No one else ever came in, as though the library were made for me alone. I never heard any sound except, from time to time, the distant noise of the trams going down Ştefan cel Mare, vibrating the walls. I would pass my fingers over the books' ragged spines, with their torn dustcovers and yellowed pages, I would drown in clouds of dust when I took a book from the shelf, I would peer curiously at the small insects, also yellow, that hid among the pages that abraded their tough skins. The air there was as stale as Palamar's house, stale and sad like a hypogeum. I would choose, finally, three books and take them to the librarian's room. In all those years that I borrowed books, I never heard his voice. He would just raise his head from his book (the same book with strange plates that he seemed to read eternally), look at me with deep, brown eyes, arrange a strand of his then brown hair, combed back against his skull, write the books down in a register, and not respond to my goodbye. He would just lower his gaze back to his book.

I never chose books by their author, cover, or even their titles. I would choose them for a certain quality that, using the wrong word (but lacking an adequate one), I would call their "tactility." Simply the touch of my fingertips to the spine of the book. Some books "burned," other seemed "frozen" to me. But these are metaphors. Something would click, like coins to a magnet. I felt I could tell in a flash if the book was for me, just as later I could intuit, in a single glance into the eyes of a woman with whom I might live, whether we were compatible, if she could open the path, through her body and climate and perfume, to paradise. I felt, without error, the books that would make me happy/unhappy, and even if I didn't actually read some (*The Castle, Shameless Death, Hinterland, Malpertuis*) at that time, I was still right, because they became my favorites later. Once I got home, I would go in my room, the one from which I could see the whole city from my triple window, all the way to the horizon, with the complicated architecture of the clouds above, and I would lie over my bed, in the transfinite light, and read until it was dark, until I couldn't see the letters.

"You are the librarian," I said. The words sounded crude and obscene in the musty chiaroscuro of his study, in that photographic silence. "You put the card with the Voynich manuscript in . . ." "Yes, of course I did. Who else? I don't think there's anyone else in the city who knows about the manuscript. I fear there's no one who would even want to know. I simply put a message in a bottle and threw it into the ocean, years ago, when there was a meeting in the Letters lecture hall of all the librarians in the area. I knew, of course, that it would, sooner or later, end up with you, because everything ends up with you, as though you were an antlion hidden in its paranoid nest, but somehow I hoped that our world's determinism would prove less rigid, that vibrations and reverberations might change history, destiny, even if very slowly, with only a minuscule deviation at every crossroad. Because it is horrible to be frozen within the block of a definite world that flows like a book from its first page to its last, without its characters being able to say or do anything besides what was written (what was written for them) once and for all. I hoped that someone else, some confused student, perhaps, someone writing her doctorate on *The Gadfly*, some vagabond mercifully sheltered in the library during a bitter January, would come across my card, would wonder what this Voynich manuscript was, would become so intrigued that they would examine every mark on the rectangular card and find my telephone number.

"For ten years, however, no one has called. The card has sat there, hidden, virtual, like a foreign sequence in the genetic code of the great libraries, like the account of Tlön inserted in the Encyclopedia Britannica, a spore, a structure without life or energy yet which still unfurls like a paper lotus under the eyes of whoever is predestined to see it. The code written on it activated immediately when it met your face, engrammed in its memory, and its first action was to send you to me. It unleashed, that is, a chain of events, one flowing into the next, which had been planned in times immemorial and which cannot (any longer) be stopped. You are here, before me, as you were so many times in your childhood, when you brought me books without knowing how well I knew you and how much certainty you brought into my world. I knew that we would meet again, and not only so that I could open, before your eyes, the Voynich manuscript."

Some people are functions, they live along one edge of the world for the sake of a single gesture, a single reply, lacking their own life or psychology, like doormen or elevator operators in big hotels. I was now, perhaps, waiting in front of a gigantic gate, one as high as the sky. But Palamar stood in front of it, and without his blessing I could not cross the threshold. "So, what is this manuscript? Do you have it?"

"Yes, I do—a copy of it, of course, the original is in America."

"And why am I supposed to know about it? Why am I here?"

"That I cannot know. Maybe because you borrowed books from the B. P. Hasdeu Library (you know that you were, for seven years, my only client? After you stopped coming, the library was shut down. Now it's a coffee shop), or because you found the card in the drawer . . ." Or because I cried for the first time reading a book, one written by this same Ethel Lilian Voynich. Or maybe because I learned that the author was George Boole's daughter and grew up around Hinton. Through what impossible coincidence did the mysterious manuscript, the one Palamar was about to show me, carry the name of the writer and her husband, the former Polish revolutionary?

"I have a very good copy, in color and the original size. It came to me along a complicated route, with which I wouldn't want to bore you. When you look at a field full of flowers, you don't care about the pale roots stretching into the ground, among the beetles and worms. I am only the person who puts it in your hands."

The old man stood up and opened a cupboard on the wall opposite the metal locker. He removed a box that appeared to be made from yellowed ivory. For a moment it seemed as though he was, in fact, holding a skull. He placed the box on the desk between us, and, still standing, he removed the lid. With infinite delicacy, he slid his pale fingers into the box and lifted, like a newborn, the dusty manuscript into the light. Rigid and solemn, he placed it before me. It was professionally copied, hard to tell it was not the original. Even the paper, shining dully like parchment, gave the impression of authenticity. I wanted to leaf through the pages, but Palamar stopped me. "Later. For the moment, I want to tell you what I have discovered about the manuscript, over several years of effort. Because you have before you one of the most obscure—and yet most brilliant—books on the face of the earth, a true mine flower, as yet unexcavated . . ."

The Voynich manuscript, as Palamar told me that evening, is perhaps five hundred years old. It is written on parchment in an unknown tongue and illustrated with images of plants, likewise unidentified. Further illustrations show constellations and zodiac signs, diagrams that seem to have to do with alchemy. Strange are the images of pale, plantlike women, who bathe naked in tubs of green liquid, supplied by networks of canals and pipes that seem vegetable, as though the liquid were the sap of a gigantic plant, and the women—the fat and immobile females of woolly lice, hidden under their protective carapaces. The oldest information about this strange work appeared two hundred years after, as is supposed, it was written and illustrated somewhere in northern Italy by a yet unknown master. Although the text seems to belong to the Renaissance, it does not seem by chance that it was actually discovered in the period in which princes had garden labyrinths, cabinets of curiosities and horrors, and the taste for enigmas and catacombs was formed by writings full of ciphers, allegories, hermetic and cabalistic signs, for example, Colonna's *Hypnerotomachia Poliphili* or *Mundus Subterraneus* by the scholar, monastic, and polygraph Athanasius Kircher. Fed with alchemy, *Sefer Ha-Bahir*, and meditations on all-devouring time and the opulent desolation of life, the seventeenth century received this indecipherable manuscript as new evidence of the world's baroque monstrosity. In a letter to Kircher, the Bohemian Marcus Marci, author of *Labyrinthus, in quo via ad circuli quadraturam pluribus modis exhibetur,* communicated, to the best of his knowledge, the manuscript's fragmentary history.

One century earlier, it had been in the possession of Emperor Rudolf II, who was said to have bought it from an unknown person for six hundred guilders. The next owner was, it seems, the emperor's botanist, who created the wonder of the imperial park in Prague, with greenhouses and cages of exotic animals, with peacocks and pheasants that strutted across the flower-glazed grass. The botanist passed the codex to Georg Baresch, one of the alchemists in Prague who multiplied like rabbits under the emperor's patronage, and who called his library's new book an eternally indecipherable "sphinx." Baresch was so haunted by the abstruse nature of the book that he sent a copy of one of its pages to be deciphered by the greatest cryptographer of the age, the same Jesuit monk, Kircher, who claimed to have deciphered the Egyptian hieroglyphs and who, in addition, knew Chinese, Coptic, and various other exotic languages. Only after the alchemist's death did the codex come into Marci's possession, who, as the Jesuit's disciple, fulfilled his long-standing desire to see the manuscript with his own eyes. Anthanasius Kircher was in the middle of his great book *Ars magna lucis et umbrae* when he received it, accompanied by Marci's letter. They say that he dropped his work in progress, as well as the bric-a-brac of his work on minerology, crystallography, physics, and biology (he had just begun to look through his microscope at the transparent animalcules never before seen by human eyes), in order to occupy himself, in the following weeks from dawn to dusk, with nothing, nothing but the wheels, flowers, large-bellied women, and lists of meaningless letters—were they even letters?—of the codex. He identified, in the 240 pages that survived from the original book, sections on cosmology, botany, aphorisms, and others hard to define, but most interestingly he found a text that ran for pages without erasures or additions, monotonous, separated into words of differing lengths, but apparently without any linguistic features that would serve as clues for a real language, even one you didn't know and couldn't name. A hoax by the great Leonardo? the master wondered. In his youth the divine painter had written backward, from right to left, but you didn't need more than a mirror to make as plain as the back of your hand the writing that appeared beside a drawing of a man's erect organ sticking into the fleshly sheath of a female womb, or another that demonstrates the blue of the mountains as effect of the air between them and the eye that sees, or yet another of hydraulic machines, alongside which he had written, "O Lionardo, perche tanto penate?" But it seemed impossible that a hack writer, even were he a genius, could write a meaningless text so fluently, in which some letters appeared only at the start of the words, others only at the end, some words appeared only in certain sections—clearly some rules, at least of statistics if not linguistics, seemed to be strictly respected. If it were not an elaborate con, done for money, betting on the oddness of the book (otherwise what craftsman of sound mind would have worked to invent a language; types of plants that do not exist on Earth, with their flowers, leaves, stems, and roots; unintelligible zodiacs and calendars; rather than using his talent to describe the works left to us by God in his great glory?), and Kircher was forced to reject this possibility categorically, then there was no other choice—excluding the possibility of an insane craftsman—but to see the whole as a document in code, hiding revelations, perhaps demonic, perhaps divine, but one which could be deciphered using the instruments of human ingenuity.

The monk engaged the manuscript with all the cryptographical tricks of his age. He wrote the text on strips of paper and wound them around sticks of different widths, he arranged them in boxes of magic squares, under the weighty gaze of the angel leaning his head in his hand, he read the pages through grids cut from heavy paper. He moved the letters through simple and compound permutations, but without his knowing the alphabet in which the text was written, or any parallel text in a known language, or any other sign, the text resisted his efforts, and the monk was not able to decipher even a single word, with the exception of a few Latin and Greek words scattered parsimoniously above the illustrations. In the end, the master declared himself bested and left the text to collect dust in the shelves of the Collegio Romano library.

In the heat of Italian unification movements (precisely those that serve as the backdrop for *The Gadfly*), the library was taken over by Vittorio Emanuele II's soldiers, who moved the old manuscripts to the Villa Mondragone, near

Rome. In 1912, the Jesuit brotherhood sold, discreetly, some manuscripts to private parties, including the Polish rare book dealer Wilfrid Voynich, then ten years married to Ethel Lilian Boole, daughter of the great English mathematician and logician, and author of *The Gadfly.*

The Pole was noble, born to a well-known family, his full name was Wilfrid Michał Habdank-Wojnicz. He had studied chemistry in Moscow and had a degree in pharmacy. He looked like an eggheaded badger with round glasses, a fact which reduced his successes with women to zero. Returning from Warsaw, the young man, for whom it seemed all roads were closed, frequented high-society balls, and the proud female offspring—who turned across the polished floors in dresses foaming with the colors of saffron and lavender, glittering with the thousands of facets of the diamonds on their ears, neck, and wrists—seemed to prefer slightly less noble and less well-known young men who were yet endowed with a dancer's grace, strong shoulders, and an arrogant gaze. He tried for a while to make his way as a pharmacist, but even though his knowledge of chemistry later brought him fame as a maker of artisanal explosives, he didn't do too well in tiled interiors full of shelves of intricately painted porcelain jars in which nux vomica, laudanum, tinctures and iodines, pills for impotence and pills for abortions, suppositories wrapped in paraffin, and other countless substances and preparations waited to assuage suffering bodies. His fingers were too thick for the fine silver scale on the counter, and he was too honest to prescribe to the vicious the ambrosia and nectar for which their hands trembled, that is, the morphine so widely used at the time, the tincture of opium and ether. "Get drunk on anything," an eccentric poet had recently written, "on wine, poetry, virtue, it doesn't matter . . ."

Once he encountered, by chance, on his way to care for a patient in a dank attic apartment, people who got drunk on revolutionary ideals, Wilfrid felt how small, how petty, how chaotic his life had been up to that moment. Ludwik, a man even more hapless than the pharmacist, placed in his hands the capital works of the socialists. Clandestine works, primitively printed, bearing the dirt of the hands through which they had passed, signed with names Wilfrid had scarcely heard before then: Louis Blanc, Saint-Simon, Fourier, Engels, Marx, and the writings of the enfants terribles, the Russian nihilists, Bakunin, Kropotkin, and the demonical Nechayev, whose *Catechism* brought him sleepless nights of feverish chills. He understood his destiny had little to do with balls and apothecaries. The world was a corrupt and unjust inferno that needed to be razed to the ground. The final exterminating archangel and the hero of the times to come was the revolutionary. "A revolutionary is cursed. He has no private occupations, no businesses, no feelings, no connections, no properties, not even a world. His entire being is consumed by a single purpose, a single thought, a single passion: revolution. In body and soul, not just in words and deeds, he has broken all his connections with social order and with the entire civilized world, with the world's laws, manners, conventions, and morals. He is their merciless enemy that continues to live in the world with a single goal: to destroy it," wrote the terrible Nechayev. At the age of twenty, Wilfrid had found the most important book of his life, his older and wiser comrade, and the path for which he felt more and more prepared. He entered, through a ritual that seemed rather in bad taste (but good taste was one of those values that must be denounced and mistrusted), Ludwik Waryński's Proletariat organization, and he immediately took on the most hazardous of revolutionary actions. As consequence of one of them, an attempt to free two condemned men from the Warsaw citadel, he was caught by the Okhrana and sent to Siberia. After three years' hard labor, he escaped and spent the following year wandering through forests, feeding on mulberries and bread he stole from the village, often meeting murderers on the run and peasants over whom holiness descended through prayer of the heart. He was finally saved, more dead than alive, by his fellow conspirators, who sent him to China to cover his tracks.

In Beijing, he had time to study the hidden, twisted paths of revolution. Perhaps its violent side, however, did not fit his style. Maybe it was not worthy of the ascesis and martyrdom that the frightening catechism demanded of them. He was still young (although worn to threads from years of imprisonment and wandering) when he returned to Europe, first to Hamburg, then settling in London. A meeting with Sergey Stepnyak, who militated for the transformation of Russia through revolutionary, but peaceful, means, confirmed his wanderings had been in error. The newly founded Society of Friends of Russian Freedom was attended by wise people who accepted gradual change, through political means, of the testy troika.

At the Society's London meetings, he met Ethel Lilian, an old revolutionary of long residences in Russia and ample Narodnik activity. She was ugly, and a year older than Wilfrid, but just as educated and just as devoted to Mother Russia. They married in 1902, in a small ceremony with their circle of ex-revolutionaries, now graying slightly, a bit bougie, their ideals transformed into memories. Voynich Anglicized his name, took British citizenship, and became an antiques dealer, following an old and long-forgotten passion for rare books. As the years passed, the couple dropped their revolutionary activities and lived in the world of books, she writing novels (*The Gadfly* was already published in the States and England and had brought her some fame), he opening bookstores and trading in old manuscripts and printed matter. Once their New York store, opened in 1914, started doing well, the ex-revolutionary couple moved across the ocean, where the two lived until Wilfrid's death in 1930 and Ethel's in 1960, when the author of *The Gadfly* was of the advanced age of ninety-six, and I—under the rainbow cupola of my Floreasca, on the other side of the world—was only four.

"You can take it," Palamar said, wearily passing his hand over his combed-back gray hair, pressing it against his skull. "It is the last book I will ever lend you, now, after my library hasn't existed for a long time." He stood and looked at me impersonally: our meeting had ended. Before leaving the room, I glanced toward the pearly gray metal cabinet occupying the entire left wall. It was such a contrast with the rest of what I had seen in the librarian's house that I couldn't stop myself from asking, in passing, out of the side of my mouth, "What's locked in the cabinet?"

"Ah, more papers," he answered without surprise, "when you bring back the manuscript (and let's follow the old rule: three weeks), I'll show it to you. But maybe you already know, maybe you've seen it. Or maybe your eyes fell over my desk back then, in the library, and you noticed the book plates. That's where I usually worked, during the long hours I spent waiting for you."

He walked me to the door and shook my hand, looking at me with his brown eyes shadowed in the foyer's penumbra. "I'll be expecting you," he said, and it occurred to me that he had been expecting me his whole life. I left down the dark road, I heard the door close, then I turned to look once more at the large house, the flow of pitch that obliterated the stars, paling in the cold night wind. The only lit window went out after a few minutes, and then the dragon's-head lantern did, as well. That surprised me, so I waited a few more minutes, my hair ravished by the wind. I expected to see a light in another window, somewhere in the house's facade; surely Palamar wouldn't sit there in the dark, he had to eat, get ready for bed, go to the bathroom . . . I looked down a side street, I walked around the house: no light at all. Only a large, black building, surrounded by stars.

When I was walking back toward the entrance along the right-hand wall, I heard the buzzing. Barely audible, but for me unmistakable. The ground under my feet vibrated, because the electric noise, like a factory on the night shift, came from deep below the house. "It follows that, like me, he also has a solenoid under his foundation. It follows that, Mr. Palamar, you are a larger part of the story than I thought," I whispered to myself, and after a few minutes, I turned back toward the main road. Passing the Titan movie theater, I heard Fernandel's throaty *rs*, then the delicate reply of who knows which actress. The theater was probably full—I could hear occasional bursts of loud laughter. At the tram stop, there was no one at all. I waited for over an hour. In the end, the tram came clattering down the line. I climbed into the second car, completely empty, like the first. As I sat on the chair, I saw my reflection in the window: a ghost in a sickly world. Then I put my head against the headrest and fell asleep. I woke in a depot in an unknown part of the city and had to wait until morning to get home.

42

Irina is pregnant. It is as unthinkable and unimaginable as the world itself, and just as frightening for me, because "every angel is terrifying" and "the third I cannot bear to look at." I hide behind quotes because I don't know what to do or what to think. Ştefana never got pregnant, although we didn't try to prevent this parade of Russian dolls, we couldn't even if we'd wanted to: the condoms from the tobacconist broke as soon as you put them on, and there were no spermicides or birth control pills. With Irina, I never thought that our moments of extreme pleasure, whether the paradisial, floating knotted together in the middle of the bedroom, one meter above the carefully made bed, or the dark and perverse, between the sweat-dampened sheets, could take part in the chain of causation, equally obscure for primitives and libertines, that ends in a fruit curled up inside a person who gives birth and provides milk. When I think about pregnancy, any reality of the maternity ward and obstetricians, of the birthing tables and the blood- and meconium-covered child, is utterly forbidden to me. A pregnant woman—those you can see so often on the street, especially in the spring, stepping heavily among the puddles reflecting the sky—never meant for me a woman who would give birth: she existed as she was, as she had always been and would always be, without any connection to men, children, or other, not-pregnant women. It was a condition of human existence that my holonic mind could only imagine as an eternal matryoshka doll: in the womb of every pregnant woman is a pregnant woman who carries in her womb a pregnant woman, until the end of the end of this line, on the Planck scale, where everything stops being divided: space, time, causality, pregnancy. Whenever I actually saw a pregnant woman, I imagined her womb as transparent, so I could see, there, *inter urinam et faeces,* the small woman with a transparent womb connected umbilically to the giant around her, and feeding, in turn, the woman in her own womb. Our child, therefore, could only, can only be, for me, a girl. A boy expelled from a womb couldn't be anything but a melancholy monster, worthy of expulsion, floating in a jar full of formaldehyde in an evil museum, like the one at the morgue.

"Irina is pregnant" means, for me, therefore, that we will have a child. She told me yesterday in the teachers' lounge, when both of us were at the window looking at the abandoned factory and water tower through the thin fog descending over our periphery of the end of the world. I recalled from the depths of time that moment when we went onto the roof of my house and stood in the winds and smells of a storm that transformed us into autumnal daimons; when, battered and beaten by the wind like flags, we spun around together, mixing our clothes and hair, and when she, my blonde and dream-filled woman, shouted through the full and round gusts of wind that she would also save the child from the burning building, even if it would become the Antichrist, even Hitler, even Lucrezia Borgia or Messalina. I thought that if there were ever a moment of insemination, when the twilit sperm penetrated her ivory, organic receptacle, it did not happen during our floating entanglements or when we were crushed between the sheets by an absurd gravity, but then, when we spun joyfully, like glittering weathervanes under the stormy skies. That was when we conceived the being who would later be pulled from the flaming pieces of building that fell everywhere, through the smoke that blinded and suffocated you, through the rending cries of those being burned alive, leaving behind, condemned in the center of the house, the deaf and blind and senseless painting, *"ce seul objet dont le néant s'honore."*

Since we were alone, I held her hand, and we stood in silence a few more moments, feeling how unreal were the room, the window, the scene outside, and the world. From this moment on, everything changes, I thought, without managing to imagine the change. Her fingers were dry and cold. Her hand lay in mine passively, with a kind of resignation. Then we walked, without feeling the need to say anything, to the registers, where only ours were left. We took them under our arms into the empty halls, where we were each alone, as we had been, as we would always be, even as the parents of our child, who, as yet, was only a minuscule larva, elastic, pulsing, feeding on her body, where it was both parasite and blessing. I took the stairs to the upper floor, those stairs of ordinary tile, with oil painted Nile-green walls that extended upward and down through an indefinite number of floors, but when I came to 7-S to teach my Romanian class, I found the door wide open and a single student cleaning the blackboard with a sponge soaked in vinegar.

Nothing has ever seemed more desolate to me than an empty classroom, abandoned by its population of minute people with disproportionately large skulls and eyes that could swallow you whole. When the *Mary Celeste* was discovered drifting across the endless ocean, on the icy cetacean path, what was shocking and frightening was the disappearance of the crew, the emptiness of the cabins, the inhumanity of a human construction emptied of the inhabitants who had given it a use and purpose. Every empty classroom, with coats still hanging on hooks and heaps of books and notebooks on the writing-covered desks, with a window open and the breeze giving the curtain a ghostly swell, would always bring tears to my eyes, because it reminded me of a day from the depths of time when I went to the school I attended in the middle of summer and I found it vacant, melancholy, and deserted, frozen under the glaze of time like a photo with poorly reproduced colors.

The student, a boy who, no one knows why, wore a Pioneer's tie at his neck, told me that his classmates had all been called for a dental checkup. There wasn't going to be any Romanian class today. I didn't know what to do, my mind was completely occupied with Irina and my child, as though I were the one having it, as though I had her curled up inside my skull. I went into the room anyway and walked to the window. On the sill, a few tin cans were being used for flowerpots, with geraniums and fuchsia leaning against the window. From here, I could see the area behind the school much better and much farther. I saw the curved and colossal spine of Şoseaua Colentina lined with trams, small cars, and buses, the water tower with its great sphere on top, the tracks where tram 21 turned around, and especially—shining within an eternal fog, as though it itself emanated, with all its powers, a yellow, crepuscular gas—the abandoned factory, in whose unforgettable catacombs I had not been for years. I remembered as though it were yesterday my trip with Goia, the math teacher—the same one who would tell me about Hinton, because nothing happens by chance in this world of enigmas and dreams—through the fantastic hall and among the unearthly machines of that building; and the image of the colossal girl sleeping in a round room still seemed so vivid, so imperious, that I decided to go back there, in the free hour I now had. Especially because, looking directly at the outline of the building cut out against the sky, it seemed that the tall, circular window in the middle of the brick pediment was flashing crazily, like a lighthouse, like hypnotized eyes in an old, discolored film.

I left the school and walked again down the neighborhood streets, I passed the grocery and the propane center, I turned at the warehouse and found myself, again—my hair standing on end all over, my body just as frightened as my soul—face-to-face with the enormous building in the middle of the trash-filled field. Blind brick walls bore the traces of old fires. At a dizzying height, the oval windows were framed with spasmodic and chipped stucco figures, emerging from the melancholy soul of who knows which abstract sculptor; they didn't seem attached to the building but rather to float around it, in the tender and sad spring air. Slowly, I walked around to the front of the building. The gate still had its lock as big as a child's head, and thirty meters above, the chimera still extended its bat wings, screaming inaudibly, a visual scream, a tactile scream, an osmic scream, above the entire universe.

I found the entrance and sank again, this time alone and without a light, into the slanted tunnel that took me into the edifice's depths. I found the deep pit in the middle of the hall, the graves and tombs made of marble, chalcedony, and malachite, affixed with ancient copper plates. I found myself lingering among them, I read the inscriptions written in unknown languages, yet with symbols that I knew so well: crosses, stars, gears, crescents, rings . . . On the plaque over the largest tomb's door, among the channels chiseled into the rosy marble, I could make out, more with my fingertips than my eyes, a bizarre line I hadn't noticed the first time:

SIGNA TE SIGNA TEMERE ME TANGIS ET ANGIS

Signs, fear, and touching, I thought, without imagining that I could translate it correctly, but I had a moment of pleasure, feeling overwhelmed by the olive-and-wilted-rose-colored immensity above, when I noticed that the Latin verse was a palindrome: it read just as well from its end to the beginning.

Next, I climbed one of the large girders that crossed this area diagonally, with one end leaning on the upper edge of the pit, and I found myself again in the large and melancholy industrial hall. Wide shards of light fell here and there from the oval windows, from their colossal height over the shining squares of the floor, wavy and deformed by the veins pulsing underneath, the way the ground undulates when a nearby tree fills it with roots. Lines of dust, billions of minuscule, inhabited worlds, twisted in slow waves in that precise, crystalline light. Clouds darted across the spring sky, visible through gaps in the roof. But the air was still dark and gelatinous in the giant enclosure, and the dominant color was a desolate olive, evoking irrepressible loneliness. I walked along the rails and conveyor belts until I found myself again facing the five complex mechanisms of shiny metal, rising two-thirds the height of the room, and whose cylindrical bases were painted, like a children's game, in the colors and order I found on Valeria's fingernails: dirty pink, dark blue, scarlet, ocher-orange, bright yellow. I walked around each of them, as I had the first time, amazed by their lonely and intangible atmosphere and the immemorial patina of their enigma. You could touch them with your fingers, their tips picking up a light oil, but you could not touch them with human understanding, stunned by the five technological angels that rose toward the broken roof. Chilled by the cold of the hall, I thought to look for the azure entrance, when I saw, from the corner of my eye, something I hadn't noticed before.

It was—framed in the same metal that looked like solidified mercury, yet somehow still as liquid as thick honey—five rose-colored circles that drew my attention. I looked at them more closely and saw they were somehow alive. They might have been as large as a circle made with your fingers of both hands, when you touch your index fingers and thumbs. Or the diameter of a completely dilated vagina during birth, I thought. The circles were skin-colored and had a domed, braided structure. Since they were right in front of my face, I couldn't have any doubts: they were giant navels made of living flesh, installed in the metal. You could clearly see how they had been tied off, how the pale flesh had folded over the surgical thread—or maybe, as at my birth, just simple packing twine—it was sweet in a way, and moving, since each of the belly buttons wasn't simply the diameter of a large rose, and didn't seem just endearingly pink in pallor, but it also smelled like mystical roses. By these proportions, the human fruits that would have these navels in their center, the way apples preserve the impression and stem from where they hung from the branch, would have to be giants.

Something within me immediately understood— I knew what I had to do. I spread my fingers and placed my hand on the first hemisphere of living, warm flesh. Suddenly, all around the metal lip, a fluorescent circle of light appeared, a sad pink, and at the same moment (I could tell it was coming and I had already turned my head toward the other end of the hall) the concatenated pieces of the first mechanism slowly began to unfurl, exposing cracks of strong, homogeneous light. The metal retracted more and more toward the base and top, between which appeared, in all its purity, an enormous cylindrical vial with thick glass walls filled with a clear, golden liquid resembling cerebrospinal fluid. In the center of the vial, I thought I could make out a large, solid sphere, white and crisscrossed with fine channels. "It's a morula," I said to myself, a sphere of a living cell, created by the first few divisions of the primordial egg. Once it grows enough, its walls will turn inward, following the divine plan, forming embryonic layers, the way you make the first folds of paper in that art closest to embryology: origami. As yet, however, the wondrous egg seemed sunken in sleep and, perhaps, incomprehensible dreams.

Next, I pressed on the second hemisphere, and as I felt its texture with my hand, the second cylinder unfurled, in the same utter silence. But this time, I moved closer, so I wouldn't miss any of the details of the compact object pulsating in its center. Rolling my head far back, I saw it in a foreshortening that shrank it slightly, deforming it, the way the statues look on the roof of a temple. It must have been two meters long, and it was, unmistakably, a human embryo at the age of two months, when you can already see the giant, truncated head bent far over, pressing the face, with its eyes still buried in the whitish, translucid flesh, against the thorax, and the stumpy limbs, with fingers and toes already formed, rising on either side of its trunk, like large Latimeria fish lost anachronistically within our oceans. It looked, furthermore, like precisely this kind of concrete animal, elastic and complete, a saturnine monster that lacked nothing and had no reason to evolve, the kind you could find in swamps full of carnivorous plants, or in warm tropical waters, tangled in marine algae, feeding on ciliated, transparent creatures.

The following two gigantic tubes revealed—limpid in the intersecting, slanted columns of light falling from the high windows, once I had pressed the third and the fourth warm, soft, rose-colored buttons—the ravishing image of a human fetus, at four months and at six months, alive and throbbing, hanging from a wrinkled umbilical cord that wound through the golden liquid to disappear somewhere in the vial's base. Phantasmagoric creatures, with their foreheads further bent toward their chests, with enigmatic, insectoid eyes under the transparent skin of their eyelids, the buds of their ears already formed, their limbs thinner but their heads even more fascinatingly massive, disproportionate to their lengthening bodies, much more developed than in the first cylinders: they looked like baby whales, but dreamy and anemic, with hyaline flesh like that of jellyfish. Their organs and cartilage were darkly transparent, in all the bodies of the giant fetuses, and their soft skulls were furrowed with the ramifying nodes of blue and purple arteries. Seen from beneath, from the feet of the colossal test tubes (the walls must have been as thick as a hand, made from colorless sapphire or mine flower), it was easy to tell that the embryos were girls.

The last creature, whose thickness filled the cylinder closest to the locked entryway, under the frozen flight and mute scream of the great chimera, was as massive as a white-rose elephant, and her head had turned toward the floor. Curled up, head between her legs, dressed in a puffy fur that shone in the light like a dandelion globe, and already dissolved in the glittering liquid, the girl was ready to be born. Impossible to imagine a more delicate little girl, limbs more graceful, fingers more supple, enchanting the liquid air of the cylinder, a spine more delicately curved, with the dull gold islands of her vertebrae showing here and there through the smooth, flat skin. Under her eyelids, human eyes, but as big as half her face, were twitching and batting, proof that she was dreaming.

I turned toward the metal plates in time to see the organic buttons retreat into the honey-thick mercury, disappearing bit by bit below the slow invasion of the shiny, ashen substance. In a few minutes, only the luminous circles, colored in the five hues, remained as blind witnesses of the umbilical switches. The hall fell absolutely quiet, unmoving in the gelatin of musty air. I looked around: the large chamber had felt strange enough before. When I explored it with Goia, we had been charmed and horrified by its combination of ancient temple and industrial space, by its architecture mixing angled iron with allegorical stucco statuettes, by the yellow clouds that passed over the cracks in the ceiling as though they were painted on its curvature by a melancholic Tiepolo. Now, however, with the six cylinders stripped of their xenotechnological crust and with giant fetuses flowing in their unmoving waters, the hall suddenly showed another side, one of rending emotions, the end of the world, a space where it was impossible to breathe or live. I began to cry, leaning my head against the yellow cement base of the last cylinder.

It is hard to guess how much time passed, but when I lifted my head, I thought I saw a subtle change in the structure of light. The day inclined, imperceptibly, toward evening. The columns of light adopted an amber hue. The thick veins under the floor full of swarf and oil seemed to gurgle, peristaltically, in the quiet of the abandoned building: "If this hall is truly something like an old radio, with tubes and crystal detectors," I thought, "now it's turned on, receiving messages from somewhere, across an unimaginable distance, and soon it will begin to play." That grand and overwhelming song, springing from the cylinders of the abandoned factory, might not be made for our minuscule cochlea in their petrous pyramids, asymptotic spirals stopping only after two turns around the column, the second twice as long as the first.

I passed the mechanism closest to me and walked to the opposite side of the hall, there where I remembered finding the student number that had come unstitched, and then the door that glowed, pale blue, in the penumbra. I found, on the wall, the frames full of mechanisms, levers, ratchets, rods, and flywheels, dials that slowly changed shape, switches that puffed up like spongy mushrooms, all made of the fluid metal omnipresent in that room. I found, much more quickly this time, the tumblers where the code had to be entered. Pointlessly, I put in the old combination, the one that had been engraved in who knows what shining synaptic folds of my brain. I tried others. The blue outline of the door remained motionless. And yet, it wasn't just that I must go in, since that was why I was here instead of teaching my Romanian class, but also I knew for sure that I would, even if it took days, without eating or sleeping, of trying various five-number combinations. I was no longer so naïve as to think I could fail, that I could make aleatory moves, that anything was inconsequential. It would have been as though the pen in an author's hand began to oppose the fingers that guided it, began to cover the immaculate page with its own story, different from the one the mind had initiated, poured into the delta of motorial nerves in the arm, and then transformed into the small, precise motions that guided, without the possibility of objection, the writing implement across the page. The combination was scattered through my memory, perhaps it came from even farther away, like an inborn fear of snakes and spiders. Since all knowledge is anamnesis, I just had to recall, like my earliest images from childhood, like the shape of the clouds over Floreasca, and like Ştefana's cracked lips, the five numbers, each click resounding in the room's silence. And so it was, a half hour didn't pass before I was standing in front of an open door. The number was 96105. They were the numbers that appeared to me in gold when I visualized the long line of digits on the paper in the briefcase of the porter kidnapped into the sky, when the first and last three digits had remained erased and ashen. I was on the right path. I glanced one more time over my shoulder, at the five gigantic test tubes in the hall where glass and metal embraced so strangely, and I turned again toward the Holy of Holies of this decrepit temple.

I was worried, while walking through the labyrinth of aquaria, terraria, and dioramas packed with monstrous creatures from treatises on parasitology, that the change of combination would bring a change in the being who filled the semicircular hall that stood, as I knew, at the end of my nightmarish descent. It seemed probable, because I hadn't been walking for more than a quarter hour—through the rooms packed with exhibits floating in their liquid, at once placental and cerebrospinal: tapeworms, roundworms, mites, amoebas, gigantic ticks, centipedes, antlions, and horrible dragonfly larvae—when I noticed, along with the change of light, a modification in plated and spiky creatures behind the glass walls. Here and there, among the dioramas with beasts whose gazes carbonized your mind, I saw some containers with nothing but an unshaped, human-sized lump of dough stuck to a tree trunk or onto a cliff face. They were woven from a kind of whitish felt, ectoplasmic, you might say, like in doctored photos of séance mediums who pulled these kinds of cobwebby waves from their mouths, thick and blindingly white, a dismaying psychic vomit. Bit by bit as I walked, these pods, which pulsed with some living thing, appeared more and more often, while the menagerie of hells diminished in number and strength. Soon I moved as though hypnotized in a single direction, among dozens of glass boxes with a larva, each as large as a person, hanging in the middle, like sick people wrapped in wet sheets, all bending toward one side or the other, as though the creatures inside wanted their tense limbs to burst through the hard wrappings of their chrysalis. An almost total silence had fallen, the dark rose color took control of this museum below who knows what skull, that now seemed to be a single, vast chamber, across whose windows someone had pulled the wavy, pink drapes.

I, myself, felt changed. I walked, it seemed, more softly across the hall's soft tiles, and my hand, which sometimes touched the cold face of the glass layers, seemed now thin, pale, with unusually long fingers. My clothes started to feel awkward—these cumbersome fig leaves that we wore over our blessed, warm, and supple skin—so in the end I pulled them off, letting them fall one by one onto the tiles that mirrored their slow floating, thinking I would get them on the way back, one by one. By the time I saw the first chrysalis cracking, I was already naked. My body, as reflected vaguely in the glass cases, was now thin and pale, with a disproportionately large head, like a two- or three-year-old child, and it had large, black, hypnotic eyes, like a wise and sad insect, while my face's other features were small, barely sketched out. Those creatures came to mind, that wander for millennia on their paths beyond death, the bleached creatures that search out their series of monsters, the ones Traian told us about while we sat on the warm windowsill above the radiators at Voila. I remembered how afraid I had been on that distant night, how I ran to my bed and pulled the blanket over my head so the full moon and the creatures in Traian's story wouldn't devour my brain. But this thought was banished from my mind when I saw the first eclosion, followed quickly by others and still others.

Out of the cracked pupae, livid moths with human faces and hands writhed free, they were human-sized, with feminine cheeks, with mouths like a sleeping child, but with firm, blue gazes, with an intelligence umbilically connected to logical space. Their ringed, insectoid abdomens were covered in fur, and they pumped a liquid into the greedy fibers of their wings to straighten and smooth them out. Still hanging from the fibrous cocoons with the little claws of their feet, they slowly dried off their velvety coats, while their wings, covered with cryptic patterns, emitted a dust of minuscule scales barely darker than the rest of the white-gray wings. They were crepuscular and beautiful beyond imagining, and when they began to rise from the terraria and to meet above in dense groups, like the saints who crush their halos together on the walls of churches, lazily beating their great owl wings, you could only feel a great and rending regret that you couldn't return their smiles, so much consolation and light did theirs project. I left the abandoned dioramas behind as I arrived, shadowed by the flocks of human moths, at the entrance to the womb of the world. The moths crossed the narrow space between the cavern and the hemispheric window that encapsulated it, there where the crimson worms had once made their winding coils, and they spread along the cupola, covering it with their faces and wings and abdomens, looking down into the chamber like hundreds and thousands of spectators from their opera boxes. I paused on the threshold, shaken by the sight that unrolled before me, by the dreamlike brilliance of the hall in the center of the world.

The cavern was spherical, not a half sphere, as I had imagined it. The floor was a giant depression, symmetrical to the curving ceiling above, and together they formed a perfectly round and unique chamber. It might have been multiple kilometers in diameter, and it was lined with a single wall of glass, like a soap bubble through which gazed thousands and tens of thousands of winged creatures, with their wings clinging electrostatically to the curved wall and their faces gathered in the single azure hue. I stood on the edge of the cavern, where I could see them, to the end of my sight, above and below, spread uniformly over the spherical diorama, completely covering it with an Escherian mosaic of wings and faces.

The sphere was a cranium and a uterus at the same time, and it was meant to house a fetus and a brain. Under its skull, our brain houses the curled-up motor-sensorial homunculus, which is just as deformed, its proportions just as inhuman, as the infant curled up in the womb, and the latter is in turn the product of a supreme intelligence. In this way, time and space, the somatic and the cerebral, light and dark, man and woman, dream and reality, the animal pole and the vegetable pole of our manifold symmetrical bodies, hell and heaven, ecstasy and abjection, the luminous and the shadowy, corpuscle and wave all fuse, here, in an object-notion, un-understandable and unnameable because it transcends our eternal dualisms. Here, there was no more up and down, no past and future, but only a perfect creature that, like a crystal globe, reflected all without being anything. Yes, in the center of the spherical cavern was a sphere. Like a planet made of lava, like a sun that slowly extinguishes itself. Its rays of liquid amber filled the enormous cavity. Images of the world slid across its surface, like a skin with constantly changing tattoos. It wasn't beautiful, it was beauty. But that beauty that burns and tortures us like the flames of hell. "I am in the forbidden room," I thought, and that thought was my last.

While standing there, I had changed again. My arms shrank into my body, and my legs pressed together, until they were a long, twitching tail. My domed head was much larger than my entire body, and it was full of an ivory substance. I was now floating in that gelatinous air, under the gaze of angel choirs. And I suddenly felt love, at once sexual and cerebral, the love that moves the sun and other stars, the love that is higher than belief or hope. Like a golden sap, like a photon tide, like a protuberance popping out from the central sphere, from the central brain, from the central infant, from the bride in the middle of the world. Wiggling my vibrating cilia, I advanced; I was attracted, across the empty, love-filled space, toward the lazy and constantly changing ball of fire from which, ever more powerfully, resounded the chemical call, the desperate drug, the desperate addiction of Godliness. I now saw through all of my superdimensional brain, as though I were an eyeball hanging from the tail of its optic nerve, and what I saw filled me with joy and terror.

The central sun was an unimaginable complexity. The human mind could neither comprehend nor understand it; the mind could only love it as no one on Earth had ever loved. I moved toward him, toward her, toward the unthinkable fourth person, feeling triumphant and resigned: I had been chosen, I was the one chosen from billions like me, because all those who had ever lived were the single ejaculation of a supreme god. All had perished, all who had begun this journey with me, they had been devoured by our corrosive universe, falling prey one by one to happiness and to sadness, blind to the signs, incapable of assembling the puzzle pieces scattered everywhere, wandering in circles in the three-dimensional labyrinth, with its piece of cheese in the middle. I was the last one, ready for divine martyrdom in the encounter with the ovum, and now I was face-to-face and eye to eye with it, like a mosquito before a white elephant, decorated for battle. The eye could not encompass it, and you lacked the tens of thousands of senses that could perceive it as it was. A tongue of fire stretched toward me and pulled me into that body of melted gold, giving me the death that leads to life. I remember the supreme scream of our melding, not pulled from my long-vanished mouth, but from my brain as it burst suddenly into splinters.

Afterward, all that remained was the blinding light of beginnings.

43

I woke up late this morning, my head heavy with too much sleep, the way I've woken on each of these past ten days I have spent on medical leave. It's as though they gave me this leave on purpose, so I can be as sick as I please. I don't feel right. I sleep too much, dream too much, but no dream, however hopeless, can compare with the vast and repetitive dream that lasts from when I open my eyes, at eleven in the morning or even noon, until I close them again, long after midnight. The dream where it seems I am in my house on

Maica Domnului, where I was yesterday, exploring its undefined number of rooms, and where I will be tomorrow and every day until the end of my life. The dream where I am alone in my world in a minuscule imperfection of infinite, dense night. An unobservable bubble of air inside a pitchy sludge the same diameter as eternity. Here is Bucharest, the most melancholic city in the world, infested with wood lice, worn away by the strong acids of time and nostalgia, here is the neighborhood of School 86 and the bottle plant and the auto mechanic, here Floreasca, intact under its bell jar, here the model of Ştefan cel Mare. Voila is also here, with its pavilions and houses in the grove of flowering apple trees. Everything that I have dreamed I have experienced, everything that has seemed to have happened to me. Each morning, before opening my eyes, I feel the same anxiety: This again? *This* is what's called reality? This is what my life will be: home–school–home–school, with no chance of breaking this vicious and destructive circle? Why was I given, like everyone else like me, a god's mind, if it had to come with a mite's body? Why can I think, when I can think of nothing but how I will perish in my hallway, buried in the skin of a creature I will never come to know? Why can I understand everything, if I can do nothing?

Then I get out of bed, go to the bathroom, and look at myself in the mirror: a man long past the age of thirty who has done nothing in the world. Black eyes, tight lips, unshaven, with weak cheekbones; old and discolored pajamas covering his shoulders. "Efimov," I say, in my morning ritual. Efimov with his out-of-tune, diabolical violin. After he heard what real music sounds like.

I said it again this morning, with more reason than ever before, because toward dawn, still not awake enough, I had a kind of hallucination that I felt I needed to write down in my diary. I did so quickly and carelessly, afraid I'd lose the peculiar vision, but I'll copy it here anyway, as my ever more unintelligible manuscript continues.

I'm in a deep well or, better put, inside an enormous, hollow bell. Countless strings hang down toward me from above, some as thin as cobwebs, and some are ropes as thick as my palm. If I pull any of the hundreds of cords and threads, high above me a bell rings, a little copper bell or an enormous cathedral bell. But this isn't what I'm thinking about. I have to escape this dirty, sinister well. There is no other way but up, toward the invisible sky above, full of invisible bells.

So I begin, like an unskilled spider, to climb up the threads, creating a terrible cacophony of clinking and clanging and sounds vibrating from the copper. With time, climbing higher, I notice that I can climb more efficiently if I take certain threads in order, instinctively moving from the thinnest to the thickest and back again. I start to play scales and arpeggios, then little melodies; I discover harmony and counterpoint and uncover the hidden forms of the first fugues. When I begin to compose more complicated pieces, I feel like I'm flying up through the tube of the bell, like I have wings.

After years of climbing the rope, cords, strings, and threads that cut my hands, I am able to create a supreme form of music. Now I rise upon it, at a fantastic speed, like a bullet of melted gold through a rifled barrel. The sounds solidify, they become material. High up, I make them into a plate of pure light and frozen photons, hard as a diamond, with which I collide, splattering my blood and brain, my urine and broken teeth, over the wonder.

And only in this way, freed of the husk of my organs, of my skin and senses, do I penetrate into the world above.

"Exactly," I said to myself after I woke up, and I say it again now, nodding in agreement with each phrase. "Art has no meaning if it's not an escape. If it's not born of a prisoner's despair. I can't respect any art that comforts and relieves, those novels and music and paintings designed to make your prison more bearable. I don't want to paint miniature Tuileries Gardens on the bulging walls, and I don't want to paint the barrel in the corner some particular shade of pink. I want to see the circus horsewoman as she is: tubercular and flea-infested, sleeping with anyone who gives her a glass of absinthe. I want to be able to see the grates on the high transom, through which no sunray falls to destroy the vision. I want to understand my situation lucidly and cynically. We are all prisoners inside multiple concentric prisons. I am the prisoner of my mind, which is the prisoner of my body, which is the prisoner of the world. My writing is a reflex of my dignity, it is my need to search for the world promised by my own mind, just as perfume is the promise of the many-layered rose. I want to write not like a writer, even a writer of genius, but the way Efimov plays, with unmeasurable pride and sublime imperfection. He found the way, not through tradition but through spirit, because art will be belief or will not be at all. I am a dilettante, I know, I don't have the millennia-old tricks of my art—as I am sure the other knows, in his world where he has success and money and glory and women—but in my obscurity I feel free to see the truth a thousand times more acutely. I understand better than anyone why Efimov left his violin to rot, why Virgil and Kafka wanted to turn their masterpieces into ash. Because silence and ash are straight paths, while music and books set free in the world are divagations. Ash is the final fate, in any case, of all writing, and because of that I will not suffer when my manuscript meets the fire. It is not a book, even less so a novel: it is an escape plan. And after escape its natural destiny is ash."

"How alone I am," I say to myself every moment of my life. How ghostly my life is! Like a craps player, I rattle its derisory vestiges in my palm: baby teeth that grew in my gums, mummified pieces of thread from my navel. I toss them onto the table and try to read my future in the aleatory configuration, like constellations that they make at random, never to be repeated. And my future is like my past, seen in a mirror whose silver nitrate is more and more worn away by time. I don't care. The mirror needs to break. The catoptromancer's mission is to break all the mirrors and end the art of divination. And the painting's canvas should not be weighed down with colors—its immaculate woven fibers are heavy enough—but ripped, like Fontana did to his, in his only exasperated act of liberation. As I do now, right now, on this lined notebook where I write, which I have already rent with the tip of my pen. Now I will take the lips of the wound and part them, to see the writing on the previous page through this hole. I read between the dry labia of my page, mixing time and writing: "Why can I understand everything, if I can do nothing?" A book shot through, its thickness stabbed by a pen that crosses to the other side, a perpendicular writing on the inextricable volume, made up of hundreds of surfaces of my desperate scribbling—this is what my book would be, if it ever were: writing into the deep, *through* the pages, and not scattered across their surfaces: writing as never before seen nor lived.

They found me in the abandoned factory, lying in the pit of mausoleums, under the wall of the large, rose-colored tomb, the one with SIGNA TE SIGNA . . . I had probably been unconscious for a few hours, because a group of kids snuck in through the tunnel and found me that evening; they tried to bring me back to my senses there, in the funereal combination of marble and twilight. When they couldn't, they dragged me out into the cool of the evening, and I woke under the stars in the field, alongside the large building. They were standing around me, trembling, with large, expressionless heads and eyes, with their differences of sex annulled in the darkness. They got me to my feet and walked me down Str. Puiandrului, toward the house of the one who lived closest. His parents called an ambulance.

I don't know how I got to the hospital, but I woke up the next day in a small, narrow room, one with just four beds, probably a spare room. Of course, I had never been there, as far as I knew, but at the same time I had a familiar sensation, as though I could feel a force field around me and could remember not images but my orientation within it. The space here hummed with a certain tone, to which I listened to try to figure out where I was. I wasn't at the Emergency Hospital, but, surely, at the Mașina de Pâine Clinic, where my parents had taken me countless times when I was little for batteries of injections and to torture me, shaking and innocent, on dental chairs. Beside my bed was a stand with two soft plastic bags hanging up high, one scarlet and the other half full of a vaguely yellow liquid. I sat up and saw I was dressed in pajamas that were not mine, and two large, thick needles attached to transparent tubes were stuck in my arm. The other three beds were made, the sheets and blankets were perfectly smooth, not like they would be in an actual spare room in a hospital, but the way they would be in a drawing. The only living and moving thing, as though it were traversing a large photo, was a cockroach that hauled its ringed abdomen over the white footboard of the bed across from mine.

I lay there, watching the flowering branches of a cherry tree outside rock gently in the spring wind, daydreaming, perhaps for hours, but no one entered my little box. Only that evening did a nurse come and put a thermometer in me and change the bags on the stand. Then I was alone again. Although it was now completely dark and the sky had taken on the cherry tree's pinkish color, such that the blooms seemed to have suddenly burst, obscuring the entire window, the neon tubes above the bed remained unlit. Little by little, I found myself within shadow. The world darkened and disappeared. It dissolved into nothing and into never. Afraid, I sat up: did I still exist? Could it be said I was alive? I yanked the needles from my veins and stepped to the middle of the room. I opened the door and went into the hall.

There was no one there, probably there wasn't anyone in the entire building surrounded by falling dusk. A few windows at the end of the hall glinted like pieces of amber. No sound at all, aside from my footsteps, the soles of my shoeless feet sticking to the cold floor tiles. The Nile-green paint, going halfway up the walls, seemed inhuman and sinister to me in that eternal penumbra. The grimy, vinyl benches against the walls in front of the examination rooms still held the impressions of the hips that had pressed into them during the day. I opened a door made of matte glass—it screeched terribly in the complete silence—and found myself suddenly minuscule, standing in a hallway where monumental stairways of frozen stone led both upward and down. The clinic building was one of those massive, imposing constructions, with walls so thick that, like the interior of a pyramid, the spaces between the walls seemed like mere fissures, galleries through which you had to creep forward on your stomach. But from time to time the architectonic insanity produced, inside them, karstic pockets, chambers of a wild and absurd grandeur, such as the one that presented itself to me in this stairwell. The steps and railings, with pillars of the same shiny travertine, were too tall for a normal person. Climbing, I felt like a child who has to lift his knees up high to reach the next step, and to rise onto his tiptoes to touch the railing. I went up several floors in that lonesome, petrified photographic emulsion, I passed floors whose entryways were marked INTERNAL MEDICINE, CARDIOLOGY, GYNECOLOGY, OSTEOLOGY, LABORATORY, along corridors that extended far into the darkness. I remembered the cold glass plates on either side of my half-naked body, where I stood for X-rays, and how the doctor's office could suddenly fill with the moldy damp odor of penicillin when the nurse brought her syringe toward my bare buttocks. I was cold and hungry, I hadn't eaten anything for an entire day, but I kept climbing the stairs, without knowing what I was doing, and after I had passed three landings, twisting along with the enormous staircase around a void big enough for a building, I came to the vast attic, the dentistry floor.

Because the light could not reach here, in the wide, windowless space of the attic, the dark brown shadow of the rest of the building should have congealed here into total darkness. Still, I could safely climb the last steps of the spiral staircase, with its massive, shiny stone sections, and I found the attic filled with a chestnut light, unexpectedly golden in some places. It came from one end, through the matte windows of the office's four doors; they shone dimly like four gold bars. A vague sound, a pulsing, like a cat purring, came from behind the doors. This meant, I told myself in fear, that the clinic was not completely empty, that in the middle of the night the dentists were still working. When my eyes adjusted to the low light coming from the corners of the long, dark hall, I spied a few patients patiently waiting their turns on vinyl benches. Their eyes shone yellow in the semishadow. They paid no attention to me, as though they hadn't seen me climb from the depths of the monumental staircase. I didn't know what to do, I didn't understand why I had come. Was I supposed to sit and wait with the others, just as I had done dozens of times as a terrified child, letting everyone else go first, hoping a miracle would save me from the inevitable torture? Did I have to go inside to see what would happen? I stood undecided for a while in the middle of the hall, lit like a salt statue by the office's matte windows, until in the end, my heart in my throat, I walked to the first door on the left, knocked gently, and waited. None of the waiting patients objected. No one inside the office answered. So I turned the handle and went in.

The light inside came solely from the large examination lights above the dental chairs. It was a dirty yellow, like the concentrated urine of dawn. The office was empty, there were no doctors or patients, only four identical chairs, motionless within their enigma, in quiet and solitude. Their large metal frames, the brown vinyl lining of their back and headrests, the little spatulas and mirrors on the tray, everything seemed familiar to me, so familiar from other times that I had the powerful feeling that stepping into the office, I had stepped back in time. There was a lag of about two decades between the age of the awkward, massive chairs—fixed to the floor by giant bolts, ancient models, hideous fossils of the dental arts—and the time that flowed outside the office, one fresher and more fluid.

Suddenly I had the feeling, as I have so often when I close the door behind me and find myself in isolated rooms, that everyone outside had disappeared, forever, that I was locked inside, forever. I looked in fear toward the door, in the wall of glass cabinets full of sadistic torture instruments and diagrams of molars and gums: it was the spider's nest, the hole at the bottom of the web where the white fabric thickens into canvas and where two articulated legs poke out, a sign that the horrifying insect is there, waiting for you. So far, the door was still closed.

I wandered for a while around the dental chairs, and then, overcome with trembling, I sat down in one, resting my head on the hard vinyl pillow. I opened my mouth wide, under the blinding light, I clenched my eyes shut and waited. I felt I was a child again, I felt, in the flesh of my gums, each nerve running through the root canal: a flower of nerves, an anemone pulsing its filaments in the ocean's rocking waters. Someone would come, as they had come so many times in the past, someone, like a harpist of pain, would come to play a song of agony on the strings of my dental nerves. I awaited the scream of the drill and the moans of the brush, the metal hooks on the rods, the bitter metal taste of the saliva vacuum. I awaited a fat animal in a white dentist's coat to deposit his stomach on top of me, to feel his heart beat and his bowels gurgle, to see his merciless eyes lock onto mine, feel his breathing mix with mine, the sweat from his forehead dripping into my wide-open mouth, while for an undefined time I would be erased by the substance of pain, the clearest and most intense substance in the world. I was crucified on a pain extraction machine, one of billions that milk the world's suffering and screams, all connected by swollen, organic cables, snaking under the foundations of reality. And there had to be a place where all the conduits of pulsing flesh, like the roots of old trees, converged into a single enormous pipe, where all the screams of fear from humanity mixed together, the despair and hopelessness of a madrepore with thousands and millions of living creatures with red mouths hanging wide open, screaming with clenched eyes, for eternity, in the hands of blind and deaf and impersonal executioners, the instruments of our terrifying destiny. Where did it go, the vertical conduit of human suffering? Who fed on our crying and unhappiness and helplessness and annihilation and mortality? Who enjoyed the crack of our bones, the pain of unrequited love, of the ravages of cancer and the death of the people we love, of burned skin, of torn-out eyes, of exploding veins? Who needed our ill-fated substance as clear as tears, like we needed air and water? I imagined a vertical pipe, like the needle of a syringe but with the diameter of the oldest baobab tree, descending to the center of the earth and feeding there, in the empty, spherical hypogeum, a people of necromancers and telepaths related to bedbugs, ticks, and mites. Hedonists of pain, visionaries of terror, archangels of being crushed alive, kings of destruction and hate . . .

I was a child again, waiting with a lump in my throat for my torturer's arrival, and when I suddenly heard the door at the end of the office open, I started violently, as before. I jumped out of the dental chair, and when I saw who was coming, slowly, out of the shadow, I could not believe it.

He wasn't a dentist at all, but a shabby old man barely able to drag his feet across the cold tile floor. I recognized him, even though I hadn't seen him for a long time: he was our porter, Ispas, the one who had been "taken to the sky," then had showed up again, at the bottom of a ditch, filthy as a pig and reeking of cheap booze. I had thought so often about the connections between his story and Valeria's, the special spot—once an oasis of flowers and butterflies, now a gray wart on the ground where, according to his famous declaration to the militia, the porter had been sucked up by an unstoppable force, after which he found himself suspended within a complete and endless night. And in that darkness, he had felt his body opened and mechanical instruments moving around in it, trepanning and modifying it, binding it to other bodies, making his blood, lymph, urine, and other liquids go into tubes that led out of him and into somewhere, who knows where . . . And more than anything, he had claimed in his illiterate declaration, written in chemical pencil, that they had messed with his brain, stuck something in there that made him hear voices and commandments, while every thought of his was captured and sent somewhere where it was conscientiously recorded. Thus transformed into a new creature and full of the Holy Spirit (as written in the affidavit), he had descended to Earth to dwell among people again.

Ispas was not surprised to see me. He only greeted me the way he usually did when the teachers passed through the school door: he put his fingers to his temple in a parody of a military salute. Then, with empty eyes, he walked on, with his usual odor of salami and cheap țuica. He went out the office door, leaving it open behind him, allowing, to my surprise, a loud murmur of voices, many voices, to come in. Through the doorway, I saw the hall was packed with people. I crossed the threshold as well and I found myself among hundreds of women and men, of every sort, of every age and condition. You couldn't swing a cat in the building's large attic, and this crowd also flooded the travertine stairway, down as far as the eye could see. People were crowded on the stairs and even on the large railing that twisted in a wide curve toward the depths. When Ispas appeared, the white noise of voices grew suddenly into a kind of shout or, better put, a moan of agony, and the Picketists (in their mourning black and with covered heads, they could be no one else) suddenly raised their crude signs made of Masonite or poster board, where they had written their objections to suffering and death: "Stop the human tragedy!", "Boycott agony!", "Rage against the dying of the light!", "NO to daily slaughter!", "Down with leukemia!", "Down with the billions of centuries we will not see!", "NO to falling down an elevator shaft!", "Stop derailments!", "Stop plane crashes!", "No more cerebral hemorrhages!" "No more death in any form!" And scattered among hundreds of such slogans, scribbled in pen on a cardboard box here and there, in bad handwriting and worse grammar, in blood-colored letters the color of poppies in a wheat field, was the most painful word that ever passed though the human larynx, making it burst in sputum and blood: "Help!" "Help!" "Help!" "Help!"

When had they arrived? And why here? Because Resurrection Cemetery was nearby? Were they planning to protest there all night? The porter, crowded on all sides because everyone wanted to touch him, motioned for everyone to sit, and, squeezing together to take up as little space as possible, everyone sat like submissive peasants in the shadows and livid, already scarce air of the attic. The crowd now looked like a dark coral reef packed with eyes, all fixed on the porter. I sat down, too, pulling my oversized pajamas against my chest, now looking up at Ispas from below; perhaps that is why he seemed, as jaundiced, unshaven, and dirty as he was, to be wrapped in a mantle of pale light.

"Brothers," the old man began, in an alcoholic's unsteady voice, in the grave-like silence that had fallen, "Brothers, you were all witnesses to my abduction from the world, and you know that what I said is true. This, good people, took place on April sixteenth of last year, when the heavens opened up over my head. I . . . was coming back from the bar, from Ocean Magic, three sheets, out of sorts, not myself. I was drunk, brothers, to say it straight, but I wasn't totally out of it. I don't know how I rode the tram to the end of the line and I don't know why I went into the field. It was like something was calling me, like something inside me was saying, "Ispas, go in the field on the other side of the tracks, you're expected." I went past the school, I took Dimitrie Herescu, I bumped into a fence, I tripped on a pothole—it was nighttime, and scary!—and when I got to the end, I heard that call even louder, and I was scared, but the bear doesn't dance when it feels like it. I thought there was something there, you see, even then they were telling me what they wanted me to do, they moved me around, and I knew, brothers, that the people from the sky, the ones with the flying saucers, they had had their eyes on me since I was a kid. Yes, on me, the way you're looking at me now, because they don't look at a person like they're a drunk or a whore, they look for something else . . . for what they need. I kept telling the cleaning ladies and the teachers that one day they'd come and take me, but even little kids laughed at me. Eh, they'd still laugh today, if I still talked to them. Those guys didn't want them, the smart people, the rich people, they wanted me, Ispas, from the front door of the school, for their experiments.

"So I crossed the tramline, brothers, and it was a dark night, the clouds swirling like they were in a cauldron. You couldn't see where the ground stopped and the sky started. And there was mud everywhere up to your knees, your boots went plop plop and you could barely pull them back out again. I went across the field, because that's what the voice said to do, and I fell a couple of times, made a pig of myself. And that big suitcase got in the way, I wanted to drop it, but I was smart enough at least to keep it, because I had some food in it. How was I supposed to know I didn't need any? I walked about a hundred meters and then I found the spot. I stopped there, and I dropped the case in the mud and did the combination. What, like this was the first time? I had felt sure of myself like this, before, when I was drunk, and I'd stand in the intersection and wait for them to take me. But all my shouting and arm swinging was in vain—"Look! I'm ready! Come and take me!"—because nothing had happened, some people just swore at me. I did the same thing now. I leaned all the way back and howled into the wind as loud as I could, "I'm here! Come on!" I screamed like that for maybe fifteen minutes, since there in the field no one could hear a damn thing. I was getting ready to go home, and I was already thinking of how good it was going to be in my little basement, on my mattress, when suddenly, brothers, something completely strange happened."

At that, the human madrepore held its breath. The utter silence was frightening, as though never before in the world had there been vibrations that the cochlea could perceive, could resonate with. The world became compact again, without moving parts to rub together to make even the diaphanous sound of breath, even the adhesion of the petal of a blinking eyelid. Every eye was fixed on the face of the one who had been abducted and had returned miraculously to his own kind, as though he himself were a cherubim covered with eyes from top to bottom. I recognized some faces in the crowd, people who had been around me during the night at the morgue, a night buried deep in time and in the hyaline material of my brain, when the fantastical statue of Damnation had climbed down from the cupola, pulling itself from the sky, and had sat on the throne of judgment. Caty wasn't there, or maybe she had come late and was listening to the old man's words somewhere at the bottom of the stairs (since the crowd seemed to fill the stairway all the way down to the first floor), instead a rosy wart caught my eye, the one between the biology teacher's eyebrows, and I recognized the silvery hair, pressed to his skull, of the librarian Palamar, who gave me a small wave when our gazes crossed. I startled without wanting to when I spotted, in the chiaroscuro of a dark corner, the lunatic face of Ştefana. Others, too, seemed familiar. Perhaps I had only seen them once, on the street or in the tram, or perhaps I saw them every day, as I did the shopkeeper who sold me milk and bread near the Teiul Doamnei station, without my paying them any more attention than I did the cars on the street or the dusty bushes on the side of the road. For example, the guy who refilled cigarette lighters was there, in his corner stinking of lighter fluid, full of all kinds of tubes and rusty, broken lighters, from the entrance of the furniture store on Teiul Doamnei.

"While I was standing in the middle of the field and shouting at the sky, while I beat my fists against my chest, while the wind beat on me, I saw a black cloud gather and kind of flicker over my head. It got thicker and turned around and around, like you stir a spoon in your coffee. And there were silver stripes in it: they appeared and disappeared like ghosts, good people, it was beautiful and it made your flesh quiver. I knew the moment had come, that they had finally shown themselves. I knew they could see me from up there. And suddenly there was a light all around me, coming from the cloud, and I heard some words, but I couldn't understand them. And something grabbed me and pulled me up, it sucked me up like you suck the soup out of your spoon. Brothers, I saw the ground going away from me, I saw the suitcase still in the mud, and the lights from houses in the neighborhood receding. The wind was heavy, it whipped my clothes around me, it blew my hair. While I was going up, I felt scared, I could barely see the city, the field, anything below me in the night. I screamed, I was scared, then suddenly I wasn't going up anymore and it was dark. Darkness, good people, not even in the basement at the bottom of the earth there's not darkness like that. And silence. Brothers, it was like death. There was nothing in the whole world. I couldn't feel my body, I couldn't touch myself, I couldn't yell. It was like I was in a pine box, but alive. And I stayed like that, but so afraid, I don't know for how long. Days, months—God knows. It wasn't night, wasn't day. It was nothing, nothing, nothing."

Ispas stopped for a moment with his eyes wide, as though he had lost the thread; he looked around confusedly and then burst into tears. He put his face in his hands, sobbing, and sank to the cold floor, alongside everyone else. He cried in a ball on the floor for a long time, then he wiped his eyes and nose on his sleeve. The face of this man of pain, already devastated by alcohol and weathered to the color of dry dirt, now bathed in tears, looked like an ancient prophet.

"They didn't treat me right," he moaned in between tears and sobs. "It wasn't what I wanted. It wasn't like they cared about what's wrong with this world that gets worse every day, where no one can survive. They didn't ask me what had to be done, how things could be put right. I had been thinking for a long time of what to say, so they would let us live with them. I thought they would show me their powers, their wonders, that they'd take me to another planet or wherever they had their cities. I thought that they would tell me the cure for all the diseases and how to make yourself immortal. And I, brothers, this is my cross to bear, I would have come back down to the people and I would have told you everything, absolutely everything, for free, for no money . . . Just to make things good in the world, so we'd be like them, you know how people suffer all their lives . . . And instead—look what they did to me, brothers, look what a fool they made of me!"

And just as Virgil had once done, the old man began to tear his clothes off, and then he stood there, naked, gnarled, disgusting. There was a general shout of horror, and the first rows of people scurried away with animal fear on their faces. Ispas's chest and stomach were covered by a transparent carapace, through which, as though he were a plaster anatomical model, everyone could see his internal organs, all soft and warm, bathed in a blue light. From his throat down to his pubis, his skin, bones, and muscles had been removed and replaced with this flexible plating, perfectly woven, without a stitch, into his surrounding skin. We could see his heart beating rhythmically in between his elastic lungs; his diaphragm rose and fell to the rhythm of his breath; and his intestines and bladder, their soft, greenish flesh, housed the lobes of his plainly engorged and diseased liver. Who had changed the poor porter into an anatomical model, and for what otherworldly pedagogical need? The sight was pathetic and devoid of hope. "Ecce homo," you would have said, looking at the knot of flesh, bones, guts, and tissue that is inside all of us, and which the old man, victim of cynical creatures with another kind of mind and feeling, revealed now within his own martyred body.

"I sensed them ahead of time. I don't know how, but I knew when they appeared. I mean, they didn't appear, but they were there, with me, that night. I started to scream and there was no sound, I couldn't even tell if my mouth was open. But when they started into me, started to cut me and sew me up, I felt it. Terrible pain, my brothers, terrible pain! Like no one's ever felt! Like bandits they worked me over without mercy. I thought I was in Hell, in boiling pitch, and that demons were sticking me with their pitchforks! Awful pain: kidneys ripped out of my flesh and my liver stabbed with a red-hot poker. And it lasted an eternity." Ispas raised his arms out from his sides, so that everyone could more easily see what "the merciless ones" had done to him, and he stayed like that, silent, his chin on his chest, for a few minutes, and then he began to pull his underpants back on, and his shirt and shoes. Only when he was dressed again did he resume his speech.

"An eternity passed like that, good people, until suddenly there was a light, there inside. Yes, a light suddenly, after the darkness. White, white, blinding, you couldn't see a thing in all the shining light. I just felt myself going down, little by little, the way I had gone up before, until I dropped to the ground, ground as cold as a grave. And the light went out and I was left in a harsh daylight, while the roosters were crowing. I was in the field on the other side of the tracks, there where they had taken me, but no mud . . . I'd escaped. I was so happy, and so scared, thinking about what I'd been through. I looked up: nothing, clear sky, some stars, and at the end of the field, the first light of dawn. Then I dared to get up, and I started walking toward my neighborhood. I walked home, I went to the basement, and there was no one there. I had my bottle hidden behind the . . . And I got good and wasted, and I went out again to see what was going on, but I fell in a ditch. And that's where I stayed, since I was a bit . . . tired. That's where the militia found me. They took me to the station and made me write down everything that happened, and right when I was doing that, I saw what they did to me, and I started yelling like crazy, and I didn't stop for three nights. After that, the Securitate came, then some foreigners, they hooked me up to a bunch of machines . . . What they didn't do to me before they let me go . . . In the end, Comrade Gherghina from Centrocoop, who's a Picketist like the rest of us, he took me to his house and he was the one who brought me here, to meet with you, my brothers, I was at the Laromet factory, at the Eagle of the Sea, at Casa Scânteii, and now I'm here, at the Mașina de Pâine Clinic, so that as many people as possible can hear what I went through. And listen to what I say! Everywhere there's hundreds and thousands of people, people like you, who can't stand this stupid game we get in life. Who want a reckoning. Who rise up, brothers, against getting old, against diseases and death, because it's too much, it cuts to the bone. How much longer are we going to lie down, like cows in the slaughterhouse, good people? How much longer are we going to eat the bitter bread of our lives? Why are we on Earth? To be torn up and buried alive and drowned like cats and sacrificed like sheep? For death to cut us down, with a scythe, like sheaves of wheat? Shout, good people, shout until your throat breaks! Shout, good people, from the bottom of your lungs, shout like pigs getting stuck, shout out your pain and fear, now, good people! Let them hear you, good people!"

The hair on my arms was standing up. The last words had been spoken not by our lowly and filthy porter, but by an ancient prophet, as beautiful as a decrepit god, an unshaven archangel with dirty fingernails. People pressed against him, they put their hands on his hunched body, they pulled at his clothes like children, in tears or in stone-faced pain. He looked like the patriarch from whom everyone descended, the hopeless father of the children of the void, the children of waste and sacrifice. At his signal, everyone in the attic, everyone in the building—which I imagined was packed with people I couldn't see, dressed in black and waving signs over their heads—resounded with a single shout, so powerful that it seemed to burst out of a million tracheae, from all the pipes of the organ of human suffering. The horror, the limitless terror, the demented panic, the crazed hysteria, the vomitous nausea, the vertigo and pain and disorientation were set loose in space with the powerless despair of someone abandoned in an underground oubliette with no food or water, who bangs on the iron door for days on end until his hands are nothing but bloody flesh. It was the cry of those in the final phase of cancer, of those on the seat of torture, of those who have lost a child, of those who are falling from a great height. People slapped their hands against their faces and screamed, their faces bathed in tears, the veins of their necks swollen, their eyes red with sobbing. And if at the beginning each larynx shouted its own pain until it tore, soon in a frightening confusion, like on the signs with scribbled slogans against Alzheimer's and insanity, one word began to sound more often, more dominant, more burning, the word that embodied hopelessness, the word of hell, of black eternal flames and regret and self-hatred: help! Like someone drowning in the midst of dark waters, the gathered crowd shouted the word more and more often, the word that called, that called for Mom, that called for God, the word of unbearable separation from comfort and light. At first in groups scattered throughout the chaos of screams, then together, in a chorus of hundreds and thousands of voices, pulsing suddenly with the pulse of the heart and ejaculation and the intestinal snakes of cerebral chemicals, it sounded throughout our daily prison, from the microevents on the Planck scale to the clusters of metagalaxies, from the sensual touch of skin and moisture to the mathematical structure of space, time, and consciousness, the only word that encompassed all the deceit of our loneliness: help! The human madrepore shouted this word for minutes or hours on end, always deeper within itself and obsessed by itself, the final prayer, when all other prayers have failed. I found myself shouting along with them, in the chorus, in self-forgetting, dissolving into the cry, releasing, like a fountain, the black jet of my unhappiness: help! help! help! help! Soon the great choir that joined within a single pulsation, man and woman, slave and free person, rich and poor, smart and lost, honest and wrong, writer and reader, all lifted up, perpendicular to our world, the song of our fearful agony: help!

help! help!

help! help!

help! help!

help! help!

help! help!

help! help!

help! help!

We came down slowly, as though from a mystical experience or a heroin trip, we collapsed into ourselves like after a desolating orgasm, burnt out and devastated inside. The old man, who had raged, along with the rest of us, against the dying of the light, looked around with stunned eyes, and when the cries for help were almost completely extinguished, he raised his hand and complete silence fell again. We looked at the faces—half-sunken in shadow, half-golden in the light of the dentist office transoms—of those who had protested the almighty tyranny of illusion and impermanence. People had come back to their senses, and now determination took the place of fear and hopelessness: they would fight to the end. Ispas sat down, and his sallow face looked no different than the others. For a few minutes there was complete silence, and then, unexpectedly and without knowing how, we all received the message.

We felt it like a spherical wave jetting from Ispas's transformed brain, an almost visible wave, like an ultradiaphanous, prismatic soap bubble that incorporated all of us in the dream of its fluctuation, passing through the walls, through the attic, through the marble stairway, and finally engulfing the entire building of the Mașina de Pâine Clinic, while it was drowsing in the night, under the moon reflected by the tramlines. No one heard a word, the message didn't have anything to do with the mechanism of the tympanum, hammer, ladder, and anvil, or the oval window, or the trembling snail of the temporal lobe; I would almost say it didn't even have anything to do with the zones for the decryption of language in the left hemisphere. It was only the palpitation of a butterfly's wing, a quiet and unmistakable, "I know," the way it must be in the mind of someone hypnotized who wakes up and then, without knowing why, climbs onto a table and poses like a statue. Ispas didn't transfer suggestions, orders, or commandments, but a piece of the future, just as certain as the past. We knew, we saw, we understood what had to happen, the same way we can remember one detail from the voluminous contortions of our childhood. And each of us would fulfill the prophecy-memory as though it were already done and behind us, because in the end belief is no doubt just this: the future seen as though it were the past, as though in complete illumination, frozen in a single movement of the dance, and not as a bouquet of infinite possibilities. We could do nothing but go, one year from that time, back to the morgue, we could only avenge the crushing of Virgil like a cockroach, the confrontation could not be avoided, none of us could avoid the confrontation with the obsidian god of Damnation. But what she and we would do, what had to happen to our world, sadder than any of those ever imagined under the black sun of melancholy, could not be seen: the undoing of the enigma, the response to the Sphinx, the final arrangement of the puzzle pieces were outside the frame of the immaterial soap bubble, because they didn't, at that moment, have anything to do with the seven blessed wavelengths permitted to our interior sight and arching over the curve of the soap bottle, but they were infra-life and ultra-destiny, the hand that draws the other hand that comes out of the page and draws the first, in an endless cycle.

As though the cerebral impulse had completely exhausted him, the porter collapsed to one side and stayed like that, his face ashen-sallow, until a few women in black clothes and black headscarves helped him up and bore him away, supporting him as though he had been wounded on a battlefield. People, beginning with those deep in the bowels of the building, began to leave, taking small steps, as though they were walking out of a movie theater. It took more than a half hour to empty the steps of the monumental stairway, much too sumptuous for the poor little clinic, and only then could those who had packed the attic follow. After another half hour, I was left alone, in the petrified photographic silence where everything had begun. I picked up a sign that read, "Help!" left behind by someone in the departed crowd. The word might have been scrawled onto the cardboard with a bloody finger, by one inscribing the secret name of each of us and of our species. "We live for a nanosecond on a speck of dust lost in the cosmos," I said to myself, and I returned to the dentist's office, where the four chairs glowed, pure and fulfilled, in the light of their own panels of bulbs. I wanted to see where Ispas had come from, through what secret tunnel hollowed out inside the building's massive walls. I opened the door at the end of the office, between two metal and glass cases full of dental instruments and molds, and I found a room the size of closet, with walls of rough brick, barely big enough for a person standing up. In the gaps between the bricks were dusty cobwebs, and everything smelled like debris and filth. A yellowed newspaper spread on the floor was covered with a thick layer of dust, except for two boot prints, within whose outlines the columns of type and photos were clearly visible. Nothing else, no tunnel, no trapdoor, no secret door. The anatomical model-person had stood there like a mannequin, for who knows how long, until who knows what force activated him. At Voila, Comrade Nistor at least had a bed where he could rest, to regenerate his bestiality overnight.

Frightened, I closed the door and left the office. I walked down the marble stairway, floor after floor, in the monstrous loneliness of the dark edifice. I wandered through corridors looking for my room for a long time, opening doors to labs and abandoned offices, until I could finally throw myself onto my bed. I don't know when I fell asleep, because for the first time I felt I was passing from one dream into another. The next day a doctor came in, examined me, and ran some tests, and I stayed in the clinic two more nights. I was released with a diagnosis of neurasthenia and a prescription for Quilibrex, along with some smoky vials whose glass throats I had to cut with a tiny saw to swallow the oily liquid, and a two-week medical leave, including the ten days that had already passed.

I wrote here all day, from the time I woke up to now, 4:00 AM the next morning. I feel, with my whole body, that the end is coming, or an end. An end, at least, of some of our multiple and multidimensional lives. But I can't think or write. Not another line. Tomorrow is another day. Now I'm going to bed. Good night, sweet prince, good night.

44

I was eating at the auto mechanic's by school, as usual, when a memory flashed through my mind. On this page, I want to be very calm, very rational, I want to look things right in the eyes. After the Romanian test for class 6-Ω, I stacked up the thin notebooks, without their slipcovers—so they wouldn't be too heavy when I took them home—I tied them with string and left them on the table in the teachers' lounge. I saw Irina for a moment, we smiled, then Gheară, Agripina, and Băjenaru came in together, registers under their arms and strangely well disposed. The woman was laughing, she had also given her kids a test, and she had just glanced at the fifth-graders' agrammatical scribblings. "Listen to this, dom profesor, you've never heard anything like it. You're going to die laughing! Hee hee! I was crying I was laughing so hard, there at the front of the room. Look what Haralambescu wrote for 'Describe the protagonist of *Prâslea the Brave and the Golden Apples*.' Listen to this, dom profesor! 'The king had a big garden with an apple tree in his bottom!' In his bottom, dom profesor, look at it, there it is in black and white . . ." The whole group was falling over with laughter. "That's a good one, dear, but wait 'til you hear what I got while marking the entrance exams for Iulia Hasdeu. I come to an essay that starts like this: 'Many vaivodes dug the foundations of our nation, but only one put in the tombstone: Comrade . . .'" Here, doamna Rădulescu whispered a name, then, sweating, she broke into hysterical laughter. "Yes, girls, a tombstone, how was the poor kid to know what a *cornerstone* was, just from reading it in the textbook?" More laughter, titters, and bellows, but all in an odd muteness, because walls have ears, and you never know . . . I was hungry and didn't stay to hear any more. I left the school with a herd of older kids and went upstairs to the mechanic's, above the filthy workshop full of ancient cars on blocks and tools scattered across the tile floor: hoses, wrenches, and jacks, all greased with fuel oil. I waited in line for my usual portion of stewed meatballs and sodas with bizarre impurities in sweaty bottles, and I took my tray to a table. The workers in stinking work coats, which had probably never been washed, tore their rolls at the next table, their hands black with grease.

But there was a happy, early spring light in the room, and the trimester was ending, and the food, even cafeteria food, looked good, because hunger is the best cook—so the memory of the dream that was in no way a dream took me by surprise, shattering the beautiful day as though you would slash a beautiful face with a straight razor.

Maybe that expression, "hunger is the best cook," triggered the memory, because my mother used to say it a lot; perhaps it sounded in my mind, for a moment, the way my mother said it, in our dark kitchen, in the depths of time, at the window that showed the fantastical brick pediment of Moara Dâmbovița. Perhaps what flashed through my mind was my oldest dream, the one where I'm holding my mother's hand, walking through an unknown place with ditches crossed by little footbridges, under a rosy dawn. Perhaps it was the link to a nightmare. Because two years ago, when I wrote down in my notebook my series of dreams that were inexplicable, yet precious to me, as though carved in high relief on the interior concavity of my brow, I didn't dare to write down the most penetrating, most unforgettable of them, the one that I push away with desperate gestures whenever it rises to my mind, the way I push away ghosts whose eyeballs are sliced by the edge of a piece of paper, or the spider that wraps me in his web and devours me . . . Today, now, I want to write it down, because I sense it's the puzzle piece with Snow White or the princess in the story of the eleven swans, the piece that the rest of the puzzle—even with all the other pieces of cardboard put together correctly—needs in order to make sense.

The recollection of my "Mama" dream hit me right in the heart. I got up from the table, leaving my rolls almost untouched. I went downstairs and stared, forgetting myself completely, at the desolation of the workshop, with its flaking walls and old workplace safety posters stuck crookedly here and there. I stared blankly at the three or four cars with their hoods up and wheels missing, rims bent, and at the dirty rags and metal shavings on the floor. I would have stayed there forever, because my reality was all the same and there was no reason to make the effort of going anywhere else. My entire reality might have been just that grimy hall, with small windows stuck in sheet metal doors, with unpainted auto body pieces leaning on the walls, with crude mechanics covered in grease up to their elbows. I shook myself out of this trance, and I taught the afternoon classes as though in a dream.

I want to be very calm, very descriptive, very rational. I don't know when I had the dream—although I seem to remember November 12 (but what year?), I don't have the patience to check my diary, and anyway it wouldn't help—this dream is the only one I didn't write down when I woke up in the morning, for shame and for horror. Like the dream in which I was grabbed by the ankles and thrown out of the bed, to be hit with extraordinary violence against the opposite wall, like in the one in which I spun in my bed like a propeller, with the sheets and everything, and like in a few others (the one with my aunt, for example, who grinned at me from the foot of the bed), I experienced a third state in the "Mama" dream—I wasn't awake or asleep. It was as though I was awake and lucid, but drugged, unable to resist, unable to feel emotions, doubled, dissociated, looking at my body from outside with a gentle kind of knowledge and compassion. I didn't experience what happened as though it were a dream or a memory: it was real, immediate, but my consciousness seemed narrow and passive. A long time ago, when I had my tonsils out, they gave me a blue pill, after which I witnessed the extraction of pieces of flesh from my throat without fear and without participating, in spite of the otherwise unbearably sharp pain, which I didn't perceive as my own pain. This is the state in which the dream occurred, the most painful dream of my life.

I found myself inside a bitter knot of hallucinations that made no sense. It was night, I was in my room on Ştefan cel Mare, the one with the panoramic window showing all of Bucharest spread out in nocturnal illumination, as neon lights flicked on and off. It was never completely dark in my room, and rarely quiet. A tram was always roaring by and casting bands of light across the ceiling. The distant houses were lit up, like the billboards in the center of town, and like the cross-shaped posts between the two tramlines bearing crucified Christs, their tilting heads crowned with thorns. But instead of lying on a bed, I was on a kind of table covered with a rubber mat. It had appeared there, in the otherwise unaltered room, between the bed and the desk where I did my homework. I was cold, perhaps because I was completely naked. My shoulder blades and hips felt the cool of the sheet. I lifted my hand and looked at it: I wasn't dreaming. What was happening to me? I sat up, but I suddenly heard an interior voice, sure of itself and clear as a drop of water into a karstic basin, that ordered me to lie back down. What was going on? I didn't recall, at that moment, the scene from my childhood, when my mother took me to the hospital for an operation, one I find no trace of anywhere on my skin, during which I heard the same voice, but I did later, without daring to follow the thought to its end. I lay my head back down on the table but turned it toward the door, because, in the illuminated darkness of the room, I suddenly saw it.

I advised myself to stay calm, but the hair on my arms was standing up and I felt the approach of madness. The fact is that I saw her, without any possible doubt, concrete and indescribable. She was there, in the half shadow, feminine but inhuman. The female of a grotesque species similar to our own. Pale, without clothes. With the same grimace that had scared me a few months before, when a grinning dwarf appeared at the foot of my bed. This one's face had the same twisted mouth, the same caricatured smile. Even the limbs lacked human proportions: she looked deformed, maimed, somehow infirm. She limped slowly. You felt, on top of everything, like you could see through her whitish body. Her large breasts and the fiery red hair of her pubis didn't at all match that unearthly, chlorotic body, with an extended skull, a thin neck, and eyes filled by their enormous pupils. I don't know what else to say, in that moment I didn't have the concentration and inspired observations I needed to understand and describe her. If I had actually been awake, I would have gone mad with fear. As it was, I looked at her impersonally, feeling something like resignation. Something inside me called her "Mama," but that didn't mean she was my own mother. She was a mother, pure and simple, who looked at me with dark eyes, an embryo's eyes, or an insect's. She came nearer and lay on the operating table beside me. Then we made love in a manner I don't understand and can't describe. She made love, in fact, below my eyes, in the center of my skull. The teenager ejaculated, for the first time in his life, inside the womb of that creature. With the sense that his sperm was being milked, his sperm extracted, the way your blood is taken for tests.

That's all I know. I probably fell asleep right afterward. In the morning, I woke with the memory of the dream that didn't feel like a dream, it felt like an awful reality. In my room there hung a faint smell, like medicine or an unknown chemical substance. I went to the bathroom and looked at myself in the mirror. I wore a strange expression, showing a cruelty I didn't recognize, that had nothing to do with me.

I don't want to write even one line too much. There isn't anything much to write. There, in my room on Ştefan cel Mare, in the whirring of the trams and magic of the city spread out upon the window, something happened of supreme importance, but incomprehensible to my poor brain, the prisoner of its stupid skull.

45

The essential ambiguity of my writing. Its irreducible insanity. I was in a world that cannot be described, and definitely not understood, through any other kind of writing, insofar as it can be truly comprehended. Revealing is one thing, and the painful process of reverse engineering, which is true understanding, quite another. You have before your eyes an artifact of another world, with other dawns and other gods, an enigmatic Antikythera mechanism that shines, floating in the air, in all the details of its metal brackets covered with symbols and gears. It was difficult to retrieve it from the bottom of the sea, from all its oyster beds and undulating algae, to meticulously clean off the crust of petrified sand and rust, to grease it with glittering oil, to set every gear in place so all the teeth fit together, and *this* is what my manuscript has done, up to this point: it has revealed, brought to light, unveiled what was hidden behind veils, it has decrypted what was locked in the crypt, it has deciphered the cipher of the box where it lay, without even a dash of the unknown object's shadow and melancholy dripping into our world. The more details we see, the less we understand, because understanding means penetrating the meaning of the mechanism, and that only exists in the mind of its inventor. Understanding means penetrating another mind; any object that asks to be understood is a portal on that mind, and the terror and endless enigma begin the moment when, looking at an object, you are sucked inside it and deposited within an inhuman mind, completely different than your own, a world you call, with all of the word's ambiguity, *sacred*, which is to say, foreign, apparently arbitrary, capable of miracles and absurdities, that can feed you or crush you for equally obscure reasons. You can learn this mind's mannerisms, you can use prayer to receive, invocation to make manifest, the way a cat licks its master at dinnertime, but *how* the master leads his life, how he built the house, turned on the lights, drove the car, how he learned that the sun will rise tomorrow, how he knows that there is a tomorrow, in what way he deciphers mathematical symbols and their ghostlike movements across the logical field, and countless other details of an unimaginable life within a world and within a mind of another level of complexity—all of this, for the cat, is camouflaged inside another dimension, on another spiral arm of existence. When the master points at something with his finger, the cat looks at the finger, sniffs it, licks it. That is how we understand the Godly: incomprehensible beyond good and evil, lost for us in an unreachable dimension. Religions are, and should be, the mindless contemplation of God's finger, in our inability to understand that the finger is not the message, it only *points* toward something else. We think with the ganglion of flesh inside our skull, we are censured by its limitations, just as the fly uses its own ganglion within its world, as the cat uses its brain in its little skull to ask for food and affection from a foreign and incomprehensible creature.

☼

I went to give the librarian his manuscript back. During my convalescence, not a day passed without me removing it from its ivory-colored box and leafing through it, in a pointless effort to find even a partial solution to its mystery. Page after page written in the same unknown language, with constants as clear as they were obscure, with a meticulousness of transcription that made the idea of it being a hoax or a demented person's raving almost totally implausible. How many linguists and how many obsessed amateurs had lost their minds, so they said, using statistics, divination, cryptology, or astrology to understand even a few words, just as it happened in another moment of *The Gadfly*–Voynich manuscript trajectory, for those using the kit of colored cubes that Hinton hoped would make the fourth dimension tangible to our minds. Because in a strange way, although they didn't seem similar, Hinton's kit, the Voynich manuscript, Nicolae Minovici's post-hanging drawings, the ultramarine pitcher Valeria received from the sky, and my manuscript, written in a tiny hand between the covers of these three notebooks, are all the same kind of object, the same finger points toward all of them; they constitute a mental crutch, perhaps, just like classical calculations with exponential spirals whose whirling arms quickly exceed our mind's visual field, and which drive themselves, like degraded drill bits, into the Cantorian infinity: fold a piece of paper fifteen times and its thickness will reach from the earth to the moon; put a speck of grain on the first square of a chessboard, two on the second, four on the third, eight on the fourth, and all the harvests of the world won't equal the sixty-fourth square; a cell divides only eighty times to create the entire human body. In this same way we pour our brain over the world—the way a starfish eviscerates its stomach to comprehend the crustaceans on which it feeds.

fachys ykal ar ataiin shd shory cthres y kor sholdy
sory cthar or y kair chtaiin shar are chtar olan
syaiir skey or ikaiin shadlcthoary chtes daraiin sa
o'oiin oteey oteor roloty cthar daiin otaiin or okan
sair y chear cthaiin cphar cfaiin ydaraishi

The whole text is like this, clear as day and completely unintelligible, the way any piece of writing appears to an illiterate person. It is interrupted by splendid plates showing unknown plants with green and gold leaves, with spiky blossoms and blue buds, with strange and powerful roots that sometimes end in bizarre tubercles. It is plagued by lines of naked women, white as milk, bathing in tubs and tubes, in green and turquoise blue liquids. Dozens of naked women with prominent stomachs, women holding, arms outstretched in a kind of horror, something that sometimes looks like a fish, sometimes an embryo, sometimes a flower. Rubicund, vegetative women, shoving their hands into sinuous, ramifying pipes, standing up in the same blue water, in receptacles shaped like cornucopia that extend through pipes that look like veins or intestines. It is a labyrinthine system of ponds and tubs, spread over dozens of manuscript pages and surrounded at each turn by the same writing: calm, elaborate, orderly, without hesitations or erasures, but defying intelligibility in any language on Earth.

Then there are plates that unfold, three times wider than the rest of the manuscript, showing unimaginably complex concentric spheres, like the cellular structures under a microscope, with seemingly organic pipes and compartments, with unpredictable symmetries and asymmetries, with a legend written in words from the same unintelligible language. Protozoa? Fetuses? Energies with rotating auras like peacocks? I looked at them tens and hundreds of times, squinting, trying to go inside the hidden design, the deep wisdom. Always the same hopeless obscurity, the same glass wall separating me from the fascinating axolotl with an Aztec face, the same inability to find something in common with the Xipéhuz, the elves, the strangers from another place and time who watch me at night from the edge of my bed.

Then there are plates that show—in concentric, Jungian circles infested with letters from the same illegible alphabet—anthropomorphic images: suns (maybe), zodiac signs (maybe), the stars and moon (probably). With indiscernible extensions between the technical and the floral. With carousels of faces arranged in allegories just as obscure as their surrounding commentaries. A half millennium ago, some unknown person, who had never before made anything like it (because nothing like the Voynich manuscript exists anywhere in the world), constructed, with what must have been a clear and powerful motivation, the perfect labyrinth, and placed a complete enigma in its center. Like all prophecies, this one regards the future, when we will see not through a glass darkly, but face-to-face. There are whole pages of these rotating spheres, full of stars and faces. I have actually seen some of these before: passing overhead in marvelous brilliance in the circular room where I was operated on; some of these were the stars that terrified me whenever I went out in the middle of the night. There are skies from other worlds, with other constellations and unknown apparatuses moving silently among them. The most fascinating of these toothed gears, crescents, crosses, and crossed triangles of an ad hoc language are inhabited, in each of their concentric circles, like a Dantean paradise, by these same naked, plantlike women wearing crowns and holding scepters and stars. Judging by the figures in the center, these are zodiac signs; by the imagery, this is the Garden of Earthly Delights; by their deep enigma, the women are a bolted door frantically searching for their own key.

Dusk descended over the pages of the manuscript, and I still couldn't bear to leave it, to stop leafing through it in the hope that precisely this darkening purple light would blur the ornamentation and reveal, in all its murderous splendor, the judgment. Then night fell completely, and the sounds of Maica Domnului became quieter, and not a dram of the book's mystery dissolved into the air. "Who knows," I said to myself, leaning my head on my hand and tracing my fingertip around the largest and most ornate circle of the ancient parchment, "perhaps the sign isn't in this book, the sign that could transport you to the depths of the soul, into real worlds that shape themselves according to your desires, in spaces illuminated by a splendid blue, damp and flowing . . ."

❊

Palamar opened the door—he was home alone, as always. I followed him through the same series of somber, high-ceilinged rooms, and I was just as surprised by the large, pearly gray metal cabinet that occupied one full wall of his office. We spoke about the manuscript for a bit, as it lay between us once again in its ivory box, then we fell silent, as happens when your host has nothing more to talk about and waits for you to understand that it's time to take your leave. But I couldn't leave until I understood what was truly going on in that house on the edge of the city.

"Last time," I said without looking in his eyes, "when I left, I heard a sound coming from the basement . . ."

"Well, that's the solenoid," Palamar told me right away, with a verve and naturalness I hadn't expected, as though he had been wanting to talk to me about the large coil and hadn't found the right moment to do so until then. "Our houses, like a few others in the city, were built on nodes of the city's energy network, and each one has this thing buzzing in the basement, which, sometimes, you could do without. I would bet you use your coil to levitate over your bed, and I wouldn't blame you, it's nicer to sleep like that, instead of being crushed against a lumpy mattress by the attraction of the earth. For me, it is even more important, as a joke I'd call it a 'work tool,' even 'one of the most refined.' In my job, I couldn't do without this lens of energy, this gate between worlds that, although they coexist over a few square meters, are as foreign to each other as if they were on different planets or different dimensions."

"In your job as a librarian?"

Palamar looked at me as though he had just awoken from a dream. "No, I was only a librarian for you. You were never curious enough to ask what I was reading, for hours on end, in the front room of the Holy of Holies where you chose your books (not even arbitrarily, as you still think even today, but selected with great care so that reading them would lead you here, to this moment, without any chance of mistake. You didn't choose *The Black Museum* at random, or *Malpertuis,* not Nerval's poetry, not *Malte Laurids Brigge,* not *Le Horla,* not *Maldoror*, not the astounding writings of Judge Schreber, not Blecher, not Cavafy, not Kafka, the master of dreams), the sole book, open on the desk in front of me, that you saw without seeing all those years you visited the B. P. Hasdeu Library. Look, here, this is your one chance."

I looked at him in fear: the sepia photograph had come to life and looked almost like a real creature. What was with Palamar? He had become persuasive, enthusiastic, as though this one chance were his. He was like a merchant hawking his wares, desperate to pull in a customer. I saw him stand, walk over to the gray file cabinet, and unlock it, throwing the doors back with large, demonstrative gestures, like a magician: see, nothing up my sleeves . . . Inside were dozens, hundreds of small drawers coded with of numbers and letters, like card catalogs in large libraries. Palamar, with a wide, almost ravenous smile pulled one of them out: instead of the index cards I was expecting, it was full of glass slides, microscope slides holding biological preparations. They were yellowed along their edges, apparently empty and clean, set at a diagonal, parallel to each other. On another shelf were little, round boxes and test tubes of differing sizes, but three-quarters of the cabinet was taken up by drawers of slides. On the lowest shelf, there was a book with some small author names on the upper part of the cover, followed by an enormous title, taking up half the remaining area: *MITES*. Palamar slowly leaned down, bending at his knees as though he had back trouble, he grabbed the massive volume and brought it to his desk, plopping it down beside the ivory box. "Take a look at this book and you'll understand my true profession, vocation, passion, or whatever you want to call it. But it is so much more."

I ran my thumb up the block of pages before opening it at random. It was amazing. Among pages covered with small print, the volume had perhaps thirty plates showing nightmarish creatures, more bizarre, adorned with more unreal appendages, and assembled more fantastically than any known insect by a few orders of magnitude, at least. And furthermore, according to the scale under each illustration, they were just as minute as insects were in comparison to mammals. The sight of this animalcule, part of the criminal underworld and absolute abomination of the animal kingdom, kin to spiders, ticks, and mange, to bloodsuckers and devourers of living flesh, surprised me less for nature's blind cruelty than for its endless imagination. On one of the plates, I found the crepuscular vision Irina and I had had a year ago, when, after we had discussed our school porter's disappearance and made love in the disheveled bed, forgetting to float in the bedroom's musty air, we entered the tower with the dental chair and looked through the porthole. They were the same species of mites, the leprous elephants with long legs in multiple articulations, like those that Saint Anthony, in Dalí's painting, protects himself against with his pathetic crucifix. Brownish-yellow, slow-moving, and blind, with long, curving strands of hair on their giant spines and with enormous claws, on parade through mounds of dead skin, the pudgy creatures looked like the creation of an impossibly saturnine, demonic spirit. On other plates were violet or purple mites, with screaming yellow tongues, with hair on the joints of their legs like tarantulas, others were smooth as ivory, with spines and horns that looked absurdly dangerous, others soft as waterdrops, with black claws turned upward, others were mottled and translucent like aspic, but all were blind, weaving their way through another kind of world, one that emerged from the void through other kinds of senses. "The insects of insects," I said to myself, the third spiral of organic, world-carrying containers, the numberless legion of creatures smaller than the human eye can perceive and yet living and real and made from the same organic substance and the same sad body that houses us as well, soma-sema, carrying us through our mortal world.

"Each slide in the file contains one of every known species. Some are unique, not to be found in even the largest natural science museums. All of us who study mites—there are a few hundred of us in the world—maintain a correspondence, we know each other well, we often send specimens to each other, make exchanges . . . I have always been surprised by how small our sect is, because I can't imagine any more fascinating area of knowledge. Why don't all entomologists study mites and only mites? Why are myrmecologists wasting their time? What could you possibly find interesting about a bee or a spider—and the pathetic kitsch of lepidopterists goes without saying. Look at this scabies mite, this jewel of creation, with its sublime, chubby little legs, look at the fists on the ends, it knows how to cut a path through the human derma, with who knows what thoughts housed in its head. Look at this bed mite, with its feather-shaped muzzle, look at this rose-colored spider mite that sucks the blood from ticks while they are busy sucking blood from humans. So much variation, so much imagination, what floral colors, what azure and metallic green and brazen pink and what cadaverous lividity . . . My dear man, if I were a poet, I would trade a decade of my life to write the epic of these unrecognized lives, their loves and their wars, their turpitude and their glory, their empires of just a few square centimeters, but just as rich in tactile, auditory, thermal, and vibratory scenes as those in our realm. As for their number, I'll just say that mites make up a quarter of the weight of every pillow where those who labor on this earth lay their heads night after night; mites who, night after night, invade us like the Lilliputians did Gulliver, but as many as the grains of sand on the beach and the stars in the sky, entire nations, legions, and phalanxes, to devour the dead skin our bodies shed. You will find them, invisible as the atoms of the air you breathe, in every part of the earth, from the poles to the equator, in every climate, at every altitude, in tens of thousands of corporal levels, in atrocious colors and repulsive habits. A quarter of the living mass of the planet is formed by their minuscule bodies. Sometimes I read newspaper articles about the feverish search for life that might exist everywhere in the universe. If it is so, and it could not be otherwise, then the planets of all solar systems, of all galaxies, even the farthest away, are infested, teeming, being eaten alive by mites. They are absolutely packed with them. Like mange, they dig their channels through the universal mantle, crawling and swarming, on top of each other, inside of each other, devouring each other, planting eggs in their own bodies, suffocating and unbearable and ineffable. What Dantean vision, what a multitude of worlds colliding, endlessly, hopelessly, in one minuscule region of the great void! Where can you find the exobiologists, the exosociologists, the exopsychologists of this universal swarm? Where are the paleontologists and historians of these societies? Where the ethnologists, where the philosophers, where the theologians?"

Palamar took slides out, one after another, and looked at them in the light, as though he could see the invisible creature crushed between the two glass plates, their eight legs spread out pathetically, like a little biological sun, like a Krishna with multiple arms dancing the dance of creation and destruction. I looked at some of them: there was nothing, aside from my reflection, flashing on the transparent slide. "Most of the species don't even have names," the collector continued, "they are known only by a code of numbers and letters, like supernovas and quasars. But as there are so many kinds, angelology and demonology would have been too impoverished to name them in their abstruse Latin. What's strange to me, and incredible, is the fact that mites have the same makeup that we do. A colleague in Latin America specializes in their dissection: they are organic constructions made of systems and apparatuses. All the organs of our bodies have equivalents in theirs, while, of course, their skeleton is external, like that of insects. The cells from which they are formed are no different than our own. They feed and reproduce in their minuscule worlds just as we do, which leads one to wonder—isn't the question inevitable?—whether we are not mites inside a superior world, one so enormous that it surpasses our powers of perception. If it isn't somehow the case that the Gigantism of this world is not just another degree of three-dimensional magnitude, but rather another dimension, given our allegiance to logical space . . . What other kind of space, unimaginable to our skull-sheltered ganglion, could belong to the creature who is just as large and as complete in comparison to me as I am to—see, to the invisible microbug on this slide? If at this very moment, some god who exceeds my sight like a vast edifice doesn't look at my martyred body, flattened out in my dimension on an endlessly large slide? And if he is unaware that he, too, is crucified on a slide held between the fingers of an even larger god, even more incomprehensible, and so on, and so on, without end? And we cannot imagine a final god, who transcends the endless scale of dimensions, because it is itself that scale, itself the divine chessboard, with squares where the kernels of grain keep doubling? . . . Let me show you something else."

Palamar put the slides away carefully and locked the large cabinet. He sat back down, and I sat down again across from him. He turned his lamp on and placed one hand in the circle of light, palm down. He spread his fingers and whispered to me, "Look carefully at the triangle between my thumb and index finger. Do you see anything?" In the raking light, the skin on the back of the old man's hand looked as scaly as a lizard's, with varicose veins and white strands of hair and brown spots showing his age. On the triangle of skin between his fingers I did, in fact, perceive something unusual. There were fine, barely visible, white lines that formed a network, like the runways of an airport. They didn't cover more than two square centimeters. Among the straight, intersecting lines, I thought I saw some figures—a monkey, a bird with outstretched wings and fanned tail, a chameleon—all vaguely sketched. My eyes had to strain to see, however, and they soon began to tear up. "Is it a tattoo?" I asked him. "It's mange," he responded, smiling happily. "It is a scabies colony I have grown on my own skin. I started with a single female full of eggs. Now there has to be a small nation of millions of individuals. The lines are the passages they've dug in my dermis. At night, the itching can be almost unbearable, but I endure it happily, and I wouldn't destroy the colony for anything in the world. They are my creation, in a way they are made in my image, because the same amino acids, the same purine and pyrimidine bases, the same functions and the same organs, the same physical laws, the same matter and the same fields that animate my body also animate theirs, generating the improbable, inexplicable, and inextricable phenomenon of life. I created a world inside my very body, a network of channels through my dermis, constantly inhabited, explored, and expanded by a people that believes, as we do, that it is alone in the universe. Hundreds of generations have already passed since their Genesis, there must have already appeared, in their world, a chemical glory: myths of their origins, of their totemic ancestors, of the perplexing creatures who gave them face and name only to then retreat into the imperceptible and incomprehensible. I often wonder if, as they live and die, as they copulate and defecate, as they rend and devour the organic material of my body and blood, whether they ever intuit their solitude, their helplessness. If they ever shout, from the depths, unto me. If, as they torture me with such tremendous itching, such that sometimes I feel like pouring acid over my martyred hand, they have ever thought of their unforgivable sin. It's almost certain they haven't developed a science of me, not yet, or of the asymptotic levels, from the depths to the heights, of worlds screwed into other worlds, into other worlds, and so on, each one twice as vast as the one before . . . They think they are alone, without a purpose and without a destiny, sprung from who knows where into a world of passages dug inside an elastic and firm dermis. They perceive vibrations, smells and tastes, and sensations we cannot imagine, just as they cannot imagine sight. Thinking of my people, in my torturous nights of insomnia, I have begun to love them with a great love, much more than I love myself . . ."

Was he insane? Over the course of the evening, his eyes had acquired a more than bizarre glint. It reminded me of the way the windows flashed dementedly at the top of the water tower. He kept his hand in the same position the entire time, his palm downward and his fingers spread. The white lines between the thumb and index looked like the map of an Incan settlement, as seen from a monoplane flying over the endless desert. From time to time, he passed the fingers of his other hand over the lines, with a kind of tenderness, as though caressing the invisible, innocent subjects of their heavenly emperor. Once, he slowly brought his hand toward his eyes, just a few millimeters away, perhaps hoping that, from their transparent trenches, the citizens of the mite catacombs might observe the double system of colossal, brown suns.

"I began to feel sorry for them, to pity their lack of knowledge and their darkness. I mourned the dark sadness of their fate, the fact that they die in their misfortune, without any hope or any help. I wondered how I could open the eyes they do not have, how to speak to the ears that did not extend into the flesh of their temples. How I could address a people that doesn't understand my words, who has other senses and lives on a different spiral of our world? How could the good news of my existence, of my love for them, of my desire for sacrifice reach them? I tried for months on end to imagine a chemical swab, a vibration, a ray of light that could transmit my message: rejoice! You are not alone! You have a purpose in the world, you have a creator who has not forgotten you. You will all be saved in the end, you will know new heavens and new earths, in a life more radiant and vast! Or to tell them just this: do not be afraid! Because on this commandment hang all the law and the prophets.

"Night after night I struggled until, in a flash, I realized how simple it was. Now I know I can reveal myself to them at any time, all the instruments have been given to me, everything is here, in this house. I just need you to help me. So I'm asking you, as though you were my son. Come see what I have in the basement."

Palamar got up from his chair with an unexpected elan and opened—toward the corner of the office, across from the metal cabinet—a door I had not noticed before, narrow and white like for a toilet or closet. Right behind it, a steep cement stairway descended somewhere into the house's basement. "It goes to the solenoid, naturally," he said to me, reminding me of the soft buzzing I had heard last time. "Watch the ceiling," Palamar said, going down first, his head tilted to one side, since the stairs fell at a pronounced angle. I followed him until we came to a circular room, not that large (it fit within the square of the building), circled along its walls by a large coil of thick copper wire, greased and glistening, complexly woven, difficult to describe, like a redheaded girl's braid in a bun on the top of her head. The copper torus must have been more than a meter thick. In the middle of the otherwise empty and white hypogeum, lit by a window near the ceiling, there was a console with dials and levers, and a few stands holding things I could not identify. In the center of the room, like a pillar from the floor to the ceiling, was a thick cylinder of blue glass, wide enough to encompass a person standing up. Our footsteps echoed loudly and clearly off the dull glass floor tiles.

The old man sat on the stool before the console, adjusted the height of a stand that held a black, horizontal plaque under a plexiglass sheet, then, with a certain impatience, he moved a finger toward a button on the panel. He hesitated and pulled his hand back. He sat thinking for a while, like a person who wants to start an important discussion but doesn't know how to, and then he turned toward me. He told me firmly, almost brutally, what he had to say, with the determined courage of one who knows ahead of time he will be denied, but cannot turn back: "You will be my messenger. I will send you to them with my message of redemption. Do not be afraid, everything will last only a few hours here, and a few years there. I can transfer, through the power of my solenoid, a human's entire interior being into the body of a blind mite, born and raised there in the blind world of its tunnels, among heaps of eggs and droppings. It will be a flawless mite, chosen by me even while it was in its mother's womb, just as I chose you, without your knowing. You came to the old library, lured by the print smell of my lair on Ştefan cel Mare, and from there you traced the pheromones to *The Gadfly*, which led you to the Voynich manuscript. It was the right trajectory, as predictable as the course of a bullet, the metaphysical arc that led you into the center of my solenoid. You are at the frontier of the holarchy, where two worlds mirror each other along an asymptotic spiral on a scale neither one of us can imagine. Even though I know you will do it, still I ask you to do so; even though you will go, still I ask you to go, traveler with staff in hand, go toward their world thirsting for the truth. Please go, my friend."

I listened to him with the greatest calm. I also knew that I would go. I couldn't let myself be ignorant of even one pore of the enormous sponge in which I lived: every pore could be the Exit. So, without speaking a word, I walked toward the cylinder which, I imagined, would surround my body and keep it in a vegetative state as long as the journey lasted. "Exactly, exactly," murmured Palamar, as though he had read my thoughts. "But first I want to show you your new body, I hope you find it comfortable and worthy. Look here, with the magnifying glass."

The librarian placed his right hand on the black marble plate and adjusted the dome above it, that now looked like an eyeball's lens, until its center was directly above the area crisscrossed with white stripes between his thumb and index finger. I leaned over to look through the lens, which seemed to be not just cold glass but an intelligent and selective viewfinder. What I saw at that moment would imprint itself deep within my memory. Through his translucid skin the channels were quite visible, and in the channels, like on the boulevards of a large and melancholic city, were unending processions of mites, teeming crowds intersecting, interweaving, knocking into each other and scattering, only to gather again and again in large piațas and to move down cross streets and into the dead ends and courtyards of the magnified city. Constructions the size of cyclopes, made from something black and shiny like pitch, rose on the edges of underground chambers, their windows and balconies and patios populated with small animals in slow, eternal agitation. Thickening like an organic lens over scratches as clear as seawater, the domed lens focused on one of the tunnels, then zoomed in on the closest building. Finally, out of the group of mites that surrounded the base of the edifice, only one remained within the clear circle of the lens, visible in all his details, as though he were drawn in ink on an anatomical plate and then colored in with the most delicate of watercolor brushstrokes. It was *Sarcoptes scabiei,* just as I had seen as a teenager in the parasitology treatise, a creature whose every feature and every organ was differently shaped, at that microscopic scale, in an altered proportion between surface, gravity, and volume. The thinnest of spiderlike legs could hold up the paunchiest of creatures, like the elephants loaded with all the temptations of the world in Dalí's famous painting. The body which I would control when I renounced my own was perfect, even poignant, in its every feature. A great ivory-rose bead, with folds and commissures that outlined rhinoceros-like cuirass plates, with faint striations and lines, with tender crosshatches and timid shadows, was lined on its edges with little buds, the one in front being the head. On his bizarre surface, like Aztec hieroglyphics, the only members visible, for lack of any eyes, were his massive buccal pieces. The other buds growing on the spherical body were only slightly different from the head: four forward legs and four backward looked more like tubercles spouting a long, curved hair, thicker than the rest of the hairs scattered over the body. The rows of orifices, as they opened and closed spasmodically on each side of the large stomach, created the image of a body just as monstrous and as beautiful as my own, as your own. That creature, albeit minuscule, was complete and alive. Its movements were barely visible, because time itself below the lens thickened and flowed like honey.

"You will go inside it like the driver of a tank's narrow, armored cell, you will accustom yourself to your neural control panel, you will explore its possibilities, you will adapt to a different sensorial system than ours, and a strange world will unfurl around you, you will have its needs, you will move according to the logic of its being. You will think with a few rudimentary ganglions, you will communicate through chemical traces and pheromones, you will touch and perceive clouds of the inexhaustible material that human creatures cannot even dream of. You will be like them, but you will know that you are not one of them. You will live with them, but like one descended from heaven, incomprehensible and unattainable. And in spite of the chasms between worlds on other levels and other dimensions, you will need to transmit to them, through a tunnel effect, the message. The escape plan. The annunciation without which they are living dead, buried beneath their sins."

"I have to try," I said, trembling, but he didn't seem to hear me, because he had something else to add.

"And then I will remove you from there, and you will be once more the one you always were, yourself in your rightful body of flesh, the one you are not proud of, but which is all you were given. Flesh like theirs, no nobler or purer, because our differences are not fleshly. We are, all of us, digestive tracts with a brain at one end and a sex at the other, spirals of material that exist, like tops, only as long as the spinning keeps us upright . . ."

"Of course," I said again, looking at him calmly. "I am ready to go whenever you want." And at that moment, I didn't even care if I died in the mite scientist's bizarre experiment, I didn't care if I stayed in my new body, among new people, and in new world forever, never finding a way back, living their life, procreating with them, eating with them (eating them and letting myself be eaten), sharing chemical beliefs and vibrating ideas with them, or if I would come back to the blank world, one surely burrowed inside the skin of an incomprehensible god who endures all of us, in spite of the pains and sleepless nights we cause him.

My aim was to discover, even if I had only a slim chance, whether salvation were possible. If the message could pass from one spiral to another, in spite of the tragic differences between worlds on different scales, perceived with other senses, in spite of belonging to different ontological fields, other instincts, other loves and other morals, other paradises and other gods . . . I wanted to know if the cat would ever look in the direction the finger is pointing. If we would ever perceive the code in the tapping on the cell wall, if we would ever be taken up into the sky from the middle of our snow-filled yard. If we would ever get out of here, ever be saved by being given this day our daily fear. I wanted a drop of certainty, even if it meant abandoning all hope. Can You hear my voice, You, who have no tympanum or internal ear? Can You see me from heaven, without a cornea, or lens, or retina, or optic nerves; can You see me, me, the one living for a nanosecond on a speck of dust in a world with billions and billions of stars? And if You could talk to me, how could I hear You? Because Your voice could speak not in words but in bodies, things, clouds, and maybe whole universes, for which we lack sensory organs. You could belong to a hyperlogical and ultrametaphysical space, one that would rend my poor world like a spider's diaphanous web . . . Could we ever go into the world outside, leaving behind billions of bloodstained chrysalides?

The old man pulled a lever and the glass cylinder began to descend slowly, until its lip reached the floor. I stepped inside the blue circle, allowing the curved walls to surround me as they rose again, just as smoothly, toward the ceiling. Through its blurry husk, I saw the room under Palamar's house in a slight deformation, and sounds became as soft and calm as in a dream. That is how I heard the great coil buzzing, first almost imperceptibly, like the breath of a sleeping child, then louder and more acute. After a minute, its buzzing became just as intense as that of the Dâmbovița mill that vibrated its electric sifters day and night behind our block on Ştefan cel Mare. It grew louder, imperative and oscillating like a police siren, it amplified until it wounded my eardrums, until it moved beyond hearing, after which, without any connection to my poor little ears, it grew louder, asymptotic, insane, devastating, like my epileptic dream; it became a yellow hurricane, a sea of flames of unbelievable fury, in the middle of which my skin was torn away, my vertebrae blown apart, my blood, lymph, and bile were splattered, my neck broken. Only the stubborn bone of my cranium resisted for a moment, before bursting into splinters, leaving my brain to howl for eons, in the deepest of hells.

Then, suddenly, there was silence.

❋

I found myself in the night of a mite's body, with my mental substance inserted into its appendages and organs, with my desires dissolved into its desires, with my senses dead, as though they never were, while the world was illuminated with sights from other portals, both wonderful and incommunicable. How can you show a blind person the blessedness of light, the grand landscapes of the world, how can you explain to him that your body perceives things from a great distance, things covered in colors, flashes, shimmers, and shadows that make them miraculous and rendingly beautiful? And to someone deaf since birth who will never understand the blessing of music, the delicate fingers that wander across the keyboard of the mind? I cannot express or really remember, now lacking my mite senses, the abstruse and incredible landscapes in the middle of which, a Gulliver in the microscopic locale in the dermis of a hand, I was pleased by the inequivalent equivalences of the forests and fields and grasslands and smells and trilling birds, but also frightened by that which I might translate, unfaithfully and ineffectively, as extreme suffering and agony, as being buried alive and flayed of my skin, as a sadistic impalement and being crushed by monstrous mandibles. Landscapes of smells and tastes, panoramas of gastric acid, objects felt with the air around the hairs, with the electromagnetic aura of stomach gurgles. I learned to take my bearings from mipliogvnv and quznzdz, to feel shrnv in my mouth, to follow a primitive but effective algebra with my eight legs. My motor and sensorial homunculus was remodeled on the pattern of the cockroach, spider, and tick.

I lived among them, inside their tunnels full of trash and stench, formaldehydes and hydrocyanic acid; with them I explored the edifice of fat and bitumen, with them I devoured the trembling hyaline substance that was space itself, in the same way the constant rustling of those around me was time; I copulated with their monstrous females, and this produced in me the pleasure of a million shots of pure heroin, I left my traces behind me, my own traces, written at first awkwardly, then more and more surely, in bizarre chemicals, combined in my filthy cloaca and ejaculated in short spurts or in interminable flows through posterior teats. I stumbled blindly over my hairs, tumbling and turning until I learned to walk. I tangled my sensorial strands with those of the mites around me, whom I began to distinguish from each other and to recognize each in part, as though they had odor faces, just as expressive as human faces. I understood, over time, their ecstasy and unhappiness, their tenderness and abjection, their pitiless cruelty and villainous tolerance, the fate of their flesh from the moment they emerged from the egg until their common end: those closest tear the aged bodies into bits. I shared their disputes, I fought their wars, I understood their beliefs, passed from generation to generation through delicate and complicated contacts like a rose petal rocking on a spider's web, but also filthy, perverse, and sadistic like a libertine orgy: their gods with tens of thousands of legs, vibrating continuously in sulfur and saltpeter sanctuaries, their saints wet with an unknown substance called light, their martyrs slit open from top to bottom, their gigantic ovaries hanging out, like wings covered in transparent eggs.

I began my mission by leaving my unimportant tunnel, at the edge of a city of crossing corridors, and traveling through many districts teeming with lowly mobs whose ignorance stirred a deep pity within me. I spoke my sermons while being crushed by mites in a large piața, where three giant tunnels set off into the deep, where a legend said that you could find blood. I used the Sqwiwhtl language, whose phonemes are the subtly rhymed waves of my own stomach, transmitted by placing it against other stomachs, and so on and so on, to the edges of the mass that surrounds you. And I used the language of Haaslaaslaah, which speaks in magnetic fields like enchanted harps, and which does not express concepts but rather pains, from the pain of a leg being pulled off to the abandonment of a belief. And I used the lofty language of flatulence and belching, suited to manipulating the crowds of the agora, like the flowery language of panders and sophists. It was difficult to tell them about the world outside, because the mites had no intuition of "outside." I replaced it with the image of a far-off tunnel, populated with gigantic mites. I failed to explain their participation in a hyaline dome called "logical space." I didn't figure out how to transmit to them the infinite love of the one who had created them and who was for them their watchman and their caretaker, an ever-constant guardian of their world. I inspired in them an attitude they hadn't felt before, a longing toward what is impossible to imagine, toward what is absurd and opposed to all their previous beliefs, a need to leave, to abandon the metropole in search of the other, in another dimension, where they may meet their creative imagination. Which, in spite of all my efforts, they could not imagine except as an endlessly lazy and indescribably sad mite, wrapped in baroque-fetid scents, in whom putridness and sandalwood, formaldehyde and oleander, cinnamon and hydrogen sulfide, as well as for us inconceivable smells of eyes, sky, spider, scream, hunger, claw, bronze, god, near, and, nor, probably weave together into a metaphysical robe of an endless grandeur.

Then I performed miracles, because my human spirit, enveloped in my new body's pulpy bead of fat, radiated a gnostic field that could close wounds and cure asthma. In the time it was given to me to remain in the midst of the minuscule people, I brought all of them the good news that in this world they were not alone; they were not buried in an ephemeral and ill-fated homeland but were watched over by a lofty and unseen power, that none of their sensorial hairs on their oily, blind carcasses ever bent without his knowledge, that each part is precious and would not perish. To my disappointment, however, I saw how everything was misinterpreted, retranslated, not from one language to another, but from one world to another, until love became yivringzw and belief became sumnmnmao and God became Ialdabaoth and life and death and dreams and murder became symbols whose decryption would take more than a thousand lifetimes. In the end I became afraid. This, at least, they did understand, because fear is the shared thread of worlds, the string that holds pearls together in a necklace.

I communicated to a few of those who had been with me since the beginning that soon I would leave them. I promised I would be back, though I knew that this would increase their fear. I foretold the martyrdom I would undergo in that risible world, which yet permitted itself the luxury of suffering. Then I was captured and, with the typical lack of imagination of worlds in which the spirit resides in flesh, my flesh was mortified to wound my spirit. And my pitiful, disgusting, suppurating mite flesh pained me more than I will ever be able to express. Around me I smelled the stench of tens and hundreds of other mites, and this stench was unforgiving.

My martyrdom took place in one of the city's largest piațas. Dozens of tunnels led there and drove farther in the thick and stratified skin of the unknown god. There, in the center, my eight legs were pulled off and devoured, and then my body was dismantled. I waited in terrible suffering and disappointment and hopelessness to be pulled out of there, for the heavens to open and to hear the thundering voice of the living and faraway One. But nothing happened until the end. I died being devoured by those I tried to awaken from their slumber, to pull from their world, as though they could survive, with their grotesque bodies, in our world, to unlock the cell door, only to reveal to them a much, much vaster cell.

And then I was back in my own body, inside the cylinder where it had been waiting, unconscious and useless like a hunk of meat, for a few hours, not the years as I had lived them in the labyrinthine tunnels. It was still hard to penetrate my brain, heart, intestines, liver, scrotum, limbs, the way you put on the clothes waiting for you in the morning on the back of your chair. The cylinder descended and I collapsed onto the floor, unable to stand up for some time. But I pulled myself along on my stomach, using my hands and feet like paddles. Palamar lifted me up and held me under my arms so I wouldn't fall again. We stood face-to-face, both shaking all over, as though he had also gone down there, as though he had also lived through the terrible drama that had been produced. His eyes were full of tears, they also held an enormous question, perhaps the greatest question that our cerebral ganglion can ask.

In response, making an almost imperceptible motion with my head, I said no.

46

Our daughter will also be named Irina. We understood each other at a glance, smiling calmly, as if we could see the future just as clearly as we could see the past. Yes, we saw one line of the future, thickened by thousands and hundreds of thousands of individual lines, dancing around this matrix of everyone and of no one. What was is what will be, we said to ourselves, the sun will rise tomorrow, because it has always risen at dawn, and those before us left their testimony that it rose every day in their time, too. People were born, they lived, they procreated, and they died. Their lives lasted seventy years, or for the strong, eighty. That's how it will be from here on, as long as the earth shall last. We all see this future woven from millions of examples, strengthened by millions of phantomatic lines. It is as though we could see before our eyes a bridge over a river, but only because it was there yesterday, and in the past, and for dozens of good years ahead. So we can walk across the river with the certainty that we have a firm earth beneath our feet.

I've asked myself many times what belief without doubt could be, the faith that could move mountains, the one that knows that all is possible. What it's like to pray for something and have the complete assurance your prayer will be accepted. In fact, prayer and certainty are the same thing; both mean the power to truly see into the future, the true future, not the image of the eternal return of the past: no one prays for the sun to come up tomorrow. Through belief, we see the future and already inhabit it. And we have the power of belief because we are from the future, such that we cannot be saved unless we have already been saved, if we already live on the new earth under a new sky. We see paradise only because we are already living there, otherwise we could not be given the power to see it, the power of belief without doubt. No one will be saved if he is not already saved from the beginning of time, not in our ephemeral present in this world, but in our real being conducted in the fourth dimension.

We see the future like a church elder who can only make out thick lines, patterns, and forms, whose eye with its rigid lens can no longer perceive fine lines, deviations from the monotony of eternal repetition. From one day to the next, all plans may change. Certainty is always worn away by the flickering coin tossed in the air by our stochastic universe. The coin projected upward, the ghostly globe like a butterfly fluttering toward the ceiling, falls on heads or tails unpredictably, and only with a very large number of throws does the line between the two faces, like the needle on a scale, settle, with ever greater precision, in between the two results. In spite of this statistical equality, no one can ever foretell which way the coin will fall with the next toss.

We cannot know this because we are in the same world as the coin. We cannot discern our future because it is part of our world, because it adheres without a gap to the present and past, which make up the same block, the same monolithic world, frozen in its riddle. If we lived in two dimensions, we could never cross a simple line drawn in front of us. We could never see anything inside a square. To see everything inside the drawing, including ourselves, we would need to be able to see from above, in the third dimension. The extra dimension is the perspective necessary for complete knowledge. Anyone in a world of four dimensions will always know which way the coin will fall in our world, will know all of the future just as well as the past. The becoming of our world will be for him a simple spatial dimension. For him, I, the one in a world with one dimension less, will seem like an elongated creature who will begin with my birth and end with death, just as here we begin with the soles of our feet and end with the tops of our heads. For him, my body, the objects around me, and all the other presences of our world will be transparent. He will be able to look inside my body and tell me at any moment what illnesses I have, and he will be able to heal them. He will be able to remove valuable things locked inside unopenable safes, to enter rooms with sealed doors. He will be able to raise me from the dead, because he will see that in the future, I will be raised from the dead by him. For him, my world will be eternally frozen, without freedom of movement or conscience, without free will—the most inhumane of oubliettes a sadistic and perverse demon could imagine. He will see me closed within the amber of my destiny, locked in my own statue, a living mind in an eternally paralyzed body, like those inside a photo or a film where, no matter how often you see them, nothing new ever happens. It is the frightening world you must escape, the tomb where you rot while living, the chrysalis from which you must break out to become a butterfly.

For this to happen, a crack must appear somewhere in the block of amber that encases you. A defect in the machinery of statistical predictions. The coin falls almost half the time on one side and almost half the time on the other. But it is not a disk with only two sides, rather, it is a very short cylinder, hiding another dimension between its faces, hiding its thickness, slight but not completely negligible. Every few thousand or tens of thousands of tosses, the coin lands on its edge, even on a surface as uniform as endless marble. It stays there, standing up, after it twists and turns a while, clinking against the soft surface, fighting against all the statistical demons. Sometimes, very rarely, you wrestle with the angel and emerge unscathed. All our hopes hang from this impossibility, this crack in the world's enamel, otherwise so unforgivingly uniform. Whenever we flip a coin, we hope it will land on its edge. Irina, like all the other children that come into the world from love and chance, are the cruel, blind coin landing on its edge, impossibilities becoming realities, miracles that prove escape is possible. Encrusted within the amber of the big Irina, little Irina is already there, she already devours her mother from within, like an ichneumon larva, and, in six months, she will emerge triumphant, tender, and sweet, with shining eyes, leaving big Irina behind like a snake shedding its skin. This is the story of our people: women coming out of women coming out of women coming out of women, in a chain of explosions of life and beauty, but also of endless cruelty. It is an uninterrupted line of goddesses with two faces: one of a child regarding the future, the other of an old woman, wearing a tragic mask, rent and bleeding from parturition, who strains to read our fortune in the stains of our aleatory past.

Whenever I think about this, levitating in the summer heat over the rumpled sheets of my bed and surrounded, as though I have been swallowed by an enormous shark, by my baby teeth once extracted from my childhood gums, now outlining my body with their pebbles of polished calcium, I have unkind thoughts about the other one, the author of novels, books of poetry, essays, Lord knows what else, who peeled away from me in that distant autumn, in the Workshop of the Moon, my conjoined twin separated from me in an invasive operation, a traumatic mutilation. I see him, I know him, I sense him on the other side of the coin, I hear him through the cold metal pellet stamped "heads" on one side and "tails" on the other. I try, tapping rhythmically, to send him an escape plan. But he is deaf, blind, and thick, as his cursed need for glory would lead you to expect. The only things you can talk to him about are festivals, tours, print runs, autographs, interviews. He is satisfied with the false escapes he promises to his readers, the false, illusory doors painted on the thick walls of the museum of literature. He is the professional, master of his medium, the Moscow virtuoso who shows the run-down, alcoholic, and vain Efimov what real art is. The one who, with the sounds of his violin, paints grand portals on the walls of the mind, incomparable with the bizarreries produced by the musician lost in his province. But with Efimov's ugly and tortuously painted doors, you can get out. You can grasp the knob firmly, you can turn it, and you can pull it toward you. And that's when the real miracle happens. Not the one made of utter beauty that remains on the level of the door, fooling our mind's naïve eye, but the one made by opening the door, breaking through the wall, and leaving the museum, with all of the risk of leaving literature behind, as well.

Only the eternal Efimov, the eternal dilettante, has anything to say, in the sad world of our impostures. Only the one who, far from the grand whirlpool of glory, fills notebooks with the bizarreries and anomalies of the soft animal between the clam's valves, writing only for himself; except he understands his situation, his position outside of the rules and customs of his art, outside of the mammoth mausoleum. Only the amateur, who doesn't even know what he will do with his manuscript, who doesn't even know if it really exists (how many times have I dreamed of thick notebooks, full of stories, written by me in other dreams, enthusiastically turning through dozens of pages, only for morning to come and everything to turn to ash . . .); only the disdained janitor, grouchy and taciturn, who leaves behind thousands of pages, illustrated with amazing girls, dragons, butterflies, and bloodshed; the lathe worker who keeps a diary meticulously describing his factory shift, how he uses condoms, what he eats and how he defecates; the hairdresser who compulsively details the terrible pains of her fertility treatments; the hebephrenic student who writes the world's longest composition about what he did on his summer vacation, throwing in pirates and aliens; all these nutcases, who can't put a sentence together, who are ignorant of high culture, who make art out of patches, trash, and nothing, only they know the best-kept secret of any art: the blind man's battle and the lame man's flight—everything else is barren ritual and Pharisaism. Their books are destined for fires and forgetting. That's good, that's real. There comes a moment when each of us must decide to rescue either the work of art or the child from the burning building. With only one of those two will we depict Judgment, and it is the only way we will be judged. The professional, every time, will save the masterpiece. The very one he wrote, painted, composed. The dilettante will save the child and let his own writing burn, along with his body and his mind.

So, we will call her Irina, like her mother, and she will have blond hair and blue eyes, like her mother. By now, after more than six months, she is well formed in the womb, heavy and compact like a river stone. Her pregnancy is showing, and Irina does nothing to hide it. Gossip is riding high in the teachers' lounge, and since no one suspects me, I get an earful. But we keep quiet, we keep quiet together, like statues on a plinth whose connection only we know. We don't stand next to each other even as little as we did before; we don't allow ourselves, for example, to be seen together at the window, looking absently at the vast and melancholy industrial landscape of the end of Colentina. We go into the lounge, we leave the registers on the table, and each with a different group, we sink into the endless daily chatter, the conversations that include even the Bulgarians in the paintings lining the walls. Teachers come and go on the dusty, provincial stage where we act our grotesque play. Chemistry, history, math, art, music, biology—in old clothes, always with the same gestures, always in the same words about the same television shows from Saturday evening and Sunday morning. About the food that's getting harder to find. About the kids who are spending more than half their time in the old factory. They all came back to school in September with the feeling it would be their last year teaching, maybe the last of their life and of the world. They all feel it's too much, too sad, too suffocating to keep on like this.

And over the summer, the school has become even more run-down: no one has painted it, no one has cleaned the benches or mopped the floors like in other summers. If you look at it from the street, your eyes will fill with tears: under a high, harsh sky, between trees whose leaves are beginning to turn, the school looks crooked, tilted to one side, with its plaster flaking off and blowing down the sidewalk. The roof is missing shingles, and, at the peak, on the chimneys left over from when the building was wood-heated, an unknown type of bird has built a nest. In back, the new wing lies in shadow and looks more than ever like a prison. Looking at the building that has already stolen more than nine years of my life, I feel lonely and unhappy, like a kid on his first day of school, when he knows full well that the best part of his life is gone. He stands in front of a sinister slaughterhouse, his spine bent under the weight of his leaden backpack. In front of a ruined school, you are always alone, more alone than if you were the last person on Earth.

The cold September light brought Irina to my house, twice. First to give me two books by Krishnamurti, found who knows where and which she knows I will not read. We levitated naked that afternoon, floating over the bed in the delicate, cool gold that came through the window, allowing me to contemplate her round stomach, her pushed-out navel, the hemisphere of delicate flesh, under which, curled up like a little sprite under a bell jar, our daughter slept. I kissed that stomach, where a few strands of hair showed, then I put my hands on her, one over the other, as a kind of blessing. We made love with a special tenderness, the way only a pregnant woman can, turning and rocking on the invisible, elastic, magical magnetic surface over the wrinkled, sunlit sheets.

The second time was last night, when she came, nervous and smiling, to bring me "a bit of hope," as she said the moment she came in. I wasn't in the best shape to receive it. I had just written in my journal that the gods of dreams had abandoned me: for months on end, I hadn't seen more than a tangle of faces, arms, and movements in a sepia light, in the stunning absence of enigma.

"Look what a wonderful story I found! Do you remember the fragment from Herodotus, with Emperor Xerxes, the one that the Picketists liked to spread around and that Virgil put on his paper?"

"Of course, the one where the king sits on a high stone throne and watches his troops cross the Hellespont."

"And first he enjoys the sight of his military, but then he begins to cry, because he suddenly realizes that all this countless host, and he himself, will be dead in a hundred years. And that the life of a person, even the life of a great king, is an endless line of misfortunes, sufferings, and trials. All the story of humanity, in *Histories*, seems to come down to this, the image of the crying king. And still, even in Herodotus I found a little light, a bit of hope, an utterly tender page. In fact, not directly in his book: I came upon the fragment about the infant in a footnote in Helena Blavatsky, you know, *The Secret Doctrine*, where she is talking about the founding of Corinth. She's talking about a kid named Cypselus, the son of Aetion and Labda (I wrote this name down on the back of the page), who an oracle prophesizes will become king. Like in fairy tales and Scripture, the king sends soldiers to find the infant and kill him. A predictable and boring story, but look at the beautiful part that comes next—apologies for my doctor's handwriting."

I unfolded the piece of paper and we both read together, like twins conjoined only at their eyes:

> Then, as soon as his wife was delivered, they sent ten men of their clan to the township where Eetion dwelt, to kill the child. These men came to Petra and passing into Eetion's courtyard asked for the child; and Labda, knowing nothing of the purpose of their coming, and thinking that they asked out of friendliness to the child's father, brought it and gave it into the hands of one of them. Now they had planned on their way (as the story goes) that the first of them who received the child should dash it to the ground. So then when Labda brought and gave the child, by heaven's providence it smiled at the man who took it, and he saw that, and compassion forbade him to kill it, and in that compassion he delivered it to a second, and he again to a third; and thus it passed from hand to hand to

each of the ten, for none would make an end of it. So they gave the child back to its mother and went out, and stood before the door reproaching and upbraiding one another . . .

"Do you get it? Think of the warriors back then: barbarians, killing machines. I don't think we can even imagine today the cruelty and mercilessness they showed in war. Each of the ten had flayed people, had plucked out their eyes and cut off their hands. The more they showed how little they cared about others' sufferings, and their own, the more they were respected. And their superiors' orders were the word of God. For them it would have been no more than a joke to throw a newborn to the ground in front of his mother. But the infant smiled. He smiled at each of them, 'to his face.' Even these old executioners melted with pity and pleasure, and their guilty, bloodstained hands became weak and helpless."

"So it wasn't the infant that made them kind, but his smile. The child's smile tamed them . . ."

"Let's stop talking about it," Irina said to me, putting a finger on my lips, "Whatever we can say will diminish the beauty of the story. It's so beautiful, not like a tale, but like a cloud or a flower . . ."

She burst into tears and cried, sobbing for a long time, in my arms. She stayed overnight and left today, at dawn, as she had never done before, even though we've been together for years. I watched her dream: she twitched and turned like someone tied down by silk threads, who couldn't move any more than her fingers, lips, eyelids. After she left, I made some coffee and reread, in the ice-cold autumn, the story from Herodotus, come to us across thousands of years. An infant dead long ago, a mother dead long ago, anonymous soldiers dead just as long ago, as though they had never lived. But an immortal smile arched like a rainbow over the world, turning it transparent, giving it cause and being, across time, substance, life, suffering, and other illusions.

Faced with the terrible gods of death and of rending, the child smiled. Just as miraculous and counterintuitive as the way our improbable consciousness opposes brute matter. A smile is a special arrangement of matter, a fold of our mouth, the way consciousness is a special disposition of our brain's synapses. We are all a smile of the void, of the night, a fold of the frightening, silent Pascaline spaces. We are an impossible formation of the aleatory, endless world; we are the coin landing on an edge so thin that it cuts itself in half a billion times per second. This continual self-drawing and self-quartering is our pathetic being. Only Simmias got it right in the great debate over immortality, he who called the spirit a harmony, impossible without the lyre, because it came from the special, unique combination of its parts: the ivory frame and sheep-gut strings, so finely tuned that it will always defy the monstrous roar of matter. We are chords made of chords made of chords, layer upon layer of folds of space and time and energy, from the smile of quarks impossibly isolated from each other to the smile of bosons and pheromones, from the atomic smile to the molecular, with their three-dimensional contortions, from the smile of ultra-hyper-superorganized living substances, their inflorescence wonderfully unfolding in spite of the laws of statistics and thermodynamics, to the great and overwhelming smile of self-knowledge. A holarchy of smiles, miracles, and impossibilities that led to the infant who was us all, passed from hand to hand by the angels of destruction and yet surviving, with a smile, the long line of horrors that is our life in the world. Human consciousness ("*ce seul objet dont le néant s'honore*") is a smile, the smile of providence. Its death is absolute murder, it cannot be accepted and never excused. It is that against which you must rage, with all your might: "Rage, rage against the dying of the light!"

47

I haven't written anything here for more than two months, and in all this time I haven't done more than deepen the same rut between school and home that my footsteps have worn for a decade. A ditch that now goes over my head. I'm not that into my classes, or into anything, in fact. All I do all day is imagine her, still hidden in Irina's stomach, the one who turned around just a couple of days ago, ready to come down the channel where once my sperm swam upstream, like salmon, searching for the bride of the world, who came to them as a scorching globe, in welcome. I have imagined her, again and again, a girl with golden hair, with a body full of a substance as dense as honey, with shining eyes and a rose between her fingers, as though she would be born holding it, as an extension of her body. Last night I went through my entire library looking for a piece of paper (I have it in front of me now, friable and ragged) where I had once scribbled a few lines, without understanding what they meant, but knowing that they were important. When I left it mixed in with some homework I was grading, I ran to the end of the neighborhood, to the Bazavans', to get it back. When I came back home I put the paper inside a book, but which one? I spent an entire day looking through them all, one by one, almost suffocating in their dust, until I found it in the last one I would have expected—a tattered copy, almost rotted away, eaten by minuscule, transparent insects, of *Hebdomeros*:

> *When I dream, a girl leaps up from her bed, goes to the window, and, pressing her cheek against the glass, watches the sun set over the pink and yellow houses. She turns toward the bloodred bedroom and curls up again under her damp blanket.*
>
> *Something, when I dream, approaches my paralyzed body, it takes my head in its hands and bites it, like a translucid fruit. I open my eyes, but I don't dare move. I jump from the bed and run to the window. The sky is all stars.*

Yes, I remembered that nausea again, that vertigo: I had been raised as a girl, with long, soft braids my mother didn't cut until I was four. Since then I've kept them in a paper envelope, by now yellowed with time. I had somehow passed, even now I don't know in what way, from one side of the mountain of sex and humanity to the other. Somewhere in my interior palace of frozen marble, perhaps in its forbidden chamber, the little prisoner was still living, a dirty and starving little girl, her dress in tatters, her lips sewn shut, her black eyes glaring insanely: my eyes. At night I could hear her desperate fists against the cold wall that separated us, thumps that I converted into crosses, stars, gears, and other symbols that eventually spelled out the great escape plan. For my captive sister (or, perhaps, for my daughter), I wrote, over the course of last night, a kind of story; I finished it only at dawn, after which I decided to not go to school and slept until afternoon. I am copying it down here, not from pride, but from the feeling that this is where it is meant to be:

Once, in a suffocating and incomprehensible world, a woman became pregnant. Since it was not a man but a kind of foreboding whose shadow she felt, she knew from the start that she would bear a girl. The woman had once inhabited a creature like her, and now she was also inhabited. Out of the four hundred transparent eggs she carried, like an insect, in her abdomen, one had filled her stomach like an enormous grape.

Just after the girl was born, at a hospital in a distant neighborhood, her mother told the doctors to wait, because she felt something else in her womb. And under their amazed eyes, she gave birth to a sack of ivory skin, like a fish bladder, but the size of a child. There were unclear markings on the soft skin, scribbled in chemical pencil. The doctors resected the sack with a shining scalpel and took it apart on the birthing table, next to the exhausted mother. An unbelievable sight appeared before them. Inside, nicely arranged in little pockets, there were warm, living organs. Fingers, teeth, an eye with a brown gaze, some little bones, some soft tubes, a kidney . . . And in three larger pockets, made of the same rosy skin, three hearts beat lazily: one made of crystal, one of iron, and one of lead. "This is the first child to come into the world with spare parts," one of the doctors said, suddenly calm. In fact, it was a good idea, he repeated with a smile. You don't have to be a doctor to understand that one of the biggest mistakes in the divine plan was to let the delicate human body go through life without its delicate little features—braided into a complicated, soft machine—being able to regenerate. Maybe from now on all children will be born like this, the doctor thought, full of hope. But neither before nor after did another child appear with such enhancements.

The child grew up on the edge of town, in the yard of a house with yellow walls. She had no heart. In the sole tree in the yard, a pear tree loaded with juicy fruits, her mother made a little swing. But the girl preferred to torture the critters that lived in the grass and dirt. She never looked anyone in the eyes. She only spoke when she was alone. For hours, she would stand at the wrought iron gate, watching the rust slowly advance over the rain-wet metal.

Despairing, her mother remembered the hearts from the skin packet. One afternoon, while the girl napped faceup, as she always did, in her room filled with useless toys, her mother approached and unfastened two of the skin buttons, like little navels, on the left side of her chest. An organic door opened and an oval space, lined in pink and violet, appeared behind her ribs. Her mother, with infinite delicacy, inserted the heart made of warm, soft crystal.

The girl woke overcome with a happiness she had never known before. Her skin and hair glowed, her eyes became lively and quick. For the first time, she saw the dolls that literally filled the room. For the first time, too, she saw her mother, the biggest doll of all, and she hugged her with all her heart. They went outside, and suddenly the blue sky, full of summer clouds, and the giant flowers overwhelmed her. She smelled the tree sap, she touched the crumbs of the earth. For the first time, she opened the door of the house and saw the street that went from the house to the neighborhood school.

After a few years, she went to that school; she looked at her classmates through the prism of her plastic ruler. She tasted bitter ink on her tongue. She drew letters in chalk that screeched terribly on the glass-covered blackboard. At lunch, she ate her sandwich and grapes, then she played with her classmates, in a daze, in the schoolyard with melancholy basketball hoops.

As she grew, her girl's body changed in subtle ways. In the afternoons after school, she closed herself in her room and began a strange ritual. She opened the cooler at the head of her bed, kept in the chest with sheets and blankets, and she took out the old sack of spare organs, and she began to attach them to certain specially shaped places on her body. She became the girl with seven fingers on each hand, the girl with an eye in her forehead, the girl with ears on her knees, the girl with lips on her stomach. She looked at herself in the mirror with the amusement of a child wearing her mother's dress and high heels.

This is how she came to change her heart. First, she put the iron one in, and, inside her chest, the iron turned red, like in a forge. It burned, it stunned her, it made her long for an unknown thing, unwanted but as necessary as air, the lack of which suffocated her. She immediately pulled this raw and ravishing heart from her chest, determined to never use it again. Next she put in the lead heart, and it became a sack of thick, gray liquid, with somber glints of indigo. An unbelievable sadness and a rending, dark melancholy, without horizon and without a future, overwhelmed her. Nothing really existed, the world was absurd, bound in infinite night and oblivion. Better you had never been born, better to get through your days as fast as possible. It was unbearable. She took out the new heart with the last of her strength and decided to leave it forever in the sack with organic pockets. Only the crystal heart was real. That was the only one she wanted ever to feel in her chest.

But the spare hearts didn't last forever. In the fall, when the schoolyard chestnuts hung low under a stormy sky, the girl felt the light from the crystal heart grow dim. As the days went on, it beat more and more quietly. When she held it in her hands, in front of the mirror, she could clearly see a kind of salt, a kind of calcium cloud over what was once clear, like pearls aging inside a jewelry box. In the end, the crystal heart turned dull and cracked.

Since anything was better than an inhuman life without a heart, the girl started to wear the incandescent iron heart. She lived with her new heart through her adolescence and youth. She fell in love, and from love she suffered terribly. She married, had children, then divorced. She remarried. Happiness and unhappiness alternated rapidly with this restless heart, both of them pushed to the threshold where they became unbearable pain. As an adult, she who had been a girl gave birth in turn to two children and raised them until they grew and left her as well. A confused life dragged her to the bottom of the river, without a straw to cling to.

After the woman's second child married, the incandescence of the iron heart burned out, little by little. The metal had been cooling for years, but now it became a heavy, dark sludge under her left breast. Looking at her second heart in the mirror, the woman saw it was covered in ash. She didn't dare to look any higher up her body, afraid to see a face devastated by time. Resigned, she knew that there was nothing left but the fearsome heart of lead.

She returned to her childhood house. The lead heart hung heavy in its place in her chest. It spread a black light around her body, a light of extinction and erasure. She lay down on her mother's old bed and waited for the end. Images from her childhood and her adolescence flashed through her mind. She lived for years in complete solitude, in the stale air, in the scent of medication. Rarely would she rise from the sheets to look in the mirror at the heart she held in her hands. One evening when she felt more abandoned and more unhappy than ever, she pulled out her heart, determined to break it against the floor. But one unexpected twitch made her stop. She suddenly felt how her lead heart, instead of destroying itself like the others, had become as fleshy and heavy as a fruit. Frightened, she put it back inside her weak, emaciated chest. Now she knew that the miracle would happen, that a fourth, unearthly heart would be given to her, from now on, forever.

The fist-sized organ, fed with her suffering and disappointment, metamorphosed little by little, it took on soft corners and curves like the ends of a growing fern. The old woman could hardly wait for the end of her days to see how her heart had changed. Soon she saw a little head with its chin on its chest, eyes still veiled in mist, with soft and transparent skin. Her hands came to hold a heavy, palpitating infant, well formed and resting, a child the size of an orange. "Blessed be my last birth," the old woman said, and she pushed the new body, full of a tender light, into the waters of the mirror. There, her minuscule, frail daughter swam away toward the kingdom from which we all came and to which we all return.

Only then, in a quiet she had never before felt with any of her other hearts, the old woman closed her eyes forever. At that same moment, in a hospital in a far-off neighborhood, a wonderful girl was born.

I don't know what this story means or how it connects with all the others, the same way I know nothing about any of them. In only ten days a girl will flow from another girl, descending between her legs, wet and clinging with her little claws to the gnarled, cracked branch and throbbing in the wind that moves the clusters of leaves. Her wings will unfurl little by little, then spread smoothly and stiffly into the air. While the new Irina takes flight, proficient even from the first beats of her wings, I will remain beside the empty shell of the old Irina, as moving as a mutilated statue, until, inevitably, the wind scatters her being.

48

There wasn't enough room on the table, so I spread the map of Bucharest out on the floor, between the table and bed. One corner folded over like a cat's ear because of the ladder that led to the hatch in the ceiling. But I didn't need that part. I have owned the map for a long time, I bought it downtown, from the bookstore at Sala Dalles (I don't remember the name; I haven't been downtown for a long time) in 1976, in that luminous, exalted autumn when the air was full of cobwebs, when I went to college for the first time. Soon I would amaze my classmates and professors with monstrous works, fall madly in love, and go to the Workshop of the Moon to read my unhappy *Fall*, but as yet I was wandering aimlessly among the buildings (whose state of advanced ruin I had yet to notice) and through the crowds on the street (whose deep melancholy I did not see). I needed to know the city better, the chaos where my parents, coming from the country, had remade their village in the area defined by three movie theaters. That's why I bought the map and studied it for entire evenings, enchanted and frightened by Bucharest's labyrinth, in an advanced state of ruin, drawn there so meticulously that you could see not only the streets, rivers, and lakes, as on normal maps, but also every building, with its apartments, kitchens, and bathrooms, the mold on the walls, shoes by the door, clothes in the wardrobes, lint on the clothes, and the microscopic fibers in the lint, and every tree down to its branches and leaves, with the veins of every leaf and their petals with tannin stains shaped like faces, clouds, or distant African countries. I was waiting for the dusk to turn to liquid amber and for the wavy paper, with its creases intersecting at right angles, to come truly alive. Then Bucharest would also come back from the dead, like an ultra-flat animal, a fluke against the bottom of the sea. I leaned over the map to look at the traffic on the boulevards and to spy on intertwined couples through the windows. I saw the broad semicircle of Ştefan cel Mare, which turned into Mihai Bravu, following the curving tracks of tram 26 around the city. There I had a room, on the street side, in my parents' apartment. With my eye practically touching the map's porous paper, I could see myself through the window: a bony kid leaning deeply over a map, his eye practically touching the map's porous paper.

Since then, so much folding and unfolding has worn through the map's creases. There are rhomboid gaps, like those on the Turin Shroud, and some sections barely cling to the others. Now it is an old map, worn away, barely legible, if at all. I use it—and this will be the last time before I fold it up and throw it away—only to mark the locations of the solenoids. Their symmetry and coherence in the putrid space of the great city have long been clear to me. I always knew there would be five, like small coins in a circle surrounding a much more powerful sixth, the way we once made coin flowers on the glare of the kitchen table: one leu in the middle and five twenty-five-bani pieces around it. I also knew that, despite Borina's palaver, the solenoids must be eternal and indestructible, placed more firmly in the structure of reality than in the foundations of the city. Not just Tesla, but also Newton and da Vinci (descendants of the mythical Bezalel, womanless men visited by visions and inspired by doves) seemed somehow involved in their miracle. In my world you could not doubt them, just as in another world, perhaps, you would have sworn that something like this could not exist. But isn't it so easy to imagine worlds differing only in one detail from other, almost identical worlds: in the world in the mirror, I wore my ring on my right hand . . .

To mark the map I chose the method I had at hand. In my journal, pressed between the pages to bookmark the most important dreams, I have dozens of the bonbon wrappers my parents would hang on the holiday tree. After I ate a candy, I would smooth out the foil wrapper until it was perfectly flat, crinkling a bit at each touch. On the back they were all the same, their silver printed with squares or minuscule flowers. But on the other side were the most tender, soft, enigmatic colors, so moving I could faint, because the metal backing gave them a shine and a liveliness that a colored pencil could never create on paper. I would look at them for hours on end in a painful daze: the emerald green and lacquered blue, the pink animated by the repeated pattern, the lavender of the crocus and columbine . . . Dozens of distinct hues, but all sparkling in the same, slow way at the touch of a finger, and shaking with my breath or any breeze from the window.

I cut dots out of them, the size of a milk bottle cap for the central solenoid and the size of a fingernail for the others, around the first. For the Mina

Minovici Institute of Forensic Medicine, in the center of the city, I chose a black dot with indigo highlights, cut from the only wrapper of this color I ever found in a bag of bonbons. Pressed to the map, it looked like a large amethyst scattering its stars of light around it. For my boat-shaped house on Maica Domnului I used a dirty-pink wrapper, like from a paint bucket, the color of plastic recycled dozens of times that they use for Aradeanca dolls. I put a light blue dot on the solenoid around the throat of the enormous skeleton buried standing up in Ferentari, so that even now you can see the grassy hill over his skull. For the great bobbin under Palamar's house at the end of Pantelimon, the color scarlet seemed best. For the one under our school in Colentina (perhaps I've mentioned that, one day when a blizzard, a truly apocalyptic storm, kept everyone away from school, I went down the cement staircase to the basement, and near the school's dentist office I moved a bookcase over, one swelling from the damp and teeming with rotting books full of insects feeding on their gray cellulose, and I went down another stairway, leading deeper into a grimy room full of broken benches, coatracks falling apart, rank-smelling erasers, and starving rats, where, barely glinting here and there along the cobweb-covered walls, ran the glorious, giant copper ring? When I turned it on and climbed back up to the surface, I found myself in an empty field, with the auto mechanic on one end and on the other, the house of the idiot who always sat on his fence and shook everyone's hand. I only found the school when I looked up, to see it floating in the blizzard several meters over its own bare foundation, obliterated by gusts of snow . . .) I chose ocher, a more powerful color than I would have thought. But the bright yellow I saved for . . .

I never once doubted the location of the sixth solenoid. Even without my strong intuition, bordering on certainty, I could have guessed its location, because the other centers of energy were arranged symmetrically around the center, so that the empty spot in the southwest of the map and city was so obvious, it might have been already marked with an invisible dot. It was in the Dudești-Cioplea neighborhood, where my aunt lived, my mother's older sister. She had a brick-faced house that soaked up heat and sunlight during the day, to release it timidly and tenderly at night. In the yard, surrounded by staked vegetables, there was a truck without tires in whose cabin I loved to play, turning the wheel surrounded by the smell of warm plastic and imaging I was driving across wide, fantastic places that could never exist in the real world. There was also a cherry tree, with its shiny, smooth bark; I would climb to the top and look at the field, because my aunt lived at another edge of the city. In the field behind her house, there was a shed that always fascinated me. I could see it from the top of the cherry tree, and in the evening it seemed to shine, as though it were painted with light. There, under the old fruit cellar, was the last solenoid. I had always felt it, but it became clear to me three weeks ago, when I made the trip to my aunt's, in Dudești-Cioplea, for the first time in more than ten years.

How strange it was to climb onto tram 4 again, to go down the streets that were so familiar to me, so like me, so organically worn into my brain! How strange it was to travel under yellow skies, under a dome that could be nothing other than my own skull! I changed at Rond, the circular piața with an imposing statue of a hero from who knows which war, to the 27, which led, like before, like in another life, past the C. I. Parhon Institute of Endocrinology, and then into a part of town of fields, lumberyards, seltzer shops, and ramshackle bars, an endless and winding area that lasted more than ten tram stops. I got off at the station closest to Dudești-Cioplea, and after a few minutes of brisk walking I came to my aunt's street. Nothing, at least for me, was more melancholic than these empty and abandoned streets on the edge of town, with kites tangled in the power lines and grass growing up through the pavement. With plum trees and stunted mulberries along the fences. With the smell of slop tossed into the ditch, with strange houses exiled at the end of their yards. This time I went past my aunt's house and walked across the field toward the shed. On its whitewashed wooden door, eaten away by time, there was a heavy lock, covered with a shapeless mass of rust. I held it, felt its weight against my lifeline, luckline, and loveline, over the M written on everyone's palm, which in this world could only stand for Mors, and I rubbed it between my fingers like a dry leaf. The door opened and I found the shed full of rusty tools, buckets with petrified paint, mounds of lime and brick. Spiders had woven their webs over the gray, wooden walls, covering them almost completely with their immaterial silk. A dull hum, like the vibration of an underground being, made the walls tremble. It was there, under the floor. I didn't need to see it with my eyes—organs to which we give, in any case, too much weight.

On the map spread out in my bedroom, I can place the last dot, yellow like the shining light of September, over the place in Dudeşti-Coplea where REM is.

49

The little one turned a month old today, and over the past few days she had been levitating over our bed like a little turtle, with her hands up around her bald head, with her legs bent, while we slept across a constantly different bed in a different room, never to be found again, however much we wander the hallways and however many doors we open. When the child cried in the middle of the night, Irina would jump up, terrified she wouldn't find the way back to the bedroom, but after doubling back and fumbling through icy hallways, bathrooms with two doors, rooms lined with books, kitchens with linen tablecloths and yellow silverware, greenhouses with flowers impossible to find in botanical atlases (but familiar to me, because I always recognized them as the delicate chimeras from the pages of the Voynich manuscript), sordid closets and toilets with cracked porcelain, following the girl's quiet cries as though spooling a shiny silk thread, she always reached the little Irina, picked her up, pulling her out of the invisible water where she floated, and putting her against her breast, her left hand covering her little head, she would dance through the room in a whirlpool of weariness and happiness, two exhausting and inhuman emotions. The milk of her body entered the child's, where, like a Eucharist, it became body and blood, spinal fluid and endorphins, through a magic and mystery the mind cannot comprehend. The little girl, in those moments, was her mother's external organ, a vital organ, any wound to which would have turned their diptych to ash.

Irina's eyes have never had a moment of the cloudy, inchoate chaos often found between the drowsy, half-open eyelids of babies. From the first moment I held her in my arms, stained like her with blood and meconium, amazed that she was a girl although I had known she would be, I saw the color of her eyes: the triumphant azure of her mother's eyes, lapis lazuli disks placed between the eyelids of antic statues. The rest of her body was also wonderful, as she emerged like an elastic fruit, luminous and dense at the end of the umbilical cord that hung between her mother's thighs. Each member of her body was perfect, each little pocket and each golden hair, but her face wasn't sweet: it was firm and calm, as though her being, so new to the earth, wasn't an entity in itself but part of an irresistible, incorporeal will. Through her pink chest, still dirty with mixed liquids, you could see the quick beating, like a small animal, of her heart. From the start, the child I was holding didn't seem a biological creature like other newborns, she seemed like an idol, heavy as a river stone of the same size, beyond good and evil, pulled out of time and the three dimensions of our world. In the first minutes I held her, I didn't feel an animal, instinctual warmth, as I expected, but a kind of frightened adulation.

I was there, really there, for the birth of our daughter. As we knew the horror of the maternity ward, we decided Irina would give birth at home, aided only by me. Here, in our boat-shaped house. Not in the bedroom and not in one of the constantly changing rooms, but in a place that had already known rending physical suffering and torture, in the same way that in the past, monuments were raised on the ruins of other monuments. She had been there before, she had lain back, as a joke—but jokes often prove deathly serious—in the chair that transformed so easily into an operating table; I had already leaned over her, holding a whirring metal instrument, I had already heard the lazy gurgling of the veins under the floor that so resembled the damp, knotted, blue veins under the tongue. We had often been to that atemporal place, dematerialized and blinded by the unforgiving light that filled the small chamber.

Irina, thus, gave birth in the tower, crucified on the fully reclined dental chair, her head supported by the two round leather disks, her hair hanging toward the ground. Without anything to support them, her legs hung painfully on either side of the chair, the interrupted blood flow turning them purple. She lay there for hours, crying out and convulsively scratching my arms bloody. After an entire night of barbarous torture, during which I could clearly see, through the thick and now translucid metal root that supported the improvised metal bed, the long, fluorescent spurts of pure pain being captured in hyaline tubes and shot through pipes into the root system rippling under the floor tiles, and after I had crushed many of them under my feet in hate, crazed by the abject, porcine gurgling of her birth pains coursing into the earth, the child emerged, slowly, into my hands, tearing the tissue of her mother, crowned with the tongues of fire of her supreme screams.

Now she is sleeping quietly, her eyelids closed and mouth half-open, while I blacken the pages of my fourth notebook, feeling in full the pleasures of winter and of the end.

Because my world will soon end, along with my manuscript. No hiatus ever separated them. Reality was never more embedded in fiction, more one with it, more desperately lacking space to move, space to hope. Like a fish inside an aquarium that presses without a gap against every scale, every soft curve of its white abdomen. Like an actor in a film forced to say the same words every time, like a relative in a photo, frozen with the same grin. If I screamed in hate and helplessness, my scream would be foretold from the beginning of time. If I took my own life, I would be following a script letter by letter, laid out on paper long ago. My thoughts are prethought, my gestures preconceived, the murder of my life premeditated. I read and reread Kafka's diary, only so I can come to the passage where, in the depths of my adolescence, I underlined in pencil what I thought was the highest of literary ideas: "The master of dreams, the great Issachar, sat in front of the mirror, his spine against its surface, his head hanging far back, deeply sunk into the mirror. Then Hermana appeared, master of the twilight, and she melted into Issachar's chest, until she completely disappeared." Never, however often I reread this fragment, will the master of the twilight take the great Issachar in her arms, pull his head from the mirror, touch her long fingers across the vertebrae of his fractured neck, the sectioned marrow, and lay him, naked, on the ground. To mourn him, throwing herself onto his body, in her black clothes. My manuscript and my world embrace like the man and reptile in the Dantean circle: they pass through each other, they change into each other after their intestines have been completely mixed.

I have readied my arms for the final confrontation. I have them right here, on the right-hand, immaculate page of my notebook (while the left-hand is three-quarters covered by my anankastic writing): my baby teeth, taken from their Tic-Tac box and arranged in order, just as they were in my mouth. Each casts a vague shadow over the page, each is unnaturally shiny and white, like a drop of petrified milk. As though my mother hadn't squeezed flowing milk from her nipples but my polished teeth instead. Also on the table, in an old ashtray, are the pieces of packing twine that, until about five or six years ago, I regularly pulled out of my navel; they lay there like burnt candlewicks. I have the school ID tag with the insane number Goia found in the old factory. I also have the plates with Nicolae Minovici's visions, from when he was the world champion of controlled hanging (a single glance at the plates would make you ill for a week). Then the box with the Voynich manuscript, which didn't end up with Palamar: the last time we parted the old man put it in my arms as a superlative gift or as a consolation for my immersion in the world of the mites. I also have my diaries and a small box of photos, the old ones with serrated edges, yellow with the passage of time. And finally, I have my braids from when I was a child.

With these heterotypical and absurd knickknacks, with these jigsaw puzzle pieces, I will go to be judged. But I would be just as well prepared if I carried *Critique of Pure Reason* or *The Virgin of the Rocks* or *Principia Mathematica*. There would be no difference. The chessboard is infinite, its squares are narrow and flow like water, each one a different color. The king and queen on the other side are so great you cannot hope to ever see more than an atom of their ebony. But you, like all the other pieces, occupy only the point of a needle in the corner of a single square.

Irina is up, hungry and crying. I press a button and she comes down slowly, as though enchanted, to the sheets. I pick her up, protecting her little body, sweaty from effort, I touch her cotton diaper where her legs stick out, I look at her little, red, indignant face, and I suddenly, with an extraordinary power, feel all of reality, as though a shock wave has hit me in the face. The fractals of the stiff curtain. The olive semidarkness. The ladder. The cupboard. The bed. My maniacal writing, never revised, already extending below my baby teeth on the right-hand page, floating them on a sea of signs. My face, mirrored in the window, bent over Irina's. The pink sky. The snow that falls and falls.

50

It would seem that the powers of the skies were shaken, because in a single day of intense heat, intense heat in April, unnatural and overwhelming, the heavy snow under which the city had lain dormant melted, as though it had never been. A blinding sun woke us in the morning, coming in through our windows earlier than it should have, and by lunch the streets were flooded, traffic was a mess, buses turned into boats, people were forced to climb fences and gape at the lakes reflecting the sky. To switch from the overcoats and heavy hats of an endless winter, the worst since the start of the century, to shirts and sleeveless dresses, to be drenched with sweat as soon as you stepped out from a building's shadow—there was, as people said at tram stops and cafeterias, nothing like it. Phaeton had dropped the bridle of the horses of the sun and cried with his face in his hands, curled up in the bottom of the chariot that collapsed over the world. Black tree branches scraped against the intensely blue sky, and all the trees were dead—as though they had never lived. But the change was greater and more amazing than the spectacle of cars sunk up to their windows in the deluge, it was visible in the desolation and decay of the buildings throughout the city.

Once the mounds of snow disappeared, Bucharest revealed itself to your gaze as a skeleton with scattered bones. You would not have believed that its customary decrepitude—the sinister baroque of its ruins—could have become twice as sad and hopeless. The three of us went out that afternoon, to give the little girl some air, and we first walked, as we seldom did, not toward the school's old neighborhood but in the opposite direction, toward downtown. We took Teiul Doamnei, and on that very street, one that had never been all that well cared for, we were shocked by what we found: in the blind walls that sectioned the mercantile buildings, two stories tall, there were big holes, as though there had been an earthquake. The walls, buckling for decades and held up precariously by planks of wood, were falling down; you could see inside people's living rooms and bathrooms, into their miserable kitchens. The rotted window frames, the broken panes covered over with newspaper, the ornaments on the facades—a people of mythological figures that infested the city from times immemorial—had almost all fallen. At the feet of these old houses you could see heaps of arms, chipped heads, bits of plaster wings, chubby thighs, braids of serpents, crushed lyres and flutes; all in pink, blue, and olive; lying like the remains of an ancient massacre in a common grave. Sinister, sinister hecatomb!

At Lizeanu, the trams drove through the water, ringing as loud as they could as they passed the clothing stores, donut shops, seltzer shops, shoemakers, all unimpressive storefronts with loudly painted signs. We turned, as we were able, down Moșilor, slapping our feet through the puddles, taking turns carrying the girl, looking over our shoulders with large eyes. Soon, I took off her little hat—the sun was burning like in the middle of July—and when we saw ourselves reflected in the dirty window of the Miorița movie theater, with its rotted signs and buckling movie stills, just for a moment I had the clear feeling that I was looking at my own parents carrying me thirty-seven years ago. "He could not doubt it," I suddenly remembered lines from Eminescu, "an unseen hand pulled him into the past . . ."

The city center was empty and desolate. The giant neoclassical buildings, with their cupolas that looked like astronomical observatories, stood like the memorials of a devastating war, still standing by some miracle. I would have cried at the lugubrious sight, if I hadn't known that it had been planned and built like this on purpose, in its abandonment and ruin, as an eternal protest against the war that time wages on people and objects. As fragile as cardboard, shaking in any breath of wind, scattering flakes of plaster like snow over the empty boulevards and abandoned parks, the constructions behind Children's Romarta, all the way toward Kogălniceanu, looked to our gazes like Persepolis half-buried in sand: crooked balconies, walls about to fall down over the few automobiles parked imprudently underneath, facades with great chunks of plaster fallen and shattered on the sidewalk. The sagging lampposts, the disgusting carcasses with blue guts coming out of their stomachs thrown beside trash bins, the walled over or boarded up windows—everything made you wish not just that you'd die the next moment, but that you had never existed in the world. And at the same time you knew, and this is strange and incomprehensible, that it had to be like this, that only in this kind of world were people given to live, because nothing defines us better than the sweet torture of nostalgia.

To take a rest, we went inside one of the dozens of movie theaters that lined the boulevard. How well did we know them all, with their crooked stages and absurd names! Corso, Festival, Bucharest, Capitol, and the many others where we had seen, after waiting in ticket lines for hours, movies with Indians and Vikings, afterward not remembering anything but the quantities of sunflower seeds people around you were crunching. Each theater was different, bizarrely decorated, always pompous and kitschy, with vandalized chairs, everything bent and tilted, and the screen material patched in a dozen places. To go inside one of the most obscure theaters, you went down a corridor that also housed a photo studio and a store that repaired pantyhose. At the end was a little piața, and the theater was opposite, its doors framed by two narrow showcases full of ancient photographs. The doors were wide open, like all the others downtown, apparently abandoned forever. The name of this theater, which I had never noticed before, was Chimera.

We walked into the solemn quiet of the hall's shadows, as heavy and thick as if we were in a tomb. There was no one else there. It smelled strongly of the kerosene cleaner that had once scoured the wood floors. The hall was dressed in violet velvet. The dome of the ceiling was fantastically painted with naked women and men, animated by passion, frozen in unintelligible poses. We stretched our necks to decipher the complicated allegory, despite the fragments that had fallen to reveal bits of somber cement. We sat in the last row of chairs, like people who might have come to see a film. In front of us, framed by two large, identical, plaster statues of winged young men looking toward each other, stood the screen, a blotchy canvas like a sweat-stained sheet. Irina opened her blouse and placed the child on her breast.

I suddenly felt this had happened to me before. In the dawn of my childhood, I would go with my parents, simple workers, to the cinema. The crowd of unknown people who squirmed in their seats in such a somber light frightened me. My mother held me so I could see better. Suddenly, it was dark and giant heads appeared on the screen. The speakers screamed so loud your ears would burst. I was afraid, I started to whimper, and the people around us tsk-tsked and turned around: "You can't bring a kid to the movie! He won't sit still, you see?" "What am I supposed to do with him, smart guy? Can I leave him at your house?" My mother snapped back at them, bouncing me on her knees. The ghosts kept pacing the screen, I slipped out of my mother's arms, I ran, screaming, through the knees that came up to my neck... We never lasted more than fifteen minutes. We'd go home in silence, under the full moon, my parents carrying me. I felt like I was levitating over the stone-paved streets.

I watched our girl nurse contentedly for half an hour. Our every whisper echoed in the hall, disturbing the cool, immobile air. The theater was a reservoir filled to the top with a dark liquid. Our eyes stung with the smell of the petrosin rising from the floor covered with old sunflower seed shells. We didn't even notice as the last lights turned off quietly, and across the dirty screen, scratches and dots began to march, numbers wet with typographic sap, ectoplasms leaping from one side to the other. Maybe because the sound was broken, we didn't pay attention to the first black-and-white images, drowning so pathetically in ponds of ink, barely discernible. Irina was the first to turn toward the back wall, where blue beams of light jetted out of a small window. "There's a movie," she said, curious, "why in the world, when the place is empty?" Did all these run-down theaters, their ceilings ready to cave in, still show movies? Our daughter latched off Irina and rested her cheek against her shoulder. We stood up and moved toward the exit, ready to leave the theater, when a great light from behind, a feeling-light or an intuition that didn't need feeling, made me turn around. I walked up the aisle and dropped into one of the chairs in the first row, in front of the suddenly fantastic screen. I stayed there, paralyzed, as though in front of a giant portal toward another world.

The screen suddenly cleared up, and now it spread a liquid, amber light over the entire theater. It became a large window onto a nighttime panorama, a gulf full of ships with billowing sails, lit by a dozen bloodred moons hanging like scarlet balloons in the endless sky. The waters of the gulf crinkled with shiny waves, mixing their dark green with the bright moons and the white lace of seafoam. At the end of this diorama rose a cliff teeming with palaces, full to the top with facades and rows of columns and marble capitals, one on top of the other, pink and transparent in the crepuscular light. I sank suddenly into my dream from when I was a teenager. I floated on the deck of a felucca toward the shore with svelte colonnades, with minuscule windows scattered across transparent facades, like the gaps in a friable madrepore. The gulf was so vast that, along with the hundreds of fishing vessels trailing wakes of blood, I reached the shore just as the moons were about to descend below the lip of the horizon. I walked the esplanade lined with ornamental facades and countless, convulsive statues, and I sank into the cold streets that rose toward the peak. I reached an empty piața, in the center of which was a stone pool full of a black water, too dense to ripple. Around me—temples and cathedrals worn into the same pink, crystalline marble. I leaned over and gazed deeply into the waters of the pool. I saw a face that was not my own. I suddenly remembered the livid wanderers, with giant, black eyes, from Traian's story about what follows death.

A child came from the cathedral doors toward the pool. When he reached me, he smiled as though he knew me well and for a long time. He raised his right hand toward me, a fist fingers up, then he opened it slowly, while looking in my eyes. In his palm there was a large, heavy beetle, with shiny, deep blue armor that reflected the colors around it. Rising on its thin, pitch-black legs, the beetle slowly waved its short antennae with tufts of feathers at their ends. I froze. "It had to be this way," I whispered to myself, "this is the sign, this is what I've been waiting for." The boy took me by the hand and, led like two blind men by the scarab in his hand, we walked toward the great cathedral. Its porphyry facade was adorned with an enormous stained-glass rosette.

After we passed the doorway, we found ourselves in a tall space, but it was so narrow between the walls that it was like being at the bottom of a well. The church's wide facade had fooled us, as many places of worship do. The room was solely occupied by a large, rose-colored marble tomb, around which there was barely enough room to pass. I recognized it immediately, it was the one from the old factory. Over its door, closed by a padlock with five tumblers, these upper-case letters were chiseled into the stone:

SIGNA TE SIGNA TEMERE ME TANGIS ET ANGIS

Signs, fear, and contact, it all came back into my mind, while I worked the metal parallelepiped with movable letters. What was the combination for the tomb? And, if I could ever find it, what awaited me inside the grooved marble? "You'll be trapped for an eternity," I said to myself. Billions of years of nothing but trying different combinations, billions of combinations, under the Angel's ironic but also encouraging eyes. Until, in a moment identical and interchangeable with any other, the mystical word will shine forth, each of the five letters in its place, the way it had been from the beginning of time. The child closed his hand again and looked at me inquisitively. The metronome of my heart started, and woe to me if I didn't give the right answer before it beat its last.

I didn't have to wait until the threshold of death. My sure fingers turned the tumblers to the combination on the first try. In fact, there was no try, just a pure and unswerving certainty. Because now, excited and yet calmer than I had ever been, I understood, as though I were already there, what was inside the rose-colored tomb. The word I formed without hesitation was MARIA. And the lock opened, and the child stayed outside with his head bowed, leaving me to enter the secret chamber, alone.

There, on the catafalque, straight and young and brunette and beautiful, eyes open, filling the entire chamber with her oleander scent, my mother slept; in her modest dress, a dress from the 1960s, white with black circles; with her string of cheap pearls on her chest; with her unimpressive sandals and unpainted toenails. Looking at her, as I stood beside her, I remembered the sound of her voice, unlike any other on Earth. I always knew she was in the forbidden chamber of my castle. I leaned over her, and, suddenly sobbing like a child, I whispered, "Mama, I never lit a candle for you!" I sat on the cold floor, my head against the catafalque, and I cried until I had no more tears, begging, through my sobs and gasps, over and over, for forgiveness.

I eventually calmed down. I stood up and looked at her one more time, sleeping with her eyes open, breathing calmly. I leaned over and kissed her forehead. Then I walked out of the tomb and the cathedral and back into the movie theater, while I saw, trembling on the black screen, as in the films of my childhood, the word

FIN

Irina was waiting for me at the exit. We walked back through the flooded center, where cars cut through the water like boats. I was drained from so much crying. But now the little one smiled at me from her mother's arms, her few strands of blond hair glinting in the sun. "She looks like me," I thought and smiled back. I took her from Irina's arms and we walked on, toward the Armenian church, then up Moşilor. From there, it was not more than an hour's walk home.

We found ourselves finally in front of the boat-shaped house, looking at it with an endless sadness, as though we knew we were seeing it for the last time: my poor little shell, my body's refuge, broken by time and weather. The round window in the tower glowed yellow in the falling dusk, and the hornbeam tree beside it, with black, bare branches, leaning to the left, scratched the plaster of the walls that supported it. The girls went inside, but I walked around to the back, along the timeworn walls. The brick wall that cut off the house had no window. Instead, in the middle of the large, blind wall there was an entrance, bricked over with bricks of a different color, mortared with the same crumbling gray mortar, full of spider holes; the walled over door I had seen the first time I came, before buying the house, and which, I remember, moved me deeply even then. Now I was facing it again. High above my head, a rusty iron support held up the bulging wall.

I put my ear against the bricked-over door and listened carefully, until, after a long time, I could hear the tapping. Groups of two. Groups of three. Loud and soft in alternation. Long pauses and very short ones. Long scratches and little knocks all over the wall. The escape plan.

I didn't go inside the house until dawn.

51

I crawled down the slope to the edge of the cliff, through air the color of kerosene, and, with my heart trembling (was anything left of my poor heart?), I looked into the abyss. The measureless depth of the gaping funnel, as though the crust of the earth had been struck by a gigantic meteor; the size, thirty kilometers wide; the oven-hot smoke rising from the pit to dissolve in the yellow air of the morning—all this made my hair stand up on my head and arms. Before pulling myself back in fear and before rolling away over the grass, greasy from heating oil, beyond the Voluntari bridge, I managed to understand, through my senses more than my useless, from now on, logical space, the limitless desolation of that forever damned place.

The bridge at Voluntari was torn in two and hung crookedly in space, but on its end a crowd of people swarmed. All those who had fled from the fantastic ascension. Those who, like us, had been able to get ourselves outside the ring. Hordes of people, like after a soccer game, crowded the field around the cliff as far as you could see, and the same sights could probably be seen on all sides of the place where the melancholic grandeur of Bucharest once stood. Its former inhabitants now made a human circle, extending from the pit toward the surrounding towns: Cernica, Glina, Jilava, Popeşti-Leordeni, Bragadiru, Ciorogârla, Chiajna, Chitila, Aergistal, Ştefăneşti, Pantelimon, all of which had escaped whole, with their bars, propane stations, and lots for parking cars and tractors, with their People's Councils painted white, their plaster statues of World War One heroes, and their cultural centers with padlocks on the gate. Few of those that I could see—the elderly and students, housewives and workers, Gypsy girls with floral skirts and men's hats, shady types in leather jackets, uselessly worked-up police—thought it meet and right to go near the edge of the giant gorge. In fact, the crowds, thousands and thousands of people shoulder to shoulder, just as amazed now as they had been in the first hours of the uprooting, looked up, only up, as though imploring the city where they had lived their lowly lives to not leave them orphans, to not leave them behind like nobody's children. But the city from the heart of the Bărăgan, beaten by its winds for centuries, seemed now to have other plans.

When I recovered my senses after the terrible vision, I went back to the shadow of the bridge, where I had left the girls lying on a sweater spread across the weeds. I slowly picked up our daughter, careful not to wake her, but she opened her eyes and put her arms around my neck. Then with a finger pointing up, she showed me, giggling in delight, the city. As we stood together, cheek to cheek, looking at the unbelievable icon motionless against the sky, filling it with an endless grandeur, with waves of unearthly light, I suddenly felt overcome with love and nostalgia, without knowing if it was in fact for the golden-haired girl in my arms or for the funereal, unhappy city that now floated hundreds of meters above us, like a Laputa among the clouds.

Because Bucharest, my world, now hung in the air over the hellish pit it had always hidden, like a scab over a purulent wound, and which now, through an unparalleled uprooting, it finally brought to light. Bucharest looked like a gigantic plate loaded with fragile, decrepit edifices, with thousands of windows shining in the sun from above. The cupolas shone in the sun like crystal and silver goblets, as did the city's steeples and bell towers. The enormous platter was surrounded by wonderful, glowing clouds, as though made of kaolin, floating inoffensively in the April sky. The buildings' foundations hung down below, tangling with the sewer pipes and electric cables, metro tunnels, and the underground levels of Casa Poporului, like hairy roots, like a dusty spiderweb. On the western end you could clearly see, even though at that distance it was minuscule, the skeleton from Ferentari, hanging down from its shoulders. In a few places, this underground fabric seemed to burn in red metal rings. And there was a flaming ring in the center, surrounded by five other ones along the city's perimeter. Their crystalline light, jetting out of these powerful nozzles, lifted Bucharest toward the heavens.

But now, what made it most resemble a solemn, floating jellyfish wasn't the frameworks and cables, or the roots of the great trees hanging into the air, but a fantastic system of flexible tubes, like gray veins and arteries, which at that distance looked like filaments waving lazily underneath, some hanging free, but most linked up with a colossal central tube that reached down almost to the surface of the earth. "The aorta of pain," I said to myself when I first saw it, "the sewer where all of human suffering runs." Each filament sucked up the pain of the city's residents, crucified on dental chairs and hospital beds and torture tables, insane with unhappiness in minimally habitable studio apartments, spitting their lungs out in fabric or rubber factories, being beaten at school, beaten by the militia, beaten by fate, standing in endless lines for propane or groceries, blind, numb, without a purpose, without a home, without a destiny. It sucked up the pains of women having illegal abortions, of beggars kneeling in the wind, of drunks sleeping in bushes and caves, of starving children, of poets with destroyed lives. Each tube gurgled with the most precious substance in the world, the brain extract, the concentrate of fate which weaves our stupid, deceitful reality. Collected from all parts, the sparkling substance of pain flowed down the great tube, at the end of which was a sphere of translucent ivory skin, flexible as a fish bladder, waving like ectoplasm back and forth, half-stuck in the infernal crater underneath. The sphere was many kilometers in diameter, and it wobbled gently under the motionless city in the air. We all saw them now, in their round receptacle, those who were fed with the daily bread of our suffering: the crepuscular people from the center of the earth, fragile, lunatic, weak, with huge insectoid eyes, those who climbed up the tubes at night, like salmon going upstream, to appear in our hallucinations and in our dreams. Now, in their great, devastated city, pulled from the earth that had sheltered and warmed them, deprived suddenly of the portion of psychic sap springing from our flesh, they pressed their foreheads to the milky glass and made slow, imploring gestures toward us. There were tens of thousands, like wasp larvae filling the recesses of their paper nests. Irina pointed at them from time to time, amused by their writhing, their pale heads, all eyes, by the crooked smiles sketched across their faces, that wanted to show, perhaps, a well-meaning servility. I had seen them, in my restless nights on Ştefan cel Mare, poking up their lunatic heads at the window, even though I was on the fifth story. I had sat on the floor, paralyzed and abulic, my back against the wardrobe, while they danced sensually and grotesquely in the dark room.

While I looked at the incredible panorama with those around me—the parents of the kids from School 86, the shopkeepers I knew, the drivers of the trams that had plummeted into the funnel—the solenoids suddenly glowed even brighter, like inflorescences of blue flame. The city began to ascend again, slowly and solemnly, like one of those ancient elevators in the stores downtown, obscured more and more by clouds and heated by the sun, whose disk now appeared beyond the edge of the flying city. Bucharest became smaller and smaller, taking away all those who hadn't been able to get to the edge of town, all those who didn't want to abandon their houses, now collapsing by the hundreds with the vibration of ascension, leading the demons toward the stratosphere, as the ivory sphere swelled more and more, as though it soon would burst. In the end, all that was left was a ghost, a white cloud that melted into the dusty sky bent over the Bărăgan plains.

I imagined the statue of Damnation, the pitiless obsidian goddess, seated in the morgue's giant dental chair in the center of the flying disk like the pilot of a celestial ship, waving her fingers over the round buttons on the console, inputting combinations that maneuvered the city, torn from the earth and its antiquity, toward the cosmic dust. I saw my city wrapped in cosmos. Little by little, the edges of the enormous platter crumbled and dropped off—the school neighborhood, the old factory, and the water tower, the turnaround for tram 21, Pantelimon and Palamar's house, Ferentari with the skeleton, Dudeşti-Cioplea with the REM shed. They all were islands tumbling through the endless night, eroding as they were swallowed by the cold of the end. On one piece of earth floating in nothingness, with its tram tracks brutally broken and the crucified Christs on the streetlights looking dumbly around them, Ştefan cel Mare still stretched, with my parents' apartment block tilting over as though it had been bombed, with the Dâmboviţa mill, with the grocery across the street and the newsstands, with the B. P. Hasdeu Library, and with, toward the edge of the island, the strange cathedral of the tram depot I once visited. Many other parts of the city broke away from their precarious connection and were lost in nothingness, with their houses and theaters, their centenary trees and insalubrious train stations growing on them like beds of clams on a rock. Each piece broke further apart, house by house, furniture by piece of furniture, dropping the pieces to float alone: broken chairs, coins, combs, sign letters, shards of brick, dead dogs with dirty fur, upholstery springs, dolls with rag dresses . . . The pulverization continued down to the rubble and dust and molecules and atoms and bosons and fermions and quarks, until all of these were reabsorbed into the fabric of space, time, and thought, on the Planck scale of the world and of my mind.

The core of the city lasted the longest, the massive boulder where the university was still visible, with the room where I had read *The Fall*, the National Theater and the street with the movie theaters, the morgue, and Casa Poporului, more and more masticated and diminished by the destructive power of time. I saw myself there, in front of the Danube apartment block on one of my first days as a student, in the air thick with cobwebs, a crazy kid with his books and dreams, who still had a future on Earth. Now, however, the piece of rock floating in the cosmos was as rough as a meteor, and the plaster figures from the university facade had already been reduced to rubble. Below this piece of the city, the skin sphere still hung, intact, like a monstrous cherry, and I imagined the sudden explosion of the sinister capsule and the freeing of all the creatures from inside it like a dandelion's tiny parachutes, like spores of fear spread throughout the measureless and risible universe. They would take root in other worlds, absorbing the substance of other pains, from which they would weave the cloth of other illusory realities.

The last part was the morgue and its large central hall, whose roof, gaping like a mouth screaming at the eternal night, revealed the woman sitting like a heap of pitch on the dental chair. Untroubled and straight on her throne, she looked like an Assyrian deity, a cosmic object that only by chance had a human form. Around her, the walls fell one after another, the floor cracked, and the stone tiles scattered, until at the end of an endless age, only she, Damnation, would remain on her metal throne, surrounded by the twelve black statues that ornamented the cupola: Sadness, Despair, Fear, Nostalgia, Bitterness, Mania, Revulsion, Melancholy, Nausea, Horror, Grief, and Resignation, her entourage, the dark states of the soul. There in the depths, in the uncreated, in the most secret fold of the world and the mind, their black apple seeds would glitter, the sole and indestructible monogram of those 10,500 universes.

I am crying and I am writing, indistinguishably, as though I were writing with tears and crying ink. My manuscript perished in flames long ago: I always knew that fire would be its only reader. I am now writing a few final pages, so my world will not be left unfinished. And these, too, will be read, passionately or indifferently, after my death, by the same fire, the great reader of all the libraries of the world. Then I will take my daughter on my shoulders and, with Irina beside me, we will walk, in the ever-bloodier dusk, wherever our eyes take us, walking out of the book and the story.

One year, not a day more or less, after the meeting at the Mașina de Pâine Clinic, when we all felt the shock wave of the message Ispas's tortured mind emitted, we found ourselves in front of the grand fortress of the morgue. There were all of us who had filled the attic and the monumental staircase, holding against our chests our signs bent and torn from so much protest against heaven, letters half-erased from rain and moldy at the edges, who still were shouting with all our rage and indignation. It was a night full of stars, against which the building stood out like a cliff made of pitch. With every hard gust of spring wind, the trees swept the luminous stardust, waving from one corner to the other of the Bucharest sky.

Irina was next to me, holding our child, as she had been day after day, beside me, in me, in my mind and heart, ever since our girl came into the world. It was as though the entire chapel of my skull had been filled with a single statue of transparent marble, carved and polished, with pink and gray veins in its mineral, sugary flesh: Irina holding our girl, both of them with large eyes and the same smile. Watching them when they play together, for hours and hours, without ever getting bored of each other, when they laugh cheek to cheek, or when we give Irina a bath in her little pink plastic tub, pushing warm water over her chest, or when we stand her up, holding her little hands, and watch her step on the tips of her toes with the grace of a translucid tendril of vine, I have so often wished that time would freeze, in a pearl of supreme splendor, that there would be no future or history or illusion or life or death. I have so often felt—in those moments I never thought I would experience—that I did escape in the end, that I flew through all dimensions in an unexpected escape from self.

I walked over to the group of my colleagues from 86. This time, almost the whole school was there: Goia with his tragic face, doamna Rădulescu with the terrifying gemstone on her ring, Florabela, the charming redhead full of gold and freckles, Caty, with her mouth like a poppy, Eftene with his golden teeth gone, and Gheară, whose laughter never returned to his lips. The lower school teachers were there, too, crowded together like sheep, the filthy Zarzăre and perfidious Higena, doamna Mototolescu, and doamna Călătorescu with her knitting needles still hanging around her neck. They looked like the frightened survivors of a shipwreck: on their faces, so different and so familiar to me, a single expression showed: deep and inconsolable loss, like after the loss of a spouse, like after the loss of a child. Then I knew that in the circles under my eyes, in the furrows between my eyebrows, in my feverish and bloodshot eyes, in my pale lips, I wore the same expression of deep mourning, of inconsolable mourning. We were all lost, our values wasted away, with no reason left to live, people reduced to their cry for help. What could the rest of our lives hold? What more disappointments, sufferings, terrible illnesses, and pains impossible to assuage? How would we bear the passage of time that dragged pieces of our body and our world along? That robbed us of the distant paradise of childhood? Old age, agony, and death were waiting for us. We were standing in a long line at the entrance of the slaughterhouse. There was no one who would guide us through the inferno, now that Virgil had been crushed, carelessly and without hate, like a fly. No one would open the doors, with their pathetic high relief carvings, no one would take us to the central hall. We had to stay there all night, in front of the giant building, walking in a circle and waving our ridiculous, powerless signs. "Down with death!" But death was up, at the zenith, burning like a black sun. "NO to insanity!" But, if there were any gods left on Earth, they were the gods of those contorted by paranoia, schizophrenia, and depression. "Stop human carnage!" But people continued to kill each other; it was the only thing they had known how to do from the start, and their skills were only improving. People didn't die one at a time, pierced by steel blades or arrows, they perished en masse, whole peoples injected with the substance of universal hate drained from the ocean of metaphysical evil that surrounded us. "Help!" we all screamed in the end, swimming in the limitless, black, frozen waters.

This is what we did for a few hours, we picketed the morgue, glancing up from time to time at the statues around the cupola. Their black arms raised toward the sky looked, at that distance, like a tick's thin legs ending in powerful claws. The statue levitating on top was visible only from the chest up, the rest was covered by the high cornice of the funereal temple. The night turned cold, and we walked in a circle, several abreast, huddled together, when suddenly we felt the pulse with which everything began. It wasn't coming from inside of me. It was as though a filament or a ray came from another world and touched my brain. I suddenly felt myself filled with a thought that was not my own, but that couldn't penetrate any mind but mine, the way inspiration takes hold of an artist, like the rapture that can make an epileptic kill. Beside me, with a black scarf over her head, with a sign saying "Stop the massacre of children!" raised higher than all the others, walked Florabela, whose mourning couldn't cover the exuberance of her godlike body. When the thought from another dimension shot into me, I looked at her face framed in locks of fiery red hair, and Florabela, as though she knew, nodded in approval.

Then I had no doubt. I stepped, in the very dim light of the solitary bulb hanging over the piața, into the center of the wheel in which, like Dantean creations of shadow and light, the Picketists walked. The wheel stopped, the people gathered around me (there were hundreds), and they waited, obviously they waited for me to talk to them, looking at me as though they all knew, the way they had once looked at Virgil, the way they had surrounded Ispas with their appalling adulation. Virgil, Ispas, Palamar, I thought. We all had our prophets, those who spoke to us with voices that were not their own. I had to do the same thing, because the most obscene act on Earth was to speak from yourself, from your own mind, pretending that a god put words in your mouth. The false prophets were the other subtle painters who put doors on the walls of your cranium. Baroque, gothic, classical, or art nouveau doors, but all with the same property: they never opened.

I didn't speak with my own words. I took a crumpled piece of paper from my pocket, the one Virgil had once given me, and I read out loud the poem by Dylan Thomas:

Do not go gentle into that good night,
Old age should burn and rave at close of day;
Rage, rage against the dying of the light.

Though wise men at their end know dark is right,
Because their words had forked no lightning they
Do not go gentle into that good night.

Good men, the last wave by, crying how bright
Their frail deeds might have danced in a green bay,
Rage, rage against the dying of the light.

Wild men who caught and sang the sun in flight,
And learn, too late, they grieved it on its way,
Do not go gentle into that good night.

Grave men, near death, who see with blinding sight
Blind eyes could blaze like meteors and be gay,
Rage, rage against the dying of the light.

And you, my father, there on the sad height,
Curse, bless, me now with your fierce tears, I pray.
Do not go gentle into that good night.
Rage, rage against the dying of the light.

Then, followed by the Picketists, we set off toward the grand doorway. Irina walked beside me, carrying our daughter. Out of the massive, high relief carving, countless human hands reached toward us, desperate to escape their two-dimensional prison. We had only to interlace our fingers with theirs, as Virgil had once done, for the massive doors to open. And we all went inside, into a museum-like silence, into the corridor leading to the central hall.

Everything was so changed there that shivers of overwhelming emotions shot through me. Along the walls were the same glass cases, but they no longer held the ancient and rusted torture instruments. The cases were now full . . . of things from my life, of things that had once belonged to me. I saw my parents' photographs, aged with the passage of time into a pale, crackled sepia: the one from when they met at Govora and the one from their wedding. They were enlarged, over a meter tall, and underneath was a text so small you couldn't make it out. I saw the picture of my parents smiling happily, my mother holding me, and my father holding my twin brother, or perhaps it was the other way around: two identical children, smiling at each other like in a mirror. Then I saw yellowed pacifiers, clothes from when I was one, my first photo—me crying, little fists in my eyes, at the photographer, a piece of paper from a herbarium with a pressed oleander blossom, a little bell I dropped in a puddle on Str. Silistra. I saw my poor toys, the deformed horse with its red saddle and thread mane, its eyes fallen out long ago, and the wagon pulled by metal horses. I saw the plastic ruler I looked through in class to make rainbows on everything, the Papagal-brand pencil with a four-color tip, my frayed Pioneer tie that my mother made into a dust rag. I saw the two sandals, one black and one brown, that I wore by mistake when I went to the cafeteria for a packet of ground coffee. I saw some worn-out books borrowed from the B. P. Hasdeu Library and a few issues of *Science-Fantasy Stories* and *Adventure Club*. In another case was a heavy, bent bicycle, missing spokes, its metal rusted. I recognized it right away: it was the one from Herăstrău, where I made thousands of pathetic circles, without ever wanting to stop, until night fell and a peacock cried loud enough to break your eardrums. I saw my first little poems, scrawled in student notebooks, then a lock of Esther's hair, my first love in high school. In the last case I saw college courses, a sweater my mother knitted and dyed red with automobile paint. I saw my first-year seminar paper on the Psalms, and the paper officially assigning me to School 86 at the end of Colentina. Registers from the school, homework scrawled over in red, a picture of me in the center of a group of bizarre-looking students, and bunches of other paraphernalia of a teacher's life, the saddest in the world, occupied the penultimate case. The last one seemed empty and threatening, as though waiting for items that had yet to arrive. But when I looked closer, I saw a massive, black insect with huge horns, like deer antlers. It was a living stag beetle, standing on its pitch-black legs, and it seemed to be looking at me. I lifted the lid of the case, the only one left unlocked, and I picked up the beetle. It was heavier than I had imagined, as though made of metal. With him in my open hand, palm up, I walked into the next room, which I remembered was full of cadavers on zinc tables. But my surprise, which had grown over the course of the day to an uncontrollable tension, now turned into panic and horror. I put the beetle in my pocket, as though this were something it shouldn't see.

And now, on the dozens of tables through which I passed in amazement, there were cadavers, but they all were mine, from different ages, like pieces of my being over time! I saw myself stiff on a morgue table as a tiny newborn with bent legs, as a six-month-old in a blue shirt, then as a one-year-old, all in rigor mortis, all with their eyes open, all with their hands folded over their chests. I saw the velvet suit and the shirt with two mushrooms that I had when I was five, now on the dead child with mild brown eyes on the next table. I saw my school uniform with polka-dotted shorts from when I was seven, and my Pioneer uniform on my nine-year-old cadaver. And on and on, to the end of the room, there were dozens of bodies, each one taller than the previous, the adolescent and then the young man I once was, dressed with the clothes I knew well, all as rigid as in photographs, all looking at the ceiling with empty eyes, all with their arms on their chests, a long line of dead bodies, because we all die every moment that we move, like hermit crabs, from one cell into a larger cell. It was my museum, the museum of my life, I walked through it at the head of a line of Picketists who spread out among the dozens of my bodies, looking at them curiously, pointing out details to each other: the student number on an arm, the lunula on a finger, the bitter smile in the corner of a mouth. We stayed there a long time, as though we had to keep vigil over them, as though we were mourning each of them, the boys, the teenagers, and the men who all died at once in who knows what terrifying cataclysm. The last one was an exact copy of me, dressed in black as I was that night, with one shoe untied, as mine was at that moment. A little below his chin I saw the nick I gave myself shaving yesterday morning, which I stanched with a piece of toilet paper.

The hair on my arms standing on end, and certain the end was coming, I rushed toward the ordinary white door at the other end, causing a little snowfall of plaster. Such that, before going into the next space, I could see the number that had been covered. It was the unimaginable *α* raised to the power of *α*, the number of the Divine, the number that included all. I opened the door, and, like a minuscule population of fleas, we all entered the inordinately large room. Even though we had been there once already, nothing prepared us for that closed space, larger than the mind itself, supported by columns of a thickness at a nonhuman scale. In the center of the room, we again contemplated the dental chair, like a mastodon of metal bolted to the floor that miraculously held its weight. We approached and surrounded it on every side, with our heads tilting back to see, at the height of an eight-story block of apartments, the headrest of twin leather disks, the chair arms, the tray with the same dental instruments as before, the horrible metal snakes of the drills and motors. Our heads came up to the footrests and to the pedals that raised and lowered the chair. We all walked around the giant throne a few times, waving our signs in silence, because we all expected, with wide eyes, the monstrous miracle to come again: the descent of Damnation from the heavens to take her seat on the chair of judgment.

This time, I was the priest in his ephod—the gold diadem on his forehead, the hem of his vestment lined with bells and tassels, so that the divine creature would hear the clinking and tolerate my presence in its sacred space, in its beastly breath. I was the one who, following Virgil's footsteps, walked between the footrests and found the console with hemispheric buttons. I entered a combination my mind did not know but my fingers seemed to have always known, and, as before, the paneling along the curved walls rose to reveal a copper solenoid, like the braids of a giant redheaded woman, a large coil of thick copper wire that gave the impression of supreme perfection. It ran, shining, along the walls of the room until it disappeared into the fog at the other end. Another fluttering of fingers and the solenoid, flowing with electric current, began to hum gently, filling the greenish air with a continuous tremor. Then the slow and solemn buzzing grew louder, until it reached the intensity of a cloud of locusts, then to the intolerable level of an airplane engine. We felt our lungs vibrating in our thoracic cavities, we felt our teeth rattling in our mouths. My hand reached again for the rounded, multicolor buttons, each a different texture and clarity, and it picked out, like the sharp sounds of a zither, a little melody floating like a silk thread released from the bass noise of the solenoid. And the dome opened again, gathering its petals in a spiral, and I saw the sky turning above us again, bearing its plentiful harvest of stars. Enough to remind us of what we often forget: that we are children of the cosmos, living for a nanosecond on a speck of dust in the infinite depths of the night.

With what grand leisure, with what fluttering of her obsidian dress and hair, with what nobility in her blind and inexpressive face, like that of an insect, did the colossal statue descend from the sky, covering and uncovering the golden, astral dust scattered across the dome of heaven. How gracefully she levitated above us, in the wind of an April night that had suddenly entered the hall, with its cool air and sounds of distant trams! And yet, when her body, covered in waves that looked not like clothes but like the excrescence of her pitch-black skin, settled into the dental chair, it moaned and sank toward the earth as though loaded with a measureless burden. Now, the goddess again waited on her imperial throne, turning her head slowly like a praying mantis. And the Picketists, who a year ago screamed as loudly as they could against the dying of the light, now stood silent and spiritless, their jaws clenched, their tongues stuck to the roofs of their mouths, forgetting themselves, fascinated by the statue's blind eyes. The people were sheep led into the slaughterhouse, the doomed on the road to death. The petals of the cupola closed slowly overhead, like those of a hungry, carnivorous plant, and there was no longer any escape.

I stepped back about ten paces across the glassy tiles, and the panel of spherical buttons was reabsorbed into the floor as though it had never existed. The statue of Damnation was now above me, foreshortened in a way that accentuated her imperious form. Soon, she noticed me at her feet, and she leaned far over from the chair toward me, like a large shadow falling over my heart. I looked into her impersonal eyes, eyes without pupils, the empty eyes of children who pull the wings off flies and the legs off grasshoppers, or who crush an anthill under their heel. I expected at any moment to suffer Virgil's fate, and I wouldn't have tried to escape it. Everything seemed lost, lost for all of us, lost forever. But the night before, my fingers had known much more than I did. I took the beetle from my pocket, and, holding it in the palm of my hand, I lifted it up as far as I could, toward the dark goddess. And in the immense silence of the circular hall, we all saw her lift her right hand from the armrest of the dental chair and bring it close, palm up and fingers spread, toward me. Soon, her longest finger touched mine, and the heavy beetle, with its horns of pitch, began its journey toward the statue's hand. It was the mystery of the space between synapses, it was the drop of serotonin that crosses the minuscule gap like an angel or a messenger. The bug stopped, smaller than a flea, in the middle of her black, uncreased palm, and there it was reabsorbed. Contact had been made.

Then I kneeled and took my collection of objects out of my bag. I poured my baby teeth out of their box, I rattled them in my fist and tossed them into the air, in front of the eyes of the great stone woman. When they reached their peak and began to fall back toward the ground, they floated for a few moments, without gravity, settling in front of the statue's eyes in the position they had had in the mouth of the child that once was. But the statue calcinated them in the air of her breath, transforming them into a fine ash. My locks and braids suffered the same fate, as did the little bits of twine that, until a few years ago, I would pull from my navel. I lifted up to the void the few photos I had of my parents and me, faded with broken perforations and writing in chemical pencil on the back, and soon in the chalice of my fingers were brief tongues of fire that left only dust. Bit by bit, I remained without life and without fate.

I set the plates showing the visions Nicolae Minovici had during his controlled hanging next to Vaschide's *Sleep and Dreams* and the Voynich manuscript I received from Palamar. The statue leaned down even more deeply, looking at them, it seemed, not with her eyes but with her entire face. She made a small motion with the tips of her fingers, and the pages rose slowly in the air, they separated from their spines and mixed together, creating a new, magnificent work, more intense, more profound, more poetic than anything that had ever adorned a bookshelf, where each page mirrored the others and each word generated an illuminated icon, which in turn generated the word. It was the gospel of my mind and the stamp sweetly and brutally imprinted upon the wax of the world in which I had lived. On its massive paperboard cover was one of the concentric plates from the Voynich manuscript: planets, zodiac signs, plantlike women with diadems on their heads. And then, ah, wretched Dionysus, I knew how I could bring them to life. Without hesitating, I placed my right index finger in the center of the diagram, which burned me like a red-hot wire. The book rose, floating slowly toward the ceiling, and the gigantic statue straightened until she again sat upright with her back against the chair. Before her eyes, the book melted into a single substance, a white-gray mass, which quickly separated into eight cubes. Emptying themselves of the milky cloud, they soon glittered like mine flowers and together formed a kind of hopscotch shape in space, a crucifix with two transverse beams interpenetrating the vertical one. Then, under our gazes, the cubic sides closed one over the other, in a way that the human mind cannot perceive, cannot observe, cannot describe, so that in the end what sparkled before us was the unearthly object that Hinton dreamed of, the prophet of the fourth dimension: the mystical tesseract. We looked at it, even though it was not possible to see, just as you cannot see, from the side of a cube, anything but a square that hides the volume extending behind it into another world. The hypervolume of the tesseract, its secret history, was forever forbidden to us. The light of the inconceivable object projected a handful of rays onto the curved walls, and there it painted a door. Not a simple door, nor a highly decorated door, but a door pure and simple, without features, a conceptual door, a door from the world of ideas untouched by the dirt and pus of the world. It was the promised door, the door of the grand egress.

Then, only then, the statue had no doubt. I was the one on the other side of the wall, listening to the taps, translating them feverishly into crosses, crescents, and gears. I was the one in the middle of the immaculate snow, ready to rise to the sky for beatification or damnation. I was the one destined to escape, the one who was to leave. She quickly stood up from the chair and stepped in front of me. The Picketists, pressed to the wall, screamed as loud as they could. Would they see my body break open and splatter them with my guts, my skull bursting like an old clay urn under the goddess's vengeful foot? Instead of all this, standing straight and immeasurably tall, Damnation began to speak.

It was a long speech, in a language not just foreign but unconnected with any phonic apparatus, with lungs and trachea and larynx and vocal cords and tongue and teeth and lips which, damped with saliva and the bitterness of taste buds, passed the word into the world. It was the kind of cicada chirps, of guitar flourishes, of a saw wilting while stroked with a bow, of the high staccato "Queen of the Night" aria. If you could transcribe in our alphabet those sounds not enunciated with a human mouth, I thought with a shiver, perhaps the lines would look like this:

ychtaiis aiichy dol aiin otaiin aiidy okchd otor daiin
poar keeo daiin qoair ar aiphhey qoeed eody qokaiin qotedais aporair apy
lsheody tair oteey oteeo ol otaiin okeey qokaiin ar aiir al dal
dcheo fcheeody ckheey dar aiin al dar ar daiiidy otedy oteody ytaiin

Then, with a wide movement of her arm, she opened in the floor between us a large pit of spitting flames. There were tongues of fire, dragons of fire twisting their necks together, vipers of liquid fire, alive, terrifyingly furious, hell fire, unquenchable fire. From its core, we thought we heard the cries of the eternally damned. The statue then held out both its hands toward me, palms up: Choose!

I looked back and saw Irina holding our daughter. I motioned them to come closer. Then I took from my bag my last object, my last possession, my last justification for my presence on Earth. My manuscript, the humble notebooks, swollen with the weight of ink, with circular coffee stains, where I had written for years in the effort to understand my anomalies, my mind, and my life. I broke into sobs and dampened the last page with tears, a fitting addition of salt to a sacrifice before the altar. Irina, pale as death, was now shoulder to shoulder with me. At the same moment, we held them both over the fire, the girl and the manuscript. One by one, I let the notebooks fall into the flames, while the woman I loved pulled our child back to her chest. We embraced, with our daughter between us, suddenly incredibly happy, without a care for any statue or any door. Now the statue could raise her foot and crush us: we were living in love, and no one could take that from us.

The tesseract dimmed and melted into the air, and the door painted on the wall stopped glowing. I would stay, forever, the prisoner of this valley. I knew now that I could not have left alone, that I was bound in brotherhood and in love to all of my kind, to all of those standing in the line of death, to all of those who would soon be erased from the world. To the Picketists, to my colleagues, to every face I had ever seen. I would not have left without my Irina, who gave my life light. Because only as my manuscript disappeared into the flames did I begin to feel I truly had a life.

The pit in the floor closed like an eye, and the statue, satisfied with the scent of our sacrifice, sat back down in the chair. Waking from the collective hallucination, the Picketists began to flow out the door where they had come in. Most of them grumbled and smacked their signs onto the ground: they had been expecting to avenge Virgil, to somehow annihilate the deity of destruction and death. But they didn't have much time to think about this, because the earth suddenly began to shake and a rain of plaster and stone fell over them. The earth was moving, it seemed to pull itself up by the roots, it was trying to tear itself away from the depths beneath. As the last ones in the hall of the morgue, we understood: it was the solenoid. Sitting in her chair, the obsidian statue had turned the enormous coil to its highest power. Probably the others along the periphery had also turned on. Now all the earth was shaking, the underground cables were breaking, the sewer pipes cracking, the frames of the foundations moaned in their joints. A sinister sound had filled the morgue, and an unexpectedly powerful fear rose within us. "It's exploding!" I shouted to Irina, pulling the child from her arms. "Exploding!" And we fled down the hall, without a glance at the museum. When we all poured outside, it was fully day.

We ran through the streets of the city for two hours, driven mad by the tramlines breaking and rising toward the sky, the houses collapsing with apocalyptic noises, the desperate crowds running toward the edge of town, the roar in the air like bombing raids. We went first up Moşilor, near Armenească, stopping to catch our breath for a moment in an abandoned grocery, we reached Obor, the enormous, stone-paved market that the fish hall made stink, and we crossed Colentina at Ziduri-Moşi to get home. But we changed our plan: the city had begun, extremely slowly, to rise, taking off like a scab peeling from a wound. We had to, at any cost, get outside the city. We ran as fast as we could, our daughter crying in our arms, but after making stops as frequent as the tram stations—the cars had derailed and were turned over, blocking the street—we finally reached the end of line 21. The water tower shook like the mast of a ship in a storm. All the windows of the pipe factory had shattered. We didn't go down Dimitrie Herescu, there was no point, we would only be safe outside the belt road. When we crossed the bridge at Voluntari, we heard a sound behind us like an extended bolt of lightning: the bridge broke in two and the Bucharest side rose visibly into the air. We collapsed, gasping, our faces red, into the weeds under the bridge. From this spot we watched, alongside all the others who had saved themselves, the unreal ascension. The last roots and cables were pulled up, the last automobiles slid into the ravine, and Bucharest, my world, rose toward the sky. Where it once had been, there was the cone of a bottomless pit, leading perhaps to the center of the earth, with, in the other hemisphere, a corresponding mountain as white as milk, rising perhaps from green, clear waves. When the great flying city had ascended high enough, we saw the horrifying sack of hell our pain had fed: the legions of parasitic demons, like trichinella larvae, feeding on our interior life.

And now, in a few moments, I will set these last pages on fire over the chasm. I will watch the feathers of ash descend, in wide spirals, toward its unsoundable depth. Then we will leave toward the east. I've spoken with Irina; we know what we will do. We will follow along the edge of the road, beyond the village of Voluntari, and toward Afumați, we will find the oak grove where we once collected acorns. A ruined chapel is waiting for us there, and, as we knew when we first found it, this will be our last home. There, within its rickety, fresco-covered walls, we will grow old together. There, I will push my head deeply into the waters of dream, and Irina will melt like the dusk into my chest.

We will stay there forever, sheltered from the frightening stars.

END

Acknowledgments

Solenoid includes quotes from the following:

Arghezi, Tudor. *Cuvinte potrivite*. 1927.[*]

Borges, Jorge Luis. *Collected Fictions*. Translated by Andrew Hurley. New York: Penguin, 1999.

Herodotus, *The Histories*. Translated by A. D. Godley. Cambridge: Harvard University Press. 1920.

Kafka, Franz. *Tagebücher 1910–1923*.[*]

Mallarmé, Stéphane. *Poésies*. 1887.

Thomas, Dylan. *The Poems of Dylan Thomas*. New York: New Directions, 1953.

* The translations that appear in the text are by Sean Cotter.

Thank you all
for your support.
We do this for you,
and could not do
it without you.

PARTNERS

FIRST EDITION MEMBERSHIP

Anonymous (9)
Donna Wilhelm

TRANSLATOR'S CIRCLE

Ben & Sharon Fountain
Meriwether Evans

PRINTER'S PRESS MEMBERSHIP

Allred Capital Management
Robert Appel
Charles Dee Mitchell
Cullen Schaar
David Tomlinson & Kathryn Berry
Jeff Leuschel
Judy Pollock
Loretta Siciliano
Lori Feathers
Mary Ann Thompson-Frenk & Joshua Frenk
Matthew Rittmayer
Nick Storch
Pixel and Texel
Social Venture Partners Dallas
Stephen Bullock

AUTHOR'S LEAGUE

Christie Tull
Farley Houston
Jacob Seifring
Lissa Dunlay
Stephen Bullock
Steven Kornajcik
Thomas DiPiero

PUBLISHER'S LEAGUE

Adam Rekerdres
Christie Tull
Justin Childress
Kay Cattarulla
KMGMT
Olga Kislova

EDITOR'S LEAGUE

Amrit Dhir
Brandon Kennedy
Dallas Sonnier
Garth Hallberg
Greg McConeghy
Linda Nell Evans
Mary Moore Grimaldi
Mike Kaminsky
Patricia Storace
Ryan Todd
Steven Harding
Suejean Kim
Symphonic Source
Wendy Belcher

READER'S LEAGUE

Caitlin Baker
Caroline Casey
Carolyn Mulligan
Chilton Thomson
Cody Cosmic & Jeremy Hays
Jeff Waxman
Joseph Milazzo
Kayla Finstein
Kelly Britson
Kelly & Corby Baxter
Marian Schwartz & Reid Minot
Marlo D. Cruz Pagan
Maryam Baig
Peggy Carr
Susan Ernst

ADDITIONAL DONORS

Alan Shockley
Amanda & Bjorn Beer
Andrew Yorke
Anonymous (10)
Anthony Messenger
Ashley Milne Shadoin
Bob & Katherine Penn
Brandon Childress
Charley Mitcherson
Charley Rejsek
Cheryl Thompson
Chloe Pak
Cone Johnson
CS Maynard
Daniel J. Hale
Daniela Hurezanu
Dori Boone-Costantino
Ed Nawotka
Elizabeth Gillette
Erin Kubatzky
Ester & Matt Harrison
Grace Kenney
Hillary Richards
JJ Italiano
Jeremy Hughes
John Darnielle
Julie Janicke Muhsmann
Kelly Falconer
Laura Thomson
Lea Courington
Leigh Ann Pike
Lowell Frye
Maaza Mengiste

pixel texel

ADDITIONAL DONORS, CONT'D

Mark Haber
Mary Cline
Maynard Thomson
Michael Reklis
Mike Soto
Mokhtar Ramadan
Nikki & Dennis Gibson
Patrick Kukucka
Patrick Kutcher
Rev. Elizabeth & Neil Moseley
Richard Meyer
Scott & Katy Nimmons
Sherry Perry
Sydneyann Binion
Stephen Harding
Stephen Williamson
Susan Carp
Susan Ernst
Theater Jones
Tim Perttula
Tony Thomson

SUBSCRIBERS

Alan Glazer
Amber Williams
Angela Schlegel
Austin Dearborn
Carole Hailey
Caroline West
Courtney Sheedy
Damon Copeland
Dauphin Ewart
Donald Morrison
Elizabeth Simpson
Emily Beck
Erin Kubatzky
Hannah Good
Heath Dollar
Heustis Whiteside
Hillary Richards
Jane Gerhard
Jarratt Willis
Jennifer Owen
Jessica Sirs
John Andrew Margrave
John Mitchell
John Tenny
Joseph Rebella
Josh Rubenoff
Katarzyna Bartoszynska
Kenneth McClain
Kyle Trimmer
Matt Ammon
Matt Bucher
Matthew LaBarbera
Melanie Nicholls
Michael Binkley
Michael Lighty
Nancy Allen
Nancy Keaton
Nicole Yurcaba
Petra Hendrickson
Ryan Todd
Samuel Herrera
Scott Chiddister
Sian Valvis
Sonam Vashi
Tania Rodriguez

AVAILABLE NOW FROM DEEP VELLUM

SHANE ANDERSON • *After the Oracle* • USA

MICHÈLE AUDIN • *One Hundred Twenty-One Days* • translated by Christiana Hills • FRANCE

BAE SUAH • *Recitation* • translated by Deborah Smith • SOUTH KOREA

MARIO BELLATIN • *Mrs. Murakami's Garden* • translated by Heather Cleary • *Beauty Salon* • translated by Shook • MEXICO

EDUARDO BERTI • *The Imagined Land* • translated by Charlotte Coombe • ARGENTINA

CARMEN BOULLOSA • *Texas: The Great Theft* • translated by Samantha Schnee • *Before* • translated by Peter Bush • *Heavens on Earth* • translated by Shelby Vincent • MEXICO

CAYLIN CAPRA-THOMAS • *Iguana Iguana* • USA

MAGDA CÂRNECI • *FEM* • translated by Sean Cotter • ROMANIA

LEILA S. CHUDORI • *Home* • translated by John H. McGlynn • INDONESIA

MATHILDE WALTER CLARK • *Lone Star* • translated by Martin Aitken & K. E. Semmel • DENMARK

SARAH CLEAVE, ed. • *Banthology: Stories from Banned Nations* • IRAN, IRAQ, LIBYA, SOMALIA, SUDAN, SYRIA & YEMEN

TIM COURSEY • *Driving Lessons* • USA

LOGEN CURE • *Welcome to Midland: Poems* • USA

ANANDA DEVI • *Eve Out of Her Ruins* • translated by Jeffrey Zuckerman • *When the Night Agrees to Speak to Me* • translated by Kazim Ali MAURITIUS

DHUMKETU • *The Shehnai Virtuoso* • translated by Jenny Bhatt • INDIA

PETER DIMOCK • *Daybook from Sheep Meadow* • USA

CLAUDIA ULLOA DONOSO • *Little Bird,* translated by Lily Meyer • PERU/NORWAY

LEYLÂ ERBIL • *A Strange Woman* • translated by Nermin Menemencioğlu & Amy Marie Spangler • TURKEY

RADNA FABIAS • *Habitus* • translated by David Colmer • CURAÇAO/NETHERLANDS

ROSS FARRAR • *Ross Sings Cheree & the Animated Dark: Poems* • USA

ALISA GANIEVA • *Bride and Groom* • *The Mountain and the Wall* • translated by Carol Apollonio • RUSSIA

FERNANDA GARCÍA LAO • *Out of the Cage* • translated by Will Vanderhyden • ARGENTINA

ANNE GARRÉTA • *Sphinx* • *Not One Day* • *In Concrete* • translated by Emma Ramadan • FRANCE

NIVEN GOVINDEN • *Diary of a Film* • GREAT BRITAIN

JÓN GNARR • *The Indian* • *The Pirate* • *The Outlaw* • translated by Lytton Smith • ICELAND

GOETHE • *The Golden Goblet: Selected Poems* • *Faust, Part One* • translated by Zsuzsanna Ozsváth and Frederick Turner • GERMANY

SARA GOUDARZI • *The Almond in the Apricot* • USA

NOEMI JAFFE • *What Are the Blind Men Dreaming?* • translated by Julia Sanches & Ellen Elias-Bursac • BRAZIL

CLAUDIA SALAZAR JIMÉNEZ • *Blood of the Dawn* • translated by Elizabeth Bryer • PERU

PERGENTINO JOSÉ • *Red Ants* • MEXICO

TAISIA KITAISKAIA • *The Nightgown & Other Poems* • USA

SONG LIN • *The Gleaner Song: Selected Poems* • translated by Dong Li • CHINA

GYULA JENEI • *Always Different* • translated by Diana Senechal • HUNGARY

DIA JUBAILI • *No Windmills in Basra* • translated by Chip Rossetti • IRAQ

JUNG YOUNG MOON • *Seven Samurai Swept Away in a River* • *Vaseline Buddha* • translated by Yewon Jung • SOUTH KOREA

ELENI KEFALA • *Time Stitches* • translated by Peter Constantine • CYPRUS

UZMA ASLAM KHAN • *The Miraculous True History of Nomi Ali* • PAKISTAN

KIM YIDEUM • *Blood Sisters* • translated by Jiyoon Lee • SOUTH KOREA

JOSEFINE KLOUGART • *Of Darkness* • translated by Martin Aitken • DENMARK

ANDREY KURKOV • *Grey Bees* • translated by Boris Dralyuk • UKRAINE

YANICK LAHENS • *Moonbath* • translated by Emily Gogolak • HAITI

JORGE ENRIQUE LAGE • *Freeway: La Movie* • translated by Lourdes Molina • CUBA

FOUAD LAROUI • *The Curious Case of Dassoukine's Trousers* • translated by Emma Ramadan • MOROCCO

MARIA GABRIELA LLANSOL • *The Geography of Rebels Trilogy: The Book of Communities; The Remaining Life; In the House of July & August* • translated by Audrey Young • PORTUGAL

TEDI LÓPEZ MILLS • *The Book of Explanations* • translated by Robin Myers • MEXICO

PABLO MARTÍN SÁNCHEZ • *The Anarchist Who Shared My Name* • translated by Jeff Diteman • SPAIN

DOROTA MASŁOWSKA • *Honey, I Killed the Cats* • translated by Benjamin Paloff • POLAND

BRICE MATTHIEUSSENT • *Revenge of the Translator* • translated by Emma Ramadan • FRANCE

LINA MERUANE • *Seeing Red* • translated by Megan McDowell • CHILE

ANTONIO MORESCO • *Clandestinity* • translated by Richard Dixon • ITALY

VALÉRIE MRÉJEN • *Black Forest* • translated by Katie Shireen Assef • FRANCE

FISTON MWANZA MUJILA • *Tram 83* • translated by Roland Glasser • *The River in the Belly: Poems* • translated by J. Bret Maney • DEMOCRATIC REPUBLIC OF CONGO

GORAN PETROVIĆ • *At the Lucky Hand, aka The Sixty-Nine Drawers* • translated by Peter Agnone • SERBIA

LUDMILLA PETRUSHEVSKAYA • *The New Adventures of Helen: Magical Tales* • translated by Jane Bugaeva • RUSSIA

ILJA LEONARD PFEIJFFER • *La Superba* • translated by Michele Hutchison • NETHERLANDS

RICARDO PIGLIA • *Target in the Night* • translated by Sergio Waisman • ARGENTINA

SERGIO PITOL • *The Art of Flight* • *The Journey* • *The Magician of Vienna* • *Mephisto's Waltz: Selected Short Stories* • *The Love Parade* • translated by George Henson • MEXICO

JULIE POOLE • *Bright Specimen* • USA

EDUARDO RABASA • *A Zero-Sum Game* • translated by Christina MacSweeney • MEXICO

ZAHIA RAHMANI • *"Muslim": A Novel* • translated by Matt Reeck • FRANCE/ALGERIA

MANON STEFFAN ROS • *The Blue Book of Nebo* • WALES

JUAN RULFO • *The Golden Cockerel & Other Writings* • translated by Douglas J. Weatherford • MEXICO

IGNACIO RUIZ-PÉREZ • *Isles of Firm Ground* • translated by Mike Soto • MEXICO

ETHAN RUTHERFORD • *Farthest South & Other Stories* • USA

TATIANA RYCKMAN • *Ancestry of Objects* • USA

JIM SCHUTZE • *The Accommodation* • USA

OLEG SENTSOV • *Life Went On Anyway* • translated by Uilleam Blacker • UKRAINE

MIKHAIL SHISHKIN • *Calligraphy Lesson: The Collected Stories* • translated by Marian Schwartz, Leo Shtutin, Mariya Bashkatova, Sylvia Maizell • RUSSIA

ÓFEIGUR SIGURÐSSON • *Öræfi: The Wasteland* • translated by Lytton Smith • ICELAND

NOAH SIMBLIST, ed. • *Tania Bruguera: The Francis Effect* • CUBA

DANIEL SIMON, ed. • *Dispatches from the Republic of Letters* • USA

MUSTAFA STITOU • *Two Half Faces* • translated by David Colmer • NETHERLANDS

SOPHIA TERAZAWA • *Winter Phoenix: Testimonies in Verse* • USA

MÄRTA TIKKANEN • *The Love Story of the Century* • translated by Stina Katchadourian • SWEDEN

ROBERT TRAMMELL • *Jack Ruby & the Origins of the Avant-Garde in Dallas & Other Stories* • USA

BENJAMIN VILLEGAS • *ELPASO: A Punk Story* • translated by Jay Noden • SPAIN

S. YARBERRY • *A Boy in the City* • USA

SERHIY ZHADAN • *Voroshilovgrad* • translated by Reilly Costigan-Humes & Isaac Wheeler • UKRAINE

FORTHCOMING FROM DEEP VELLUM

CHARLES ALCORN • *Beneath the Sands of Monahans* • USA
MARIO BELLATIN • *Etchapare* • translated by Shook • MEXICO
CARMEN BOULLOSA • *The Book of Eve* • translated by Samantha Schnee • MEXICO
CHRISTINE BYL • *Lookout* • USA
MIRCEA CĂRTĂRESCU • *Solenoid* • translated by Sean Cotter • ROMANIA
TIM CLOWARD • *The City that Killed the President* • USA
JULIA CIMAFIEJEVA • *Motherfield* • translated by Valzhyna Mort & Hanif Abdurraqib • BELARUS
PETER CONSTANTINE • *The Purchased Bride* • USA
FREDERIKA AMALIA FINKELSTEIN • *Forgetting* • translated by Isabel Cout & Christopher Elson • FRANCE
EMILIAN GALAICU-PĂUN • *Canting Arms* • translated by Adam J. Sorkin, Diana Manole, & Stefania Hirtopanu • MOLDOVA
ALISA GANIEVA • *Offended Sensibilities* • translated by Carol Apollonio • RUSSIA
ALLA GORBUNOVA • *It's the End of the World, My Love* • translated by Elina Alter • RUSSIA
GISELA HEFFES • *Ischia* • translated by Grady C. Ray • ARGENTINA
TOSHIKO HIRATA • *Is It Poetry?* • translated by Eric E. Hyett & Spencer Thurlow • JAPAN
KB • *Freedom House* • USA
YANICK LAHENS • *Sweet Undoings* • translated by Kaiama Glover • HAITI
ERNEST MCMILLAN • *Standing: One Man's Odyssey through the Turbulent Sixties* • USA
FISTON MWANZA MUJILA • *The Villain's Dance* • translated by Roland Glasser • DEMOCRATIC REPUBLIC OF CONGO
LUDMILLA PETRUSHEVSKAYA • *Kidnapped: A Story in Crimes* • translated by Marian Schwartz • RUSSIA
SERGIO PITOL • *Taming the Divine Heron* • translated by George Henson • MEXICO
N. PRABHAKARAN • *Diary of a Mālayali Madman* • translated by Jayasree Kalathil • INDIA
THOMAS ROSS • *Miss Abracadabra* • USA
JANE SAGINAW • *Because the World Is Round* • USA
SHUMONA SINHA • *Down with the Poor!* • translated by Teresa Fagan • INDIA/FRANCE
KIM SOUSA, MALCOLM FRIEND, & ALAN CHAZARO, eds. • *Até Mas: Until More—An Anthology of LatinX Futurisms* • USA
MARIANA SPADA • *The Law of Conservation* • translated by Robin Myers • ARGENTINA
SOPHIA TERAZAWA • *Anon* • USA
KRISTÍN SVAVA TÓMASDÓTTIR • *Herostories* • translated by K. B. Thors • ICELAND
YANA VAGNER • *To the Lake* • translated by Maria Wiltshire • RUSSIA
SYLVIA AGUILAR ZÉLENY • *Trash* • translated by JD Pluecker • MEXICO
LIU ZONGYUAN • *The Poetic Garden of Liu Zongyuan* • translated by Nathaniel Dolton-Thornton & Yu Yuanyuan • CHINA